REFLECTIONS OF DEATH

A John England story

By

R. A. JORDAN

ISBN-13: 9798862577150

As time passes, I rely more on my wife, Caro, for love and support. My family and grandchildren remain a constant source of joy. I hope they don't mind being associated with fiction of this genre. I constantly think of each of them, especially when the younger ones sit examinations; I know they work so hard.

OTHER NOVELS BY R A JORDAN

THE WALLS SAGA:

Time's Up
England's Wall
Laundry
Cracks in the Wall
Secret Side

CHARITY BOOKS IN AID OF NHS CHARITIES:

Match Day Murder
The Family Lie

A JOHN ENGLAND STORY

Tower of Strength
Failed Redemption

A NEW NOVEL DUE TO BE PUBLISHED IN AUTUMN 2024

Head in the sand

All my books can be obtained from Amazon
Visit my website – www.rajordan.uk

CONTENTS

ACKNOWLEDGEMENTS

In writing my book, help and advice are required on various technical aspects which are not within the scope of my knowledge. *Reflections of Death* is no exception. Those who have helped me with information include Robert at Paleros Yacht Services of Lefkas, Greece; the Maritime and Coastguard Agency of the UK; and the archives of the British Army, information about whose service in Bosnia I have been able to access with the help of the War Museum North.

The front cover shows the Citadel over Corfu Town. It was built by the Venetians in 1386 at the request of the people of Corfu to protect the Island. The Venetians occupied the island for four centuries., The British took control after the Napoleonic Wars in 1813. In 1863 Corfu and other islands were ceded to the Greeks. A fondness for Cricket remained in Corfu, where a cricket square exists to this day.

I also want to thank Vanessa, who read the first transcript. Her invaluable comments are greatly appreciated. Finally, for the detailed proofread and cover design, thank you to my publishing team at Kindle Book Publishing.

PROLOGUE

On 4th January 2000, John England, who had been working at the firm of solicitors, Bennetts in Chester, over the Christmas period, received an urgent call from Sandra Wall asking him to meet her at Long Acre Farm in Tarporley. The death of Peter Wall, her father, had been discovered on New Year's Day. Peter's decapitated body was lying in his old Land Rover which had run into the gate post of the access to the farm. Initial investigations indicated the cause of death to be suicide.

John England went to Long Acre Farm as soon as possible to meet Peter's two daughters: Sandra, a commercial lawyer, and Sienna, a chartered surveyor. John felt a tingle of attraction with the latter daughter, despite the nature of the visit, and maintained prolonged eye contact with her when they shook hands, despite the necessity for propriety.

John was hardly away from Long Acre in the following days and weeks. Peter Wall's estate was complex. The initial belief was that he had committed suicide. However, the police, aided by forensic examinations, eventually decided a murder had been committed. This was a great help to John; the life insurance policies which could not be claimed against in the event of suicide were now in play.

The police discovered the murderer was Peter's business partner, Roger Whiteside. He, too, was eventually found dead floating in the River Dee. So, Sandra left her job in Liverpool to take over the running of Wall's Civil Engineers. Sienna likewise left her career with a firm of chartered surveyors in Chester to start and run Wall's Developments. Peter had purchased land, which was a helpful starting point for Sienna's venture.

After a romantic holiday skiing in the Swiss Alps, John and Sienna became even more attracted to one another. A wedding was in the offing. Frank Stringer, the family doctor, was available to give Sienna away as his goddaughter, despite being imprisoned for murdering Roger Whiteside.

The property market was on fire in the early twenty-first century, especially for houses and flats. The enthusiasm for buy-to-let by private individuals was a great help to increase sales of properties constructed and developed by the now renamed group Walls Holdings.

The demand for buy-to-let property was such that two local estate agent negotiators and entrepreneurs spotted an opportunity in the market. Michael Fitzallen and Wayne Lamb formed a new company to buy, furnish and let property for new landlords who had purchased properties as an investment. They teamed up with Wall's Holdings and offered package deals for the inexperienced investor. What the pair needed most was finance to get them going. Michael recalled he had once met an Irishman at a professional dinner who had invited him to make contact if he had any deals that would interest him.

During a phone call to his contact in Ireland, Niall Phelan, who lived at Dunmore Hall, the two men were invited to come to Ireland to discuss the deal. A deal was struck, but it was not what the boys ideally wanted. However, beggars can't be choosers. Phelan was to take 75% of the profit. The arrangement was that all proceeds had to be sent the day they received money from a sale transferred to a new bank account in southern Spain. Wayne or Michael, and Niall Phelan were signatories to the bank account. Only one signature was required and the deal allowed many new houses and flats to be sold to investors. After commencing this new enterprise, over five million pounds were sent to the Spanish bank account. As time passed, more money was transferred and Wayne was posted permanently to Spain. He kept an eye on the bank account and any withdrawals and credits.

Then, Wayne was killed in a car crash in Malaga. Michael Fitzallen was getting tired of doing all the work. He visited Phelan in Ireland to try and renegotiate the deal. He was unsuccessful. Michael wanted to withdraw a significant amount of cash from the Spanish bank but, when he went to Spain, he discovered that Phelan had transferred all the money to his account in Ireland. It soon became known that Phelan, who pretended to be helping drug addicts, was a drug supplier and was pocketing a small fortune from his drug trading. Michael was at a loss to know how he might recover his money. He was concerned that he might be liable for money laundering if he went to the authorities.

Michael was introduced to a man called 'Goose'. He owned a superyacht and was often thought to be a smuggler of contraband of one sort or another. Michael told Goose of his predicament. Goose said he would help. Goose arranged to sell Niall Phelan a significant amount of cocaine and heroin. He needed to be paid five million euros in cash for the load. It was agreed that the drugs would be transferred to Phelan at sea, in a location to be decided inside the fishing zone known as the Irish Box. The drugs would be loaded onto Phelan's boat with cash at handover to Goose. Once the deed was done, Goose sped off in his superyacht, *Flying Goose*, to Turkey. In a roundabout fashion, Michael had received three-and-a-half million pounds and Niall Phelan got his drugs. However, on opening the packets of drugs, Niall Phelan and his chemist were killed by an exploding package of fake drugs.

Michael sold up in the UK and moved to Puerto Banus. He had briefly been in touch with Goose, who said he had sent most of the money, three million pounds, to his bank in the Cayman Islands as, he explained to Michael, it was impossible to swan into a European bank and deposit millions of pounds or euros.

Michael received three hundred thousand euros which enabled him to live in Spain. A financial crisis hit the UK and most of Europe but Wall's Holdings was fortunate that they had sold most of their property, except Peter's Tower in Manchester which wasn't yet finished. The bank to Wall's Holdings demanded repayment of the £3m loan secured on Peters Tower. After numerous failed attempts to raise the money to pay off the bank, Sandra Wall placed an advert in the Sunday Times. Michael Fitzallen responded from Spain. Fitzallen agreed to pay the £3m for half the tower and half the rent.

As a lawyer, and not entirely trusting Michael, Sandra drew up a contract for the loan, embodying the payments due to Michael Fitzallen. To be safe, she included a clause which protected her from Michael: if he committed a crime and was sentenced to over ten years in jail, he would forfeit his share of Peter's Tower and lose the money he had paid into the scheme.

One afternoon, under severe pressure from the authorities, Michael arranged to collect an extra £10,000 from Sandra to enable him to leave the country and avoid jail for a recent crime. Sandra thought she knew what he was up to and said she would tell the police if he absconded. No one was around as they were on her farm, which was currently being renovated. Michael murdered Sandra to prevent her from telling the authorities.

John was the remaining beneficiary: following Peter's death, his widow, Ann Wall, had died, Sandra had been murdered, and then Sienna had died with the children in a car crash with a tram in Manchester. He inherited considerable sums of money, insurance pay-outs, and Peter's Tower. It was fully tenanted and debt-free, and now belonged to him. He had sold the family home. As a consequence of all these deaths, John became extremely wealthy.

Through his legal training, he decided to operate as a pro bono lawyer and leave the solicitor's practice in Chester. One day, having been summoned to court for using excessive force on a man who attacked him in the underground car park of Peter's Towe, John met Fiona in the court waiting area, where she was sobbing, having been accused of committing a crime. Acting as her lawyer, John was able to get Fiona acquitted and she was, of course, delighted.

They kept in touch with Goose who had now purchased a new superyacht, *Brave Goose*. John and Fiona accepted an invitation to go to Ireland on holiday with Goose on *Brave Goose*. Relatives of Michael

Fitzallen pursued them, intending to recover on his behalf the £3m he had lent Sandra years before.

John and Fiona were preparing to fly back to Manchester from Cork when a rogue taxi driver offered them a lift to see the countryside – what they thought was a sightseeing trip. Instead, they were taken to Dunmore Hall where they soon realised the inhabitants intended to lock them up. When a gun was drawn by one of them, John tried to fight him off. Fiona picked it up and fired it at the attacker; John thought she had killed him but the small calibre round had run out of power when it found its way through the man's wax jacket and mobile phone and he merely collapsed.

The inhabitants of Dunmore Hall were imprisoned, and John and Fiona were allowed home. Fiona was fined €1000 and bound over to keep the peace. They returned to Manchester on the next plane.

Due to a complex set of circumstances ending with the assassination of Goose, John, who had acted as Goose's lawyer, found that he was able to purchase the superyacht *Brave Goose.* Various failed attempts to recover the money on behalf of Michael Fitzallen persuaded John and Fiona to move the boat and her crew to Corfu, where they planned to join them. The route from Mallorca to Corfu took the boat and her crew via Sicily, the home of Georgio, one of the assistants to the Fitzallen family who were still trying to recover the €3m from John England. Sicily was also the home of the Cosa Nostra, who came to the aid of the Fitzallen family. Georgio orchestrated the capture of *Brave Goose* and the Mafia team he assembled held *Brave Goose* and the crew hostage until John England paid the ransom of £3m, less £200,000 which had been extorted from a group of pensioners in Manchester by Georgio which John used to pay them back.

Finally, John and Fiona believed they were safe from the extortion rackets and free to continue cruising in *Brave Goose.*

CHAPTER 1

The threat of further kidnappings was ringing in John's head. He was anxious not to let the news of the phone calls and emails he had received from Georgio in Sicily become known. A quarter of a million euros was now demanded. John had paid the two million eight hundred thousand of the three million euros demanded. He had held back the two hundred thousand to pay the four pensioners whom Georgio had robbed of their pension pots using his fake finance company based in Manchester. John had reimbursed the pensioners from the two hundred thousand pounds he retained from the payment to Brandon Phelan, Michael Fitzallen's helper on the 'outside'.

Jon Kim, John's contact and now friend in the Greater Manchester Police, was interested to hear of the developments.

'Are you going away soon, John?' Kim enquired.

Kim was the descendant of a Chinese couple who had died some years ago. He was originally from Hong Kong. He looked the part and spoke perfect English and Cantonese, always smartly dressed in one of the many suits he had made for him in Hong Kong before the handover which had allowed Kim to get a lifetime visa and passport to come to the UK after leaving the Royal Hong Kong Police.

'Yes, we're going to Greece; the boat is on its way to Corfu with the crew. Fiona and I will meet *Brave Goose* there. We fly from Manchester on Sunday.'

'Interesting you should tell me this, John. I just came from a briefing with the Assistant Chief Constable of GMP. He is concerned about a growing trend in trafficking girls, usually from Albania, to work in the sex trade in the UK.'

'We're not going to Albania, Jon.'

'Albania is cheek by jowl to Corfu. The distance from the island to the Albanian coast is only a mile. There is a little bay called Ftelia, right on the border with Albania. If you by chance come across a potential kidnap or, more likely, the transportation of girls to an island in Greece, possibly Ionia, then can you let me know, please?'

'Yes, we can do that, Jon, but as we have no specific details, we could be informing on totally innocent people.'

'Don't worry about that, John, that isn't what I am asking. What seems to happen is these young girls, all certainly under twenty, sixteen to eighteen mainly, seek a free trip in exchange for working on a large boat to get to the island of Ionia. We gather there is a Russian Mafia enclave on one of the islands, which would appear to be the holding base for the girls, and they trickle them out little by little to the UK and other European destinations.'

'How do they get them there?'

'Well, as soon as they are in Greece, the Schengen area rules allow free movement, so it's easy. The UK is tricky; apparently, they get UK passports for some girls, though it's a puzzle how they achieve this.'

'I see; so, if we were approached by someone wanting to work and have a free trip to Ionia, do you want us to take them?'

'If they seem suitable and you have room for them, yes; ideally you should take only one girl. Then please tell me the details.'

'Okay, Jon. I was going to tell you that Georgio rang me earlier today. He told me I could expect further kidnappings of our crew – or us – with the help of the Greek and Russian Mafia. That is why fifty thousand has been added to pay for their services. He now needs two hundred and fifty thousand Euros.'

'Okay, John, I have noted that, but until there is a definite threat, I cannot justify involving the Greek authorities.'

'I understand that entirely, Jon. We'll be cruising around the Ionian and other parts of Greece onboard *Brave Goose*. I'm determined not to pay or even tell Fiona about it. It would spoil the holiday.'

'I fully understand, John. I hope nothing happens, but you know where I am should something occur. Have a great holiday, my friend.'

At 3pm on Sunday, 1st September 2019, the plane touched down at Kerkira Airport, Corfu. A queue for the toilet was not helpful. The Greek toilets are basic: a toilet pan in a cubicle without a seat, a door with no lock or catch, an overflowing waste bin to collect the toilet paper which Greek drains cannot cope with. Patience was required. John was in stitches with laughter. Some wag had added to the official warning notice about not dropping toilet paper in the pan. *No, just chuck it in*! said the amended sign.

John extracted himself from the loo. He joined Fiona, who had collected their baggage from the carousel, and told her the amusing story.

'Leaving clothes onboard *Brave Goose* has been a definite advantage. I guess the wardrobes will be full by the time this current load of clothes has been stored.'

'You are a tease, John. Are you going to tell Noel we are here?'

John phoned the captain of *Brave Goose*.

'Just to let you know, Noel, we are about to get a taxi. We should be with you in about half an hour.'

'Okay, John, we are on dock E.'

The air-conditioned Mercedes taxi protected them from thirty-two degrees Celsius of late summer heat. It took more than half an hour, winding through Corfu town and the Corfu traffic, to reach the Gouvia Marina. The taxi dropped them at the end of E dock. José, the deckhand on *Brave Goose*, welcomed John and Fiona and took the first load of bags to their cabin.

As he paid the driver, John was conscious of two men standing on the other side of the taxi. The cab pulled away, and he realised he knew the two men but couldn't recollect where they were from.

'John? It's Bill and Tony, from Oxford days.'

'Good heavens, sorry, I didn't recognise you! The years have passed. How are you both?'

'Just fine, John. We are about to set sail to Lefkas in our forty-five-foot Bénéteau yacht.'

'Great! As you can see, I'm a bit busy right now. We may see you in Lefkas, as that's our destination as well. We will be there in a week.'

'Wonderful,' said Tony. 'Is this your boat, John?'

'Yes. Let's try and meet. In Lefkas.'

'That would be great, John, thank you. We certainly won't need any directions to find you!'

John waved the pair farewell and joined Fiona on the quarterdeck of *Brave Goose* where the whole crew was in attendance to greet their owners. Noel, the captain, Sally the stewardess, and Jock, the engineer, were lined up on the deck as a welcoming party. They were all dressed in beige shorts and white polo shirts, and white deck shoes. *Brave Goose,* was embroidered on the breast of each shirt. Once they had dealt with the formalities, John and Fiona went to the stateroom, their cabin as the new owners.

Fiona was delighted with the cabin. Despite all the trauma on the voyage there, Sally had re-made attractive curtains, re-lined drawers and polished everything. A large vase of fresh flowers adorned the dressing table. The two of them couldn't wait to change into shorts and polo shirts and repair to the quarter deck for a drink and relaxation. Sally had always produced iced lemonade in a lovely cut glass jug with matching tumblers. It was always a hit.

'Sally, you have worked wonders on our cabin. It is beautiful. So different to the décor when dear old Goose occupied it.'

'I love sewing. I have to admit to purchasing a sewing machine on ship's expenses. Noel said it would be fine. The boys helped put up the new curtains and polish the panelling. I am so glad you like it.'

'Who were those men, John?' enquired Fiona, referring to the two men John had spoken to as they left the taxi.

'I knew them when I was at university. They wanted to chat, but I said we would meet them in Lefkas as they're sailing there too. How are things on *Brave Goose*, Noel?'

'Nothing more than you already know, John,' said Noel. 'We have just about recovered from the invasion by the Italian Mafia. We were held hostage in the port of Catania in Sicily. Thank you for organising the payment of the ransom so quickly, John. We were all convinced we were going to be killed.'

'Well, I have some compensation for you all, so I hope that will be the end of the dangerous and frightening attempts to recover the three million which was paid back, despite the fact the Fitzallen and Phelan families were not entitled to it. The killing of Goose when we were in Puerto Pollenca was unforgivable. I will always have a soft spot in my heart for Goose. He was a rebel and capable of all sorts of dubious activities. He was a modern pirate, that's for sure, but a likeable rogue. God bless him.'

'I loved him, John,' chipped in Fiona.

'Me too,' added Sally.

'Sally, thank you so much for all your work on our cabin and the flowers. Everything is beautiful.'

John knew his statement was not true. He had only paid £2.8m and Georgio had threatened to recover the outstanding balance of £200,000. John was convinced it was Georgio's commission for collecting the nearly three million. The balance had been demanded, plus fifty thousand to pay the Mafia troops, who Georgio had employed for the next attack. John had paid the pensioners back the money Georgio had stolen from them;. He believed the two hundred thousand must be paid back at Georgio's cost; it was only right. Had they been in the UK, Georgio would have been arrested and charged with theft. He could be in jail now.

'A man was hanging around yesterday, trying to find out who owned *Brave Goose.* I asked the marina not to divulge the information, of course.'

'A man?' John had the words of Jon Kim ringing in his head. He had been expecting a young lady to seek passage.

'Did he have a name, Noel?' John assumed it was a member of Georgio's Mafia team.

'Yes, he said he was called Azmir. We didn't expect for a moment you would know him. He was trying to get to the island of Kalamos and hoped we could give him a lift. I explained it could be at least two weeks before we went there. I told him there was a bus service from the mainland to Mitika. From there there's a ferry to Kalamos. That would be the only way of getting there by public transport. I explained he would need to go to the port of Corfu and catch a ferry to Igoumenitsa, where he could catch a bus to Mitika.'

'Azmir, you say? Was he Croatian?' John suddenly felt uneasy. He began to feel sweat running down his back. He was sure his face had turned red. His heart started to beat faster.

'Yes, John. I believe he did say he was Croatian. He said you would remember him.'

'That is remarkable. Someone must have told him *Brave Goose* was my boat. I met Azmir when I was in the Army Legal Services in Bosnia. He was my interpreter.'

'Good heavens! I had no idea you were in the army, John.'

'Neither did I,' said Fiona.

'It's a long story, but I was in the army for less than two years, due to certain events. Perhaps it would be appropriate if I explained my time in the army after we've unpacked.'

CHAPTER 2

John and Fiona returned to the quarterdeck, having unpacked their clothes. John was surprised there was sufficient space in the wardrobes which were much larger in the main cabin. The wardrobes, opposite a king-sized bed, were illuminated by internal lights which came on automatically when the doors opened. The whole cabin had been cleaned to perfection. It was spotless.

On the quarterdeck, Sally had laid out some crisps and nuts. John said he would have a beer, while the others poured some of Sally's homemade lemonade.

'So, please tell us all about your army exploits,' insisted Fiona.

'Very well. I suspect there won't be time to cover it all, but I can always continue another time. I am happy for you all to listen in. To go back even further, I read law at Balliol College, Oxford. That is where I met Bill and Tony, the two guys who were on the quay earlier. When I graduated, I studied at the College of Law in Chester. I then decided I would like some excitement before settling down to become a country solicitor and I joined the Army Legal Services. Once I had completed a six-month initiation course, including physical fitness, I was sent to Sandhurst at the Royal Military Academy. I was taught military skills, tactics, and the legal skills required in conflict zones. Skills to lead and take command. I left Sandhurst with the rank of captain and re-joined the Legal Services Directorate.'

'Wow, that must have been quite an initiation, John! So, what does a solicitor in the army do? And what happened next?' Fiona was fascinated by what she had heard and desperate to know more.

'I was sent to Bosnia the year after the war had ended. I was involved in all sorts of issues. One of the more interesting ones was assisting the Bosnian government, such as it was, with preparing documents and voting arrangements for an election to their parliament.'

'Were you involved with the conflict, John?' Fiona enquired.

'Not really in Bosnia – the conflict had ended, but the country's NATO troops were now the de-facto security service. A NATO soldier had arrested one of the fighters involved in the massacre in Srebrenica. It was a nasty war. Ethnic cleansing, rape, torture and summary assassinations were commonplace. I had to interrogate a soldier with the assistance of Azmir. The Bosnian fighter had only just been captured and his gun and hand grenades had been taken from him. Azmir and I walked out of our office to cross the parade ground. The fighter was ahead of us by a reasonable distance. He was being escorted to the interrogation suite by a NATO soldier. That's when it happened. The fighter exploded. There was an enormous explosion. He had been wearing a suicide vest under his clothes. He wasn't wearing a uniform; they all wore free-flowing robes, sandals, and a hat like a beret but different. There were body parts all over the place. The ground turned red with blood. The NATO soldier escort was very severely injured. Azmir and I were hit by shrapnel. The Bosnian fighter was in pieces all over the square. Before we knew what had happened, Azmir and I were sprawled on the ground. We'd both been hit by shrapnel – odds and sods of metal, nails, nuts and bolts. The fighter had disintegrated in front of us. I could see his body parts all over the place. An arm, complete with a hand attached, was close by. I was afraid it was mine. The smell was awful – a mixture of cordite from the explosion and human remains. I never want to smell an odour like it again. The ground had turned red from the massive blood loss from the Bosnian and the NATO guard. Azmir and I were bleeding profusely from the shrapnel wounds.

I couldn't hear a thing. Blood was dripping from my body. Azmir was in a similar state. I began to shake uncontrollably. It wasn't long, but it seemed an age before medics came with a stretcher and took us both to the first-aid area where we had our wounds dressed. I was taken by helicopter to Sarajevo airport but I'm not sure where Azmir went.

That evening, I was operated on to remove numerous pieces of shrapnel. The following day I was a medivac patient, flown to the UK. Two injured soldiers were on the same flight. I didn't talk to them as I couldn't hear anything – I was deaf.'

'Oh, John, how terrible!'

'It could have been much worse, darling; I could have been killed. I suspect that was the lot of the soldier.'

'So, John, the opportunity to become a solicitor in Chester must have seemed very peaceful after the trauma of Bosnia?'

'You are so right, Noel. I left the army about six months later. My hearing had returned. Despite my three-year commitment at the outset, I only served just under two years. I took a long holiday, mainly in the Mediterranean, quite a bit here in Greece.'

'You never told me that, John.'

'You never asked. I have had a few injuries since, but my Krav Magar training on top of my army training has been my saviour.'

'And mine,' added Fiona.

'Krav Magar?' enquired Noel.

'Yes, I have learnt how to protect myself using their system. It is the official unarmed fighting system of the Israeli Defence Forces. It has been battle-tested and proved successful. I decided in these days of street attacks to learn Krav Magar to protect myself and my loved ones.'

'Did Azmir say why he wanted to go to Kalamos? From my recollection, there is nothing much there.'

'No, John, I kept the conversation short, not knowing what he wanted.'

'Good. I guess when we get to Kalamos, we may discover what it's all about.'

'Gosh, John. I had no idea about all this.'

'Well, my love, you do now. Does it make any difference to our relationship?'

'No, of course not. I don't know why I should even express surprise. It's just you don't think of the army having solicitors.'

'Well, there you are. I might tell you all about it one day. Noel, what are the plans for this week?'

'Well, John and Fiona, I have a reservation in Lefkas Marina to moor *Brave Goose* for the evening of Friday 6th September. We are expected to leave by Monday the 10th, giving time for your three friends to arrive, come on board and settle in before we leave. They are to return on Saturday 15th September, as I understand? This week is very casual. We can do anything you like.'

'That's a good plan, Noel. I guess Fiona would like to look at the shops in the marina. Perhaps we could eat ashore tonight. Would you all like to come? I'll stroll over and book a table now.'

'We could then head to Corfu town tomorrow, John, and moor under the castle. It's a lovely anchorage. It is possible we may be able to get on the outside of the mole of the small marina. It is part of the NAOK Corfu Rowing Club. We can easily access the shore using the passerelle.'

'I am sure Fiona would love a walk around the town, and we will eat out tomorrow evening as well.'

'That's all fine, John. We will be pleased to join you for dinner tonight. Thank you.'

John returned to their cabin to find Fiona re-hanging all her clothes in her allocated wardrobes.

'John, I am sorry if I upset you by asking about your time in the army. I wasn't prying. It was a surprise, that's all.'

'Don't worry, darling. There is nothing to it. It's all behind me now. It's a closed book as far as I am concerned.'

'Will you let me into more of your secrets one day?'

'Well, if you *need* to know. There is nothing important. So, now let's get on with our holiday. I have booked a table for six at the restaurant opposite at eight-thirty. We can have drinks here before we go.'

'That's great, John. What are we going to do tomorrow?'

'Well, my love, I thought you would like to wander around the shops here. Then we could anchor in the bay under the castle near Corfu town. There are a great many interesting shops and buildings in town. You and I can have dinner in town, just the two of us.'

'Have you any more thoughts on what we do after Corfu?'

'Yes, but it will be a surprise.'

It was early evening. John asked Sally to bring some champagne flutes to the quarter deck and he opened a bottle of Goose's champagne with a loud bang. Once they all had a glass of champagne, John toasted everyone's good health and said he looked forward to a happy and relaxed cruise.

'Now, here are some envelopes, one each. My thanks go to you all. In the envelope is compensation for the trauma you suffered on your way here. What happened was highly illegal and very dangerous – being held hostage by a group of Mafia men with guns for a day. However, I suspect the Sicilian police might have a different view. I hope the contents of the envelopes go a small way to compensate you for the outrage. It is unlikely we shall have Sicily on our itinerary any time soon! The cash is in euros, which I thought would be the most useful. Everyone has the same amount. Enjoy it.'

A chorus of thanks erupted from the crew. They realised their release and *Brave Goose* must have cost John three million pounds. The protagonists had been keen to collect this money for some time. All of the crew had experienced a traumatic time one way or another, helping

John avoid the fraudulent demands of the Irish families. The Irish were not entitled to the money but persisted with more dangerous stunts to recover what they believed was rightfully theirs.

They all returned to *Brave Goose* at eleven o'clock in the evening. José withdrew the passerelle and the crew retired.

'You know, it is such a beautiful evening. I fancy sitting here for a while with a glass of brandy. Will you join me, darling?'

'Yes, I would love to, John. The brandy speaks of being on holiday in the Mediterranean."

Just after midnight, John had finished explaining to Fiona what else he had done in the Army and why he had left. She gave him a huge kiss and suggested they go to bed.

'Will you tell me more about your exploits in the army and other adventures?'

'It was some time ago and not very interesting. Let's leave it.'

John knew that if he explained his activities in the army, particularly his time in Bosnia from 1996 to 1998, he would regret it as it was most distressing. Yes, he did have an interpreter called Azmir. He was a great guy, but it became problematic when Azmir's friend was arrested for laying an IED, killing a colleague and wounding two other soldiers. He had had to prosecute the friend, which put Azmir in a difficult position.

CHAPTER 3

Sally could offer a range of breakfasts. They always included a full English or a Greek breakfast with its stiff yoghurt and honey, cornflakes, Weetabix and shredded wheat. She could also offer special breakfasts if she obtained the right products from a local shop. For example, fish but not kippers in the Mediterranean. Her breakfast set you up for the day. After a magnificent feed, John and Fiona headed for the marina shops – a mixture of hairdressers, clothes shops and jewellers in one, excellent chandlers and two restaurants. Strolling around, nothing was purchased, much to John's amazement, in the chandlery shop, which he found to be the most interesting. The range of products available for boats was terrific – a fascinating selection, including lengths of rope of various types, and boating clothing. John was surprised Fiona didn't fancy any nautical clothing. Appearing from behind a display stand of marine cleaning materials, John ran straight into Tony and Bill.

'Well, not seen you both for twenty years and now twice in as many days! What are you up to?'

'We needed some cleaning materials as we want to leave our yacht spick and span. We leave her ashore in Lefkas.'

'Well, we will be in Lefkas certainly on Saturday, so you must come over for a beer.'

'We will, thanks, John,' the pair responded in unison.

John and Fiona left the Chandlery shop empty-handed.

'Life is amazing, John. You don't see someone for years, and suddenly, you meet friends from years back in an unexpected location.'

'I wouldn't say they were friends, Fiona. We had some issues at uni, but nothing serious.'

'What was that, darling?'

'Despite the fact I was not a qualified lawyer then, they asked me to intercede following the theft of two bikes. Essential transport at university. Two Irish lads who were not at uni had stolen them. I helped Bill and Tony report the issue to the police, who then prosecuted the bike thieves.'

'You were always cut out to be a lawyer!'

'These two lads were just thugs, and they intimidated all three of us until I managed to get them arrested and bound over.'

'Bound over? What does that mean, John?'

'It was clear they had pinched the bikes. Either Bill or Tony found a constable to I explained the circumstances and he agreed with me that a PND – Penalty Notice for Disorder – should be issued. He explained to the two Irish thugs that they could be arrested and taken to court if they didn't pay the fine in time. The constable took down the offenders' particulars and gave each one a PND and a fine payment slip. They took the slips and shouted at me, Bill and Tony, calling us 'fucking wankers' and saying that if they saw us again, we would be sorry. Then they ran off. I said, "Will you kindly put that parting comment in your report, constable? You might have chosen a different penalty for those two had they said that before you issued the PND". I don't know what happened next, but I have hated people like that ever since.'

John was angry. His eyes widened. He didn't know how or when any attempt might occur to try and recover the residual money Georgio had demanded. His recollection of the incident in Oxford reminded him that he considered Georgio a criminal and thug, too.

'What's the matter, John? You look angry.'

'I am. I cannot get the thought of Brandon and Georgio out of my mind. People like that are a scourge on society, just like the bike thieves.'

'Why is that, darling? I thought all that was behind us.'

'I don't think it is.'

'What makes you think that, John?'

'I have been silly, so I am cross with myself. I could have put this whole holiday in jeopardy.'

'Oh John, what is it? Tell me, please. A trouble shared is a trouble halved.'

'It is all to do with Georgio. I don't want anyone else to know. If I tell you, you must promise not to tell anyone. The time may come when I must come clean, but it's a secret for now. Okay?'

'Of course, darling, I must help you. You are in a state about something. Please let me help. I promise not to tell a soul.'

'Okay, well, when Georgio and the Mafia held the crew hostage at gunpoint when they moored in Catania, I was so angry that I was determined to take out my revenge on Georgio. I paid the lion's share of the money Brandon demanded and I withheld two hundred thousand pounds.'

'Why did you do that?'

'Don't question my actions, Fiona. I did it for an excellent reason,' John responded in a firm and somewhat angry voice. He was not used to being questioned on his judgement.

'Oh John, don't be cross with me. If you don't want to tell me, fair enough, but as we are partners now, I have a right to know what is troubling you. I haven't seen you like this before. You worry me, darling.'

'Sorry, you are right. I discovered that Georgio was running an illegal money-lending business in Manchester. I was about to prosecute him, but he left the country before I could get him in court.'

'So why is that worrying you?'

'I paid Brandon two million eight hundred thousand pounds, two hundred thousand short.'

'Why, what happened to the two hundred thousand?'

'The business Georgio was running had taken the pension pots of four pensioners and he used that money to lend to people desperate for cash, with excessive interest rates. The pensioners were persuaded to give him their pension pots as he guaranteed a higher interest rate than their pension fund insurers would pay. Yes, it was too good to be true, but people who don't know any better are persuaded to go with these schemes due to the higher interest rates. The old adage is that *if it is too good to be true, it probably is.* The pensioners gave him their pension pots.'

'I understand that. What did you do with the money you held back?'

'I found the pensioners and paid them back their pension money.'

'That was very noble; so why are you getting all het-up about Georgio? Is Georgio threatening you?'

'You are correct. He is threatening some form of action. I don't know what. He is upset because I told Brandon he should collect the two hundred thousand from Geogio.'

'So?'

'So Georgio hasn't got any money, which is why he escaped to Sicily. He needs the cash. That is why he is threatening me, or us, and *Brave Goose.*'

'Oh John, what a mess. Why not just give him the money?'

'It would be immoral. I am determined he should not benefit from a bent enterprise in the UK. He might have gone to jail if he had remained in the UK.'

'Well, my love, I understand your anger, but don't let it spoil things. We have other people to help. It is unlikely Georgio, without any cash, can mount an assault on *Brave Goose.*'

'Possibly. I hope you are right.' John smiled now. Fiona was feeling happier.

When they returned to *Brave Goose* a little more than an hour after leaving her, she was made ready to sail.

CHAPTER 4

About seven kilometres south of Catania was the airport and Georgio's home. Regular bus service to the airport from the centre of Catania was available. Georgio lived on the city's outskirts in a bedsit with a shared bathroom. It was a neglected building. Built of brick and rendered, much of which was flaking off and what was left needed repainting. The building housed ten bedsits. Georgio shared the bathroom with four other tenants. The building was owned by one of Georgio's cousins, a leading light in the Cosa Nostra, as they called the Mafia then. The landlord's occupation ensured that there were no arrears of rent. Georgio could live there rent-free so long as he worked washing up every evening in one of his cousin's restaurants.

The shabby bedsit reflected Georgio's lifestyle perfectly. He wore the same pair of dark trousers day after day; a once white, now pale grey shirt with sleeves rolled up to the elbow; black shoes laced up which had never seen a cleaning cloth in their life. He had thick black hair and his tanned complexion was his natural skin colour.

His family connections in Sicily were invaluable. He could not have managed to hold the crew of *Brave Goose* hostage without the help of the Mafia. They were also pleased to receive cash for their work. The payment was to Brandon Phelan, the Irish man acting for his cousin, who was still in an English jail for the murder of Sandra Wall. John England had paid two hundred thousand pounds short of the three million Phelan said was owed. John England had explained to Phelan that the two hundred thousand pounds shortfall was used to repay four pensioners who had been tricked out of their pension pots by Georgio. So, John suggested that Phelan ask Georgio for the two hundred thousand to make up the shortfall.

The crew and *Brave Goose* were released in Catania when Phelan notified Georgio that John England had received payment. The Cosa Nostra men left immediately, allowing *Brave Goose* to leave Catania. Georgio was pleased to hear that the money had been paid over. His Mafia friends had done their bit. It was costly, so Brandon had to send a hundred thousand euros to Georgio for the services of the Mafia. Georgio was unable to pay Brandon his missing two hundred thousand. to allow him to live. Brandon was not worried about the shortfall. He did a disappearing act as soon as the money was his.

Georgio was still short of funds. He made calls to his Mafia friends in Athens. He explained that the deal was to stop the motor yacht *Brave Goose* and extract two hundred and fifty thousand Euros now that they were in Europe.

'Georgio, that will be a difficult thing to do. Do you know their route to Athens?'

'Yes, Vova, they will be going via the Corinth Canal. I am not sure when they will be there.'

'I will come back to you within the day to tell you what we will do to hold this superyacht to ransom.'

'Brilliant, Vova. Thank you.'

'There will be a fee, probably fifty thousand euros.'

'Yes, yes, of course,' Georgio confirmed although he wasn't sure where he would get that money if funds were demanded in advance; he was going to be in a mess.

CHAPTER 5

Vova was trying to access the task that Georgio had set him: how to stop a superyacht in the Corinth Canal. Vova was half Russian and half Greek. His father was one of the leaders of the Moscow collective known throughout Russia as 'Bratva'. It consisted of six thousand branches. The main activities were the same as the Cosa Nostra; Bratva was the Russian Mafia branch. It was associated with extortion, sex trafficking, and money laundering. Vova's father, Vladimir, was ex-KGB, a fierce bully of a man. Nothing was too extreme to assist him in extorting funds or girls into his web.

Vladimir was such an evil man the majority of the leaders of the Russian cells of Bratva feared him. Vlad, as he was known, rarely received a call from his son. This afternoon was a rare occasion. Vova explained the task he had been set and that achieving it was causing him difficulties.

'We've all heard of the Corinth Canal, of course, but I don't know what it is like. What are the dimensions?'

Vova went to his papers and read them out to Vlad.

'The sides are very tall and nearly vertical. The canal at the bottom is narrow. Only small cruise ships, ferries and private motor yachts can get through.'

'The height is your friend. Throw a few rocks down onto the boat and be ready to collect the money or board the boat with arms, insisting the owner transfers the money to your account. Check it's in your account before you leave, then get out of there.'

Vova thought long and hard about the suggested tactic. He decided to go to the canal and look for himself. He had the dimensions but could not comprehend the size of the canal. The walls were very high. The canal was like a ribbon of water feeding its way through the limestone walls. How on earth could he throw large rocks over the edge of such massive walls?

'Hey, Spiros. I have a job. It will need some big boulders and a 'Hymac' to lift them into place. Is that something you could do?'

'I have no idea. I need to meet with you and go to the site where you plan to do this operation.'

'Okay, Spiros, I will arrange a meet!'

The two men met on the banks of the Corinth Canal.

'I need to halt the progress of a superyacht called *Brave Goose* through the canal while I get the owner to pay me what he owes me.'

'It's a long way down but it is possible. The rocks might bounce on the bank then into the canal or onto the boat!'

'Fine, that is just what I need. Can you organise that, please?'

'I will arrange it, Georgio, but it will be expensive. I will ring you when I can get things organised, and I'll let you know the cost.'

CHAPTER 6

Once the passerelle had been withdrawn, the stern lines were taken in. The anchor was hauled, and *Brave Goose* started her short sail from Gouvia marina to Corfu's old town, past the citadel, Ormos Garitas, protruding from the island and on which stood the magnificent fortress. On their way, they passed the cruise liner terminal. Three colossal cruise ships were in port, either waiting for their guests to return or for new guests to arrive after flying into Corfu.

'These cruise ships are so tall, Noel,' John commented as they sailed past the vessels.

'They look unstable to me.'

'It has happened, John. As soon as things go wrong, they can turn over. Do you recall the Costa Concordia which capsized?'

'Yes, I remember,' John said and looked upward in a disparaging way.

Noel was concerned that John was not his usual self. Not his worry, but John's demeanour was far from happy.

They set a course to the rear of the large fortress and the NAOK Yacht Club's small marina which housed Corfu's rowing club.

'It's remarkable, John – the rowing club can put out the fleet of rowing boats on a still day for training and practice. I am surprised there are none out at the moment.'

'That's quite a chance to take in narrow rowing boats.'

'Yes, it's their marina where I want to moor stern-to at the quay. It's around the corner.'

Their marina was too small to accommodate *Brave Goose*. However, she could moor stern-to on the outer section of the mole. Noel had radioed the yacht club, obtaining permission to do so. A marinara appeared on the quay. Noel positioned the yacht perfectly with two anchors deployed. Stern lines were secured, and the passerelle was run out.

'What a wonderful view of the old castle,' said Fiona.

'Yes, Fiona, it's called a citadel,' Noel said. 'It has substantial fortifications. Its origins date back to the Romans in 200BC, who built the first smaller fortification. Many years later, a Turkish invasion in the 15th century saw the need for even greater fortifications. The Venetians had taken over this part of Corfu and there were regular invasions by different factions. The whole history of the place is recorded in the pilot book. If you want to read it, there's a copy on board.

John, Fiona – if you walk around the quay towards the land, take the steps up behind the clubhouse, walk right until you cross the road and walk into a park, on the opposite side you can access the old town, shops, restaurants, museums, etcetera. It is a lovely place to visit.'

'Okay, Noel, we will change and go ashore. We will have our meal in the town, Sally. We'll see you later.'

John and Fiona did as suggested and walked into Corfu town.

'Darling, this is beautiful!' exclaimed Fiona as they entered the park through the open ornate cast iron gates. They walked past the Victorian cast iron bandstand with its glazed roof and perimeter balustrade, looking as if it belonged in Brighton or some English seaside resort.

'We could be in any English seaside town. Pity there isn't a band playing. It is a beautiful sylvan setting.'

Perspiration was dripping down their faces and backs. John's shirt was marked with dark patches where the shirt had absorbed the sweat. The early afternoon sun was beating down. All they had done was walk from the boat but the temperature was in the thirties. The late morning saw the wind abate, unusually. The stone buildings and footpaths gave out heat like a storage heater. Their lightweight shoes let the pavements heat their feet, which added to their discomfort.

John was still outraged but attempted to hide his anger.

They left the park, crossing over a road servicing a car park, and avoiding getting knocked over by Greek traffic. Suddenly, there was loud bang and both John and Fiona jumped at the sound.

'I thought that was a gunshot,' said John, breathing a sigh of relief when he realised it was a car backfiring.

'So did I!' retorted Fiona. 'Our nerves must be highly strung at the moment.'

John was sweating even more. They were now in the old town where arched colonnades provided some shade. Cafés had taken over the shady areas. Customers were fanning themselves in the heat. Iced tea, coffee, and ice cream seemed to be most popular. There were many empty tables and it was very tempting to have a cold drink, but they didn't. The town was full of honey-coloured buildings, interesting little streets, and attractive squares. The stone-paved pavements had been polished smooth; they shone in the sunshine. There were plenty of shops to keep Fiona occupied for ages.

'Whoops, watch out,' said Fiona as a man on a bicycle nearly ran them down. She was in and out of almost every shop they passed. John, on high alert, was very aware of the potential conflict. A bicycle was not what he was expecting.

'Do you need anything, or are you just stocktaking for the shops?' enquired John.

Some postcards were purchased, complete with stamps.

'I can send these home.'

'Oh, who have you got at home you haven't told me about?'

'I have a sister and a mum. I also have a niece, but they all live in Croydon, so I rarely see them.'

'So, Miss Superyacht Owner, you have some secrets you haven't told me about!'

'We are equal now, John. Do we need to have a session of frankness, or shall we carry on not knowing anything about one another?'

'We can have a revealing session. I don't have anything to hide.'

'Neither do I, so let's forget about it now, and when a moment seems appropriate, we agree to have a heart-to-heart. Agreed?'

'Agreed.'

Walking hand-in-hand along Corfu Town's small back streets, they saw a small taverna in a beautiful square with a large jacaranda tree in full bloom. It was magnificent, with its bluey-purple blossom filling every branch, providing much-needed shade.

'John, this is gorgeous! Could we have imagined seeing such a sight as this magnificent tree? You know, they are very difficult trees to make bloom. They have a mind of their own. A bit like someone I know. The important thing is that they are protected from the wind. They love full sun and poor soil. They have it all here.'

'I didn't know you were a botanist.'

'I think there is a great deal we don't know about one another. As we have agreed, a heart-to-heart is required. A full reveal.'

'I like the idea of a full reveal … if you get my meaning?' John retorted with a cheeky smile.

'Clever! You *are* a little rascal! Okay, I will agree to that, not directly, though. I will have another glass of that lovely white wine. Will you join me? If so, should we buy a bottle?'

They slowly consumed a bottle of the excellent wine, sitting at a round, cream-painted metal table in a patch of shade outside the taverna. They ordered two meze platters, including dolmades, olives, aubergine, tomatoes, tzatziki, small fish and olive oil. They could taste the sunshine in the food. Lunch lasted for two hours and more.

CHAPTER 7

After lunch, the question was, 'What now, my lovely?'

Before Fiona could answer, there was a voice from behind her.

'Hello, Captain. Fancy seeing you here!'

John nearly fainted. He had to respond despite the fact he didn't want to engage with this man. Not now, anyway.

'Azmir! Good heavens! What are *you* doing here?'

'I was just out for a stroll before I catch a ferry to Ingoumitsa this evening.'

'Oh, sorry, let me introduce my partner, Fiona. Darling, this is Azmir. He was my interpreter in Bosnia. So, why are you going to Ingoumitsa?'

'Oh, it's a way of getting to Kalamos. My wife is working on the island in a taverna just now. I left a few days ago to get to the British Consulate. I caught the ferry from Kalamos to Mitika and then the bus to Lefkada. I discovered that there is no British Consulate in Lefkada so I have to go to Athens to the British Embassy. I'm here in Corfu to get the ferry to the mainland this evening. Are you here on holiday, Captain?'

'We're not in the Army now, Azmir; call me John. Yes, in answer to your question, we are on holiday. We have a boat and are about to sail around the Greek Islands. I know where Kalamos is, but it is miles from where we are going. You will be quicker going your way. Otherwise, I would have offered you a lift.'

'Kind of you, John. What are you doing with yourself now you are out of the army?'

'Here, have a seat. Would you like a drink?' said John, pulling a chair across to their table from the empty adjoining table.

'If there is a beer, that would be excellent.'

John asked the waiter for a beer, which arrived quickly with a glass taken from the fridge, ice drizzling down the outside.

'To answer your question, I still work in law, to help people.'

'That's typical of you, John. Always helping others.'

This man intrigued Fiona. He had smooth black hair and could have been mistaken for African, except his hair and complexion were bronze, not black, typical of his Arabic roots. There was no beard or moustache. He was clean-shaven with dark eyes like pools of still water. He wore a blue shirt, a Greek blue – the colour they paint their shutters. His sleeves were rolled up and he wore fawn, lightweight trousers and deck shoes, and a light-weight blue scarf around his neck completed the outfit. He spoke perfect English.

'You speak perfect English, Azmir!' complemented Fiona.

'Thank you, dear lady. I went to school in England until I was thirteen. My parents returned to the family home when my grandfather died. He had a wonderful house on the Island of Korcula in Croatia. It was a wonderful time being at school in England. English was my first language but it didn't take me long to speak Croatian and Arabic. I was hoping I could go to university to read medicine but the Bosnian war got in the way. I managed to get a job with first the British Army and then the NATO contingent as an interpreter. I recently married my wife and decided to get out of Bosnia. The British Army promised me I would be given a British passport, but it must have been overlooked in the chaos.'

'Oh, that's terrible. Is that why you needed the British Embassy?'

'Yes, Fiona. I hope they will agree, as previously discussed with the army, that my wife and I can get a British passport and transfer to the UK.

'Have you only recently left Bosnia?'

'No, not really, but when we were there, NATO had started a big hunt for the leaders of the terrible war. The main protagonists were captured. NATO kept me on to assist in translations. Radovan Karadzic and Ratko Mladic were arrested and put on trial. They were awful men. I translated for NATO during their interrogation, which took ages. We left when they were moved to the Hague for trial. The country is now at peace, and apologies are given to one side and the other. My wife and I then moved to Greece. NATO suggested I could help with the repatriation of refugees. The Greeks were not happy to have the refugees, so my services were not required. We liked Greece, so we thought we would stay a while, but the Greek financial crisis with the EU meant jobs were hard to find. We were lucky to get temporary work on Kalamos, helping in a taverna. Nothing will help us more than UK passports.'

'Well, Azmir, good luck with your endeavours. Time is marching on. We need to get back to the boat. I hope you succeed at the embassy in Athens. We may see you in Kalamos in a few weeks or so. Keep well. Come on, Fiona, we need to make tracks.'

John paid the bill and the two walked back to the park, John leading the way briskly. Cooler now.

They walked in silence until they were well into the park.

'You were not very forthcoming in helping Azmir, John.'

'Darling, the whole Bosnia thing was a mess from beginning to end. I will tell you all about it on our heart-to-heart day.'

John had the terrible thought he might have been responsible for not placing Azmir on the register of interpreters which could have caused him not to be considered for a visa. *Azmir should have realised that before we both left the Balkans, we had been subject to that bomb attack by the Serbian fighter on the parade ground. I was not in any fit state to put names on a list, even if I recalled the requirement.*

Back onboard *Brave Goose*, John and Fiona showered and changed, ready for a night out.

*

Azmir was pleased he had met John again, though slightly taken aback that he was not more forthcoming. John could be the person to help him the most. He could confirm to the authorities that he was an employee of the British Army. Azmir had thought long and hard about how he might contact John. If he came to Kalamos, that would be the time to try and solicit his help. The incident in Bosnia was not his fault, but as it had injured John and nearly killed a soldier, there had been quite a few hurdles to cross first.

*

Before a meal at Rex, a restaurant on the main street in Corfu town, John and Fiona watched the swallows' acrobatics provide cabaret before dinner. It was a sight to behold. The street was lined with tall stone buildings. The swallows caught insects in mid-air. The flying display would have impressed the Red Arrows. Their aerobatics held the attention of diners and passers-by until the last of the evening sun was gone, and then the birds returned to their roosts. Following an excellent meal at one of the many tables on the main street, John and Fiona made tracks again for *Brave Goose.*

CHAPTER 8

The couple boarded their superyacht via the quay at NAOK Yacht Club using the passerelle. Once onboard, assuming that everyone was on board, John pressed the button to retract the passerelle, which disappeared into the body of the boat.

Feeling tired and irritated by John's reluctance to help Azmir, Fiona went straight to bed. John said he wanted to sit and have a brandy. They had consumed a quantity of wine in the afternoon and evening so sleep came quickly to Fiona.

John sat with a bottle of five-star Metaxa – a beautiful mellow taste. The town's distant lights illuminated the view from the quarterdeck across the bay. The castle ramparts were floodlit. A moonbeam reflected onto the still water of the bay, mingling with the lights from hotels and other buildings around the bay. Meeting Azmir was an unexpected event. Had Azmir been trying to find him, or was it chance? The last time John had seen him, they were both in the same ambulance going to the camp's medical centre. Their bodies covered in blood from the blast of the suicide belt activated by the rebel.

John recalled all the events in his mind. The arrested man activated the suicide vest and the soldier escorting him was severely injured. John was convinced the NATO soldier would die. John and Azmir were both hit by shrapnel, John's wounds on his upper legs and two injuries to his chest. Azmir had taken more of the blast, which had injured his upper body.

Once inside the medical facility, they were separated and never met again. John was sent as a medical evacuee back to the UK that evening. He was joined by the NATO soldier and two other soldiers who had been hit by an exploding land mine (IED) elsewhere earlier in the day.

The whole episode brought the horror of war and the Bosnia insurgency to a personal level. The situation was hard to understand as an Englishman.

The stillness of the night, the pools of light reflected in the water now, were in total contrast to his Bosnia days. What, he wondered, did Azmir want from him? John was confident he had not seen the last of him. Draining his glass, he decided he had best retire.

He slipped under the single sheet, which was more than sufficient in the heat of this Greek night. He put his head on the soft pillow and closed his eyes, expecting to drift off in a soothing alcoholic-induced sleep.

However, he tossed and turned. His mind was back in Bosnia. He discussed a simple disciplinary situation with Azmir regarding one of the soldiers under training. The scheme created by NATO anticipated handing the region's security back to the indigenous troops one day.

Why didn't Azmir consider the fact that the insurgent could easily blow himself up and injure them both? Was he a Sunni? Why didn't Azmir say something? John would have recognised the arrested man's potential risk if he had known his ethnicity.

Azmir may have said something after the blast, but he couldn't hear. The noise, the smell, the sight of the explosion and of blood everywhere had stayed with John.

He tossed from side to side as he remembered the medics moving him onto a stretcher and into the medical facility. He was sweating profusely. Did Azmir, his interpreter and friend, know the land mine was planted, and where? He never said. A good man with evil relatives who blew up an army Land Rover. The stench of death, blood, human body parts, and organs splattered everywhere. He could still see an arm with its hand attached not many feet away. John recalls having to check his arms and hands were still there. Then, as his mind began racing, he could see Sienna's car being hit by the tram, turned upside down and crashing against a wall; he remembered when he discovered that his two beautiful children had been killed in the crash. Sienna was in hospital, just alive, connected to tubes and machines. She died in the hospital when surgeons attempted to remove a clot from her brain. He tossed and turned again and again. He could hear a nurse talking to him in the hospital in the UK where he had been treated for his wounds.

'Are you alright, John? Where is the worst pain? Are you alright, John?'

His heart was beating quickly in his chest; he had pain there.

'Are you alright, John?'

He was bathed in sweat.

'Are you alright, John?' the voice asked again.

He woke with a start to find Fiona bending over him, saying, 'Are you alright, John?'

'What are you doing here?' said John.

Fiona realised he was having a nightmare. Everything was jumbled up in his mind. He was sweating profusely. It was a hot night, but even so, he was drenched.

'John, it's me. Fiona, darling. Are you alright?'

John was awake now.

'Sorry, darling, what are you doing? Can't you sleep?' John asked.

'Oh, my love, you were having a nightmare, tossing and turning. You are drenched in sweat. Do you want a drink of water? Let me get a towel to dry you. Shall I put a new sheet on the bed?'

'Yes, to water and towel. We can sort the bed out in the morning.'

'Okay, have a couple of paracetamol. They will help you sleep.'

Half an hour later, the two were back in bed, and Fiona was sure John was asleep. She tried to go back to sleep but felt as though she had been awake all night.

It was eight-thirty when they both awoke. Fiona thought she hadn't slept at all, but she had.

'John darling, how do you feel this morning?'

'I feel worn out. I don't know what happened last night. I had a terrible nightmare.'

'You certainly did, darling. It must have been triggered by meeting Azmir. All of the terrible things you have endured came back at once. You were covered in sweat. Can I tempt you to a shower?'

'You can so long as you join me?'

'It's a deal; come on then.'

It was nine-fifteen when the pair appeared on the quarterdeck.

'Sorry, we are so late for breakfast, Sally. I had a bad night.'

'Oh, I am sorry. Would you like a fry-up or flakes and fruit?'

Fiona and John replied as one: 'Flakes and fruit.'

'Another beautiful day, Sally. Do you know where Noel is planning to go today? Is it really Wednesday already?'

They were finishing their breakfast when Noel joined them.

'I hope you both slept well?'

'Yes, fine, they both lied. 'Though it was sweltering. I was sweating like a pig. I need to change the sheets.'

'Give them Sally, and she will wash them in no time. The laundry will dry quickly in this heat with a light breeze. Just a thought, John – it would be the ideal time to consider installing air conditioning when the interior re-fit is carried out. If you plan on keeping her in the Mediterranean, the heat can be quite a problem, especially when trying to sleep.'

'That is certainly one to add to the list, Noel. Can you keep a list of things to have a good idea of what is required when we visit a boatyard that could tackle the refit?

'Yes, certainly, John.'

'Where do you plan on going today, Noel?'

'Well. Joint owners, where would *you* like to go? Remember we must be in Lefkas by the latest Saturday, preferably Friday, as Saturday is usually a change-over day for charters, and the marinas can be bustling.'

'So, what is your recommendation, Noel?'

'Well, I think it would be good to sail to Gaios. It is an exciting place on the island of Paxos. The harbour is behind a small island with a relatively narrow channel forming the port. We cannot get in, but there's a good anchorage on the island's south side. It is a short RIB journey to the town of Gaios. It's trendy, so take that as busy. Lots of restaurants and bars. It's an attractive little town.'

'I will go for that, said John. 'What do you think, Madam owner?'

'I am with you all the way. It all sounds wonderful. Thank you, Noel.'

Brave Goose left Corfu and sailed south to Paxos, the larger of the two accompanying islands to Corfu. To the south of Gaios, two islands plug the entrance to the sea. A channel runs between the central island Paxos and two small uninhabited islands forming the port of Gaios. Noel had studied the charts and spotted a recommended anchorage south of the main 'plug' island. It was here he brought *Brave Goose* to anchor. The side steps on the port side were lowered and the RIB was hoisted from the boat deck and launched close to the bathing platform at the bottom of the side steps.

'Shall we go for a swim, John?'

'Yes, let's.'

They changed into bathers and dived into the warm blue water from the platform at the end of the port boarding steps.

'This is just beautiful, John. Pity there isn't a beach on the island.'

'I'm not so keen on visiting beaches since the last episode when I was attacked in Mahon, on Minorca.'

'I understand, John. Why is the water so warm?'

'It's the time of the year, darling. It has been warmed up all summer and is probably at its warmest now.'

'Race you to the anchor chain.'

John arrived first, despite giving Fiona a start.

'Beaten you.'

'Yes, the winner gets a big kiss and a cuddle.'

'Better than a silver cup any day. Let me give you the biggest hug and kiss I can manage while staying afloat.'

The two of them were like young seals playing in the water.

'Shall we take the RIB for a trip around?'

'Yes, why not?'

They motioned to Noel that they were going on a trip in the RIB.

'Should be back within the hour,' John called.

They followed the coast south and entered another bay. There was a small cove on the westerly side of the inlet to the bay, devoid of people. It was a sandy inlet, so John steered the boat to the beach in the cove. They both jumped out and pulled the RIB a short way up the beach.

'God, this is beautiful, John. Let me kiss you again. You have changed my life. I love you so much.'

They both collapsed in one another's arms onto the beach. They were in love.

'I love you, John.'

His hand behind her back deftly undid the clip to her bikini top, which fell away. They became intensely intimate.

'I love you, little one,' whispered John into her ear.

After a short while, they enjoyed one another in having even more sex. They ran naked into the sea with the exhilaration of being free like children playing in the sand. They put their swimmers back on and motored slowly back to *Brave Goose.*

'You know, darling, I would like to buy another little RIB so you and I can explore without denying *Brave Goose* use of the large RIB, which is needed for shopping and trips ashore for essential marine items. What do you think?'

'I think that would be fantastic, John, and we could sometimes take a picnic. We could take a little radio just in case we get stuck?' Fiona was excited at the prospect.

'Yes, that is a possibility. Let's chat with Noel and see what he has to say.'

'Could we store it on the boat deck? Would there be room?'

Back onboard *Brave Goose*, with smiles as broad as a Cheshire cat, they were invited to partake of Sally's excellent lemonade. As they sipped the thirst-quenching drink, Noel came to check everything was alright.

Sally was always dressed immaculately in either beige or navy-blue shorts. Beige today. She wore a blue or white polo shirt. She was a quiet girl. She would go about her many duties without any fuss or complaint. Her naturally blond hair had been cut short in a bob to make it easy to look after in the heat. There was always a smile on her lips. Her ability with first-aid didn't need any explanation, having dealt with numerous situations since John had bought the boat. Goose had been shot three times and Sally had always been there to administer to his needs. She had been on an advanced first-aid course which allowed her to carry oxygen, Entonox, antibiotics and certain drugs which would need injecting in the event of need. She never complained. She just got on with the many jobs on her list. John realised what an asset she was.

'Yes, Noel, we had a great time. The only thing was we felt we were potentially preventing you, Sally or others from going ashore for whatever reason.'

'Don't even think about it. We can always get stuff early or late. This is the Mediterranean. There are always supermarkets open.'

'Well, that's good, but Fiona and I wondered if there would be room on the boat deck for a smaller RIB we could use. We could go off on little expeditions, leaving you at anchor with transport available should you need it.'

'I am sure there will be room for a smaller RIB. I was hoping you were not going to mention getting a jet ski. They're dangerous and not practical. When we haul the RIB, would you like to inspect the remaining space with me, and we can decide what size of a boat could be accommodated.'

CHAPTER 9

Azmir returned to George's taverna on Kalamos, situated at the end of what had been a small square harbour. It used to accommodate a few private boats and several small fishing boats. It was a stop for the pass boat or ferry, which made regular daily journeys between Kalamos and Kastos islands and the mainland at Mitika. The island of Kalamos had a church and several small shops scattered on the side of the wooded hill, with a road that rose from the harbour side to the church and beyond. Over the years, 'George' had assisted the few boats that originally found their way to the harbour. The harbour had been extended about twenty years ago to twice its size. It now accommodated forty or fifty boats each evening during the sailing season between Easter and the end of September. George was quite an entrepreneur, extending his taverna to accommodate flotillas of yachts daily. He had foreseen the boom in yachting in the Ionian. He was right. Hundreds of boats were sailing this lovely area, with its turquoise sea, beautiful harbours and taverners. Just what the cruising yachts wanted. Staff had always been an issue for George. He would employ anyone who sailed in, looking for work, so long as they seemed honest and preferably able to speak English, some Greek and any other European language that would attract the crews of yachts.

Ulrika and Azmir fitted the bill. George had a few rooms he could let out to accommodate some of his staff. Stepping from the pass boat, Azmir saw Ulrika, his wife, waiting for him, hopefully with good news.

*

Ulrika was apprehensive when she saw Azmir walking down the quay from the pass boat. She threw her arms around him but was downcast when he said he had been unable to secure UK passports.

'Why, what have we done wrong to be treated like this?'

'The consulate said they were there to assist visitors from the UK; passports are an Embassy issue. I need to go to Athens. But, I did meet John England and his partner, Fiona. They bought me a beer in Corfu.'

'Oh, that's great,' Ulrika responded with an ironic smile. 'Perhaps John can help with the passport thing?'

'Don't know. He was very cagey but he may help. They have a boat and they're going to call into Kalamos during their holiday.'

'Let's hope they come. We can take them for dinner. I am sure John will help you if he can.'

Azmir wandered off to their one-room apartment provided by the generous George. He was worried that the season had only a month to go. He and Ulrika would have to leave then. Where would they go? They had no idea. There was no work available on Kalamos.

*

It was Friday, and it was time to go to Lefkas, advised Noel.

'Fiona, would you like to see where we are going?'

'Yes, I would.'

'So would I,' added John.

The location of Lefkas marina was in a pool created at the northern end of the Lefkas canal, a canal that the Romans initially constructed. It also gave access to the now unused large salt pans on either side of the channel. It obviated the need to circumnavigate the island, making the trip into the inland sea much shorter. Noel explained the route. It was straightforward from Gaios.

'You see, we have to go to the buoyed channel, and then we may have to wait until the swinging bridge opens. However, they may open the bridge especially for us, due to our size.'

At three in the afternoon, *Brave Goose* approached the Lefkas canal entrance. Noel navigated around the buoys at the end of the spit, indicating shallow water. As he approached, he called the swing-bridge operator on Channel 12 to request the bridge be opened.

Noel could see the operator in his little box perched on the edge of the bridge. He had his binoculars out, checking the size of the boat that had called.

'*Brave Goose*, please proceed slowly. I will open the bridge for you.'

The bridge operator realised that keeping *Brave Goose* in a holding position while the bridge was closed would be difficult. The size of the boat would create a blockage for smaller craft. Best to go against the established timings for bridge openings and let *Brave Goose* go through now.

The bridge operator did as promised. On the flybridge of *Brave Goose,* Noel, John and Fiona could see that the road traffic had stopped on both sides. Eventually, the bridge lifted the ramps on the causeway into Lefkas town, as well as on the mainland side. Then the whole structure began to swing. Noel had edged *Brave Goose* very slowly towards the bridge.

'The so-called 'bridge' is, in fact, a ship – a floating bridge,' explained Noel. 'It is moored on the mainland side, but not permanently. It is possible to uncouple the bridge from its moorings and remove it for maintenance. However, on this occasion, the car ramps will fold up, and the bridge will clear the channel, allowing *Brave Goose* to pass through.'

'That's fantastic, Noel, but why go to all the trouble of making a floating bridge – or ship, I should say?'

'There is a grant from the EU, I assume, for all islands. Lefkas, as an island, qualifies for the grant. They would lose it if the bridge were a permanent structure. That's the story I have heard, John.'

'Sounds feasible, Noel. Clever idea.'

There was plenty of room on either side as they went through the bridge ramparts, but it looked very close to the inexperienced eye. They all waved their thanks to the bridge operator.

Noel picked up the microphone for the ship's intercom system.

'Here this, we shall be in Lefkas shortly. I will need both anchors out at angles and then the stern lines. Please set fenders on both sides as we do not know where we will be placed.'

'Lefkas Marina, Lefkas Marina, this is *Brave Goose.* I have a mooring reserved for today. Over,' said Noel on the VHF.

'*Brave Goose*, this is Lefkas Marina. Your berth is stern-to on the concrete mole beyond the fuelling dock. You will need to deploy anchors. There will be two marineras on the quay to greet you. Over.'

'Lefkas Marina, this is *Brave Goose.* Understood, out.'

Noel manoeuvred her along the canal past the marina's outer pontoon, passing the fuelling dock. Two marineras were standing roughly halfway along the quay, waving their arms. There were three other large boats moored stern-to. Noel worked out that *Brave Goose* was longer than the others which pleased him.

'As we are longer than the boats already moored, I can set my anchors further out, and not tangle with them.'

Noel set the port anchor and then the starboard so that the chains formed a V shape when the boat was squared off to the quay. The stern heaving lines were passed to the marineras on the quay, who hauled the main lines, set them around the bollards, and threw them back. Jock and José pulled the end of the heaving lines until the main lines arrived on board, ready to be wound onto the stern capstans. They made up the lines until *Brave Goose* was the appropriate distance from the quay then moved back to the bow and tightened the anchor lines.

'Okay, Noel, we are moored.'

José rang the bell, then set the passerelle, the handrails, and the 'No Entry' notice advising visitors that it was private. CCTV cameras were established on the passerelle.

Noel made a detailed inspection of the mooring lines, anchors and fenders.

'Thanks, José and Jock, well done.'

Brave Goose was six to ten feet away from the nearest boats. Fenders were not required but were left in place in case there was bad weather.

'Well done, Noel, you've done this before!' smiled John.

'Thanks, John. Oh, I was looking at the space needed for your dinghy. I think a ten-foot RIB would fit nicely. There is room alongside the large RIB, and there will still be plenty of room for people to walk around. Do you want to have a look?'

John and Fiona went with Noel to inspect the space.

'Will the crane manage to pick it up from here?'

'Yes, Fiona, I am certain it will. The smaller boat will not be as heavy as this big RIB.'

'What space is there, Noel, if we see one?'

'I think a boat 3.5 meters long and no wider than 2 meters will be ideal.'

'Okay, thanks, Noel, we will look around.'

'Shall we go to the chandlers on the dock? They look quite a big outfit.'

'Sally, Fiona and I are off for a wander around.'

*

They came to the big chandlers called Paleros which had a few dinghies blown up outside, so the two went in to see what they could find.

The interior of the chandlers was an Aladdin's cave for any yachtsman. They seemed to have everything from anchors to paint, pictures to portholes. Nautical clothing caught the attention of Fiona. John approached the counter and addressed the mature gentleman who looked like he owned the place. It transpired he did.

'Good afternoon, sir. Can I help you?'

'Yes, my name is John England. We have just arrived on our motor yacht. My partner Fiona and I have decided we would like a second tender so we can explore, leaving the large RIB for the crew to use for supplies and so on. Do you have anything that would suit us?'

'We could have, sir. What size do you require?'

'Something no longer than 3.5 meters and no wider than 2 meters. Have you anything in stock?'

'Is the large blue superyacht yours?'

'Yes, she is,' John said with pride.

'I saw her come in. She looks like a beautiful boat.'

'She is.'

'Do you want a brand-new tender, or would you consider a second-hand one?'

'Don't mind, so long as the second-hand boat is in reasonable condition.'

'Yes, I fully understand that. I have a boat in the big shed which was taken in exchange for a new one of the same make but longer. It's a Williams Jet. Are you familiar with the marque?'

'No, I am not.'

'Let me show you. They are RIBs in the traditional style but have an inboard engine that drives a water jet. They are very safe, with no propellers to catch the unwary. They were designed as tenders for motor yachts, so this could be just the job.'

'Sorry, I didn't catch your name?'

'Robert. And you are?'

I am John, and this is Fiona, the joint owner of *Brave Goose*.'

While chatting, Robert had invited them to accompany him to the large shed beyond the quay where *Brave Goose* was moored. Robert certainly did have a 'large shed'.

'I have a new name for the tender when we find it,' said Fiona, smiling.

'Oh, that's forward-thinking, Fiona. What are you thinking?'

'*Gosling*.'

'Excellent!' said Robert. 'We don't see many goslings in Greece, but I am Dutch, so I am used to seeing them on the inland waters of the Netherlands.' He pulled open the massive door to the shed and removed the cover on a small boat, declaring that this was the Williams tender he had in mind. It measured 3.5 meters long and 1.8 meters wide.'

'Oh my goodness, that is just what we need. It looks in good condition, Robert. How old is it?'

'Six months old. I supplied it to the current owner for his superyacht in March. They decided in August they needed the larger version. They have just taken that one away, and we took it in part exchange.'

'Well, it looks brand new, Robert. How much is it?'

'New they are forty-five thousand. I only want forty-one thousand for it.'

'What do you think, Fiona?'

'I think it's excellent, John; better than an outboard motor.'

'I will say we will have it, subject to my skipper and engineer having a look, and us having a trial run in her. We shall also need chocks so she can sit securely on the boat deck. 'Oh yes, we will also need a VHF radio. Can you do all that?'

'The chocks are easy. We had to make new ones for the larger boat for the previous owner. Here are the chocks for this boat which you can have. We will just have to charge for fitting.'

'That's brilliant, Robert. Is the cover with the boat?'

'Yes, it is.'

'It's a deal, Robert. I cannot believe it was that easy. We only decided yesterday to buy another tender.'

'Well, if you had been here earlier in the week, the boat would not have been here. We only supplied the new boat on Wednesday.'

Robert, John and Fiona all shook hands. Robert said he would have the boat cleaned and ready for a trial in the morning any time after nine-thirty.

'Here is a brochure on the Williams range. See you in the morning.'

John and Fiona nearly skipped back to *Brave Goose* like a couple of children on their birthday.

'What a stroke of luck. That is terrific! We will have a great deal of fun with that.'

They couldn't wait to tell the others. Noel and Jock were delighted. Williams was a very well-thought-of make. John and Fiona would have a reliable and safe little boat to explore with. Everyone on board was thrilled that *Gosling* would join the ship.

John sat on the quarterdeck to read the brochure about the manufacture of *Gosling*. She was made in Britain and had a water jet power unit and an inboard petrol motor. She had white tubes in the same configuration as a RIB and grey highlights on the seats and tubes. There were twin seats to the front with two seats behind facing aft. The steering wheel had a hand throttle and engine and fuel level instruments. On the stern was a bathing ladder off the rear of the RIB. Fiona had a flip-through, looking at the pictures. Like a child on Christmas morning, she was thrilled to think they would have this little boat tomorrow.

Saturday morning was hectic. The men from the boatyard arrived at nine with *Gosling* on a trailer. John, Fiona, Noel and Jock were all crowded around while Sally and José observed from the quarterdeck.

'Shall we launch it now?' asked one of the red T-shirted men from the yard.

'Yes, but we'll need a strop to fit the crane to lift her on board and the chocks.'

'Don't worry, sir, all those items come with this boat. We took the chocks from the previous owner's boat, so we know they fit. The strop for lifting is also with the boat.'

'Can you let Jock look at the engine and water jet before launching?'

The senior red T-shirt explained all the workings to Jock. He pointed out that the water intake had a filter that had to be kept clean. Without a clean water supply, the jet would not work efficiently. He showed him the sea cock, which should be closed if towing the tender behind the motor yacht.

'If you don't close it, the boat will flood,' he said.

'I understand that, said Jock. 'Can the filter be accessed from inside the boat?'

'Yes, lift this locker and there is the filter. Close the sea cock here, and then the filter can be removed for cleaning.'

'That all looks very straightforward. I am sure I can keep that in full working order.'

'Okay,' said John. 'Let's get it in the water and go for a trip.'

Fiona, John and Noel got on board with the chief engineer in the red T-shirt. He turned the key to start the engine. It started the first time.

'First time starting is always a good sign,' John commented.

Gosling made stately progress down the canal with its load of four adults, speeding up once away from the marina. When the channel's last marker buoy was passed, he gave it some welly!

'Wow!' shrieked Fiona. 'This is fantastic!'

Gosling flew over the calm water, leaving a big groove and wash behind her.

'We could water-ski behind this,' remarked John.

'That assumes you can ski,' retorted Fiona.

'Cheek! I used to be good at it.'

Once back at *Brave Goose*, John and Fiona got out. Jock and José had anticipated the next move and had the crane ready. The wire was dangling just over the top of *Gosling*. The hoisting strop was attached to the manufacturers' special loops built into the hull of *Gosling*. *Gosling* was then allowed to float back to the bathing platform at the stern of *Brave Goose* so the occupants could get out. *Gosling* was then allowed to float back until she was under the crane. Then up she came.

Once on the boat deck dangling from the crane, two red T-shirts positioned the chocks so she would sit perfectly on them. They marked the location by checking with Noel. Once he was happy, *Gosling* was swung away so the engineers could secure the chocks to the deck.

Within two hours, *Gosling* was secure on her chocks and looked as if she had been on *Brave Goose* for years.

John and Fiona went to see Robert in the office and paid for *Gosling*.

'The cover wasn't in the boat so please can you arrange delivery of it as soon as possible, Robert? Also, no VHF is fitted.'

'My advice is that you buy a handheld VHF set. I will get the cover delivered.'

'Okay, can you sell me a handheld VHF set, preferably waterproof?'

'Yes, John, I have an excellent VHF handset here. It's waterproof and it's the model the professionals use.'

The radio was supplied in its box. John and Fiona were delighted with their morning's work. John realised that *Gosling* should have some lifejackets, which could be stored under one of the seats so four jackets were purchased.

'Before you go, having a small pack of emergency flares might be useful in case you are in trouble. VHF radios can run out of battery at the wrong moment.'

'Good idea, Robert.'

Flares were added to the pile of shopping.

'I feel like you look, Fiona, when you return from your shopping trips.'

'Cheek! At least this is all good advice.'

'Before we go, Robert, can your yard carry out a refit of the interior of *Brave Goose*?'

'Yes, we could. I would love to be considered to carry out the work for you. From the size of our main building, you can see that we can get her inside and work on her over winter.'

'Okay, Robert. We have some friends joining us tomorrow. When we come back in a week, can we meet up? I will create a schedule of work. You can look around, and before we go home in October, perhaps we can get a price?'

'Sounds like a plan, John. See you in a week?'

'Thanks, Robert,' they said in unison as they struggled out of the shop, then up the passerelle with the armfuls of their shopping.

CHAPTER 10

As a solicitor, it occurred to John that he had overlooked obtaining insurance for *Gosling*. It was not registered as a small ship under the Royal Yachting Association (RYA) scheme. He emailed Ian Birch, his insurance broker, requesting that he insure it immediately, ideally backdated to Saturday. John provided the details and the value.

Assuming the RYA would deal with the registration, John was surprised that it couldn't, as a government agency did this now. He was able to register *Gosling* online for £35 for five years. That wasn't going to break the bank. John crawled over and under the little boat to get the hull's registration and engine numbers for the form. Soon it was all done. Registration was complete. One step closer to complying with the rules.

'Fiona, do you want to go for a trip in *Gosling*?'

'Ooh! Yes, please, are we going now?'

'Yes, I will get one of the team to get her back into the water. I guess you will be changing?'

'Got it in one. I will be down shortly.'

Gosling was back in the water. John told Noel the VHF needed charging up. John said that in the meantime he should take the ship's mobile VHF set.

'No problem, John. If we get an incoming VHF call, I can use the boat's static radio. Also, we need to get *Gosling* a small red ensign to signify her country of registration. In the winter, we can get the yard to have the name sign written on the stern,' said Noel.

Fiona arrived in a new swimming costume, beach top, and baseball cap. She had brought John's Tilley hat. John had prepared the life jackets which they both put on before leaving the side of *Brave Goose.*

'We need to stop at the fuel dock. If this gauge shows the correct fuel level, we need more petrol.'

*

'I just need to come alongside for fuel,' John said to the attendant who was waiting for instructions.

'Hey, this isn't as easy as it looks.'

John threw the bowline to the man on the dock and then the stern line. He undid the fuel cap behind the driver's seat.

'We need about 40 litres of petrol. We've just purchased the boat, so I'm not sure how much she takes,' John advised the fuel pump attendant.

John paid for the fuel with his credit card.

'I guess the capacity of the tank is 50 litres, Fiona,' John commented, looking at the fuel gauge which showed 'full'.

John gently increased the speed by moving the throttle lever forward. The boat was creaming along even at ten knots, faster than *Brave Goose* cruised. Fiona was excited by the speed. They were still in the canal and John felt they shouldn't go any quicker.

'Go on, John, just a bit faster.'

As they reached the end of the canal, John was about to increase speed when Fiona alerted him to something in the water ahead.

'John, what is that in the water?' Fiona pointed a little to the right. There was a yellow shape. As they approached, they saw arms and a head.

'God, it's a child. I think they're floating in a buoyancy ring.'

John throttled back and came to a dead stop. As *Gosling* approached the person in the life-ring, it was instantly apparent the arms belonged to a little girl. Thanks to the water jet propulsion system, John was confident he couldn't hurt anyone in the water.

The little girl was in floods of tears and shivering. Despite the warm weather, exposure to water can cause hypothermia if the person is exposed to the water for a long time.

Fiona leant over the side to catch the girl's hands. She pulled the little girl into *Gosling*, sliding over the round tube of the hull like a young seal. She was crying. John leant over and collected the lifebuoy.

'Hello, don't cry. You are safe now. Why are you out here?'

'I fell off our boat. I don't think daddy could turn round.'

'I'm John, and this is Fiona. So, what is your name?'

'I'm Mel, Melanie. Everyone calls me Mel.'

'That is a pretty name, Mel. Which way did your mummy and daddy go in their boat? Does it have sails?'

'Yes, it has sails. That was the problem. Daddy put up the sails, the boat immediately leaned to one side, and I fell off. I screamed. Mummy said they would be back in a minute. Fortunately, she threw me the life ring.'

'Did they turn round, Mel, or are they up ahead?'

'They didn't turn round; I don't think Daddy knew how to do that.'

'Okay, let's see if we can catch them up.'

Mel, dressed only in a lightweight swimming costume, was still shivering. There was no blanket to warm her up. Her costume was soaking wet, as was her blond hair. She had beautiful pale blue eyes and a lovely smile, displayed now and again between bouts of shivering.

'Just a minute, John, let me put this lifejacket on Mel. Just in case she wants to repeat the falling-out manoeuvre. It will help her warm up.'

'Good idea, Fiona.'

John engaged nearly full speed once all the safety precautions had been taken.

'Whee, this is fun!' cried Mel, suddenly far more cheerful at the speed of *Gosling*. Fiona hoped John would slow down when they got to her parents' boat. Mel pointed out the family's yacht and they came alongside. Mel cried out to her parents.

'It's me! It's me! I'm safe!'

'Hi there, I'm John. We found Mel adrift in her lifebelt. We have brought her back to you.'

'Thank goodness for that!' said Mel's father. 'We chartered this boat but it will not turn round, and the sails won't come down.'

'Oh, I'm sorry I can't help you. Are you stuck?'

The father shouted that he was.

'The bloody thing will not turn around.'

'Would you like me to call for some help?'

'Yes, we are going to run out of sea soon.'

'Noel, it's John. We have rescued a little girl, and her parents have chartered a yacht they cannot sail. We are about a mile or so from the end of the canal. Can you please come out and bring José with you, and a beach towel? We need you to take over the yacht.'

'I'm on my way, John.'

About ten minutes later, the big RIB arrived. Noel jumped onto the yacht, leaving José in charge of the RIB. The beach towel was handed to Fiona, who wrapped it around the still-shivering Mel.

'May I help you, sir?' enquired Noel, now onboard the yacht.

'We can't turn the yacht around or get the sails down.'

'Okay, can you let the sheets go?'

'Sorry, mate, I have no idea what they are or what you want me to do.'

Noel realised this could be a disaster about to happen unless he took immediate control. *How did these people get to charter a yacht when they didn't know the first thing about it?* Noel said to himself. He set about bringing the thirty-five-foot yacht under control. Looking at the condition of the boat, it was pretty new. He eased the main and jib sheets. He furled the jib using the roller reefing. The in-mast reefing for the main was a similar system. He had the main folded away in no time.

'Now, let's start the engine.'

'How do you do that? It was explained to me once, but that was earlier. I don't recall the process.'

Noel decided it would be better to explain the process in the marina. It wasn't his job to train someone with no knowledge of boats. Noel had averted a disaster in minutes.

'Do you want to go back to the marina? Maybe get someone to come with you so you can learn the ropes, so to speak?'

'They wanted €400 for someone to be with us. It will take a lot of our spending money.'

'Well, not knowing what to do could have cost you far more than that.'

'Do you want to go with Mummy and Daddy, Mel?' enquired John.

'No, I am staying with my new best friends. I will see Mummy and Daddy at the harbour.'

Fiona grinned at the little girl's insightful remark.

Noel insisted on taking the yacht back into the marina. He explained to Mel's parents that she would be safe with John and Fiona. He turned the yacht around and took it back to the marina, mooring it with the other charter boats of the same company. Once tied up, a wooden plank was set on the stern to the pontoon so everyone could get off the yacht and onto dry land.

Mel was excited and wanted to stay with John and Fiona. José took the RIB around to the marina and back alongside *Brave Goose*. Noel and the parents descended from the yacht and walked to the charter company's office. John and Fiona motored *Gosling* to that part of the marina, where they both went on shore with Mel.

'I will take you to Mummy and Daddy, Mel, so you will all be back together again.'

Mel insisted she go with Fiona and John, returning to *Brave Goose* on *Gosling*. Mel was small enough to sit between them in the front seat of *Gosling*. When they arrived at the side of *Brave Goose*, the starboard passerelle and boarding platform had been lowered. Fiona and Mel boarded *Brave Goose*, followed by Mel's parents and Noel. José remained with *Gosling*, requesting Jock to assist in returning both RIBs to the boat deck by crane.

'Is this your boat, Fiona?' the little girl asked, incredulous.

'Yes, Mel, this boat belongs to John and me. Would you like to have a look around?'

'Yes, please,' retorted an excited Mel.

'How old are you, Mel?'

'I am eight.'

'You are a good swimmer. You managed to stay afloat with the life-ring. You were courageous.'

'Sally, do you think you could find some lemonade and biscuits – unless you prefer coffee or tea?' Fiona addressed Mel's parents. 'Sorry, I don't know your names?'

'Oh, yes, sure. Brian and Jill. We live in Liverpool. So, this is your boat, John and Fiona?'

'Yes. We'd just bought the little RIB and it was our first run-out. Fiona luckily spotted Mel. There are not so many boats about as the schools have gone back. All the families with children have gone home,' John said to Brian, embedding a question in his remark about schools.

'That is why we are here now, John. It's so much cheaper at this time of the year. We might get a fine for taking Mel off school. However, the penalty is much less than the extra cost of coming here during school holidays.'

Sally delivered her lemonade, biscuits, and two black coffees, a jug of milk and a bowl of sugar.

'So, what are your plans now, Brian?'

'Well, John, I will enquire if the charter company has a spare crew to help us so we don't get into a tangle again.'

'Good idea, Brian. These boats require training and experience to sail them.'

'Did the charter company ask about your sailing experience, Brian, when you booked?'

'Yes, they did. They said this area was ideal for those with little experience. The question asked if I could sail, so I ticked it. How hard can it be? No tides, light winds and sunshine?'

'Mm, well, you know a little more than you did. But having someone with you for a day or two is essential. How did little Mel fall off the boat?'

'She was sitting on the step at the back of the boat. It was all calm and gentle. I decided to put the sails up. I told everyone to hold on. Once the big sail went up, the boat leaned alarmingly to one side, and Mel fell off. Luckily, Jill spotted what had happened and threw out the lifebelt. I couldn't make the boat turn. I couldn't get the sails down. I don't know what we would have done if you hadn't turned up, John.'

'We weren't prepared for what happened. At least we had our life jackets on.'

'Yes, perhaps we should have worn ours, but it's hot, and we wanted to catch the rays.'

'Mum, Dad, this boat is fantastic. There are bedrooms and bathrooms! It's great. Can you get one like this, please, Daddy?'

'It would be too expensive for us, darling. You have to be a millionaire like John to own a boat like this.'

John smiled to himself. He went to the galley to speak with Sally.

Returning to the quarterdeck, John invited Mel and her family to stay for a barbecue lunch.

'Oh, say yes, Daddy, please?' demanded Mel.

John received unanimous approval for the idea.

'Shall we all walk around the marina so Sally and the crew can get organised for lunch? We might be able to meet the charter company to discuss the availability of a crew for you, maybe for a week? You know, Brian, if you have no idea how to sail, you're taking a huge risk. It is perilous. You will have no idea what to do in the event of an incident.'

'You're right, John. I have been on the canal in a boat but not proper sailing. The boat would not respond to my efforts to turn her around.'

The charter manager of the company gave Brian a mild rebuke.

'I will not permit you to leave the dock unless you have a competent person with you. I will get a team member to accompany you for the rest of the week. You will come back here at the end of the week, and subject to my staff's report, I will decide if you can take the boat out again. I hope you understand?'

'Yes, I do.'

'One more thing, Brian; everyone on board must wear a life jacket while you are at sea.'

Feeling suitably told off, Brian agreed and paid the excess fee for the extra crew member.

CHAPTER 11

Sunday morning broke with a cloudy sky. Could it possibly rain today? John and Fiona wore a sweater at breakfast on the quarterdeck.

'This is not what was ordered. The girls will not be happy with this weather. Why are we always obsessed with the weather? Here in Greece, it should be sunny nearly all the time.'

'It's forecast for rain later, then clearing. It should be good tomorrow, John,' said Noel.

'Let's hope so, Noel. Have you a plan for our travels next week?'

'No, John, I wasn't sure what you would like to do?'

'Noel, knowing the girls as I do, I think they would like sunbathing, swimming trips, beaches and food! If there are some shops nearby, that would be ideal.'

'So not long distances?'

'Correct. It might be good to go to a few islands. I will leave it up to you, Noel.'

'Fiona, remind me of the names of the girls and what they do for a job?'

'Yes, of course. Emily, the youngest, is a nursery nurse. Then Tracey is a travel agent. The third is Joy. She is a civil servant working in a branch of the Home Office in Manchester.'

'Interesting set of jobs. How did you meet them?'

'We met in a pub near the flats where we all live. Or should I say where I used to live until my prince charming arrived. Their flight is supposed to land in Preveza tomorrow at three in the afternoon.

Depending on the number of flights the airport is dealing with, they should be with us by four to four-thirty.'

'That sounds fine. Shall we eat out tonight, perhaps at the restaurant on the marina?'

'I'm getting cold out here, John. I think I will watch some TV in the saloon.'

She switched on BBC; the news was about to be broadcast.

'John, you must come and watch this. The main news item was about refugees escaping to Europe through Greece. They arrived from Iraq, Iran, Syria, and Afghanistan. The Greek residents of the island of Lesvos, the closest to Turkey, were fed up with rubber boats full of refugees landing on the beaches. Matters reached boiling point. There was a BBC reporter and cameraman on Lesvos. The report was gruesome. I've recorded it. Let me play it back to you.'

'A boat holding 49 people, including 18 children, has been attacked twice by a speed boat with black-masked men near the southern village of Mitilini on Lesvos, roughly ten miles from the coast of Turkey. With clear Greek Coast Guard signs on the side, the speed boat was harassing the overloaded rubber boat. The rubber boat's engine was put out of action, having been submerged by the wash from the Coast Guard boat. Shots were fired near the rubber boat. The Coast Guard boat crew attempted to puncture the rubber boat with hooks. It was a shameful scene. Children were screaming, and men and women were forced to row the boat using their hands. We could not film the end of this encounter as the police moved us on.

This is Tom Starling for the BBC News on Lesvos.'

'This is terrible, darling. Is there anything we can do to help?'

'Fiona, you are forever the good Samaritan. I don't see what we could do to help. It needs international condemnation and the EU to get member countries together to stop it.'

'Couldn't we provide support for these people?'

'Well, yes, but put fifty people on here? *Brave Goose* would be overloaded. The Greeks would turn us away at every port. It isn't a simple situation.'

'It's terrible; those poor people. This surely is criminal behaviour by the Greek Coast Guard?'

'Yes, I am sure you are correct. The BBC are the best people to help as their harrowing report will be seen in the EU, Brussels, and other places, including the Greek government.'

'Do you think so, John? It is appalling the way these immigrants are being treated.'

'I agree, Fiona, but we can do nothing. Well, I hope I might be able to help Azmir and his wife. I look forward to chatting with your friend Joy, who works in the Home Office.'

'You know, when she first said she worked in the home office, I thought she meant she was working from home!'

'You are a goon, Fiona Homes!'

'Noel, any idea what the forecast is for today and tomorrow?'

'Yes, John. The forecast is clear later today and fine and sunny tomorrow. That's from the Greek weather service for shipping. I record it daily as it is broadcast at six in the morning.'

'Thanks, Noel, that is helpful. Good idea to record it. It's too early to be up and about. You can always listen to it again if there is a bad forecast.'

*

It was hot when the sun was still blazing at four in the afternoon. A taxi with three pretty girls onboard appeared on the quay. They all spilled out of the cab, waving and shouting for Fiona, who raced down the passerelle to meet them.

'Hi, hun!' the girls chorused.

They all crowded around each other, oblivious to the taxi driver unloading their cases. José ushered them onboard and John paid for the taxi. He checked there was nothing left in the cab before it departed.

'Hello, girls; lovely to see you all again.'

'My word, is this your boat, John? It's the biggest in the harbour!'

'It might be. Are you Joy?'

'No, John, I'm Tracey. This is Joy.'

'Okay, I will get you all sorted out by tonight. Let's have a drink.'

The girls were in full conversation mode. Sally had made supper so everyone, including the crew, could get to know one another. John cancelled the booking at the restaurant.

The girls and Fiona assembled on the quarterdeck; Sally was on hand to deliver drinks. John wondered if he should get some ear defenders due to the constant chatter from the girls, full of joy and laughter. He was delighted Fiona had her friends around her. As the evening had turned out so pleasant, John decided to take himself off to wander around the extensive marina and look at the boats and whatever else the place offered. There was a watchtower in the central piazza of the marina, with the marina office on the first floor. He decided to go up and explore.

Opening the door to the open-plan office, he realised there were several individual offices and an open-plan general office. Two helpful young ladies staffed it. It soon became apparent to John that they were extremely efficient at dealing with VHF calls on the radio, mainly boats asking if there was a berth for the night.

'My, you two are busy!'

'Yes, it's a busy time as yachts come through the canal and decide to stop for the night. Do you have a boat with us, sir? How can we help you?'

'My boat is *Brave Goose*, on the quay behind the fuel dock. I wondered if you had a berth I could rent for a few years?'

'We do, sir. It would probably be where you are now. It would help if you spoke with the port captain, who will be here in the morning from eight o'clock.'

'Okay, I think I may leave the boat here when we leave in October, as I think I will get Paleros to do the refit.'

'We don't usually charge when a boat is out of the water and undergoing work with one of the yards on the marina. However, there may be a charge for storage on land when they finish until you want the boat putting back in the water.

'That sounds a reasonable arrangement. We will leave tomorrow because my partner has three girlfriends onboard, so we shall be sailing around the area for a week.

'I can ask the captain to call on you, sir, if you wish. Would nine o'clock be acceptable?'

'Thank you. I look forward to speaking with him.'

John had a marvellous view of the marina while in the office. He saw an area at the back, full of shops and businesses that serviced the boats in the marina. He decided to head over in that direction.

CHAPTER 12

The football was showing at the first bar he came to, so he found a place away from the TV set, sat down, and ordered a beer, which arrived with complimentary nuts. *Always a nice touch*, John said to himself. Two Englishmen were sitting nearby, chatting. It was Tony and Bill – again! John shook hands with them.

'I see you've avoided the TV?' Bill said.

'Yes, I don't mind football, but on my terms. I don't like to have a quiet beer with the background of foreign commentary I don't understand. Is that why you are on this side of the bar? I could see you were deep in conversation, so I decided to sit here.

'What do you two do here, then?'

'We work together. It's a long time since we were all at Oxford together. Are you pleased with your fantastic boat, John?

'Yes, I am. As you saw, it's a motor boat. Much easier – not like you clever people, sailing.'

'We often wish we had a bigger engine when there's no wind.'

'Does that happen often?'

'Yes, the Greek summer weather is known for calm mornings, windy afternoons and calm evenings and nights.'

'That must be very convenient, Bill.'

'Yes, it is. We jointly own the yacht. This marina is its home. We are here to clean and tidy her as it's the end of our sailing for this year.'

'It is a beautiful place to be. I would invite you to come on board for a drink, but my partner has invited her three girlfriends who will monopolise the place. I will be back here in a week. You are welcome to come on board, at least for a drink if you are still here.'

'Thanks, John, we shall be here. We have a few chores to complete but we will accept your kind offer.'

'Okay, look out for the blue motor boat: *Brave Goose*. We are moored on the fuelling quay.'

'Thanks, John. I recall seeing your boat in Corfu. It's a super yacht, not a motor boat. You are seriously underselling her.'

'I don't want to appear fustian speaking about my boat.'

'Fair enough. How are sailing conditions here in general?'

'Well, John, sometimes the wind forgets to blow or blows too strongly. In those cases, getting to a sheltered mooring or harbour is wise. There are very few marinas in Greece.'

'I believe so, Tony. I think we will be unable to get into many harbours.'

'How big is your boat, John?'

'Too big for me to handle. She is lovely, but I need a crew with her length of thirty meters. I have four wonderful people who keep the ship going.'

'I think we are in a different league to you,' said Bill enviously, realising they were talking to their old university colleague who had done well for himself.

John smiled.

'What did you do, John, to be able to afford your ship?'

'I'm a solicitor. Depending on how you look at it, I have been very unfortunate or fortunate.

'How's that?' enquired Tony.

'My wife's family owned a very successful business – building and development. A series of misfortunes, accidents, and three murders meant all the money trickled down through the family until it landed in my wife's account. She and my children were killed in an extraordinary accident two years ago. So, my recent history has been filled with sadness. *Brave Goose* helps a bit.'

'Oh dear, I am sorry, John. I hadn't meant to pry. You would rather have a wife and children than the boat.'

'Don't worry. I am over the worst now. I had a client I managed to get acquitted in a court case, and we struck up a friendship. We're now in a relationship. Three of her friends have just joined us on the boat this afternoon. Are you alone, or do you have partners on your boat?'

'We would normally have our wives with us, John. They are back in England looking after relatives. We have come out to tidy the boat and put her away, so to speak.'

'John, it was odd, but Bill and I were not friends at Oxford. We were brought together by the Security Services, who asked us what we intended to do next, and if we would like to go for an interview. Independent of one another, we thought there could be no harm in it, so we met at the round-robin series of interviews and tests. It seemed at the time to take ages, but we were both successful.'

Bill carried on the story, which included their success with languages.

'We ended up working for MI6.'

'Sounds like university stood you both in good stead. How long have you been with MI6?'

'Twenty years or so now, John. The fantastic thing is that we both love sailing and so do our wives. As we are currently on missions involving Mediterranean countries, the yacht provides excellent accommodation and a reason for being somewhere. Our bosses like it a lot,' Tony explained.

'I can see that. So, are you involved in a case in Greece?'

'We might be,' said Bill, 'but that is as much as we can tell you.'

'You both must come for that drink when we return in a week.

Look, chaps, I must make tracks back to my *motor boat*,' said John with a smile.

'John, one more thing – what is your planned route from here?'

'Well, after a week cruising around the Ionian, we will eventually end up in Athens.'

'Ah, well, we could do with having a chat with you. We will still be here in Lefkas when you get back next week. Perhaps we can have a chat then.'

'Yes, certainly; you intrigue me. Is there anything I should be aware of in the immediate future?'

The two men shook their heads as John rose from the taverna table, leaving a five euro note for the three-euro beer.

*

'He must have done well for himself, Bill,' Tony commented as soon as John was out of earshot. 'It will be fascinating to have a look around his boat.'

'You are at it now, Tony, underselling the *superyacht*'. They both laughed, paid their drinks bill and moved off in the opposite direction to John.

*

Onboard *Brave Goose*, the girls were enjoying the last of the sun's rays on the flybridge.

Sally was hovering around the dining table.

'Sally, are we in your way? I guess you want to lay the table?'

Sally smiled, but John got the message.

'Look, girls, let me give you a quick tour. We are in Sally's way.

John gave the three friends a tour of the boat. The engine room was not the highlight as far as they were concerned. They thanked John and told him they were looking forward to their cruise.

*

The following morning as people began to emerge, some later than others, the previous night of merrymaking had taken its toll.

'What we need now is a swim,' announced Fiona. 'Is there a bay we could go to, Noel? Preferably with a beach, where we could all go and swim and chill out?'

'There is Fiona. I know just the place. Ormos Varko is just around the corner once we get out of the canal. Shall we go?'

'Ooh, yes, please.'

''The man approaching us now is the captain of the marina. I need to have a chat with him first,' said John. 'Why don't you girls catch some rays on the boat deck? I won't be long.'

John and the captain had a very fruitful discussion. John asked him to provide a three-year costing for mooring to be paid in advance. John agreed they would meet when *Brave Goose* returned a week after completing their little cruise.

Noel was on the ship's intercom, advising the crew what would happen.

'We will be anchoring until mid-afternoon in Ormos Varko. We're leaving in twenty minutes.'

Brave Goose left her berth at Lefkas Marina at ten in the morning.

As they started their journey, Fiona explained to the girls that they were sailing down a canal. On either side were the disused salt pans, where salt was extracted from the sea in Roman times. They let seawater into the lagoons, the sun evaporated the water, and the salt remained and was then collected. The men who scooped up the salt were paid in salt. The origination of the word 'salary'. The salt pans were enormous. Hugh quantities of salt would be made available to the Romans.

John was relaxing in his chair on the quarter deck. Tony and Bill had offered him a sail, but despite being on holiday, time prevented it. *Pity*, he muttered to himself. He thought he would enjoy finding out how to sail. Once *Brave Goose* was in the bay of Varko, famous for the oak tree at the centre of the arc of the beach, the water was turquoise and flat, completely calm. They anchored *Brave Goose* in ten meters of water. Most of the other boats at anchor were mainly yachts, midway between the beach and *Brave Goose's* location.

Noel had arranged for *Gosling* to be launched. Fiona and the girls zoomed off to the beach, leaving John and the crew on board. Jock and José launched the big RIB as it was required at the following mooring location. Noel had arranged a mooring in the Vathi harbour entrance on Ionia Island.

CHAPTER 13

'Is everything in order, Noel?' enquired John.

'It is, John. May I ask you a personal question? Please don't think me impertinent, but I have been wondering what you have done in your life to be able to amass what appears to be a considerable fortune?'

'Sit down, Noel. I owe you this if nothing else. Shall we have a coffee?'

'That would be good, John.'

John returned to his chair on the quarter-deck without any coffee. Shortly after he sat down without giving Noel an explanation for the missing coffee, Sally appeared with a tray bearing cups and a jug of coffee, cream, a bowl of sugar, and a plate full of biscuits.

'I was about to make the coffee when Sally appeared and chastised me for making coffee! When I explained, she asked if she could listen to the story. So here we are. What a beautiful spot. I bet those girls will be on the beach for ages. I will give you as much of the story as possible before the girls return. My story is not confidential, but I am not habitually trotting it out to anyone. As you have been involved far more than anyone else this year in the recovery of money by the Irish connection, you at least deserve an explanation.'

'Thank you, John. I hope it won't be too painful. Do you mind if Jock and José listen as well?'

'No, Sally, it's life and in the past. I will reflect on many deaths. I have never counted how many. The story is one of unexpected death. I need to reflect on them all.'

'Sounds very intriguing, John.'

At that moment, Fiona walked onto the quarter-deck and enquired as to the purpose of the meeting. John explained he was going to tell them how he had managed to amass his money and whatever else that cropped up.

'It sounds like I should be part of this, simply to listen; you do owe me an explanation about your past, don't you, John?'

'Of course, darling, you are most welcome. I didn't hear you come back.'

'No, I wanted to use the loo. I am due back to collect the girls shortly.'

'Coffee or tea, Fiona?' enquired Sally.

'Coffee, please, Sally.'

Once the six of them were fully ready, John commenced the potted history of his recent life.

'It may, in retrospect, sound intriguing, but my thoughts are very mixed. Extreme happiness and sadness are all intertwined. Families can be complex, especially when there are numerous siblings and a family business with significant sums of money generated, and directors and other business operators who are not family, all of which can lead to turmoil. Then, due to unforeseen circumstances in the economy, all plans can be interrupted without an obvious way out of the situation. I will let you decide when you have heard the story. I doubt I will do justice to the whole story before the girls are collected from the beach for lunch. We can always carry on later from where I leave off.'

'Okay, John, we are all ears.'

Noel, Sally and Fiona sat close to John around the table. John was sitting in his favourite wicker armchair, which Goose had favoured. His audience was keen to hear the story of how he achieved his wealth.

'It all started for me on 4th January 2000. Most people were still celebrating or recovering from monumental hangovers. The celebration of letting in a new millennium was exceptional indeed. As the new junior partner solicitor at Bennett and Bennett solicitors in Chester, I had drawn the short straw to be on duty in the office in case of emergencies.

The other issue I needed to deal with was ensuring the computer system was working correctly. As most computers worked on the last two digits of the current year, there was a genuine concern that the computers would not work with zero- zero. In the year two thousand with one number, two and three zeros, there was a fear that computers in all walks of life might not work at the stroke of midnight as the new millennium dawned. It is hard to appreciate now, but computer engineers who had developed ever more complex machines had given little or no thought to what might happen when the year two thousand arrived. Computer engineers were making a fortune out of preparing computers for the millennium. Airlines stopped flying over the change of date because of the real fear aircraft would drop out of the sky. Trains, traffic signals, hospital operations, and numerous other activities were curtailed until the computers were shown to work correctly on and after New Year's Day.

Solicitors' offices and every machine used in commerce or the professions needed to work without a hitch after the New Year holiday. I was the youngest member of the firm, so I was tasked with ensuring the computer system was working correctly. In Bennett's office, the computer system checked out just fine. I decided to catch up on some work I had left unfinished before the holiday. Donna, our receptionist, had volunteered to keep me company for the half-day we were open. Late morning, Donna buzzed me to say there was a call for me.

Once the call was put through, I discovered Sandra Wall was on the phone. I had forgotten that I had dealings with her sister Sienna, a surveyor acting for the vendors of a property one of my clients was purchasing. However, property dealing was not what the call was about. Sandra and the Wall family were distraught: Peter Wall, the founder of Walls' Civil Engineers, Sandra and Sienna's father and the husband of Ann, had apparently committed suicide on New Year's Day.

The suicide was most unusual. Peter had taken the old Land Rover, which was used as a runabout on the farm. It was called 'Jumbo'. There were no roofs or side windows on this Land Rover. All these had been removed to enable ease of use of the vehicle. It appeared that Peter had driven Jumbo to the top of the sloping meadow known as Long Meadow early on New Year's Day. He had untied the cable from the winch at the front of the vehicle, tied one end around the old oak tree at the top of the rise, and made a noose at the other end. Peter then placed the noose around his neck. Sitting in the driver's seat, he set Jumbo to drive down the hill with a hand throttle. The cable at some point became tight and decapitated him. At the bottom of the hill, Jumbo became impaled in the gate post at the entrance to the field.

Ann Wall eventually found Peter, or what was left of him. She was distraught and hysterical, as you could imagine. She called the girls who had spent the night living it up in Chester. When they arrived home, the police, who had been called by Ann, were everywhere around the farm, and an officer positioned at the gate. Eventually, Peter's body was removed for forensic investigations, and the Land Rover was taken for investigation.

Three days later, despite Sandra being a solicitor, she had decided that she didn't want to have the family affairs dealt with by a firm of commercial lawyers in Liverpool. She asked if I would handle the legal matters in dealing with the estate of Peter Wall. I agreed.

So, I turned up at Long Meadow Farm. It had a very noisy cattle grid at the entrance to the farmyard, so no doorbell was required as everyone knew when someone had arrived.

Long Meadow Farm had been bought by Peter and Ann Wall when it was a wreck. He used his company, which was a construction business, to modernise and refurbish the farm. He also converted the space over some of the barns into two flats for the Wall sisters. I was asked to help with arrangements for the funeral of Peter Wall and subsequently deal with a grant of probate and other financial matters. The Walls' family firm became quite an issue. The other shareholder and Peter's business partner was a man called Roger Whiteside. He had started the firm with Peter. He was the office-based organiser of all their projects while Peter was the salesman who got the jobs. Whiteside was a strange man, not easy to comprehend. When Peter died, Whiteside was skiing in Switzerland for the New Year's holiday.

For the previous two years, myself and several friends from the Chester area had gone skiing in Switzerland for a week. By coincidence, that year Roger Whiteside was staying at the same hotel we would be going to in February.

Over the next six weeks, I was hardly away from Long Meadow and the Walls. I became very fond of Sienna. She was attracted to me and I invited her on the skiing trip with the rest of my friends.

A further tragedy occurred when Fred Appleyard, the Walls' long-term retainer who looked after the farm gardens, yard and fences, was knocked off his bike by a car near the farm and died. It was a gruesome affair. The vehicle made sure Fred was dead – it reversed over the body again.

I was so busy sorting out Peter's affairs that I didn't get involved with the Fred episode.

Sienna told me that Fred had confided in her before his death that he was confident he saw Roger Whiteside drive out of the farm in the morning on New Year's Day – the day Peter Wall committed suicide. It eventually transpired that Roger Whiteside was the culprit.

Ann Wall, the matriarch of the Wall family, was a delightful lady. I had a great affection for her. She was very upset about Fred.

I was keen to pursue my friendship with Sienna. She joined me and others on the skiing trip to Switzerland. That trip cemented our relationship. Sienna discovered in conversation with the receptionist in the hotel that Whiteside had *not* been at the hotel's New Year's Eve party, despite having told her he had been there celebrating with friends.

At Manchester Airport, Sienna spotted daily flights to and from

Zurich on the indicator boards. It could have been possible for Whiteside to come to England, kill Peter Wall, and fly back to Switzerland. This information was passed to the police. On further detailed forensic examination, they confirmed Whiteside's DNA had been found on the cable leading from Jumbo that decapitated Peter Wall. Cheshire police issued a warrant for the arrest of Whiteside.

Frank Stringer, the family doctor, had been incredible throughout all these events. He was a personal friend of Peter's and the family. Unknown to everyone, he had leukaemia and didn't have long to live. He was furious when he heard that it had been established Whiteside was the killer of his great friend, Peter. It was also discovered that Whiteside was the car driver that had killed Fred. Frank decided to take things into his own hands. Whiteside was hiding in Chester but needed to return from time to time to his flat which had been kept under guard by the police until they realised it was a futile exercise as Whiteside had never returned.

Frank Stringer thought he knew Whiteside's route to get to his flat. Through Grosvenor Park, then along the riverside path, crossing the River Dee over the pedestrian suspension bridge and down the footpath on the opposite side. Frank followed him one evening and, once Whiteside was on the bridge, Frank hit him with his old police truncheon. He then tipped Whiteside over the edge of the bridge and he drowned. Frank was convicted of Whiteside's murder and died in prison of leukaemia. But before his death he was permitted to give Sienna away as her godfather on our wedding day to John England – me!'

'John, I must go and get the girls,' José said as she made off to get into *Gosling*.

'Okay, remind me where I was up to when I resume my tale.'

*

'Oh darling, we have had such fun!' said Fiona as she dripped water over the deck on her way to hug and kiss John. The other girls followed her.

'I am delighted you had a great time. Did *Gosling* work well?'

'Yes, perfectly, but she wanted to return to the sea. We had her on the shore, but we had to keep pulling her back up onto the beach. We couldn't get her too far as she is quite heavy.'

'I will arrange for a small anchor and warp so you can anchor her on or near the beach, and she won't float away,' advised Noel.

'That would be good, Noel. Girls, before you come onto the quarter-deck, please hose off your feet and legs on the platform at the bottom of the steps or the swimming deck,' said John.

'Oh, John, isn't that a bit hard?'

'No, darling, saltwater and sand are a pain on the deck. When saltwater dries, it leaves white marks all over the deck, which then need cleaning. It doesn't take a minute and saves a lot of work.'

'Aye, aye, captain, message understood.'

'Lunch will be served here in about twenty minutes,' advised Sally.

John retired to his office to check there was no email he needed to attend to. There was an unexpected email from Brandon Phelan. John had hoped he had heard the last of this man.

Mr England,

When you paid back the three million pounds Michael Fitzallen had lent to your sister-in-law, you only repaid two million eight hundred thousand pounds. The basis of this underpayment was that you returned the two hundred to re-pay the retired customers of Georgio, the financier in Manchester. You suggested I recover the two hundred thousand directly from Georgio. He has refused. He said you had no right to pay his customers back.

Please complete your obligation and pay me the two hundred thousand pounds this week. I know where you are, and I have many friends to assist me.

Brandon Phelan.

John was furious. He penned a response simply saying: '*Never*'. He then went to join the others for lunch; Fiona could tell something was wrong, but she knew enough about John not to embarrass him in front of the others. She was dying to know what the problem was.

When lunch was over and two bottles of rosé wine consumed, the three girls took themselves to the boat deck to sunbathe and snooze.

'What's the matter, darling?' Fiona enquired.

'You will not believe it, but you will recall that I paid £2.8m to Brandon, telling him to collect the shortfall of £200,000 from Georgio, who had pinched that money from pensioners. As I said, I returned to the pensioners the money I had retained. Brandon has now emailed me saying Georgio says I had no right to interfere and I should pay the balance of the money.'

'Are you going to pay him, John?'

'I am not. Georgio swindled those pensioners out of their life savings. He had no right to do what he was doing. He's not registered anywhere as a money broker. He's a fraudster.'

'Could this cause more trouble, John?'

'I hope not. I guess they will go away. What legal case can they bring to support their claim?'

'I wasn't thinking legal I was thinking kidnap and guns.'

'Don't you worry your pretty little head over this.'

'It's my little head that has been the subject of attack. I am worried, John. These people seem to have contacts all over the place!'

'If it gets serious, I will get the Greek authorities involved. You go and join your friends. I am going to have a nap.'

CHAPTER 14

'What time do you want to head to our mooring for the night, Noel?'

'It's not far to go, John. Probably around four this afternoon.'

'That will be fine. I am off to my office. I have some work to do.'

John decided to email his great friend Jon in the Greater Manchester Police Force (GMP) to identify a Greek police force or department that might be able to help them out. John explained that the money paid out to Brandon Phelan was two hundred thousand pounds short and the reason why.

'Jon, I am attaching a copy of Phelan's email. As a lawyer, I see the last sentence as blackmail – demanding money with menaces. I seem to recall that has been an illegal act on the statute book since Victorian times.'

John had looked up the Greek Special Police Force on Wikipedia who worked with the Hellenic Coast Guard. That made sense to him as Greece is a country of hundreds of islands. The force was called EKAM – a specialist anti-terrorist unit.

'Jon, I wondered if you could discover the person I should speak with to obtain assistance should *Brave Goose* or any of her crew or guests be the subject of an attack?'

'Yes, John, I will get approval from the powers that be to speak with the Greek police. I will also consider the issue you raise about Phelan's email.'

'Thanks, Jon. Because of our recent experiences in Spain, I am concerned by this recent email. It's not a fortune, but any mafia-style organisation would seek more money to pay for their activities.'

'I understand, John. Leave it with me. I will be back as soon as I can. Good luck.'

*

José and Jock got ready to leave. Jock was hoisting the side boarding steps and platform while José prepared to weigh the anchor. *Brave Goose* moved slowly over the anchor chain to reduce pressure on the winch. The automatic chain-wash operated, cleaning the chain as it was hauled in. José rang the bell on a stainless steel loop over the anchor winch area. Ringing the bell once was the signal that the anchor was up, while two bells sounded on deploying the anchor. *Brave Goose* now moved slowly and turned around to face the opposite way so she could travel back south towards the island of Ionia.

'What was the bell for Fiona?' enquired Joy.

'Oh, it's a signal from José on the foredeck to indicate the anchor is up.'

'Where are we going next?'

'We will be mooring in a bay on Ionia. I guess we shall all be going on shore for dinner.'

'That sounds like fun.' Joy seemed delighted at the change of mooring.

According to the pilot book, *Brave Goose* had ample space to anchor in Vathi. The harbour in the new marina would not be used by *Brave Goose* as she would block the entrance to the port so an anchorage before the breakwater to the marina was the preferred location.

Noel was watching the instruments. The radar ensured he was far enough from the shore. The depth sounder would reassure him that there was sufficient water to anchor. He could also check the chain required to hold *Brave Goose* fast in a depth of twenty meters.

'José , fifty meters, please?' Noel announced through the intercom. José gave him the thumbs up.

Eventually, *Brave Goose* came to her anchor and sat comfortably still, having already established the anchor had bitten. Two bells sounded. José didn't need to ask. He raised the black anchor ball, an indication to all other vessels that she was anchored. The engines were stopped but one of the generators remained running.

The RIB had remained afloat and was towed by *Brave Goose* to their new anchorage.

'Can we go onshore, John?' enquired Fiona excitedly.

'Darling, this is as much your boat as mine. So, if you and the girls want to go ashore, why not ask José to take you or, preferably, launch *Gosling*? Then you will be self-sufficient. Take the mobile so you can call if you need us. While you are onshore, can you choose a restaurant for this evening? Let's aim for eight-thirty to nine o'clock.'

'Great. Will you join us, John?'

'No, I have a few things to deal with here. Make sure you have some money, as there are quite a few shops along the front. I like the look of the taverna with the green canopy but I will leave it up to you. Noel, please let me know when you hear the girls returning. I will be working in my office.'

There was nothing from Jon Kim. The reminder to pay up was still there from Brandon Phelan.

John decided to ignore the threat.

*

Nikos, the son of the owner of the taverna with the green awning, was delighted to book a table for five people at eight-thirty.

'Please have a drink with me on the house now!'

'Ooh, yes, please!' went up the cry from the four girls.

Nikos brought a small metal carafe of white wine and four small glasses like small tumblers. He filled each glass.

'Yamas,' he said. 'We look forward to seeing you tonight. Which is your boat?' He'd assumed the girls were off one of the yachts moored on the town quay.

'Our boat is hard to see from here, Nikos. It's a big motor yacht with a blue hull.'

'Wow, that's what I call a boat. I saw it coming in. I have some lobster tonight. Would that be welcome?'

'Yes, please!' was the unanimous response. Nikos grinned and went to tell his mother. She was in the kitchen, separated from the restaurant area by the narrow harbour road, the original road that had to be crossed to get to the kitchen. Many restaurants were separated from the kitchen by a road. Some streets were bustling but this little road saw very little traffic.

While Nikos was gone, a man who'd been sitting on his own at a table overlooking the harbour with a glass of beer came across to speak to the girls.

'I will see you all later tonight. I am Yannis. I, too, am eating here. Excellent food. Good choice. What are your names?'

Fiona announced her name and the other three went around the table: Joy, Tracey and Emily.

'Lovely! See you later, girls. I'll pay for my beer tonight.'

*

'Oh, Yannis has gone. He didn't pay for his beer,' said Nikos when he returned.

'He said he would pay for it when he comes to eat here tonight,' said, Fiona.

Nikos was hesitant to accept the promise: Yannis had never eaten here before.

*

'Aleksandre, it's Yannis. The target will be eating at Nikos's Taverna after eight-thirty this evening. It will be necessary to get her off the island quickly. You will need some troops.'

'Okay, Yannis, I will get organised.'

'I assume you have her mobile. When you are organised with your escape arrangements, text her about when she will join you on the road at the rear of the restaurant.'

*

Fiona and her friends had drunk all the wine Nikos had given them. They were giggling, their shopping bags in tow as they walked the short distance to the area of the dock where they had left *Gosling*.

Nikos came to say goodbye. He held the painter as the girls got into the little boat. Once Fiona had started the engine, it was ready to go. He let the line fall back into the boat.

'See you later!' They all waved at Nikos as they left.

'He's a smooth character,' said Tracey, 'and handsome.'

Back at *Brave Goose*, the peace was shattered by a cacophony of chatter from the four girls; Noel didn't need to advise John they were back. It was obvious. John was regaled by the story of the taverna, the shopping trophies, the wine, and what a wonderful little place it was.

Amid the excitement, John's mobile rang.

'Jon, any luck?' he asked, walking back to his office.

'Yes, I think so, John. I have asked someone from EKAM to phone you. They are the anti-terrorist special unit of the Hellenic Police. They deal with piracy, hostage-taking, VIP escorts, etcetera. It is very similar to the GEO in Spain. I don't know the name of the man who will phone you, but I have asked that an English-speaking person should make the call.'

'Jon, that is fantastic. Thank you so much.'

'I have arranged to take a constable with me to interview Brendon. Of course, you are correct that the 'demanding money with menaces' crime is still on the statute books; dating, as you correctly stated, from Victorian times. I will let you know how I get on.'

Fiona, the girls, and John chatted about the shops, the taverna for dinner and Nikos. Then John's mobile rang.

'I need to take this call. I'm going to my office.'

'Whoever heard of an office on a boat!' remarked Tracey. They all giggled again.

'John England speaking.'

'Mr England, my name is Miron. I am a commandant in EKAM based in Athens. How can we help you?'

'It is rather a long story, so bear with me.'

'That's okay, sir. We should know the full facts.'

John spelt out the latest strand of the story. The two hundred thousand had now increased to a quarter of a million. Based on the previous attacks in Spain, John was confident that a further attempt at kidnap to recover this additional amount was likely to occur.

'Where are you now, sir?'

'We have just moored in the bay outside the marina at Vathi, on the island of Ionia.'

'Yes, I know the location. It is some distance from our base. I would be happier if you were not in Vathi. However, I know arrangements will have been made. I will get a couple of officers from the local police in Nidri to come over on the ferry. Not sure about the time of the last one. Let's hope they can get to the island this evening. They will patrol the area where you will be dining. Tomorrow we should try and meet somewhere.'

'You sound pretty concerned about Vathi, Miron. Are the officers necessary?'

'A Russian property company owns half the island of Ionia. They purchased the land a few years ago when Greece had severe financial difficulties, greater than they are now. It seemed sensible to raise much-needed cash to sell unwanted islands or parts of them. We have had some issues with the Russian purchasers. They seem to think they are not subject to Greek law. All the difficulties have been handled well by the Nidri police. Let me go now. I will ring you again to advise you on the arrangements I make.'

John joined the others. Fiona could tell by the look on John's face there was something going on.

CHAPTER 15

Miron was as good as his word. He spoke with the police officer in charge at Nidri. Miron was satisfied that there was a credible threat against John England, his guests and the crew aboard *Brave Goose.* There was a degree of reluctance by the police in Nidri to jump to it and rush out to Vathi but they would see what they could organise. The officer promised to call Miron back with the plan.

The girls and John all went to shower and change for their night out. No one other than John knew the potential problems that could lie ahead. Once in their cabin, Fiona was keen to understand what was happening.

'So, what is the problem, John?'

'Brandon Phelan is demanding a quarter of a million pounds payment in league with Georgio because I paid two hundred thousand less than the three million to the pensioners who had their pensions stolen by Georgio. I told Brandon to get the money from Georgio. He says he hasn't any money. There's an extra fifty thousand for the cost of the troops to kidnap and extort money from me. Some of the money will go to Georgio, I assume.'

'Oh no. Here we go again. What are we going to do?'

'I have spoken to the Greek special services group EKAM. They are, of course, in Athens. They hope to get a couple of police officers onshore in Vathi tonight. Did you meet anyone when you went ashore?'

'Just a lovely man who was drinking a beer. He said he would see us all later.'

'Did he have a name?'

'Yes, he said he was Yannis.'

'Okay. I expect a call back from EKAM to tell me what they have managed to arrange.'

Once showered and changed, all the girls dried their hair with hair dryers on full power. Jock was keeping an eye on the electrical demand – the generator was at full stretch. At one point, he started the second generator to avoid burnout. The crew were due to join John and Fiona on the quarter-deck. John had decided not to tell Noel about the potential issues ahead. He asked Sally to organise a bottle of prosecco and some glasses for pre-dinner drinks.

Sally was already ahead of the request. Bowls of nuts and crisps had been placed on the table with five champagne flutes. As soon as everyone was gathered, Sally produced a cold bottle of prosecco and John poured out the drinks. His mobile rang as he was about to put his glass to his lips. Without explanation, he returned to his office.

'Hi Miron, what news?'

'John, two police officers are on their way to Vathi. They will be armed, and they will be patrolling the port area.'

'Thanks, Miron, that is excellent news. It is reassuring you have some cover for us. We are due in Athens in about a week or so. I'll call you when we get there. I can add a name of a local who has already made contact with my partner and her friends who went ashore earlier. They chatted with a man drinking beer in Nickos's Taverna whose name was Yannis.'

'Oh, how did this meeting take place?

'The four went ashore and chose a taverna for dinner tonight. This Yannis chap approached them and said he looked forward to meeting them again tonight! He left without paying.'

'That's helpful, sir. The trouble is that thousands of people are called Yannis in that area.'

*

John and his brood took the RIB, skippered by Jose, to the shore. They all arrived at Nikos's Taverna at the appointed hour. As John left the RIB, José passed him the handheld VHF radio.

'If you have any problems, sir, or when you want collecting, call me.

The welcome they received from Nikos could not have been more friendly. It was as if they were regular customers in his taverna. Before discussing their menu choices, carafes of red and white wine arrived.

'With our compliments,' Nikos said.

'Nikos, that is terrific. I gather you mentioned lobster would be on the menu. Is that still a possibility?'

'It certainly is, sir.'

'My name is John. That's all you need to know. Have you any starters, Niko?'

'Yes, John. We have tzatziki and yemista, my mother's speciality stuffed tomatoes and peppers, cheese pies, grilled haloumi cheese, and taramasalata.'

'Wow, Nikos, that is fantastic. I love tzatziki. All that yoghurt and garlic though! I hope you'll have some, Fiona, as well as me?'

'I guess I better have some as well.' Fiona said, laughing.

The other three girls all ordered the stuffed tomatoes.

'Perfect, and then lobster for you all?'

'I believe so, Nikos. I've heard no objection!'

The wine flowed and the starters arrived, which were delicious. John appreciated the suggestion that both he and Fiona should eat the tzatziki; if he embraced Fiona tonight, the garlic would be shared, not rejected. An hour later, John ordered more wine. Five whole lobsters or, more accurately, crayfish, the Mediterranean version of the crustacean, arrived.

The lobsters were accompanied by some delicious chips cooked in olive oil. The party shared a couple of Greek salads as they extracted the flesh from the shells. Soft sweet, succulent white meat – it was all very delicious.

John was conscious that two police officers had taken a table at the other end of the taverna. John called Nikos over to say whatever the police officers wanted, he was to put the cost on his bill. On hearing this news, the officers acknowledged John.

Once the lobster had been eaten, the police officers' food was delivered.

'Sorry, I just need to go to the loo,' announced Joy.

'Nikos, where is the WC?'

'Ah, follow me, dear lady.'

They walked over the narrow road, into a lobby area before the kitchen, then out of the kitchen to a WC in a small building set against the narrow road at the back of the taverna.

'It's odd, but Yannis said he would see us tonight and pay for the beer he drank earlier. But he hasn't turned up,' remarked Tracey.

Nikos returned and started to take orders for sweets. Baklava, ice-cream, Greek yogurt and honey were all offered this evening. There was an animated discussion. Tracey knew Joy would love the yoghurt and honey. The others ordered Baklava and an ice-cream for John. The sweets were delivered and consumed. Honey dribbled down the chins for those who had chosen baklava.

John, realising that Joy must have left the table some twenty minutes ago, asked Fiona to go and see if she was okay. Fiona was back in no time.

'She isn't there, John.'

'She must be. Have you looked in the right place?'

'Yes, darling, in the loo which is outside at the back.'

John immediately alerted the two police officers and told them what had happened. They got up and were up and away in seconds, running down the narrow street which followed the buildings facing the harbour. They burst out at the end of the narrow road to the original harbour's edge beyond the breakwater. A motorboat was leaving the port at some speed. One of the officers was on his radio to the base in Nidri, stating what had happened. Within minutes, two police RIBs were racing to the scene, hoping to spot the motorboat with Joy on board.

'John, what is going on?' enquired Noel over the VHF radio.

'I think this is another attempt to recover some money I held back when I paid Brandon.'

'My god, will there be no end to this? It is very worrying, John.'

'I agree, but what can I do?'

'Pay them the money.'

'That is where you are wrong. The more we give these people, the more they will want. It will never end.'

'So, what do we do?'

The two police officers returned to their table to discuss what they had seen, telling John that two police patrol boats were out looking for the launch. As the officer in charge was talking, his mobile went off. He detached himself from the party. Coming back to the table, the officer made an announcement.

'Sir, we have been advised that your friend Joy is likely to be on a helicopter that took off from the far end of this island a few moments ago. That area is all owned by Russians. We don't go there; they have their own private security guards.'

Fiona was about to speak when her mobile pinged to indicate a text had been received.

'My God, everyone. You will not believe the content of this text!'

CHAPTER 16

A uniformed army officer met with Joy as she stepped into the helicopter.

'We will have you on a plane and back in Moscow before you know it. You will have a diplomatic transfer at Athens Airport. You will literally step off this helicopter and walk up the boarding ladder for the flight to Moscow. It is scheduled to take off in about an hour.'

Speaking in fluent Russian, Joy thanked her comrade.

'It will be good to be back home. I gather I was close to being arrested in the UK, which would have been difficult.'

'Yes, and not pleasant. We discovered two MI6 operatives on Ionia, pretending to be amateur sailors. We think they had orders to remove you back to the UK. It's likely they spotted your 'extra' passports for our comrades. The comrade who allowed us to access you owns half of the island. He allowed us to land the helicopter there. The local police have been chasing an empty speedboat, thinking you were on board.'

The Russian official laughed loudly at the foolishness of the Greek police.

'Can I send a text to my friends who will be worried that I am not with them? I don't want them to be spending ages looking for me.'

'Yes, that will be fine, but wait until you are on the plane and send it before taking off.'

'Okay.'

Fiona, John, Tracey and Emily.

I am sorry I had to leave but be assured I am safe. When you receive this message, I will be flying back home to Moscow. You see, my name is Roksanda, *a*

Russian name. I chose Joy in England because it was a name everyone could remember and spell easily.

I have been working as a clerk in England. Firstly, in London in the Home Office, then the Foreign Office in Manchester. That was a dreary job. Nothing exciting going on there. My handlers decided it was time I left the UK.

I am looking forward to seeing my mother and two younger sisters. My father is dead. Chechens shot him when he was in the army fighting them. My mother gets his pension. I expect to get assistance in Russia. We will not meet again. I have enjoyed your company.

My love and best wishes, Joy/Roksanda

*

'Well, whatever next! I didn't see that coming! Did any of you?' said John.

'No, John,' Tracey and Emily spoke as one.

The two police officers approached their table to report they had lost the scent in their pursuit of Joy.

'The search will resume tomorrow at first light.'

'We know where she is or will be at first thing tomorrow – Moscow. It was a put-up job. She never got into a speed boat; she was taken to a waiting helicopter on this island. Then she flew to Athens airport, where a diplomatic transfer put her onto a Russian plane. We have just received the text. I can send you a copy if you wish?' John said.

'I will tell my boss, senor. We will take a copy of the text, please?'

'Of course, let me send it to your phone now.'

'Thank you. My boss may wish to come and speak with you all. Please do not leave tomorrow until that has happened.'

'Okay, but please ask your boss to radio *Brave Goose* with a time he wishes to come.'

'Girls,' said John, shaking his head. 'I was not expecting this interlude. I will do my utmost to make the remaining days of your holiday incredibly special. I am certain there will be some further questions from the Greek authorities. Then we can holiday!'

*

Joy landed in Domodedovo Airport, Moscow, after a three-and-a-half-hour flight. It was very early in the morning, and despite the early hour, there were large queues of passengers. They were mainly jetting off on holiday to the Black Sea resorts. Joy had to wait a moment or two to pass through arrivals and present her documents for scrutiny. Then two officials escorted her to a private room off the main concourse. Joy knew this was routine. She only had her UK passport with her.

After an hour of questions that she was able to answer – in Russian – it was established she was a member of the KGB. She had expected a car to collect her from the airport. She was dismayed when a police van appeared and took her to a building in Moscow. She couldn't see out as the van didn't have windows. She was taken from the van once it was inside and, after a body search and the removal of all her belongings, including her mobile phone, she was taken to a holding cell – a small tiled room with artificial light. There was a concrete slab pretending to be a bed and a rough blanket, which Joy wrapped around her to keep warm. What had she done to warrant this treatment?

Joy protested, to no avail. She was held for two or three days; she lost track of time. Food and water were supplied and a rough mattress had been placed on the concrete base. There was a washbasin and a toilet but no window. It was airless. At some time in the evening, the light was turned off.

Eventually, she was collected by two guards and taken up about four floors to a room occupied by three uniformed military types. The room was unfurnished except for a metal table in the centre.

The three men picked her up. No one spoke. One on each arm, the third held her feet. She was placed on the table, struggling now and unsure what would happen.

'What are you doing? I am a KGB officer.'

Still, no one spoke.

Her hands were tied by what seemed to be handcuffs. One strap round her wrists, and another underneath the table. Her feet were bound together and strapped to the table at the other end. Straps were tied and tightened around her thighs and upper body. She couldn't move. She screamed at the men as they left the room but they didn't speak. She realised she was wasting her breath. What was to happen now? The table was in an empty room with no windows, just strip lights fastened to the dirty ceiling.

After what seemed an age, two white-coated men and one woman entered the room, pushing a surgical trolley with some objects on the top tray. One white-coated man inserted a cannula into a vein on her right arm.

No one spoke.

He then injected Joy with a substance.

'What are you doing? What do you want from me? Don't poison me! Stop!'

Still no one spoke.

She was sure she was being treated with the truth serum, Sodium Pentathol. It didn't take long before she was drowsy. This was a regular procedure undertaken by KGB agents when they wanted to interrogate someone, especially when they had returned to the mother land.

The man who injected her started to ask questions in Russian.

What did you do in London?

What did you do in Manchester?

Do you know the names of the British spies acting against Russia?

Do you know where they live?

Where are they now?

Half asleep, she chatted about her time in London's Home Office and Foreign Office. She also talked about the dreary time she spent in Manchester issuing passports. She was pleased to have helped comrades who needed UK passports to obtain them. She spoke of her visits to

Greece. The two men she knew were spies, Tony Franks and Bill Edwards. They had a yacht in Lefkas. She also confirmed that she supplied UK passports for young girls who appeared to be of Albanian parentage.

How many passports for young girls did you issue?

Who received these passports?

She was screaming and shouting, demanding to know why she was being treated like this. What was the liquid? She received no response. Another dose of Sodium Pentathol was administered. There was a burning sensation in her arm where the liquid entered.

She continued with her tirade against Russia.

'The regime's a failure. Everyone would be destitute and starving if Russia failed, which it will. Putin is a failure, a tyrant and a dictator. Russia was supposed to be a democracy. It isn't. It's a police state.'

She was soon asleep, passing out under the influence of the drug she'd been given.

She woke up, not knowing what time it was or how long she had been under the influence of the drug, and with no recollection of what she had said to the Russian minders.

*

'Did any of you suspect Joy was a Russian spy?'

'No, John. We didn't, but we suspect the Home Office didn't know either.'

'What makes you say that, Tracey?'

'Well, she had been on holiday several times, always booking through me. She had a British Passport. She went all over Europe. She was a regular customer.'

'So, Tracey, you say that because she was able to travel unhindered?'

'Yes, John. She would have been stopped if there had been any suspicion of spying or other irregular activities. I am sure HM Government would have withdrawn her passport or expelled her from the UK.'

'Yes, I get that,' said John. 'We can only assume they were unaware. But presumably they will know by now that she has escaped back to Russia. Well, what a tangled web we weave. An unexpected event for us all.'

*

The following day, John's mobile phone rang at half past nine in the morning.

'Senor, it's Miron.'

'Ah, do you want to come over to us? I can send the RIB.'

'No, I am still in Athens. Enquiries are continuing. I will report back to you when I know more. What is your next port?'

'Sorry, I don't know, but we will be in the Ionian for the week. We will be back in Lefkas next weekend. Then we may go to Athens via the Corinth Canal.'

'Okay, sir. I will contact you before you come to Athens.'

'Noel, due to the unexpected situation where Joy disappeared so suddenly, I think we need to find an anchorage where the girls can relax, sunbathe and perhaps have a barbecue on board this evening, if Sally can manage that?'

'Yes, John, I can arrange that. The best place would be the bay before Vathi on Ithaca. It has room to moor, with beautiful wooded slopes down to the sea. A perfect place to explore in *Gosling*.'

'Sounds like a plan. No one is up yet, so let's make ready, and before they know it, we will be there.'

CHAPTER 17

Within half an hour, *Brave Goose* was underway. It was about twenty miles to the mooring. They would be there in two hours. While underway, people began to appear. Sally produced breakfast on a conveyor belt system. No sooner was one breakfast served than another was required.

By quarter-past eleven, the main anchor was dropped in a beautiful bay, Ormos Skhoinos. There were buildings at the head of the bay, which they later discovered were a school. The other shores of this square bay were wooded with narrow sandy beaches, small coves, and promontories protruding into the bay. No other boat was moored here; it was probably too deep for smaller craft. Jock and José launched *Gosling,* knowing she would be required here. The large RIB followed as it was only a short distance around the corner to the town of Vathi. Sally was bound to want some shopping.

José took Sally in the RIB to the supermarket in Vathi to secure some supplies for the barbecue. Unlike many markets in Greece, this had a wide variety of food, delicacies and wines. The front of the shop was open; at night, it was secured with shutters. Boxes of fruit and vegetables were piled up, leaving passageways for customers to browse the goods while getting into the shop. Chatting with the lady who must have been the owner, Sally discovered that the shop had a delivery service. An opportunity too good to miss. Sally's shopping order suddenly increased. Trolleys full of groceries, fresh vegetables, fruit and a significant quantity of wine and beer. There was a final request for two bottles of five-star Metaxa brandy.

Christos, the van driver, packed everything into four large boxes, which he placed carefully in the back of his van. Sally was offered a ride to the quay. Christos took his precious load to the harbourside. Jose was surprised when the van arrived. He helped the driver with offloading the van into the RIB.

José and Sally returned to *Brave Goose*, feeling satisfied with their purchases. Once everything had been transported to the galley, Sally stored and refrigerated some items. The wine and brandy were placed in the wine lockers, the beer in the fridge on the quarterdeck.

No sooner had this been undertaken than Fiona, Tracey, and Emily returned from their trip in *Gosling*.

John was convinced he could hear the animated chatter of the girls before he heard the engine's note. He welcomed the girls back, reserving a kiss for Fiona.

'Sally has been shopping. We're eating onboard tonight if that suits you?' Acclamation all around. The girls told Sally they'd help with everything Sally needed to do, an offer that she gladly accepted.

Noel and John sat on the bridge, looking at charts. The decision was made to have a meal at Sami tomorrow in Cephalonia, having first stopped for swimming and sunbathing at the southern end of Ithaca. From Sami, they could then travel to Kalamos, to the east of Ionia. There John expected to meet with Azmir and his wife. From Kalamos, it would be a simple trip to Lefkas.

'We would get back there on Saturday, giving the girls time to prepare to leave. We can eat out on the last night.'

'Do you intend to go to Athens, John?'

'Only if it seems like the most appropriate place for Azmir and his wife to obtain visas.'

'Okay, John. I guess we will have to play that one by ear.'

'Yes, much depends on how Azmir has got on.'

CHAPTER 18

The following day was Wednesday. Lots of swimming and trips in *Gosling* before lunch. Once lunch had been consumed, Noel advised it was time to leave. The journey to Sami was a stately voyage, with no hurry, towards the locations John and Noel had agreed on. Noel was in his element, making all the calculations for the course, which he fed into the chart plotter.

The entrance to the small port from the sea was unusual: it was through an opening in the quay parallel to the shoreline. They were to moor alongside the harbour wall but on the inside of the port, facing into the hinterland. *Brave Goose* came alongside the main quay inside the port. She was aided by a marinara whose primary job was putting the lines on bollards for ferries. He did the same job for *Brave Goose.* Once tied up, Noel threw him a can of beer in appreciation of his assistance.

Brave Goose was now secure against the quay. The opposite side of the quay was open to the sea, where the car and passenger ferries tied up, stern-to, allowing their cargo to be discharged and take on new people and vehicles.

'Hi folks, the pilot book has given me some information about this port. When the ferry comes in, the place goes ballistic. The pilot book advises that it is quite a sight, not to be missed. The marinara who took our lines said he expects a ferry to arrive shortly.'

'Thanks, Noel. It looks like we will have a grandstand seat. If we sit on the flybridge, we will see everything.'

José had lowered the port side boarding ladder to allow access to the quay. Gradually cars and trucks started to appear and parked along the quay's edge. The lorries made a parking area in the turning area at the end of the broad pier.

The police had a plan, which reckoned without the temperament and urgency of the Greeks and Italians. Three local police stood on the pier, intending to make order out of the chaos when it occurred.

As soon as the ferry appeared in the bay, it dropped its port anchor. The ferry captain used the anchor as a fulcrum to swing the stern around, ready to reverse to the pier. The bow anchor also prevented the afternoon wind from blowing the ship sideways. Soon, vehicles of all descriptions, cars, motorbikes, lorries, petrol tankers, and large and small RVs, started to move down the pier from the small town. They intended to be first in the queue to board the ferry.

Once in range, the heaving lines were thrown to two waiting dockers. They pulled the lines from the ferry, putting the loops at the end of the main mooring lines over the bollards. The heaving lines were untied before the main lines were winched in by the ferry. Once the stern lines were tight, the crew moved to the bow winch to tighten the anchor cable. The stern ramp was lowered. The ferry could now commence unloading.

Cars of friends and relatives had parked their vehicles on the road to the pier. These cars made the available space to reach the pier one vehicle wide. The police had to sort this out. The three officers started to blow their whistles. There was a cacophony of sound. The engine and the turbulence of the ferry's propellers made the police instructions inaudible.

The docking of the ferry was going to be such fun to watch. Everyone on board *Brave Goose,* moored directly opposite the ferry's position, couldn't wait to witness what would happen next.

'José, can you please pull in the port gangway, as a vehicle will likely hit it?' Noel asked.

Once that was achieved, the crew and guests on *Brave Goose* could watch the entertainment.

Sure enough, the first vehicles off the ferry were two large identical coaches. The coach passengers, carrying their belongings, trouped off the ferry as foot passengers. They could board their coach as soon as the coaches were off the ship. Passengers were not allowed to board the coaches on the ferry. The next amusement was watching the passengers trying to decide which coach they were on. According to the courier shouting her head off, it was essential for the passengers to board the correct one. Eventually, most foot passengers were seated in one or the other coach, while the rest, carrying all sorts of baggage and parcels, met their relatives waiting on the pier road. The two coaches could move off now that most of the parked vehicles had gone. Other vehicles left the ferry, with much whistling from the police designed to hurry them up. As the traffic was virtually stationary, no amount of whistling would hurry things up. After half an hour, the disembarkation was complete. The empty places were soon filled by large tankers and lorries first, much to the annoyance of the waiting private traffic.

'Look, folks,' said John.' That little yellow car is at the end of the queue to get on board. I am certain it has just disembarked. He must have thought he was somewhere else!'

'That's not unusual, John. He was asked to do that to be in the correct position in the next port of call.'

'Thanks, Noel. What a spectacle this has been! I wouldn't have missed it for the world.'

The stop in Sami was a great success, and the theatre of the ferry was undoubtedly a high point.

John, Tracey, Fiona and Emily made their way to a taverna overlooking the port. An aristocratic Greek who ran the Lighthouse restaurant told John that previously he had been a steward on P&O cruise ships.

The diners were extremely well-fed. Many opted for Cephalonia pie – a local delicacy. The meal was delicious. After dinner, they had drinks in a different taverna overlooking the bay. The four of them found a table where they were served coffee and brandy. One of the girls asked the waitress if this was the location for the film *Captain Corelli's Mandolin*. She said it was. She brought over a photograph album showing all the stars and the changes that had taken place to the location to fit the film's script.

As they talked, another large ferry docked stern-to on another part of the quay opposite where the party was sitting. Large fuel tankers, whose purpose was to supply the island with fuel, were disgorged from the ship and drove off into the island.

With a degree of sadness, the last leg of the girl's holiday meant they would fly home to the UK the following day. Brave Goose left Sami mid-morning and made her way back to Lefkas.

Brave Goose moored on the jetty at Lefkas marina in the early afternoon on Saturday. Tracey and Emily started to pack their bags in preparation for their return to the UK. John took the opportunity to visit Paleros boatyard to discuss with Robert the potential refit. He had prepared a work schedule and invited Robert to board on Monday to look at the boat and see what the refurbishment would involve.

He ran into Tony and Bill on his way back to *Brave Goose.*

'Hello, you two. Sorry we never got together last time. Coming for a coffee or a beer – or something stronger?'

'We were just strolling around the marina, looking at boats.'

'Good, come on, we are nearly at *Brave Goose*.'

The three men took the passerelle to the quarterdeck.

'What would you like to drink?'

'Coffee for me, John,' said Tony.

'And me', said Bill.

John called Sally and placed the order.

'While Sally does her thing, would you like to have another look around?'

John escorted the men around the boat, starting at the bow and taking in the foredeck and anchoring equipment. Then they went down to the accommodation and engine room, where Jock was introduced. He was busy cleaning the engines and the bilges to maintain the high standard of the mechanical aspects. The final part of the tour was to visit the flybridge and boat deck.

'She's a very impressive boat, John. You must be very proud of her. It was good to have another look as I didn't take it all in on the first visit.'

'I am proud of her, but the crew is the essential element. I wouldn't have bought the boat without the crew who came with her. As you saw in the engine room, that is not a space for amateurs to play.'

'I can see that. We're not engineers.'

'Yes, MI6 wasn't it?'

'Yes, that's right, John.'

'We could have done with having you onboard. One of our numbers, it transpired, was a double agent and was returned to Russia. She left the dining table to go to the loo and we never saw her again.'

'Good heavens. Have you had any help from the authorities to find her?'

'Yes and no. The local police were involved at the request of EKAM. Not sure if you know of them?'

'We do. What happened, John?'

'Hang on. I will get a copy of the text we received.'

A moment later, John returned with a copy of Joy's text.

'Here, you can have this. According to the local police, she was taken by car to a private helipad at the end of the island of Ionia. I gather Russians own half the island. Then she was flown to Athens, so the police tell us, and transferred to a waiting Russian plane under diplomatic immunity.'

'Despite being on holiday, we must transfer this information to London. It looks on the face of it that Joy could have been a double agent, as you say. She possibly thought she would be safe and secure in Russia. I doubt that very much. She will be interrogated for some time so they can learn as much as possible from her. Once she has finished her interrogation, she will be held for a few months, so she learns not to change sides. She will never be let out of Russia again.'

'That's interesting, Bill. I guess you come across this sort of thing quite often.'

'No, John, it's not as common as people think. Finding a double agent is always tricky.'

'Well, Tony, it was something of a shock. She made an excuse to go to the toilet. After twenty minutes, Fiona went to see if she was alright. It was then we realised she had disappeared. I was convinced she had been kidnapped.'

'London may know about this already, but I will tell them later in case it's news to them.'

'What puzzled me, Bill, was what possible use would a spy be in the Home Office?'

'John, you would be amazed what use such a person could be. This will trigger a significant enquiry into all her work. She could have approved visas for other Russian spies. Equally, Russia will want to know what she has told the UK authorities about Russia and their intelligence set-up.'

'Quite a tangled web. Are you two going back to the UK soon?'

In unison, they confirmed that they were going back tomorrow.

'Sunday is the day for UK flights to Preveza and vice-versa. We will have a busy day on Monday as we'll have to give all the detail to the team back in London.'

'Are the other girls going back tomorrow?'

'Yes, Tony. Tracey and Emily. Good friends of Fiona. One's a travel agent, and one's a nursery nurse. They're flying to Manchester.'

'Are they onboard now, John?'

'Don't think so. They all went into town to purchase goodness knows what to take home as souvenirs.'

'Would you mind if we chatted with them later before you go out for dinner?'

'Not at all. Come for a sundowner, say six o'clock, and you can chat with them then.'

*

At the appointed hour, Tony and Bill returned to *Brave Goose*. Beers were provided, and other drinks for the girls.

'Look, we are sorry to have to ask you some questions, but the apparent disappearance of your friend Joy has raised questions with us. To be clear, we are officers in Special Branch in the UK. We must get involved as soon as a spy or terrorist is uncovered. I hope you don't mind, but we need to ask you some questions.'

The next half hour involved essential information gathering: names, addresses, phone numbers and email addresses, not just for Tracey and Emily but also Fiona, as they were all friends.

'Can you please show us where Joy slept? As she left after dinner onshore, I assume everything will still be in her cabin?'

'Yes, Tony, I can show you,' volunteered Fiona.

Bill, Tony and Fiona left the party to search Joy's possessions. They returned carrying a lot of clothes, some papers, a book and a notebook.

'This is all that Joy left behind.'

'We'll take these items if you don't mind, John?'

'Can anyone tell me if you ever had suspicions that Joy Jackson was not who she made out to be?'

'I did have a few thoughts about her. I was wrong, of course. When

I first asked her what she did, she explained that she was a clerk in the Home Office. I responded, saying it must be an unusual job if she worked from home for the government.'

'Why did you say that, Emily?'

'I misunderstood. When she said Home Office, I thought she was working from home. Daft, I know now, but at the time my mind was not on espionage or anything very much. We were chatting.'

'Think back, Tracey. Did Joy ever give you details of her job? Furthermore, did she ever ask *you* any probing questions?'

'Gosh, that's difficult. If I think of something, I will let you know. She said her employer paid her rent and council tax. I have been there, and it is a beautiful two-bedroom flat. It would be worth seven or eight hundred a month. At the time, I didn't think anything of it, but the government wouldn't do that, would they?'

'I doubt it. Did she tell you what her job was in the Home Office?'

'Yes, she said it was very boring. She allocated visas to people coming to stay or on holiday to the UK.'

'Did she now!' said Bill. 'That would be very useful for a foreign power to access the UK.'

'Well, now you mention it, I can see how useful she might be to help other spies enter the country,' said Fiona.

'Do you know her address?'

'Yes, I have it written down. My diary is in my cabin. I will be back in a minute.'

Fiona gave the two men all the details she had.

'Tracey's right; it was a lovely, beautifully furnished flat.'

'Thanks. I don't suppose you were ever given a key, Tracey?'

'No, sorry, but the concierge has a master key.'

'Did Joy have any other friends, like a boyfriend?'

'Strange you should mention that, Bill. I saw her in a pub we go to quite often with a man. She waved to me but never came over. The two of them left when she saw me there.'

'Okay, girls, thanks for all your help. Here are our cards in case you think of something else. We need to go now.'

Bill and Tony left and walked briskly away.

'Well, that was interesting. It certainly throws some light on what Joy was up to.'

'It does, John. How were we to know though?'

'You weren't to know; how could you? Let's go for dinner,' suggested John.

CHAPTER 19

Back on their boat, Tony and Bill phoned London and explained to their handler what had happened. They advised him Joy was apparently a double agent, primarily working for Moscow. They reported on who she was and what she had said in a text to her friends, a copy of which had been despatched to London.

Within an hour, uniformed and plainclothes officers arrived at Joy's flat. The concierge opened up for them. A full-scale search of the premises was undertaken, including a forensic investigation by SOCO on behalf of MI6.

Speaking to their handler in London, Tony explained they had recovered all Joy's belongings from the boat on which she had been staying.

'Tony and I made a thorough search of her cabin. We have gathered up every last item of hers. There was no mobile phone. She must have had that with her at the restaurant. She and the others were out for a meal, and Joy excused herself to go to the toilet. Twenty minutes later, she was not to be found. This was a Greek taverna on the island of Ionia. From the information gathered from her friends, all four spent some time in the taverna in the afternoon to book a table for the evening. They were approached by an unknown man named Yanis, who managed to find out their names. He said he would see them later but didn't materialise.'

'Okay, Tony. It sounds like Joy had her repatriation to Russia all organised. We were going to arrest her when she returned to the UK. We suspected she was issuing passports to Albanian females who were being trafficked by a Russian gang in Greece.'

'Okay, do you want us to see if we can find out who the Russians are on Ionia and what they are up to?'

'Yes, but please be careful. By all accounts, they are ruthless. It may not be the Russian government they are working for. It could be the Russian mafia.'

*

In Moscow, Joy was oblivious to what was happening in her flat. She was oblivious to what was happening to her. She was in an induced coma. Eventually, she came round and realised she was still restrained. She was still pretty sure she'd been injected with Sodium Pentathol, the truth drug. She could do nothing about it. What she said to the KGB while under the influence was known only to the KGB. Was it the truth, or had Joy just said what her subconscious ordered? She fell asleep again into a semi-coma.

*

Tony and Bill had a good rummage through Joy's possessions, anxious to find anything that might cause an issue with customs or immigration. However, they were more keen to find anything confirming the suspicion she was a double agent.

'All seems fine, but forensics must look at all this as well.'

'I agree, Tony. Let us assemble a report and put all this stuff in a sealed plastic bag.'

The two men purchased pizzas from a nearby taverna and returned them to their boat. The margaritas were delicious with a thin, crusty base. The two men spent the evening reflecting on what had happened and drafting their reports for their boss at MI6.

Their yacht was a Bénéteau Oceanis 450, a lovely sailing boat that was easy to handle and excellent in a seaway. They had improved the boat considerably since they had purchased her second-hand three years earlier. The electronics had been updated and a new radar with a dome was fitted halfway up the mast facing forward; they'd also bought a new autohelm. The gas pipework needed an upgrade to the gas cooker. Gas was lethal on a boat; they knew that if propane leaked on a boat, it would go into the bilge, as gas is heavier than air. If that were the case, an explosion would be inevitable at some point. There was a gas monitor on board but it had shown no signs of any gas leak. They put the gas pipe renewal on the list for work to be carried out by the boatyard over the winter.

They were half-packed, ready to fly home the following day. They had prepared their report for London. The pizza had been eaten, and the remaining two bottles of *Land of Lefkas* red wine had been consumed. By half-past midnight, they were both sound asleep, assisted in their slumbers by a bottle each of the local red wine.

They were to fly back to the UK at 21:00 hours. It was only just Sunday, nearly one o'clock in the morning. Both men were fast asleep in their alcohol-induced sleep. Then they both woke, half asleep, half awake, thinking the boat was moving. Ridiculous – there was no wind, no tide, and the bow and two stern lines secured the vessel very well. The wash from a passing boat in the main channel had probably caused the yacht's movement

'Did you feel that, Bill?'

'Yes, Tony, but it was probably the stern wave from a big fishing boat. Go back to sleep.'

Sleep didn't come to either of them. Eventually, they decided that they *were* afloat but moving.

'Sod it, we must have broken free somehow. I'll go and have a look, Bill.'

*

Tony poked his head out of the companionway whilst balancing on the steps leading from the saloon to the cockpit. There was a tremendous crash in the saloon, then silence. Bill got up to investigate. There was no response from Tony. Bill was not surprised – Tony, lying at the foot of the steps, looked concussed. He was slumped onto the companionway with blood oozing from a wound to his head.

'What the hell? Tony, are you okay?'

There was no response to Bill's urgent enquiry. Turning on the cabin lights, he saw that Tony had fallen backwards from the steps, banging his head on the corner of the galley unit. The unit was bloodstained and blood trickled down Tony's head and face. He was out cold. Believing the boat was still attached to the marina pontoon, Bill rushed up the saloon steps to get help. He didn't get beyond the top step. He was pushed unceremoniously back down the steps again, hitting his head on the opposite side, catching the corner of the chart table.

Their yacht was under tow from a workboat and a member of its crew was at her helm.

The marina lights faded as the two vessels exited the canal, joined by a tow line. Both red and green buoys flashed their little lights marking the boundary of the channel. The convoy was unlit. No other vessels were in sight. The convoy headed due south towards Ionia. Once out of the canal, the workboat helmsman went to sort out the two men who were in a pile at the bottom of the steps. He pulled the two men apart, tied their hands behind their backs with cable ties, and then tied their legs together.

Once clear of the canal and roughly in the spot where John and Fiona had rescued little Mel, the tow was shortened so the yacht could lie alongside the tug. The sea was flat. The vessels were securely tied together. The skipper of the motor launch, the helmsman of the yacht, and another two crew members on the launch manhandled Tony and Bill from the yacht to the launch.

After an hour, Bill woke with a start, realising he had been hit, nursing a massive headache. He tried to see if Tony was okay; he realised they were tied up, unable to move. More to the point, they were no longer in their yacht. Bill realised they'd been stuffed in the bottom of a launch-type boat.

The launch progressed towards Ionia. The yacht had been turned around by the helmsman, who was taking it back to the marina to put onto its mooring. It was daylight, so he hailed the marina office to ask for assistance in mooring. Once moored securely, the helmsman trashed the yacht, picked up keys that he found on the chart table and, leaving the yacht unlocked, but the hatch and hatch boards in place, he walked to the office and left the keys on the steps.

He left the marina and walked around the old port quay to a point near the floating restaurant. He joined the inter-island ferry that moored on the quay. It would take him straight to the dock on Ionia.

*

The launch took Tony and Bill to its mooring in the small marina behind the main wharf on Ionia. Quite a few people were milling about now. Getting the two men to their base could be difficult, without questions, so two of the crew gagged them with duct tape to prevent them from shouting out.

The launch skipper and the two crew members led Tony and Bill, each covered in a blanket to obscure their features, to a van with a side-opening door. Once the two men were secured, the driver drove up the hill to the road that would take them to the entrance of the fenced-off section of the island owned by the Russian oligarch.

*

Life was stirring on *Brave Goose.* Sally was, as always, busy preparing the quarterdeck in the bright sunshine for breakfast. It was half-past nine when the first guests appeared. Tracey and Emily took the Greek option for breakfast – a bowl of Greek yoghurt, honey and fresh figs.

'We might as well enjoy this for one last time, Tracey. I hope Joy is enjoying her breakfast in Russia.'

'I feel betrayed by Joy. She might have let on what she does for a living,' said Emily.

'I guess in espionage, that is not what you do. Your head must be full of secrets that no one is allowed to know.'

John and Fiona joined the pair who were eating their last breakfast in Greece. While they chatted, a man from the marina office appeared, dressed in a T-shirt emblazoned with the marina logo. He stood at the bottom of the gangplank and started asking questions about Bill and Tony.

'We had a night out with them last night. They returned here for a drink, then returned to their boat. Why?' said John.

'They seemed to have disappeared, sir. They ordered a taxi for nine o'clock this morning. Their boat keys were left on the steps of the marina office. I have been to check the boat. They're not there and the place is in a state. Their beds had been used and their holdalls are still on the boat, but there are clothes everywhere. There would appear to be several bloodstains on the side of the galley and chart table.'

'Sorry, they were just casual friends. We don't know where they live. If there are suspicious signs, you should call the police.'

'John, what is going on?'

'Darling, I have no idea. Events like this usually have a straightforward explanation. For instance, it is possible one or the other tripped and cut his face, so blood was everywhere, and the other friend took him to the hospital for treatment.'

'As usual, John, you are possibly correct in your assumption. What time will your taxi be here, girls? I am not trying to get rid of you, just planning the day.'

'We ordered a taxi for two this afternoon. The flight is at five o'clock, but knowing airports, it can take ages to get through security.'

'Great, how about taking *Gosling* out for a last swim and sunbathe on the beach?'

'Great idea, Fiona. I don't have much to pack; what about you, Emily?'

'That would be excellent. Like you, Tracey, I have very little to pack. Where has a week gone?'

'I know the days fly when we are onboard. We have another three or four weeks before we go home. I will miss *Brave Goose* when I get home.'

'You are right, Fiona, to wonder where all the days go,' remarked John. 'I will get *Gosling* launched for you. Then you can go as soon as you are ready.'

The three girls motored *Gosling* out of the Lefkas canal to Ormos Palairo, an undeveloped bay with a beautiful beach. It was only a short motor from the end of the Lefkas canal. Just what the girls needed for their last day.

John and Noel took the opportunity to discuss the next part of their voyage and the refit.

'What do you say to me instructing Paleros, at Lefkas marina, to carry out the refit, Noel?'

'They certainly have the facilities. There is no reason I can think of why you shouldn't use them. Are you planning on staying in Greece for next season, John?'

'Yes, Noel, I think there is more to explore. It will give you and the crew at least three months' leave. I will, of course, pay you during that time. If you want to return during or after the refit but before she is launched, you can fly to Athens and get a bus to Lefkas. Get a hotel in the marina to put you and the rest of the crew up. Put any bills on the boat's credit card. It would be reassuring to know you and Jock are watching everything during her refurbishment.'

'I'll discuss it with the rest of the crew, John. I suspect they will be thrilled at the prospect.'

'Good, so let's discuss what we will do next.'

'I suspect you would like to go to Kalamos to meet your ex-army friend and then to Athens? Am I right, John?'

'Yes, that is spot on, Noel.'

'That's terrific, John. I can sail to two places I have wanted to sail but have never done so. I am keen to traverse the Corinth Canal. We'll sail to the Gulf of Patras once we leave Kalamos. There is a spectacular road bridge over the gulf. We need consent to pass under and decide which span we can use. Control centre allocates when and where to pass under the bridge. Then we motor on to transit to the Corinth Canal. A sight not to be missed. Cameras at the ready. We then motor on to Piraeus, where we will moor in a marina. I will book a berth when I know when we will be there.'

'That all sounds very exciting, Noel. Fiona will be thrilled at the prospect.'

John was leaving the bridge when Sally came to tidy the quarterdeck.

'Sally, Fiona and I will eat out this evening, so you can do as you wish. If you want a night off, you can all eat out if that would be helpful. I will leave a hundred euros with you to supplement the cost if you eat out. I will take a spare set of control buttons for the passerelle. Can you please do the same so that *Brave Goose* will be secure?'

'That is extremely kind of you, John.'

Fiona and the girls were back with *Gosling* by twelve-thirty. Sally provided a light lunch. All the girls' belongings were packed up. They discussed what would happen to Joy's things. John confirmed that Tony and Bill had taken everything so they would return to the UK, presumably for forensic examination.

At two o'clock, the taxi arrived to transport the two girls to Preveza airport; kisses and thanks, a wave from the taxi window, and they were gone.

John explained to Fiona the itinerary for the next few days. They would eventually go to Athens, with Azmir and Ulrika aboard, so Azmir could visit the British Embassy, hoping to persuade them to grant the two of them visas to stay and work in the UK.

John and Fiona had a relaxing afternoon on the sun deck, and a snooze prepared them both for a night out in Lefkas.

CHAPTER 20

'Hi, Brandon, it's Georgio. 'I wanted to let you know that I am about to tackle John England again to recover the £200,000 he failed to pay you. In fact, I plan on recovering a quarter of a million as I need to pay the troops.'

'Be careful, Georgio. England has contacts in high places. The last lot who tried are in prison or dead.'

'The people I used in Sicily were better than England's team, and you got your money back except for the £200,000. John England suggested I had stolen it from some pensioners to finance my business.'

'Well, Georgio, that's a true statement. You *did* steal the money from the pensioners.'

'I would have paid them an enhanced pension, but I never got to do that.'

'If you get the money, you know it belongs to me.'

'In theory, yes, but I am taking the risk to recover it. Will you cut me a deal, Brandon?'

'I would say we go fifty-fifty on what you collect. Don't involve me or my name.'

'Okay, Brandon, that's a deal. I will keep you posted on events. I am about to fly to Greece.'

Georgio ended the call. He would succeed this time. He was sure of it. He didn't plan on being in Greece for too long. Just long enough to gather his troops and prepare the ground for an attack on *Brave Goose.* It would be a sufficiently damaging attack. England would have no choice but to pay. The Air Italia plane took off half-full, landing in Preveza on time in mid-afternoon. A taxi deposited him at the pick-up point for the local ferry on the quay in Lefkas town. The boat would not go for two hours.

'Dima, it's Georgio. From Sicily. I have a job. Would you be prepared to help?' Georgio was speaking to his first team member, a Greek national and a member of the Greek Mafia. The Sicilian branch of Cosa Nostra was accepted as the leading organisation. Any Mafia branch would double down to assist a Sicilian branch member.

'Yes, sure, if there is money in it. Where are you now?'

'I am about to check into the marina hotel in Lefkas.'

'That's a useful location. I have your number now. I will ring you tomorrow about a meeting.'

Georgio decided he would not get the ferry to Ionia this afternoon as he discovered no return before tomorrow. Needing a base from which he could operate, the modern hotel in the marina would be ideal. It would allow him to watch the boats in the harbour. Georgio checked into the hotel and requested a room overlooking the marina.

'They all look over the marina, sir,' the young man in reception advised. Georgio was charged €400 for a five-night stay. He definitely needed to get the money from England now, as he would run out of cash by the end of the week. He dialled a number on his phone.

'Is that Vladimir?'

'Who wants to know?'

'It's Georgio, from Siciliy. I have a job to do in Greece. Would you be interested in helping?'

'I might be able to help. Call me Vova.'

Georgio was delighted he could assemble a team to recover the money from John England. Georgio also knew he needed a bank for the money exchange; his Greek friends would be able to suggest a suitable one.

The day after he checked in and settled in the hotel, he phoned his contacts, Dima and Vova. They agreed to meet at eleven o'clock in the port café in Ionia. They told Georgio that there was a ferry from Lefkas port to Ionia.

Before he had something to eat, he walked around the port. He found the little green ferry moored alongside the quay. The timetable indicated it would leave the port at nine-thirty each morning. The arrival time in Ionia was stated to be ten-thirty.

He was ready.

CHAPTER 21

It was mid-morning on Monday when *Brave Goose* slipped her mooring at Lefkas marina en- route to the island of Kalamos. The sky, as it had been for the last two weeks, was a bright blue with only one or two small clouds, which dissipated as the day wore on. José and Jock were busy with lines, anchors and fenders. The twin anchor deployment meant that one anchor had to be raised first. The starboard anchor was last down so that it would be first up. It took Noel some controlling the boat as the head was secured now by one anchor as soon as the starboard anchor had been recovered. Once the port anchor was weighed, the two-deck crew returned to the stern, withdrawing the stern lines. *Brave Goose* was now free to commence her next voyage.

Noel on the bridge activated the bow thruster, which pushed the vessel's bow to port. Noel now triggered a slight movement in reverse of the port engine. The bow thruster and the activation of the port engine in reverse pushed the bow to port and the stern to starboard, allowing *Brave Goose* to have an uninterrupted view of the canal and their passageway to it.

John and Fiona had become accustomed to the activities of the crew. They were always spellbound whenever they manoeuvred *Brave Goose* in a tight spot. It took real skill to achieve.

They had become accustomed to the beautiful end-of-summer weather. A flat sea, bright sunshine and no wind. It was, without doubt, the correct choice to buy a motor yacht and not rely on sails.

'You know John, I enjoyed having my friends on board, thank you.'

'Hey, this boat is half yours. You can invite whoever you like, whenever you want.'

'I find it difficult to imagine that I own half of *Brave Goose*. She is worth more than I have earned in my life.'

'That's fine. You have been a real help to me at one of the most difficult times in my life. It hasn't been easy staying onboard with all the trials we have had. I know you enjoy her as much as I do.'

'Thank you, John. I think I am living a dream.' Fiona gave him a peck on the cheek.

'When we get to Kalamos, we'll collect Azmir and his wife immediately. His priority is a visa to get him and his wife to the UK. He won't have a job here soon. The tourist trade will end here at the end of October in a few weeks.'

'Is it difficult to get a visa, John?'

'A tourist visa is easy, but a permanent stay visa is not easy. He will need a sponsor, so I guess that will be me.'

'What will that mean, John?'.

'I will have to help him find a job, possibly provide a financial guarantee. He may need help finding a place to live.'

Fiona contemplated the implications of assisting Azmir and his wife. She couldn't think how she might help.

Once underway sailing down the Lefkas canal, Noel carefully avoided oncoming traffic. Luckily, they were all small vessels. It would have been challenging had a *Brave Goose*-type boat been coming up. While the authorities had spent a great deal of money widening and deepening the canal and laying new marker buoys, it could still be challenging. Noel liked to keep to the centre of the canal, allowing space for smaller boats to pass from ahead or astern. They passed the last of the buoys that marked the deep-water entrance to the channel. Once in the Ionian Sea, a south-easterly course was set to take *Brave Goose* to the island of Kalamos. In the final stages of the short voyage, they passed the little agricultural town of Mitika. As *Brave Goose* entered the sound between the islands of Kalamos and Kastos, a voice from the bridge asked, 'Would you like to stop for a swim?'

'Oh yes, please, Noel,' replied Fiona.

Noel sailed *Brave Goose* beyond the port at Kalamos to a stop in Port Leone, passing their ultimate destination. Further along, the coast was Port Leone, not a port but a wide bay. The anchor was laid in the centre of the bay with plenty of scope to swing under what wind and depth were available for *Brave Goose.*

'Look, John, there is a village over there with a little jetty. Could we go there in *Gosling*?'

'We could. Noel OK to crane her over?'

'Yes, I will get the boys to launch *Gosling* for you. I will establish stairs and the bathing platform. The village is deserted. The only building which is maintained is the church. People come from the mainland to look after it, especially families with relatives buried in the graveyard. The bell in the courtyard still works,' advised Noel.

John and Fiona changed into swimmers. A towel each, and they were down to the water in seconds. A few laps of *Brave Goose* provided enough exercise for the day.

'The water is so warm, John.'

'Yes, my love. It will cool down shortly.'

Grabbing a towel and some beach shoes once they were on *Gosling,* they were away. Fiona took the helm and John appreciated how well she had taken to helming the little boat. She was very proficient. They came alongside the short jetty. John took a line ashore and made it fast.

'You *are* getting good at this boating stuff!'

'Thanks, John. I love it. *Gosling* is the perfect little boat for me.'

It transpired they would not be the only people in the deserted village. A fibreglass rowing boat was tied to the opposite side of the jetty. The oars were in the boat, so someone must be around.

The pair walked up the rough track, passing half-derelict houses and buildings towards the church. As they rounded the corner towards the church, the bell rang. John could now make out a man pulling on the bell rope. Two, three chimes. That was enough. The bell's voice echoed around the bay for some time.

'Hello,' John spoke loudly to the man who had been bell ringing.

'Heavens, it's *you*! Azmir?'

'Hello, John, Fiona. I wondered if it was your boat in the bay. You haven't met my wife, Ulrika, have you?'

Ulrika was a tall blond girl, unlikely to be Iranian or Greek. She waved to John and Fiona. The campanile was a single bell held aloft by an arched stone bell tower. The bell was hung from the apex of the arch. A lever protruded from the bell's yoke, which allowed a bell rope to be attached. Pulling the rope, the bell swung, which made the clapper hit the lip of the bell, making the familiar sound of a bell tuned to middle C.

'It is a beautiful sound on this lovely day,' commented Ulrika in her Scandinavian accent.

'It is. Hello, Ulrika. My name is Fiona. This is John, who was Azmir's boss in Bosnia.'

'Hi, Fiona. Great to meet you. Isn't it a pity this village is abandoned? I wonder what happened?'

'I don't know, but I am sure our boat captain will know. I will find out when I go back aboard.'

'Have you two girls finished here?'

'I think so, John. Why?'

'Well, I was thinking of offering Ulrika and Azmir a lift back to Kalamos port. We can tow their dinghy there. What do you think?'

'Now the wind has increased somewhat, I think that is an excellent idea, John. It would be quite a row.'

'Okay, Azmir, that's agreed. Let's all go to *Brave Goose*. You will find a gangway and platform for boarding on the starboard side.'

José arranged a long tow line for both Azmir's dinghy and *Gosling.*

Brave Goose lifted her anchor.

'STOP!' shouted Jock. 'I need to turn off the stop valve in *Gosling* before we tow her, or she will sink.'

'Good thinking, Jock.'

José went to help. It didn't take a minute for Jock to turn the inlet stop valve off. 'Okay now.'

Noel waited until the two men were back on board.

Brave Goose motored slowly down the two miles to the port of Kalamos. Noel laid the anchor, and the boat sat comfortably under the cliff outside the harbour. This left space for other boats to gain access to the port. The starboard passerelle and bathing platform remained deployed.

'Noel, I have a question for you?'

'Yes, Fiona, what can I help you with?'

'That deserted village in Port Leone, where we met Azmir and Ulrika. Why was it deserted?'

'Ah, well, according to the pilot, in 1953 a large earthquake broke the pipeline supplying the village with water. In this climate, you can't live without water. Crops need watering and animals need water, as do humans. I believe the cost of replacing the pipe would have been very high. Consequently, the villagers decided to go to Port Kalamos or the mainland. So, there it stands. The church has a dedicated following who come over occasionally to look after it.'

'There you are, Ulrika. I knew Noel would know. Thanks, Noel.'

'What time do you have to report for duty at the taverna, Ulrika?'

'No, I don't work on Mondays. Azmir and I took the little boat for a trip out.'

Fiona consulted with John about inviting the pair to join them onboard *Brave Goose* for dinner. He agreed and Fiona went to speak with Sally to see if she could cope with four for dinner.

All was arranged. Once the rowing dinghy had been released from its tow, the two couples took *Gosling* into the port where the men had a beer and a chat, while the girls did whatever girls do before a night out!

John and Azmir chatted about anything and everything but not the subject uppermost in Azmir's mind: the visa and the British Embassy's help to get it. Their conversation was interrupted by a noisy RIB entering the harbour. It was a UN RIB with large inboard diesel engines, hence the noise. Three men dressed in black came onshore, leaving one on board.

The three men approached John and Azmir. They had UN embroidered on their uniforms and wore light blue berets. The notation of their rank was embroidered on their uniform, an officer and two ratings.

The officer in charge addressed John first, in English.

'Good afternoon, sir. I gather the motor yacht at anchor outside the harbour is yours?'

'That's correct, officer.'

'I wonder if you have encountered two gentlemen with a yacht moored in Lefkas marina. Their names are Tony Franks and Bill Edward?'

'I do know Bill and Tony. They boarded my boat for a meal and a drink the other evening. We met the first time for a beer in one of the cafés on the marina. We were all at the same university together many years ago.'

'Have you seen them since, sir?'

'No, I haven't. Once our guests departed on Sunday, we arranged to leave Lefkas this morning. We came straight here."

'Sir,' addressing Azmir, 'are you travelling with this gentleman on his boat?'

John took over before Azmir had a chance to answer.

'Yes, he and his wife will accompany us to Athens. We need to go to the British Consul. Azmir was my interpreter in the army in Bosnia. I am a solicitor and will stand surety for him and his wife until they are settled in the UK.'

'I see, sir. I understand the Russians took a young lady travelling with you and removed her to Moscow. Is that correct?'

'Yes. You are very well-informed, officer.'

'Thank you, sir. We do try and get the relevant information before we set out on a search for individuals.'

'I know 'Joy' was taken at dinner in Ionia. We tried to find her. I have connections with EKAM in Athens. I advised them that she had gone missing. They reported that she had effectively transited Athens airport in the Russian diplomatic bag.'

'You seem to be having quite a trip, sir. Not the sort of thing you expect to happen on holiday?'

'No, officer, I agree. But events occur, and there is little I can do. Sorry, I don't know anything about Tony and Bill. What is your interest in them?'

'They are employees of the British Government and seem to have disappeared. Their boat is on its mooring. They never made their flight home.'

'What can I do to help, officer?'

'Here is a card with our contact details. We want to know if you have heard anything about these three missing persons. In addition, we would like to search your boat.'

'I have no objection to that, officer. I will be returning to *Brave Goose* as soon as the ladies return. If you want to go now, I will call Noel, my captain and authorise your visit.'

'No, please do not give advance notice of our visit, sir. We shall escort you back to your boat and come on board.'

'Okay but this all sounds very strange. I assume you must be satisfied that we are not holding anyone or anything you seek.'

The senior officer just grinned at John.

When the girls returned, they boarded *Gosling* with the men. The UN RIB, with its four crew, followed. They boarded *Brave Goose* by the boarding platform and stairs on the starboard side. Once onboard, John introduced Azmir and Ulrika to the crew and the UN crew was told they could search wherever they liked.

The senior UN officer asked if Joy had left any belongings behind. John explained that Bill and Tony had taken them as they were supposed to return to Manchester yesterday. They intended to submit her belongings for forensic examination in the UK. John suggested the crew join the four on the quarterdeck for a drink. Some of Sally's lemonade was served and the boys all had a beer.

The UN officer returned to the quarterdeck after an hour of methodical searching.

'All's well, sir; nothing here could interest the British authorities.'

'Thank you, officer. We will advise you if we have any information on any of our three missing friends.'

CHAPTER 22

'Hi Vova, I am now on Ionia. I am staying in the hotel at the back of the port. A friend who runs a taverna on the quay advised me, without realising it, that when *Brave Goose* leaves here, they will be sailing to Athens via the Corinth Canal.'

'That's useful, but we still don't have a date?'

'No, but we can estimate a date when she leaves here. We can plan for, say, about ten days from now. The plan must be flexible to work sooner or later.'

'Okay, let's go and look at the lie of the land.'

'Look, Vova. I have my laptop with me. If you get over to Ionia, we can discuss the issues. With the aid of Google Earth, I can see the details of the Corinth Canal. Once we have done that, we can see if the proposed site is suitable.'

'It sounds like a plan, Georgio, but as I am in Lefkas and can be on the mainland quickly from here; you come over on the ferry, and I will meet you on the quay, where it docks. Phone me back and tell me when you will likely be here.'

Later that day, Georgio stepped off the Ionia ferry to meet with Vova in Lefkada. He was always struck by the narrow passageways that eventually led to the town square. They made their way to the square, choosing a bar from the many to discuss the project. They ordered two beers and Georgio opened his laptop and showed Vova the Google Earth satellite photograph of the canal.

'We need to consider a site about two nautical miles from the western end and one mile from the canal entrance in the east. It has cover on both sides of the canal with a small copse on either side. The camouflage will be in our favour. Against us will be the principal office of the canal at the eastern end. I don't know if they have security on the canal's edges.'

'Seems like an ideal plan, Georgio. Let's go and look. It will be a two-hour drive for sure.'

Vova had come in his beaten-up Citroen with more bangs and scratches than anyone could count. They went to the southern side of the canal in the first instance. According to the photograph, there was a small track through the copse to the side of the canal. This apparently was duplicated on the facing northern bank. They would only know for sure when they inspected both sides.

'Look, Georgio. It's getting dark now. Let's find a taverna with a room somewhere and get going first thing tomorrow so that we can check the plan against the terrain.'

They found just what they needed on the outskirts of Corinth. The Athenian Bar and Taverna with beds, as advertised on the sign outside. The place was run down. The owner was pleased to see them, nevertheless.

'We want two beds for the night, a meal this evening, and breakfast tomorrow.'

'Okay, I only have burgers tonight. I will show you your rooms.' They each had a small bag with minimal personal kit. The rooms were basic, with a wash basin, a single bed and a wardrobe. The WC was in a small room accessed from the landing. The two men met within minutes of inspecting the rooms in the bar.

'Yes, that will do the job. A beer would be good, Georgio.'

The two men sat at the small table near the door, and their beers were delivered.

Vova confirmed to Georgio that Hymacs could do the job but would be highly inaccurate. 'They are not like bullets. They cannot be aimed at the target. I still don't understand why you don't use a gun or similar?'

'A .22 round would make no impression. It might kill someone, which would cause all sorts of difficulties, not least arrest and prison for a long time.'

Georgio motioned to Vova to stop this line of conversation as the taverna owner reappeared.

The owner went into the back again. Vova continued.

'I wasn't thinking bullets. I have in mind a portable shoulder defence weapon. They were invented in the fifties. There must be several out-of-date unused items which will never be used again as more accurate, modern Manpads have replaced the older units. I am sure the Greek mafia group could find a couple for you.'

'If you know where to get two at a price we could afford, that would be an excellent idea.'

Vova went to the centre of the square with his mobile phone. He was requesting help to obtain two Manpads.

'I should have a call back,' Vova said, 'in a couple of hours; and a price.'

'Are they difficult to use, Vova?'

'It takes some skill, but as they are self-seeking, the aim is not that essential.'

'What do they use as their target?'

'Heat is the target for these items. They are designed to home in on the exhaust plume from aircraft.'

'Would the exhaust from two marine diesel engines be sufficient?'

Vova's phone rang. 'Yes, don't know, I will ring you back.'

Georgio was keen to know the answer.

'Yes, they can supply two with two projectiles. They would cost five hundred euros for the pair.'

'How much would the Hymacs cost?'

'I guess a €1000 for the pair and €200 for the rocks to be delivered.'

'I think we should have one of the Manpad's rocket launchers as a standby in case the rocks don't do the job.'

'Okay, I will arrange for the Hymacs, the rocks and one Manpad.'

Georgio's phone rang from his contact on Ionia.

'Georgio, *Brave Goose* is planning on leaving tomorrow, Tuesday. They will moor overnight at Galaxhidi on the northern shore of the Gulf of Corinth.'

'Okay, Vova, I have just heard they will set off tomorrow. It will be a day's sail to Galaxidie. Then on Wednesday, I expect they will motor the forty miles or so to the easterly entrance of the Corinth Canal. I assume they will take that easy and probably moor off the northern shore just before the entrance to the canal. Then they will request transit of the canal, being able to enter at a moment's notice. They will be close enough to wait and see the traffic lights change to green, signifying their permission to enter. That will be Thursday. Once through the canal, they will head for Zea Marina. So, we need everything in place by Tuesday night at the latest. We need the drivers and the rocket launcher on standby from Tuesday night.'

'Okay, I will make arrangements.'

*

On board *Brave Goose,* Azmir and his wife were making last-minute preparations to leave for Athens.

'George. Would you mind if we leave today as we need to go to Athens to obtain new passports?' Ulrika asked her boss.

'Can you leave it a week? It's nearly the end of the season, but I know of two flotillas coming in next week. I would like you to stay if you can, Ulrika.'

Ulrika went to discuss it with Azmir and John. It was agreed that *Brave Goose* would return in a week to collect Azmir and Ulrika. If they wanted to put some belongings on board now, they could.

As it was Sunday, the whole crew plus Azmir and Ulrika joined at George's taverna for a large Sunday lunch at one o'clock. The food, roast leg of lamb, was delicious. Once the main course had been cleared away, George, arrived with an unopened bottle of Metaxa brandy and nine glasses. He joined the party, dispensing the brandy.

CHAPTER 23

Tony and Bill were locked inside an airless room in what seemed to be a villa. It was hot. They realised they must be on the island of Ionia. Despite their concussion, they had recognised certain aspects of the landscape on the way to their incarceration.

Bill started to speak.

'Hey, this place might be bugged. I bet they can hear every word,' whispered Bill.

'Okay,' responded Tony softly, a whisper but loud enough for Bill to hear.

'Despite the instructions not to answer questions, we do need to discover what is happening here.'

'Yes, the instructions have been not to speak. I don't see how we can discover much about the activities here without engaging?'

Two tough-looking men with Rugby Union front-row physiques then burst into the room, flooding the room with sunlight. Their unannounced entry made both men jump. They could only see their silhouettes as their exceptional size acted to block the doorway.

They wore beige trousers, black T-shirts and black corps boots; the ensemble was completed by dark sunglasses. They had very muscular arms, as though they pumped iron daily.

Bill and Tony stood up, albeit a bit unsteady on their legs.

'Come' was the monosyllabic instruction. The detainees had not been shackled but they would be unlikely to attempt a breakout with gorillas like these two. They followed one of the men; the second brought up the rear. They walked along a passageway with windows at a high level – no view out. Finally, the lead guard opened a door ahead and forced the pair to enter. They were instructed to sit down on two plastic patio-type chairs. There was a desk in front of them.

Behind the desk was a casually dressed man. He looked smart with a short-sleeved, white shirt and long trousers in a dusty pink colour. He wore a cravat at his neck. He certainly looked English to the two men.

'Good afternoon,' he greeted them in an Oxford accent. 'I am sorry you have not been welcomed onto this island properly. I hope you are both feeling in good order?' The man spoke perfect English.

Neither Bill nor Tony responded.

'Now, I understand you must be a bit shaken up, but I have some questions that need answering. We will start now. Okay, so let's sort out who is who. Are you Tony?' he asked, pointing at Bill, who didn't answer.

'So,' pointing at Tony, their inquisitor said again: '*You* must be Tony?'

This time, a slight twitch of the lips revealed that the name was correct.

'So, you are Bill,' he said. 'I know the British Secret Service, for whom you both work. They will have trained you not to divulge information under interrogation.'

Neither answered.

'So be it. The questions are simple. So should be the answers. Shall we try?'

Nothing was forthcoming from the two. The guards who had accompanied them from their room stood behind them, but closer now.

'Now, what is your position in the British Secret Service? Which country do you specialise in?'

No response.

'Look, gentlemen, I am afraid you may never see England again unless I get some information from you. There are two ways to go about this interrogation. You cooperate, or you *don't* cooperate, and we have to try and persuade you to talk.'

No response.

'I take your silence to indicate that you will not cooperate. So, we will take Tony to another room. You will stay here, Bill.'

Their interrogator pressed a bell button on the desk. After a few moments, three more heavily built men, wearing the same uniform as the earlier guards, entered the room from a door behind the desk.

'Best to say farewell to Bill. You may never see him again unless you cooperate. Take Bill back to his room.'

The two men took Bill, much against his will, back to the airless room they had been in before this ordeal. Bill did not cooperate on the trip back. He kept sitting down until, eventually, the guards had had enough of his antics. They lifted him by his legs and arms and dragged him to the room where they dropped him from waist height onto the concrete floor. The guards retreated and locked the door.

Tony was taken to a room behind the interrogator's desk. It, too, was an airless room. There were no windows. In the centre stood an old dentist's chair. It differed from the chair Tony could recall from his own dentist. It had arms, feet, legs, body, and neck bindings. Two men held him fast in the chair as the third man tied him to it with the straps. The bindings were tight but not painful. He was able to move slightly so it wasn't particularly uncomfortable.

Once he was bound without any prospect of escape, the three men retired. The lights were turned off.

Tony had little recollection of how long he had been sitting in the chair. It felt like hours. Then without warning, blinding lights started to flash in his face. Then deafening, awful pop music began to play at maximum decibels. He tried to keep his eyes shut to protect them from the lights but they were so powerful that he couldn't overcome the penetration to his eyes. He could see the flashes through his eyelids and his ears were painful from the loud music.

Tony had no way of working out how long this ordeal would continue. It seemed never-ending. The sound appeared to be getting louder and the lights brighter as time passed; his head was screaming for it all to stop.

*

Meanwhile, on *Brave Goose,* a convivial evening was enjoyed as the four sat down to an excellent dinner prepared by Sally. John did the honours with the wine – two bottles of an excellent French claret were consumed.

The pudding, crème brulé, was delicious. Coffee was served, and then Azmir broke his silence. He addressed John on his expectations about the visit to the British Ambassador in Athens.

'Do you think you can support my application for a permanent visa to enter the UK, John? I want to seek employment in the UK, as would Ulrika.'

Ulrika smiled as if to confirm Azmir's statement.

'We understand there is a shortage of people willing to work in hospitality. I know Ulrika would be a great asset to any hotel. If the establishment were based in one of the great cities, my interpreter skills would benefit them. I am, of course, happy to work in whatever capacity is available.'

'Azmir, you can be assured that I will offer whatever support I can to help you.'

'Thanks, John, that is a great relief to us both. When are you planning to leave for Athens?'

'Well, we thought we could leave any day now we are here. Would that suit you?'

'George wants us to work another week as some flotillas are due this week. He has no problem about us leaving next weekend.'

'Well, we can accommodate that. We will cruise around this area and return in a week, Azmir.'

'That's fantastic, John, thank you.'

The four chatted until eleven o'clock when John asked José to take them back to the shore. They would meet again in a week when *Brave Goose* returned. Azmir and Ulrika would fulfil their obligations to George and then they would leave in a week. They wanted to leave on good terms.

John and Fiona watched them go on board *Gosling* and waved goodbye.

Breakfast on *Brave Goose* was taken, as it was every day, on the quarter deck. It was a day the pair had come to expect: cloudless blue sky and flat sea.

'That was an enjoyable little dinner party last night, John. They are a lovely couple.'

'Yes, darling, I agree. I was wondering what possibly could have happened to Tony and Bill. It's all very odd. I hope they are okay. Nevertheless, whilst it is lovely to have guests on board, it is equally good to have the boat to ourselves.'

'Where shall we go today, John?'

'Noel, have you a moment? Where should we go for a few days before returning to collect Azmir and Ulrika?'

'I would recommend sailing to Cephalonia and moor off at Fiskardo. It is a beautiful yet busy harbour with lots of interesting shops. Places to explore in *Gosling* and lovely swimming at anchor.'

'What do you think, Fiona?'

'Ooh, yes, please, sounds fantastic.'

'There you have it. You mentioned the magic word – shops, Noel! That's where we should go today. Is it far?'

'About four hours at the most, John, without pushing it.'

'Well, let's go.'

Brave Goose established its average cruising speed of nine knots soon after leaving the anchorage outside the harbour of Kalamos. Noel had estimated it would take them about four and a half hours to reach their destination anchorage at Fiskardo. The route took *Brave Goose* from the tip of Kalamos to Fiskardo. They would pass the island of Atakos roughly halfway through the journey. A small white chapel was at the back of the only beach on the island. The bay would be teeming with yachts and boats of all kinds so there would be nowhere for *Brave Goose* to moor. Hence, they would continue to Fiskardo.

Noel had decided to helm from the flybridge. It was sunny, but a brisk wind had blown up from the north. The course they were taking took them across the shipping lane taken by ferries and cruise ships travelling from Corfu or Italy in the north, down to the Corinth Canal or to Patras. The ferry boats would berth at Patras. Vehicles could then drive to Athens using the bridge over the Corinth Canal or the Gulf of Patras.

The wind was whipping up some waves, many with white crests. The wind instrument showed twenty-nine knots. Deducting boat speed meant the wind blew at twenty knots – a force five on the Beaufort scale. Strong enough to give small yachts something to think about. There were a few small yachts, thirty-five feet or so, which Noel assumed were on course to Fiskardo. It would take all their effort to maintain a course in a force five. He noticed that there were no reefs in their sails, so they were at the limit of their abilities.

Noel kept a keen eye out for other small boats, especially the local fishermen, who often would be out single-handed. They became engrossed in fishing and didn't look out for other vessels. As he scanned the sea ahead of *Brave Goose,* he spotted a small rubber dinghy holding two people. It didn't appear to have an engine or oars and was being tossed around in the moderate sea, breaking waves washing over the top. On his second look, they were clearly in trouble, a hand waving when he got were closer. It was not the usual international signal for distress.

'John, there's a small boat in distress just ahead. We should go and help. I trust you don't have any objection?'

'No, you press on, Noel. What can we do to help?'

'I think José and Jock can deal with this. I will alert Sally as there may be an injury.'

Noel alerted the crew to the potential incident. Jock and José came to the bow. Sally was watching from the quarterdeck. John and Fiona, with binoculars in hand, remained on the flybridge.

Noel brought *Brave Goose* alongside the little craft, positioning her to windward, creating a calm patch of sea to rescue the dinghy and occupants. The port side boarding ladder and bathing platform had been lowered, providing access to *Brave Goose*. Noel had stopped the main engines from driving forward and maintained a safe distance from the dinghy and its occupants by using the bow and stern thrusters against the prevailing wind.

'Noel, we have the dinghy tied up, but we can't get the two men out as they are tied up with cable ties. Can you bring some snips, Jock?' said José.

John looked over the rail on the boat deck to see what was happening. He realised he knew the occupants of the dinghy.

'Hey, Bill! Tony! I know these men! Can I do anything to help?'

'Look, please do not go down to the dinghy without wearing a life jacket. Can you fetch four, one each for the two men in the dinghy and for Jock and José, please, John?

John did as directed. The two men looked to be in a terrible state. One by one, they were brought on deck and sat down. Sally took control and gave them a glass of water. They were very dehydrated.

'I think you both need a hot shower and a change of clothes. Then we can feed you, repair your bruises and you can tell us what happened and what to do next.'

CHAPTER 24

Somewhere close to Moscow, Joy realised she was still a hostage of the state. The small flat she was in was on an upper floor, but she couldn't tell which floor of the tower block it occupied. It was better than a cell, but only just. She had a minder, Oleg. The apartment was sparsely furnished with old, worn-out furniture to provide the minimum required. There were two bedrooms. Joy had the smaller room, with a single bed with metal springs, a worn-out mattress and iron bedsteads. The bedclothes were old and tattered. Two sheets, a blanket and an old eiderdown. With no heating, it was cold even though it wasn't winter. There was no carpet anywhere. The wooden floorboards were uncomfortable to walk on in bare feet and the boards were full of splinters. There were hooks on the back of the door and a shelf had been placed along one wall. Joy had no idea how Oleg's bedroom was furnished. She always kept her door locked.

The main entrance to the flat was kept locked. Again, the living area was sparsely furnished without carpet or curtains. The square Formica-topped table and two chairs were the limits of the furnishings. There was no settee or creature comforts of any kind. Along one wall was a china sink with a pot cupboard beneath. A gas geyser gave some hot water. There was a cold tap and an old refrigerator which was noisy and not very effective. The toilet was in a small area off the living room. It had a sink and a hand shower ran from it, and a drain in the floor – no separate shower as such. A small tabletop cooker adjoined the sink on top of the work surface. The cooker was electric and had two rings and a small oven and provided the only heat for the flat.

Joy wondered what she had done to deserve all this awful treatment. She couldn't go outside or open a window for ventilation. All the windows had been screwed shut.

Olga, her minder, or jailer as Joy referred to her in her mind, was small, her black hair scraped into a bun at the back of her head. She wore a full-length black dress splattered with food stains. She wore the same clothes every day. Her face was white and devoid of any makeup. She had cruel eyes that seemed to stare right through Joy. Olga hardly spoke. She gave instructions but refused to enter into a conversation. Joy was anxious to know why she was being kept here. No response from Olga.

Olga went out every day at ten o'clock, returning at four in the afternoon. The door to the landing outside the flat remained locked at all times. Joy found some scraps from yesterday, the remains of a hard loaf of bread and some soup in a pan. That amounted to her daily rations until Olga returned with some more rations. There was no paper or writing equipment; no newspapers, books or magazines. The place was sparse. Food – served once a day – would usually be potatoes, pasta, some small tomatoes, or a small tin of beef stew, a hard loaf a day (probably baked the previous day), shared between the two.

There was no radio or TV. Joy had no idea what was going on in the outside world. She just wished she could escape this incarceration.

*

On *Brave Goose*, Sally had taken control of the two rescued men.

'John, would you have a set of clothes that you could let Bill and Tony borrow while I launder their clothes? They will have them back tomorrow.'

'You are an angel, Sally. While you give them some refreshments, I'll set out dry clothes for them in the guest cabin.'

Once the two men had recovered their equilibrium, Sally showed them the guest cabin with ensuite heads and a shower. She asked them to leave their wet clothes in the galley when they had freshened up.

'God, this shower is lovely, Bill. I began to think at one point we would never see civilisation again.'

Noel called the UN officer who had been on board a few days ago. He told him what had happened and that the two men were safe and onboard *Brave Goose*. He advised the UN officer that they would be at anchor off Fiskardo by sixteen hundred hours.

'Please do not let the two men leave your boat until we have been to meet and interview them,' the officer instructed.

Bill and Tony arrived back on the quarterdeck, looking in better shape and more relaxed.

'That was wonderful, Sally, and thank you, John, for lending us your clothes.'

'There's tea and coffee and cake. Please help yourselves.'

'Well done, Sally, you have done an excellent job,' said John.

'Thank you, John. Tony and Bill, you have both been hit on the head. Can I examine your wounds and, if necessary, clean them and dress them with some antiseptic cream?'

'Yes, please, Sally. That would be helpful; I have a severe headache. A paracetamol would be good, too.'

'Okay, Bill. Are you in a similar condition, Tony?'

'Yes, Sally.'

Following her medical administrations, Sally returned to the galley to start with the laundry. *Brave Goose*, having recovered the rubber dinghy and lashed it on top of the boat deck's RIB, was underway again. José had retrieved the boarding steps and platform.

'Tony, Bill, I am so glad we came along when we did and were able to rescue you. Noel tells me some UN officers will join us when we get to Fiskardo. They have requested that you remain on board until you meet with them. When we know the timings, I will hopefully make an appointment for you to join Fiona and me for dinner onshore. I hope that will be satisfactory?'

'John, you are our saviour. Thank you so much. It will be interesting to know what concerns the UN. I guess the goings-on at Ionia and the unauthorised private army the Russians have established. Thank you so much for the hot shower and clothes. A luxury we both expected to be far out of reach for some time.'

'I am certain there will be a list of enquiries. Please make yourselves comfortable. We will let you know when we arrive in Friskardho. If you prefer, you can snooze in the two available cabins.'

'John, that would be wonderful; we are, to say the least, short on sleep.'

John and Fiona resumed their relaxation on the boat deck.

'What happened to Bill and Tony, John?'

'I don't know, darling. It isn't for me to discuss with them. We will know the full story when they are ready.'

'Will they remain on board tonight?'

'Yes, darling, if you are happy with that. It seems the least we can do.'

'Okay, I had hoped to go ashore and look around.'

It was a quarter to four when *Brave Goose* picked her spot outside the harbour of Fiskardo. The ship's main port anchor was deployed, and the boarding ladder and bathing platform on the port side permitted boarding once *Gosling* and the large RIB were deployed.

'No problem, we can leave the two men here with our crew. I will get *Gosling* launched,' said Noel.

John requested that Noel call him on his mobile if the UN officers arrived before they were back on board. The two owners soon headed for the quay to look around the pretty little port. *Gosling* was tied up on the pontoon, against which were yachts and motorboats. The pontoon had been set about ten feet from the old stone harbour wall, leaving a canal between it and the old harbour wall. It was ideal for dinghy mooring.

'How about this restaurant, John? It looks lovely!'

'Yes, I guess that will do perfectly. I will book for say nine o'clock?'

'Yes, darling, I am getting used to the late dining favoured by the locals.'

Having achieved what they came for, a walk around the much improved and developed harbour village came next. Some would say it wasn't really much of an improvement but it suited Fiona. The old and the new extra buildings were constructed around a stone circular planter with an ancient olive tree in the centre. The rounded lip on the planter's edges was an excellent spot for John to sit while Fiona occupied herself in the numerous boutiques and gift shops nearby.

'Look, John, what a fabulous boutique.'

'Okay, in you go!'

John sat on the edge of the circular planter. There were plenty of people around, but he assumed it would be very crowded in the height of summer. The source of so many people was a large trip boat while the local car ferry had arrived at the other side of the harbour. John's peace was about to be shattered. He was just contemplating what would happen next with Bill and Tony when a shout came from the shop.

'John, what do you think about this?'

He was shaken out of his daydream. Fiona modelled a new dress in powder blue, slit at the front with not much material at the back. Little imagination was required to work out what was concealed by the dress.

'It suits you, especially now you have a tan. I can see most of the tan from here!'

'Cheek! You think it's a bit too daring?'

'No, you can carry it off. Go for it – if there is enough wardrobe space!'

'Okay, John, I will.'

Moments later, Fiona came skipping out of the shop with a bag on her arm and a wide grin.

John plotted a course through the now very crowded little port.

They eventually returned to *Gosling.*

'Mind you, don't get your bag wet,' said John as he untied their rib and made sedate progress back to *Brave Goose.*

The large UN black RIB was tied alongside the boarding ladder and platform.

'The UN officers must be on board. Hope they will release Tony and Bill to carry on and, I suppose, fly back to Manchester.'

Little *Gosling* looked overwhelmed by the UN boat. There was just enough room for John to tie up and reach the platform.

'Hello, everyone. I see the UN officers have arrived, Noel.'

'Yes, John, the two are interviewing Bill and Tony now in the saloon.'

The two men and two UN officers appeared on the quarterdeck as they spoke.

'Is everything okay, officer?' enquired John.

'Yes, sir. Bill and Tony are required to return to the UK straight away. They must get to Lefkas to sort out their yacht and then fly home.'

'Okay, we will get them back to their boat.'

The UN officers thanked John and all the crew on *Brave Goose* for their help. At that moment, the ferry to Vassiliki on Lefkada was leaving from the slipway on the far side of the harbour.

'There's the solution, Bill, Tony. We can get you on that ferry tomorrow. Once back in Lefkada, you can get a taxi from Vassiliki to the marina in Lefkas. How are you off for money?'

'John, thank you, that will be excellent. Look, we don't have any money. Our wallets were not with us. They are still on our yacht with our passports. Well, we hope they are.'

'That's no problem, let me give you €500. That should be sufficient to get the ferry, a taxi ride and even a flight home.'

'Let us have your bank details, John, and we will reimburse you as soon as we get home.'

'Okay, all good. Now, I have a table booked for this evening in the port. We four can go in on *Gosling*.'

'You are too kind, John. We would love to come.'

'Good, we are eating at Greek time – the table is booked for nine.'

Tony and Bill joined Fiona and John on the boat deck. They each occupied a sun lounger. John and Fiona read their books, and Tony and Bill conversed before taking a siesta. On waking around six, the temperature had dropped slightly, but it was still hot by UK standards.

'What will you two do when you get home?'

'That's is for others to decide, John. The Secret Service is not as secret as you might think. We shall be debriefed about our time in captivity on Ionia Island.'

'Tony, it would be interesting to know why you and Bill were in Lefkas. It would seem that your roles were known to the Russians?'

'I don't know who could have shopped us other than Joy – the obvious choice.'

'So, what did you do daily? Am I allowed to know?'

'That's no problem. We are MI6 employees, mainly monitoring known terrorists or suspected terrorists who have arrived legally or illegally in the UK.'

'So, what is the end goal, and why are you in Greece?'

'To make the UK safer and more prosperous for its citizens.'

'That sounds like a line from a brochure, Bill! I was really looking for details about how you achieve those ends, not what the ends are.'

'Okay, we have three core aims: stopping terrorism, disrupting the activity of hostile states, and giving the UK a cyber advantage.

We work closely with MI5, GCHQ, HM Armed Forces, law enforcement, and other international partners. We are tasked and authorised by senior government ministers and overseen by Parliament and independent judges. People who work for MI6 come from all walks of life with different skills, interests and backgrounds. We are not James Bond characters. We keep it in the background.

MI6 is an organisation where integrity, courage and respect are central to our actions. We encourage and admire difference. Many MI6 staff are overseas, while others work from our headquarters in Vauxhall, London. Although our work is secret, everything we do is legal and underpinned by the values that define the UK.

We are SIS – the UK's Secret Intelligence Service – or MI6. SIS has ensured the UK and our allies keep one step ahead of our adversaries. We are creative and determined – using cutting-edge technology and espionage.'

'That sounds like a well-rehearsed speech, Bill. You must have some James Bond moments?'

'Well, yes, but only due to diligent work behind the scenes. Only when a bad guy is flushed out do we find ourselves in a situation that could be reminiscent of James Bond!'

'I gather you have had a few Bond moments, John. How did you cope?'

'A few years back, I was attacked from behind, waiting for the lift in my apartment block in the basement. A great friend advised me well before that incident to take some lessons in Krav Maga, which is Mossad's self-defence method. I guess you know them. Adding it to my Army training has proved to be extremely helpful.'

'So, why are you not applying to work for MI6? There are vacancies.'

'It never occurred to me, and we have a very happy life. I am not sure I want to spoil what we have.'

'I understand. I could always put a good word in the right ear at Vauxhall.'

'Not just now, Tony, it's kind of you, and let's keep in touch. You never know how things can change. Why were the Russians keen to capture you two? What have you been up to that caused them to take you?'

'Difficult to explain. They are causing issues with immigrants. We think they are behind a significant human trafficking racket to get girls into prostitution in the UK.'

'How do they do that?'

'Issuing UK passports to pretty girls in exchange for work when they arrived in the UK. The work nearly always involved drugs and prostitution.'

'So, how do they get the passports?'

'A double agent in the Home Office has been providing them.'

'Could we possibly know this person?'

'You might,' said Tony with a broad smile. John was sure they were referring to Joy.

'Had your actions anything to do with Joy hopping off to Moscow and then your capture by the Russians?'

'It might have,' said Bill.'

'I suspect the sex business is a very lucrative enterprise. Hence the human trafficking of pretty girls from Albania. Enver Hoxha was a horrific dictator. A cruel man. He died in 1985, leaving Albania in grinding poverty. The proximity of Greece enabled the criminal fraternities to plunder Greece. They were assisted by Russians who were keen to exploit this small and helpless country. The Russian mafia chose to extract all the pretty girls for their own purposes, exporting them to the UK and other parts of Europe for exploitation.

'Yes, we think that is what the Russians are doing here in Ionia. Anyway, we think we have seen an end to their game.'

'Good. Look boys, Fiona and I need to change. Sorry, I don't have any more spare clothes. Sally will have your clothes available for you in the morning. There is a notice board on the slipway on the other side of the harbour. I suspect it has the times of ferries. It's the ferry to Vasiliki you will need. When we go for dinner, I will take *Gosling* over there, and you can see what time they run.'

Once John had requested that *Gosling* be launched for their trip ashore, John and Fiona retired to change.

At half past eight, the three men and Fiona went ashore on *Gosling*. The timetable pinned to the notice board on the slipway indicated that the ferry would leave for Vassiliki at ten o'clock in the morning.

'That's perfect,' announced Bill.

After a sumptuous dinner and joviality between the four, they all returned to *Brave Goose* just after eleven o'clock.

On returning to the boat and arriving on the quarter deck, brandy was offered but refused by Bill and Tony. They were delighted to see their laundered clothes awaiting them, beautifully folded, ironed and laid out on one of the sofas.

'Sally is a marvel, John. We will see her to say thank you in the morning.'

CHAPTER 25

After a full English breakfast, the two MI6 men were chauffeured across the harbour in good time to board the ferry to Vasiliki. John had given them the €500 he'd promised and his details and bank account. Sally received kisses for all her hard work.

At 09:45, the sizeable white ferry with a drop-down ramp at the bow entered the harbour. All on *Brave Goose* had a great view of the activities. It was a still morning. The diesel engines of the ferry maintained position on the slipway without the requirement to tie up to the quay.

'That's clever, Noel.'

'Yes, John, it's the way they do it. Saves time, I suppose.'

A small crowd of locals and tourists alighted, as did the vehicles – everything, from a fuel tanker to bicycles; lorries once loaded with building materials but empty now, private cars; small vans delivering foodstuffs; motorcycles; and people. Once the last vehicle had been safely manoeuvred on board, all on *Brave Goose* could see Tony and Bill walk up the bow ramp to the passenger area. The ferry had been in gear throughout this procedure, keeping her tight against the slipway. The engines were put into neutral as the bow ramp was hoisted when the captain gave the signal. During that process, the ferry reversed from the quay into the open water to the side of the slipway. She turned through one hundred and eighty degrees. Once she had cleared the slipway, she could move out of the port.

'Quite a trick to manoeuvring that ferry. I bet it isn't as easy as it seems if the wind blows, Noel?'

'You're correct, John. However, they do this three or four times daily, so it's second nature. They do rope the ferry in heavy weather, mind you.'

As the ferry moved out of the port, two figures on the upper deck on the starboard side waved furiously at all those on *Brave Goose* who had lined the rail to see them go.

*

'Well, that was an unexpected diversion.'

'Yes, John. I would love to go to the shops again. Do you need anything, Sally?' enquired Fiona.

Nothing was required, so John and Fiona took *Gosling* to allow Fiona to inspect all the shops thoroughly. She eventually found the shop she wanted and dived in. There was no request from John to look at the clothes she'd bought; her bag was tiny. He knew he would be told what it was when Fiona was ready.

*

Tony and Bill disembarked their ferry in Vasiliki. They were fortunate to find a taxi that had not been pre-booked waiting on the quayside. Within the hour, the two men were back at Lefkas marina. Tony paid for the cab, saying he would go and see in what state the Russians had left the boat.

'Can you collect the keys from the harbour office, Bill?'

'Will do, Tony.'

The two men went about their tasks.

Bill explained to the girls in the office that they had been delayed. They would give the boat's keys to the boatyard so it could be put on dry land in preparation for the winter.

Maria, one of the office girls, went to collect the keys.

'Which yard will she be in over winter, Mr Edwards?'

'It will be Paleros. I'll give them the keys. Thanks, Maria.'

As Bill was handed the keys, there was a massive explosion from the marina …

*

When Tony had reached the boat, the hatch was unlocked so he pushed it into its housing; there was a flash of light and he could smell gas. He was blown out of the cockpit into the water.

*

'Bloody hell! That sounded like a bomb, Maria!'

Bill and the girls in the office looked out from the elevated position of the marina office as smoke and flames rose from the pontoon where their yacht was moored. He shot down the stairs joining several marineras, some carrying portable fire extinguishers. Others were preparing a hose and connecting it to the raw water supply in anticipation of dowsing the boat and possibly more boats nearby.

'My god, it's our boat! Tony, Tony, where are you?' Bill shouted, fearing the worst.

There was now a fire raging on his yacht and boats on either side. The office staff called the fire brigade, the police and an ambulance. The marina was in full alert mode, with alarm bells ringing full blast. The standing orders were that the marina would now be closed to incoming or outgoing vessels. The team at the fuel dock had closed down and laid a line across the entrance.

Bill couldn't get near his boat as a cordon of rope had been deployed, preventing anyone from getting onto the pontoon. There was no doubt it was their boat. The severely damaged yacht was on fire at the centre of a group of boats. Even from a distance, Bill could tell their craft was severely damaged. Tony must have been on board when the bomb exploded. Could the Russians have planted a booby trap? Bill could not get close to the burning boats but he called as loudly as he could for Tony.

'Tony, Tony, are you there?'

The ferocity of the fire and subsequent explosions from gas bottles, petrol cans, and diesel tanks for the engines on their boat and neighbouring craft created an inferno the likes of which Bill had never seen before. Modern yachts and boats constructed of fibreglass and wood with fuel tanks, gas bottles and the like were a dangerous mixture. The flames were ferocious, spreading rapidly due to the strengthening north-west wind and yet more boats on either side of the conflagration caught fire.

It took only minutes for the fire brigade to arrive on the scene and start quelling the flames. The acrid black smoke could be seen from all around Lefkas town. The fire brigade managed to get the fire engine to the end of pontoon E. The pump on the fire truck could suck up seawater from the harbour through the big pump on the engine, providing significantly increased water pressure. Within half an hour of arriving, the fires had been extinguished.

A police officer had been conscious of Bill calling the name Tony.

'Is there someone you know on one of the boats?'

'Yes, my partner. He would have been in the middle boat. Tony went to board her while I got the keys from the harbour office.'

'Was he onboard, do you think, when your yacht exploded?'

'I am confident he would have been. There was so much smoke and flames I couldn't see. I fear the worst.'

An ambulance had arrived. Several police officers were asking for witnesses. *Were there any people on the boats, and had anyone seen anything suspicious recently?* Bill was beside himself. The police officer brought the chief police officer to Bill, who was distraught. With tears running down his face, he did his best to explain what Tony could have been doing.

'Do you think he could have been inside the boat when it exploded?'

'I don't know. He might have dived or been blasted overboard. I couldn't see.'

The police officer instructed the fire brigade to conduct a detailed search of the area to try and find a body. There was debris and charred wood, parts of boats, masts and sails everywhere. Several firefighters were on their hands and knees looking for a survivor.

Bill knew that Tony must have triggered a booby trap device left by the Russians. Given the enormous blast that had been set off, it was hard to see how he could have survived. If he did survive the blast, could he have survived the subsequent fire?

'Was anyone on board, sir?' asked the senior officer, judging by the embroidery on his cap and lapels.

'Yes,' responded Bill, hardly able to speak. 'My partner in the boat, Tony, had just gone on board.'

'Do you know why the boat could have exploded as it did?'

'Yes, sir, I have a very good idea. I need to discuss this with you in a private place.' Bill had become aware that a local TV crew had arrived, and several reporters were around. One was keen to speak to Bill, who refused the invitation.

'Okay, sir, let's go to the marina office. We can speak there.'

Bill was shaken as they were about to leave the fire-damaged pontoon. He knew that his best friend must have been killed.

'Over here, over here, quick!' shouted a firefighter. He had found a man's body. It was submerged under the floating jetty. 'I think he is still alive!'

This signalled for more fire officers, a medic, paramedics with a stretcher and police helpers to all run to the spot identified by the firefighter. Bill joined the stampede to see if it was Tony. It was! *Was he still alive?* He was hard to recognise. The explosion had blackened his face and body.

Bill's mobile rang. A cheery voice enquired if they had arrived at the boat and had they made arrangements to get home …

'Oh Fiona, I can hardly speak. Tony has been killed!'

Bill burst into tears. He was shaking and red in the face. He bent double; he couldn't communicate. He tried to say what had happened, but the words wouldn't come.

'Bill! How awful! What happened? I don't believe this! Oh, I'm mortified. Tony has gone? He was here only a matter of hours ago.' Fiona began to cry; tears were running down her cheeks.

'Look, I am with a police officer. I will ring you later.'

*

Fiona ran to find John and told him what little she knew.

'John, John, there has been a terrible accident!' Fiona was weeping and hyperventilating. She struggled to get the words out.

'Fiona, whatever is the matter, sit down, darling and tell me all.'

Sitting in a wicker chair on the quarterdeck, she tried through sobs to repeat the content of the phone call she had received from Bill.

'Oh no. The bomb must have been a booby trap left by the Russian captors.'

'Do you think so, John?'

'Yes, there is no other explanation. I need to go and see Bill as soon as I can.'

'Oh, please be careful, darling.'

'The damage has been done. Bill will need some help. Tony had all the money. Bill needs help.'

*

'Please,' said the senior officer. 'Can I have your name and the name of your partner who was on the yacht when it exploded?'

'Yes, I am Bill Edwards, and the man killed was Tony Franks. I need to speak to you confidentially – Tony and I are officers in MI6, the British Secret Service –'

Just then, a shout went up from the pontoon.

'He's alive! Get a helicopter! He will need to be flown to the hospital. He's in a bad way.'

Bill was allowed to go and see his friend, now lying on the pontoon covered in black ash and soot, with blood streaming down his face, his clothes in tatters.

'Yes, that's Tony. Tony Franks. Let me know where he will be. I want to be with him.'

Bill realised there was nothing he could do to help his friend. He would be in the best place. A helicopter overhead alerted the ambulance and fire crews to prepare Tony for a rapid transfer. The helicopter landed on an empty area in the marina where boats were stored in the winter. As he watched in stunned silence, his friend was picked up on a stretcher and loaded into the helicopter to be flown to the hospital.

'Can we have a chat about what happened, please, sir?'

'Yes, okay. I am badly shaken but I will do my best. Tony and I are, as I have indicated, officers of the British Secret Service. We have been trying to identify the individuals, possibly Russians, smuggling young girls from Albania to Greece. They then take them to Europe and the UK. The girls are captured to work in the sex trade in the cities of Europe. We were due to fly home a week ago, but whilst we were asleep one night, we were hijacked after we were knocked unconscious by our Russian captors. Our boat was towed out of the marina with us onboard. We eventually found ourselves in a building which we now know was on Ionia. We discovered pretty quickly some Russians had taken us. We were subject to interrogation techniques, and after about a week, we were released. They tied us up, put us in a small rubber dinghy, and set us adrift. We were rescued by a motor yacht –*Brave Goose*. They couldn't have been more helpful. We were interrogated by the UN and advised we were free to return home. Our yacht must have been returned to its berth by the Russians so it could be them who left a booby trap bomb. I came up to the marina office to collect the spare keys. While I was here, I saw and heard the explosion.'

'Have you reported this to your employers yet?'

'No, I have only just come around enough from the shock to talk to you. They will be the next on the list. I need them to send me money as my credit cards and cash have been blown up.'

'I understand, sir. I am sorry for your loss. Please don't leave the area without contacting us first.'

'Okay, but I suspect I must go to the British Embassy in Athens. Thanks for your card. I will let you know what is happening.'

Bill rang his contact at MI6. He made arrangements for some cash to be available later that day at Alpha Bank. All he had to do was to give his name and pick up €1000.

'Can you come back as soon as you can, Bill? We have some serious issues to sort out.'

*

John decided to return to Lefkas to see if he could help. The big RIB would be the quickest with its one-hundred horsepower motor.

'Noel, can you please bring *Brave Goose* to the marina? I will shoot off in the RIB. It will take an hour so I will see you later. Fiona, do you want to come with me?'

'Yes, I will get a sweater and a waterproof jacket. '

'Would you get something for me, darling? I will get the lifejackets.'

They raced to Lefkas, leaving the crew to travel with *Brave Goose.*

CHAPTER 26

John and Fiona left *Brave Goose* at high speed in the big RIB. The entrance to the marina had been closed, a large rope strung across the entrance. A sign attached to the centre of the rope stated 'Marina closed'. There was only one way for them to get in. They berthed at *Brave Goose*'s mooring on the opposite side of the fuelling berth. The pair climbed out, half ran and half walked to where the activity was opposite the marina office. John could see Bill at the centre of a clutch of people, including several police officers.

Walking over to the group, John requested access to Bill.

'Sorry, sir, he is busy with the police.'

'I am a friend and his solicitor.'

'I will see what I can do, sir.'

Bill broke away from the group and approached John and Fiona.

'Please come in, John.'

Fiona stayed outside the cordon. The area had been secured by police tape. Bill introduced John as a friend and John added again that he was Bill's solicitor. A police officer addressed him and took him to one side.

'Ah, Mr England. I think we have met. *Brave Goose* is your superyacht?'

'Yes, that is correct. Have you managed to establish what happened here?' John enquired of the senior police officer.

'There was a large explosion on the yacht jointly owned by Mr Edwards and Mr Franks. We are sorry to say Mr Franks was caught up in the blast. He was discovered under a pontoon, barely alive. He is in a helicopter on his way to the hospital now. The subsequent fire set alight the adjoining boats. It is quite a tragedy. How do you know the two men, sir?'

'We were at university together years ago. We found one another only the other day when we met in the bar.' John pointed out the location. 'We got caught up in conversation, they were on their own, so I invited them on board my boat. We got on like old friends. We met about two weeks later when we picked them both up from a dinghy floating adrift midway between Ionia Island and Ithaka. They had been bound hand and foot. Upon further enquiry, we discovered they had been tortured and released in the dinghy. They told us all this once we had them onboard.'

'Why would they be tortured?'

'Well, officer, I assume Mr Edwards has disclosed that he and Mr Franks are field operatives for MI6 in the UK?'

'Yes, but he has been somewhat distraught.'

'I can imagine.'

'With that information, what do you plan on doing now, inspector?'

'I need to speak with my superiors. We can then make arrangements for Mr Edwards.'

'I am not sure what you mean by that, but my yacht will be here soon. We can arrange accommodation for him. We plan to visit Athens, and we can get him to the British Embassy there. They are the best people to help him.'

'That would be very helpful, sir. I will explain that to him. Our forensic teams are working on what is left of the three damaged boats. We have arranged for them to be retrieved from the marina. It will make examination easier.'

'I understand. Once my boat is back here, we will be onboard should you wish to speak to me again.'

'Bill, *Brave Goose* is on her way here,' John addressed Bill now. 'I have just told the inspector that we can provide you with accommodation. I can also help you buy some clothes etcetera.'

'That is very kind, John. I need to get to the British Embassy in Athens so they can provide me with an emergency passport.'

'No worries, we are sailing to Athens next. Why don't you come with us?'

'I guess it depends on what the police want to do here.' Bill's face was screwed up. His whole body was shaking. Tears were cascading down his face.

'I am devastated, John. The interrogation by those Russians was bad enough, but this is terrible. It could have been me who set the bomb off if Tony had gone to get the keys.'

As they were talking, *Brave Goose* appeared beyond the fuelling dock. Her berth could easily be accessed from the canal. Noel brought her in and made her fast. The passerelle was rigged.

'Fiona, please ask Sally to make up the bunk cabin. We will have another guest for our trip to Athens.'

Fiona was delighted to move away from the gruesome scene at the marina. Once onboard, Fiona explained to everyone what had happened. The whole crew were incredulous.

'I find it unbelievable this sort of thing can happen these days.'

'I agree, Noel. There is far more to this than we have heard so far.'

'John hopes Bill will come and stay onboard and we'll take him, Azmir and his wife to the British Embassy in Athens.'

With the consent of the police, the marina staff were moving five damaged yachts and a motorboat. The yacht owned by Bill and Tony was little more than a charred shell. The two yachts on either side were severely damaged, while the other three vessels were damaged but repairable. The boats were hoisted out of the marina and taken on cradles to an area of the marina away from other vessels. The police would then be able to establish a secure compound while the forensic investigation continued.

The marina captain inspected the pontoons where the fire had taken hold. It was clear two sections of the pontoon would require replacing. He arranged for divers and engineers to remove the damaged sections and close the gap by attaching the rest of the pontoon to the remaining pontoon, allowing full access to the shore. It shortened the pontoon, but it wasn't that much of a problem as it was the end of the season. Several boat yards were involved as the boats moored on the furthest section beyond the fire and were requested to move as they had no damage.

Eventually, it transpired that eight boats in all required moving. They were to be temporarily moored alongside the outer pontoon,

The police allowed Bill to go onboard *Brave Goose,* but she was not permitted to sail until the local police had completed their enquiries. The marina was opened again, and the business of boats coming and going resumed.

*

Bill was a shadow of his former self. He found it challenging to communicate. He was a mental wreck.

'Bill, I understand your distress, but communicating with family, work, and the British Embassy in Athens is required. I can help you if you like. I can start the conversation and then allow you to speak. Would that help?'

'It would, John. I need to ring my wife first.'

'Well, let's go into my office.' The two men headed to John's office to start the conversation. John knew they would be brutal and harrowing conversations. He requested Sally bring them some coffee and lemonade.

Realising the phone calls would be lengthy and complex, Fiona suggested to Sally that they go into town to purchase some clothes for Bill. As he had managed to fit into John's clothes when he had been rescued from the rubber dinghy, she had a good idea of size.

The two girls advised Noel what they were going to do and where. They would be a couple of hours or so. If they were going to be longer, Fiona promised to phone.

The two women found their way out of the marina and, crossing the main access road into Lefkas town, moved into the labyrinth of narrow streets. Eventually, they could hear the babble of humanity. They realised they were close to the town square as the noise became louder.

An attractive town square appeared as they exited from a narrow street, surrounded by restaurants and cafés. They spread their awnings, tables and chairs into the square. The area was paved with stone flags which had become highly polished from the hundreds of feet walking over them for years.

'Look, let's go down here, Sally. Most of the shops seem to be down this street.'

It took an hour and two shops to find suitable clothes, mainly casual, for Bill. The third and final one was a tourist shop selling a mixture of items from umbrellas to models of the Parthenon, tiny dolls in traditional Greek costume and, importantly for Sally and Fiona, suitcases. They purchased a grey lightweight case. On a bench in the street, they undid all their parcels and carefully packed all the clothes from underpants, socks and handkerchiefs to trousers, shirts, T-shirts, a pair of swimmers, and one sweater. Finally, they purchased a lightweight anorak in case of rain.

'Job done, Sally. Let's get back to the boat.'

'Hang on, Fiona. We need to get Bill some toiletries: a razor and all that sort of stuff.'

'You are right.'

A large perfume shop was opposite the bench they had used to pack the suitcase. They sold men's toiletries and a massive collection of perfumes.

*

Back on the boat, to the girls' astonishment, John and Bill were still on the phone when they arrived with the case full of clothes for Bill.

'Cup of tea, Fiona?'

'What a good idea. While you make the tea, Sally I will put the case in Bill's cabin.'

When Fiona and Sally returned, John and Bill went. to the quarterdeck to explain what had been happening.

'Is that a cup of tea you have there, Fiona?' enquired John.

'Yes, my love, would you like a cup?'

'Well, I would prefer a beer. What would you like, Bill?'

'I will join you in a beer, John, after that marathon.'

As soon as beer was mentioned, Sally was on her feet, glasses and bottles straight from the fridge placed on the table, the crown tops removed.

'Thanks, Sally.'

'There's a suitcase in the cabin you have been allocated, so you have two changes of clothes and a waterproof, as well as toiletries and a razor etcetera. We hope you like our choices, Bill.'

'Sally, Fiona, what can I say? Just a big thank you. As I have no money, I will send the money to you when I return to the UK.'

'That will not be necessary, Bill; it's our little offering. The least we can do considering the circumstances.'

'Have you managed to contact everyone, most importantly your wife, Bill?'

'Yes, thanks, Fiona. As it transpired, it was the easiest call. The difficult one was to MI6. However, they are sending three operatives here to liaise with the police. Interestingly, the Russian connection on the island of Ionia is tentative. A Russian oligarch purchased half of the island from the Greek government during the country's severe financial problems. It would appear that this oligarch thinks he can run half the island as his kingdom and do what he likes.'

'I guess that will not sit well with the Greek government?'

'No, especially as they had no idea what was going on. Once we are in Athens to consider the wording of the land transfer document, we can indicate to MI6 what was permitted. The document was housed in the National Archive legal section. The Greek government have invited John as a lawyer to visit the estate's department and give advice on the terms of the sale.

'Oh, good. That will keep you busy, John, won't it?'

'Cheeky!'

John's mobile rang as they were talking.

'Thank you, inspector, that is excellent. I appreciate your help.'

'That was the Greek police inspector. We can make our way to Athens as soon as we like. We have to speak to a man in the Athens police and someone from EKAM, their anti-terrorist group.'

'They will want to look into what is happening on the island of Ionia. I guess they suspect there is a terrorist cell on the island.'

'Well, you wouldn't bet against that, Bill.'

'I would like to get my hands on those people. I haven't told you what went on. I will tell you all very soon. I cannot help thinking about Tony.'

'Okay, let's consider what we will do in the next few days,' said John. 'My thoughts are that we leave Lefkas tomorrow and sail to Kalamos. We can anchor off there. Once Azmir and Ulrika are on board with their stuff, we will leave for Athens.'

'Is that okay by you, Noel?'

'Yes, John, so let's work it out. I need to get a mooring in Zea marina. It is Tuesday today; my calculations say we will be in Kalamos on Wednesday. I suspect it will be Friday before we leave Kalamos. It is about 150 nautical miles to Zea marina. There could be hold-ups in the

Corinth Canal. So, an extra six hours would make the journey to Zea Marina about 24 hours. I suggest we don't go through the canal at night. We can anchor in several places in the Gulf of Corinth. From memory, the trip through the canal must be at a speed no faster than four knots. So, if we are in the Gulf of Corinth on Saturday, we would get to Zea Marina on Sunday afternoon. That will be ideal.'

'That sounds perfect. How are you off for supplies, Sally?'

'I will go this afternoon and top up, as we will then have three more people on board. I will go to the supermarket that has the van. Can you come with me, José?'

'Yes, Sally, I will have finished the cleaning by then.'

'Good, that's all arranged. Is that okay with you, Bill?'

'I will phone London now and advise on our movements. I will ask if they can make an appointment for Azmir and me on Monday afternoon at the embassy in Athens.'

'Fiona darling, would you like to go into Lefkas? We could have lunch, and there may be some shops that appeal?'

'Thanks, John, that would be excellent. I did see some boutiques when I was shopping for Bill. Oh, Bill, if there is anything you don't like or want to change, let me have it now, and I will take it back. I have kept the receipts.'

'No, Fiona, you and Sally did a splendid job. I like it all.'

CHAPTER 27

It was four in the afternoon when *Brave Goose* dropped anchor off Kalamos. John had already phoned Azmir to see if their plans fit with him and Ulrika. Azmir had been delighted. He now stood on the top of the harbour wall at Kalamos, waving his hat in the air to greet *Brave Goose.*

The two RIBs were ready, and the boarding ladder and platform were established. *Gosling* was the first boat away to the harbour, with John and Fiona at the wheel and Bill sitting behind in the 'shotgun' position. Fiona expertly brought *Gosling* to a halt alongside the quay. Azmir took the bow line and helped the passengers out. Fiona was the last to find dry land. There was much hugging and hand-shaking in greeting. It was again a perfect day.

The four walked to the taverna to be greeted by George. He was delighted to see them, but he always was. Even if he had never met a customer before, George would treat them as a long-lost friend. Ulrika joined Azmir, who introduced her to the rest of the party. John introduced Fiona to George. He was the de-facto harbour master. No one knew if he was the paid harbour master or not. During the season, shortly to end, George would be there standing in his white fibreglass dinghy with a thirty-horsepower engine. He always had a smile on his face. He wore a straw hat, a shirt with rolled-up sleeves and a beige pair of trousers which could do with a wash. George's Taverna, established at the head of the small harbour, had been extended. When all the yachts and flotillas appeared during the summer, George would zoom around in his little boat, ensuring people were. moored safely and in the correct place. An important task was placing the anchor properly to ensure anchors did not become tangled. This allowed the yachts to moor 'stern to' the quay, allowing occupants to step off their boat onto the quay. Apparently, in the summer, there were so many yachts in the harbour that you could walk from side to side of the harbour on moored boats.

The first building they came to was George's Taverna.

'Is that your beautiful boat at anchor?'

'It is George. Fiona, and I own it. We are very fortunate.'

'Well, you have a beautiful boat. Will you be eating with us this evening?'

'We shall, George. Can you manage with nine people if it is okay for Azmir and Ulrika to join us for dinner before taking them away from you?'

'Of course, we will be delighted. Your table will be set here for the nine of you.' George indicated the undercover dining area overlooking the sea.'

'Perfect. What time do you suggest, George?'

'Eight-thirty to nine this evening?'

'Excellent. Shall we sit down there now and have some beers?'

'That's fine; I will get someone to take your order.'

The group sat at a long table close to the harbourside: beers and a glass of wine each for Ulrika and Fiona. John began introducing their fellow shipmates.

'Noel, can you please ask José to come to the end of the harbour? Azmir and Ulrika will have some suitcases and packages to load onto *Brave Goose.*'

'He is just completing the washdown after the trip here. Will it be okay if he comes in half an hour, John?'

'Yes, sure, no rush.'

'Azmir, Ulrika, and the ship's RIB will be here in about three-quarters of an hour. If all your belongings and clothes could be on the harbourside, we can get you settled onto *Brave Goose.'*

By seven o'clock in the evening, everyone was back onboard *Brave Goose*, settling in and getting ready for the trip back to the harbour for dinner. John advised Noel and the crew that they were all invited to come for dinner.

'We need to lock her up but leave the boarding ladder and platform down so we can get back on board after dinner.'

Although it was near the end of September, plenty of yachts were coming into the harbour. John was fascinated by all the activities and how George dealt with the complexity of anchors and mooring lines. He stood at the controls of the outboard motor, the engine on tick-over, with the tiller ready to twist the accelerator and rush off to sort out another yacht. He welcomed all the boats entering the harbour, giving precise instructions on where to drop their anchor and to have stern lines ready to be given to him. The majority of boats coming in were charter boats and flotillas. Boats were double-banked; George knew where every anchor was laid. He managed to get every boat moored that appeared at the entrance. It was a sight to behold.

John and Fiona watched on with great amusement at some of the boats. One of the skippers clearly had a serious lack of experience. The instruction to drop the anchor was given to the crew on the foredeck, who lowered the anchor with the electric winch. At the same time, the inexperienced skipper started moving back towards the quay. The result of this premature move was that the anchor only found ground and held about the time the yacht met the dock.

'Sorry, that won't do. You have no anchor down. Leave it where it is,' George said, but before he could complete the instruction, the crew on the foredeck had raised the anchor, and the yacht moved forward. A breeze inevitably blew the boat sideways, so they were not set up correctly to reverse into the slot.

On the third attempt, with a queue of boats waiting to moor,

George jumped into his dinghy and, coming alongside, tied the yacht to his dinghy. He positioned the yacht and instructed the crew to drop the anchor. After a short while, as the chain was going out, George moved the yacht back. To everyone's amusement and George's frustration, the crew on the foredeck stopped letting the anchor out.

'No, No, keep letting the chain out until I say stop!'

Eventually, with the aid of a flotilla leader on the quay to take the stern lines, George had the yacht moored.

'Okay, you can tighten the anchor chain now you are secure at the stern. The chain will become tight. Then stop.'

*

John, Fiona and the crew on *Brave Goose* prepared to take the RIB and *Gosling* to the harbour for dinner. As this was happening, Jock asked to speak to John.

'Yes, Jock, is there an issue?'

'No, sir, but I am concerned at leaving *Brave Goose* on her mooring without someone on board. We have had some strange experiences lately, so if you don't mind, sir, I will stay on board. I will be the security man on duty.'

'That is a very generous act, Jock. Now I am sure we can get some food sent out to you. What would you like to eat?'

'Mousaka would be excellent, sir.'

'Okay, Jock, so be it. Oh, and please call me John. We are a family when we are onboard. I will ask José to bring your meal to you. Noel will take the handheld VHF, so if you have any concerns, you must call, okay?'

As it was the last days of September, the anchor light needed to be lit by seven o'clock. Jock also had all the ship's other illumination lit. She looked a picture. José took Jock's mousaka back to *Brave Goose*. At John's suggestion, José used *Gosling*. It was easier to handle on his own and he was back quite soon. The others ate their way through a banquet of homemade food and local wine. The evening was warm, the sea flat, with not a whisper of a breeze. John was concerned about Bill, who had not said very much. He was absorbed in his inner thoughts – the massive injuries to Tony and the loss of their beloved yacht. Bill had spoken to his wife and Tony's wife. That was the most difficult conversation of all.

Bill reflected on the fun times the two families had enjoyed on their yacht. The Ionian was and always had been a perfect place to sail. Flat seas, mainly, lovely little harbours and bays. Everything the yachtsman could want. Eating his dinner, Bill realised that all the adventures and fun would be over. A tear trickled down his cheek, noticed by Fiona and John. They knowingly looked at one another, wondering how to help this man.

'John,' said Noel. 'I plan on leaving here by eleven on Sunday morning, and anchoring in the Gulf of Corinth Saturday night. We could go through the canal at night, but pilotage is not as easy as in the daytime. At night it could be challenging.'

'Okay, Noel, I am in your hands. You have far more experience navigating this boat than anyone else.'

Friday was full of activity. People were coming and going. Ulrika and Azmir were bringing all their belongings onto *Brave Goose.* José and Jock were deployed as baggage handlers. When it came onboard, Ulrika, Fiona and Sally moved suitcases and packages from the quarterdeck to their double cabin. Fortunately, there was ample room for everything. There would be no obstructions if everything were unpacked and placed in wardrobes, cupboards and drawers. However, as they would be onboard for just a short time, or so it was intended, there was no point in decanting everything to repack in a few days.

John arranged lunch at George's Taverna, a gesture that everyone greatly appreciated.

George was delighted to see everyone but realised this would be the last time this year. The season was closing down, though the weather was still as beautiful as ever.

Fiona and Sally took *Gosling* to the harbour on Sunday morning at eight o'clock to get breakfast stuff. They were chatting so loudly they could be heard all the way to the quay. The bakery was halfway up the hill out of the port – a very steep walk with a severe left-hand turn partway up. Then past the church, which had woken Fiona and Sally by the call to prayers at seven.

Two widows, dressed from head to toe in black with a few marks of white, which was baker's flour from where they had brushed against the counter, were purchasing bread in the bakery shop. Sally ordered bread, but Fiona decided the pastries looked excellent, so a quantity of them was purchased. Then as Fiona's eyes wandered around the little shop where everything had a light dusting of flour, she spotted some baklava.

'This will be a treat at supper,' she said to Sally.

The two women had many bags full of their purchases. Luckily, it was a downhill walk.

Back on *Gosling,* Sally protected their purchases with her body to prevent the packages from being covered in spray. Fiona expertly navigated *Gosling* to the boarding platform at the bottom of the side boarding steps to get back on *Brave Goose.*

Fiona and Sally set about laying the table for breakfast. Nine places were laid. A chair from the saloon was redeployed on the quarterdeck, so everyone had a seat.

There were baskets of fresh bread, croissants and pastries. A basket of boiled eggs was added to the feast, several pots of preserves, a large bowl of Greek yoghurt and a honey pot.

'Wow, what a spread,' announced John as he joined the others for breakfast. 'Does all this mean we won't be having lunch?'

'What cheek, John – you will have a salad lunch and dinner tonight.'

'Okay, Fiona, that's great. I will be swimming after breakfast, so anyone who wants to join in must be quick about it as I know Noel is keen to leave.'

Jock was completing his engine checks as well as the number two generator. Once everything was checked and passed, Jock started the number two generator and stopped the number one generator. Electricity was always required, so the generators were changed occasionally to avoid overuse. Everything was checked and was just fine. The electric current had been switched over from generator one to two so that the generator that had run all night could rest.

The RIBs were recovered by the crane and placed on their chocks on the boat deck. José then retrieved the boarding ladder and the platform. All items were stowed away carefully, ready for the next adventure.

Jock advised Noel everything was in order; should he start the main engines? He received the go-ahead. Everyone on board could feel the vibration from the main engines as they began to run and then brought down to idle speed. There was a gentle purr from the main engines now.

John, Fiona, Bill, Azmir and Ulrika went to the flybridge to wave goodbye to George and other people who had gathered on the end of the quay forming the outer edge of the harbour.

'Bye, bye!' was shouted by all as they waved. José was finalising raising the anchor and washing down the foredeck from the dark muddy sand brought up by the anchor chain.

Leaving Kalamos, *Brave Goose* travelled in an easterly direction to round the end of the island of Kastos. She then travelled in a southerly direction for 23 nautical miles rounding the tiny island of Oxia, then entered the Gulf of Patras. The next excitement was to shoot under the new Rion-Andirrion Bridge, which provided a road link from the port of Patras, where ferries berthed, to connect with the motorway, eventually leading to Athens.

Once the new road bridge was in sight, Noel moved himself to the bridge where he called Bridge Control and requested permission to shoot the bridge. Noel received instructions on which section of the bridge he should use. Everyone on the flybridge followed Noel down to the main deck level.

'I didn't realise that getting to the Corinth Canal would be so complicated,' commented Fiona.

'This new bridge is magnificent. There has to be control of the traffic passing under it to avoid a collision with other vessels and the supports,' advised Noel.

'Yes, you are right. We must shoot the bridge by the second section towards the centre, maintaining a course of 067 degrees true. We are to set this course two miles out from the bridge. It has been nominated for us by Bridge Control.'

There was a degree of tension as *Brave Goose* shot the bridge. As they closed the bridge, it looked at one point she might not pass underneath.

'Will we make it under the bridge Noel?'

'Yes, John, we will have a lot of space to spare. I hope so. It doesn't look like it from this distance, but we will be fine if all the calculations are correct.'

'Well done, Noel. I don't know why we should have had any concerns. There was space above us for another boat!'

'Thanks, John. I haven't shot that bridge before. It helps when all the ship's dimensions are on a chart pinned above the chart table.'

'Where now, Noel?'

'I propose to anchor in the bay of Galaxidi, roughly 35 miles away. It is also 35 miles to the entrance of the canal.'

'Good, we can be off after breakfast and get through the canal.'

'It isn't as simple as that, John. We have to obtain permission to go, and exactly what time. We will have to pay a considerable amount to traverse the canal.'

'That's fine, Noel. I am sure it will be less than the cost of fuel to go around the Peloponnese, which I know is a journey of over 400 miles.'

'That was the reason for building this canal. I will drop anchor near the entrance to the canal to be ready to go when we are given the signal. There are traffic lights to control traffic so we must wait for the green.'

By ten o'clock on Monday, *Brave Goose* was lying at anchor about half a mile from the entrance to the Corinth Canal. Noel had asked for permission to transit. He was instructed to wait and enter the canal on the green light.

CHAPTER 28

'Hi Belov, it's Georgio from Sicily. How are things in Greece?'

'Ah, my little Mafia friend. We have been busy. Our bosses in Moscow gave us a snatch – an English woman working for both sides. We were to send her back to the fatherland. She must have had some information they were looking for. Then we received an instruction to capture two men on their yacht. They, too, were both spies – for MI6. They had been sailing around Ionia looking for information on what we did in our Russian enclave.'

'You have been busy. Did you get your men?'

'We did; we had to interrogate them here and then release them. We tied them up and put them afloat in a small rubber dinghy. Moscow said if they died from drowning, that would be a fitting end.'

'So, your MI6 spies are dead?'

'No, one is dead, but the other is alive.'

'So, your drowning idea didn't work?'

'No thanks to the interference from a boat that I think you know – *Brave Goose*.'

'Yes, I know only too well this vessel. More to the point, the owner owes me a quarter of a million pounds. As usual, he is sailing in areas that make approaching the boat difficult without being seen by the authorities.'

'You are correct, Georgio, but we will try again to stop him with a view to payment being made to you. Don't worry. We have a plan.'

'Thanks, Belov. I am running out of ideas to catch this man and get my money back.'

'Will you be coming to Greece?'

'I am already in Greece. Shall I come over now to your location? I want to get my hands on these people.'

'Okay, Georgio, come over to the westerly end of the Corinth Canal. I am there with some excavators.

Belov shouted over the wall of the fortified villa to Vova as loudly as he could.

'Hi, I have just been speaking to our Sicilian friend about stopping *Brave Goose* and extracting a quarter of a million pounds from the owner.'

'Okay, sounds like fun. What scheme do you have in mind?'

'The problem is that the Greek authorities are keen to keep all pleasure craft safe, as they provide significant income to the country. Our plan is to attack the boat in the canal and get the money transferred to Georgio's account.'

'It seems the bomb on the yacht in Lefkas marina only killed one of the spies. The other is reported to be on *Brave Goose.* I believe they are going to Athens.'

'Is that our contact on Kalamos who has given you that information?'

'Yes, Vova. I am certain it is genuine.'

'Well, Belov. We could create a landslide in the Corinth Canal, damaging *Brave Goose* and hopefully stopping her. If the owner doesn't send the money to Georgio while stopped in the canal, we will continue to bombard the boat.'

'Sounds like a plan. We must get organised quickly and look out for the ship's transit.'

'Agreed; let's get some troops organised.'

Vova had a plan. He needed to get his plan ready to 'pull the trigger' when *Brave Goose* started to transit the Corinth Canal.

Vova thought he was a good engineer. He went online to get the statistics on the canal. It was 17.5m wide at water level. The height of the banks was 90m, and the angle of the bank from the water level to the top of the bank was ten degrees. He made some calculations to establish how far the rocks would need to be thrown to get to *Brave Goose*. He calculated that the edge of the top of the limestone embankment was 15m from the canal's edge at water level. There would have to be a significant amount of power behind releasing the large stones to get them to the centre of the canal, where they should hit *Brave Goose* fair and square.

Georgio was on his mobile to Vova, enquiring about exactly where the attack was to be launched. He had hired a car and wished to be present when the missiles were thrown at *Brave Goose* as she transited the canal.

'Belov, I have just taken a call from our contact on Kalamos. She says that *Brave Goose* will set off tomorrow morning, anchor in the Gulf of Corinth for the night, and travel through the canal during Monday.'

'Thanks, Vova. No indication of when they expect to be through the canal?'

'No, but they will surely contact the canal control room on Monday morning, and then they will be given a time to transit. If we had someone with a VHF set at the top of the canal's banks, they would certainly hear the conversation and nominated time.'

'Good thinking. I will arrange that along with my other arrangements for that area.'

Vova, waiting at the top of the canal bank on Sunday about two miles along the canal bank from the Gulf of Corinth, kept a keen lookout for his prey. He could see a reasonable distance but could not yet see *Brave Goose*. He couldn't see the traffic lights controlling passage along the canal. When they went green, he would know *Brave Goose* could transit the canal. He gave a mobile phone and €50 to a teenage boy who had been hanging around. His job was to go on his moped to a Posidhonia where the signal mast was located. His task was to phone Vova when the light went green and a superyacht painted dark blue entered the canal, and tell him the name of the boat if he could read it.

'Morning, Vova.' A voice interrupted his lookout.

'Hi, it's Georgio. I wasn't sure which side you would be on. My guess was correct. Can you see anything?'

'Hi, Georgio. No, nothing to be seen yet. Off you go, boy. Don't forget your primary task is to phone me when the vessel enters the canal.'

The boy shot off on his red and cream Honda moped. He went to the end of the canal and then walked along the path over the breakwater on the Corinth side to the signal mast, which housed the red and green lights. He could see the signal lights at the entrance to the canal, currently showing red.

'Is the excavator with the long arm part of the plan?' enquired Georgio.

'Yes, there is one on each side. It is part of the whole plan. See these big rocks?'

'Yes, the large ones?'

'The excavator on this side and the one on the other side will pick up these stones and drop them onto *Brave Goose*.'

'That should make them stop and think.'

'I hope so. I am not aware of this having been done before. If it works, we can stop *Brave Goose* in her tracks. In case of a problem, I have also brought a Manpad rocket launcher. It was left over from the previous activity against this boat. The rocks may frighten the boat's skipper. But the rocket will hit the boat. It is a heat-seeking rocket that detects the exhaust heat and hits the boat. Did you bring a laptop computer or mobile to communicate with the vessel and also to see if the money has been sent to your account?'

'Yes, I am ready. How will the bombardment work, Vova?'

'Okay, when the time is right, an excavator on each side will pick up a rock and drive to the ravine's edge. They will be side-on to the canal. This will give the excavators the maximum distance over the edge, making it easier to hit the ship.'

'Okay, sounds like a plan. Will the rocks go straight down onto *Brave Goose*?'

'No, I don't think so. The canal's edge up here is about 15m from the canal's edge. We expect the rocks to hit the edge of the sloping side. Once they have fallen about 60m, they will hit the rock face and bounce towards the canal, hopefully hitting the boat.'

'It's an excellent plan, Vova.'

'By the way, Georgio, we will need €100,00. This is an expensive exercise.'

'Oh, well, I better up my demand to €300,000.'

'Do you agree to that, Georgio? No matter what happens, we need €100,000.'

'It looks like this should work, so I am happy.'

Georgio was hoping against hope it would work and that nothing would go wrong. He didn't have €100,00 or anything near it.

'Before we start the exercise, I need €50,000 now.'

Before Georgio could reply, the boy phoned Vova to advise the lights were on green and a big blue motor yacht was coming around the northern breakwater.

'I can't see her name. It must be on the stern. As soon as I see it, I will call back.'

Georgio thought this was a perfectly timed call as Vova leaped into action and notified the Hymac drivers to load up and be ready to discharge the rocks.

'Vova,' said the boy. 'She is called *Brave Goose.* I will bring your radio back.'

Vova drove to the Hymac on the southern bank. Georgio followed him in his hired Fiat 500.

*

It was eleven forty-five when the light went green on Monday morning. There was no voice communication on *Brave Goose*. The main engines were started, and José struck anchor. *Brave Goose* made a sedate entry into the four-mile-long canal carved out of limestone rock, finally opened to traffic after numerous failed attempts in July 1893. Noel wondered how many vessels had sailed down this canal before them.

Everyone on board was standing on the flybridge to get the perfect view of the ribbon of water stretching ahead of them. Just as John didn't think *Brave Goose* would fit under the road bridge, he thought it looked unlikely she would fit down the length of the canal.

'There must be repairs in progress,' said Bill. 'There are machines on the top of. the banks top on either side of the canal. It's Monday so they will be working today.'

Noel never spoke. He was concentrating like mad to keep *Brave Goose* in the centre of the canal and not drift over to one side or the other. He had calculated that, at the maximum, there would be a 5m gap on either side of *Brave Goose* to the canal's edge.

'Amazingly,' he said, 'smaller cruise ships travel down with only a meter of space on either side. I have five meters on either side, and it's still tricky to keep straight. There is a current coming towards us, which is making steering difficult.'

*

Belov's mobile phone rang. It was Vova.

'*Brave Goose* has just entered the canal. There are no other vessels with her.'

'Yes, we can see her. The machines are ready. Let me know when you want us to start.'

John's mobile rang when *Brave Goose* was in the canal and beyond the point of no return.

'John, it's Georgio. Put £300,000 into my account now. I have texted you my bank details. Failure to do so may mean your boat will be in danger within the next half hour.'

'What on earth are you talking about?'

'I am sure you can see the big excavators on the top of the banks. They are ready to hurl three-ton rocks over the bank on top of *Brave Goose*. Good luck if you don't pay. You will be sunk.'

John went white with fear. He started to shake uncontrollably.

'Whatever is the matter, John?' said Fiona.

'I have just had a terrible phone call from Georgio. I don't know what to do, darling!'

'Tell me what he said?'

'He is demanding the final payment from the ransom. He said €300,000 this time. I have to pay in the next thirty minutes, or we will get bombarded by rocks from the top. I assume that is what those machines are doing. Getting ready to hurl rocks from the top of the walls which are about 90m. The rocks will cause a lot of serious damage from that height.'

Noel could hear this interchange. He immediately throttled back to two knots.

'Canal control, this is *Brave Goose*. We have just received a threat to our vessel. In the next half hour, we are threatened with falling rocks if my owner doesn't pay €300,000. This is a legitimate threat, as we can see earth-moving equipment on the top of the banks about a mile and a half ahead. I have reduced speed to two knots.'

'*Brave Goose*', we have your message. We have despatched some of our security guards. Which side of the canal are the excavators?'

'There is one on each side.'

'Okay, sir, we will advise when we have intercepted the blackmailers. You may see activities.'

'Corinth Canal Control. Please communicate by way of my mobile phone. Others can hear the VHF. I will text you my number.'

Everyone on *Brave Goose* was now in a state of anxiety. The thought of rocks coming down from the top onto the boat was terrifying. If someone was hit by one of these rocks, it could be curtains for them.

Unusually, Jock joined the ship's company on the flybridge. He realised there must be something wrong as the speed had dropped to two knots, effectively standing still against the two-knot current flowing towards them.

'Can I borrow your binoculars, John?'

John passed them over to Jock. He could see the machines that. would be brought into action to pick up rocks and send them over the side.

'They are a pair of thirteen-ton JCB excavators.'

'How do you know that, Jock?' enquired John.

'I used to work as a site engineer on motorway construction in the UK. I had to keep all the machinery running. I looked after JCB, Caterpillar and other similar machines.'

'Will they be able to send down large boulders, Jock?'

'Yes, they will. I will be interested to see how expert the drivers are.'

'What are you looking out for, Jock?'

'Well, the issue will be that the jib and the smaller arm reach only eight meters maximum, from memory. That would be possible, but they must not be alongside the bank's edge. With a three-ton rock in their bucket, they could become unstable. If they did the correct manoeuvre, so the tracks were at ninety degrees to the edge of the cut, the reach would be reduced to about three meters.'

'That's interesting, Jock. I have just figured out that to the water's edge from the top would be about fifteen and a half meters.'

'How did you arrive at that, Noel?'

'Oh, the pilot book gives me the information – I didn't need to work it out. The rocks will likely bounce off the rock face and then rebound into the canal – or us.'

'Look!' shouted Jock. 'There are white vans with blue flashing lights. Could it be the police?'

'Quite possible. The canal authorities will have called them in.'

As they were watching, getting ever closer to the location of the excavators, one of the machines swung violently around.

'It's very close to the banks edge,' said Jock.

The excavator turned the jib around so the rock in its bucket was hovering over the canal.

Then it happened.

Some earth and small rocks were dislodged from the top of the bank. On the side of the excavator, its track on the canal side had dislodged some of the earth. The excavator began to change its angle. It slipped towards the canal, and then with a loud shout from the driver and a thunderous bang, the excavator, with a large rock in its bucket, started to slide over the side. The driver shouted for help.

Too late.

The machine, its driver, and the rock descended quickly towards the canal surface.

Fiona was videoing the whole event. Screams and shouts went up from *Brave Goose.*

Two police officers looked carefully over the edge. Noel reversed *Brave Goose*, hoping the excavator would not make contact with her. She stopped almost instantly when the excavator splashed into the canal at the waterway's edge.

'My god, is the driver okay? Can you see him?' asked John; Jock still had his binoculars.

Nothing hit *Brave Goose*, but the driver couldn't be seen. Then, a man floated to the surface close to the excavator as if by some miracle. The machine was submerged. Just the jib, without its rock, was visible, breaking the surface.

'José, can you throw the man a life belt?' asked John.

José did as instructed, but the lifebelt fell short of the excavator and driver who held on to the jib, which was still poking out of the water.

The audience to this tragedy was stunned into silence until Noel announced a high-speed RIB coming towards them from the Athens end of the canal. There were shouts from *Brave Goose* and signals indicating the driver's location. The crew on the RIB found him and had him onboard in no time.

The JCB excavator on the other bank decided not to copy the one in the water, and backed away. The driver of this Hymac was soon seen running away from the canal.

'Look, Vova,' said Georgio. 'This has not worked. See if you can fire the rocket at *Brave Goose*.'

Noel phoned canal control.

'This is *Brave Goose*. We are stationary in the canal; we should be able to get past the excavator that has fallen into the canal. Is it safe for us to continue our journey?'

'Yes, *Brave Goose*, please proceed at four knots. We need to speak with you at this end of the canal. Please be ready to moor alongside the Canal Control building.'

When Noel finished his call, the rocket from the Manpad, balanced on the shoulder of one of Georgio's helpers at the canal's edge, was launched. It flew at a low arc, and then, as if by some unseen hand, the rocket pulled itself out of the ravine and flew straight at the excavator on the other bank. There was a massive explosion, and the excavator split in two. The various bits of the excavator landed on the bank, and the boom fell over the edge into the canal. The driver escaped and so avoided being killed.

'My god, I hope they don't have more of those. We would be sunk if a rocket hit us. Why did the rocket hit the excavator, Jock, not us?'

'John, those are heat-seeking rockets, and the heat from *Brave Goose*'s exhaust at the stern, which is water-cooled, is much cooler than the exhaust from the excavator, which is air discharged. The rocket would have homed in on that.'

There were police cars all over the place, their blue lights flashing. The police RIB started trying to get the first Hymac driver to shore. The only way they had was to return to the office at the easterly end of the canal. Control called *Brave Goose.*

'Are you all okay?' was the question.

'This is *Brave Goose.* We are all unharmed but badly shaken and concerned for the operatives of the machines. We think the man on the northern bank must be dead, having received a direct hit from a Manpad rocket.'

'*Brave Goose*, please continue travelling down the canal towards us, and be ready to moor starboard side to the quay, outside our control room and office. The canal is currently closed both ways.'

Noel did as requested but at three knots, as he was not in a great hurry to take on the Greek authorities who were anxious to discuss the reason behind the attempt to damage or sink *Brave Goose.*

Jock and José prepared warps and fenders for the mooring that was to come. Sally enquired if anyone wanted tea or coffee … or perhaps something stronger. Everyone placed an order. John ordered a coffee and a small brandy; Fiona followed suit, as did Azmir.

CHAPTER 29

'Miron. It's John England.'

'Hello, John! Are you in Athens?'

'No, not quite, Miron. We are stopped in the Corinth Canal. We have just been the subject of a blackmail attempt. We were threatened with a bombardment of rocks in the canal if I didn't pay the funds demanded within half an hour. We reported the attempt to Canal Control. The proposed threat was to be carried out by two excavators, one on each bank. One excavator has fallen into the canal. They switched to a man-held rocket launcher, which blew up the excavator on the northern bank, and we assume killed the driver.'

'Heavens, that was a massive attempt to get to you. You don't know if the driver survived?'

'Don't know yet, Miron. A police RIB is at the scene now. The driver of the. excavator that fell into the canal might be alive but the other excavator chap was hit by the rocket so we reckon he must be dead.'

'Okay, I will make some enquiries at my end.'

'Thanks. I received a call from Georgio once we had entered the canal and could not turn around, warning me that if I hadn't paid €300,000 within thirty minutes of his call.'

'That seems clear cut, John. We need to get hold of this Georgio character.'

'The police have arrived. The excavator fell from the Peloponnese bank with the driver. I guess the police RIB will try to rescue the driver. I thought you should be aware of these people as they are something to do with the Mafia mob who held *Brave Goose* when in Sicily.'

'Thanks, John. We will talk with Canal Control and go and arrest all the participants in this dangerous manoeuvre.'

*

'Darling, who was that?'

'It was Miron of the Greek special forces in Athens. We were due to meet him anyway to discuss the previous threats against us. He will ensure everyone involved with the issue in the canal is arrested. He will visit us when I advise him of our location when we get to Athens. We will moor in Zea marina, I believe.'

Noel carefully manoeuvred *Brave Goose* past the submerged excavator. They could see the policemen in the RIB recovering the driver. Was he still alive? They placed the body carefully into the RIB and returned in the direction of Athens at full speed.

'I guess he will be off to the hospital, John.'

'You are probably correct, Noel. He can't have fallen that far without breaking something.'

As *Brave Goose* continued her journey down the canal at the prescribed four knots, another police RIB hurtled past them in the opposite direction with what seemed to be two divers and two police officers on board. They gave an acknowledgement, not a wave.

The magic of the canal had been lost on the passengers and crew due to the incident. Noel commented that it had been an ambition of his to navigate the canal, but today's events had spoilt the journey. With the assistance of José and Jock, he made *Brave Goose* fast alongside the quay outside the canal Control Centre. José established the starboard side boarding ladder, permitting people to come and go as required.

Noel and John went together to the control office.

'John, wait a minute. I have something you might need.'

John turned to see Fiona leaning over the starboard rail.

'What is it?'

'My phone. I took a video of the whole event.'

'Great, I will meet you halfway to collect it. Well done, that will be very useful, I am sure.'

'Good morning, sir,' came the greeting from the officer behind the counter. 'Do you have the ship's papers, transit log, a crew and visitor list plus passports for everyone on board?'

'Yes, to the first two. I will leave Noel, my captain, with the ship's papers. I'll go and get the passports,' explained John. 'Noel, do you have a crew list?'

'Don't look for my passport, John. I have it with me. The other three passports are in the drawer under the chart table: Sally, Jock and José. As for Azmir and Ulrika, theirs will be with them. They will need to explain why they're onboard. Bill of course doesn't have one but I think he has an email from the British Embassy. There's a crew list on the chart table. It will be helpful if you can make a copy as I will need it again at Zea Marina.'

Back onboard *Brave Goose*, John explained to his guests what he needed while he went to his safe to collect the passports for himself and Fiona.

'Here are the passports for Ulrika and me. Please don't indicate we have been working. We only have tourist visas.'

'John,' said Bill. 'As you know, my papers and passport were lost in the fire on my boat. Part of the reason for visiting Athens is to acquire a new passport. I have an email from the embassy. Let's make a copy, and then you can explain.'

'Don't worry, Bill, there will be a method to deal with such a situation.'

Back in the office, Noel told John that the ship's papers were all in order. The fee of €650 had been paid.

'What I can't provide you with is the passport for Bill Edwards. Fire in Lefkas Marina sank his boat and all his belongings.'

'I recall reading about that event. So, what is his intention now, sir?'

'We are going to the British Embassy in Athens to acquire a new temporary passport. The other two, Ulrika and Azmir, have their passports. They also need visas for the UK, so we offered them a lift as we were all going to the same place,' said John.

'I understand, sir. We have received a call from EKAM. We have been asked if you would call the commandant at the Athens HQ – a man called Miron?'

'Yes, I know him. I will call him now. I have his number on my phone.'

John called Miron.

'Miron, it's John England. I am in the control office of the Corinth Canal. You wanted to speak to me?'

'Yes, John. Where do you intend to moor when you are through the canal?'

'Zea marina; our ETA is sixteen hundred hours today.'

'Okay, John. You will be requested to berth in the outer harbour initially. Be careful on entering as hydrofoils race in and out. They seem to believe they have special navigational privileges but they don't. There will be a police RIB to escort you to your initial berth. Please do not disembark before we have come on board.'

'Okay, Miron, all understood. I will pass the message on to Noel, our captain. Look forward to seeing you later.'

Miron hung up, thinking that John's delight in meeting him would be short-lived.

'What are your intentions when you leave here, sir?'

'Ah, we have a berth in Zea marina; we intend to arrive at about 1600 hours today. Miron at EKAM has just told me a police RIB will escort us to our temporary mooring. When the officers board, they will want to know what has been happening and why, so they can take appropriate action as required.'

‘I see, sir. What are your intentions when you leave Athens?’

‘I thought once we had conducted all our business in Athens, we would return eventually to Lefkas, which will be the permanent mooring for *Brave Goose* for a couple of years or so.’

‘So, do I assume you will not return via the canal?’

‘That’s correct, officer.’

‘Well, then I will have to ask Mr Edwards to go to a police station in Athens and ask them to phone here to confirm he is in possession of a valid UK passport. That needs to be done in the next seven days.’

‘Can you please write that instruction down in Greek with your name and telephone number? I will need to speak with someone at the Embassy and a local police station who can inspect the document and confirm that everything is in order.’

*

During the commotion at the top of the bank from where the excavator had fallen, Georgio decided it was time to leave as quickly as possible. At that point, he had not paid Vova the €50,000 down payment. Luckily, he had parked his hire car on the side of the road outside the field. The field gate was open. The police had been using the access to arrest anyone in sight for the attempted attack on *Brave Goose*. And the crashing of an excavator into the canal.

Vova had been arrested and put in a police van. The same fate fell to Belov. The excavator driver on the opposite bank was thought to be dead. Police officers were in attendance on the opposite bank. The driver whose excavator fell into the canal was taken to Athens in a police RIB. He needed medical attention and his injuries were yet to be assessed.

Georgio walked calmly to the field gate. He squeezed between the police cars, got into the hired Fiat, and drove off.

*

Canal Control decided the canal would have to be closed for some time. A salvage tug would be required, a floating pontoon, a floating crane and some divers to extract the excavator and the rock from the canal.

The director of the canal instructed his staff to issue a 'Notice to Mariners' that the canal would be closed for ten days due to an incident that would impede navigation. The director contacted the police to discover who was behind the attack on shipping and the canal. He was pleased the operatives in charge of the bombardment had been arrested. He expected them to be charged and jailed. He advised the police that he would like to interview them. He was awaiting confirmation from the police to get his lawyers on the case. The question was whether the canal authorities could extract a financial settlement for the damage and loss of traffic and who was to blame. That would be one for the lawyers.

Georgio drove back to Athens and then down to Zea marina, as he was confident that was where *Brave Goose* would be moored. He was delighted not to have paid the Russians but equally distraught that he had not been able to collect all the money he believed John England owed him.

*

John, Azmir and Noel, along with Bill Edwards, went into the canal office, as the director required details as to why *Brave Goose* had been subject to attack.

'Come this way, gentlemen,' was the invitation from a staff member.

Hardly a boardroom, but a meeting room nevertheless. A white-topped long table surrounded by ten chairs. Nothing on the walls. Not the most comfortable meeting room, John thought to himself. He hoped the meeting would not take too long.

Clearly of high rank in the marine police, an officer came in with a female officer and one other officer. They sat down opposite the three men from *Brave Goose.*

'Gentlemen, please allow me to introduce ourselves. I am

Konstantinos Makris, people call me Kostas. I am a captain in the Marine Police. My secretary, Agnetha, and my assistant, Christos. This meeting aims to discover what happened in the canal, why you were travelling down in the first place, and what issues you experienced which put lives at risk and potentially your vessel, *Brave Goose.* Please introduce yourselves, your role on the ship, and your reason for being on board.'

John was impressed by Kostas. A tall man in a beige, military-style uniform. He had two pips on his shoulder and a collection of medal ribbons sewn to his jacket. He had black hair, a bronze face, dark eyes and a kind smile. He spoke perfect English. His associates were also dressed in the khaki uniform but no insignia of rank or medal ribbons earned on previous missions.

'My name is John England. I am the joint owner of *Brave Goose*; my partner owns half. I am on holiday. My profession is a solicitor.'

'My name is Noel Gallagher; I am a professional seaman and captain of *Brave Goose.* My employer is Mr England.'

'My name is Azmir Karimi, my wife is Swedish, and her name is Ulrika. Her maiden name was Bjork.'

'I am Bill Edwards. I am a British citizen and a civil servant.'

'Very well, so we have an interesting selection of people on board your boat, Mr England. Are you all friends?'

'Yes, I think it is fair to say that. Noel, of course, is not just a friend but a paid employee. There are three other crew members on board: Sally, the stewardess, Jock, the engineer, and José, a deckhand.'

'You seem to have a trail of serious issues following you about in your vessel, Mr England. Can you please reflect on the issues that caused at least one death in the canal?'

'Yes, I can do all that, but I want to be sure you have managed to arrest the five men, well, at least five as far as I am aware, who were responsible. According to the phone message I received from the ringleader, Georgio, it would seem that the excavators were there to throw large rocks on top of *Brave Goose* if payment of €300,000 ransom was not made. The threat was that if the ransom were not paid within half an hour of his call, severe damage would be inflicted on *Brave Goose* and her occupants. I contacted your control room to report the threat as soon as his call ended.'

'You say five people? We have only four men, two Russians and two Greeks, in custody.'

'No, there was a fifth, the ring leader. His name is Georgio, and he comes from Sicily.'

'We have no one of that name or nationality. I think you had best explain.'

'I will explain the context in greater detail, but I am anxious that Georgio should not escape your jurisdiction as he has been the root cause of our problems.'

'Okay, sir, I will arrange an alert for this man. Any idea what sort of car he was driving?'

'No, it was out of our sight.'

'Okay, let me investigate and issue a warrant to arrest this man.'

'As I mentioned, I am a solicitor. I operate only on a *pro bono* basis for clients. I acted for a client of Georgio's illegal finance company in Manchester. I think he has been behind all our troubles. He is a criminal and needs arresting. Can you please activate a search for him now? Then I will explain why he should not be on the loose.'

'Coming from you, Mr England, and your professional standing, I will do that. I need some details about him first, if you can do that now.'

'That is the problem. I don't know his real name or how to recognise him. The Russians will know more about him than I do.'

Kostas left the meeting to give instructions for Georgio's arrest.

*

The Russian detainees were questioned about where Georgio might be and how he might be recognised.

'We were doing a job for him. He is Sicilian; his cousins are in the Cosa Nostra. He needed to collect money from the owner of *Brave Goose*.'

'What does Georgio look like?' demanded Kostas.

'Like a small Italian,' responded Vova. 'Black hair, tanned complexion but quite rotund. He was wearing a white shirt and dark trousers. He had a black Fiat 500, which he had parked on the road. When the excavator went over the edge, he left very quickly. This was the only time I have seen him. We were busy deciding what to do when your lot arrived.'

'Okay, I will deal with you all as soon as I have more information.'

'Is the excavator driver dead?'

'No, but he is in hospital in a bad way.'

*

Kostas returned to the meeting.

'Noel, can you tell me where you will head when you leave the canal?'

'Yes, sir, we have a berth arranged for this afternoon at Zea marina.'

'Excellent. Would Georgio know that?'

'If he does, I don't know how. But he seemed to know where and when we would be going.'

'Excuse me for a moment. I need to alert the police officers at Zea so if Georgio turns up, they can arrest him. Christos, please speak with the traffic officers who attended the scene on the Peloponnese side. They may have a picture of Georgio on his dashcam. And arrange for copies to be circulated.'

Christos left the meeting.

'Okay, Mr England, please can you explain what is going on?'

John then spent at least half an hour telling the story of the murder of Sandra, a solicitor, and his wife's sister, murdered by Michael Fitzallen, the property developer who had lent £3m to Sandra, the Managing Director of Wall's Holdings. Due to the financial crisis, the bank was pressing to repay a loan on a block of fifty apartments in Manchester. Fitzallen agreed to lend enough money to pay off the bank. The deal was that the money paid to Sandra, three million or so, would give Fitzallen half the block.

'For an unknown reason, Fitzallen murdered Sandra. The loan agreement had a clause that Fitzallen should be in jail for more than ten years. Fitzallen was proven guilty of the murder and was sentenced to a minimum of twenty-five years. The time clause in the agreement came into effect that no money would be refunded if Fitzallen were convicted of a crime which put him in jail for more than ten years. He would lose all his money.

'Two years ago, my wife Sienna, the other shareholder in Wall's Holdings, was killed in an accident with a tram in Manchester, which also killed both of my children.

'As a consequence of all the deaths, which I reflect on regularly, I was the 'last man standing', as far as the company and family were concerned. The money from all the estates and the business became mine and ownership of the apartment block. Sitting in jail, Fitzallen decided he wanted his money back, contrary to his signed agreement.

'I have become a target of Fitzallen's for the money. He uses agents to achieve his aim. Georgio was one such agent. As a solicitor, I was instructed to take action against Georgio on a separate matter. He was borrowing money from pensioners and lending it to dubious borrowers at significant margins. Georgio's business was not registered and was an illegal operation. When he arranged to kidnap the crew of *Brave Goose* during a stop in Sicily on our way here to Greece, I paid the ransom to Fitzallen's accomplice, Brandon Phelan.'

'Why did you pay then and not previously?'

'My crew's life was in danger. There was a group of Mafia operatives, heavily armed, onboard. The lives of all my crew were in imminent danger.

'I paid £2.750m. The balance I told Phelan would have to be collected from Georgio, as I had paid the four pensioners the money he had stolen from their pension pots. So, you see, I did repay the three million, but Georgio is trying to get his hands on what he considers to be 'missing money, as he does not have any money. I am afraid that the excavators and rocks are Georgio's latest attempt to get the missing £250,000. Yes, I could pay him without any problem. Money is not an issue. I would have paid twice, once to the pensioners and once to the man who stole the money from the pensioners, though in my book, that is very wrong. Further, there would be no guarantee that payment of this ransom would see an end to the issues with this man. Sorry, it is such a long saga, but these things are never easy.'

'Thank you, Mr England. That does make sense. It seems that despite trying to do the right thing, you were being harried for the money.'

'That's correct.'

'Thank you, Mr England. I don't see how the Canal Company could hold you responsible for the illegal deeds of those who caused the excavator to fall into the canal. I know you have paid the fee for transiting the canal, so I am pleased to say you are free to go and continue your voyage.'

'Thank you, Kostas. I am sorry you have had so much trouble from the rogues trying to blackmail me.'

'Have a good trip.' Smiling, Kostas waved them away.

CHAPTER 30

It was just before four in the afternoon. *Brave Goose* entered Zea marina, taking heed of the busy jet foil boats travelling at high speed in the area.

Following the instructions of the harbour authorities, *Brave Goose* came alongside the quay outside the captain's office. Noel hadn't spotted it so a police RIB escorted *Brave Goose* to her temporary berth. Fortunately, there were willing hands on the quay to take the fore and aft lines and the springs. As soon as she was berthed, the port side gangway was lowered to facilitate access to the quay and the office. Following the instructions from Miron, no one left *Brave Goose* until the police had boarded.

Within ten minutes of berthing, three marine police officers, or so John thought, came up the gangway to the side deck of *Brave Goose.* These men were not in uniform. Who were they?

'I assume you are John England, the owner of the boat?'

'Yes, and you are?'

'Miron, of EKAM, Mr England.'

'Ah, it's good to meet you. Would you and your colleagues like something to drink? Why don't we sit down here,' said John, gesturing to the quarterdeck table.

'Thank you, Mr England, just a coffee for me, please.'

'Same for everyone?'

There was a group 'yes' to the invitation.

'Call me John, please, Miron.'

Sally was summoned to provide the refreshments. On delivery of the coffee, she reminded John that she had to go shopping with José.

'Would that be in order?'

John looked at Miron, asking permission to allow José and Sally to go shopping.

'Yes, of course.'

'Now, John, I have spoken with the Guardia Civil in Spain and a detective called Jon Kim at the Greater Manchester Police Department. Kim gave me all the details of your travails over the last few years. As you say in the UK, you have been put through 'the ringer'. The commandant at the canal has filled me in on the details of the attempted blackmail there. So, what are your next steps?'

Sally placed a tray of coffee, milk, sugar and a plate of biscuits on the table.

'I am going now, John, with José.'

'Just be careful, Sally.'

'So, yes, I am glad you have the details of our problems. I hope to relax once Georgio has been arrested, and get on with our holiday.'

'The passengers you have, Bill Edwards and Azmir and his wife. Will they all be leaving you here?'

'Yes, I believe so, Miron. The issue is passports. I will go with them all tomorrow to try and sort out them out at the British Embassy.'

'What's the issue, John?'

'The easy one is a replacement passport for Bill and, I guess we will need one for Tony. They lost their passports in the fire when their yacht was blown up in the marina at Lefkas. Tony, the other partner on the yacht with Bill, was badly injured and is in a hospital in Lefkada. As for Azmir and his wife Ulrika, that is a little more complex. As a lawyer in the British Army in Bosnia, Azmir was my interpreter. He was promised a full British passport, so he and his wife could move to the UK and work. However, for whatever reason, no passport has been forthcoming. As he worked for me, I will represent him to try and correct this oversight.'

'Good luck with that. I suspect all sorts of promises get lost in the fog of war.'

'Yes, I am sure that is the case. I hope it wasn't my fault for not completing some paperwork on his behalf. We were both wounded due to an unexpected explosion. I left by way of medical evacuation back to the UK. I don't know what happened to Azmir. I guess that is the nub of the problem – missing papers!'

'These things can so easily happen. Let's keep in touch. I hope we can secure the capture of Georgio. I also have to investigate the goings-on on the island of Ionia.'

'Oh, I had forgotten, but I think you asked me to look at the paperwork that transferred ownership of half of Ionia to someone. I don't think anyone knows who that is?'

'That's correct. The documents are held in the Greek government archive. I have brought with me the address of the library and a letter of introduction to allow you to see the documents.'

'Okay, Miron. When we have relocated to our berth, I will get a taxi to the archive building. Once I have studied the document, I will let you have the information you need and my legal interpretation of what it says. There is just one more thing. Do you know where I can get an interpreter to read Greek to me in English?'

'That won't be necessary, John. The EU regulations stipulate that all document acts and laws must be written in the language of the country they apply to, in this case, Greek, and also in English.'

'Now that is excellent news. Do you know which language takes precedence? Will someone have checked that the English version is the same as the Greek?

'Yes, John, there will be a certificate of compliance as to the translation attached to the front of the legal document written in Greek and English.'

'Thanks, Miron; I will examine the document soon. We won't leave here until we have spoken.'

Miron and his companions left. John turned to Fiona.

'Fiona, have you seen Sally and José return? They have been gone ages.'

'No, darling, shall I go and try and find them? Do you know where they were heading?'

'Well, other than food shopping, I don't know. There must be a supermarket close by.'

'Look, John, isn't that José?'

The person Fiona had pointed out was half running, stumbling, avoiding falling, and then back to his jogging as best he could. The nearer he came, it was clear it was José.

'José!' Fiona went to meet him at the foot of the passerelle. 'Whatever has happened?'

'It's Sally. She has been kidnapped.'

'What? What happened?'

'They tried to kidnap me as well. I had to fight them off. The men were bigger than me and gave me a beating but left me on the pavement. I don't know where Sally is. He began to cry. 'I am so sorry. Where could she be?'

John joined Fiona on the dock. He soon realised what had happened.

'Noel, Jock, can you help, please? Can you get José back on board? Fiona will look after him. I will get hold of the police. Noel, see if you can get an indication of the location of the attack and if a vehicle was used to cart Sally away. Does José know what sort, the colour of the vehicle, etcetera? Licence plate, if he can recall. I appreciate that it is a long shot.'

The two men, unused to hearing John call out like this, ran to the passerelle and down onto the dock. Meanwhile, John ran to catch up with Miron who was still in the marina.

'Miron, Miron, stop, please! We have a problem. Our stewardess has been kidnapped. The deckhand who was with her got beaten up. They went to a local supermarket for food.'

'Okay, John. I am on the case you will get some officers coming to you soon. They will need the deckhand to recall where they were and the type of vehicle used if there was one; as soon as we know that, we can commence an all-points search. Don't worry, we will find her.

The commotion on deck soon attracted Azmir and Ulrika's attention, including Bill, who had also heard the noise. After speaking to Miron, John met them all in the saloon and explained what had happened.

'Seems to me that until this money is paid, John, you will be subject to attack one way or the other.'

'My concern, Bill, is that once the money is paid, what will stop them from coming for more?'

'I understand your thinking John, but it is less likely than the certainty of them coming for the money now.'

As they were talking, John's mobile rang. He returned to his office to answer it.

'Mr England. Will you never learn? Until you pay me the money I am owed, you will be harassed wherever you are. You will be without crew, as I will attack them. So how do you propose to move your boat then? Paper and pen are needed to take down my bank details.

If the money is in my bank before four o'clock this afternoon, then Sally will be returned to you. If not, you may never see her again.'

'Georgio! Words fail me. I will pay the money now, so as soon as the money is in your account within the hour, you must deliver Sally back to us.'

'Okay, you do as agreed, and I will release her.'

'Agreed,' said John. He turned his phone off and crashed his fist onto his desk. He was in a rage, shaking with anger. He wanted to tear Georgio limb from limb, but they were unlikely to ever meet.

John fired up his computer and transferred €300,000 to the bank account Georgio had nominated. He checked the money had left his account then joined the others, trying to make José feel better. John explained what had just happened and that he had paid the money.

'I think and hope your advice is correct, Bill. It's more your territory than mine.'

'Yes, John. I am sure you will not hear from him again other than to say he has released Sally.'

As they were talking, two plain-clothes police officers came on board.

'Mr England?' said one of the officers. John acknowledged him.

'I have further news for you since my call to Miron.'

'And what is that, sir?'

'I had a call from the kidnapper, Georgio, who instructed me to pay the money directly to his bank, which I have done. He said my stewardess, Sally, would be released back to us when he had the money.'

'I hope your faith in this man is justified, sir.'

'So do I. Do you have any suggestions?'

'I am going to phone my boss for further instructions. Do you have the phone number for Georgio?'

'Yes, it will be on my phone recorded under 'recent calls'. John gave the officers the number. The officer wandered off to the foredeck, and John assumed he was speaking with Miron.

*

Sally was petrified. Her hands and feet were tied, and her head was covered with an old sack previously used for onions going by the smell.

So far, she had not been ill-treated other than being tied up. Sally had no idea where she was. She was sobbing and shivering, not from cold but from a nervous reaction to what had just happened. She was sitting on a wooden floor in a small room which echoed. She could see some light through the sack.

She was thirsty in the oppressive heat and her wrists were sore where the bindings were cutting into her flesh. She tried not to move, but she suffered from cramps, which were more painful than the bindings. There was no one in the room; she had no idea where she was. She had been picked up on the pavement and thrown into the back of a van without windows. She could hear José shouting at her kidnappers. She was sure they had struck him, as he had suddenly stopped screaming, and the men got into the van and drove off. The sack was placed over her head before she was allowed out of the van. She was dragged and pushed up some old wooden stairs so she thought she must be in a room on the first floor, which she assumed was unfurnished as she sat there on the floor.

Sally had no idea of the time. It was going dark, so she assumed she had been in her 'cell' for several hours. As the hood had not been removed, she was unaware of anyone else there.

*

John tried to phone Georgio to discover if he had received the money and was bringing Sally back. The mobile number John had captured on his mobile didn't ring. It had to be a 'burner' phone. Georgio had probably thrown it away.

'Miron, you asked me to call if there had been any developments. There have been no developments. The money has left my bank. Georgio must have it now. We have still. not seen Sally. We are very worried.'

'John, within the last few moments, I received an email from the bank you sent the money to, with Georgio's address, when he opened the account less than a week ago. They confirmed that the account had been emptied of cash save for ten euros. The customer withdrew the money in cash this afternoon.'

'Did you arrest him?'

'No, as I say, I have just received the bank's information. They have not co-operated at all.'

'So, do you have an address for the customer?'

'Yes, we are about to visit the address. I will let you know what we find.'

*

Georgio had discovered an Alitalia flight to Catania Airport in Sicily at six in the evening. He bought a one-way ticket from an agent in Athens. The timing was perfect. He left for the airport as soon as he had bought his ticket. He reckoned he would be in Sicily by seven-thirty this evening. Job done.

While he was waiting for the flight, he thought about Sally. He was confident the authorities would trace the address and go there to remove her from her incarceration. It saved him a great deal of trouble. He couldn't help thinking what a wonderful service the tourist information provided. He had asked to rent one room and a bathroom as cheaply as possible. The tourist information administrator had such a place – she explained they were about to remove it from their list as the standard was very poor. However, if he wanted a cheap place for a week, then this would suffice. Fifty euros for the week seemed like a bargain until he went there. He then understood why it was to be removed from the list.

His flight was called. It was five-thirty. He joined a small queue of ten people waiting to board the flight to Sicily. The passengers were requested to have their boarding cards ready and to have their passports open at the picture page. The passengers ahead of him were allowed through and onto the tarmac, directed by airline staff to a set of steps to the plane at the front of the aircraft. Georgio had no luggage of any kind.

He boarded the plane quickly once his passport had been checked.

He settled into his seat roughly halfway down the plane, over a wing. He couldn't help noticing there was only a small number of passengers. Once everyone was onboard, the steps were withdrawn into the aircraft's body, and the door closed.

Georgio was inwardly delighted. He was on his way home now without even paying the Russians who had made a pig's ear of the operation. How could they have got it so wrong? There were no magazines in the seat pocket in front of him. He didn't have anything to look at. There was no cinema on board, so he decided to sleep. The aircraft moved off the stand and taxied down the taxiway, ready to take its turn to take off on the main runway. By the time the plane reached the taxiway's end, Georgio was asleep.

'Wake up, wake up, please, sir.'

Georgio woke with a start. He had been fast asleep. His recent exertions had knocked him out.

'Yes, yes, are we there already?' He woke to find an air hostess bending over him to wake him up.

'What's the matter?'

Unbeknown to Georgio, the plane had been recalled to the stand. Once back on the stand, the engines were turned off, and the door opened. Two uniformed officials boarded the plane, walked down the aisle and stopped at Georgio's seat.

'Come with us, please, sir.'

'Why? I have a valid ticket? Why are we not taking off?'

'Can I see your passport, please, sir?'

'Thank you, sir.' The passport confirmed to the police officer that Georgio was the person they wanted to interview.

'I need you to come with us, sir. Do you have any hand baggage?'

'No, I don't have any baggage at all.'

'Why is that, sir?'

'I like to travel light, and I am going home.'

'Not on this aircraft you're not. Come with us.'

Georgio didn't move. The two police officers hauled him out of his seat and immediately handcuffed his wrists. He was helped down the boarding steps and marched into the terminal. The plane went through its pre-flight checks once again and moved off down the taxiway. This time it would take off, minus one passenger.

Georgio demanded an explanation. No response was forthcoming from the police but he knew what was happening. How unlucky could he be? He had been minutes away from escaping Greece!

CHAPTER 31

The marina office shared its offices with the customs and port police. It was busy with people from different vessels coming and going, obtaining the essential rubber stamp on the cruising log. It became apparent that many were on their second or third visit. The issue seemed to be that they had failed to bring all the paperwork demanded of the port officials. There was no queue jumping.

'Some computerisation would make everyone's life so much easier, don't you think, Noel?'

'Yes, you are right, John, but the old-fashioned methods have been used for so long, employing many people. I think there is more to it than efficiency saving. I think it is a job creation scheme.'

A senior police officer dressed in a white shirt and shorts approached. The shirt had two pips on the epaulettes. He addressed John, assuming he was in charge of *Brave Goose,* which was blocking up the visitors' quay.

'Mr England, your ships papers, please? Nine people are on the crew manifest; four are your professional crew, and the other five are friends, but I only have eight passports. Please can you return to the vessel and bring me the missing passport.'

'Sorry, sir, we cannot do that; Bill Edwards's passport was destroyed in a fire on his yacht in Lefkas marina. You might have seen it on TV? I did explain that before.'

'Yes, we did. I still have to have a passport for our records.'

'One of the reasons for coming here is to allow Mr Edwards to visit the British Embassy to get a temporary passport. We have an appointment tomorrow morning. I can assure you that we will not leave here until you have seen the new passport for Mr Edwards.'

'Okay, sir, under the circumstances, you may do that. I will put an appropriate note on the file. Also, Mr England, we will hold your passport as surety.'

'I think that is excessive. You have my boat moored here. As a solicitor, I promise we will return with the temporary passport. I may need mine as I have to go to a bank.'

'Very well, sir, I will agree to that. I will need your signature on an undertaking to do as you suggest.'

*

'John, it's Miron.'

'Hi, Miron, any news?'

'In part, John. We have Georgio in custody. We still have not yet discovered the whereabouts of Sally. We're working on it.'

'That sounds like progress, Miron but I am very concerned that you have been unsuccessful in recovering Sally. Let me know as soon as you have some news.'

Miron put his phone down, only for it to ring within a minute.

*

'John, we have found Sally.'

'Brilliant, Miron. How is she?'

'As far as I know, she is fine, but they are taking her to the hospital for a check-over. Just to be sure, there is nothing serious. I hope José is beginning to feel better.

*

As they were leaving the office, Bill's mobile phone rang.

'Yes, yes, can I today? Okay, I will be there in an hour or so.'

'It sounds like you need to be somewhere in an hour, Bill,' remarked John.

'Yes, it was a most encouraging call. It was from the hospital where they have taken Tony. It is apparently a specialist hospital for burns. He is alive and wants to speak to me. I was concerned they were ringing me to say he had died.'

'Look, Bill, I will give you some cash, and you can pick up a taxi here; there are a few around. We will be thinking of you. Let's hope he recovers.'

Noel made arrangements with the port manager for a berth for *Brave Goose* not far from the entrance. As they were short of José, Noel arranged for a marinera to be on hand to assist with the berthing. Within the hour, she was berthed stern-to. The passerelle was run out, Bill was given funds, and he was away.

'Well, folks, we will be eating on board tonight if that's okay with everyone?'

'Yes, John, that isn't a problem. I will do the cooking tonight,' said Fiona.

'Well, I thought that if a taverna is nearby, we could ask them if they can do a takeaway and deliver it to us.'

'That sounds like a good idea, John.'

*

Bill took a taxi to Agios Panteleimon Hospital, Piraeus. Despite the searing heat, the taxi – a Mercedes – was cool. Its air conditioning was just the job. Stepping out at the hospital was like hitting a hot wall. Bill paid the driver and took a card so he could call another cab for his return journey. The air conditioning inside the hospital was good but not as good as the taxi.

Bill enquired at reception and was given directions to the burns ward. It was three floors up, so he took the elevator. The air con was not quite as good up there. Walking along a wide corridor, clearly looking lost, a young nurse enquired what he wanted. She spoke perfect English. How did she know? Do Englishmen stand out?

'I am looking for the burns unit.'

'What is the patient's name?'

'Tony Franks.'

'I know the gentleman. He has had terrible burns. I am going that way. I will show you. Is he a relative?'

'No, we are great friends, and we work together. Our yacht exploded in Lefkas the other day. I feel guilty as Tony had the keys and went to the boat. I was in the marina office, looking out towards our boat, when there was a massive explosion. I thought he had been killed.'

'I shouldn't say this, but it was touch and go for a while. He will get better, I am sure. Here is his room. I will tell the sister on duty that you are here.'

'Thank you. You are very kind.'

Bill pushed the door open carefully so as not to make a noise. What greeted him was a horror show. Tony was wrapped from top to toe in white bandages. His face was visible. The visible skin was red and burnt. Bill wasn't sure what to do. Should he speak or wait for Tony to say something?

'Bill is that you?' he said slowly in an indistinct voice.

'Yes, mate, it is. You have taken a pounding, my friend. Are you in a lot of pain?'

'No, I am full of morphine. Why are you in Athens, Bill?'

'I came to see you and get a new passport. I am going to the embassy tomorrow. Not sure if I can get a new passport for you, but I will try.'

'Why don't you take a video of me asking you to do that for me?'

'Okay, that sounds like an idea. Okay, Tony, you can speak now. My phone is ready.'

'Bill, can you ask for a new passport for me? I don't have an up-to-date picture. I guess I am not photogenic at the moment. I want to get transferred home as soon as I can. A new passport would be required, I am sure. Thank you.'

'That's great. I will do that for you. I will also talk to the office about a transfer back to the UK.'

Bill sat and chatted with Tony for about an hour. Mainly about the boat and making an insurance claim. Bill said he would do all that and get the latest information from the police and the forensic team.

'I will phone Mary when I leave the hospital and then ring the office. I will also tell Judy to have a chat with Mary. Keep up your spirits. We will be back on a boat quite soon. You'll see.'

'Thanks for calling in, Bill. I feel much more hopeful now. There is something I should tell you.'

'Oh, business?'

'Yes. The trafficking of girls and young women from Greece and Albania is happening almost daily. I forgot to tell you about my chat with an Albanian girl. She was in Greece, but she had been sent there by some men from Athens. After 'testing her out,' they managed to get her a British passport. It wouldn't surprise me to find Joy was behind that. Once they had the passport, they promised to send her to London. They explained that she would have to work the brothels in London until she had earned enough money to reimburse the men for all their costs.'

'Did you document this, Tony?'

'Yes, but I didn't get it to London, and of course, it will be destroyed now. The girl couldn't wait to leave Albania as she was being abused by her father, uncle and their friends. No one seemed to take any notice of her terrible situation. The prospect of going to London was wonderful, no matter the cost.'

'Who told you all this, Tony?'

'The girl's brother whom I met while wandering around the Lefkas marina. Someone had told him we were police from England. We know that is not true, but adequate for the purpose.'

Bill walked from Tony's room to the nurses' station. He asked to speak to the senior nurse.

'Yes, Mr Edwards, I believe you are a friend of Tony's, and you have been visiting?'

'Correct. Tony seemed a little more cheerful when I left. Are you able to give me a prognosis? Would it be sensible in his current condition to seek a medivac back to the UK? Or should we wait longer?'

'Mr Edwards – I think it's Bill? Tony said you might come.'

'Yes, it's Bill.'

'It would be possible to get him back to the UK. Maybe in a week, depending on progress. He has fifty per cent burns.'

'Okay. We work together and our employer may assist in returning him and maybe me to the UK. Here is my number in case you need me for anything. I shall be staying in Athens for a while. I need to speak with our employer.'

*

'We are trying to discover where Georgio has got Sally. An interrogation is underway to see if he will say where she is.'

'That is good news, Miron. He has the money, so I guess it will stay in his bank unless he has already taken it out in cash.'

'Okay, John, the bank in Athens has confirmed Georgio has removed the money in cash, leaving a minimal sum to keep the account open – just a moment …'

A police officer interrupted Miron's call to say they had finally found Sally.

John returned to the team to look after José. He told Noel and Fiona that the police had found Sally. They have taken her to the hospital for a check-up.

'The police have arrested Georgio.'

John went to the port office to get a contact number for a doctor and one arrived at *Brave Goose* within the hour. The doctor immediately realised this could be a beneficial call. He went up the passerelle and introduced himself.

'Hello, I am Dr Emanuelle. Where is the patient?'

'In here, doctor.'

John brought him to José, who had been kept on the sofa in the saloon. He had been given water as he was dehydrated. John and Fiona left the doctor to his ministrations and returned to Noel.

'John, I am devastated; Sally will be in a state. I hope they have not hurt her,' said Noel.

'I am sure she will be okay.'

'You can't know that, John. If the money had been paid sooner, we would not have had all these troubles.'

'I told you, Noel, why I didn't pay; there can be no end to blackmail if you make the initial payment.'

'You may be right, John. What will we do if Sally won't work for us anymore?'

'Look, let's cross one bridge at a time. The first job is to get Sally back.'

John's mobile rang.

'John, it's Miron. We have found nearly €300,000 in cash on Georgio's person.'

'Thanks, Miron, but that is the least of my worries. Where is Sally?'

'We will use some of the money we have found on Georgio's person to pay for a taxi to get Sally back to *Brave Goose*.'

'Thanks, Miron. That's great.'

John approached Fiona.

'How is José? What does the doctor say?'

'He said without X-rays it is hard to determine precisely what is wrong. José explained that when the two men grabbed Sally and threw her into the van, he tried to get her back. He was pulled back by the second man, who was as big as a house. He struck José in the stomach, and as he bent over with the pain, he was hit again with an uppercut to the chin, which knocked him out for a moment. When he recovered, the van, the two men and Sally were gone. A local shop worker and a passer-by came to his aid. They gave him water. Once he had recovered slightly, he insisted on returning to the boat. He is pretty cut up about the whole thing.'

'I think we all are. Does the doctor suggest we do anything or give him twenty-four hours to see how he gets on?'

'The latter, John. Oh, I can't get poor Sally out of my mind.'

Noel asked to speak with John.

'Is this going to be the resignation of the whole crew?' thought John.

'John, I don't know at the moment what the rest of the crew will want to do, but on their behalf, we are all extremely concerned by the criminal activities that have befallen the boat and crew. I am sure it isn't something you have sought. Some major issue or another seems to be at the root of these problems. I am extremely concerned for Sally's welfare. José is in a bad way, after having been beaten up. Who knows what would have happened if the excavator had hit *Brave Goose*? What can you tell me that will alleviate my concerns for the future of all the crew?'

'Noel, as always, being the good man you are, you are concerned for the people you employ on our behalf. The last thing I had expected was this attack on Sally and José. I will make whatever reparations are thought to be appropriate. Let's wait until we get Sally back, have a relaxing couple of days and see how people feel then, having had time to consider events.'

'Okay, John. I know none of this is your fault, but as crew, we seem to be getting the brunt of it.'

'Okay, Noel. Let's concentrate on Sally and getting José back in good form. We can discuss everything later.'

'José has been given some strong painkillers,' said Fiona. 'We have a supply for the next week. The doctor says nothing more needs to be done. He should make a recovery within seven days. The doctor has a bill he needs paying. Do you have any cash?'

'Yes, darling, I will go and see him and sort out the payment.'

CHAPTER 32

'Fiona, I must go to the Embassy with Azmir, Ulrika and Bill. I think their appointment is at two this afternoon.'

'Okay, darling, would you like some lunch before you go?'

'No, I don't think so. We will get a tapas lunch once we have found the embassy.'

'Okay, I will stay here with Jock and Noel and await developments, and of course, look after José, who is asleep and may well be for some time.'

'Thanks, darling. We may have a severe problem. Noel is considering whether they should all continue working on *Brave Goose*.'

'I know; I don't know what to say. I will do what I can. Hope all goes well at the embassy.'

John and the others departed for the embassy at noon in a taxi. No sooner had they left than two police officers arrived to take a statement from José. He woke up feeling very light-headed but was able to give them a statement about how Sally was abducted. With Fiona in attendance, a call came on the police officers' radios as they were talking. The message was in Greek, but the word 'Sally' was uttered. When they finished, they turned to Fiona to explain what was happening.

'Senora, the lady Sally has been taken in an ambulance to the hospital.'

'Can you please tell me the name of the hospital?'

'Yes, she has been taken to the intensive care suite at the Athens Limestone Hospital. A nearly new hospital on the outskirts of the city. It is a very good hospital.'

'Thank you, officer. I will go and see her when you have finished here. Is there anything else you need, officers?'.

Fiona went off in a taxi. During the journey, she sent a text to John, explaining about Sally.

*

John, Azmir, Ulrika and Bill turned up at the embassy at one-fifty in the afternoon. A modern office building, the British Embassy was easily recognised by the Union Jack flying from a flagstaff at the entrance. It had its gable end onto the street. The pavement was lined with large stainless-steel bollards, preventing any vehicle from getting close to the Embassy.

Bill was singled out immediately as he had no passport and required 'special treatment'. A clerk asked him to accompany him, and he disappeared into the bowls of the modern building. Bill explained he needed an emergency travel document. He told the clerk it had been destroyed in a fire on his jointly owned yacht with Tony Franks. Bill explained that he and Tony were both operatives in MI6. The clerk confirmed they had received a request from the Secret Service to issue emergency travel documents, one for himself and one for Tony, who they knew was currently in hospital. The clerk understood the urgency and why their passports had been destroyed. New emergency travel documents had been prepared in advance. Bill signed for his receipt for the document. He also signed Tony's document, but Tony would have to try and sign the document himself in due course.

He was out and back in reception in half an hour. He explained to the receptionist that he was waiting for friends who had a different type of request. He sat on the leather sofas and read the Daily Telegraph. He expected to be there for some time.

*

When the three friends arrived at the reception, Bill had managed to get to the editorial comment in the paper.

'Hi, how did it go?'

'We are delighted with the outcome but shall return to collect some documents in two days.'

'That sounds like a result, Azmir?'

'It was, thanks to John; without his help, I think we could have been waiting for years.'

'I wouldn't say that, Azmir, but I am pleased to have been some help.'

John's mobile made a chime indicating a text message.

John, not sure how she is, but Sally has been taken to Athens Limestone Hospital. A nearly new hospital on the outskirts of the city. If you need me, that is where I will be. F.

'Oh, Sally is now in hospital. Fiona has gone to see her. I plan on doing the same. Can you three find your way to *Brave Goose?* Help yourselves to food and drink. I will see you all later.'

The taxi delivered John outside the front reception area of the hospital. The helpful receptionist directed John to the ward where Sally was being treated. The first person he saw was Fiona.

'Hi, where is Sally? Is she okay?'

'She is in this ward but has just been taken for some tests, and then she will be allowed home if that is the applicable word for *Brave Goose*?'

'Yes, I think so, darling.'

'She is pretty well except for bruising and scars on her wrists and ankles, where she had been restrained. She was very dehydrated, so they are checking that no lasting damage has been caused.'

*

John and Fiona brought Sally back to *Brave Goose* in a taxi from the hospital later that afternoon. She said she felt alright but was unsteady on her legs and held tightly to the guard rails on the passerelle getting back on board. José staggered out of the saloon to greet her. They both sat down on the quarterdeck. Fiona invited them both to have a drink, perhaps Sally's lemonade. The suggestion went down well. There wasn't much conversation until Noel and Jock appeared to welcome their colleagues back home.

'I suggest we stay here for several days until you two are back in good health,' said John. 'Fiona will be the chief cook for the next few days without argument! She and I will do the shopping.'

'Yes, we have had a tumultuous time. Let's hope it's all over with now,' said Fiona.

Noel projected impatience. He let out a long breath but did not speak. He was angry and sweating. His face was red.

'We all need to have a serious discussion, John, about recent events, which are unacceptable.'

'Yes, Noel.' John wondered what he might say next.

Noel stomped off to his cabin in the crew's quarters.

'Jock, we have an unexpected stay in the harbour for the next few days or weeks so we should draft a refit specification between us. So, by the time we return to Lefkas, we will have a work schedule that Robert at Paleros can price. The passports will take a day or two.'

'That would be a good plan, John. Shall we start in the morning?'

'Yes, Jock, but it all depends on the condition of José and Sally. Your input on the technical side will be helpful.'

As John and Jock agreed a work plan for the following days, Azmir, Ulrika and Bill arrived back on board.

'Hello, you three. Are you all feeling better now the passport issues have been sorted out?'

'Yes, John, thank you. We can pick up our passports tomorrow or Thursday. We will check into a hotel as we don't want to delay you here.'

'You will do no such thing. We'll stay in the harbour until Sally and Jose recover from their ordeals. So, you are most welcome to stay on board.'

'That's very kind, John. Especially as we have ordered a meal for us all to be delivered to the boat, here in the marina, this evening at about eight-thirty! A gift from us for your kindness and help.'

Sally was the first to say how thrilled she was to hear that, coupled with thanks from John, Fiona and Jock.

'The goodwill and friendship that we have struck up is wonderful. I suspect José and Sally would like to rest. It's just gone four o'clock. I think a siesta is called for, so I will join them in a snooze.'

'So will I,' added Fiona.

*

Later in the day, one by one, the occupants of *Brave Goose* began to reappear. They had all showered and changed. José and Sally looked a great deal better following their ordeals. At seven forty-five, Miron came up the passerelle to see how everyone was. The news he brought was very welcome.

'I am pleased to tell you that a magistrate has interrogated Georgio who was in no position to excuse his behaviour, not just his part in instructing the Russian Mafia to hurl rocks down onto *Brave Goose*, and we all know how that ended, but furthermore, he admitted to hiring thugs, who we have also arrested, to take a crew member into hiding to assist him in his blackmailing of John England.'

'That is a very successful outcome, Miron. Your men have done well.'

'Thank you, John. The magistrate has sent all the accused to custody pending a full trial, which could take six months to come to court. However, the magistrate has made a temporary order, which cannot be challenged. The proceeds of the kidnapping attempt, €300,000, should be awarded equally to Sally and Jose. The magistrate will inform the court that these payments are an advance on any further compensation for their distress. As the court sees it, there may be an award for further compensation.'

'Wow, that was unexpected. Thank you, Miron,' said Sally. José confirmed his acceptance as well.

Drinks were then poured. Ulrika and Fiona acted as waitresses and passed glasses of wine and beer around to thank everyone involved. As promised, Miron finished his beer, giving the bundles of notes to Sally and José. He explained that this would not have been possible if Georgio had not taken cash out of his bank.

'That is swift justice, Miron, well done and thank you.'

'Well, it is only right those who have suffered for no fault receive compensation swiftly. It helps to take the pain away.'

'Thank you, Miron. We will be here for a few more days as we await some documents from the British Embassy for our friends here,' said John. 'Tomorrow, I will have time to go to the Greek archives and inspect the transfer document for half the island of Ionia. Once I have been, I will let you have my thoughts.'

Miron left to finish his excellent day's work.

The restaurant providing dinner appeared at the end of the passerelle. There were two waiters, a chef and a kitchen assistant.

'Good evening, everyone. My name is Costas. We are here to provide you with a special dinner. Can someone please direct us to the kitchen? No, *galley*! I forgot we were on a ship,' said Costas with a grin.

Fiona jumped at the request and escorted Costas to the galley. She explained all the equipment on board and requested that everything be cleaned and washed when used. She explained where the dishwasher was, the oven, the grill microwave, the pots and pans, cutlery and crockery.

'That is perfect, madam. It is a better-equipped kitchen than we have in our restaurant. Where shall we serve dinner?'

'Oh, on the quarterdeck, where we were all sitting. There are nine of us. We will need to bring an extra chair in from the saloon.'

'That is excellent, madam. Are you all going out for, say, an hour? So, we can set up?'

'No, we will be on the top deck having champagne. I need to get out some nibbles.'

'Please don't bother yourself in that area. We have some special appetisers for you. I will bring them up to you, and the glasses and the champagne, which I assume will be in a fridge somewhere?'

'Yes, I will show you when I've got everyone onto the upper deck.'

Fiona couldn't believe the transformation in the onboard atmosphere, from a gloomy and worrying morning to a happy evening. Everyone was chatting. They all moved up to the flybridge. Sitting around the table, the conversation became even more animated.

Carlos appeared with champagne flutes, and two bottles of champagne followed in the capable hands of his assistant. Loud cork pops sounded then the golden liquid was poured. Costas's assistant went below and reappeared with two silver salvers laden with canapés which everyone agreed were delicious.

'Tony would have loved this. It is such a shame he is stuck in the hospital. I fear he will be out of action for some time.'

'Have you spoken to your employers, Bill?'

'Yes, I have John. They are arranging for Tony to be flown home so he can recover in the UK'.

'What about you, Bill? Will you be going home soon as well?'

'I am waiting for instructions. The office wants to see the forensic reports on the explosion on our yacht. They also are keen to see police reports on the people involved. We have noticed increased Russian surveillance since Joy defected to Russia.'

After a splendid dinner, Fiona and Ulrika helped the restaurant team return the clean crockery and glasses to their rightful places. The crew had been dismissed from all duties. By midnight everything was back in place. The restaurant team had disappeared. John and Fiona awarded them accolades.

John withdrew the passerelle to add to the security of the boat. Everyone retired for a well-earned sleep after a very unusual and, at times, traumatic day.

CHAPTER 33

It was pretty late on a beautiful sunny Wednesday morning in Zea marina where *Brave Goose* had been moored securely since her arrival. Sally, despite her ordeal of the previous two days, was up and about, making breakfast, laying the table on the quarterdeck. There was a choice of Greek breakfast with yoghurt and honey or a full English.

The men of the party went for the full English. Five were ordered, while the girls preferred the Greek option. Usually, the crew would eat their breakfast in their mess off the galley. It was quite a task cooking breakfast for nine when five were having the full English. Fiona stepped in to help Sally. She prepared the Greek option, while Sally made the full English. She had eggs, bacon, tomatoes, beans and potato roasties. The smell wafting from the galley was terrific. The men were eager to be served.

During the break in activity, Noel took his opportunity to request a meeting between the crew and John and Fiona.

'We have endured more than our share of unexpected violent events. Fortunately, we are all still here to discuss these issues.'

'Look, folks, Ulrika and I want to do some shopping. It seems that after breakfast would be an opportune moment to discuss that, if that is acceptable to all?' said Fiona.

'And I thought I might have a wander around the shops now. I will leave you to your meeting,' said Bill.

Everyone was settled except Sally, who appeared a few moments after Bill, Ulrika and Azmir had gone down the passerelle to the dockside and into town. Sally brought a tray with cups and saucers, a coffee pot, a teapot, and a plate of biscuits.

All six of them were seated with their preferred beverage in front of them.

'Now, what is all this about Noel?' John commenced proceedings with a degree of impatience in his voice.

'John, Fiona, I believe that unless we can have a frank and open discussion about all the issues that have engulfed *Brave Goose* and her paid crew, an understanding for the future, and formal contracts of employment with a compensation clause for further disruptions, I believe you will find you have a boat but no crew.'

'I see, Noel. That is an opening statement. What has led you to make that statement?'

'Unless you have shut your ears and eyes, you cannot fail to know that this boat has been marked. Someone is trying to extort money from you that they believe is theirs. Your apparent reluctance to pay them has led to major confrontations with the most unsavoury characters. To involve the Mafia in Sicily would normally only end one way. We could have all been killed. Since Sicily, we have been spied on and the final straw was the latest attempt to sink *Brave Goose* in the Corinth Canal. I am surprised the Greek authorities have not sought to obtain damages from you. I believe we, as a crew, need an explanation and why all this hassle has occurred.'

'Noel, I understand your concern, but all monies due have been paid.'

'Those were the words you uttered as we left Corfu. It appears not to be the case. You seem unwilling to meet your obligations until you are forced to.'

'That is untrue.'

'How do you explain the attack in the Corinth Canal and your payment to Georgio of €300,000?'

'£200,000 was the sum Georgio had extorted from four pensioners. I acted for them as their solicitor. When the £3m was paid back to the representative of Michael Fitzallen, who is in prison in Manchester, £200,000 was retained by me. However, as Georgio was part of the plot and ran an illegal finance company in Manchester, my deduction of £200,000 allowed me to pay the pensioners their life savings back. I advised the representative of Fitzallen to get Georgio to produce the missing £200,000, and I explained why.'

'I see, so the true recipient of this £200,000, which seems to have grown to €300,000, is still Georgio, who has not been paid. We could expect future dealings with him or his cohorts, which is a worry.'

'I understand your concern, but Georgio will be in prison shortly.'

'I don't think that will restrict the abilities of him and his friends to collect the money. Indeed, they might be looking for more cash due to the damage to their equipment in the canal.'

'You may have a point, but we must see.'

'That's where this meeting started, John. We are not prepared as a crew to put ourselves in jeopardy by sailing this boat for you to who knows where with the potential of a further attack pending. Someone is going to get killed. It is a too high a price to pay.'

'Are you all of the same mind regarding this?'

'We are,' said the rest of the crew as one.

As the latest victim of the attempts to collect money from John, Sally said:

'I am terrified, John. I love this boat and the two of you, but my experience at the hands of these hooligans has scared me. I am not willing to sail again until I have the reassurance that there are no outstanding obligations.'

'I fully understand, Sally,' said Fiona. 'Don't forget I was kidnapped as well. Let John and me chat about this. Can we come back to you tomorrow?'

The crew agreed, and the meeting broke up without a resolution.

CHAPTER 34

'So, Bill, I assume we shall be waving goodbye to you today or tomorrow? You have temporary passports. Am I right in thinking you need to visit the local police for them to conform with the Corinth Canal control?

'That's correct, John. I was planning on doing that today while on my way to visit Tony. I assume you will be here for one more night?'

'Correct, Bill. I need to make arrangements for our departure; much will depend on the production of the passports for Azmir and Ulrika. I also have some issues with the crew. We shall see when you leave.'

'Understood, John. Do you mind if I slip out soon after breakfast? I hope to be back after lunch.'

'No, that's not a problem for us. I guess you intend to fly back to the UK from Athens?'

'Yes, John. My return ticket from Preveza went up in smoke with the rest of my belongings.'

'Morning, Noel.'

'John, good morning to you and everyone. Is all well?'

'As far as I know, Noel. Azmir and Ulrika are the missing links, but I assume they will be with us soon.'

'I will need to advise the port when we intend to leave. I will check the fuel position with Jock and, of course, the price here. It may be beneficial to top up here. I must remember to fill up *Gosling* and the RIB as they may be run around a bit during the next few weeks.'

'Good thinking, Noel.'

Sally was the next to arrive at the breakfast table, shortly followed by José.

'Hello, you two. How are you both feeling today?'

'I still have bruises and the marks to prove it,' said José. 'Apart from the residual pain, I am fine. I will try and find some spray for bruises. That can be very helpful.'

Sally left the table and returned in no time with a spray can.

'Here, José, this is the stuff they use on footballers. That will draw the pain out.'

'You are wonderful, Sally. You seem to have everything in your medicine chest.'

'It is surprising how many bumps and bruises are sustained on a boat. In fact, I need to purchase another can of this magic spray.'

'How are you, Sally?'

'I feel much better, thank you, John. My abrasions are recovering. The spray is unsuitable for the abrasions, but I have applied an antiseptic cream, which has greatly helped.'

'Let me come to the point straight away. The various incidents might have been avoided if I had paid sooner. But who knows? I am conscious that some of you, or maybe all the crew, have had enough and would like to move on, leaving *Brave Goose.* If that is what you, individually or as a group, would like to do, Fiona and me will be very upset as we like you all as friends. Unfortunately, these events have happened but could not have been anticipated. If it is your wish individually or as a group you wish to leave, I would appreciate it if you could let us know in the next day or so. I hope you will still join us on our trip back to Lefkas so you can leave via Preveza.'

'John, that is most generous and shows an appreciation of the issues we have all experienced. However, having slept on my thoughts, I see *Brave Goose* as my home and wish to stay and carry on as before.'

'Thanks, Noel. Fiona and I are extremely grateful to you for that decision.'

'That is my view too, John.'

'And mine,' said Sally and José in unison.

Jock had not appeared, but when he did and was brought up to speed with the conversation, his remark was, 'Why would I want to leave my home? It has been rather. unusual, but unusual things happen. No, I would like to stay.'

'Thank you all. It confirms to us what a wonderful group of people you are. Great, let's carry on cruising.'

'One caveat, John – you must continue your story about your wealth and how you acquired it?'

'Yes, Sally, I promise to do that. Maybe this afternoon, as we will not be going anywhere until Thursday tomorrow at the earliest. To tidy things up, Georgio has not received the requested money. I have his bank details, so I will send his bank £250,000 this morning. Once done, I will show you all a copy of the payment statement; there can be no reason then for Georgio to carry on with his aggressive behaviour. I have a job to carry out for Miron at the Greek Archive here in Athens. It shouldn't take too long. I hope to be back for lunch.'

John left just after ten in the morning. *It is Wednesday already*, he mumbled to himself, hoping he could find a taxi driver who spoke English. He did, and he knew where the archive was. It was a new, heavily fortified building close to the parliament building in Athens.

Pressing the security bell, he entered the building which had a magnificent reception area with white marble flooring. Despite the modern nature of the building, the architects had built imitations of Roman or Corinthian columns. It was magnificent.

Somehow, John was addressed in English. Did he appear English even before he opened his mouth?

'Good morning, sir. Can I help you?'

'Ah, yes, you can. I wish to examine the transfer or lease between the Greek government and the purchaser or tenant of the island of Ionia. I am acting for EKAM. Here is a copy of my instructions.'

'It will take a few moments to retrieve the document. You will only be able to see a certified copy. No one except government ministers and their officials can inspect the originals.'

'I understand. It is the English translation I would like to look at.'

'It is quite a large document. Perhaps you would prefer to purchase a certified copy and take it with you?'

'I didn't know that would be possible. How much would a copy cost?'

'The price for this document is €200.'

'Can I quickly look at the English translation to ensure it will provide the required information if I purchase the copy? I am an English lawyer.'

'I will get the copy sent up, sir. It may take ten minutes. Please have a seat over there. I will bring the document over to you as soon as it arrives.'

By eleven thirty, John had purchased a full copy of the text of the long lease of the island of Ionia. He paid €200, obtained a receipt, and left to find a taxi. To his delight, there was a queue of ten or more white Mercedes taxis waiting for customers.

At noon John walked up the passerelle with a folder of documents under his arm.

'That didn't take long, John?'

'It was so efficient; I was in and out within half an hour, and I have purchased a copy of the deed of transfer and lease between the Hellenic government and a man called Zhukova.'

*

While the crew, John and Fiona took a light lunch, Azmir and Ulrika went shopping before going to the embassy to collect their new passports, suitably stamped with a visa so they could work in the UK.

'We have been fortunate in running into John, darling. We will be ready to start work somewhere in the UK as soon as we arrive. It could be as early as the end of this week.'

'Yes, my love. I know there are issues in the UK, but I am sure we can find a suitable calling for our talents?'

'Have you any idea, Azmir, what kind of work we should look for?

'Hospitality, I think. It seems to fit our experience.'

'What part of the UK would be best to find work?'

'I wondered if the Lake District might be a suitable area. It is full of beautiful scenery, mountains, and plentiful hotels and guest houses.'

'That sounds like a good idea, Azmir. My childhood, like yours, was spent in the mountains, and the Lake District shouldn't be any different.'

'Okay, Ulrika, let's head up to the Lakes, as they call it, to see what we can find.'

*

Surrounded by his flock, John sat in his wicker armchair on the quarterdeck, ready to continue his life story about the Wall family. Jock, José and Sally joined Noel and Fiona to listen to the enthralling events of part of John's past life.

'I think I ended the last part of my story with Roger Whiteside, Peter Wall's business partner, being recovered from the River Dee as he floated along the river bank alongside the Roodee Race Course. A dog walker had found him. It transpired Whiteside had been murdered. Eventually, Dr Frank Stringer was shown to have been the murderer. He had been keen to right a wrong. Peter Wall was a long-standing friend and Frank was the godfather to Sienna. He was very close to the family. Frank was found guilty and sent to jail. He had leukaemia, and as a doctor, he knew he would not have that long to live, hence his actions.

'I was faced with the monumental task of unravelling the estates of the deceased parties. The business had a complicated ownership structure which would have been helpful if just one of the partners had died. In this case, I faced the death of both business partners. They were the identified beneficiaries of Peter Wall. Having discovered that he had been murdered and had not committed suicide as initially thought, we could proceed to call in cash from life insurance companies.'

'Do you mean if he had committed suicide, the policies would not have been helpful?

'Yes, that is correct, Noel. There are time limits. So, if he had committed suicide, say three years after the policies had been taken out, they could have been used. As it was, one of the biggest policies was less than a year old.

'Working out if Roger Whiteside had any dependent relatives was difficult. He has an estranged wife, but she didn't qualify for any of Whitesides's estate. Did he have any children? I managed to speak to his ex-wife, who confirmed they had no children. She would know, wouldn't she?' A ripple of laughter rang around the audience.

'Usually, you could accept the situation as presented. Still, as I couldn't be sure, I put an advert in the local paper and circulated local solicitors to see if anyone had any information for me.

'The answer, I discovered, was that many years earlier when, casual, drunken sex had consequences, not least of which was an unwanted pregnancy, Roger Whiteside and others became drunk at a rugby club dance in Wrexham. On the way home, Roger and his friend, who had a van with a mattress in the back, spotted a girl – called Gwyneth – on the roadside walking home. The boys offered her a lift from Wrexham, where the dance had been held, back to her house in Mold. Before arriving in Mold, the boys had illicit sex with the girl. No more was said until the girl, Gwyneth, discovered she was pregnant. She was shipped off to a relative during her confinement. Her father was furious and determined to find the responsible man's identity. She eventually gave him the name of the father of her baby boy. Gwyneth died in childbirth after receiving her father's forgiveness in the hospital. The child was named after his grandfather, Rhys.

Her grandparents raised young Rhys Williams. He did well at school and university, ending up with a job in the North Wales police forensic laboratory. Rhys was involved with helping to identify DNA residue from items found at crime scenes. Eventually, I found him and, through a DNA sample, was able to declare Rhys was the legal heir to Whiteside and should inherit his fortune.

'Sandra and Sienna were concerned that Whitesides's inheritance was a substantial shareholding of Wall's Holdings. If Rhys Williams was inclined to exercise his rights as a significant shareholder, it could seriously damage the company's prospects.

'I organised a meeting with Rhys, Sienna, Sandra, Anne Wall and myself. We intended to discover what Rhys wanted to do with his valuable inheritance. Fortunately, Rhys had no ambitions to become involved with commerce. Before the meeting, it had been agreed between the Wall family that they would prefer to purchase the shares from Rhys. His opening remark was that he had no interest in holding shares and could I advise him on how to transfer the shares into cash?

'So, Rhys became a very wealthy young man and went on a globe-trotting adventure. There was to be a complicated transfer of properties between the family. I was in love with Sienna, and getting married while all the changes took place was interesting. Frank Stringer was permitted a day's release to give Sienna away as a proxy for her father, Peter.

'I purchased the farm from Ann Wall, so Sienna and I lived there. Sandra bought my flat in Chester with magnificent views over Chester Racecourse, and Ann purchased a cottage near the church in Tarporley, which she converted to a lovely home.'

'That is quite a story, John, and I bet it was far more complex than you have made it sound?'

'You are right, Noel, but I didn't want to take the rest of the year, which it would if all the details had to be laid out.'

'Sandra became chairman and managing director of Walls' Holdings. Wall Developments was Sienna's company. They were both incredibly successful and made a great deal of money. Sienna and I had two lovely children, Peter and Anne. I was the solicitor of the group. There was extensive legal work from acquiring sites for development, company purchases, and the sale of property.

'In the mid-1980s, a financial crisis led to the banks being very nervous and calling in outstanding overdrafts. That was the situation for Walls' Developments. The construction of Peter's Tower was all finished, but detailed finishing was required. Sales were slow. Some flats had been sold before they were built. Sales off-plan as the scheme was known. However, I discovered that most of the contracts exchanged for about five flats were never going to complete. So, Sienna and I agreed to return the contracts and deposits, finish the apartments and let them. During this situation, the bank pressured Walls' Holdings, insisting the overdraft be paid off within thirty days.

'The largest customer of Walls' Developments was Michael Fitzallen; his business partner and financier was Niall Phelan, an Irish businessman, racehorse owner, and trainer. Michael spotted an advert in the Sunday Times that Sandra had placed to sell a fifty per cent share in Peter's Tower. Michael had acquired significant cash from his development and buy-to-let scheme. Niall Phelan had double-crossed a man whose nickname was Goose, an acquaintance of Fitzallen. Goose managed to recover three and a half million pounds from Phelan by selling his five million pounds worth of drugs which were fake packages. One package was armed with a booby trap bomb, which killed Phelan and his chemist. Phelan had tried to suggest he was helping drug addicts kick the habit, but the reverse was the case. He was one of the biggest drug dealers in Ireland.

'Fitzallen, now possessing just over three million pounds, called Sandra and offered to help. He paid the sum requested by Sandra. She knew Michael Fitzallen was a rogue, so she drafted an agreement which stated that if Fitzallen were found guilty of a crime that put him in jail for more than ten years, he would lose his right to recover the money. The bank was paid off, and the future looked rosy. However, Fitzallen became involved in drug dealing and needed some cash urgently. He demanded some of the rent Sandra had collected. He had ten thousand in mind, going to the continent to avoid the police. Sandra agreed and met him on a Sunday at her stables in Tarporley. The farmhouse was being renovated. Builders' materials were all over the place. Sandra insisted on knowing what the money was for, suspecting it was to purchase drugs, and she said so. When she leaned into the car to recover the envelope containing ten thousand pounds in cash funds, Fitzallen hit her head with a brick.

'He then put her body in a tonne bag that was lying around. He also placed some bricks in the bag with Sandra; then he threw her into the midden, a large plastic tank with an open top. Anchored with bricks in the sack, she sank slowly beneath the rancid liquid manure. She was declared drowned by forensic examination. Fitzallen was found guilty and sent to jail on a life sentence. Significantly more protracted than the ten-year limit in the agreement.

'Various attempts on behalf of Fitzallen were made to get his money back, even though he was in jail. He used the offices of a cousin to recover the money; some of these efforts you have had the misfortune to become involved in. The hijack of *Brave Goose* and all of you in Sicily got most of the money paid. I withheld £200,000.

'When I was in Manchester as a solicitor, I came across Georgio. He was running an illegal finance company. He got hold of the pension pots of pensioners and offered to pay them a higher interest rate than their current pension provider. Georgio then lent the money to a desperate family man at excessive interest rates. He was very much in debt, made worse by Georgio's loan. The scheme failed when the repayments stopped. Georgio's plan was in tatters. The pensioners had lost all their pensions and had no income. I retained £200,000 from the £3m and repaid the capital to the pensioners. It is that money Georgio has been trying to recover.

'Reflecting on this current scheme, I will have repaid the pension money three times. It's my fault. If I had not been so cross with Georgio and the implications for the four pensioner families, I would have paid the whole amount to Fitzallen, which would have been its end.

'During all this, but not in chronological order, a big fire at Peter's Tower turned out to be arson. It had been set by the Fitzallen team, to try and recover the pensioners' money which had been held in a tin in one of the wardrobes of the flat that was set alight. On that day, I was in court on a case in Chester. Sienna had collected both children from school. On her way home, Sienna had to visit the flat at the request of the fire service. She came to some unfamiliar traffic lights to control traffic crossing the Manchester tram tracks. At this point, the trams travelled quickly to go up an incline. A man in his car lost his temper when Sienna didn't move and blew his horn hard. It shook Sienna out of her trance. She set off right in front of a tram. She was severely injured, and the children were killed.'

'John, what a story. I suspect you would rather have your wife and children and your home in Tarporley than sailing in *Brave Goose*?'

'You would have been correct a few years ago, but now I have come to terms with all that has happened. I was so lucky to meet Fiona; we are both content. I hope *you* are all content. I am so sorry for the various attacks. I am certain that it is all over now.'

'How did you meet Fiona?'

Fiona intervened and explained that she had met John in the crown court in Manchester.

'I was waiting to be called in a case I would almost certainly lose, as I couldn't afford a lawyer. John saw my distress, took over my case, and he won it; that's how we met. I have been so lucky. How was I to know it would all lead to this?'

CHAPTER 35

'Hello, you two.' John acknowledged the return of Azmir and Ulrika. 'Is everything okay?'

'Yes, John, all is well. We have our documents, and we are ready to depart. I wondered if I could use your computer to purchase some flight tickets to London?'

'Yes, of course.'

John took Azmir to his office, and between them, two tickets were purchased for a flight to Heathrow tomorrow, leaving Athens at noon. As Azmir didn't have a credit card, John paid for the tickets and gave Azmir €200 to help them on their way.

'Look, Azmir. I may have caused you frustration by not completing the paperwork in Bosnia. However, my excuse is that I had been partly blown up, like you. I don't want any money back. Please accept the tickets and the cash as a helping hand with my best wishes. We need to celebrate on board tonight.'

'Thank you, John. You are very kind.'

When Bill appeared on the passerelle, the two men had just returned to the saloon. Bill's face was odd. He looked confused and as if he were in pain.

'Ah, Bill. Welcome back. I expect you managed to get some lunch while you were out?'

'Yes, thank you, John.'

John was concerned. Bill looked leached of colour. Bill rubbed his face with both hands. When he dropped his hands to his side, his hair was sticking up where he had ruffled it. His eyes were wide, if not a little manic.

'Did you see Tony, Bill?'

'Er. Yes, I did, John, thank you. Arrangements are being made to fly him home in the next few days.'

'That sounds like progress, Bill. Will you be going as well?'

'I wish. But alas, no.'

John was not sure how to continue this conversation. John thought Bill looked fearful, if not frightened.

'Well, Bill, you are welcome to stay with us until you are ready to depart or come with us around the Peloponnese?'

'I am not quite sure about my arrangements yet, John. I have to return to the embassy tomorrow. Once I have been there again, I will know more about my immediate future.'

'Okay, Bill. Would you like a drink?'

'Kind of you, John, but not just at the moment. I think I will have a siesta as I didn't sleep well last night.'

'Okay, see you later.'

Bill opened the door of the small Pullman bunk cabin he had occupied for the last few days. He flopped onto the bottom bunk. His head was splitting with a headache. His headache was a hostile squatter occupying every inch of his head. He had to close his eyes to expel the light as best he could. The light made the ache even more painful. He had pain in his neck, down his spine and in all his joints. He wanted to sleep and put this dreadful pain out of his mind and feeling.

'Fiona, did you see Bill when he came back?'

'Yes, John, but only briefly. He was not very communicative. I don't think he is very well.'

'You may be right. It could be a reaction to the events of the last few days. He has had a battering with the Russians torturing him and Tony, the ordeal in the dinghy, and the accident Tony had on their yacht. It has probably caught up with him!'

'Oh dear, we are all having a bad time.'

'As always, you are correct, my love. Our systems need to relax to get over the damage caused to our mental faculties.'

Her eyes narrowed, and her eyebrows pulled together.

'Are you feeling alright, darling?'

'No, not really. Again, it is a psychological effect.'

'Okay, darling, why don't you have a siesta and relax? That is what we should all be doing.'

Sally had overheard the conversation Bill had had with John. She went to Bill's cabin and gently knocked on the door, opening it quietly.

'Bill, it's Sally. Can I get you anything??'

He groaned and indicated some paracetamol or other pain killer to help relieve his headache and pain.

'Okay, I will be back in a minute.'

Sally extracted two co-codamol from her vast array of medications. Bill swallowed two 8mg of the medication in no time with a glass of water. She closed the cabin door quietly and left Bill to it.

*

Azmir and Ulrika sat in a bar just a short distance from *Brave Goose* and the entrance to the marina. It was in a small square, adorned with floral displays outside the houses, restaurants, and bars.

'How do you think we should find a job, Azmir?'

'Well, my love, I guess it will depend largely on where we would like to settle down. City, town or country. What is your preference?

'I have loved working on Kalamos. It is a small village community which has been wonderful. That is the sort of place I would prefer. I expect the issue will be whether you can find work in such a community?'

'Mm. I suppose a large hotel would be able to provide us both work. I am happy to do any task a hotel requires, from carrying bags to bar work. I guess you have talents in housekeeping, restaurant service and the like. I am sure a larger hotel could find us both work.'

'So, we're still agreed on the Lake District?'

'Well yes, Ulrika. There are numerous hotels there, so one of those could be the target location. Maybe I should ask John if I could search for hotels in the Lake District and send them an email with our CVs. Let's wander back to *Brave Goose* and chat with John, shall we?'

Back at the marina, they walked to the dock walkway and the passerelle for *Brave Goose.* There was a man following them. He pushed his way to the gate to gain access to the marina. Ulrika was first up the pasereelle. Azmir was about to place a foot on the bottom of the passerelle when the stranger asked if he lived on this boat.

'Yes, I do. Do I know you?'

'I doubt it. I am a friend of Tony and Bill. Is Bill on board?'

'I don't know. As you can see, I have only just arrived back. I will make some enquiries if you hang on here.'

Azmir and Ulrika moved up the passerelle with the stranger following them. Azmir spun around.

'Just a minute, can you please wait here? This is not my boat. I don't have the authority to invite you on board.'

'Oh, Bill, won't mind.'

'This isn't Bill's boat either. It would be best if you stayed here while I enquire,' said Azmir, pointing to a chair on the quarterdeck. 'What is your name?'

'Charles Eccles.'

'Oh, you are English. If you wait here, I will return as soon as possible.'

Azmir tapped on Bill's cabin door. There was a delay until a muffled response came: 'Who's that?'

'Azmir; there is someone here to see you.'

Bill opened the door, virtually asleep.

'Did you say there was someone here to see me?'

'Yes, Bill. Charles Eccles. He says he knows you.'

'Never heard of him in my life. What does he look like?'

'He looked smart with a short-sleeved white shirt and long trousers in a dusty pink colour. He wore a cravat at the neck. He had a dark complexion and dark eyes. He is English, judging by his accent.'

Bill stepped out into the corridor. He could see Ulrika speaking to Eccles. He looked very familiar – then the penny dropped. Bill pulled Azmir back into his cabin.

'Bloody hell, Azmir. This guy interrogated and tortured us when the Russians captured us. I am not walking out to greet him. Who knows what he will do? He could be armed.'

'Okay, leave this with me; lock the door and don't open it until you recognise our voice, okay?'

Azmir knocked on John's cabin door. John poked his head out.

'Can I come in, John? It's urgent?'

'Whatever is the matter?'

Azmir explained what had just occurred.

'Okay, leave it with me. Don't go back to him just yet. Come in. I need to make a call.'

John called Miron of EKAM and explained the situation. Miron realised this could play right into their hands. It should be easy enough to arrest this man in the marina.

'I will have some troops with you within minutes.'

'Okay, Miron, he is sitting on the quarterdeck. If your men come as policemen, he may be armed, and there could be dreadful consequences.'

'Understood, John. Send him off *Brave Goose* to the café on the quay in ten minutes. We will arrest him there.'

John and Azmir walked together to the quarterdeck. Azmir had been tasked with taking Ulrika to their cabin.

'Good afternoon, Mr Eccles. Should I know you?'

'No, because you are not Bill Edwards.'

'Well, I have told Bill you are here, but he has been asleep for some time. He is still in bedclothes. He is getting up and will have a shower and come and see you.'

'That doesn't matter. I don't care how he is dressed.'

'Well, Bill does. Would you like a drink, coffee, beer, whatever?'

'Yes, that would be good.'

'My staff need to prepare this area for a dinner party this evening. Let me escort you to the taverna on the quay. We can have a drink and chat there. I told Bill that's where we would be. He promised to join us in ten minutes.'

'Can I join you, John?' requested Azmir.

'Why not? Let's go and leave Sally, Ulrika and the team to get started on the dinner.'

Azmir led the way, and John brought up the rear behind Charles Eccles.

Mid-afternoon and the marina taverna was not busy. It became busy when boats arrived either to stay on their moorings or overnight when the crew might enjoy a meal there. Coffee and beer now were easy for them.

'So, Charles, how is it, you know, Bill?'

'We go back a long way.'

'Oh, how long and what context?'

'John, it's Bill I have come to see. Are you trying to make sure I don't get to see him?'

'You sound a suspicious character. I'm not too fond of your tone and the fact you made your way onto my boat without an invitation. You were specifically asked to remain on the quay.'

'When the waiter arrives, I would like a beer, John. I am just going to the toilet.'

'Bloody cheek. Who does he think he is?' said John to Azmir.

'He's a pushy sod, John. I told him to wait on the quay, but he came up anyway.'

Two men in jeans and polo shirts, who looked fit and athletic, arrived at the side of the table.

'Are you John England, sir?' one of the two men addressed John.

'Yes, I am. Did Miron send you?'

'He did, sir. Are you the gentleman seeking to speak to Bill Edwards?' he said, addressing Azmir.

'No, he has gone to the toilet.'

The two police officers raced off to the toilets. There was no one there. They had missed him. He must have guessed he was in a trap.

Bill joined John and Azmir in the taverna. The two police officers returned to advise John that he was not there; he had presumably fled to avoid a suspected trap.

'Sit down, gentlemen. Coffee, beer or anything else?'

The two officers asked for a bottle of water. John placed an order for three beers.

'What reason would this man have for seeking you out?' the officers asked Bill.

Bill explained how he was there, and his friend Tony who was now in the hospital with severe burns. It was quite a story. It took at least half an hour to be told.

'Ah, I see why Miron was keen to get his hands on this man,' said the leader of the pair. The other policeman said nothing.

'Are you staying much longer here, sir?' he continued, addressing John.

'So much depends on the British Embassy sending documents for Bill. He is the man Eccles said he wanted to see,' said Azmir.

'Oh, and how do you come to be here, sir?'

'I am on holiday. I was Mr England's interpreter in the Bosnian War. We met totally by chance in Corfu. He offered us a trip on his boat, and as we had an appointment with the British Embassy here in Athens, he said he would bring us here. So here we are.'

'Good, I hope everything works out for you in England. I will report that the man we were tasked to apprehend had left before our arrival. Safe journey, gentlemen.'

The two EKAM officers departed, leaving the three men to consume a cold beer each.

'Why do you think Charles Eccles wanted to speak to you, Bill?'

'It could be that he has discovered Tony was not killed in the blast on our yacht. He may have wanted to get rid of me to satisfy his bosses back in Moscow.'

'Were you working on something that would upset the Russians so much they needed to kill you both?'

'I would rather talk about our activities onboard; we could be overheard here.'

Once the beers had been consumed, the three men returned to *Brave Goose*. On board, they chose to sit around the table on the quarterdeck.

'As you know, Tony and I come from Manchester. Greater Manchester Police had become aware of a considerable number of girls and young women being transported to the Manchester area. They were convinced they were put to work in the sex trade. Various raids had confirmed their suspicions. Many of the girls were foreign yet had British passports. Very few of them could speak English to a standard that would assist the police. GMP needed to know how they arrived in the UK and why Manchester.

'MI5 were enlisted to discover the girls' original place of departure. In every case, it was a foreign departure point, so MI6 became involved. Between them, MI5 and GMP realised that several groups of 'exporters' seemed to be linked. Eventually, they discovered a Russian link. A Russian individual appeared to be in charge of the whole operation. No one knew their name. They were very secretive. What was known was that several thugs had joined their 'security' arm. Hence, many stabbings and deaths when some of the girls who tried to escape the organisation's clutches or their 'new' boyfriends tried to help them escape and were subsequently killed. The assassinations have become much less than initially a few years back. The fear of being killed has brought everyone under control.

'As the countries where these girls were being trafficked to were mainly in Europe, MI6 was co-opted to discover who was behind the organisation. Tony and I owning a yacht in the Mediterranean was ideal for the task. We had perfect excuses to visit places off the usual tourist routes. So that's what we have been doing for the last two years.'

'That is quite a story, Bill. Is it a correct assumption you were getting very close to exposing the people behind the racket?'

'Correct, John. What makes you say that?'

'It appears the Russians had identified you as getting too close to how their organisation works. Hence the attempted assassinations.'

'Which countries provide the majority of the girls?'

'It varies, John, but Albania, Greece, Turkey and Croatia.'

'Handy, as they are all easily accessed by sea.'

'Yes, that is the idea of using us. We have an easily established reason for being in various places.'

'So, where are you up to now, Bill?'

'Well, the interruption of our boat blowing up and Tony in hospital, I will now return to London before going home to Manchester. I expect to get some further instructions tomorrow before I go.'

CHAPTER 36

'John, I have just spotted that man Eccles, who was here earlier.'

'It's Bill the man wants. Based on previous activities, he could be out to kill Bill.'

'Let's wait and see if he comes back. If he does, should we detain him, John?'

'If you feel up to it, Azmir. I will get Jock to stand by. You and I should be able to stop him.'

'Sally, can you spare a moment? I think Bill is back in his cabin.'

'Yes, he is John. He went for another siesta.'

'Fiona, Azmir has just seen the man who called himself Charles Eccles. If he comes to the boat again, I intend inviting him up to the deck, and between Jock, Azmir and me, we intend to hold him.'

John spoke to Jock and asked if he would be happy to participate. He agreed.

Returning to the engine room, Jock knew the ideal implement to cause this guy damage without killing him. He was excited to get one of the people who had held Bill and Tony. He hovered at the entrance to the engine room with a long timber rod about two inches in diameter at one end rising to nearly four inches in diameter. He showed John his secret weapon. It was like a baseball bat.

'What on earth do you use that for, Jock?'

'It's a lever, John, which allows me to move heavy bits of the engine without damaging a casting. It will be useful on this job, assuming he returns.'

'Yes, it will, Jock. Don't hang around; he might not come.'

Jock decided to wait in the mess room of the crew's quarters, where the screen relayed pictures from the CCTV camera on the passerelle. Azmir went to the saloon to read, and John sat in his chair on the quarterdeck. There were eight chairs on the quarter deck, six set around the table, and two extra chairs in the port and starboard corners between the coaming for the quarter deck and the superstructure for the saloon. John's favourite was the starboard chair. It was Goose's favourite seat when he was alive. All the seats were identical woven wickerwork armchairs. John's had been additionally furnished with three soft cushions. Nothing happened. It was now getting dark.

Without pre-warning, about an hour after the trap had been laid, Eccles rushed up the passerelle onto the quarterdeck, surprising John. John stood up immediately he saw Eccles looking at him from the foot of his chair.

'Oh, it's you again. Bill and I came over to see you in the taverna, but you weren't there.'

'Cut the crap. Where is Bill?'

'I've been dozing here. I think he is on the boat, but I am not sure where.' said John, standing to his full height. Eccles then kicked out at John, who caught his foot in both hands, having stood back slightly out of range. Twisting Eccles's foot to the inside of his leg, John held it very tight, turning it as he did so, making him fall. He was unbalanced and went red in the face as he twisted towards the deck. On his way down, he hit his head on the table which caused his nose to bleed. He realised he was now fighting three men as Jock and Azmir jumped in to help John. Eccles tried to stand. Jock gave his left leg, on which he was standing, a massive blow with his wooden club. Eccles's white shirt rapidly changed colour to match his pink trousers due to the blood from his nose running off his chin. The man squealed like a wounded dog. He collapsed. Jock was pretty sure he had broken his leg.

'Doonna stand up again, ye sacernack. I will break your other leg in a second!' shouted Jock in a rather frightening Scottish accent.

Eccles stayed where he was. He closed his eyes against the pain. His face was red, the. veins in his neck were protruding and he kept moaning. He couldn't move.

Jock and Azmir helped John pin Eccles to the floor. John found a length of light rope from a locker. He efficiently tied the man's hands and feet and then joined the bound hands to his feet together, leaving Eccles as an immobile pile on the deck.

José, hearing the commotion, appeared on the deck.

'Lift the passerelle, please, José. That should stop any of his associates from coming on board.'

'Keep an eye on him, please, boys.'

John returned to his office and called Miron, explaining what had happened. Miron said he would despatch some of his team immediately.

Sally, Bill and Fiona appeared on the quarterdeck to see what was happening. Bill confirmed that the man was in charge of the Russian goons who had arrested him and Tony.

'Who the hell *are* you?' demanded John.

'I will tell you nothing – just like your guest here told us nothing – scum!' As he spoke, he spat spittle and blood as far as he could towards Jock.

'You sound English, but you work for the Russians. What's your game?' John once again tried to get an answer from the man.

'Okay, you hold your tongue. I will let the Greek special branch take over when they arrive. I am sure they have ways of extracting information from people like you, you bastard.'

John had hardly got the words out of his mouth when Miron and two other officers appeared on the dock.

'José, please let the passerelle down for Miron and his men, please?'

He did as requested, allowing Miron and his two officers to come onto the quarterdeck. Jock quickly retreated to the engine room with his baulk of timber and put it away in its secret place.

'Hi Miron, this is Charles Eccles of the Russian department on Ionia!'

'Is he now? I have wanted to speak to you for some time.'

Eccles said nothing. Miron ordered his minions to remove him from *Brave Goose*. 'We think he may have a broken leg, Miron.'

'How did that happen?'

'My engineer got carried away with his baseball bat as the guy was threatening us.'

'Maybe a stop at the hospital then. Thanks for catching him. We will make further investigations in Ionia. Has he said anything?'

'Only to be abusive.'

'We have some lovely ancient cells in Athens; a week or two there will loosen his tongue.'

The crew of *Brave Goose,* along with Azmir, Ulrika, John and Fiona, assembled on the quarterdeck.

'That was an unexpected interlude. Is that the end of the issues with thugs?' enquired John of the assembled company. Sally had returned to the galley with a washing-up bowl of hot water and rags and started to clean away the spilt blood.

'Here, let me help you, Sally,' demanded Fiona as she bent down with a rag in hand, helping with the clean-up.

Whilst chatting, Azmir's phone bleeped, indicating that a text message had arrived. It advised him that the papers and passports were ready for collection. His smile is as wide as the Cheshire Cat. He announced the good news to the crew and John and Fiona.

'I think we should go immediately and collect the papers. Do you mind if we shoot off now?'

Outside the marina gates, Azmir found a taxi, which was free, to take him and Ulrika to the British Embassy. The rest of the assembled company wished them good luck.

*

'Look, everyone. It's late Thursday now. Unless there are pressing requirements to visit Athens, may I suggest we leave here and head for Lefkas? Azmir and Ulrika could get a flight to Manchester from Preveza. I will check with Azmir when he returns to see if his tickets can be amended. Can you see if there is a different way of getting back to Lefkas that doesn't involve the Corinth Canal?'

'Yes, that's easy, John. I know the route. I will work out how long it will take.'

Sally and Fiona stood up. The deck and table were now as new.

'Anyone like a cup of tea?'

Everyone voted yes except John, who wanted a cup of black coffee.

'Do you want me to show you the route we could take around the Peloponnese?'

'Yes, that would be a good trip, Noel. '

'I have just calculated that it is a three hundred nautical mile trip from here to Lefkas.'

'How long would that take, Noel?'

'Taking it easy, we would be at sea for eleven hours a day for three days. We would be back at Lefkas marina Sunday evening if we left tomorrow, Friday. That would give Azmir and Ulrika time to pack and leave the boat on Sunday to catch the flight to Manchester. They thought they would initially fly to London, but considering where they would like to work, they changed the flights to Manchester.'

'How will they transport all their belongings, John?'

'They should be able to take it on the plane, but they would have to pay for considerable excess baggage. It can be done. They would need some large suitcases to fit everything in.'

'I have seen an advert for a company with a van here in Greece who travels to and from the UK once a month. He might be available; it might be cheaper. I guess cardboard boxes would do the job in that case. I will try and find the advert in the local paper I bought in Lefkas. I will phone them now if I can find the number.'

John eventually found the number and phoned the transport man who quoted a minimum fee of £100 and a maximum of £200.

'Do you want to book in?'

John advised that the person requiring his services was not here.

'He will ring you shortly.'

*

'It's been another fraught day, Noel. Have you had a chance to speak with the crew? Are they up to sailing again soon? If so, do they want to remain on *Brave Goose*?'

'No one has told me they want to leave. I will meet with them all shortly and put the proposition to them. Now that things have settled, I would love to stay involved in the refit this winter. I will let you know their views, but they will want to stay.'

'Good. Who knows what will happen next, but the money is all paid, so that should no longer be an issue.'

'It has been a bit more interesting than being held on the quay in Southampton for months, as was the case with the previous owner.'

'I can't disagree with that, John.' Noel ran his fingers through his hair, leaving it all tussled. He did have a smile on his face, which was encouraging, thought John.

Noel went to the crew's quarters. They were all enjoying tea or coffee and a cake from Sally's secret store. He joined in the relaxing repast laid out then launched into a discussion that each knew would be coming at some point.

'Look, folks, we have endured some serious issues. Some of us have been hurt. The leisurely cruise has not been as anticipated. The plan is to sail down the Peloponnese and eventually return to Lefkas. How do you each feel about remaining on board? I think John was asking for trouble, not paying all the money. But he has had to pay twice. Georgio was a pain and will suffer accordingly for the damage caused to the canal. The issues that Bill and Tony had to endure were nothing to do with John. I suspect Bill will be onboard on our way to Lefkas.'

'I don't see that as a problem,' Sally chirped.

The other two agreed.

'Hindsight is easy, but would you have paid this man Georgio if you put yourself in John's shoes?'

'You know, Jock, that is a very good question. Yes, putting yourself in John's shoes, I would likely have done the same thing. He could not have imagined the problems that followed. Okay, I will tell John that we all agreed we are still a happy crew and wish to remain. We look forward to the refit. We will take him up on his hotel accommodation offer while *Brave Goose* is laid up for refurbishment.'

*

Noel didn't hesitate to give the good news to John. The two men shook hands and decided to take the opportunity to review the schedule of works for *Brave Goose* to be carried out by Pelaros during the winter.

'John, Sally and I are off to the shops, mainly for food for the voyage, but if I spot anything else that appeals, I may have a look at the odd clothes shop!' said Fiona.

The two women walked off the boat, checking out with security, advising that they would return later in the day.

'John, would you mind if I shoot off to visit Tony?'

'Bill, it is as much your stay as anyone. Feel free to come and go as you wish, subject to Azmir and Ulrika's plans. We will probably leave on Sunday.'

Bill, carrying the anorak that had been purchased for him, set off, firstly, to the shops. There was one urgent purchase he needed to make:

a mobile phone. He planned on purchasing a basic phone but getting back in touch with friends and family was urgently required. Once equipped with a simple phone, he hailed a taxi to transport him to the hospital where Tony was being treated.

'Good morning, I have come to see Tony Franks. He is in the burns unit.'

'Just a moment, sir, I will check that it is convenient for you to visit.'

'Mr Franks was discharged yesterday, sir.'

'That's impossible. He was very poorly. Who was he released to?'

'That is all I have been told, sir.'

'Do you mind if I go to the ward to speak with the sister in charge? I guess it may be possible our employer arranged for a medical evacuation?'

The nurse in charge informed Bill that Tony had been collected in a private ambulance and was to be taken to the airport for medical repatriation to the UK.

'Did you have prior notice of this?'

'Strangely, no, but it sometimes happens when the right hand doesn't know what the left is doing.'

'Would you have the phone number of Tony's employer? They are also my employer. I need to call them as they will be the ones who authorised the repatriation.'

'Yes, sir, it is a UK Government department.'

The nurse wrote the number on a slip of paper for Bill. He then returned outside to the sunshine.

'Yes, it's Bill Edwards. I am in Athens. Tony Edwards, badly burnt in the explosion on our yacht, has been removed from the hospital, apparently, organised by you for a flight home? Is that correct?'

'Just a moment, I will put you through to the section head.'

'Bill, it's Rupert Phillips. How is Tony?'

'Don't you know, Rupert? You sent an ambulance to collect him yesterday and flew him back to the UK, didn't you?'

'We did no such thing. Why do you say that?'

'Because that is what has happened. If it isn't you, I suspect it is the Russians.'

'Oh, bloody hell, Bill. What a cock up. What can you do to try and find him?'

'We are in touch with a bloke called Miron, the head of the equivalent of our SAS.'

'Okay, Bill. I will get onto it right away. I will also call the embassy. Where are you staying?'

'I am on a friend's boat called *Brave Goose*. I can stay there as long as I wish.'

'Okay, you go back to the boat. I was hoping you could send me an email with your contact details. I will try and get the Greek authorities moving to find Tony. About what time did he leave yesterday?'

'I gather it was about five in the afternoon local time.'

'Okay, keep in touch. I need to make some calls.'

Bill hailed a taxi and returned to the marina as quickly as possible. As he exited the cab to enter the marina, Azmir and Ulrika were about to take the same path as him.

'Hi Bill, we have now got all our papers and passports. We can go to England now. Isn't that great?'

'Yes, but my dear friend Tony, who was recovering from terrible burns, has been kidnapped from the hospital. I need to tell John.'

CHAPTER 37

Tony was oblivious that he was in a private ambulance, being driven away from the Athens hospital. He knew he had received an injection from a new nurse; none of this bothered him.

A private ambulance had parked at the entrance and two young nurses in white tunics had wheeled a stretcher into the hospital. A middle-aged nurse wearing a similar tunic but with a badge from some nursing organisation, indicating her seniority, approached the nurses' station on Tony's ward. Speaking Greek, she introduced herself.

'I am Nurse Galanis. These two nurses are my assistants,' she said, pointing out the two young nurses. Galanis had a disrespectful look on her face when making this statement. She was sure the two girls knew nothing about nursing and were just cadging a lift to the UK.

The paperwork she carried looked official to the nurse on duty, so she assisted in disconnecting Tony from his tubes. She replaced the morphine drip with a bag, which hooked onto a pole that was part of the trolley brought from the ambulance. Tony needed an extra morphine boost to assist with the additional pain as he was transferred from the hospital bed.

He stirred slightly as the ambulance trundled through the capital's busy streets. They eventually found the smart new road, built for the Olympics, out to the new airport that had been constructed for the same event. More paperwork was required as they entered the secure area for access to the apron, and the air ambulance. The security guard waved the ambulance through after a cursory look at the documents. Passports of the three nurses, all Greek, were examined. Nurse Galanis explained that the patient was suffering from third-degree burns. He had been blown up on a sailing boat and was to be transported to the burns unit at Wythenshawe Hospital in Manchester. She gave his name but explained his passport had been lost in the explosion and subsequent fire.

The airport ground crew assisted in getting Tony loaded onto a small plane, ready for the journey to Manchester. Within an hour, the plane took off. It was now midday. Most holiday traffic seemed to fly first thing in the morning or late at night. The schedules in the middle of the day were quiet. Four hours was the scheduled flight time to the UK in this small plane, specially kitted out as an air ambulance with comfy seats for the medical team.

Nurse Galanis closely watched Tony, recording his vital signs regularly. The two young nurses laid back in the comfy seats reading magazines. On schedule, the plane landed at Manchester Airport four hours after take-off, but only two hours difference in time zones.

Once on the ground and marshalled to a private area of Terminal 2, a private ambulance greeted the plane and the patient was transferred. All three nurses accompanied Tony on the journey to the hospital. Wythenshawe had a specialist burns unit and should be able to administer the care he so urgently required. They took with them their bags of personal belongings.

Tony was transferred to the hospital with the minimum of bureaucracy. Nurse Galanis stayed with him. The two girls, after an hour of hanging around, conspicuous in their white tunics, were approached by an Albanian man. The girls understood him instantly. He drove them away from the airport. Nurse Galanis never saw them again.

*

Once back on *Brave Goose,* Bill told John and Noel what had happened. He had no information as to what had happened to Tony. The nurse on the ward had advised him that there were three nurses and a private ambulance. The head nurse told the hospital that Tony was to be flown back to the UK to a specialist burns unit in Wythenshawe in Manchester.

'Well, if that happens, Bill, it will be a good thing, as I understand that Wythenshawe is a specialist hospital in so far as burns are concerned.'

'Thanks for the re-assurance, John; however, I need to speak to MI6 and discover if they were behind the transfer.'

John offered Bill the phone in his office. His call was to the duty officer. Bill was back on the quarterdeck within ten minutes. Sally brought him a cup of tea.

'What news, Bill?'

'Yes, it's all above board. The department organised the flight home for Tony. Strangely, he said that the department had organised a nurse to accompany Tony the whole way. When I was at the hospital, the nurse in Tony's ward explained there were two young nurses and a far more experienced nurse as part of the team to repatriate Tony. *Three* in total. I can't see the department coughing up for more nurses than required.'

'Don't worry about it, Bill; there will be a perfectly good reason for the confusion.'

'I am sure you are right, John. So, what is going to happen now?'

'Azmir and Ulrika are leaving the boat tomorrow. They will leave two large suitcases and extra luggage with us on *Brave Goose*. We will give them to Robert at Paleros, and the carrier we have been in contact with will take the suitcases to a location currently unknown but is likely to be a hotel in the Lake District.'

Azmir and Ulrika were anxious to move on. They had swapped their airline tickets to fly to Manchester from Athens.

'We have purchased two enormous suitcases, John. They should be delivered here this afternoon. Ulrika and I will pack them. It's great that you're going to leave them at Paleros. When I know the exact address, I will text the delivery company so they know where to deliver them.'

'That's no problem. We will be pleased to do that. So, when will you be going?'

'We thought we would go tomorrow. If that is okay with you, John.'

'That's no problem at all. Shall we all go out for dinner tonight to wish you well for the future?'

'That is an offer not to be sniffed at. Thank you, John.'

As Bill was walking away, his phone rang. He stopped and dealt with the call.

'You can't imagine what I have just heard, John.'

'No, go on.'

'The department organised the senior nurse and the flight to the UK. A different division, so on my initial enquiry, no one knew what was happening. The two young girls posing as nurses have jumped ship, so to speak, and disappeared in Manchester. No one knows what has happened to them.'

'I wonder if they are Albanians, who the Russian enclave on Ionia has trafficked to the UK to work in the sex trade?'

'Quite likely, John. The office is onto it. They want a full raid on the Russians on Ionia to see what else they might be up to.'

'Looks like there is more to come from this story. At least Tony is in the right place.'

CHAPTER 38

It was eight o'clock on Sunday morning. The chapel bell in the village nearby was calling parishioners to prayer. It was a single bell and chimed for ages with its monotonous single chime. The sound echoed over the water. There didn't appear to be much movement of people towards the church. Crews on other superyachts, much larger than *Brave Goose,* were drying all the white fibreglass and stainless-steel elements before the owners woke and appeared for breakfast. The dew that had settled overnight was significant. It was as if the boats had been hosed down by some unseeing hand. Eventually, the shine on the topsides sparkled again.

John and Fiona were at the table on the quarterdeck with Azmir and Ulrika. Bill was still asleep. As far as John was concerned, he could sleep all day if he wished. The trauma this man had experienced would have killed many. He was a tough cookie.

'So when is your taxi due, Azmir?'

'I booked it for ten. The plane for Manchester is due to take off at one o'clock this afternoon. I thought it best to build in some holding time in case we were delayed by authorities regarding our luggage, passports, or anything else.'

'Very sensible, Azmir. It is impossible to tell what aspect of paperwork the authorities might require further examination. I am used to it now.'

Final preparations for their departure were hastily completed.

'Where would you like to put the surplus stuff, John?'

'Well, if they are all contained in either boxes or suitcases, they can be left in your cabin. Bill might transfer so we can put all the stuff in the Pullman cabin.'

José took the suitcases they were taking with them and placed them on the dock at the end of the passerelle. Goodbyes ensued, starting with Sally. Azmir and Ulrikka were so pleased to have met her. Then goodbyes to Jock, José and, of course, Noel.

A white Mercedes taxi swung onto the dock as the final goodbyes were made. Once the driver had established he was in the correct place, he relaxed and placed the two suitcases in the boot.

Fiona and John followed Azmir and Ulrika down the passerelle to the dock.

'Have you got your passports and visa, Azmir?'

'I certainly have, John. They are the most valuable pieces of paper we have ever had.'

'Good, well, all the very best to you both. Please keep in touch, and when you are settled, should you be working for a hotel, we will come and see you.'

John received a kiss from Ulrika, as Fiona received a kiss from Azmir. Handshakes between the men, and the two travellers got into the back seat of the taxi. Several waves from the taxi window, and they were gone. It seemed so quick. One minute they were there; the next, they were gone.

'I wonder what they will end up doing, John?'

'Who's to know, darling? They are both workers and talented in various ways. They will survive. It's not until you meet people like them that you appreciate what a wonderful country we live in and why so many people want to come to the UK.'

Bill appeared on the quarterdeck looking worn out. He had just showered, and his wet hair confirmed it.

'John and Fiona, I gather I have missed saying goodbye to Ulrika and Azmir. Good bloke, Azmir.'

'Yes, Bill, they had a plane booked for one o'clock, so they wanted to get to the airport early in case of last-minute hitches.'

'There shouldn't be. I know the embassy created a gold standard set of documents and visas for the pair.'

'That's good to hear, Bill. Are you going to have some breakfast?'

'Kind of you, John, but I need to get off to the embassy as I have a zoom call fixed for me with my boss in London. That doesn't sound great; I guess they have more work for me, and I won't be going home soon.'

'Is there a chance you might not be coming with us?'

'It's a possibility, John. I will know later. I must fly, thanks.'

Bill took off like a greyhound. He was finding the energy that earlier he seemed to have lost completely.

'So, my love, it's just you and me. Would you like to go sightseeing in Athens?'

'Normally I would love to, John, but as it's turned out to be a sunny day, I fancy sunbathing on the boat deck.'

'Could your reluctance be anything to do with the fact this is Sunday and many shops will be shut?

'Cheek! But it is a consideration!'

'Are any more breakfasts required, John, or should I clear away?'

'Bill has had to go to the embassy so he's left. We are very well fed, thanks, so that's breakfast over. I don't think Fiona and I will need lunch or dinner, so if you and the crew want to spend time ashore, feel free, Sally.'

'Thanks John. I will let them know.'

'Sally, let me help clear all this away so you can enjoy the rest of the day.'

Once Fiona had finished washing up and tidying away the breakfast things, she and John repaired to their cabin to change into swimwear and pick up a book and sunscreen. They settled down to some serious sunbathing, something they had been unable to enjoy for some time.

In the next hour, all the crew left *Brave Goose.* Noel confirmed he had a key, so if the passerelle was up, he could recover it later with the magic eye on the key ring. John confirmed they might be out for dinner. Noel was to leave the passerelle down until they returned.

'I will pull the passerelle in now, Fiona. Everyone has gone.'

'You know, John, what we need as part of the refit is an in and out board so we know which crew are on board. We could be on the board as well, as owners 1 and 2. Then there could be four more places for guests 1 to 4.'

It was half-past-three in the afternoon. John and Fiona were sound asleep on the sunbeds, getting rather sunburnt despite the lashings of factor fifty Fiona had insisted they use. John woke up to a noise on the quay. His name was being shouted. Walking to the end of the boat deck railings, Azmir and Ulrika were jumping up and down, trying to attract attention.

'Hey, you two, you should be nearly in England now. Why are you here? Hang on, and I will come down.'

Once onboard, they started to gabble out the last few hours' events. By now, Fiona had joined the gathering.

'Look, let's sit down, and you can tell us all about it.'

Fiona distributed some of Sally's famous lemonade.

'John, you can't believe what has just happened. Cheap Flights Limited, the cheapest airline we could get, could not take off as they had no fuel. The airport would not supply them unless a fuel debt was paid. So, the plane was not flying to England or anywhere today.

'Couldn't you switch to another airline?'

'We tried that, but as Cheap Flights Limited were in financial difficulties, no one would honour their tickets as they might not get their money back from Cheap Flights Limited.'

'How will you get your money back, Azmir?'

'I have spoken to Visa, and they said they still held the money we paid and would not debit our account with the airfare, so we are free to book with someone else'.

'Have you managed to do that?'

'No, not yet; we can get an EasyJet flight on Sunday from Preveza. We wondered if we might cadge a lift to Lefkas?'

'Of course. We would love to have you on board. Where are your cases?'

'On the quay.'

'Okay, let's get them back on board now, and you can settle into the double cabin again. Bill has had to go to the embassy this afternoon; not sure when he will be back.'

'That's wonderful, John and Fiona. Thank you so much. Tell us what we can do to work our passage!'

*

'Bill, it's Evans. Now, I know you have had a bad experience so far. Not as bad as Tony. He is in the right place now. The irony is that the plane we chartered for Tony had two young female trainee nurses and an experienced medic on board. These two girls spoke little English, despite holding British passports.'

'Were they fraudulent documents?'

'No, I don't think so; they were the work of a double agent – Joy. You met her, I assume?'

'No sir, we didn't. I assume the girls were Albanian?'

'Yes, you are correct. We interrogated them, but we had no reason to hold them as they were holders of genuine UK passports. Look, Bill, if I send another operative out to be with you, can you, with the help of the Greek special forces, look into how they manage to get to the UK and what they are expected to do when they get here?'

'Okay, sir. I need some funds and a new credit card. I will have to rent a car and find a hotel as I cannot ask the superyacht owner whose boat I am onboard. They have been more than kind to help me so far. I will need a new driver's licence and a new passport.'

'There is no problem with all that. It seems to us that Lefkas is the ideal location to base yourselves. I will get the documents to you via the embassy. If you are leaving for Lefkas, please let us have your address when you have one. In the meantime, I have authorised a thousand euros in advance so you can set yourself up. We will courier everything to you when we know where you are.'

'Thank you, sir. I will also need a copy of my RYA European certificate of competence, as I may need to rent a boat. I also need a mobile phone.'

'These last items will come out with the new operative. I will ask the embassy to book a hire car for you and two hotel rooms in Lefkas. You need to keep me informed, understood?'

Once the call ended, Bill went to collect the euros from the embassy. He then. returned to *Brave Goose.*

CHAPTER 39

'John, I have been looking at the charts and the pilot. I think we should stop at Porto Kheli near Spetsi. That would take us about eight hours. I assume we will leave tomorrow. We will travel on Tuesday to a most exciting place that we shouldn't miss the opportunity to visit as we will be sailing past. We can anchor in the bay north of the rock and dinghy to the shore.'

'So, what is this exciting place called, Noel?'

'Well, John. Monemvassia is its name. It is an ironstone plug, thought to be the remains of a volcano. The Byzantines built a small village on the side of the rock and a lookout on the top. There are small shops, restaurants and a church. Regrettably, the shops in the main square have been converted to gift shops or ice cream parlours. However, you can see through the tat to the most imaginative village. There are no cars or motorbikes. Donkey power is the only form of transport. When you see the street paving, you will understand why.'

'Can't wait to see this place. That sounds like an excellent idea. Once we have done that, where next?

'We will go non-stop to Fiskardo. It will be a twenty-four-hour passage at ten knots. I am assuming good weather like we have enjoyed so far. That will take us to the northern side of Cephalonia. After a rest at anchor there, we will then motor to Lafkas and our mooring at the marina.'

'You mentioned the weather. You've never done that before. Are you expecting some bad weather?'

'Well, it's forecast to be a southerly wind, as it is now, and building slightly. You will notice the boats on the north side of the marina. They are working their mooring ropes. We are the opposite. We are keeping a close eye as we don't want any chaffing of the lines.'

'Okay. Do you think we will see much stronger winds?'

'No, based on the information available at the moment. However, we are at the turn of the seasons, summer into autumn. Anything could occur. There are often signs that tell you we are in for a blow. Dense clouds hugging the tops of the hills on the islands is a clue to strong winds on the way.'

'That's interesting, Noel. I will keep a look out.'

'It shouldn't concern you, John. If we get rain and strong winds, *Brave Goose* can cope. Do you recall the weather we had in the mouth of Cork estuary? That was extremely rough, but she dealt with it easily.'

'Yes, I do recall, for all the wrong reasons. That is when Sean Fitzallen fell overboard and drowned despite every effort to save him. You gave him a life jacket, plus a helicopter, and a lifeboat were all involved in the rescue. He was taken to Cork General Hospital where he died. On reflection, that's another death to add to our ever-growing list.'

'Hmmm. So, anyway, that's what I plan, John. We will be fine with whatever is thrown at us. *Brave Goose* is an extremely good boat in bad weather.'

At that moment, Bill appeared on the deck.

'Ah! Bill. Good to see you back. I hope all went well at the embassy?'

'Yes, John, I have my instructions. I am not permitted to discuss them, but I am not happy.'

'Sorry to hear that, Bill. Will you be going back to the UK?'

'No, they need me here. I must discover how the Russians operate on Ionia island, where the girls come from, and how they are transported. Oh hell, I have told you my mission. Please keep it to yourself. Not very professional of me.'

'Don't worry, Bill. It won't go any further. I assume you would like to have a lift back to Lefkas tomorrow?'

'Would that be possible, John?'

'Of course. Azmir and Ulrika are coming as well. It's a long story, but essentially the airline they were due to fly with has gone bust. They need to fly now from Preveza.'

'Oh, so it will be a full ship again.'

'Yes, depending on the weather, it will be Wednesday afternoon before we get to Lefkas. The worst case will be Thursday.'

'That is no issue for me, John. Thank you so much.'

Despite the late hour, Bill phoned Mary, his wife. The signal was not great but adequate.

'I have been told by London I have to remain here, at least for a month or so, until I have indoctrinated a new agent as to what has been occurring.'

'That's all very well for London to lay the law down. What about us, Bill? I haven't seen you for ages. There's all sorts to do here. I am fed up with you disappearing for months on end. I am at my wits' end.'

'Mary, don't be like that; it's my job. I can't just down tools and return. Look at what happened to Tony.'

'I don't want to meet a package at the airport. I want you back now, Bill. If I am not here when you decide to eventually return, it will be your own fault.'

'Don't be like that, Mary. Please.'

'Don't try and soft soap me on the phone. I am fed up with these arrangements. You think more of your job than me. If you are not back when agreed last time we spoke, I won't be here, so you can decide what you want to do, but don't involve me.' Mary ended the phone call. Bill tried calling back, but she had switched her phone off.

The crew were up early Monday morning, preparing *Brave Goose* for the journey ahead. The marina fees were paid. Noel manoeuvred the boat to the fuelling dock. Two thousand litres were taken on board. Jock wanted to ensure the new load of fuel was in good condition so he started the fuel polishing mechanism, which would ensure any particles in the fuel would be excluded before it went to the day tanks. Each day tank held seven hundred and fifty litres. John was intrigued by what Jock was up to in the engine room and made a rare visit.

'How are things, Jock?'

'Everything is just fine, sir.'

'My name is John, Jock. While we are on our own, I insist we operate as one big family. So, what are you doing?'

'Well, sir, sorry, John. When we take on fuel from a new source, I always polish the fuel.'

'You have me there, Jock; what on earth does that mean?'

'We have just taken fuel on board from a new source. It's nearly October. Their tanks will be getting low as it's almost the end of the season. It is extremely unlikely any fuel quay will have a new fuel delivery until next year. So, with the fuel getting low in their tanks, we could pick up unwanted particles. So 'polishing' is a way to stop fuel filters getting clogged, so there are two methods of cleaning the fuel: the filters and the polishing plant.'

'Clever. What happens when you run short of fuel in the day tanks?'

'We only use the diesel in one day tank and then switch to another. It is done without anyone being aware of what is happening. I then polish a new fuel supply for the now nearly empty day tank.'

'Jock, I must say I wondered what you could find to do all day down here. There is far more to this than I had expected. Well done, Jock, keep us going.'

John returned to the quarterdeck where breakfast was being served. It was half-past eight. Noel was ready to leave. Sally was willing to continue serving breakfast while *Brave Goose* was in still water. John,

Fiona, Azmir, Ulrika and Bill sat around the table and tucked into a hearty breakfast. By this time, Noel had navigated *Brave Goose* through the harbour entrance, passing the hydrofoil dock, and was headed towards the island of Aigina.

*

Charles Eccles, the Englishman working for the Russians on Ionia, returned to the island and the Russian enclave with his damaged leg in plaster. Speaking in Russian, he told the other men back at base, assisted by his driver, to help get him into the bungalow. This had become not just a dwelling but an interrogation suite and holding unit for Albanian girls.

'How are you doing, boss?' enquired one of the guards.

'It will mend. The UK have emailed me that they need four more girls.'

'Do you want me to see if four are ready to travel?'

'Yes, that would be a great help.'

'How was it the Greeks let you go?'

'They recognised that the UK's fight with the Russians and the importation of girls was not a Greek issue, so they let me go. I have a bad leg, so I assume they thought I had been punished enough.'

*

'Bill, as you have decided to come with us back to Lefkas, will you be going home to the UK when we dock?'

'No, John. London has insisted that as I know the territory, I must stay here and help root out the issues surrounding the Russian enclave. The one that tortured Tony and me.'

'That seems harsh. You would have thought you could have a couple of weeks compassionate leave.'

'My thoughts exactly, John, but I must obey my superiors.'

'What did your wife think of that?'

'She was upset, annoyed and downright angry, to put it simply.'

'That's not very good. Are things generally tricky at home?'

'No, but frankly, my wife and I have been moving further away from each other for some time now.'

'If there is anything we could do to help, just ask.'

'Thanks, John, you have been very kind already saving our lives.'

'Noel hasn't said as much, but there is a chance of some bad weather up the western coast of the Western Peloponnese.'

'No worries, John, I have been in stuff like that out here before, but *Brave Goose* will go through anything, I should think. In fact, it could be quite exciting.'

'Noel, what is the island dead ahead?' asked Fiona.

'It's Aigina, Fiona; we will be leaving it to starboard. There is a bit of piloting before we get to our mooring for the night.'

'Where will that be, Noel?'

'Once we are further south, we will pass between Dhokos island and the mainland. We will then motor southwest and pass between the mainland and Spetsi before turning north to the horseshoe bay to Porto Kheli. There should be space to anchor in the centre of this secluded bay in ten meters of water.'

'Gosh, that's quite a bit of navigation, Noel.'

'Yes, but *Brave Goose* is great at close pilotage. I love it.'

'You have to keep your wits about you. There seems to be lots of little fishing boats out. We don't want any more nets around the prop.'

'I will try and avoid them all.'

'I know you will. I love this island hopping. It's a shame we will not have time to explore.'

'We have various tasks to perform and we have to get three guests to shore so they can fly back to the UK.'

'No, I understand.'

*

Once in the sheltered bay of Porto Khelei, Noel brought *Brave Goose* head to wind, motored forward a few meters and then instructed José to let out thirty meters of chain from the starboard anchor.

Once the anchor splashed and the chain rattled over the roller built into the starboard bow, José rang the bell once to indicate the chain had been fully discharged.

Noel maintained his position on the bridge with a few spurts of both engines in reverse. This gave a slight momentum to the vessel astern. She stopped gradually without asking as she dug the anchor into the sea bed. The pilot advised that the holding was good in sticky mud.

Once the anchor had gripped, there was a slight check on the chain, and *Brave Goose* came to her anchor. José rang the bell twice and erected the black anchor ball, which indicated to other craft that she was at anchor.

Being a secluded horseshoe-shaped bay, the sea was calm, and the bay was virtually empty of boats as it was nearly the end of the holiday season. As was typical on *Brave Goose* in a new anchorage with turquoise water, the five non-crew adults took to the water using the side boarding ladder and platform. Races around the boat, first to the anchor chair, made for a happy and laughter-filled hour while supper was prepared.

CHAPTER 40

'How are your plans working out, Noel?'

'Fine. I have calculated the trip from here to Fiskardo will be about one hundred and ninety nautical miles. That will take about twenty-two hours. That assumes we can maintain nine knots all the way, John. I don't think we will have time to stop at Momanvasia, but you can't help seeing it as we pass. I would rather press on as I now suspect we will get bad weather. It will be best to keep moving at sea rather than be at anchor in an exposed spot which would be the case if we stopped there.'

'I hope we can do that. Fiona and I would like to come up on deck later as we have never sailed at night. We are very excited at the prospect.'

'Good, you should enjoy it. In my mind, night sailing is very often easier than daylight sailing. That is so long as the navigational lights are lit, and they can be identified.'

'Why wouldn't they be lit, Noel?'

'This is Greece, John. They have no organisation like the British Trinity House, who are responsible for the lights around the UK. Many of our lighthouses are now automatic, so they are monitored electronically. They have three magnificent ships: THV Galatea, TVH Patricia, and THV Alert, which check navigation marks, and move or replace marks that need servicing or replaced in the correct position. Greece does its best but nothing like the UK.'

'How do you know all this, Noel?'

'I studied to become a commercial ship's officer at the Naval College in Southampton, where they train Merchant Navy Officers. Trinity House and navigation aids internationally and around the UK were essential study areas, Fiona.'

'Gosh, so how long has Trinity House been going?'

'It's a very old British institution. It was formed by Henry VIII in 1514. The captain of the *Mary Rose* was one of two seafarers to be appointed to the board of the organisation, now with the shortened name of Trinity House. I'll just go and check on my laptop for the full name.'

A few minutes later, Noel called out the full title of Trinity House and read out the information he had found on the website:

'On 20 May 1514, a Royal Charter was presented to *The Master Wardens and Assistants of the Guild Fraternity or Brotherhood of the Most Glorious and Undivided Trinity and of Saint Clement in the Parish of Deptford Strond in the County of Kent,* the corporation's full name to this day; Sir Thomas Spert, Master of the *Mary Rose* and the *Henri Grace a Dieu*, became the first Master. So, I hope that answers the question and has whet your appetite to know more?'

'Gosh, Noel. I understand why they shortened the name to Trinity House. So, let's hope the lights are accurate as we go north.'

'Indeed, Fiona. It will be an overnight voyage. It can go cold at night so you need a sweater and maybe a waterproof. Oh, one further point for everyone. No one is permitted on deck without a life jacket. They are all stored in this cupboard here.'

'What time tomorrow will we be leaving Noel?'

'I would like to leave here by ten in the morning. Breakfast needs to be cleared away. Sally, can you prepare sandwiches for lunch as we may find it a bit choppy for the first hundred miles when we leave the shelter of this bay.'

'That sounds a bit ominous, Noel.'

'No, not ominous, John. Just sensible precautions, as sailing at night makes everything that bit harder, including moving around the boat.'

'I see. Are we being sensible heading out knowing it will be rough?

Have you spotted some bad weather coming in, Noel?'

'This little ship of yours will cope with the weather here and in most other places. It will be choppy and we'll roll a bit as we head west to begin with, and then we head north straight into the wind and swell. The boat will be fine, and so will the crew and passengers. There's a depression moving from the south in the area of Crete. Much will depend on the track it takes. If it does what I think it will, it will head north over the Peloponnese. In this case, we will be on the western edge of the depression. As winds around a depression move in an anticlockwise direction in the Northern Hemisphere, the wind will become north westerly backing north and possibly increase in strength. I am not sure how quickly the depression will move north.'

'Thanks, Noel. Looks like an interesting trip.'

Noel instructed José to weigh anchor on the dot of ten o'clock on Tuesday morning. The log was set at zero so Noel could closely check the distance travelled; *Brave Goose* eased her way out of the bay where she had been anchored. A gentle breeze began to freshen once they rounded Cape Tainaron, the most southerly tip of the Peloponnese. It became a beam wind which, when further out into the Ionian Sea, caused a small rock to port and starboard. Nine knots were established, the autopilot set. Noel phoned Jock in the engine room to check all was well. It was.

By five o'clock in the afternoon, Brave Goose rounded the final southerly point of the Peloponnese. The westerly wind that had sprung up as a consequence of the low pressure passing to the east and travelling over the Peloponnese became a northerly with a slight emphasis to the west. Noel expected the wind to veer in the direction of a northerly or north easterly. *Brave Goose* settled into a long leg in a north-westerly direction bearing 335 degrees on the compass as the wind changed direction. Every other wave broke over the bow, and spray hit the bridge windows so the wipers were switched on. The strength of the wind had increased to a Beaufort force 6. There was a great deal of seawater splashing over the bow. The log still indicated nine knots of boat speed. Checking the GPS (Global Positioning

System), Noel noted that *Brave Goose* was making eight knots instead of nine. He studiously recorded all the vital information every hour throughout the trip.

At about seven o'clock in the evening, a sea mist along with the spray started to make observations by sight difficult. Noel had the radar running with a guard ring of two miles. Anything within two miles of *Brave Goose* would cause the radar to issue an alarm. The alarm was sounded as they passed within less than two miles of an isolated pair of islands, the Nisidhes Strofadhes islands. These islands had been occupied since the 13th century. A tall building on the main island was a monastery constructed by Byzantine monks. Apparently, only one monk remained. The weather was so foul that no attempt to get closer was considered.

It was now ten in the evening. Navigation lights were on. The internal lights were switched to 'red running', so the lookout and skipper could still see if they had to go into the accommodation areas.

Fiona and John said they were going to bed. Bill, who had gone to his bunk two hours previously, had said he was happy to be woken at two or three in the morning if Noel needed an extra hand on the bridge. The offer was gratefully received. Once the radar alarm issue had been cleared up, Noel also went to his bunk, although he suspected he wouldn't sleep much. Jock and José were the main watch. Sally had retired, having provided all the crew on board with a warming stew in bowls.

Azmir and Ulrika sat in the saloon, ready to help if help was required. They were both asleep within half an hour.

At five in the morning, Noel had woken, showered, and resumed his position on the bridge. He shook Azmir and Ulrika and suggested they go to their cabin. Before they disappeared, Noel asked if anyone had seen Bill. Ulrika said that she recalled saying goodnight to him at around half-past ten last evening.

'Okay, he was very tired, he will join us when he feels the boat's motion even out. We are not far off entering the straight between Zakinthos and the Peloponnese. The wind strength might increase as it is channelled between the two land masses, but the seas will be lower as there is less scope to build up large waves.'

Noel guided *Brave Goose* into the middle of the channel between the two land masses. He checked the log and the fuel. They had travelled 140 nautical miles; the log was reading nearer 150 nautical miles. That is the effect of water over the log impeller, which maintained a higher speed due to the passage of the water. The GPS was the accurate instrument giving the 140 nautical miles distance. It had been a noisy night with the crashing and banging of the steel hull riding the waves.

It was six-thirty when Noel and Fiona appeared on the bridge. They exchanged pleasantries with Noel, asking where they were. Noel pointed to the chart where they were, with fifty nautical miles to go.

'Is there anything we can do to help?'

Noel had dismissed Jock and José when he came on watch.

'I would love a cup of coffee, Fiona, if I may.'

Fiona made three cups and brought the Tupperware box of biscuits. They would have flown off a plate the way the boat was moving.

'The waves will abate shortly the further north we go, as they will have little scope to get to be large waves. I suspect you have felt one or two big waves since we passed over the one-hundredth wave.'

'How do you know it was the hundredth?'

'I don't, but it's a well-used sailor's expression.'

The next to appear were Ulrika and Azmir, at seven-thirty. They looked tired but were quite content.

'Coffee?' asked Fiona.

'Ooh, yes, please. Let me help you.'

'Okay, Ulrika.'

As Sally appeared from the crew's quarters, the two girls disappeared into the galley to make coffee.

'The box of biscuits is on the bridge. They may have all been eaten by now!' remarked Fiona.

Fiona and Ulrika returned to the bridge, followed closely by Sally, holding two cups of coffee.

'Would you all like breakfast in half an hour?'

A unanimous 'yes please' came forth. Breakfast would be served at eight o'clock. Noel reckoned on anchoring in Fiskardho, mooring outside the harbour. The weather might improve, and they could relax before moving to Lefkas marina the next day.

They were about fifteen miles from their destination when they sat down for breakfast. The wind had abated and the sun was shining through the clouds. *Brave Goose*'s slight movement across the sea was not quite smooth but not rough enough to make the boat rock.

'Has anyone seen Bill?' enquired John.

'No, he went to his cabin shortly after you last night. He didn't say much.'

'Okay, I will pop my head round the door quietly.'

John returned to the breakfast table looking like he had seen a ghost. He sat down and read from the document in his hand.

CHAPTER 41

'John, whatever is the matter?'

'Oh, Fiona! And all of you … I have terrible news.'

'Is it Bill, John?'

'Yes, my love. He left this paper, which I will read to you.'

'Dear all on Brave Goose.

Having rescued Tony and me once, I don't want you to try and find me for a second time.

Tony is in a bad way. I understand the medics have indicated he will be in the hospital for at least a year. They say he has some prospect of recovering but will never work again.

As for me, the last few months have been the worst ever. The best bits have been with all of you on Brave Goose. I wanted peace for a month or so, but London refused my request to travel home and told me that I should help the new men they were sending out to assist in the work investigating the Russian enclave on Ionia. When I told my wife, she went berserk. She would have none of it. I have never heard her so cross. She demanded I return home, or there would be no home for me to return to. She wants a divorce from me.

I am so sorry, but the actions I am about to take will cause all sorts of trouble and extra paperwork for you on Brave Goose, for which I sincerely apologise. I hope the authorities will accept that I am writing this note with a sound mind. The decision to end my life is mine and mine only. I have had no assistance from anyone. My employer's intransigence, requiring me to remain in Greece working for the UK Government, has caused a rift in my marriage. There is nothing left for me.

I see no point in continuing to live. I know the authorities will want to know when I jumped overboard. I think it will be midnight when I leave. I know the excellent captain of Brave Goose, Noel, will be able to identify the location from this time.

No one on Brave Goose has helped or assisted me in any way regarding my decision and how I will end it all. No one will hear me slip over the side because the weather is bad and the sea rough.

I wish you all the very best for the future. To Azmir and Ulrika, lots of luck in the UK, and I hope you find the employment you seek. As for the most generous owners of Brave Goose, John and Fiona and the professional crew, Noel, Jock, Jose and Sally, I wish you all the luck in the world. It has been a privilege knowing you all.

As always, my best wishes.

Bill

Fiona and Sally burst into tears.

'Oh my god John. What do we do now?'

'I'll need to tell Noel. He will have to notify the authorities, so they can come on board and interview us. I have shut Bill's cabin door. Please do not open it, as the police will have to search the room.'

John notified Noel of the situation, who was very upset, yet kept his cool.

'I will notify the marine police in Fiskadho who will wish to board us. We cannot leave the boat until we are given the all-clear. Does your printer make copies? If so, taking a few copies of Bill's note would be helpful.

'Do you know the contact details of his employer and wife?'

'Sorry, John, I don't. I suspect he has left his mobile phone behind, which could have the contact details. But I think you should leave that to the police.'

Noel advised the police that they would be at anchor just outside Fiskardho at ten o'clock that morning. If required, *Brave Goose* could send a boat to collect an officer. Noel was told to stand by the radio and await instructions.

Just before ten o'clock, Brave Goose dropped her anchor outside Fiskardo Harbour.

José lowered the side gangway and bathing platform. José and Jock launched the ship's RIB, suitable for travelling in and out of the harbour. *Gosling* could be lowered later if John and Fiona wanted to go off, but they could not leave until the police had concluded their enquiries.

Two police officers came onboard, first taking down the details of everyone on board. Then, the officers were taken to Bill's cabin. A copy of the note which he had left on the bunk was handed to the officers. They needed a translation into Greek before they could fully understand.

John realised the problem and invited an officer to sit in the saloon beside him and moved his iPhone to translation mode – English to Greek. He started to read Bill's note. The officer was then able to make notes. By the time John had finished reading, the officer had noted the note's full content.

The police officer smiled at John.

'Okay, thank you.' Then went to speak with his partner and explain the note.

'I understand. I have the man's passport, some euros and various other documents.' Returning to the saloon, the officer who had sat with John asked if he could start the translation app again for some of the papers that had been found.

There was a pile of six pieces of paper. The note from the British embassy was constructive, explaining what London wanted Bill to do next – the fact that a partner would be joining him. The RYA certificate was easy as it had a Greek translation on the front cover as to what the document was. An email from his wife, which had not been printed but was still held in his mobile phone clearly explained the rift between Bill and his wife.

The police officers explained they would be taking several documents and personal effects. Their intention was not clear. John moved his phone to translation conversation mode. The police officer repeated what they were about to do, and John was able to reply appropriately.

'Are we able to leave the boat now?'

'Yes,' was the response, but the boat had to remain there until an officer familiar with navigation could come on board to check the ship's records of the journey they had just made.

'My friends, Azmil and Ulrika, must catch a plane from Preveza on Sunday. Can they leave the ship and travel by ferry to Lefkada and then by taxi to Prevesa?'

'Only when we have run our checks by lunchtime tomorrow!'

'Okay,' said John. 'We can manage that, but they must fly to England no later than Sunday.'

The two officers left *Brave Goose.* John was not much further along relating to what they could do.

'Noel, I think I am going to ring Miron in Athens. You know, the commandant in EKAM based in Athens. He will be helpful, I am sure.'

'Good idea.'

'Miron, it's John England – *Brave Goose.*'

'John! Do you have a problem?'

'Why do you think that?'

'People only phone me when they have a problem.'

'Well, *Brave Goose* gave the surviving British MI6 operative, Bill Edwards, a lift back to Lefkas, so he could meet with a new operative who is to replace Tony Franks. The new man is expected in Lefkas sometime next week. Bill left a note on his bunk. He was occupying a cabin on his own. The weather was pretty rough last night, so it was noisy onboard. According to the note left, he jumped overboard at around midnight. We were unaware of this until I checked on him at eight o'clock this morning to see if he wanted breakfast. He wasn't there, just his note. Is there anything I need to do beyond informing the local authorities here in Fiskardo, where we are at anchor?'

'Goodness, John, you certainly have many problems in your voyages around Greece.'

'Yes, Miron. It isn't what we wanted.'

'Yes, I am sure. Let me make a few enquiries. I will come back to you later today.'

John was pleased he'd told Miron as he was familiar with the previous situations, and thus he was the ideal man to advise what to do next.

'Noel, I have spoken to Miron; he will return to me later in the day.'

'Good John. Can we go ashore?'

'Yes, there are no restrictions. I am just waiting for the police to say if the cabin can be cleaned.'

'John, I have been looking at my log. Midnight was the time I went off watch, and Jock and José took over until we reached the coast of Cephalonia. Neither Jock nor I heard a thing that was out of the ordinary. We are sure we would have heard the cabin door opening and being shut.'

'It was noisy, Noel, so it would have been difficult to hear.'

'I know what you mean, John, but I have been at sea for many years, and you get attuned to unusual noises even in a gale.'

Sally joined the pair butting into the conversation.

'Has anyone been into the life jacket locker? I found it partially open this morning.'

'Oh, what do you mean, partially open?'

'It's a two-click process to close the locker door properly. It was held on the first click only.'

'Has anyone checked if a life jacket is missing?'

No one said they had, so they all went to the locker.

'Did the jackets we lent to Tony and Bill when we found them in the dinghy get put away?'

'Yes, John. I dried them in the engine room. Jock will remember as he chastised me for using his engine room as a drying space.'

'That sounds like Jock. There should be ten life jackets in there.'

Between them, they emptied the locker and counted the jackets as they were replaced in the locker. There were only nine.

'Are we certain?' demanded John. 'Can we count them again?'

'Yes, there were only nine jackets on the second count,' remarked Noel.

'Do you suppose Bill took a life jacket with him as he went over the side?'

'It is certainly a possibility, Noel. Taking a life jacket would indicate that he hoped to survive and find land.'

'We were more than ten miles from the coast all the way north up to the Zakynthos Channel, so why would he think as a sailor he could swim to the shore and hide away? Hang on, John, I need to check something. Do you recall the alarm going off on the radar that I had set a guard ring at two miles? We were passing a small group of islands which were hard to see, especially in the weather we had. The radar alarm went off at half-past midnight. Bill's note says he intended to go over the side around midnight.'

'Okay, let's tell the authorities that a *Brave Goose* life jacket is missing, together with a guest.'

'Okay, John, can you do that with your translation device?'

'I guess Fiona, Azmir and Ulrika would like to leave the boat for a meal this evening, so can you organise launching *Gosling* for me?

'Sure, No problem.'

The four of them went ashore to dine at what had now become a favourite restaurant in Fiskardo. Bill was the centre of the conversation, to begin with. They discussed all the ramifications of someone apparently jumping off the boat; was it suicide? No one could work out why he did what he did.

'When Bill decided to end it all, he took a life jacket which would keep him floating for hours,' remarked John.

'It's a real puzzle.'

As Fiona was about to add to her comment, John's mobile rang.

Miron told John that the Greek maritime law required the vessel from which a person went missing to undertake a detailed search of the area where they suspect the individual left the ship. The search area needed to be extensive regarding currents and wind direction. The search should be carefully recorded to give the authorities full investigation details.

When John concluded the call, he told the others what Miron had said.

'I don't want to be awkward, John, but we fly to the UK on Sunday, and it's Friday tomorrow. If we joined the search effort, which I believe we should, we would miss our flight.'

CHAPTER 42

'Azmir, I know the search would cause you a problem.'

'That is correct, John. We need to be at the airport in Prevesa by ten in the morning to catch the one o'clock flight to Manchester.'

'Okay, there is a way around this. The ferry from here to Vassiliki runs every day. On our way back to *Brave Goose*, we will take a look at the notice board on the slipway, which gives times of sailing. If you get the ferry, then a taxi to Lefkas, you could book into the hotel on the marina and then go by taxi to Prevesa airport first thing on Sunday.'

'Thanks, John.'

John could detect a level of concern in Azmir's voice.

'Is there a problem, Azmir?'

'Yes, I don't know how to say this, but we don't have enough cash for the ferry, two taxis and two nights in a hotel.'

'Don't fret about that. I can let you have some cash. Goose left a pile of cash in his safe when he died. You can have some of that.'

'That would be very kind, and we will pay it back.'

'How do you propose to pay back money to a dead man? No, you use the cash wisely and make life a little more comfortable for yourselves.'

On their way back to *Gosling*, two port police officers carrying a large piece of grey plastic approached John.

'Which is your boat, sir?'

'*Brave Goose*, she is at anchor outside the port. This is our tender.'

'Good, we have been asked by EKAM to give you this, sir.'

'What is it?'

'It's a body bag, sir. If your search is successful, you must place the body in this bag and return the body to the port police in Lefkas.'

'I understand, officer. Thank you.'

John held onto the bag. Fiona was at the helm of *Gosling* as they left the quay and made their way to the slipway. Azmir jumped out in his haste to read the board, getting his shoes and trouser bottoms wet. He ignored the discomfort and squelched his way to the notice board.

'Half-past eight tomorrow.'

'Perfect, we will transport you to the slip at eight. Shorts and beach shoes for tomorrow, I think.'

They all laughed.

Returning to *Brave Goose,* Sally offered to put Azmir's shoes and trousers into the engine room, where it was hot and would dry everything.

Azmir walked to their cabin in his boxer shorts and bare feet.

On Friday morning, everyone was up early. The cases for Azmir and Ulrika were loaded onto *Gosling,* ready to take them to the quay to await the ferry. Lots of kissing, waving and handshakes preceded the trip by *Gosling.* José took them to the slipway. As he was barefooted, he jumped out and pulled the little boat alongside the slipway so Azmir and Ulrika could escape the boat in the dry.

José passed Azmir their cases, and he was soon on his way back. As soon as he came alongside the boarding platform, Jock lowered the strops and crane hook to facilitate lifting *Gosling* onto the boat deck.

As *Brave Goose* weighed anchor, the Vassiliki ferry rounded the headland and lighthouse to dock at the slipway, allowing the vehicles and passengers to disembark. *Brave Goose* was underway as the ferry exited the harbour. Azmir and Ulrika waved from the aft deck and John and Fiona from the boat deck of *Brave Goose.*

John had explained what was required by the authorities. Noel had already calculated where they would have been at approximately midnight, the time Bill jumped off the boat.

'John, I have decided to make most of the search from a coordinate a hundred meters north of where Bill says he jumped to two miles south of our start point. The search will take all day. I am doing this because the wind and current were in the north, so Bill would have drifted with the wind and current going south.'

'Sounds sensible, Noel. How do you want us to look out? We only have three sets of binoculars. Do we need to keep a record of anything we see? Fiona and I will be on the bridge or flybridge – José on the bow and Jock on the stern. Will that be okay?'

'Yes, that is fine. I will be keeping a detailed log of what we do. In fact, we will make sweeps across the channel, about a cable or so apart, which means two cables apart taking left to right and right to left. If anyone sees anything, you must shout out immediately, and I will record our position, and then we will investigate what has been spotted.'

Brave Goose began searching, hoping to find a sighting of Bill.

After three hours, just after eleven in the morning, a helicopter with POLICE written in large on the side swooped down towards *Brave Goose.* Noel's VHF sounded.

'Police helicopter, this is *Brave Goose* over.'

'Channel 72,' was the short reply.

Noel returned the VHF radio to channel 72 and advised the helicopter that he was on channel 72 and awaiting instructions.

'*Brave Goose*, we are taking part in the search for the missing passenger. We understand that you are short of a life jacket. What colour was it?'

'Police helicopter, the lifejacket that is missing is bright orange. Over.'

'We have spotted a small dot of an orange object on the most southerly cape of Nisos Stanfani. Are you able to inspect, please, as it would appear to be only accessible by sea?'

'Yes, we will go immediately to inspect. Out.'

'Let me record our exact position now. Could you please note the content of the exchange between us and the helicopter, Fiona, so we have a record of what was said.'

Noel was now studying the chart, and the tiny island which was visible, but they didn't have a detailed chart of the island. Then it occurred to Noel that the pilot would most likely have a detailed sketch of the two islands. The index indicated pages 247 and eight. Noel flitted through the pilot but couldn't find the page.

'John, do you mind seeing if you can find the page?'

John proceeded to try and find the page.

'It isn't here, Noel. The page has been removed.'

'That's interesting. If what the helicopter saw was a lifejacket and Bill had been wearing it, the chances are that he left *Brave Goose* soon after the radar alarm went off. If he swam to land on the more northern point of the island, the wind, waves and current would have swept him down the island's coast, landing on the southerly tip. I have a note in my log about the radar alarm and the very poor visibility at the time. If he had jumped overboard, no one would have seen or heard him.'

'What will you do without the pilot book?'

'I can enlarge the picture on the GPS, which will, in effect, provide me with a chart of the islands. I will do that shortly as we near the islands. I calculate that the island is twenty-five miles away. It will be nearer three this afternoon before we are off the southerly side.'

'Okay, Noel, let's go. Shall we all have lunch on the way, Sally?'

CHAPTER 43

The Strofadhes Islands were about a mile ahead. From his recollection of the chart in the pilot book, there was an area between the islands and at each point of the main island strewn with rocks.

'John, we will have to launch the RIB to allow a search of the cape at the southern end of the first island, which is where the helicopter advised they had seen the orange speck.'

'That's okay, Noel. When you are ready, we can launch. The sea is nearly flat now. We will need the starboard boarding ladder down.'

'José and Jock, can you come to the bridge, please?' he announced over the ship's intercom.

Once they were on the bridge, Noel explained that it would be a tricky exercise to launch the RIB and motor over to the cape of the island. The area was strewn with large rocks, so they had to be careful.

'You are looking for an orange life jacket,' Noel reminded them. 'Please wear your own life jackets. Now, lower the starboard boarding ladder. Take a handheld VHF radio with you.'

The two crew didn't take long to launch and be away in the RIB. Noel manoeuvred *Brave Goose* to a position closer to the island. Everyone left on board watched keenly as José and Jock motored the RIB gingerly towards the island. John and Noel were now on the flybridge with binoculars, trying to spot the life jacket. They could see José scrabbling over the rocks. Then after a few minutes, he went behind a rock, and when he stood up, he was holding a life jacket. He waved his arms in joy. Back on the RIB, he called *Brave Goose.*

'I've got it, and it's one of ours; the name is on the jacket.'

Well done, José. Now can you please motor along the shoreline, watching out for boulders? There is a sandy inlet at the other end of the island on this coast. Once there, can you pull the RIB up the beach, and the two of you have a hunt around to see if you can find any signs of Bill?'

Noel brought *Brave Goose* opposite the RIB, standing off by half a mile. Everyone on board watched the two men as they walked up the beach, and then disappeared down a slope, eventually up again on the track to the house and monastery. After fifteen minutes, they still had not reappeared.

'I wonder what could have happened to them?'

'I don't know Fiona, but I am convinced they found Bill.'

Another quarter of an hour had passed; no news. Then José could be seen outside the house, and the ship's VHF crackled into life.

'John, it's José.'

'What has happened?'

'We have found Bill, but he is in a state. He is crying and adamant he doesn't want to return.'

'Okay, I understand. Please return to *Brave Goose* in the RIB, and I will come over to speak to him.'

The RIB was alongside in no time, leaving Jock with Bill. John donned a life jacket and hopped into the RIB for the trip back to the island. José showed John the way to the house after making sure the RIB was secure by pulling it up the beach.

They arrived at a dilapidated door which led into the ground floor of what was once a house. The place looked like a medieval prison, clay floor littered with debris and plant matter. The ceiling had fallen in in places. It was a hovel. The nasty smell became almost too much after a few minutes.

Bill was sitting on a stone near what had been a fireplace.

'Let's sit outside, Bill. The smell here is too much.'

'Okay, John.'

Bill shuffled out of the building to sit on the first rock. He felt very guilty about lying and putting the crew, owners and guests in all sorts of trouble with the authorities. They would sort something out, John was sure. Bill said he had been surprised to discover he was alone on this little island. The page he had torn from the book said that there used to be a monk living here but that he may have left. Well, he had certainly left.

Bill said he had found a big flat stone in the sun close to the monastery walls. He had picked up some small stones and laid the wet paper on the rock to dry.

Inside the first building, a three-story house with flaking rendered walls and red tiles on the roof, was where the monk had lived. The vast stone-built monastery had suffered in 2003, according to what Bill had read, due to a large earthquake in the area. Geologists had identified the epicentre of the quake to these little islands. Amazingly, just outside the monastery was a well, full of water. The bucket on a rope had allowed Bill to bring up some water and he had been delighted to discover it was sweet, clear, fresh water. He needed to discover if some edible plant life or even an animal or bird could provide sustenance. If that could be found, then he had discovered his desert island on which he could stay indefinitely. However, he couldn't find anything other than water. He assumed that was why the monk had left.

As soon as Bill saw John in the doorway, he burst into tears. He felt humiliated. He wanted to run away again, but he realised that would be a total waste of time as there was nowhere to run to on the island. He felt dreadful. His face was flushed, he was shivering uncontrollably despite it being a hot day. What was he to say or do now? What a bloody mess he had made of his life. He should have ended it all but dared not jump into the water without a life jacket. So, he was saved, but what now?

'Bill, thank goodness you are safe.'

'Oh John!' he replied, whimpering. 'I am so sorry to have put you to so much trouble.'

'Don't you worry about a thing. You have had a very rough time. Will you come back with me to *Brave Goose*, and then we can go to Lefkas and sort everything out, okay?'

'Whatever you say. It was a silly move to think I could survive here. I was hoping the monk might still be on the island, but clearly not. I realise now that I could not have survived without any method of getting to the mainland and no facilities here other than a sweet water well.'

The four men walked slowly to the RIB. José made to go first to prepare it to travel back to *Brave Goose.* They were ready to depart when Bill, wearing the life jacket that had saved his life, got on board with John.

Back at *Brave Goose*, they climbed the boarding steps onto the quarterdeck. Fiona flung her arms around Bill and gave him a big kiss.

'It's great to have you back with us, Bill. Please don't go away again!'

'No, I won't, I promise. I feel such a fool and humiliated by what I have done. How can I ever pay you back?'

'There is nothing to pay back. For us, the payback has been finding you and bringing you home.'

'I feel I owe you all so much. I have nothing. I have to start from the beginning.'

'It could have been considerably worse, Bill.'

'Yes, you are right. I could do with some of the luck you have encountered, John. But that was at considerable cost, according to the reflections of death you have mentioned.'

'You know, Bill, there have been times in my life when I was ready to end it all. The death of my wife and two children was my bleakest time. Your mental state has not been good. The torture you endured at the hands of the Russians on Ionia must have been awful. I am so pleased you are alive and well. Some of Sally's food will soon have you feeling better.'

'Thank you. Thank you. I think I need to unburden myself of all the baggage that has been haunting me and reflect on my past too.'

'Recognising that is half the battle, Bill. When we have a moment, we can all enjoy conversing with you, so your burden can be shared. What is the saying – a trouble shared is a trouble halved.'

Noel, with the aid of José and Jock, weighed anchor and motored back to Fiskardo. The journey of eighty nautical miles would take about nine hours. Noel thought this was too long, so he discussed the proposal of staying overnight in Zante harbour, the main harbour of Zakinthos, and half the distance to Fiskardo.

'John, I am planning to moor in Zakinthos harbour. We will be there at about seven this evening. It's a long way to get to Fiskardo tonight. I think we have had enough, don't you?'

John agreed. That would be their destination for tonight. He retired to his office, where he emailed Miron at EKAM and the police at Fiskardo, explaining what had happened. He thanked the police for the assistance of their helicopter which had pinpointed the life jacket. He confirmed that they would be sheltering in Zakinthos Harbour overnight. Did the Fiskardo police wish to interview Bill? If so, *Brave Goose* would anchor off and ferry Bill ashore.

Bill went for a shower and put on some dry clothes Fiona and Sally had purchased for him the last time *Brave Goose* rescued him.

John suggested that once they had moored stern-to in Zakinthos, they should all go out and have a meal in one of the many restaurants on the town quay. The passerelle could be lifted to make it difficult for anyone to get on board.

They had a very Greek meal with plenty of wine and, more importantly, a smile on Bill's face.

On returning to *Brave Goose*, John had two emails, both essentially saying the same thing. One was from the police at Fiskardo, the other from Miron at EKAM – '*No, we are delighted he has been found. Your email will be recorded as a successful conclusion to this unfortunate event.*'

'Noel, you will be delighted to know that neither the police nor EKAM needs to speak to Bill or us again.'

'Now that is excellent news, John. We can crack on to Lefkas in the morning. I will check with Jock on the fuel load, as we could refuel here if required.'

'Well, if she is going to be in a shed for the refit, surely we don't want to leave the tanks full?'

'That's a popular misconception, John. The temperatures in the Mediterranean can cause diesel bug. That is a fungus-type growth which forms in tanks. It can block fuel lines and filters. To avoid that, it's best to leave the tanks full so there is little air in them to allow the fungus to grow.'

'Just as well you run this ship. I would be in all sorts of trouble.'

'It's just experience, John.'

Brave Goose was being prepared to leave when a mini-tanker appeared on the quay asking if they would like fuel.

'Have you three thousand litres?'

'Not on board; I have about a thousand litres, but my petrol station is just the other side of the road lower down. I can refill it and bring it to you?'

'Would it be easier for us to moor nearer your station?'

'No sir, my station is on the other side of the road. The mini-tanker is the only way. I can deliver three thousand litres.'

'Good, let's do it.'

Noel notified Jock, who was pleased. It would save a great deal of trouble when they get to Lefkas. One thousand one hundred litres went in on the first filling. Being very trusting, the mini-tanker went off and was back in twenty minutes to complete the job. The attractive element of this transaction was that the tanker driver, the filling station owner, was happy to negotiate a lower price for quantity.

'Jock, we need to come back here should we be passing!'

John listened to the conversation – it was a good sign if his crew could negotiate the fuel price. John's mobile rang. He retired to his office to accept the call assuming it would be about Bill. It was Azmir from Prevesa airport.

'John, did you find Bill?'

'Yes,' John was about to go into detail but Azmir cut in.

'I can't speak long, but I thought you, Bill and Miron at EKAM should know that there are four pretty girls and a Russian chaperone on our flight to Manchester. I suspect they are part of the trafficking operation being run by the Russians. Thought you should know. Must go.'

John immediately rang Miron's office. He hoped there would be someone to answer the phone. There was, but not Miron. John explained who he was, and that Miron would need to know the information John had received. John asked him to get Miron to ring him. He returned to the rail to watch the refuelling operation. His mobile rang; it was Miron.

John recited the information he had received from Azmir. Miron agreed it sounded like the trafficking they were trying to stop. He explained he needed to contact airport security as fast as possible.

'I will let you know what happens.'

*

The passengers for the Manchester flight were requested to go to gate three. Azmir and Ulrika were in the queue, as were the four girls and their 'minder'. It was obvious to Azmir that the 'minder' held all five passports.

The line for boarding had not moved for over a quarter of an hour. Passengers were getting restless when six armed security guards and an airport official in uniform approached the line. Their target was obvious.

The airport official asked to see the group's passports. The minder held them all out. Her passport was Russian but the others were British.

'Why do you hold the passports for these young ladies?'

'In case they lose them,' she said.

With the passports in his hand, the airport official asked the girls to come out of the line and stand in a quieter area of the departures gate.

'Are you Maria Evans?' There was no answer.

'Do you speak English?'

'No.'

The officer asked the same question of all four girls, and he received the same answers.

'Madam,' he addressed the minder. 'I see you have a Russian passport. No visa is stamped on the passport, so how are you in Greece and now travelling to England without visas for either country?' There was no reply.

'Please, all of you, come with me.'

The armed security guards shepherded the five women to an office in the main airport building. Each female was placed in a separate office, and the doors were securely closed.

A Greek immigration official went to each room to interview the girls. A male immigration officer interviewed the Russian minder.

'Do you speak English?'

'A little.'

'Are you in charge of the four girls?'

'I don't understand.'

The officer knew this would be a long-winded interview. He used the telephone to speak with a Russian-speaking translator who translated all the questions.

The Russian woman responded that she was in charge of the four girls.

'How do the girls all have British passports but don't speak English?'

'I don't know. I am just doing a job.'

'Oh? Who do you work for?'

'A Russian travel agency in Greece.'

'How long have you been working in Greece for the travel company?'

'Nearly two years now.'

'You are here on a tourist visa which precludes you from working in Greece. Why have you been working here?'

'I needed the money.'

'Do you speak Albanian?'

'Yes.'

'Is that why you have been chosen to look after these four girls?'

'Possibly.'

'When you got to England, what was to happen?'

'I was to be met by a man, and he would identify himself as the transport for the girls. I was to give him the girls' passports, and he would take them to where they were to stay.'

'What would you do then?'

'I have a flight back to Prevesa from Manchester later today.'

All the interviews with the girls were virtually the same.

'What is your purpose in visiting England?'

'I am a model and will be modelling British clothes and swimwear.'

'You don't have a tourist visa to visit Britain.'

'I don't need a visa because I have a British passport.'

'I see, but you are not British. You are Albanian?'

'Yes, that is correct.'

'How did you get a British passport?'

'My boss in Greece gave it to me.'

'Wait here; the interview is suspended.'

The immigration officers met in their office, all with the same conclusion that the four girls were being trafficked for whatever reason. They certainly were not going to work as models. They would never be allowed to hold their passports. They would be prisoners of their employers in Greece and the UK.

'We need to seek advice on this,' said the senior immigration officer. As the words left his mouth, the phone rang. It was a senior officer in EKAM.

'We will be coming to Prevesa airport this afternoon to transport the five females back to Athens. We believe this is part of a people trafficking organisation based on the island of Ionia. We want to do in-depth interviews. I suspect the four girls will be returned to Albania. The woman and others we expect to round up today will be charged and held on remand in jail until there is a trial.'

CHAPTER 44

On *Brave Goose*, Bill had showered and changed into clean, dry clothes. Although he had not purchased them, they fit well and looked smart.

'Perhaps I should ask Fiona and Sally to shop for me again!'

Feeling refreshed, and feeling quite peckish, Bill appeared onto an empty quarterdeck. As he wondered where everyone had gone, he could hear John deep in conversation in his office. The RIB was missing and so were Fiona, José and Sally – a shopping trip, he assumed. Noel and Jock were in the engine room. Bill made himself a cup of coffee, and as the biscuit box had been left out on the countertop in the galley, he helped himself to a couple. He returned to the quarterdeck and had just sat down when John appeared.

'Hi Bill, are you feeling better today?'

'I am a great deal better, John, thanks to you, the crew and, I gather, the police helicopter.'

'Yes, I am glad they spotted the life jacket. Otherwise, we would never have found you.'

'John, I can't tell you how grateful I am for finding me. I find it immensely touching. With the benefit of hindsight, I would have never survived on that little island. Fresh water can keep you going for a few days, but food is essential. I could see nothing anyone would be able to eat on the island.'

'It's all over, Bill; no more needs to be said.'

'I guess my employer might want to know where I am?'

'If they do want to know, they haven't asked me. There is something

I need to discuss with you. You recall the concern that had been expressed about trafficking young Albanian girls to the UK to work in the sex trade?'

'I do, John; have there been developments?'

'There have, thanks to Azmir at Prevesa airport being very attentive. He was certain four girls and a minder were all going to the UK on the plane he and Ulrika were booked on. He rang me with the details. I then rang Miron at EKAM, who authorised the immigration officials at Prevesa airport to detain them.'

'Wow, that was good thinking by Azmir.'

'It was. It transpires his thoughts were correct. All five of the women have been arrested. Miron has authorised a raid on the Russian enclave on the island of Ionia to arrest all the people working in those premises.'

'That will be quite an operation as some are armed.'

'Miron promised to let me know later what happens. I told him we would be moving to Lefkas marina tomorrow.'

'I've lost track of the days. Is it going to be Sunday tomorrow?'

'It is Sunday today, Bill. Sally has gone food shopping. Fiona hitched a ride. I can't imagine what she will purchase, but I don't think it will be food. They'll be back in the RIB later.'

Jock and Noel appeared on the quarterdeck from the engine room.

'Hello Bill, are you feeling better?'

'Yes, Noel, thank you. Thanks for all the help to rescue me, and you too, Jock.'

Jock smiled; Noel said it was all part of the job.

'We are having a salad lunch and eating on board tonight. The BBQ will be required, Jock. We can all eat together.'

'That will be nice, John, thank you.'

The sound of an outboard motor heralded the arrival of the RIB.

'Let me help collect the shopping and bring it on deck.'

There was much joy on deck as the girls welcomed Bill back to the world again. The shopping was put away in the galley and John suggested a drink was required. Fiona disappeared into their cabin with a shopping bag; John followed to discover what she had bought.

'Ha, ha, you will never guess.'

'No, you are right. I won't try.'

She tipped the contents of the bag onto the bed. John was dumbfounded.

'These are all men's clothes?'

'Yes darling, I bought them all for Bill. He will have to present himself in due course in a business setting. I thought he would like a blazer, trousers, a couple of shirts, more underwear, and socks. I have also purchased a sailing anorak in the other bag, as the weather is so changeable.'

'That is so kind. He will be amazed. Shall I get him to come and look?'

Bill was stunned by the generosity. He took all the clothes to his cabin.

'Bill, why don't you move cabins to the one vacated by Azmir and Ulrika? There is far more room, and the ensuite is larger. You will be more comfortable and have plenty of space to hang all your clothes.'

Sally had already changed the bed linen so the larger cabin was now free.

*

As John walked back to the quarterdeck to see if there was some rosé wine in the fridge to wash down lunch, his mobile rang again.

'Hi, Miron. How can we help?'

'John, could you have a chat with Bill? We would like him to come to Athens to identify some people we arrested when we emptied the Russian enclave on Ionia.'

'Athens is a long way to sail, Miron. Corinth Canal is still out of action, I imagine?'

'Yes, it is John. No, we can send a helicopter for him.'

'It isn't easy to land a helicopter near us in the port. It would be much easier if the helicopter could come to the airport here in Zakynthos. Let us know when it's arrived, and we will ensure he is at the airport. Can you bring him back to Lefkas marina when you are finished?'

'We could pick him up at Sami. Where the ferry comes in is a large concrete quay. We could land there. We will send him back to Lefkas on Monday or Tuesday.'

'I see. Can you give me half an hour to speak with Bill and Noel?'

'No problem. I look forward to hearing from you soon.'

John invited Bill and Noel to join him on the quarterdeck. The three men sat around the table. John explained the nature of the call he had had with Miron.

'They need you in Athens, Bill, to identify the Greeks, the Englishman, and some Russians. They arrested everyone on the island of Ionia that was involved in the Russian enclave. Would you be happy to do that, Bill?'

'Certainly; it sounds as if they have all the bad guys under lock and key, and they need to stay there. If I can identify them, that will help the cause. How can I get there, John?'

'That's where Noel comes in. They say they can't land a helicopter in Zakynthos harbour so they will fly the helicopter here in Sami. You will be returned to the marina in Lefkas. There is the large concrete quay there which is a perfect landing place for a chopper.'

'Yes, we can do that, John. It would help if Miron's team could notify the port police in Lefkas for the helicopter to land when they are due back there. As you will recall, a space in the marina needs to be available.'

'I will ask, Noel. When should we go to Lefkas?'

'I can get to Sami in just over an hour. It's about ten miles to the harbour entrance.'

'Okay, Noel, I will tell Miron the plan.'

CHAPTER 45

'Is that Georgio?'

'Who wants to know?'

'It's Vova from Athens.'

'I thought you were in jail?'

'I was for a short period, but they couldn't make the charges stick. The whole complex on the island of Ionia has been raided. They are bringing the surviving MI6 operative, Bill, who was once held on Ionia, to identify people they have arrested.'

'Okay, but what can I do about it?'

'You have Mafia connections. We understand that Bill will be transported in a helicopter from Zakynthos and taken to Athens so he can carry out identifications.'

'It's not the Mafia you need. It's one of those anti-aircraft rockets we had when we attacked the Corinth Canal.'

'You are right, Vova. Can you recall where we got them from?'

'Leave it to me for half an hour. I will get back to you.'

'Vova, we obtained the shoulder-launched rockets from the Greek Mafia. I guess you know who to contact?'

'Thanks, Georgio.'

Vova made some calls. He was able to obtain the two rockets he needed. He said that payment would be made after the job concluded. Then he made arrangements with other members of the group who would assist in shooting down the helicopter which they hoped would hold the last MI6 operative, Bill.

'Vova, where do you want us to wait with the rockets?'

'I suspect the helicopter will fly over the sea and land at the airport in Zakynthos. This was confirmed by a request to the port police yesterday by EKAM on VHF. Silly people, we could all hear the request. The shortest distance to EKAM's headquarters is to fly to Piraeus, following the water the whole way.'

'So, the only land they would travel over would be the Corinth Canal? I know that it is water, but very narrow. We could get a shot away there.'

'Vova, will there be one of our lookouts at Zakynthos?'

'Yes – Spiros. If you let me have your mobile number, I will get him to ring you when the helicopter returns from Zakynthos.'

'How long will it take for them to get to our position?'

'The distance is roughly one hundred and fifty miles. If they fly at one hundred miles per hour, about an hour and a half.'

'Okay, we will be ready. We will get ready at ten in the morning. We will only get the rockets out of the car once we hear they have left Zakynthos.'

*

Noel had moored *Brave Goose* alongside the quay in Sami in time for the helicopter to pick up Bill who was ready to go, dressed in his new trousers and blazer.

'Brilliant, Bill. I hope all goes well. We will be in Lefkas when you return.'

'What sort of helicopter will they send, John?'

'It will surely be a police helicopter. It will probably fly at one hundred miles an hour, so if they leave at nine this morning, they will be here in half an hour.

'Thanks, John.'

The conversation had only just been completed when the sound of a helicopter overhead on its way to the quay in Sami drew their attention. This was not a police helicopter; it was a Greek army Sikorski Blackhawk, bristling with armaments. The pilot placed the Sikorski on the security landing pad for army helicopters. The sliding side door was opened, and the rotors continued turning. Bill walked to the helicopter and was helped into the passenger seat and asked to wear a life jacket. The sliding door was shut, and the Sikorski took off.

*

'That must be a speedy helicopter, Noel?'

'Yes, John, they are exceedingly manoeuvrable, fast and armed. I wonder if EKAM is expecting trouble?'

'Oh, I hope not.'

'I have the helicopter on my radar. It seems it will follow the sea to Piraeus.'

'Why would they do that, I wonder?'

'It would be out of range for any rocket attack. Sensible. I guess some people would like Bill not to be alive. He can identify too many Russian or Russian sympathisers.'

'You know, that had never occurred to me.'

*

Bill was amazed at how fast the helicopter flew. No one spoke to him while he was on board. It wasn't long before the Corinth Canal came into view ahead; he could see it from his seat. A crew member came and sat beside him, explaining they were expecting trouble in this area.

'The Russians would love to get their hands on you, Bill.'

'Is that why EKAM sent a military helicopter?'

'Yes, they have had intelligence that an attempt to down us might be made.'

'That is why you have all been so quiet?'

'Possibly. Just ensure your safety belt is firmly attached. If we are attacked, we will fight back. This will involve tight turns.'

'What will you fight back with?'

'We have a twenty-millimetre cannon mounted on the front of the aircraft. The co-pilot will operate this. We also have four air-to-ground rockets attached to the stub wings.'

Some moments later, as they were flying over and along the length of the Corinth Canal, a call came from the pilot.

'Rocket observed,' came the quiet comment in a steady voice from the pilot. 'Chaffe deployed.'

'Bill, that will fool the guidance system of the rocket. They are not heat seekers but magnetic.'

As his companion announced the sighting of the rocket, the helicopter banked at about forty-five degrees, returning quickly to its previous course and attitude.

'The radar has picked up the launch site of the rocket. Another one is about to be launched,' said the co-pilot, who then pressed the button to fire the cannon. A stream of bullets went searing through the undergrowth towards the rocket launcher. They have made contact with ammunition as a loud bang was heard. Smoke and flames exploded from the undergrowth beneath them. The pilot opened the throttle and shot off toward Piraeus at about two hundred miles per hour.

'Are you all right back there?'

'Yes, fine, thanks,' replied Bill, slightly shaken by what had happened and the speed involved.

'They are keen to get you, Bill. I don't think they will try again, even on our way back.'

Before Bill could understand what had happened, the helicopter landed on the large H marked out on the grounds of EKAM's headquarters. He was met by two officers and asked to follow them.

*

'Vova, this is Spiros. We have been devastated. All the rockets we had left were blown up. We have two casualties.'

'Can you get them to the hospital?'

'We are working on that now. Oh, wait, six police vehicles have just appeared from nowhere. We are all about to be arrested!'

Vova didn't reply to the VHF message. He was about to drive off in his car but was stopped by two police vehicles. Brandishing their side arms, the police officers insisted Vova get out of his car. He did as instructed and was immediately handcuffed and placed in the back of one of the police cars.

'How did you know where I was?'

'You used VHF radios. Our technicians were able to get a fix on your position. So here we are. Have a last look as I don't think you will not be seeing daylight for some time.'

*

Bill was taken to the officers' mess where he was offered coffee and refreshments, which he declined. After a few moments, he was escorted to the senior officer's office.

'This is Bill Edwards, sir,' advised the escort as the door opened to Miron's office.

'Bill, great to see you. I understand your journey went well, albeit there was a slight altercation when flying along the line of the Corinth Canal.'

'Yes, sir, I was interested to see work is still going on to repair the canal. I can report that to Noel and John when I see them again.'

'That may be some time, Bill. A small private jet belonging to the RAF awaits your arrival at Athens airport. There is a police helicopter waiting to take you there. Your boss in London is anxious to speak to you.'

'Oh, I have left so many items on *Brave Goose*. I must return to collect them.'

'There is no need, Bill. While you were in the air, another helicopter, operated by the police, landed at the port of Sami. The crew on board collected all your belongings from *Brave Goose*. The crew and John and Fiona wished you well. They hope to see you in England at some point.'

'This is all very surreal. Why all the cloak-and-dagger stuff? Don't you want me to identify the people you have arrested on Ionia?'

'No, Bill, that was an excuse to get you here. London wanted you out of the way in case you were attacked again. They were concerned for your safety and everyone on *Brave Goose*. Goodness, they have been through enough.'

'Yes, I understand, sir.'

As Bill was talking, there was a knock on the office door. A member of EKAM came in and advised that the police helicopter had arrived to take Mr Edwards to Athens International Airport. It was noon.

'Thank you, Miron. I am very grateful to you and your team.'

Bill followed the EKAM officer to the helipad. He was amazed to find all his stuff and papers in the passenger seat at the back of the helicopter, next to his seat.

'May I have your name, please, sir?'

'Yes, Bill Edwards.'

'That's fine. Please fasten your seat belt. We will soon be at the airport.'

The flight over Athens was a joy. The Acropolis was shining in the sunshine and a sight to behold despite scaffolding having been erected at one end.

At the airport, in the corner of the airfield, the police helicopter landed alongside a small executive jet with a British registration. Bill was asked to undo his belt. When the rotors had stopped, the door opened, and an RAF sergeant escorted him to the small jet. Two ratings from the RAF were busy unloading all Bill's equipment from the helicopter and placing it in the hold of the small plane. The exception was a large envelope which was passed to Bill. It contained all his personal papers, money and passport.

Bill was allotted a comfortable seat halfway along the length of the jet, complete with a table. The other members of the RAF, having completed their task, came on board. Once the door was closed, Bill looked out of the window and saw the police helicopter take off.

The pilot and co-pilot were in the flight deck. Presumably, they were talking to the tower seeking permission to taxi to the runway and then take off. Bill felt like a millionaire with this treatment. Within half an hour of landing at the airport, they were in the air heading, he assumed, for London.

Once on the flight, the captain came and spoke to Bill and told him they were to land at RAF Northolt. Bill knew it was an airport reserved for special flights, mainly by the RAF.

'However, Bill, if you want to pick up the phone next to your seat, we will connect you to *Brave Goose*. In a moment, if you look out the window, you will see her returning to Lefkas.'

'Hello, is that *Brave Goose*?'

'It is, Bill. Noel here with John, Fiona and the crew wishing you well.'

'Wow, this is surreal. I had not expected this.'

'Bill, this is John. Please get in touch when you are back in England, and we shall be back in Manchester in two weeks. If you have a pen, here is my number.'

John dictated the number, and then there was a great cheer from everyone else.

'John, if you look up, you will see my plane; the captain said he would fly a circle over *Brave Goose*. Bye, everyone and a very big thank you.'

'Look, everyone! It's Bill's private plane. Wow, that is VIP treatment!'

CHAPTER 46

'John, where do you want to go now?'

'Well, Noel, there is no point in remaining in Sami. We could go to Fiskardo and stay a night. I know Fiona would love to go there again.'

'It's getting on in the day. How about staying in Sami and Fiskardo the following day? It's a bit late for a long trip now.'

'Okay, Sami, it is then, and then we go to Fiskardo. Sally wants to buy some food.'

'Fiona, I have just been speaking with Noel. He wanted to know where we wanted to go, so I plumped for a night in Fiskardo. We will go to Fiskardo tomorrow. Is that okay, darling?'

'Wonderful! You know John, living on a boat is great. You can go to different places and not have to keep packing and unpacking. You take your home with you wherever you go!'

'Exactly. I will confirm with Noel.'

While mooring alongside the quay in Sami, the ferry from Italy arrived. The same performance ensued, but with different actors as the ferry deposited its passengers and a multitude of sundry vehicles.

Sally and José returned to the boat; José was carrying most of the purchases.

*

Unbeknown to John, Georgio was one of the foot passengers who left the ferry.

'Hi, is that Spiros?'

'Yes, who is this?

'Georgio.'

'Good to hear from you. Is there any special reason you are here?'

'Yes, but my requirements unexpectedly have been met. The boat I hoped to find is moored on the other side of the quay from where the ferry docked. My ticket is for Patras, but I have got off the ferry now.'

'That was a bit of luck; saves a trip to Athens if that is where you thought they might be?'

'Yes, can you help me? Are you in Sami?'

'No, I am in Athens.'

'Okay. I won't trouble you. Good to speak.'

*

The ferry moved off. The traffic disappeared as quickly as it had appeared.

'José, can you let the boarding ladder down, please? I need to speak with the port police.'

Noel walked off to the port police office at the head of the harbour. Georgio decided this was his moment. He walked as if he was entitled to access *Brave Goose.* John and Fiona were having a drink on the quarterdeck.

John looked up at this stranger standing on the other side of the table.

'Who are you? This is a private boat.'

'I know, John England,' Georgio responded with a rich Italian accent.

'My god, you are Georgio, aren't you?'

'Correct. You still owe me some money.'

'I don't think I do!'

'The extra cash I had to pay for the Mafia in Catania was never paid.'

'I didn't think I needed to pay for the cost of holding my crew hostage.'

'You do. It's two hundred and fifty thousand euros.'

'So that's why you have come all this way from Italy, to try and find me? It was a bit of luck your ferry berthed here. I bet you didn't think you would find me so easily?'

'No, I didn't.'

John got out of his seat. Georgio realised John was significantly taller than he was. He pulled a pistol from his trouser pocket and pointed it at him. John continued to move towards him.

'Don't come any closer, or you will be shot.'

'Yes, and you will be in jail and get no money!'

'Stand still or I will shoot, John.'

At that moment, Noel appeared at the top of the boarding ladder. The distraction saw Georgio look sideways enabling John to kick the pistol out of his hand, which went into the harbour. John then punched Geogio, at the same time kicking his legs from under him. He fell like a stone onto the deck.

'Can you bring me some rope please, José?'

José had appeared to see what was going on. Noel helped John to keep Georgio on the deck. Once they had him trussed up and bound his arms and legs, Noel returned to the police to request their assistance.

Two officers appeared to find the Italian bound and lying on the deck. They wanted proof that the man John and Noel had assaulted had threatened to shoot them.

'Well, when I kicked his hand, his gun went into the harbour,' said John.

'I saw exactly what happened. I have a video of the threat.' Fiona held up her mobile phone. 'I took a video of the whole attack.'

The police officers were convinced about the attack after seeing the video. They requested Fiona send the video to their phone.

John and Noel accompanied the police officers and Georgio to the police office, where they both made statements. Then they were allowed to leave.

'Another big excitement on *Brave Goose*!'

'Yes, Noel, but hopefully they will put this man in jail and keep him out of our way.'

'I have some lunch prepared. Would you like it before we leave Sami?'

John and Fiona answered in unison.

'Yes, please!'

Noel suggested that *Brave Goose* got underway and the meal taken while they were at sea. There was much conversation over lunch about Georgio. John said it was just luck that he had found them there.

'Shall we go to Fiskardo this afternoon? We can all go to my favourite restaurant for dinner tonight. We can go to Lefkas tomorrow. Then we can have conversations with Robert at Paleros regarding the re-fit of *Brave Goose* over the winter. I will also arrange hotel rooms for you all for the period before you return home.'

'That would be excellent, John, thank you.'

'What should I do about all my clothes over the winter while work is going on?' asked Fiona.

'I think we could arrange for the clothes to be kept safe. We can tape the doors of the wardrobes, then cover them in polythene so there will be double protection.'

'That sounds great, John. We must not forget to send the luggage to the UK on the van that goes to the UK for Azmir and Ulrika. Do we have an address for them yet?'

'I will email Azmir after lunch as we sail to Fiskardo. It's Tuesday today. Fiskhardo tonight, then we will be in Lefkas tomorrow, Wednesday. Fiona and I are flying back to the UK on Sunday.'

'Oh no, John. Where has all the time gone?'

'Yes, I am afraid so, my love.'

'Can we launch *Gosling* later, as I want to go for a few swims before we go home?'

'Of course, we won't forget.'

Brave Goose returned to Lefkas marina for the last time that season. John and Fiona were sad. Once moored and *Gosling* launched as promised, John and Noel walked to see Robert at Paleros. They arranged a visit by him, his senior maintenance engineer, and the mechanical engineer for Thursday. John arranged hotel accommodation for all four crew for the next ten days.

An email response from Azmir had arrived. Their new address was the Windermere Hotel – could John please send the luggage there? That was soon arranged. The luggage was transported to Paleros, would be collected in a couple of weeks, and taken to the UK.

John and Fiona went to the nearby beach for sunbathing and swimming. They had planned to go again on Saturday, but the weather was due to be inclement.

'John, are you going to tell Miron about Georgio?'

'Oh, Fiona, I have totally forgotten to speak to Miron about the legal position of the Russian enclave on Ionia. I must do that when I get back. I will also tell him about Georgio.'

Back onboard, he called Miron.

'Miron, it's John. I am so sorry not to have called you before. We were in Sami for twenty-four hours, and who should get off the ferry from Italy but Georgio? After he came to *Brave Goose* unannounced, he pulled a pistol on me, demanding more money. However, Noel coming back on board distracted him sufficiently and I was able to disarm him. He is now with the police there. Hopefully, he will be behind bars this time.'

'That's good news, John. Are you okay?'

'Yes, I am fine. I rang to inform you about the land on Ionia occupied by the Russians.'

'Yes, that would be helpful.'

'I went to the Greek archive, which was a most interesting experience. I returned with a copy of the transfer of the land forming half the land occupied. I will send you a full version when I return to England next week, but I can give you a heads-up now if you have a moment?'

'Yes, I am free at the moment; press on.'

'The land was transferred in 2010 to a man called Pregoznin. The money, it seems, came from a woman named Zhukova. She is a Russian. A business tycoon. She runs a fashion label, an art gallery and a magazine. She would appear to be the person with the money. However, she did not purchase a ninety-nine-year lease on the land; it was Pregoznin's name on the lease. He may be a relative somewhere along the line or Zhukova's lover. Who knows.

'The lease is very specific about not creating a separate security force or having arms on the island. So much so that if such acts occurred, the lease would be automatically forfeited without compensation.

'I gather the place has been raided, and everyone there removed as well as the armaments. I guess that is the end of the lease to Pregoznin and a great deal of money lost by Ms Zhukova. There isn't much else to say, but I will send you a more formal legal deposition relating to the occupation by the Russians. I would also like to send a copy to Bill at MI6.'

'That was easy, John. Yes, let me have the full document you are to draw up. I have no objection to MI6 having a copy. I appreciate your help.'

'If thanks are owed to anyone, it's Fiona and me to thank you for all your help with our problems. Let's hope we have a less exciting time next year!'

'I hope we don't have to meet again, and my best wishes go with you, too.'

*

On Sunday morning, farewells were exchanged, and John and Fiona returned home with a small suitcase suitable as cabin baggage.

'Sad to be leaving, John, but *Brave Goose* will look like a new boat when we come to collect her next year.'

'She will, my love. What a fantastic summer we have enjoyed despite the interruptions. There has never been a dull moment!'

THE END

ABOUT THE AUTHOR

I decided to write a book when I retired as a chartered surveyor ten years ago. A recent article in the *Sunday Times* recommended reading and writing for their older readers to help stave off the dreaded Alzheimers. *Reflections of Death* is the last in a three-book series about the exploits of John England and Fiona on their superyacht, *Brave Goose.*

I have been a keen sailor since I was eight years old, and I hold a Yacht Master ticket, allowing me to skipper a vessel up to 300 tons. Jointly, I owned a sixty-foot yacht in Mallorca, so many of the exploits with *Brave Goose* could be sailed and visited if desired. Although the names of some people and places have been changed, they are real. I now sail on the pages of my books.

To ensure you are made aware of its publication, please register for my newsletters on my website: www.rajordan.uk

Printed in Poland
by Amazon Fulfillment
Poland Sp. z o.o., Wrocław

25828643R00186

FEROCIOUS HEART

THE ANIMAL IN MAN BOOK 2

FEROCIOUS HEART

JOSEPH ASPHAHANI

4 Horsemen
Publications, Inc.

Ferocious Heart

Published By: 4 Horsemen Publications, Inc.

4 Horsemen Publications, Inc.
PO Box 417
Sylva, NC 28779
4horsemenpublications.com
info@4horsemenpublications.com

Cover & Typesetting by Autumn Skye
Edited by Laura Mita

Library of Congress Control Number: 2024933358

Paperback ISBN-13: 979-8-8232-0479-8
Hardcover ISBN-13: 979-8-8232-0480-4
Audiobook ISBN-13: 979-8-8232-0481-1
Ebook ISBN-13: 979-8-8232-0482-8

To Kus, who may not approve of all I do,
but loves me anyway.

TABLE OF CONTENTS

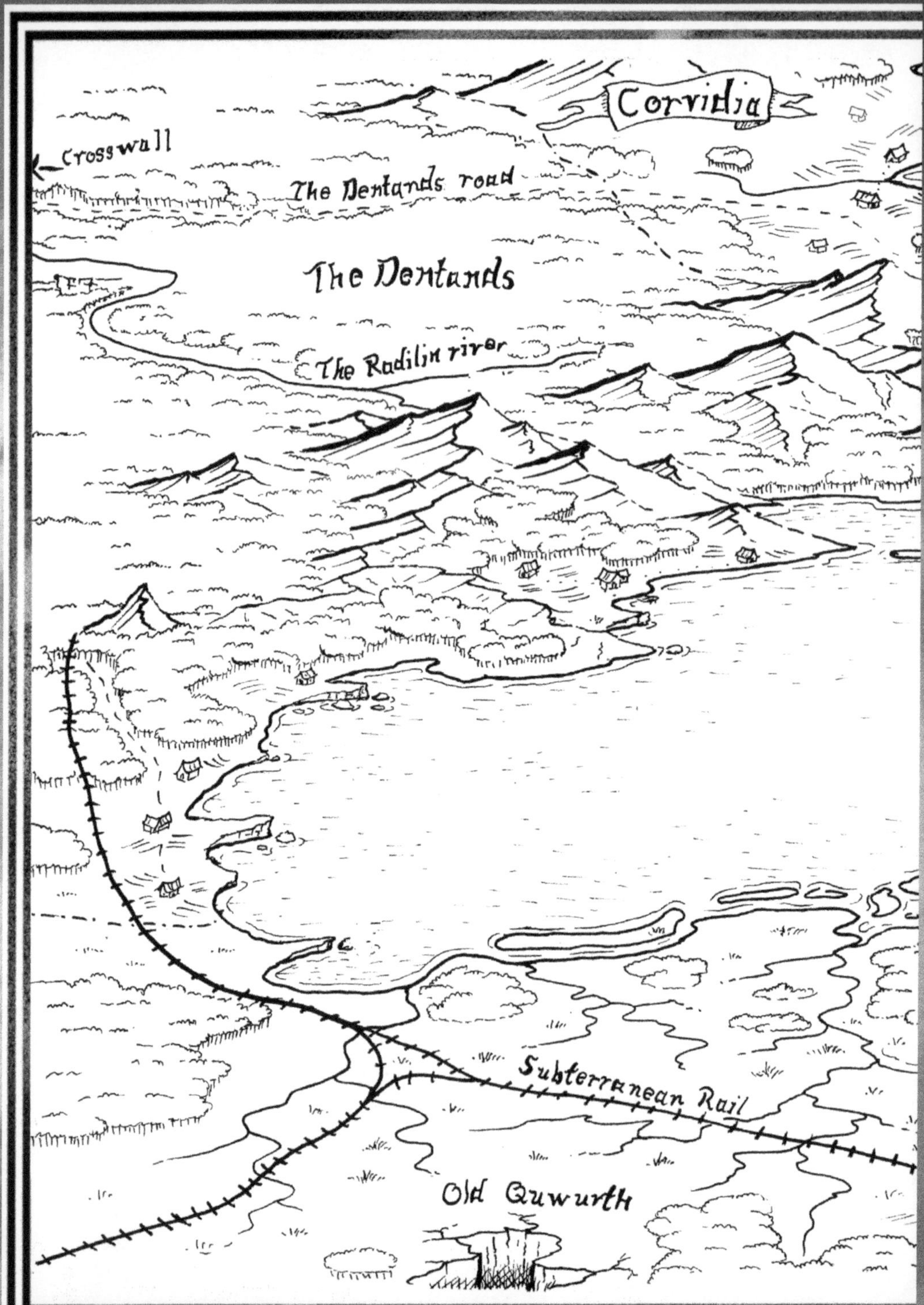
Corvidia
Crosswall
The Dentands road
The Dentands
The Radilin river
Subterranean Rail
Old Quwurth

The Spine
The Great Houses
Lake Skymere
Toicia
The Aigaion
N
W
E
S
Drakora
The vast Marshland
Castle Salstragore
New Quwurth

Prologue

THE PRISONER FELT THE FOOTSTEPS BEFORE HE HEARD them. Little shudders in the air. The prisoner's eye rolled in its socket; the pupil contracted slightly to focus his vision on the motes of dust lazily floating in the beam of afternoon light streaming from the wide crack in the steepled ceiling high overhead. The motes shifted this way and that, pushed by a whisper of force, a disturbance in the balance of air. A moment later, the thin flap of wrinkled skin that served as his species' ears picked up the vibrations. The prisoner's small leathery hand felt them too, pressed as it was against the cold stone of his prison's floor. Lying on his flat stomach, he'd had it pressed there for some time now. Three days at least, while focusing on not moving, drawing his mind inward to feel the intentional inertness of his body, finding the pulse in his brain that reminded the self of its existence, aligning his awareness to its beat. Then finally, reaching outward, reaching, reaching. Always reaching for that which the prisoner had not felt in decades. The invisible strings of power. Wanting to grasp them so badly. Once more. Just once more.

The footsteps scraped heavily against the stone stairwell just outside the slab of metal that was the circular prison's only door. The visitor on the other side slid loudly to a stop. The prisoner's eye swept to the floor, to the shadows of wide feet and the smaller shadow of the whiplike tail swaying between them.

The visitor knocked. The prisoner's hand, stiff with the rictus of prolonged immobility, curled painfully into a fist.

"May I enter?"

Every question was a trap designed to break the prisoner's will. His captor knew he had no power to turn him away. The small needlepoints of the prisoner's claws pressed into the pads of old flesh hard enough to draw blood. This would be just another moment. Pleading, placating, gloating, begging, berating, cursing, crying. Like all the other moments spanning his long imprisonment, this moment too would pass. The prisoner closed his eyes.

The key turned in the lock. The metal hinges squealed.

The visitor crossed to the cubic cage at the room's center, just inches away, then slid down to sit.

The silence hung.

"I know you're not dead. It would smell worse than it already does if you were dead." The visitor nudged the tray of uneaten food, wrapped now in a layer of fuzzy mold.

The prisoner did not move, did not relent to the sigh he so desperately wanted to sigh. He would endure. The moment would pass.

"I came up here today..." the visitor's voice trailed off. "Heh. Actually, I forgot why I came up here. Or maybe..." In the silence that followed, the prisoner imagined his captor—the red-scaled snake with his angular head at the end of the long thick neck dangling low over his lap, his expression thoughtful, his slender, black-nailed fingers flicking and rolling in the air—tortured by the desire to deliver the precise words that would make the prisoner speak.

The prisoner resisted the urge to smile.

The snake drew in a long, deep breath, then sighed.

"This is the end, I'm afraid."

Another trap? No. Something in his captor's voice was different. The bluster, the arrogance, the insanity, the usual qualities were all gone. The prisoner pressed his claws harder, held his eyes closed tight, focused on the weight of his own body pressing him down. He would not speak. He would not speak. *He would not speak.*

"The real end. I won't be coming again. You see, it's finally here. I've found it. After all this time. I mean, it's not here yet, but it's on its way. The relay."

There was a sharp hiss of victorious laughter between the snake's leering fangs. "I almost can't believe it. Can you?"

A trap.

"My ... son. And daughter. They've found it. A few mishaps, a few near losses, now they're bringing it here. Mere days away. I almost can't sit still, do you understand?"

Another trap. The prisoner focused on the pain, how it was most acute in four spots on his palm, dully threading up his short arm to the elbow. He tried to block out the snake's words. He tried not to think of what they meant.

He tried to make himself believe these were more lies. Even though the prisoner knew better.

Salastragore was telling the truth.

"Soon, this will all be over," the snake continued. "I don't think I will ever see you again. In a few minutes, I will walk out of here for the last time.

"Before that," he went on, sliding closer, wrapping his hands around the cage's bars, "there are some things I want to tell you. Things, I'm sure, you've probably already guessed. For instance... well, for the longest time, I've wanted to hear you say something. I wanted to hear you break. Just a little. Even a little. I wanted to hear you admit that your grand designs were flawed. That Epimetheus, our quest to save ourselves, this... this *game,* was useless! That even though we tried, we can't hide from what we truly are inside, because look where all the hiding got us. Anyhow, something along those lines. I've come here time and time again, showing you things, talking it through, raving like a lunatic, beating my chest, clawing my eyes out, hoping and hoping and hoping to hear you say ... *something! ANYTHING!!*"

Salastragore's voice thundered around the circle of stone wall, nearly breaking the prisoner's concentration. He felt a shudder flare along his spine, yet through his iron will he kept himself inert. In so doing, the prisoner avoided the trap. He did not move. His eye did not twitch. He focused only on the sharpness of his claws, the dull ache along his arm.

"I, ahh." The snake let out a resigned breath. "I did not mean to comport myself like this. Not for our last meeting."

Salastragore was quiet then. For a long time. The prisoner's fist began to loosen, his mind began again to drift away, and he questioned if maybe this had all been a hallucination. But then Salastragore spoke again, softly.

"Baaleb."

It was a name. His name.

"You're the only one I have left, Baaleb."

The prisoner's eye twitched, involuntarily. He hoped beyond hope the snake's gaze was elsewhere, that he had not seen the effect of his name.

"I've no one else to talk to. No one who *understands*. I know, somehow, deep inside your soul, you *understand* me. You understand why all of this must end. You understand, somehow, what we *really are*. Why ... *we* ... must end."

The prisoner felt the disturbance in the air as the snake shifted his weight. He heard the clicking of the nails on the bars of his cage as Salastragore pulled himself up to stand.

"I'm going to do it. I've come this far. You know, there's a part of me that is grateful to you, for not saying anything for all this time. Had I heard you speak, perhaps, I might have been persuaded to stop everything I've set in motion. I think there's a part of me—*was*, there *was* a part of me, now it's certainly gone, cut away like a cancer—that might have stopped, once, but not now. Never again. My will is resolute. I am set.

"I'm going now. With dignity."

The snake slid his feet loudly toward the door.

The moment would pass. The moment would pass. Soon.

"This is your last chance, Baaleb."

The slender hand lifted the latch.

"You may speak, old friend."

A tear welled in the prisoner's eye. All his will focused on holding it there. All his worry about whether the snake would see it.

The silence stretched. When he spoke next, Salastragore's voice wavered. "I see."

The snake shuffled into the hallway as he pulled the creaking metal door slowly closed. Soon after, the receding footsteps faded.

In the stillness, the prisoner thought the moment would pass, as all the snake's other moments had passed. He would let go of his feelings, feel again his body drift away, borne by time and space, as his mind would once again drift and reach for the omnipotent gifts of the Aigaion.

However, this time was different. The moment did not pass. The prisoner could not focus. The seconds of silence and stillness stretched to hours. Soon, the light of day was gone, and the chill of night breathed through the crack in the high ceiling and swirled around him while it clutched at the shell of rags piled atop his body.

What was different?

What was this new feeling settling in his heart, turning his shriveled, ancient body cold?

Fear. Like he had not felt for hundreds of years. Lifetimes. The realness of it gripped him, paralyzed him. This time it was all true. There were no tricks, no traps. The emotion had been genuine.

Salastragore would soon end the game.

I

The Cave

Chapter One

The Whole Story

THE FOX, MAXAN, AND HIS RHINOCEROS FRIEND, CHEWGAR, sat shoulder to shoulder against the cavern wall, absently watching the fire die. Perhaps the wolf, Feyn, would die alongside it. The powerful Caller and former black-robed Principal of the Mind had been scorched by a lightning strike only a few hours ago. He now lay unconscious, wracked by seizures, half of his snow-white fur burned away to show angry red, weeping blisters beneath. Feyn's apprentice Callers, Pryth and Pram, had left them only moments ago. They had disappeared into the cave passage that would take them aboveground. Feyn had lain still for several more minutes after that, as though the young squirrel twin's departure had put his mind at ease. His chest rose and fell steadily. Neither Chewgar nor Maxan had felt like filling the silence left in the twin's wake.

Not at first, anyway. Eventually, Maxan's wandering mind got the better of him, and he could no longer hold the question back. "You didn't want to go with them?"

The rhino huffed at the question that sounded more like an accusation. "They can take care of themselves."

"That's not what I meant."

"You want to know if I'm going to tell everyone … what happened." Chewgar looked away and ground his flat teeth.

What happened with Locain, Maxan's thoughts finished for him. It was the ever-present voice of reason that seemed to live a life of its own inside his mind. He could have responded; in fact, rare was the time when Maxan could resist the urge to carry on arguments with himself, but he let it go, focusing on the fact that he didn't need the voice in his head to clarify what the rhino was talking about.

Not two days before now, Chewgar had chosen to spare the life of his enemy, the lion that ruled all of Leora, the warlord hero of the Thraxian Extermination that had killed Chewgar's family, the "Golden Lord" who had stolen Chewgar's tribal birthright and claimed the crown for himself, unopposed. The King. Not two days before now, Chewgar had King Locain at his mercy, but that choice had been erased a moment later by the squirrel twins. The girl, Pram, had called upon the powers of the Aigaion to twist the lion's body from the inside, snap his bones, tear his muscles, and drown him in his own blood. When the lion's body crumpled to the dust, just like that, the great nation of Leora was left without a king.

But Chewgar could be the King. If he wanted.

Maxan let out a long sigh, agitated by the obviousness of the train of thought in his head. Chewgar must have heard it as disappointment.

"My mind's made up," Chewgar said, his gaze locked on the fire. "No. I'm not going. I'm not … as good as you think I am." He scratched at the coarse gray skin on his broad neck. "Remember what you told me about being a living coward?"

Maxan remembered. They had been sitting almost exactly as they sat now, not even one week ago. His mind drifted back to the last time he'd had a quiet moment like this one with his friend before all the chaos of the Monitors' and the Mind's secret war over control of the mysterious chrome artifact called 'the relay'. *We sat in some alley in Crosswall's center. After we'd just delivered the relay to our enemies, to Folgian—the poison-rotted bear, and Principal Harmony—the gray horned owl. We felt like we feel right now. Dreading. Not sure where to go next.*

"I said you'd made the right choice," Maxan recalled. "Not to fight Locain. To run. When your family was… That was different than now. That was about fighting an enemy that would have absolutely killed you. You weren't a coward then. And you're not a coward now."

"But this is worse than turning away from a fight. This is true cowardice. I'm afraid of … myself." Chewgar huffed at the fox's rising brow. "I mean I don't know what I am, what I'm supposed to be. A guard captain? A hero? What kind of king would I be? What gives me the right to wear the crown? There are decisions, judgments, laws, and decrees that have to be made. Lives of thousands would depend on my choices. What if I choose wrong?"

Maxan threw up his arms. "Locain was going to *burn* the Western District to the ground! A whole quarter of his capital just ashes. And all those animals, trapped. Would you have *chosen* to do the same?"

"That's the thing I keep thinking about, Max." Chewgar looked hard at the fox beside him. "What if he knew it needed to be done? What if it's the only way to stop the Stray?"

Maxan looked away, tried to resist the snarl of disgust that wanted to wrinkle along his snout. "But it's *not.* Feyn said—"

"Feyn *said*," Chewgar cut in, his booming voice battering about the small rocky chamber. "But Feyn doesn't really *know*."

Maybe it's true, Max. The fox let out another sigh. For a long time after, the only sound was the occasional popping of the dying fire. Maxan's thoughts floated back to when the white wolf had first convinced him that taking the relay to the Monitors was the only way to end the inevitability of animalkind losing their rational minds and giving in to the savage beast that seemed to be at the core of their nature. Later on, Rinnia and Saghan, the Monitor agents sent to retrieve the artifact from Crosswall, all but confirmed it: the relay was a piece of the Aigaion itself, fallen somehow from the sky perhaps. It was the reason everyone would lose their minds in time. The only way to stop the Stray was to bring it back to the Aigaion, and the Monitors were the only ones who could truly reach that city-sized, triangular object floating aimlessly in the sky.

Supposedly, the voice of reason added.

Supposedly, the fox agreed silently. *Feyn believes. But he doesn't really know.*

"Chewgar, if you're not going back, then why are you going forward? To wherever we're headed, wherever they're taking us?"

Chewgar turned away. He chewed the question over for a long moment. His flat teeth ground together, as though he was turning over an idea between them, examining what his answer meant from every angle before spitting it out. "I have to see for myself." He swung his gaze again at the fox. "What's happening across our whole world, animals losing themselves, crawling on all fours, hunting and killing each other. I don't understand any of it. Neither does he." Chewgar motioned to the white wolf on the other side of the fire. If not for the labored, raspy breaths, it would be impossible to tell if Feyn was even alive. "He's just...hoping. Or *was* hoping."

Maxan recalled what Feyn had told him on the trail just before Harmony's ambush, about the moment the wolf had lost his rational self and gave in to the violent urges within. If there was one animal in the whole of Herbridia who understood the loss of his rational mind to the beast, it was the white wolf. But Feyn had come back with the help of Folgian because she taught him to feel the connection to the Aigaion and call on its power. Feyn had divulged to Maxan that he sensed the relay had come from the Aigaion, without actual knowledge, which turned out to be true.

"He understands," Maxan said. "More than anyone. Because it happened to him. He's not just hoping to find a way to stop it. He *really does know* that this is how we stop it."

Chewgar huffed at that. "We're going in circles, Max. Put it this way—we can't wake him up and ask him to explain it to us. You talked to him. I didn't. How do you know he knows that that thing in his bag is part of the Aigaion? That bringing it back up there—forget about how crazy that sounds for a second because I'm still trying to—how is that going to stop any of this?"

Because, Maxan stopped himself from saying it, *he had the same visions I have. Floor of glass. Pillars of glass. Racing golden lights. Disappearing into shadows above. Visions of the Aigaion.*

But he was technically dead *when he saw it, Max. You? You're just going crazy.*

Maxan's fur prickled with the sudden flush of anger.

Chewgar mistook the look in his friend's eyes. "I didn't mean…"

Maxan wasn't listening.

I'm not crazy! he shouted into the void of his own mind. *They're not just visions. They're real. Did you forget? You're the one showing them to me!*

Sometimes, Maxan liked to picture the voice in his head as a mirror image of himself. Sometimes, when staring up at the starry sky, he would see this fox standing on the surface of Yerda, the enormous moon broken into a thousand pieces, with his neck craning skyward, staring back at him on the surface of Herbridia. He'd see this other self so clearly. Maxan all but gave this other fox a name because it helped him manage the insanity, keep it at bay so he could do his job as a Shadow for the Crosswall Guard.

Yet, during this last week, he'd discovered that the voice of reason wasn't just a split personality. It was another mind trapped inside his own. When Maxan had been too slow to react, it had been the voice of reason that took control of his sword arm to deflect his enemy's killing blow. When Maxan had been set on fire, panicking and dying, the voice of reason had saved him, pulled him into a deep unconsciousness. When he'd hear the secret truths about his world spoken aloud, it was the voice of reason that would show him flashes of another life, places he'd never been, though knew were real. At those times, Maxan was powerless to stop the other fox. Now, however, instead of going along with his mental neighbor's whims, Maxan was finding that speaking back directly gave him back control he never knew he had lost.

I'm not crazy, he repeated, louder now, inside his mind. *I'm only seeing what you've seen. I've never been in the Aigaion. But you have. Haven't you?*

Maxan's lungs pulled in air, suddenly and involuntarily, enough to almost burst. His eyes rolled in his head. The dark walls of the cave flaked away like ash all around him as he was flung skyward, blinded by light and frozen by wind. The luminescent glass of the Aigaion's inner chambers faded into shadow above. At the center of the room, the relay hovered inside a machine, its golden beads of light thrumming along their channels in its sides. His paw reached for it, grasped it, then pulled it away.

It was you. You're the one who stole it.

There was no answer. The other fox, wherever he was, had lowered his gaze shamefully away, staying silent.

"Max!" Chewgar crouched over the limp fox, lightly slapping the sides of his muzzle. "You all right?"

Maxan put up a paw to deflect the rhino's massive palm, which was hurting him more than reviving him.

"I'm okay. Just, maybe, blacked out for a second."

He tried to sit up and found he was shaking. The vision, the memory, had been so real, coming back to his own body disorienting.

Chewgar took Maxan's paw in his hand to lift him to a sitting position. The rhino didn't let go. Instead, he stared down at the fox's bare, scarred skin pulled tight on the back of his paw where the fur had burned away.

"You still haven't told me the whole story about this," Chewgar said. "The night you burned your arm."

When the two of them had left Crosswall behind with the Monitors days ago, Maxan had stripped off the leather sleeve he'd worn for years to cover his scars, left it on the road outside the city, and said nothing about it. A day before that, when Chewgar had told him the story of Locain and his family, Maxan had promised to match it with the story of his burned arm. Then everything spiraled out of control. He still owed his friend the whole story.

"We got to kill time somehow until the hawk and the snake get back anyway," Chewgar said, shrugging while letting go of Maxan's paw. "If they are coming back."

"Safrid," Maxan said softly as if he had just seen her face in the shadows and light cast from the fire's dying embers. "Her name was Safrid. I ... loved her. For a long time. We ran cons together. Broke into places we weren't supposed to. Stole things. Valuables, you know..." Maxan couldn't stop the smile from spreading over his fangs. "We were a good team, her and I, along with some others in the Commune. Foxes, all of us. They were my family. They saved me. I told you about my past before. You know already I was a thief and burglar. But I never told you anything about them. About her." Maxan's voice fell silent. He struggled to find the right place to start.

How do I talk about someone who was everything to me?

You start again, Max, with her name.

"Safrid," he said again. Right then, he knew what she meant to him. "After years of starving, just *surviving,* she saved me. She taught me I could still *feel.* You know what I mean?"

"No. I don't. Females of my species are..." Chewgar trailed off awkwardly, then cleared his throat. "Go on."

Maxan hardly noticed his friend's response, lost as he was in memory. He was back on the rooftops of Crosswall with Safrid, running, leaping, climbing, always smiling. Or perched at the highest points and staring off into the distance, at the stars, at Yerda, at the broken asteroids in her belt, at the twinkling gems that glowed in the sky behind them, at a thousand points of light. Maxan saw those lights living again as his eyes fixed on the dying embers at the center of the cave.

"I never told you, but before I became a thief with the Commune, I tried to find Yovan. I brought his coin once, to a guardhouse, like he told me. You remember the coin?"

"I do."

"A guard, some possum, took it from me, then kicked me into the dirt. They all laughed. Told me to scram. Well, years later, I told Safrid this story. She helped me get the coin back. She planned the whole job, led me along like it was some surprise, like a present. We cornered him, alone, in some narrow alley. When she gave me a dagger and told me to kill the one who took it, I couldn't, so she turned me away for being weak."

"What happened to the possum?"

"I made sure he remembered me, remembered my face, remembered what he'd done. He still had my coin, Yovan's coin, amazingly. I took it then told *him* to scram. When he was gone, I left Safrid there, turned my back on her, on my family, the whole Commune. Or at least I thought I had. For a couple days, all by myself, I remember turning Yovan's coin over and over in my paw, wondering if I should go back. I threw the damn thing off a building one night actually. Then I spent the next couple hours searching the ground, with nothing but moonlight to see by until I found it again. The whole time thinking, *What the hell was I doing?* Couldn't I just kill at least one of the bastards in my life that wronged me? Just once? Wasn't it my right? Wasn't it *fair?* He'd been right there in front of me, helpless, with his hands up... Maybe

Safrid was right … I could've just… Couldn't I forgive myself just that one? I thought maybe that if I could choose again, I would've chosen differently. So, I went back that same night, to the Commune's hideout, an abandoned granary in the Western District, ready to beg them to take me back, I guess. I didn't think I had anywhere else to go."

Maxan turned to Chewgar. There was so little light left in the cavern that the rhino's gray skin seemed to meld with the shade of the stone, although the fading flame reflected as tiny points in his eyes. "Yovan's coin," Maxan said. "I guess you could say it did save me. If I hadn't thrown it away and spent so much time cursing myself trying to find it—or even if I'd gone through with killing that guard in the first place—I would've already been there when… *they* came to set our granary on fire."

Maxan tried to swallow the rising lump in his throat, but instead found his mouth completely dry. He made a sound that was half sob, half retch. It was the sound of an agonized memory breaking through all the force he'd exerted for years to keep it locked away.

Chewgar covered both Maxan's shoulders with one gentle hand. Maxan felt the warmth in the gesture, the reassurance, and let go. He cried. For what happened that night, for his old friends, for Safrid. Then he couldn't hold the other memory in either, so he cried for what had happened years before Crosswall and the Commune. Maxan cried for his mother. He pulled his knees in, let his head sink low between them, huddled inside the cage of himself, then continued to sob for quite some time.

Chewgar kept his warm hand on Maxan's back. Finally, after reliving the pain of loss and surviving it all once again, Maxan at last raised his head and wiped away his tears. He took a deep breath.

Finish the story, he told himself.

"I was hiding on a rooftop, across from the granary. They were in the street. Their shadows were so long, in the firelight. A dozen of them, I don't know. All of them with long blades, and these things like torches, spitting fire. More and more fire. Dressed head to tail in dark, belted gear. I didn't get a good look at them, but I knew they were the same as the ones that killed my mother. The night you and Yovan were there in Renson's Mill, they were the same as the ones chasing me."

"I remember." Chewgar's thick brows wrinkled. "On the bridge. There were three of them. They were fast. Yovan had to let them strike his armor more than a few times before he caught on to their timing. He got two with his spear. One jumped past him and went straight at me. I… well… None of them caught you, did they?"

"Not that night, no. I didn't lose them forever, though. Just took them ten more years to catch up."

"Max," Chewgar said slowly, drawing the fox's eyes. "They didn't catch you."

He's right. It was the voice of reason, back again. Maxan realized he heard it at that moment because he'd wanted to. It comforted him. *They didn't catch you then either, Max. You're still here.*

I wouldn't be. If not for you.

It was a kind of apology. Maxan expected a snarky reply, as usual, but after a stretch of seconds, the voice only said, *Finish the story, Max.*

"They'd cut the ropes stretched out over the streets, which we'd used to reach the adjacent rooftops. There was no escape from the fire. The assassins watched it burn, until there were no more foxes running out, half on fire, screaming, just to fall on those long, thin swords. Then they left, fading back into the shadows and alleyways of the surrounding district like water trickling quietly into a drain.

"I was going to run in there…"

And die with them.

"But I was afraid."

"That fear kept you alive," Chewgar assured him. It was the same truth that the rhino had experienced himself, after all. "You know it's true. If you'd have gone in there…"

"I *did* go in there… after. I heard screaming. And I knew it was her." Maxan's right arm was trembling. The damaged nerves under the glove hadn't felt much of anything besides a fuzzy numbness for years, although the memory of the heat in the burning granary brought the pain surging through every fiber of them now. "They must've heard it too, so they left her, figuring their work was done anyway. I couldn't breathe; I couldn't see. There was so much smoke. I could barely hear her in all that roaring fire. But I found her. Safrid's legs were pinned in the wreckage. The whole place was coming down around us. I tried to pull her out, but…"

Safrid's eyes were full of tears. Both of her paws wrapped around his wrist. She called his name. Maxan pulled with everything he had, never looking away from her, even as a torrent of fire spilled from above, silencing her screams, crushing her body, and wreathing his right arm in licking flames.

You don't need to say any more, Max.

He had fulfilled his half of their deal, told Chewgar about his arm, about her. He let the long silence that followed envelop him until the twitching in his arm finally ceased, the pain along with it.

"I'm sorry, Max." He felt Chewgar's hand on his back again, then realized it had never left. It was all his friend could offer, he knew, but it was good to feel it there.

"Everything the Commune ever stole went up in flames. I guess we were sort of infamous in Crosswall. Rumors spread that nowhere was safe for foxes, no matter how well hidden we thought our little thieves' guilds were. Even beyond the city, out in the Denlands and elsewhere, word was that foxes were disappearing. Whole families and villages. I had no idea if any of it was true, or if it was just gossip left in the wake of the fire, after everyone got the chance to sift through our loot in the ash and figure out who we were. After that, I was back to how I used to be. Just surviving again. Hiding from everything. Alone. I had nothing left. Except that coin."

"Where's it now, anyway?"

"I left it in Crosswall. Ah, it's probably in the pocket of Anda or Bregg, once they figured we weren't coming back and pitched all my stuff over the wall. After a thorough inventory of my valuables, of course."

"They touch my pantry," Chewgar huffed, "and I'll bend their wrists backward 'til they stick that way for good."

Maxan smirked, very much liking the image of the leopard and the orangutan fumbling with spears in their broken hands outside their posts back in Crosswall, their paws and hands speckled with and smelling of all the various, exotic spices in the rhino's culinary hoard at the guardhouse. "Well, I didn't have anything worth much in the guardhouse anyway," he resumed. "I figure I'd already spent Yovan's coin's real value the day I brought it to you."

The two friends exchanged a nod. Maxan knew then that the bond he shared with the rhinoceros was older and stronger than anything he could have forged with him on a battlefield. The two of them shared the same story: loss and survival. Chewgar was here, now, by his side at every step of this insane quest to put an end to the Stray. He hadn't gone home because he knew, like Maxan, that the most good he could do was still ahead. Thus, he had his answer.

"Sssorry to interrupt."

The green-scaled snake Saghan squatted in the shadows at the other side of the cavern, the glint of the dying embers in his eyes like two orange gems embedded in the stone wall. His ornately weaved, dark-red Drakoran armor blended perfectly with the dull firelight cast by the low fire. Maxan saw how the leather had been scorched and scratched in some spots, not at all like it had been the very first time he'd ever seen Saghan emerge from shadow to strike off two of the Mind's soldiers' heads in one swipe of his long sword.

The armor had been impeccable days ago. However, later that same night as Maxan retrieved the relay at a Crosswall inn just before the snake's arrival, Saghan had thrown a device that blasted himself and the whole place to flaming bits, which also sent the fox crashing through a windowpane. Even in the dim, flickering firelight just now, Maxan also saw a darker stain on the armor's chest piece, where the snake's blood had splashed as one of Harmony's soldiers shot a bolt through his neck.

Yet there Saghan crouched, alive, his neck good as new, his forked tongue flicking the air, the brilles of his slitted orange eyes sliding open and closed, watching, listening to Maxan and Chewgar. Maxan understood what the snake truly was, what he was made for. Pieces of the puzzle had been falling into place right alongside the pieces that had been in Maxan's subconscious all along, truths about their tiny world of Herbridia that were half-remembered by the other resident mind in the fox's head. Saghan was a biologically engineered machine—stronger, faster, and seemingly unkillable. Rinnia had all but told Maxan so the day after Saghan had tried to kill him for the relay at the inn. It hadn't really been Saghan, she'd said. Maxan knew now that it had been the imprint of another mind invading the green snake's body, using it like a puppet.

Maxan wondered who it was right now behind those orange eyes.

"Ssseemed like a nice moment between you," the snake added a moment later. Maxan knew from the sarcasm that it was Saghan. "Pleassse, don't mind me."

When neither the fox nor the rhino replied, the snake shrugged then crossed to sit beside the wolf. Saghan produced a small vial of pink powder from one of the pouches along his belt. He pulled out the stopper delicately with two black nails.

"What is that?" Maxan asked concernedly, as he remembered how just a sliver of the green bane poison had been enough to bring the hulking rhino to the brink of death. Although he doubted the snake would poison Feyn right in front of them, the muscles in his hindlegs tensed despite the fatigue, readying to react.

"Panacea," Saghan said, tapping out half of the pink powder onto a smooth strip of cloth pulled from a different pouch. "It will ease the pain. For now. If I had more of it, plus if we had more time, this might even help him fully recover." He rubbed the cloth together to spread the medicine, then gently dabbed it on the worst of the white wolf's wounds. The trails of angry flesh sizzled briefly as the cloth passed over them, then, within seconds, the burn sores closed, the blood clotting.

The heavy, cloying scent of decay seemed to clear, swept away by something akin to berries and chalk, which tickled Maxan's snout. Feyn groaned in relief as the medicine reacted against the weeping sores. Maxan felt the tension in his body let go as he watched Saghan.

"I failed to protect him," Saghan said, looking up at the fox and the rhino. "And you."

And yourself, Maxan almost pointed out.

But look at him, Max. This is an apology.

"It's all right," Chewgar said a moment later. "We can protect ourselves." Then he rubbed the three scars on his chest where the Mind's soldiers had shot him with bolts, which Pryth had later "healed" with fire. "Most of the time," he grumbled.

Maxan said nothing as he crept over to the other side of Feyn, propping him up so Saghan could apply the remaining panacea powder to the burns on the wolf's sides and back.

"Sarovek told me about Yacub," Saghan said. "She saw you sssend him over the side of the cliff. Ssstraight down."

Maxan remembered the fading sound of the hyena's laughter as he fell. He turned away from the snake's gaze.

"You had to," Saghan told him, the blunt force of conviction in the sound of his words. "Maxan. You *had* to," he said it again, drawing Maxan's eyes back to him. Saghan's eyes flashed orange, or maybe it was the reflection of one final tongue of flame lashing from the dying fire. He smiled. "It was him. Or you. You sssee now. We're all killers, insssside."

It was the same thing Rinnia had tried to tell him, over and over. The last time she'd said it, she'd been ready to kill Maxan. And he'd been ready to die because deep inside himself, somehow, despite all the evidence written across this world's bloody history, he knew it didn't have to be true. Suddenly, just like that as his own mismatched green and gold eyes locked with the snake's flashing orange ones, he understood why.

"We don't have to enjoy it," he said, perfectly matching the force of Saghan's conviction. "Not even you."

The snake's grin vanished. The fire in his eyes died out. The Drakoran assassin seemed to be deeply considering the fox's words. Saghan withdrew the cloth with the panacea as Maxan eased Feyn back to the ground and held it limply in his hand. His slitted eyes were locked on the colors on it, pink with traces of red where it had dragged over Feyn's weeping blood, his forked tongue flicking at the conflicting, mingling scents of death and healing.

"You sssound," Saghan began slowly, still staring absently at the cave floor, "like someone who has a choice. I know you made a difficult one, taking Yacub's life. I understand that now. For Sarovek and me, and Rinnia ... killing has become too easy. Perhaps for too long. I am ...jealousss of you, you know. Your mind is *free* in a way that mine may never be.

"Don't say that I could be," Saghan quickly said, his eyes flashing again. Maxan, about to say that very thing, closed his mouth instead.

"It's not just because of how I'm made. It's because I'm a Monitor. Sssomeone has to protect this world from itself, to keep watch, to hide things that could destroy us all. The fact isss ... Rinnia, Sarovek, and I ... failed. Three times. First in Crosswall. Again in Renson's Mill. Finally, on the cliff outside this cave. You were there every time. Maxan. Chewgar. You killed those who stood in our way—Locain, Harmony, Yacub—because you had to. Ssso, because of you, we have the relay."

"What my brother means is," Sarovek said, just then stooping through the entrance to the chamber, her damaged wings tightly bound in gauze and leather cords, "Thank you."

The hawk knight had discarded her shining Corvidian plate armor, which left her with only short trousers and a loose-fitting blouse that was tattered and bloodied. Her spear was gone too, the sword slung on her hip her only weapon. She clutched the straps of a bag that looked like it had once belonged to one of the Mind's soldiers.

"I've finished staging the battle outside to look like a Denlander ambush, for what it's worth. I gathered some of their supplies, but not everything. Enough to feed us when we get to the rails. Also, the cave entrance is sealed as good as it can be."

"Hold on," Maxan started, rising on his hind paws too quickly, forgetting how low the cave's ceiling hung in some places, knocking his skull on the stone. He crashed back on his rump, massaging the soon-to-be lump under his fur while the Monitors and Chewgar exchanged awkward glances. "Wait," Maxan said again, shaking his head. "What about Rinnia? Don't we have to wait for her?"

Didn't she try to kill you, Max?

I mean, ah, yeah, he answered in his mind, recalling how she'd swiped at his throat when he'd refused to hand over the relay, how Pryth had heated the metal of her blade until it exploded in both her face and his, how she'd run, how the voice of reason had eased his panic, extinguishing his horror and panic in sleep. He hadn't told any of them about it. Hadn't told them that he'd seen her meeting with a mysterious, storm-drenched octopus with four swords strapped around his body.

Should I tell them now?

Maxan swallowed the confession instead. Cutting off the inner voice of reason's advice, if it had any to offer.

"Our sssister has made her way ahead of usss," Saghan responded. "By another route, I sussspect."

"Or she's dead," Chewgar provided. He shrugged off the withering looks the Monitors shot him, Saghan's somewhat amused, Sarovek's much harsher by degrees. "Just saying, if the Mind caught her..."

"Rinnia is fairly good at staying hidden," Saghan said. "She is also relatively unkillable."

Enough said, Maxan thought. *For now.*

Sarovek crossed to the small fire at the center of the chamber, kicked the cinders with her lower talons, scattering embers and ash across the floor, which flooded the cave with sudden darkness. Before Maxan had time to wonder why she would douse their only light, he heard a click seconds later and was blinded by a pure-white brilliance Sarovek held aloft. Another of the Monitors' technological miracles, like the gadgets he'd seen Rinnia employ back in Crosswall. "As for the little ones, Pryth and Pram, I caught them trying to slink away through the bushes. They wished to return to Leora, despite all my suggestions to the contrary. They were quite insistent. The boy, I mean. Annoyingly so. I wonder," she went on, pointing the pinlight first at the fox, then the rhino, "who gave them the idea."

"Doesn't matter," Saghan said, rising beside his sister, placing his scaled hand over her talon, lowering the light away from them. "What happens to the Mind now is of little conssssequence. Without its King, with all the Mind's principals dead or..." he glanced at Feyn, "presumed dead, then something needs to hold Leora together for a while longer. Those two squirrels can manage."

"What of the Denlander rebels?" The hawk shot back at him, clacking her beak bitingly at her brother's apparent certainty. "What if they're caught? They're children."

"One of them can control others' minds," Maxan pointed out, perhaps coming to the snake's rescue. He folded the edges of the blanket around Feyn's sides. "Barring that, the other can make everything explode."

Chewgar crept over and gently, easily cradled the unconscious wolf in his huge arms. "They'll be fine," he said with finality, rising, ready to be done with the cave. Then the serious line of his mouth crooked in puzzlement. "Did you say you sealed the entrance up there?"

The rhino and fox looked at each other.

"Ah, actually," Maxan came in, raising a finger to scratch behind his ears, "what did you say *rails* are?"

Now it was the Monitors' turn to exchange a look. Then Saghan smiled at them, and Sarovek might've done the same if a Corvidian beak could.

Chapter Two
The Abyss

SAGHAN LED THE WAY, HOLDING A PINLIGHT JUST LIKE the one Sarovek had used, fully illuminating the roughly hewn graystone walls of the tunnels. To Chewgar's relief, the space was wide enough to accommodate the frames of larger species, even when they were hauling the extra weight of wounded wolves. Maxan soon lost count of how many times the group had come to a branch of two or three more tunnels, and the snake veered them in yet another direction without any hesitation. It seemed to be a sequence designed to easily confuse a random explorer. Maxan wondered what traps and devices the Monitors may have set at the ends of the other tunnels, if there were warnings meant to discourage hapless wanderers from proceeding, or if there were heaps of animals' bones of those who did anyway.

Maxan felt they must have walked ten miles so far, if not more, the path angled ever downward so that they delved deeper underground with every step. The hours stretched. Keeping track of time and space down here was meaningless. Maxan figured they were at least as deep as Corvidia's deepest mountain quarry, from where he knew all of the solid graystone for the King Locain's palace, Crosswall's grand arena, and the Mind's Pinnacle Tower had been cut and hauled eastward centuries ago.

Maxan followed the rhino, the pads of his lower paws sinking into the soft gray dust that had settled over the gravelly path. In the unnatural white light cast by the Monitors' devices, he could see dust floating everywhere as if the ceiling and walls were constantly eroding. The surfaces were not smooth or patterned, and in fact, they appeared to have been scored and chopped violently, some of the larger gashes running for several feet at a time and crossed by others.

"Thraxians," he said aloud, running his claws gently over the rough wall as he walked. He imagined them crowding this tunnel, their hardened shells scraping together as they writhed, utterly sightless, their mandibles and pincers cutting line after line into the gray rock, churning it to chunks and gravel, while more and more behind them for miles down the line scooped and swept the debris away to some other tunnel or cavernous quarry, pitch black all around them, always breathing the dust. And all of this happening when? As the War to exterminate them started?

No, Maxan realized. *Before the war.*

It was the reason they were exterminated. They were too many. Spreading too fast. In the dark. Underneath. Uncontrollable.

"Thraxians," he said again, turning about to face Sarovek, caught in the blinding flash of her pinlight. "They made all this."

The hawk slowed and stopped beside him, sweeping the light lazily over the carvings. Her expression was mostly passive, unreadable, but Maxan thought maybe she had never really *seen* the walls before, despite having probably been through here many times. Her sharp eye darted curiously to the gentle motion of his paw, rubbing the wall, leaving a fine cloud of dust in its wake. Sarovek raised her free talon and mimed the action.

"Yes," she said after a stretch of silence. "They did."

Sarovek retracted her talon quickly, the seemingly thoughtful moment over, the seriousness fully returned. She pointed the light once more, further down the curving path where the rhino and snake had almost disappeared into the darkness.

But Maxan wasn't ready to go just yet.

They know, the inner voice echoed his thoughts. *These Monitors.*

And I want to know too.

"Why?" he asked simply, shaking his head.

Sarovek stopped short, clacked her beak, perhaps agitated at the idea of falling behind. "I don't understand what you're asking."

"Why make all these tunnels? Out here. I mean, we must be a hundred miles into the Denlands, halfway to Corvidia or Drakora. We're in the middle of nowhere. No cities or settlements. If they dug all of these tunnels to surprise attack the rest of Herbridia, like we've always been told, to wipe us all out... There's no one *out* here to attack."

"Maxan," Sarovek said as apparently gently as she could, although the sound of his name from that beak still sounded too clipped. "These are *our* tunnels."

Maxan's fanned ears flicked at the dusty air involuntarily, as if they hadn't quite heard the hawk's answer. He glanced at her talons and then again at the wall.

"The Thraxians," she said slowly, again as gently yet not so gently as possible. "They are *ours*."

Knowledge rushed in, and Maxan saw suddenly the entirety of the obscured apparatus of the Monitors' power laid out in his mind. All of the animals' tiny little world of Herbridia spun slowly beneath Yinna the blazing sun and Yerda the ruined moon, the Aigaion above casting its machine shadow over all, and the Mind—robed in brilliant green, blue, red, and black—preaching in the bright, open daylight of its wonders, whether true or fabricated in such a way as to shape history and ever expand their power. Yet underneath it all, deep in the rock and dust, hidden in the dark, *here*, the Monitors, whose number Maxan knew was four at the very least—Rinnia, Saghan, Sarovek, and their master, Salastragore—moved in the shadows that stretched between the mysterious metal stations, traveling whenever or wherever those secret places may be found to silence whoever found them, for the apparent good of all.

For twenty years, as long as Maxan had been alive, the bear Folgian had slowly built her web of influence, escaping Salastragore's purging of the Monitors' ranks which had once been one-hundred, denying stubbornly the slow agonizing death that the snake's bane poison had been inflicting upon her, finding and training callers like Feyn, Harmony, Pryth, and Pram, and who knew how many others. Folgian had undoubtedly known about the Monitors' stations, and yet, even after manipulating the power of the Leoran throne and raising her own personal army, the bear that had once told Maxan she was the very Mind herself had chosen neither to excavate these subterranean ruins nor engage the Monitors in open warfare. Not even her closest servant, Feyn, had been told about any of this.

Instead, Maxan realized, *the Mind's supreme master played the long con.* She would let all knowledge of these secrets die in time, just like her own body. All of this uncanny machinery would be buried forever in this gray dust. And all the while the Mind would educate all the animals with whatever Folgian had wanted them to believe was true. All she needed to do was hold off Salastragore long enough. To get the relay back and never let it go.

It was all part of the hidden game.

Just like Rinnia told me.

Folgian and Salastragore. The Mind and the Monitors. The puppeteers. And everyone else, the puppets.

Maxan ran his paw along a long, dusty gray cleft a final time, feeling a word that had at one time risen from the depths of his subconscious before being swept under the tide of his thoughts again. This time, there was no headache, no stinging pain behind the gold of his right eye.

"What is *Epimetheus*?"

In Maxan's experience, the often unflinching gazes of Corvidian species made them notoriously difficult to read, but he watched Sarovek closely for any sign, any tell, that she might know something yet choose to keep it secret. *Like a true Monitor would.* She stood rigid, her closely folded wings nearly in tatters, her clothing bloodied, one taloned hand clutching the pinlight shining on his face, the other resting on the pommel of the sword at her side. The hawk knight cocked her head to the side, gave him one fierce, impatient blink, and clacked her beak as she spoke.

"What?"

She hasn't heard it before, Max. The other mind in the fox's head realized it as he did. *If she had, she would demand to know how you knew.*

So how come I know? It's because of you, isn't it? In my head. But you can't tell me what Epimetheus is.

I can't.

Not because you don't know. But because you just … can't.

I don't … remember myself, Max. Who I was. What I was.

You're not even sure if you were *anything.*

I'm not sure if I'm real.

Maybe I'm just crazy.

Maybe you're just crazy.

"Ah, forget it. Just something Folgian said to me," Maxan lied. "About all this. The stations underground." In truth, it had been Maxan that had said the word to her.

They quickened their pace to catch up to Saghan and Chewgar, who had been waiting just around the next bend at yet another branch in the tunnels. This was the biggest chamber so far, with five options to choose from. Maxan spread his singed cloak on the dusty ground so Chewgar could lay Feyn down. The wolf grumbled and cracked an eye. He seemed to be in less pain now, the panacea having done its work. After Saghan had cleaned the damaged flesh, it was clear to see the permanent pink scars striping his entire body. They matched the one that ran from the corner of Feyn's mouth to his pointed ear, which had always held his face in a menacing grin.

They finished the last of the rations Sarovek had gathered from the Mind's soldiers along with the last of the Monitors' clay-like yet miraculously filling food. Sarovek had said it would all be enough to last them until the journey's end, leaving Maxan curious if the Monitors' base was concealed in the very center of Herbridia. *We have to be practically halfway there by now.*

As he gnawed on the bland food, a subtle breeze tickled the fine fur inside his fanned ears. He wandered away from the Monitors' lights at the cavern's center, following the wind's trail to the leftmost branch. His sensitive snout detected something on the air, something like the oil in the lamps at the Crosswall guardhouse, but not quite. An acrid, burning scent. He stopped at the very edge of the light and knew exactly where he'd smelled it before.

It was the burnt-metal smell of lightning, captured in the glass spheres illuminating the massive ground floor of the Mind's Pinnacle Tower, generated by the constant turning of the wheel in the canal.

Pryth called it electricity.

Maybe the Monitors' tower really is down here.

When they moved on again, it was no surprise that this was the tunnel Saghan led them to. After only a handful of minutes' journey, the ground no longer sloped downward, nor did it have the roughly scored markings left by Thraxian miners. The path was level under them, even swept of the fine gray dust, and braced by wooden planks and iron joints at regular intervals. The soft wind that had merely whispered to Maxan before had intensified enough to send his cloak flapping about beside his tail.

The tunnel ended abruptly, depositing them onto a rocky shelf overlooking a massive abyss stretching left and right as far as the Monitors' pinlights could reach. Perhaps a hundred yards away on the other side of the gap there was indeed a tower of some kind. Dozens of metal pipes of all shapes and sizes gathered into one vertical column, snaking out from random spots all along the cliff faces, above and below. Just in front of them was the largest of these pipes, jutting out like a bridge with a single chain tinkling in the wind serving as a kind of railing. The tower was studded with dim, glowing red, orange, and yellow lights. There was a constant vibration in the rock that buzzed under his paws and along the fur of his tail. The acrid electric smell was overpowering here. And it was hot.

It looks like the relay. Almost.

Chewgar nearly dropped the wolf cradled in his arms as he emerged from the tunnel. The huge rhino stood in awe. He had lived for two decades on the tiny planet of Herbridia and never imagined something like this tower could exist above ground in the light of day, let alone however far below it they were now.

"There's a ssstation just below us," Saghan hissed, sweeping his pinlight down into the chasm, where even its powerful white beam couldn't push away the darkness. There seemed to be no bottom. "One of the big ones. But we're going through." He pointed across the chasm now, and Maxan could see there was a kind of hole at the base of the tower where some of the pipes curved inward.

Another cave. Great.

Saghan again went first, demonstrating for the others how to hold the chain and splay the soles of your feet or paws outward just so over the curve of the pipe-bridge, or else risk losing your balance. "I have no idea what'sss down there," he said, loud enough for his voice to carry over the drowning thrum of power in the air. There was no echo. He had stopped halfway to light the bridge for Chewgar. The massive rhino gripped the chain in his sweaty palm tightly enough to crush the links. He had Feyn now thrown over the opposite shoulder like a sack of grain. By the time Maxan was halfway across the chasm, Chewgar had made it to the base of the tower on the other side. Having spent years racing across the dizzyingly high and sloping rooftops of Crosswall shadowing criminals, he tried to convince himself this experience wasn't all that different, with limited success.

"What is all this for?" he called out, keeping his eyes forward, locked on the pipe, and wide open despite the waves of hot, billowing air drying them out.

"Regulation," Sarovek called back from only a few paces behind. Maxan risked a glance in her direction and guessed from the way she clutched the chain with both talons that she must have known even wings wouldn't save her from the blinding dark or the wild wind in this place if she fell off. He decided it would be good for both their sakes to hurry along.

"What does she mean *regulation*?" he asked Saghan when he'd reached the other side.

"We're more than a mile underground now," the snake replied, holding the light steady at the terminus of the pipe to guide his sister along. "There are great machines below us, ssstretching around and around this world like a web, warmed by the heat from the core, converting the energy."

"Energy?" Chewgar huffed from the mouth of the next cave where the pipes bent into darkness. As soon as he had made it across, he had fallen to his knees, shaking slightly, letting Feyn fall a little more roughly than intended, and he hadn't risen yet. "Energy for what?"

Saghan flicked his tongue and smiled, holding up a single finger and twirling it around very slowly in the air. He smiled, and the twirling sped up, around and around, until finally reaching a constant rate of motion. Then he shrugged and dropped his hand. "As far as I know."

"Your master never told you?" Maxan looked from one Monitor to the other as he asked, "You're supposed to guard all of this, and you don't even know what any of it does?"

Saghan let out a dramatic sigh. "I jussst told you what it does," he hissed tiredly. His long neck stretched, bringing his face close enough to Maxan's face so his flicking tongue tickled the fox's snout.

"The fox means if you know *how* it works, Saghan." Sarovek gently pushed against the snake's neck, bringing his face away from Maxan's, then stood between them. "That knowledge died with the old Monitors. But far, far below us, there are ghosts who still know." It seemed like she would say more, maybe wanted to say more, but the silence stretched. Maxan followed Sarovek's gaze into the abyss. The dark was mesmerizing.

Ghosts. Far below.

"You're not Monitors jussst yet." Saghan had moved to the cave at the base of the tower where all the pipes converged. He gestured invitingly onward. "We can talk soon about changing that. And then, the *whole* tour."

The hot wind was at their backs now, pushing them along, which almost made the going easier. After only one minute inside the next tunnel, Maxan was already wishing he could go back to the dusty, scarred gray walls made by the Thraxians. Once, some years ago, just as the first animals in Crosswall had started going astray, before it was a widespread affliction across the whole city, Maxan had found the corpse of a rabbit in an alley, lying on its back, its ribs torn open and its slick guts pulled and twisted across the cobblestones. As he moved now between these walls of pipes—some red, some orange, most a dull gray that matched the rock—he thought this must be how the rabbit's guts had looked on the inside.

Their whole world was a body, breathing and pumping and bleeding under the surface.

Thankfully, this final length of tunnel wasn't as long or roundabout as the miles' worth they'd already traveled through. It soon exhaled them into yet another immense chamber, this one stretching again into darkness to both left and right. The ceiling was high, tall enough to fit an average building in Crosswall, and reinforced with iron columns and girders. The wind was steady here, though not as strong, pulling gently in one direction. Directly in front of them, in the center of everything, there was a machine.

It's a ... boat?

To Maxan, it looked like a Peskoran River Guild's cart, the kind used to offload the goods brought to Crosswall's docks via the Radilin. It had a sleek, angular wooden hull, heavily lacquered to resist dents and scrapes. Rising from the middle of the deck was a thick wooden mast, with something like sails folded and coiled around it. Along both sides were racks of bright copper wheels that swung down to prop the whole thing up on two metal beams riveted into the ground. On the docks, it made it possible for a Peskoran trader to transition his goods from water to street by pulling a lever just before making berth. But this thing was immense, a hundred times bigger, and just as many times heavier.

An ear-splitting crackle startled Maxan from his inspection. Saghan had moved to one of the iron columns and pulled a switch. Dozens of glowing orbs sizzled and popped to illuminating life, strung up by wires that ran every twenty feet down the tunnel, forward and back. The snake pulled another switch and crooked fingers of lightning arced across the metal beams beneath the machine's hull. A low thrumming filled the air, vibrating Maxan's clenched fangs.

"What is it?" Chewgar managed to say. He had reflexively clutched the wolf's limp body closer to his chest as the whole chamber came to electric life. "Looks like a boat," he added quietly as if to himself.

"It's called a *train,*" Sarovek said. Moving past the fox and rhino. "And those," she said, pointing to the metal beams stretching along the floor and disappearing in the distance, "are the *rails.*"

Sarovek switched off her pinlight and tossed it over her shoulder to Maxan. *A gift, I guess.* Then she yanked on a cord built into the hull to release a set of folding stairs. "Don't step on the rails," she called back without turning, disappearing onto the deck.

"This is how you move so quickly," Maxan said to Saghan, wishing his tone had sounded more objective and less fascinated, but it hadn't.

The snake moved to the stairs by the hull and again swept his hand toward the deck with the same inviting gesture.

"The tour continues."

II

The Castle

Chapter Three
All the Iron

The Monitors let Maxan do the honors. It was just like a Peskoran trader's cart. He wondered absently if they got the design from the River Guilds—*or if it's the other way around*—as he stood over the control panel at the rear of the train-boat's deck. Saghan had instructed him to watch a tiny needle behind a glass lens and wait until a green light glowed beside it, showing that the jumble of wires and glass that the snake called *the dynamo* at the very back had drawn enough electricity from the arcing rails through its hull. He pulled the lever and was surprised that it gave easily.

Both racks of copper wheels slammed the rails with a deafening *clang*, shooting waves of sparks all around as if the whole boat had crashed down upon the water. The lights strung along the passage dimmed, a few of the glass bulbs popping. Maxan felt the thrumming in his fur and fangs intensify for an instant. Then the feeling was gone.

The train lurched forward. No faster than strolling. Then a brisk walk. Within a minute, the machine was sprinting down the corridor. Maxan turned just in time to see the cave's mouth disappear from view as they rumbled around a curve.

Saghan stood beside him, with his arms folded like a teacher observing his student. At his instruction, Maxan watched the needle in the glass and flipped another switch as a second green light lit up. A flood of bright light lit up the dark passage in front just as the train reached the end of the glowing bulbs along the walls.

Maxan couldn't help but smile. It was freedom, like what he felt when he would lurk on the Crosswall rooftops, alone in knowing what the wind felt like rushing past up there. He turned to Saghan to see if the snake felt the same way, and his smile evaporated.

The snake was looking hard at him. His slitted eyes never before seemed so dull, so opaque. *Maybe it's the wind?*

We're not even going that fast.

No. We're not.

It's... He looks... sad.

Ashamed. But why?

"Saghan? What's the matter?"

Maxan had even less experience reading Drakorans' reptilian features than he had with Corvidians, but anyone could've discerned Saghan's unease, uncrossing his arms and looking down, his slender fingers fidgeting absent-mindedly at the pouches on his belt. The brilles of his eyes folded over, and then the lids closed for a long moment.

"Are you all right," Maxan prodded.

Saghan put his hand on Maxan's shoulder and held his gaze firmly. "Tell me, Maxan... That this is what you chose."

"I chose what?"

"Going forward. To the castle. With me."

"Why do you—"

"Jussst... tell me."

The fingers squeezed, not enough to hurt, but enough to emphasize the gravity in his words.

"Tell me that you know there wasss no going back."

Maxan shrugged out of the snake's grip and shot him a look he hoped matched the other's severity. After all this time, he had almost forgotten the urge he'd had once to leap at the snake and choke the life out of him. How Saghan had laughed and talked down to him, even as Chewgar was dying from the bane coursing in his veins, laid out in the broken fountain at the Monitors' safehouse in Crosswall.

After all this time, I almost forgot that we aren't friends.

But are we enemies then, Max?

"How about instead," the fox said slowly, deflecting, "you tell *me* how we're supposed to get all the way to Drakora if we're going *this* slow?"

Saghan turned his head, facing him with one narrowed eye. Deep inside it, a small orange glow sparked. He flicked his forked tongue and smiled. Apparently, it was the answer he needed.

"What're those?" Maxan said, pointing at the sails folded around the tall mast at the center of the train.

Saghan winked in response. One black nail hovered over another button on the control panel. "Hold on," he called out over the deck where Chewgar and Sarovek rested against the railing beside the wolf's prone body. Maxan instinctively gripped the side of the hull as three sails unfolded from the vertical mast and whipped outward to either side. Maxan saw that they weren't like sails at all. They faced into the wind at an angle, not flat like a sail. They were made of cloth sewn taut to tense rods, thinner and yet more pliant than any wood Maxan knew. Saghan pressed another button, and the three rods began spinning, catching the wind, and beating it back, propelling the whole machine forward faster and faster with each rotation.

Soon, they were practically flying down the tunnel.

Maxan swallowed instinctively, releasing the building pressure in his ears as the train's wheels scraped and squealed along the tracks. He was almost sorry he had criticized the machine's speed. *Almost.*

For hours, the train flew along the rails. Moving freely around the deck was rather difficult, and trying to shout over the whipping wind was utterly impossible. So Maxan settled into position beside Chewgar after clawing his way along the railings, and they all passed the time in silence. Maxan tried to count the iron columns bracing the cave walls as they flitted by, multiplying in his head how many passed every second, calculating how much of that iron went into the construction of an average building in Crosswall, and the thought of just how much time and material all of this took was overwhelming.

Light flashed behind Maxan's closed eyelids. Then it was gone. Again another flash roused him. He must have fallen asleep thinking of the scale of construction. The steady rush of wind had quieted from a roar to a gust, and the rumbling and squealing of the copper wheels was less intense.

We're slowing down. He felt it in his whole body. The train was gradually curving to the right, climbing gradually upward.

Maxan yawned, then rubbed at his snout as an odor of brine assaulted him. He stretched and grasped the side railing of the deck, pulling himself to stand. Chewgar was already up, kneeling, one big hand pressing warmly on Feyn's chest to hold him steady, the other gripping the railing.

"Look, Max." The rhino's eyes were wide with astonishment. "Have you ever seen anything like it?"

The light was gone for a few seconds as the train rumbled onward, then it returned. They were passing huge spaces where the wall of the tunnel had been mined away in the side of a cliff, like a window, revealing a breathtaking view of a cylindrical valley—or rather a gaping hole punched out of the world—with a tower of graystone and grimy iron stabbing into the world at its center, a thousand feet tall. A wide cave mouth at the waterline perpetually drank the lake, which was perpetually resupplied by a waterfall spilling and misting from the rim of land at the top.

The train passed behind another wall, and the view was gone, leaving Maxan's dazzled eyes blinking. The next window came, and he saw that the tower resembled the jumble of pipes and conduits they had seen underground, but this structure was an absolute colossus, dominating everything in view.

Its foundation was a cube-shaped monolith of dark metal sunk into a circular lake of scummy, foaming water that had to be at least a mile in circumference. Lines of blood-red rust ran along the central cube's seams a hundred feet high, and from its base where the lake waters lapped at its sides, a series of water wheels rotated in their current. A long pier extended out onto the water from an enormous doorway at the very bottom of the thing, like a tongue lolling from a yawning maw. Curiously, a set of train rails stretched from this dark opening to some sort of shed at the end of the pier.

Rising above the cube was the cluster of pipes that comprised the tower's main body. Nothing was straight. Everything seemed to be welded and bolted and twisted together to contain the chaos, as though the tower would burst if not for the corkscrewing causeways, scaffolds, stairways, and braces belting it all together. Some of the pipes shot outward, becoming sideways chimneys that belched plumes of smoke, spurts of water, and even tongues of fire in all directions. A dozen bridges extended like arms from various levels of the tower, terminating into caves all around the circular cliff. It looked tired as if it struggled to keep itself upright beneath all of its crushing weight. Some of the bridges looked unfinished, perhaps by design, jutting out over empty space. As the train looped around, Maxan saw a team of Drakorans upend a cart at the end of one of these walkways, the gravelly debris splashing into the lake far below.

The edge of the cylinder was at least a quarter mile above them, and the sky beyond was the pale-yellow glow of a new dawn. Maxan must have slept longer than he realized, although there was no telling how long they had spent below ground. Regardless, adrenaline coursed in his veins, and he felt an exhilaration as he took in the sight. He couldn't help but lean over the railing to glimpse the very top of the tower as the train rolled onward, climbing gradually higher. It was easier to see now the rails leveled flat as it neared the full tower's height. The twisted mass of pipes was crowned with solid rock, as though the excavators had left the small mountain under which all this was buried intact. And on top of the rock was a squat fortress flying the red banners of Drakora along its three tiers of ramparts. Every inch of it was solid graystone braced with crossed iron beams, and there was no discernable pattern to the innumerable windows on its side, which could leave an outside viewer guessing for days at the interior floorplan. Lightning rods and wind turbines rose from nearly every angular corner, and bundles of wires ran from these and spread over the stone surface like vines. Two more tiers rose above the first, each one taller than the one before, and rising high above all was a tower that easily rivaled the height of the Mind's Pinnacle, seemingly tall enough to scrape the bottom of the Aigaion.

And... at the top, way up...

Are those...

It looks—

Something gripped Maxan's shoulder and whirled him away from the railing just as another piece of wall closed off the view, shrouding the train in shadow again.

"Trying to bash your brains out on the wall?" Chewgar scolded him.

"The top of the tower," Maxan said, catching his breath and pointing up at the fortress and tower behind the passing wall. "It's open. Folded back, like a blooming flower or something. And there are *train rails* going straight up its side!"

When the rhino only shrugged, Maxan spun to Sarovek, then Saghan who still stood over the control panel in the back. "*Rails.* On the *wall.* Straight up the *side.* Going *nowhere!*" The rails to nowhere had been constructed alongside a massive support crane, itself hugging the tower with scaffolds at intervals. Maxan saw tiny shapes toiling away up there, sending showers of bright sparks below.

"Patience, fox," Sarovek answered. She had gathered her belongings and stood on the opposite side of the deck, clearly no stranger to the sight of the monstrous structure. She had unwound the gauze and cords binding her damaged wings and now seemed interested only in testing the glide in the easy wind along the rails. "It will all make sense soon," she said simply.

Even as he resigned to wait for an explanation, he recalled the rails on the pier at the very bottom, and how he thought that strange at the time too. *They're connected*, he reasoned. *Inside the tower. But ... why?*

Patience, fox, came the snide remark in his head.

Shut up.

The grandest of all the bridges arched over the wide expanse above at ground level, connecting the fortress to a city that rimmed the entire edge of the cylinder. They were nearing the top of the tower now, and Maxan saw that it was, in fact, two bridges stacked. Saghan flipped a switch on the control panel and the sails that had dragged them forward ceased spinning and folded themselves once again around the mast. The train rounded a final curve and rumbled across the lower portion, coasting freely as it passed through a cloud of acrid coal-black smoke billowing up from far below.

How could the Monitors build all of this? He would have asked them aloud then, but he was still choking in the smoke's aftermath.

They didn't build *any of it, Max,* the voice of reason supplied just as he realized for himself. *It's a station.*

A station.

Right below the castle.

They just dug it up.

Just days ago, Maxan had been in awe at the display of electricity and wiring and the advancement of new technologies in the ground floor of the Mind's Pinnacle, but what he saw here at the Monitors' castle surpassed all impressions of wonder that previous place had once left on him. And yet, the fox couldn't help but realize that while there was far more on display here in this cylindrical lake surrounded by cliffs, there was still an elegance to the Mind's grand hall and in the library at its top. Here, at the Monitors' castle, elegance wasn't of the slightest consideration. While the Mind was polished and extravagant, everything here was grimy and utilitarian.

The copper wheels screeched softly as Saghan engaged a braking mechanism at the control panel, and the train eased to a halt just within an arched gateway cut into the side of the station. A team of reptilian Drakoran laborers—lizards and crocodiles led by a wide-bellied brown snake—instantly went to work on a bank of levers and gears nearby, their multicolored scales glistening with condensed steam. They wore aprons and goggles and almost nothing else. The snake foreman hissed and shouted at them angrily, something about the "right sequence." The floor beneath the train's hull lifted and groaned a moment later once they figured it out, and the whole thing rotated slowly as the team spun the gears faster and faster, pointing the thing outward again, ready for a departure. And then the team was gone, rushing away back to their previous tasks.

Maxan stood at the rails, his mismatched eyes wide, taking everything in.

The voice in his head surfaced above the constant din.

Function, in this place, rules over form.

It seemed like the top levels of the station had been hollowed out, and from where the train's railing had come to rest, Maxan could see a hundred feet or more straight down. At every level of this pit, innumerable lines of spinning gears, rotating belts, and sparking wires seemed to be working on every interior surface inside, powering gigantic machines that broke, or ground, or melted cartloads of raw materials. A veritable army of Drakorans went about their work, throwing switches that spilled the white-hot liquid metal into enormous bowls at lower levels. Maxan saw a skinny skink lizard tugging at a chain the size of his own waist as though his life depended on it. This turned a series of gears and pulleys, and the crucible slowly tipped and spilled its glowing liquid contents into a mold, guided by a muscled crocodile wearing a glass mask and leather gloves, both thicker than plate armor and probably just as heavy. Further down the line, the mold went to a bath of water, which sent up gouts of hot, hissing steam. The hardest work of all, perhaps, belonged to the thick-bodied choppers at the end, who watched teams of sweating workers remove the solid metal from the mold, then brought unwieldy blades down to separate them into the rods that would later be reforged into the scaffolds and structures outside, or the thicker beams for more and more train rails.

Forging the metal for the castle's expansion wasn't the only operation being performed in the dimly lit station. Carts full of brightly colored, glossy gemstones were loaded onto belts and sent to a series of spinning grinders until only dust came out the other end. Barrels of this stuff were dumped into vats of swirling green and funneled through a branching network of pipes. The toxic runoff was vaporized and spewed at a blazing fire, the smoke from which was sucked by a fan overhead and sent away through the wall and up through a smokestack outside, all while whatever precious element emerged from the distillation was carried off to other parts of the castle's factory in even more pipes.

Across the pit along the opposite wall, a small farm of green stalks and thorny, flowering plants rose from beds of chemical-rich soil. Glass rods were arranged over each row, suspended by wires, glowing different shades of purple. A crew of squat-framed toads draped in stained robes milled about these plants, clipping leaves, dropping them into various bubbling beakers arranged atop an adjacent table, and jotting down notes about the observable changes.

At the center of everything, Maxan saw the twin rails sloping up from a hole in the factory floor, held upright by what appeared to be the iron body of the crane that stabbed through everything like a spinal cord. The rails and the crane disappeared through a massive corkscrewed pipe in the ceiling. A pile of the beams that had been forged had been braced together and stacked alongside the lower hole at the bottom of the pit, ready for the crane to retrieve them.

Everywhere Maxan looked, there was more to see. The activity was maddening. None of the Drakoran workers ever took their slitted eyes off their tasks, or else some whirling machine or toxic sludge may clamp shut or spill over, maiming or outright killing for such carelessness. Maxan hadn't noticed the two lizard guards—armored in the signature dark-red Drakoran leather like Saghan's, though much less ornate—as they approached the train with a stretcher. Chewgar's loud refusal to hand over the unconscious wolf tore his eyes finally from all the sights.

"Hey," Maxan called out, trying to shoo the lizards away with his paw. They looked to Saghan for direction, their scaled hands inching to the knives at their belts.

"These are our guesssts!" Saghan shouted, his orange eyes flaring. "Our *honored* guests!" The lizards dropped their arms and knelt, faces down. Satisfied with their compliance, Saghan gestured to Chewgar. "They will bring the wolf directly to the dispensary. Where we keep our medicines. I will attend him persssonally."

"We want to go with him," Maxan said, exchanging a look with Chewgar.

Saghan folded his hands together, striking a pose of patience and calm. "Maxan," he said, his long neck sweeping his gaze left to right, indicating all the Monitors' grand enterprise surrounding them. "You've seen ssso much, learned ssso much. Ssso many secrets. Surely by now, you must trust us." When the slitted eyes settled again on the fox, there was an unnerving glow in them.

His eyes, like that. Just like before.

Like when?

At the inn. That light in his eyes.

Or it's just the light from all the work around them?

Maxan stepped by the kneeling lizards to get a closer look, stopping just below the raised control panel at the back of the deck.

"Saghan, tell me that it's you."

The snake's forked tongue flicked the air curiously. The glow in his eyes dimmed slightly but didn't go out.

"Uhh, Max," Chewgar said behind the fox's shoulder. "Are you tired?"

A silence seemed to hang, despite all the constant clamor of the factory. Finally, Saghan smiled, then spoke as he descended onto the deck. "Hmm. I understand your hesitation… *Maxan*—"

My name. Like he almost forgot it.

"—but we've come ssso ssso far together now to start doubting each other. Haven't we?"

Saghan brushed past the fox and stood before Chewgar, who still held the wolf in his arms. His slender fingers lifted the flap of Feyn's satchel and rummaged inside, emerging holding the chrome relay. The golden beads of light raced in the looping channels, endlessly, from its top to its bottom, casting a shimmering underwater light across the snake's face. The fire in his eyes flared, for an instant, and then was gone entirely.

Saghan let out a breath, spun toward the fox, and tossed the relay playfully. "Catch!"

OH SHI—

The rod thudded on Maxan's chest and slipped through his closing claws. He pitched forward, grasping it just before his body slammed onto the deck, clutching it tightly, safely.

If I'd dropped it...

The horrific image of the factory bathed in unnatural red light, splattered in darker shades of red, vanished from his mind, even as the snake laughed uncontrollably over him.

"Not funny!" Chewgar hollered right at Saghan's leering face. The rhino looked like he might have shoved him over the railing, if not farther if he hadn't been carrying Feyn.

"Hmm. Keep it with you," Saghan offered, raising his hands defensively as he came down from his fit of laughter. "Keep it safe. On Principal Feyn's behalf. We will all bring it before the master, together. Later, after a short ressst, hmm? The wolf deserves that much."

Without waiting to see if the terms satisfied them, Saghan motioned to the two lizards. They came to Chewgar and offered their arms to take the wolf. Saghan nodded and smiled. "Principal Feyn will be perfectly fine in our care."

Maxan shrugged at the rhino.

What other choice do we have?

The thought must have been visible in his eyes because a moment later, Chewgar laid the white wolf into the attendants' arms with a sigh. They brought him to the stretcher, which upon closer look seemed like it saw a lot of use in this place, and then carried the wolf away.

If Feyn was going to die...

...he would've died already. He'll live, Max.

Sure. But he'll probably be upset next time he looks in a mirror.

Chapter Four

Tidings

SAGHAN AND SAROVEK LED THEIR TWO "HONORED" LEORAN guests through the station utterly unnoticed. Besides the team of lizards who worked the floor plate that spun the train back around, no other Drakorans in the factory could break from their routines long enough to spare them a glance. They skirted around the central pit, following the curve of the enormous factory-station's wall. The floor beneath their feet was comprised of tempered sheet metal rods, welded together as a kind of lattice so that the excess heat of industry could rise and circulate through the dozen vents around the ceiling.

The uneven footing pressed uncomfortably into the pads of his paws with every step, and he couldn't help but glance awkwardly down. At one point, he caught a glimpse through the lattice of shifting, shining metal, casting bright points of light all around like a diamond. Narrowing his eyes, he almost leapt back in sudden alarm.

A Thraxian!

The creature came into better view around the circular bend of their path. It was unlike anything Maxan had ever seen or had ever heard of in the old stories. It was twice as large by far than the scorpion that had clamped King Locain's waist in its massive claw below the Denland station, and every limb of this monster's body was plated in shining chrome, reflecting the dull lights of the place like mirrors. Its pincer-legs clattered angrily along the metal floor with a screeching and scraping that made the fur along the fox's spine stand on end. The Drakoran workers backed away at its approach.

"Maxan!"

The fox looked up at Sarovek's call. She stood in an aisle between two smelters, her talon motioning for him to catch up. When he turned back to see the creature again, it was disappearing among the whirring machinery, smoke, and steam.

He caught up with the others at an arched gate which led into a rectangular, graystone chamber. Maxan realized that this room was likely jutting out from the side of the tower, hanging over empty space a thousand or more feet over the circular lake. Crossing the threshold was like stepping into another world. Where in the factory there had been metal and machinery braced to the walls, here there were banners and tapestries tastefully adorning the walls and dangling from the sills of high windows.

The foundations of the actual castle, Maxan reasoned.

They climbed a wide circular staircase that brought them to a small box of a room. There didn't seem to be any other way forward. The two Monitors filed in as the two Leorans exchanged a puzzled look. Sarovek clacked her beak at them and motioned for them to enter. An iron fence dropped from above, closing them inside, and before the big rhino could protest about how little room he had in the corner, the floor lurched them upward.

"Aren't the stations supposed to be secret?" Maxan asked, taking in the view of the sprawling Drakoran city ringing the cliff outside through the fence and intermittent panes of glass as the box rose slowly. "This whole thing. It's on top of a station." He hadn't meant to sound accusatory.

But Sarovek seemed vexed nonetheless.

Seems she's vexed by everything...

"This site was exposed decades ago," she clipped back quickly, matter-of-factly. "Not long after the Mind began constructing its grand campus. Access to the lowest levels—*below* the lake, if you are smart enough to take my meaning, fox—remains our most closely guarded secret, even as the city of New Quwurth has grown up alongside the industry."

"I see." He bit his lip, trying to keep the rest of the questions in. He glanced at Chewgar who braced himself in the corner, bent at the waist, trying politely not to scratch the polished wooden ceiling of the elevator with the tip of his horn while also holding down his rising sense of vertigo.

Well, he's no help...

Forget it! Just ask!

"Why not share any of this with the rest of the world? The rails, the train, with all the glass lights and switches and buttons. The *electricity*."

The Mind was going to, he almost added, but clamped his fangs shut.

Were they, though?

"Think of how much we could *learn* from each other," he went on. Saghan and Sarovek exchanged a glance. "I've never been to the mountains of Corvidia. I've never seen a Peskoran beach. Or gone sailing. Imagine how close our countries could be if we just had the means to *get there*. And talk to each other. But instead, it's all underground?" Maxan shook his head and said no more.

He already knew what the Monitors' response would be.

Something to do with how all this knowledge of secret things is dangerous. What we use to create, we can use to destroy.

It's what Epimetheus tried to stop.

Maxan snarled, exposing his fangs, wincing at the sudden, searing stab of pain behind his golden right eye. But it wasn't as bad as it had been. He forced half of his mind to let go, to close off its perceptions and reach inwardly, grasping for the knowledge he knew was in there already, in the dark, somehow, since before he'd even been born.

But it was gone already. The voice of reason was silent.

The pain was gone too. *Maybe this is how I control it.*

He looked at the two Monitors behind him in the cramped space. Of course, Sarovek seemed as vexed by his ideas as he'd expected. But Saghan just seemed...

Sad.

The light behind the snake's eyes was gone again. He leaned heavily on one shoulder against the wall, his V-shaped head pointed down, looking at the floor but not seeming to *see* it. As though he wasn't actually there.

His mood changes so quickly.

The elevator rose to the castle's main floor. Another fenced gate swung open when the platform locked into place with an audible click. They'd left the clanging of machinery and hissing of molten iron far below. A new kind of maddened buzz and bustle greeted them as they came around a bend into the castle's great entrance hall.

It's like ... a prison.

Throngs of animals were crowded into pens along the walls and down the gradually sloping stairs to the towering front doors, which stood open, filling the entire chamber with daylight. Most of them were Drakorans, with assorted scales glinting all colors of the rainbow. Maxan caught glimpses of other species hailing from other countries as well, including a few damp-skinned Peskoran sharks, a handful of black-winged Corvidian crows, and even what appeared to be a family of weasels, perhaps displaced from the Denlands (Maxan guessed) and seeking refuge in the swampy nation south of their forest home. It took a long moment for Maxan to realize that the pens were bolted into the floor to guide the flow of the queue, not to imprison them.

Almost all of the animals were shouting obscenities at the castle guards, who numbered only a few. These scaly-skinned sentries yawned visibly, shifting their eyes over the mob idly, clearly bored. They let the high iron bars do all of the work for them, leaving the worst duties of all to the poor little frogs and salamanders at the end of the zig-zagging queue. These officious-looking scribes scribbled the mob's names and grievances into thick folds of paper, raising their sticky hands tiredly from time to time to hear in the riotous room.

What is it they want?

He almost asked the two Monitors beside him but thought better of it considering all the good his questions had done him so far. He then saw the slow trickle of citizens to the final destination, a short row of tables where a team of coal-stained crocodiles was being handed a coarse sack and ushered out a side exit.

Just like the western district of Crosswall, where all the animals were penned in and suffering. Where it seemed a lifetime ago he had been a guard, a shadow, a helpless observer. He recalled how the Mind's green-robed initiates had supervised a similar operation.

Food. They're here for food.

Maxan hadn't seen the squat-bodied, silk-robed Drakoran nobleman slip by the nearest pair of salamander attendants and waddle over to where he and the Monitors stood.

"Lord S*thpf*-aghan," the fat, greasy cane toad lisped. He puffed in another heavy breath, then released the next croak in a rush. "A word with you plea-*thpf*."

Maxan had never seen any creature so ugly, and he had seen a few toads in his time from the rooftops in the rich northern district of Crosswall, stealing his way through the visiting Drakoran merchants' quarters.

I might even have robbed this guy once, for all I know. The toad brought with him a cloud of sweet perfume that tickled Maxan's snout. It almost covered the pungent odor emanating from the unwashed folds in the toad's thick skin. Almost. *No, I'd recognize this one.*

The toad's face was covered with warts, most of them were pink in hue, and some of them translucent enough to show the pus sloshing around inside. One of these must have just opened into a blister, which Groak constantly wiped with a stained silk kerchief in his three-fingered hand. The worst of the toad's warts had warts of its own, and the metastasized growth of it weighed down one of his eyelids. The other gazed up expectantly at the considerably taller snake as he hissed an irritated reply.

"Lord Groak. How can I be of ssservice?"

"Tomorrow, I depart back to New Quwur-*thpf.*" A deep breath followed.

"I bid you a safe return to the capital then," Saghan cut in before the next rush of words, but Groak wasn't perturbed in the slightest.

"To the cou*nthp*f-il of Lords," Groak finished the other part of his statement, moving more swiftly than he seemed capable in front of Saghan, stopping the snake in his tracks. "I'm afraid I must tell the cou*n-thp*f-il, in full what I have witne*thpf*-ed here. The damage, the des*thpf*-peration, the acc*th-pf*-idental death, the utterly was*thpf*-ed funding!" The toad lord bent a boneless finger back as he counted each grievance. Then he threw his arms up wildly, sending another stream of pus running down his cheek. "Think of all the MONEY! Money that we've, we've just toss*thpf*-ed away on all your father's grand project*thpf*! For YEAR-*thpf*! For DECADE-*thpf*!"

Lord Groak's croaking rang out even above the din of the iron-barred queue of starving Drakorans, but still did little to silence any of it. He composed himself, wiped his face again.

Saghan folded his arms. It was obvious he seemed unmoved by the toad's bluster.

And unsurprised, Maxan understood, observing the angle of Saghan's shoulders and the rhythmic flicking of his tongue. After all the time he'd spent with Saghan and Sarovek, he was beginning to clearly see their tells. He was glad Sarovek hadn't tried to shoo him and Chewgar along elsewhere so that he could witness some of the Monitors' business firsthand, even if he didn't know all the context.

"And ssso?" Saghan hissed, examining the dirt crusted on his black nails.

Groak's head swiveled left and right, equivalent to shaking his head if he'd had a neck. He noticed the newcomers as if for the first time, eyeing the hulking rhinoceros from horn to toe, and sparing only a sidelong glance at the fox who wasn't much by comparison. His cheeks bubbled and depressed.

"New recruit-*thpf*? Leoran-*thpf,* no less. Very intere*thpf*-ting. Have you heard, young lord S*thpf*-aghan, the rumor*thpf* and here*thpf*-ay coming from Leora? They *thpf*ay the king is miss-t*hpf*ing, *thpf*-lain in the Denland rebellion..." Again, Lord Groak ran his eyes over Chewgar, surveying the damage and dried blood on his white and black Crosswall guard uniform.

Maxan recognized the look for what it was. *He's trying to read the rhino for tells of his own.*

An impulse took over. He stepped in front of the cane toad's gaze, raised his paw, and waved. "Hello," the fox said, smiling, drawing Groak's full attention. "Our host," he said, winking and cocking his head at Saghan, "is so tired from our journey that he forgot to formally introduce us. Lord Groak, may I present *Captain General Chewgar* of Crosswall, and I am but his humble squire, Maxan." He bowed, artfully and pompously sweeping his hind leg and bushy tail behind him, bending very low at the knee. Rising, he saw Sarovek's beak crack open to speak, but he spoke faster.

"We did indeed pass through the Denlands, although we skirted its southern edge and avoided most of the bloodshed. I say *most*, for as you can see..." He gestured to the three cauterized wounds in the rhino's broad chest and the one in his side. "We could not avoid the conflict. Our mission was to escort Lord Saghan and Lady Sarovek along the border safely. As you can also see..." Now he swept his paw to the hawk's damaged wings, "We were not as successful as we could have been. Denland rebels, you see, as you mentioned. But successful nonetheless!

"Lord Saghan," Maxan went on, cutting off Lord Groak's reply, "has invited us to rest before our return journey. Upon such time as we rejoin King Locain's retinue, that is, King Locain, the Golden Lord, who is very much not missing! We know exactly where we left him."

Technically not a lie. Maxan told himself inwardly. The other voice was silent, had been silent since the elevator. This impulse, maybe for the first time in a long time, was all his own. *Throwing nonsense, speculation, and unsubstantiated facts into his rumors and hearsay, the toad's as confused as he looks. Well done, fox.*

Saghan smirked, Sarovek glared, and Chewgar mouthed silently, *Captain General?*

"If there's nothing elssse then, Groak, it's as the squire says, we're very tired."

Saghan pivoted, extending an arm inviting his guests onward toward an adjacent hallway flanked by armored guards. On cue, Captain General Chewgar moved in that direction with his squire in tow, and Sarovek miraculously kept her chiding in check.

"Lord S*thpf*-aghan, you don't under*thpf*-tand," Groak again hopped more quickly than Maxan thought possible and gripped the snake's wrist tightly, physically holding him back. Saghan reeled on him, looking as though he would slash the toad's face for his insolence, but Groak was unperturbed.

"I cannot *thpf*-top what's coming. Not anymore. *Thpf*-ee for yourself." Groak's cheeks bubbled, and his gaze turned upon the caged mob of hungry animals and the maddened, constant roar of voices echoing in the hall. Saghan, it seemed, might have finally looked, really looked, at all of it.

"I've waited long enough. S*thpf*-alastragore has *thpf*-pared no time for me. Fret not, for he will have much time indeed, when the work grind-*thpf* to a halt. But that will be the leas*thpf*t of his worrie*thpf*." Groak jerked Saghan closer with surprising strength until they were eye-to-eye. "More and more are going a*thpf*-tray each day. The creature-*thpf* are taking over New Quwurth, or dragging their victim-*thpf* to the *thpf*-wamps. And all the while, your father ignore*thpf* the plea-*thpf* of the worker-*thpf*. Their meager wage*thpf* no longer match their effort. They fall to their death working on that, that… *thing*. That *ladder*. More dead every day. Washed away by the water-*thpf*, *thpf*-ucked down into that hole."

"So send the Thraxians to the ladder." Saghan tore himself out of Groak's grip, wiping at the sweaty residue the toad left on his armored forearm.

"Rrr-hrr-grrhh," Groak croaked in a lengthy, sustained note, and Maxan realized it was the little Lord's laughter. "The Thraxian-*thpf* obey only their queen, and their queen obey*thpf* only her mas*thpf*-ter. And I'm telling you, as *thpf*-traight as I can, the *thpf*o-called mas*thpf*-ter is ignoring all the warnings, is not lis*thpf*-tening to reason." Groak's cheeks bubbled ominously as he slowly raised a boneless, accusatory finger to point in Saghan's face. "I hope he will lis*thpf*-ten to hi-*thpf* own *thpf*-on."

"I already know what he'll say: *Sssend the Corvidians!*"

"Surely, young lord, you're aware it was Corvidian*thpf*s who *thpf*upplied all the money for your father to was*thpf*-te?" Groak shuffled his fat legs beneath him and turned in place to Sarovek. "Duke S*thpf*-arothorn is very dis*thpf*-pleased to learn what your great hous*thpf*e's fortune has gone to these past ten years, my dear. This*thpf*… what did your mas*thpf*-ter call it… prototype cons*thpf*-tructed here at his own cas*thpf*-tle, meanwhile the S*thpf*-pire at Lake S*thpf*-kymere s*thpf*-tands half-finished for ten years*thpf*. Mmmm, yes*thpf*… S*thpf*-arothorn is very dis*thpf*-pleased indeed."

The hawk knight had endured the cane toad's tidings as stoically as she could, until now. "What did you tell my brother?" Sarovek took a menacing step forward, the points of her talons squeezing tight as though tearing out an invisible throat. It would have taken more talons than she possessed to fit around Groak's bulbous throat though. Chewgar's hand went to her shoulder, holding her back, and Sarovek apparently recalled the part of the Corvidian code of honor that meant strangling a guest in your own house was frowned upon.

"Rrr-hrr-grrhh!" Groak's slimy hands grappled with his jiggling belly. Now he had fully won back the Monitors' attention.

All it took was threats of collapse, overthrow, open rebellion. And family.

"I told S*thpf*-arothorn the truth, my dear. That the *masthpf-ter monitor'thpf* grand design has come to nothing. That the *prototype* ha*thpf* never launched!

Not once in ten year*thpf*! All the time, was*thpf*-ted! All the grand Corvidian Houses' treasuries *emptied* to build an *airship* that's not… *air*-worthy." Lord Groak's lips warbled around the words for emphasis, but the effect was mocking. Maxan saw Sarovek straining to free herself from Chewgar's grip. He felt his legs tense, ready to spring between them.

What for? To save this toad?

"Oh, my dear. If only your true *thpf*-ire could *thpf*-ee you now with hi*thpf* own eye*thpf*. What would he *thpf*-ay ha*thpf* become of you? In *thpf*ervice to some Drakoran lunatic." Groak sighed for effect. "I *thpf*uppose your brother'*thpf* eye*thpf* will have to do."

Sarovek's eyes narrowed. If she had truly wanted them to take another step and tear into the toad's face, Maxan doubted even Chewgar could have stopped her. "Speak plainly, you slime!"

Groak pressed a hand to his chest, pantomiming shock at the insult. "Do you not know, my dear? Lord S*thpf*-arothorn is en route. He will be here soon, a few day*thpf*. I of cours*thpf* gave your mas*thpf*-ter a forewarning, but I was ignored. Repeatedly. As I've already mentioned before." Groak waddled in place to wag a finger at Saghan. "Do you think I like to wait? Does he think the mounting problem*thpf* will di*thpf*-appear if ignored? When you next *thpf*ee your father, inform him that by thi*thpf* time tomorrow, all work on the project come*thpf* to an end. If not from me, perhap-*thpf* he will heed the warning from you lot."

The little toad lord did his best to bend at the waist in a sort of bow. Had the situation not been so grave, the sight might have been comical. "At your dis*thpf*-cretion, Lord S*thpf*-aghan. I care not."

Lord Groak spun and waddled away with an entourage that had kindly waited for him by the tables. Maxan wondered why the two Monitors hadn't said anything further. He silently watched their faces carefully as they silently watched Groak disappear through the main gate. Saghan seemed as passive and apathetic as ever, unconcerned by the toad's warnings of a labor strike and even actions from the Drakoran Lords' Council.

But Sarovek's feathers were literally ruffled. She stared after the little waddling lord with murder in her eyes. Maxan figured what it was he'd said that riled her. Talk of Corvidian honor, the grand houses, the empty treasury, and some place called The Spire, which he'd first heard of when Pryth and Pram had brought him to Feyn's house on the Mind's campus. Some of it made sense.

It's a tower on the shores of Lake Skymere, nestled high in the mountains of Corvidia, unfinished for ten years. They paid Salastragore to build it, with his army of Thraxian builders. Maybe it's on top of a station, like this one. With an airship that doesn't fly.

Of course, Maxan wanted to know more, but couldn't think of the right question to ask the hawk first. So, he asked whatever came to mind.

"Ah, Sarovek, so you have a brother?"

She fixed her hard glare on him. Maxan saw the anger boiling even in the deep black pupils of her wide saucer eyes. Then he saw she wasn't angry at him. It wasn't anger at all.

She's worried.

Perhaps she recalled then the Corvidian knight code, the futility of showing emotion. Sarovek closed her eyes, clacked her beak shut, and drew a deep breath through her nostrils.

"Twin brother," she answered. "Sarothorn. We hatched from the same egg. I'd nearly already killed him before we came into this world."

"And he's a Duke?" This question was from Chewgar. "So that makes you, what, in Corvidian society… A Duchess?"

Saghan almost doubled over laughing, slapping the rhino's thick shoulder hard. "Can you imagine?" he managed to say.

The others didn't know what was so funny. "I chose to give up titles and become a knight. I chose to become a Monitor."

"No," Saghan said, getting himself under control. "You were jussst part of the deal."

"What are you saying, snake?"

Maxan was suddenly aware of the talon on the pommel of her sword, suddenly tensing into a fist. There was no way Sarovek would cut Saghan down here amid the throngs of animals in their very own castle. *Or would she?* She seemed to be containing herself well enough, for now.

Saghan threw his hands up, perhaps aware of her sword as well. "Relaxsss… I'm sssaying you weren't given a choice." The snake blinked rapidly, his forked tongue flicking wildly, suddenly realizing just how profound his words were. He looked from the hawk, to the fox, to the rhino, then shrugged at all of them.

"When were *any* of us given a choice?"

Chapter Five
Questionable Hospitality

The interior of the castle showed a consideration for decorum that the exterior entirely lacked. The angular architecture and richly colored banners of the grand entrance hall had been Maxan's first clue of the Monitors' exorbitant wealth (iron bars and starving citizenry aside). Now, they wound through passageways of dark stone polished to such a sheen that it was like being caught between endless tunnels of himself. The effect was unnerving. Maxan glanced at his side and saw the other fox staring back, and over that one's shoulder, yet another fox looking away.

Watching my back maybe? Or disgusted with all I've done?

There was no answer.

He tried to focus on the depth and softness of the red-tinged rugs, his lower paws sinking comfortably with every step, grounding him in reality. Above them, potted plants dangled from the ceiling or leaned over them from high alcoves carved into the wall. They smelled of eucalyptus and mint, a mingling of scents that relaxed his body and calmed his nerves. A pipe ran along the triangular channel where the walls bent, drip feeding the plants with water. All of a sudden, brilliant white rays of light gushed from square-cut holes in the ceiling, illuminating each plant with vibrance and casting away the semi-darkness.

Mirrors, Maxan realized, pressing himself against an opposite wall for the right angle that would let him peer into the light source. *More and more mirrors, built into the castle itself, to catch Yinna's light.*

"Amazing," he muttered.

"Indeed," Saghan agreed, coming to his side. The snake had the advantage of extending his long neck so that his face was awash with sparkling sunlight in the plant's shadow. "There are tiny motors all along the walls. They gather the heat and turn gradually to catch Yinna's rays. Providing ten hoursss of light."

Amid all the functions, here then was the *form*. While the exterior of the Monitors' castle could make a visitor choke, whether from the horrendousness of twisted metal or sulfurous chemical spew, the interior was breathtaking in a different sense.

One thing they have in common with the Mind. They don't hesitate to show off the wonders in their own houses. Maxan recalled the finely kept gardens atop the Pinnacle Tower, the rows of bookshelves in Folgian's mansion, and the carving of the behemoth looming over her fireplace.

He thought of the miles and miles of cables and wires and the distances of their spinning water wheels, all to usher electric power to the places it served them. He thought of the glowing purple lights over the farm in this station's factory, of the exotic plants there that probably made medicines like panacea or the red metabolic drops that could keep you awake for days, even the hardy rations with the consistency of tree bark. He wondered why none of these marvels were available to the common citizen.

Maybe that's all they need. The animals in the cage.

They reached another elevator, and Saghan made his goodbyes. He reminded them he had pledged to see that the white wolf was taken care of in the dispensary. "Where we dispense the medicine," Sarovek clarified as the fence-gate enclosed her and her guests in the small room. Maxan watched the snake's back as he strode away, until the rising elevator broke his line of sight.

"I imagine you have many questions," the hawk said. "The answers are coming. Know this in the meantime: the Monitors are in your debt."

"You owe the two little callers too," Chewgar said.

"The callers too," she agreed.

"Pryth and Pram," Chewgar said. The awkwardness with which he stooped in the cramped space clashed with the gravity in his voice. He looked hard at Sarovek. "When this is all done with, there will be no more hostility between you. They'll be in charge of the Mind now. All of Leora, in fact, with Locain gone. They'll have to figure out the Stray, get Crosswall under control." He raised a thick finger and pointed at the hawk's heart. "You will leave them alone."

Maxan didn't think it was fair to demand anything from Sarovek. Not then, not here, not after all the pain she'd endured. Not after the little toad lord's tidings about her brother, the Corvidian Duke. Sarovek looked so small. He could hardly believe this was the same knight that had dived through the air in shining armor and speared her enemies valiantly.

"She's not the one who can make those guarantees," Maxan said. He put his paw over the rhino's hand, pressing it down. He expected Sarovek to clack her beak and prick up her head, agitated by the idea someone could swoop in to save her. But gratitude showed in the hawk's eyes instead.

"When will we see him?" Chewgar asked. "Salastragore."

"Soon. Although I cannot say how long," she snapped quickly at Chewgar as the trio stepped off the elevator, pressing a firm taloned hand on his chest, cutting off his obvious question. "For now, the both of you have earned a long—and I hope satisfying—rest." She nodded at a pair of opposing doors at the end of the hallway. "I trust you will find the castle hospitable."

Prior to his tenure as a Crosswall guard, Maxan had found himself in affluent chambers plenty of times during his tenure as a Crosswall thief. But never before had his eyes beheld such lavish decadence.

This time, I'm even welcome *here!*

Upon first entering the suite of rooms that was to be his, his old instincts kicked in. *Those paintings, those books, those hangings, the basin, the chairs, the… that… even the bowl of fruit! There's enough loot here to overload Crosswall's black market for a month!*

The fox leapt as high as his tired legs could manage then let himself go slack as he drifted down toward the mattress. His suspicions were confirmed: the plush material molded to his form, letting him sink in slowly, gently, like how he'd imagined falling through a cloud as a young kit.

Now this, he thought, sinking deeply into the cushions, *is beyond value.*

Sarovek had shown the rhino to his rooms first across the hall. Chewgar clearly didn't have the former fox thief's knack for appraisal and only huffed at the decadence. Chewgar even frowned at the size of the bed, twice the normal Drakoran size, perhaps intended for visiting dignitaries of bulkier species. *If he ever decides to take the Leoran crown,* Maxan surmised, watching his friend's inspection of the environs, *he's probably in for disappointment.* Chewgar tossed Locain's greatsword upon the mattress and put his fists on his hips, pushing out his barrel chest and rotating his thick neck. He sighed with satisfaction as his aching joints popped. Sarovek said she would see to it that suitable clothing and trays of food would be brought up by the castle's servants. Finally, she encouraged the rhino to turn the handles over an enormous copper basin and see what happened. The smile was evident in the sound of her voice, if not in the unbending curve of her beak.

She'd told Maxan the same, and true to her word—no more than ten minutes since her departure—Maxan opened his door for two white-robed Drakoran attendants. A squat young frog boy trundled by him, balancing a covered, silver tray atop his splayed hands. A snake girl followed him, holding an assortment of neatly folded cloths, towels, and bedclothes and freshly pressed shirts and trousers. Her scales were the purest white, patterned by the deepest blood-red patterns, marking her from her brow, down her long neck, and onto her forearms.

There was no impulse in his animal nature that found her instinctually attractive, but nonetheless, Maxan knew she would be profoundly beautiful to her own species. As she laid the garments on the side table by his bed, her slitted red eyes flashed over to him. He realized then he'd been staring at her.

"Oh, ah..." He ran a paw across the amber fur on his head, between his fanned ears, and then down over his forearms. "I was just, admiring, your, ah, colors." He smiled awkwardly. "Mesmerizing."

The white snake lowered her eyes, bowing. Maxan saw then the blood-red skull written into the patterned scales of her head.

Then she stood upright again, gazing at him. "Thank you," she said quietly.

Maxan was blinking as he watched them go, not sure if what he saw was what he thought he saw. But when the door closed behind them, he quickly forgot all else in the world beside the silver tray. He practically ran to it.

His face wrinkled in revulsion, and he pinched his nostrils between two clawtips.

Eh... Drakoran food... So maybe the tales were true.

There were strings of what appeared to be some kind of swamp root arranged along the side of the plate, drizzled with a red sauce, a scoop of brown bits that could have been mistaken for mud, and a heavily spiced and thoroughly blackened wild field rodent. Everything was doused with some kind of gravy that looked—and smelled—no different than congealed blood. *It might very well BE this poor creature's blood!* The gravy was sprinkled with black lumps that might have once been flies.

Yeah... Those ARE flies...

He slammed the tray shut and raced to the door, hoping to catch the attendants. He flung it open, but there was nothing but the fragrant, sunlit hallway beyond.

Maxan returned to the tray, resolved to fill his stomach with the cloth napkin if nothing else, and he was thoroughly relieved when he found a hunk of greenish bread had been wrapped warmly in that napkin. A bowl of steaming vegetable broth appeared to be harmless as well. *Could be swamp-water...* He shrugged. Both were gone in seconds. He used the napkin to wipe the red sauce clean from the roots and downed those next, annoyed by how easily their fleshy threads wound up trapped in the gums between his fangs, but content with the taste all the same. He considered the brown scoop of *whatever that is*, but he decided there was no way he could clean the blood-fly sauce from it entirely.

He closed the lid on the crisp rodent carcass once and for all and hoped Chewgar had fared as successfully across the hall with whatever they served him. He picked at the roots in his teeth and strolled around the place, stopping at the edge of the copper basin and eyeing the handles along its rim, not much dissimilar from the control panel on the train.

A kind of euphoria like nothing he had experienced for a long time filled Maxan's very being as he watched the torrents of hot, clean water spill from the pipes under the handles. In the blink of an eye, he was stripped and plunging in.

Hours later, fed, cleaned, and dressed, Maxan sat by the tall, latticed window and took in the view. These rooms must have been at the very top of the castle's second tier, the highest level of its main structure. The flower-petal tower loomed over all, somewhere above and behind where he couldn't see, with its crane and spine-like ladder of rails. The view from the train, as it wound through the walls of the encircling cliff below, had given him no real sense of the thing's colossal scale. Judging by the length of the corridors they'd passed through to get to these rooms, and just how big these rooms were now that he was inside, Maxan realized that the tower was probably larger than the Mind's after all.

His mind wandered. His bushy tail swept lightly over the floor while his thoughts brushed lightly against concepts he'd only recently been made aware of and the impressions they'd left in his mind.

Rails, trains, towers... Wires, smoke, fire... Electricity, heat, prototype... and what exactly is an "airship?"

His window faced south, meaning little to no chance of seeing Yerda's rise as night crept slowly in. Of course, he'd been lucky enough to glimpse the

Aigaion as it passed lazily eastward, disappearing slowly over the horizon's rim. Instead of these, he was treated to an endlessly churning plume of black smoke from a huge stack below, carried thankfully away by the strong north wind at this altitude. Between the drifting curls of darkness, Maxan glimpsed the straight thoroughfares that divided the angular blocks of buildings comprising the Drakoran city surrounding the wide hole and the castle at its edge. Night was falling, and Yinna's fading light painted the sky a bloody orange and limned the whole world below in deep purple. Hundreds of windows were lighting up all across the city. Far beyond its borders, Maxan could see the brownish green Drakoran swamplands stretching flat and forever, its thousand shallow pools lighting up like eyes glowing in the fading light.

On the bridge just beneath his window, Maxan observed the day's final clusters of animals trudging across the castle's grand suspended bridge back to their city. These could be the factory workers whose shifts had ended, or the common Drakoran folk he'd seen lined up in cages, starving and waiting. For some reason, Maxan had always assumed ordinary life would be better anywhere else besides Crosswall.

But what did I really know then? About anything. What do I really know now?

He thought there would be more thoughts to follow him up. Some sarcastic comeback, then a heated debate with himself, one of his favorite pastimes. But instead, the questions lingered, stagnating in his brain, repeating again and again.

What do I really know?

What do I really know?

He could feel the presence of the other fox that lived in his mind. He was still there. But he was busy. Worried. Uneasy.

Maxan came away from the window and eased into a high-backed chair upholstered with rich-crushed velvet. An identical chair sat on the other side of an apotheosis board; the alignment of the opposing heroes' figurines suggested the two players had abandoned their match mid-game. The thick cloud of dust Maxan blew away from them suggested they'd abandoned it years and years ago. He picked up the closest hero immortally cast in pewter, a lobster or crab—Maxan wasn't sure which, only that the thing's claws were enormous—and examined the etching on the bottom.

R. N. Five.

He thought about how some animal had been made to delicately scratch the lines into the soft metal with the tip of his or her claw, probably before he was even born. Were the initials for a name? Or a title won in the arena? What did they stand for? *Maybe... Really Nice the Fifth. Renowned for his charitable contributions to the starving and destitute.* He could carry this RN back home in his pocket and ask around the center of the cross-shaped city. Maybe someone would know, someone would recall Really Nice the Fifth and his—*or her*—astonishing exploits at the center of battle on the blood-stained sands of the arena floor.

Or more likely, everyone has forgotten. The world has moved on.

Maxan scrutinized the apoth board, then set the lobster-crab hero RN the Fifth down in the safest spot he could find.

He eased back into the plush velvet and closed his eyes, felt the weight of his breath filling his body, focused on slowing his heartbeat. He searched for the line of deeper thinking that was obscured by the crowding impressions of his recent experience.

Where am I? Where are you? Where am I... Where am I really?

There it was. He heard its voice, exactly like his own voice. *I've been here before,* it said.

"Ha!" Maxan laughed aloud, feeling his grip on his subconscious unease slipping away as he did. "That's funny."

And with that, the presence was gone. He couldn't find it again.

And so I'm alone. In a room. Talking to myself.

The thoughts had gone silent. His heartbeat quickened, returning to its normal rhythm, maybe a little faster. He looked around again at his luxurious surroundings. He felt the lightness of the fresh bedclothes brush against his fur. He dug his claw points into the soft fabric of the chair's arms and breathed deep of the incense that wafted in the air from the lamps overhead.

"Nope. I've never been here before." He spoke to no one, though he wasn't sure whether he believed himself.

The room had revitalized him for a time, and it had felt good to let go. But now all of the jumbled realities surged again upon his consciousness.

Feyn. Chewgar. Rinnia. Pryth and Pram. The Monitors, the Mind, the relay. The king is dead. The Aigaion. Tomb of the gods.

Epimetheus. The game.

Folgian and bane. Harmony and the lightning. The pillars of light. The fire. The assassins. Yovan. My mother.

My father.

My father. Who I never knew.

Your father, Max.

There it was. He felt it. The voice. As if it had camouflaged itself against the patterns in his mind, and suddenly moved, detached itself. Turned to speak to him.

Was he there? Your father. Where you grew up? In your mother's den?

No. No he…

Maxan felt all the rage at his life's misfortunes rising in him. Feelings he hadn't allowed since his very first days in Crosswall. Memories he'd pushed far, far down, which he'd thought he'd crushed into nothing.

He wasn't there. When they came for it. Whoever he was, he left us there, by the river, with what they wanted. He may not have killed her, but he let her die.

Maxan shot forward and crashed his fist onto the apotheosis board, rattling all the heroes that had stood their ground for so long, toppling some, shifting others, ruining the unknown players' long-abandoned game. The sudden pain in his wrist brought him out of his dark thoughts. He rubbed at it with his other paw, let out a deep breath. He forced a smirk onto his face and laughed at his own stupidity.

"Why the hell am I thinking about this?" he asked no one. "Why now? Really, Maxan?!"

He must have realized that there had been enough talking to himself for one day. "Enough talking for a lifetime," he said aloud, then shook his head, incredulous that he had let the thought slip into sound.

"I'm just tired," he told himself, rolling his eyes.

"I'm going crazy."

If he had someone to talk to… If he wasn't alone, perhaps… He looked at the chamber door and thought of Chewgar, but then he looked at the soft bed beckoning him and thought better of it. He needed sleep. All he needed was sleep.

Hours later, when sleep would still not come, he found the relay where he had hidden it behind a row of books. He held it against his chest, staring vacantly at the high ceiling, where the thing's racing golden beads of light cast shimmering waves like light against water.

He tried to forget the same patterns on the trees by the river.

Somehow, he was in the hallway outside his own door. The scent of mint and eucalyptus, stirred by midnight air flowed through the mirror vents.

He turned the latch and flew inside. The only light was the dim glow cast by the fire, fed by gas piped in from the walls. She must have set the valve too low.

She shifted under the coverings on the bed. He'd disturbed her in his rush.

But he knew now there was no time to be quiet. No time for anything anymore.

We have to go.

He weaved through the fine furniture and stood over the bed. Her back was turned. He reached out his right paw and touched her shoulder. *The warmth of her… So familiar.* He fought back the tears, then forgot them entirely.

My fur. On my right paw. On my arm. It's not burned. How?

She woke fully, then. Turning over. Opening her eyes.

Green eyes. My mother's eyes.

It's her.

He saw then the swell of her belly.

It's… she's…

"Vess," he whispered, the sound of his own voice belonged to a stranger. He felt the panic seizing him. The sweat began to dampen and chill his fur. "We must leave. Now." He ripped the blankets away. He had not meant to be so harsh. Nor to sound so afraid.

But I am. I am afraid.

"We have to go, Vess."

"Why? Have you gone crazy?"

"We have to leave now. Tonight."

"But why?"

She sat up now. Vess. She cradled her pregnant belly with both arms, protectively.

"You're scaring me."

You should be scared. He knows. He's found out what I've done. What I've taken. But I've stopped him. I've sealed it away. I've closed the Gate. Forever. But we have to go. There's a key. He's the key, but he doesn't know it. He won't know it. I hope he never has to know it. Oh, what have I done? What was I thinking? W*e have to get out of here. This place isn't safe anymore. He may be listening right now. The machines in the walls. His eyes everywhere. He knows what I've done. That I've betrayed him. They're coming for us.*

But all he said was "Shhh… shhh… Vess, listen. Please. There's a place I've prepared. A den, where you and the boy will be safe."

Her green eyes narrowed. "Boy? How do…"

This is a dream.

No, not a dream. A memory.

Your memory. And your shame.

The greatest shame of my life.

"You, you..." Vess stammered. "The *two of you*... You *played* with him, didn't you? *The boy?* What did you do?" She moved away from his touch. He would never touch her again.

"I'm sorry, Vess. I'm so sorry." He knew she would never forgive him. He knew she would never understand if he spoke the next words. But he said them anyway. "It was the only way."

He was up a moment later, unable to stand the silence. There was no time for it. He was filling a travel sack with her clothes, medicines, maps.

And this.

The relay. He pulled it from the hidden pocket by his hip. Its light bathed the room in shimmering, shifting gold.

Without this, the signal dies. The game ends. Everything remembers its true nature. And returns.

There was a knock at the door.

They're here.

He closed his eyes tight.

But he couldn't keep out the light.

His body jerked forward, almost sending him crashing to the floor. He gripped the wooden frame of the bed, squeezing the coverings in his sweating paws. His eyes darted frantically around.

Same room. Light. Morning light.

He winced at the whiteness spilling in from the window. He raised his furless right arm, examining it like he'd never seen it before, rediscovering grooves and scars left by fire.

The knock came again. Louder. On the other side, a deep, muffled voice said something.

My name? Maxan?

He picked up the shining metal tube from where it lay beside him. Sometime in the night, the relay's yellow lights must have gone out. The only thing he saw in its chrome surface was a distorted reflection of his own mismatched eyes staring back at him. *One gold. One green, like hers...*

"Hey!" The knock became a bang. The voice shouted. "I'm coming in!"

Chewgar's fist crushed through the wood, blasting two of three hinges clean off the frame. He had enough leverage to reach in and toss the rest out into the hall behind him as he exploded into Maxan's room.

The fox had pulled the covers close under his chin, sitting upright, unsure what to do.

"Oh. That's just swell, Max." Chewgar threw up a hand in embarrassment. "Glad to see you're getting your beauty rest. Do you realize what time it is?"

Maxan peered around the room. There was the copper wash basin, still full of the filthy water he hadn't figured out how to drain. The tray of Drakoran leftovers was still on the table, still covered. His trail-worn clothing was draped on the back of the chair just beside it, still where he had left it.

It was all different. None of it the same as in the dream.

Is this the same room? Did any of it happen?

"You all right, fox?" Chewgar watched his friend pad gingerly to the fireplace without saying a word, gripping the relay tightly in one paw, the other feeling around in the soot.

Maxan dusted away the mound obscuring the pipe. He rocked back on his heels and saw the small valve set into the alcove, practically invisible. *Unless you know it was there.*

The voice of reason was silent. He urged it to respond. *Say something. Anything.* He closed his eyes and reached inside his feelings, searching for its presence like he had the day before. *Was I just imagining it all? Were you trying to warn me?* Still nothing. He reached for pieces of the dream, but they were like shards of a broken window, tumbling out into the abyss of forgetfulness. He brushed only against the fear, cold and biting. He let go and opened his eyes.

"Maxan," Chewgar said. He repeated the question slowly, one word after another. "Are you all right?"

"I..."

What do I say? Yes, I'm fine? No, I'm not? I'm not me? Or I wasn't me in a dream, but now I'm me again?

The fox inhaled deeply, then sneezed, forgetting he was kneeling in a mound of soot. Coughing and backing away, he finally said, "I'm fine." Another cough. "I mean, I have to be. Right?"

Chewgar smirked. "That makes two of us." The rhino's bulky frame seemed severely out of place in the castle's lavish accommodations. His eyes swept around the room and up to the ceiling, bringing the tip of his great horn around in an arc. Then he glanced back to the hallway behind him. "Think they'll be mad about the door?"

"Probably."

Chewgar shrugged. His footsteps shook the furniture and rattled the lid of the food tray as he crossed to the table. He scooped up the pile of fresh clothing from where the white snake had laid it and tossed it at Maxan, the trousers draping fully over the fox's head. "Get dressed. I'll wait outside." He stomped to the door and turned, still smirking. "That's an order."

Maxan followed his captain's directive to the letter. The fresh white shirt and dark trousers were incredibly comfortable, and the relay fit perfectly in a deep pocket at his hip. He frowned at the filthy drab-colored clothing that he had worn here—the shirt and trousers that Saghan had given him when they set out from the Monitors' hideout in Crosswall. He felt the same way about the tattered hooded cloak and his short sword, both remnants of the shadow's work he'd done, skulking around on the great city's rooftops.

Observe. Report. Never engage.

He'd seen too much at this point, and he'd decided to do what he could for what he knew was right. He wasn't who he used to be. And it wasn't these things that made him who he was now. But they were trophies, of a sort, that he'd earned along the way. Maxan threw the cloak around his shoulders and belted the weapon at his side.

"Did they call for us?" He fell into step behind Chewgar.

"No, surprisingly."

"Then where are we going?"

They came to a fork in the passage. Chewgar cut to the left like he knew where he was going.

"Beats me. But I guarantee you, somewhere in here there's breakfast."

Maxan felt the grumbling in his stomach and wondered if it was from hunger alone. He tugged the rhino's shirt sleeve, which was just as clean and fresh as his own, but six times larger. Chewgar came to a halt just under a massive oil painting depicting the majestic, mountain aeries of Corvidia and two grand armies viciously battling in the valley below.

"Chewgar. Something's not right."

"Tell me," the rhino breathed, taking a knee and drawing his face closer to Maxan's.

"I... don't know what..."

"We're both very far from home. Crosswall was all either of us had ever known." Chewgar laid his hand on Maxan's shoulder, drawing the fox's nervous gaze to his own. "And coming here, we barely escaped with our lives." He held up two fingers and chuckled. "Twice. But we're alive. Feyn's alive. Sarovek's alive. Pryth and Pram, I know they're alive."

And Rinnia? he wanted to say but held his tongue.

"And maybe even more important than that," Chewgar went on, "we've done it. *You've* done it."

Maxan looked quizzically at his friend. "Done what?"

"It's all because of you, Max. As your captain, I've always told you to observe, report, never engage. But more than that, as your oldest friend, I told you that because I couldn't stand to see you hurt. I know now that I should have trusted you more. Because you acted. *You* brought us here, Max. With everything you told me that happened, you could've followed your captain's orders and just given up and run back to the guardhouse."

"Limped back," Maxan corrected, feeling a little embarrassed at all this sudden praise, but unable to suppress his smile all the same.

"But you didn't. You went after it." Chewgar's eyes lowered to the pocket that held the relay. "And even after you came back, later on, you could've let Rinnia go. But you chased her. And you saved my life. And you saved Pram and Pryth and Feyn. Now we're here, and you're going to save everyone else. *Everyone* else." He squeezed Maxan's shoulder. He looked straight into the fox's eyes. "Because of you, the Stray can be who they really are again. They *will* be.

"And I want you to know something else," Chewgar went on. Now his eyes fell to the floor, contemplatively. He ground his flat teeth, chewing over his next words carefully. It was something he must've thought hard about saying, but now the time had come.

"What is it?" Maxan prompted.

"When we get home," the rhino began slowly. "I will take the crown." His gaze was serious, but there was also a plea in his eyes. "You didn't run from anything you probably wanted to run from. So I won't either. But..." He prodded the fox's chest suddenly with a thick finger. "You're going to help me. Be my *grand chancellor* or whatever. And that's an order."

Maxan felt the waves of emotion rolling through him. Gratitude, humility, pride. And of course, elation, sorrow, and fear. They washed against one another so much that he didn't know how he felt about any of this.

Grand Chancellor Maxan?

"We're going to tear down the arena, the mansions, the palace, all the barricades and walls keeping Crosswall apart, and we're going to build something new in its place. I was thinking freshwater canals. And bridges. Lots of bridges." Chewgar smiled at the vision of a new city.

Then Chewgar—*King* Chewgar—offered Maxan his hand. "I'm just as scared as you are."

Maxan nodded. He put his tiny paw in the rhino's palm. Chewgar's hand folded over it, giving it a gentle shake.

"You know," Maxan began after the solemn silence that followed. "I'd never have been able to do any this without you throwing me at rooftops and things all the time."

"Or smashing the boars and bugs about to slice your head off."

"Yeah. That too."

Chewgar turned his neck and pretended to admire the painting, working his jaw, grinding his flat teeth softly as though chewing on what else he wanted to say.

Maxan figured he knew what the rhino wanted. "I don't know about you, but I couldn't stomach half of the stuff they brought me last night. Let's find something to eat."

"Right? I think that was blood."

"And flies. Did you at least find the bread in the napkin?"

"What! There was bread?!"

Maxan laughed harder than he had in what seemed a very long time. He thought about suggesting they turn back to retrieve the starving rhino's hunk of bread, but the two pressed on through the corridors of the Drakoran castle, utterly lost, yet confident of the right direction.

Chapter Six
The Master's Workshop

MAXAN AND CHEWGAR NEVER FOUND ANYTHING RESEMbling a kitchen or even a dining hall. They went up and down stairwells, some curving around what they assumed were the castle's outer wall, while some others were set into the hall where one might think to find a door. The interior made no sense. They passed dozens of rooms of all shapes and sizes that seemed to serve no apparent purpose besides storage. Crates and boxes, tables and chairs, jars and bottles and sheets of glass, every room seemed to have a mound of junk covered by tarps so thick with dust, it was obvious they had not been moved for years.

The whole place is abandoned. As if there had once been more Monitors here.

It was quickly becoming apparent that their lavish guest chambers must have been the only two like them in the entire castle. The halls leading to them had also been one of a kind, considering the spaces they found themselves now were completely void of all decoration. There were no hanging plants, no mirrors to bring light, no scents other than the staleness of dust.

They wandered like this, back and forth through identical corridors and up and down more flights of stairs, for half an hour before Saghan abruptly materialized from around a corner and beckoned them. His dark, high-collared leather armor was the same as before, but there were no traces of the damage or dried blood. However, the snake had his long, thin sword strapped at his side. He didn't seem displeased at all to find the two Leorans wandering aimlessly in his castle. Maxan had the sense that Saghan might have even been shadowing them until just that moment.

"Ressst well?" he hissed.

"Sure," Chewgar answered. "But the food—"

"Later," Saghan cut in. "The master has asked for you." His slitted eyes fell to the short sword Maxan wore. His forked tongue lashed at the air, then he turned and strode down the hall.

Maxan realized just then that Chewgar had left Locain's greatsword behind. He didn't know if it was considered rude to bring a weapon to your host's table. Perhaps that was what Saghan's glance had been about.

The spearpoint pain pricked at the inside of his head behind his golden right eye. It had been some days since he'd last felt it, and it had been much worse then. Unbearable, in fact. He knew now that it was some sort of signal, that it meant his inner voice was trying to tell him something but couldn't find what it was it wanted to say. He lagged behind, his gaze locked vacantly on graystone bricks laid in the floor, at the flowing of the lines along their seams, like they were leading somewhere. It didn't help. He couldn't focus. The pain spread and blossomed like thick blood dripped into water.

What is it? Tell me.

He thought of the first time he'd known this pain. When he and Chewgar had crossed the Mind's bridge and stepped through the threshold of the Pinnacle Tower, and how it had screamed in his brain as he handed the relay over to the great-horned owl with the abyssal black eyes, Principal Harmony. He'd wanted so badly to be rid of it then.

Do I still want it gone? But it's not going away. It's going home. Somehow. Feyn believed the Monitors can take it back. To the Aigaion.

He remembered everything he'd said to Chewgar in the cave.

And like that, the pain was gone. He found the means to push it down.

"Max," Chewgar called back from several paces further down the hall.

"I'm right there, just..." He shook his head. "Just tired still, after everything."

"And hungry," the rhino added with a glance in his Drakoran host's direction.

The three of them walked on in silence, then descended three levels of a stairwell that the rhino and fox had somehow missed in their exploration. It was almost like the hall leading to it hadn't been there before. They landed in a corridor that seemed long enough to span the entire length of the second tier of the castle.

In fact, it is. A dozen high vertical window slits extended to the high ceiling and ran all along the left wall to the end, while the right wall was only half as tall, nothing more than a panel separating this narrow passage from the grand space behind it. They turned a sharp angle and walked another equal length. A third turn brought them around the end of the shorter panel wall and into a massive cube of a room, whose volume easily surpassed that of the castle's grand entrance hall.

None of the fox's wildest imaginings could have matched the wonders he saw in the master's workshop. Rows and rows of scratched, stained, and charred oak tables stretched the length of the immense room, some straight, some askew, a few flipped over crushing a mess of metal and glass. Fine blades, thick hammers, delicate pincers and tongs and other tools of all kinds were carelessly strewn about every surface next to piles of bolts and nails and wires of various metals. Buckets of discarded scrap and detritus were arranged regularly at the end of each table, most of which overflowed onto the floor so that Maxan had to step gingerly to avoid hurting himself. The stacks everywhere made it impossible to see over to the next row, and certainly not where they were going, but Saghan seemed to know the way by heart.

Stacks of papers spilled onto the floor, and besides these, the pages of open books flittered and turned themselves in the gusts of hot wind that rose from a series of wide chutes that opened in the floor. These were surrounded by metal rods and chain railings, perhaps to save an oblivious visitor from falling to his doom in the factories' fires below.

Several large sheets of paper had been nailed into tall wooden easels. Each of these depicted highly detailed drawings and designs in blue ink set over a square grid. Another showed the dimensions of a triangle, the Aigaion, with calculations and annotations scribbled in the margins. From this distance, one of these schematics, in particular, seemed to illustrate the rails to nowhere that rose from the station below.

There were so many machines. Everywhere he looked, it seemed that some frame or cage or wheel was riveted onto some iron beam or molded into the graystone wall itself. Thick chains from the high-vaulted ceiling draped over floor-mounted wheels. There were cranks and levers for everything, many of them marked with flaking or faded paint. Pipes and wires of all different widths and colors poked through holes in the graystone walls like hair follicles and ran away in bunches along the floor to supply power to all the workshop's technology.

Maxan saw that other tables held raised beds of soil with twisting glass pipes dripping concoctions of all different colors onto plants and fungal growths at all stages of life, from carefully scrutinized newborns to utterly neglected withering decay. Jars of clouded glass sat on shelves along the lower inside wall of the cube. These were labeled with yellowing, curling strips of paper, each filled to the brim with dull-colored, brackish liquids.

Maxan gave one of these jars a second glance as they wound their way toward an aisle that would take them to the workshop's center. He realized at once what the innumerable, spherical objects were.

Eyes.

His abdomen convulsed, tugging him forward, retching dryly. But he managed to stay standing. He was glad to have not eaten breakfast after all. He doubted he would ever want to eat again.

Before turning into what seemed to be the central aisle of the workshop, they passed one final jar so large that it rested on a wheeled platform with its tiny stepping stool beside it. Multicolored tubes and wires ran from adjacent machinery through rubber-sealed holes in its side and disappeared into the murky green liquid within. Maxan, still recovering from the previous jar he could never unsee, peered into it, sensing some solid bulk coiled up and suspended at its core.

Is that … a creature?

He rushed away, joining Chewgar and Saghan who had paused to wait.

The center of the room was clear relative to its surroundings, only because it was ringed by mountains of clutter that had been shoveled to the fringes. Four of the thickest chains were pulled taut, suspending the weight of a circular platform level with the floor. A stained canvas tarp had been thrown over most of whatever machine rested there. As Maxan drew closer, he saw several gleaming, chrome blades peeking out under the tarp's edge. There was a whirring sound, and the machine twitched. The blades scraped on the platform as they drew back beneath the tarp.

Maxan knew what it was. *The Thraxian in the factory.*

"Hmm. I didn't hear you come in."

The red-scaled snake had been bent so far over the closest oak table, blending in among all the clutter. Now he swiveled in a stool to face them and stood, his long neck extending high over his shoulders.

Besides the age of their bodies and the color of their scales, Salastragore was a copy of Saghan in every respect. But whereas Saghan's green skin was still smooth and undamaged by time, Salastragore's was mottled with deep brown age spots. Patches of his skin molted in places, and he had long ago abandoned the endeavor to keep up appearances and strip them away. A blacksmith's apron covered his otherwise bare chest, and a fur-mantled gray robe draped over his thin, bony shoulders, the sleeves of which had been rolled up while he worked. His V-shaped head dipped in a kind of bow, and when he raised it again, Maxan recognized the flicker in the Master Monitor's orange left eye, identical in every way to Saghan's. His right eye was gone. The brow above it marked by a precise surgical scar.

"I am Salastragore. Welcome to my castle." There was something unnerving about his voice, his energetic tone. Maxan realized instantly what it was.

He doesn't hiss like other snakes.

"You must be Maxan. And you Chewgar. Please consider this place your home." Salastragore followed the line of Maxan's nervous glance to the tarp. The good-eyed side of the snake's head led his sight so that he never looked at anything straight on. "Hmm? Oh, this old girl? My apologies. Her … *organic* body gave out long ago, you see, but we weren't quite ready to part ways with her. So I made her a new one."

There was a pause. Saghan had found a somewhat clutter-free side table to lean on. Salastragore nodded proudly at the thing under the tarp, while Maxan and Chewgar exchanged a glance.

"A new *body*?" Chewgar asked.

"Hmm. Yes. See for yourselves."

Salastragore paced to the tarp and flung it up with a flourish, revealing a mass of insect pincers that were half carapace, half shining steel. These were attached to layered steel plates bolted to the underside of a thorax that was at least ten times larger than the Thraxian ant soldiers Maxan had encountered at the Denland station.

"I managed to preserve the womb," Salastragore mused proudly. "Otherwise, what's the point, yes?" The red snake seemed taken aback when he noticed his guests didn't appear to share his enthusiasm for such a feat. "Hmm, my apologies, again. Perhaps we're not ready for this part of the interview."

He replaced the tarp, then threw a switch just outside the ring of the round platform. The giant motors suspended overhead whirred to life and dropped the whole thing steadily below the floor. Four triangular apertures cranked loudly into place over the gaping hole, leaving just enough space for the chains to continue their work.

"Now then," Salastragore said, barely audible against the clanking of the chains. He stood at the center of the closed aperture, rolling his eye, counting in his head until the thing stopped at last. "Now then, as I was saying, I believe you have something for me?"

Maxan swallowed. He tried to calm his nerves. He'd chosen to be here, to come this far. There was no going back. His voice of reason was silent … as he'd predicted it would be. And even if it had something clever to say, maybe he was through listening.

I have the relay.

Yet he could not say the words.

A few seconds passed while Maxan hesitated, but Salastragore's broad smile never weakened. "It's all right," he said. "Hold onto it for a while longer. Until you feel you can trust us." He motioned to a bench nearby, and after the two Leorans were seated, he took his place again on the stool. Saghan leaned on the table still, staring listlessly at the floor. "Now then, I heard one of the wolf's little twits claimed that Rinnia tried to take it from you?"

Saghan must have told him, Maxan reasoned.

"That's right," he said, finding his voice. "I was there." He hadn't anticipated ever having to explain what happened. His brain worked quickly to form a lie.

"Why would she do that?"

"Trust issues…"

Great answer. The chiding voice in his head was Maxan's own. He flashed his best smile and felt it calm his nerves.

Salastragore merely blinked, and his forked tongue whipped the air a few times. The silence hung. "Elaborate," he commanded gravely.

"Once I'd snatched the relay, she might have thought I would betray her and give it to King Locain and take the lion up on his offer. An estate. A title. Servants. Money. All that fancy stuff. He wanted to use it as a kind of weapon, some kind of leverage he could finally hold over the Mind. Rinnia must have heard him say so when we were in the station, but then the scorpion came, and the ants, and everything went crazy. And she attacked me before I could turn his offer down. I don't blame her."

Salastragore's single orange eye narrowed. The effect was unsettling.

Maxan had always found it best to just power through confidently when his old marks gave him that look of doubt. He did so now. "Ah, I suppose it didn't help matters that the squirrel set her on fire a bit before I had a chance to explain. And then she ran off, and we haven't seen her since. Do you think… maybe she's…" When a con started to tip off course, it was always best to steer it in a new direction. Maxan was gratified to see the old strategies apparently still worked.

"Rinnia's well. Resting. Here, now, in her room." He was smiling again.

Maxan focused all his will on keeping his features still upon hearing the news. Part of him was reeling, the other part was relieved.

"At least I *told* her to rest, but if foxes are anything, they're stubborn." Salastragore's lips curled then parted madly. He had an open-jaw smile, like a silent scream frozen in time. His two venomous fangs folded outward menacingly. "By their very natures, it seems. In their blood perhaps. But, if there's one thing you can *train* a fox to do well, it's watching." Salastragore's long finger pointed upward, and his orange eye shifted to the ceiling.

Maxan shuddered and craned his neck up and around, expecting to see her dangling inches above his head maybe with a blade pointed between his shoulder blades, but there was nothing. He turned back at the sound of the red snake's laughter.

"Haaa! Hmm, oh! Pardon me, friends! It has been so long since we've entertained Leoran guests here!"

Is he lying to us? Is Rinnia actually here? Maxan stole a few more glances upward while the snake finished his merriment, darting his eyes around the iron beams bracing the stone ceiling.

Chewgar was next to speak. "We're not your only Leoran guests."

"You mean Feyn. My, my. What did you boys do to my old white wolf? I'm joking of course! Another joke. Yes, I tended to Feyn immediately upon your arrival. Personally, I saw to it. Saghan did a fine job administering what we call *triage* as you were traveling. He told me everything that happened. Fine work, fine work." Salastragore twisted at his narrow waist without getting up from the stool, and he stretched his slender arm outward as if to present his son on a stage. The red-scaled snake gave his best impression of a prideful smile, but Maxan saw it easily enough for what it was. Saghan's eyes remained fixed on the floor. He picked absent-mindedly at the dirt in his long black nails.

"Eh, *lightning bolts*, was it? Nasty stuff, what these callers can do, hmm? I'm afraid there are parts of Feyn's body that will never sprout fur again. Seems, my friend, you'd know something about that, wouldn't you?"

Salastragore nodded at the fox's right paw.

Maxan didn't know what to say. *So give him a bit of the theatrical,* he decided. *He seems to enjoy it enough.*

He waved his paw around a bit, flexing his claws open and balling them into a fist. "Who needs fur anyway?"

He didn't have to see Chewgar's grimace to know it was there. Salastragore seemed to wince, the brille over his one good eye snapping shut as he stared at Maxan.

"Haa!" The sudden burst of laughter echoed around the workshop. "Haaaah! *Who needs fur* he says! Wonderful. Just wonderful. I'd've thought of that one myself if you'd given me time. I like you, fox. I really, really do. Hmm.

"Oh, well, yes. Moving on then. Or should I say, moving back to Feyn. So, yes, his condition has improved dramatically. He's talking again. Why, just this morning at dawn he asked after the both of you. He's very thankful you brought him here. We shall go see him together very soon."

"He wanted to bring it to you, you know," Maxan said. "Feyn put himself in great danger to retrieve it from the Mind. To bring it all this way himself and personally deliver it."

"Well, with the wolf out of the picture for the time being, I suppose... *you two* will just have to do." Salastragore's eye flitted eagerly over every fold in the fox's clothing. Searching.

How can I choose what's good when I don't know what's true?

The words came to mind from nowhere. He'd spoken them to Rinnia in what would be the last part of their discussion on the point of existence, or something, and she'd had her swordpoint leveled at his throat. Before that, she'd met with the mysterious octopus, the rain so loud he could not hear their words. Then they were walking, and she told him none of this was real, that his life wasn't worth anything, that he would die without making a difference.

She tried to kill me for the relay. To keep it from him. What did she know?

Maxan wished he had the courage to ask if he could see her, right now, before doing anything. He wished he could whistle and she would be there to roll her eyes at him and call him an idiot and tell him what it was about the Monitors and the relay that was just so awful anyway.

Maybe I can stall a bit. And she'll get here. Maybe...

Salastragore's forked tongue flicked the air. The tip of his whip-like tail tapped the stone floor. Chewgar rubbed his hands together. Everyone looked at Maxan. Even Saghan had stopped picking at his nails.

"Ah, I'm hoping maybe you can tell me something first, your, uh, grace."

Salastragore sneered. "Really? Grace?"

"Yeah. Is that—"

"Just, no. Don't. What is it you want?"

"I want you to tell me about Epimetheus."

A sudden fire lit in the snake's widening eye, but it wasn't fueled by fury. It was shock. Salastragore turned away, attempting and failing to seem casual. He fiddled with the dials of some instruments. Now he was stalling.

"What is it?" Maxan prodded.

"Now, now," he said at last. "I'm at a loss for words, boy. You must understand. I want to answer your question and tell you what I know. What *little* I know, of course, I mean. But, what was it you called it, *Epimetheus*, is quite literally our most closely guarded secret. Not even Saghan knows about Epimetheus. Do you, Saghan? No? See then? Why, I'd all but forgotten it myself! Ha!

"Listen," he said, spinning around on the stool, his slender hands gesticulated erratically as he rambled on. "It's something to do with the *old* Monitors, you see? Us old farts… Folgian and myself, and… It was my understanding that it was her intention to take all such knowledge we once guarded with her to the great beyond. Or whatever nonsense she believed. But no." His V-shaped head lowered ominously at Maxan, and he looked the fox straight on. A bony finger pointed accusingly at his chest. "She told *you*, didn't she? She didn't tell and of her servants who wiped her dribbling poison mouth, she didn't tell her bird friend or her wolf friend, the three of them so close after all, hmm? No, no. She told *you.* Some thief scaling her wall in the night!

"Ahh, but you two are looking at me like I'm crazy!" Salastragore threw up his hands and let out a deep sigh, then slapped them down on his knees with a kind of finality.

It's a game with him. Maxan understood, watching the red snake's unpredictable behaviors play out. Somehow, Salastragore felt familiar, as if there was no one else in this world he'd known better. Maxan *expected* the Master Monitor to be dodgy, somehow knew he *would* be even though they'd never met.

"You're not crazy," Maxan said flatly, returning Salastragore's ominous gaze as best he could. He'd emphasized the word precisely as intended. It wasn't a reassurance like the snake had baited him for. It was an observation. "You're *not* crazy," he said again. "And no, Folgian didn't tell me about Epimetheus. If you want to know the truth, I saw it scrawled on a plaque or something deep underground." It took every ounce of his willpower not to commit the most basic liar's tells, to look away, down and to the left, to quiver his lips or wiggle his snout. Maxan stared hard, straight ahead, watching the fire behind the orange eye flickering.

"Just tell me."

Salastragore returned his stare in equal measure. The two of them sat locked like that for only a few seconds, but for Maxan it was a few eternities. Then something broke open in Maxan's chest, spread like poison in his blood. *He knows.* The fire flickered brightly in the slitted orange eye. *He knows I'm lying.* Now his willpower turned against him, locking him rigid on the bench, the poison hardening in his veins like ice. *I'm afraid.*

The eye of Salastragore spoke wordlessly, saying, *Who are you, boy? To think YOU could lie to ME?*

And then it was all over. The fire went out. The snake flung his hands up and brought them slapping down again. His eye rolled; his mouth gaped its fanged, silent-scream smile. "Ahh who cares? You're going to find out anyway, aren't you? Crafty, just like a fox. Well done. First, if I may, let me tell you how utterly ironic I find it that you found the code for the entire project *scrawled* as you say on a *plaque* down there. Incredible! The bungling idiots! That's why I had to get rid of all of them.

"You want to know about Epimetheus?" Before getting an answer, he swiveled on his chair to whip his head around to Chewgar, to Saghan, and back to Maxan. "And you wanna know? And you? Great. Wonderful. We all want to know then. Here goes...

"Epimetheus was a god, my boys. He gave us all our little gifts. Do you know that I smell with my tongue?" And he flicked it wildly as if to prove it. "Hmm, yes. Saghan too. All us snakes. And you, look at your little ears. Spin them around for me. Why, I bet if you wanted to you could hear the clanging and banging far down below us as the sound wafts up through those high windows there. Good for you. And our big friend here, why... Epimetheus gave him his horn to skewer invaders and other such ne'er-do-wells. Not to mention his size, comparable to yours. So how would you survive in a fight against *all that muscle,* hmm? I mean if the two of you *had* to fight. Well, perhaps Epimetheus gave you your wits, boy!

"I know, I know. None of that tells you why his name was, again as you say, *scrawled* on the wall down there. Well then, I'll tell you that Epimetheus is also what we Monitors called this grand experiment oh so long ago when we were first building all this place up. That's right! We're far older than we look! The curves of the Peskoran beaches," the red snake lifted a hand and glided it along an imaginary vertical curve only he could see, "ahh, like that, we shaped it so. The dunes and the wind force gales that scour the Thraxian wastes," and his fingers turned some invisible dials, "we cranked those up just so! The tides. The hills and valleys. The forests and trees and rivers. The clouds. All of it! We laid it all out. That was Epimetheus too. And when we were done, we needed *people*, you know? To walk around it all and... I guess... put up fruit stalls and sell fruit. And, yeah, smile and talk...

"And stab each other to death. That is of course only if they wanted to. But it was the funnest part of the whole thing. Who wouldn't want to stab your best friend in the back and leave his body bleeding out in an alley? If you could get away with it. And I'm not talking time in jail or being executed as a punishment. No, no. I mean, if you could *really* get away with it. If you didn't have to ...*feel it* ... weighing you down.

"Now that," Salastragore spoke very slowly, "*that* was Epimetheus."

The silence was incredible. It hung so thick in the air it was hard to breathe. Gradually, the low thrumming of electricity and tinkling of chains and indeed the clanging of hammers upon iron that drifted through the windows seemed to resume.

"Okay?" Salastragore said, clapping his hands and holding them there.

No, not really, Maxan wanted to say. But he knew at this point that Salastragore would only provide non-answers to all his questions, or worse, see through all the lies he could make up to defend why he was asking.

Perhaps Chewgar knew that too, which was why he took over. "And what about the Stray then? All these animals started losing their minds and the whole thing fell apart? It's still falling apart. It's the one thing you can't control."

"Indeed, my big friend," Salastragore answered immediately. "None of us can! Not without..." The sentence hung purposefully incomplete. His long neck swung his head around, bringing the left side of his face and his one good eye to search all over Maxan yet again.

The fox brought out the relay at last. The lights were still out. It seemed so very small a thing just then.

"This will stop the Stray?"

"Oh. Yes." Salastragore's slitted eye fixated on the glimmering chrome object in the fox's paw. "And so much more, don't you see? Poverty. Famine. Pollution. Injustice. War. Hatred. With this, we can build a perfect world. A perfect galaxy." The snake reached out his hand, quivering. He seemed to forget everything else in existence for that one brief moment.

"How does it work?"

Salastragore's gaze snapped up at Maxan, the hypnosis obviously broken. His hand dropped to his side, and he cleared his throat.

"Hmm, well, there's quite a bit of science involved you see. Radiation. Magnetism. Radio waves. Neurology. Genetic manipulation. Things I'm not so sure even the Mind would be willing or able to teach you about. Even if old Folgian had wanted to. If she weren't so dead now. Well, hmm, let me try to explain anyway. Take a different approach."

Salastragore stood and whirled about, clasping his slender fingers behind his back and pacing toward the large schematic of the Aigaion nailed over a nearby bookshelf. His head was lowered beyond the fringe of fur lining the top of his robe. Maxan saw that his hands were fidgeting as he spoke.

"It's like this... Do any of you believe we have... *souls?*"

For the first time, Saghan raised his head and stared at his master's back across the space. Maxan was caught off guard as he'd been expecting more ravings to define the snake's list of so-called sciences. The definition of the "soul," and whether or not Herbridians had them, was something he and Chewgar sometimes debated on the watchtower of the guardhouse, gazing up at Yerda's Belt and a blanket of stars. Neither of them knew where the concept or even the word itself had come from.

"I do," the fox asserted, all the same. Chewgar, who often played the dissenter in their discussions, frowned at him but kept his dissent quiet.

"Hmm. And so how *many* souls do our bodies carry?"

"Just one… I suppose. Our soul is our identity. It's *who we are.*" Maxan looked at Chewgar hard, as he had so many times on those nights, trying to drive the point in once and for all.

"Hmm," Salastragore said, his back still turned. "Who we are? Identity? And what *shapes* your identity, Maxan?"

"Your choices," the fox said immediately.

"Excellent answer!" Salastragore spun around and clapped his hands together, the sound loud enough to echo throughout the workshop. "Excellent. *YOU*, boy, *you* are different from every other fox—every other Herbridian—that you've probably ever known. Because you've *chosen* differently. Our nations, our races, our species, even our *environment*—NONE of these define us. Would you agree?"

Maxan realized then that Saghan was watching him intently, his arms now crossed, holding himself perfectly still. "Not entirely," Maxan went on. "Sometimes choices are made for us. Even ones we're never aware of."

"*Especially* ones we're never aware of. Very good, Maxan. I see the old bear could put forth quite an imposing argument when you met her. Gave you maybe her whole spiel. Yes…"

Is this another non-answer? A deflection? A stall for time?

Salastragore shook his head and waved a dismissive hand, probably sensing the fox was about to put him back on point. "Hm, but I digress. You see, I've spent a hundred years asking such questions, like what is the soul, and do we actually have one, or more, and on and on. I searched for the answers, tested the limits of knowledge. I built machines that fly, that breathe underwater. I've built machines to *travel through space!* Stuff that enables your mind to *shape your reality!* Amazing technologies that turn *impossibilities* into *such trivial things!*

"And yet … the most basic truth escapes me … who are we, on the inside? In the sunless spaces between our synapses. In our veins, in our organs, our muscles. Behind our very eyes? Who are we? What are we? What is our soul?"

Salastragore moved closer to Maxan. His head dipped low, but his eye tilted up to regard the fox, and there was no denying now how it glowed with an inner light when he answered his own question.

"It's an animal."

"Ah…" Maxan, let out a slow breath. More than anything he just wanted to chuckle at how stupid the grand old Master Monitor sounded. He cleared his throat, to flush out the laughter. He nodded placatingly and simply said, "Yes. Animals is, ah, what we are."

Beyond the windows, gray clouds had obscured Yinna's light, and the entire workshop seemed to darken as the red snake spoke. In the fleeting sunshine, Salastragore's stature seemed to warp, like he was hunching over, the long claws of his hands extending like blades. The time for jokes and playfulness was over, it seemed.

"*Choices* you said before. Don't make me laugh, boy! *Choosing* to be one way or another, to go or stay, to act or to die... Choosing leads you nowhere. Your identity, and thus your soul, isn't shaped by anything you yourself think, or say, or do. It's already decided. It's in your nature. The beast inside you CAN'T be reformed. It CAN'T be expected to learn. All it knows is hunger, and destruction is all it craves.

"We are *animals,* boy. And you," he spun wildly to Chewgar, who seemed tense and ready as he watched the snake's claws, "you wanted to know about the Stray? You're right, we can't control it. Only because we can't control ourselves. We *are* the Stray. Lost, out here in all this emptiness. The Stray haven't come to remind us of that fact. They were already here! Inside us all along. In our soul. It's not a kind of ... *malfunction* that drives us to hate, to violence, to slaughter. It's just who we are inside. We're not *diseased. WE ARE THE DISEASE!!"*

Maxan knew he ought to be frightened. He knew he ought to bow his head and fold his tail between his hind legs and just endure this raving lecture. But he had endured enough already in Crosswall, in the Pinnacle tower, in Renson's Mill. Enough lectures and weary, cynical worldviews. There was only one thing he wanted to know, and he would be damned if this mad, red-scaled snake would deny him the answer.

"Nothing you just said tells us *how THIS stops it!"* He held the relay out before him and stood so abruptly that the bench would likely have toppled over if a rhino hadn't been weighing it down. "The Stray aren't who we really are. The Stray are what we become when we *lose* who we are! Hundreds of years, huh, and you haven't figured that out yet?"

What the hell am I saying? What am I doing? Please, just shut—

Maxan ignored his own better judgment to shut his mouth tight and never, ever open it again, and opted instead to charge on, blindly if need be. "If we return this to the Aigaion, we can save this world. We don't have to eat each other."

The intense light in Salastragore's eye faded. He glanced down at the thing in Maxan's grasp, just inches away. He could've reached out and touched it.

"You and I, Maxan… We want the same thing. The Stray have affected Drakora. Peskora. Corvidia, even. Though none of these other nations are afflicted to the same extent as your homeland. I know, my friend. Throughout your great city, across your golden plains, under the shade of your great forests, your species are reverting to the old dynamic, just predators or prey, without their consent. No one should be robbed of their free will, the ability to control themselves. It's like ripping their soul away, yes?

"You want to know what that relay *is*, Maxan? What it does? You have to know where it *fell* from." He turned again to the large paper tacked over the bookshelf and pointed to the massive triangular shape. "The Aigaion is control. Without its message, we don't know how to act. It gives us life. It raises us. Sustains us. It whispers to us.

"Or it used to, until there was one who betrayed us, long ago, and ripped out one of the Aigaion's many whispering tongues. And in that moment, it forgot how to speak. That tiny little indestructible tool of the gods, which you now hold in your tiny little paw. The Aigaion needs all of its tongues back, you see, or it cannot speak. Without that relay, it cannot remind the Stray *who they really are*, as you say."

"Why not?"

Salastragore shrugged. The easy smile returned. There was no trace of the grave, menacing, desperate lunacy, like none of it had ever been there this whole time. He spoke now like he'd forgotten everything they'd said. Like they were meeting for the first time and he was already bored with his new guests.

"Poor design, I guess."

"Okay, so how do we…"

Design, he said.

"Oh…" Maxan fixed his gaze on the schematic of the rail to nowhere pinned up just beside that of the Aigaion. "You mean to bring it there? Literally."

"Correct, my boy. Well… I *had* meant to. But now that you're here…" Salastragore sucked in a deep breath, his skinny chest expanding against the blacksmith apron beneath his robe, and exhaled a deep sigh of relief. "Thankfully I won't have to strap Saghan into that thing anymore! I was always more the botanist than engineer, anyway." His eyes shifted wildly about all the objects littering the place. "Despite all appearances."

"What do you mean 'now that *I'm* here?'"

Salastragore unfurled his slender finger and held out his palm.

"I mean, of course, now that you've brought me *the key*. I can finally start bringing an end to all this, this… slow suicide of man."

Maxan hesitated. *Man?* Another word, suppressed in his subconscious, tore its way to the surface. *Human.*

Salastragore droned on, ignoring the puzzlement wrinkling the fox's face. "You have a chance, here, now, to do some real good in this world, my boy. It's what you want, isn't it? You've done so much good already. You've learned so much about what's true. You've seen so many of our little secrets. But there's more yet to learn! You've earned your place as a Monitor. You belong here, with us."

Maxan felt his jaw clenching. In his mind, he was back in the Pinnacle's great round entrance hall where Principal Harmony offered her taloned hand to take it. Her words honey-sweet. It had not felt like the right thing to do then, but he had grown to trust Feyn, who had stolen it away again. The white wolf would've stolen it away from Harmony and Folgian even if Maxan hadn't been there, if he hadn't shadowed Yacub and leapt like a fool into all this little hidden war. Feyn had nothing but the best intentions.

The red snake, here, now, seemed to as well.

"To stop the Stray," Maxan said, and he let the relay go.

Salastragore's fingers closed around it. He drew it in slowly, delicately, cradling it in both hands, like a bloom that would turn to sand if he breathed. So he held his breath. He closed his one good eye. A tear streamed down the scales of his face.

"Twenty years," Salastragore whispered. "Twenty long, long years…

"Since you took it from me." He wiped the lone tear away with his sleeve.

The snake's voice had changed, lowered. The manic lunacy evaporated. Now his words seared the very air. The heat of them matched the fire raging in his eye.

Maxan saw what fueled the flame. He recognized the eye now, same as it had been when it burned in Saghan's eyes the night he stole the relay at the inn.

Power. He's more powerful than me. Than anything.

"You think I don't know who you are, boy? You think I don't know who's swimming around in there?" Salastragore's fist lashed out with unexpected speed and rapped its hard knuckles against Maxan's skull. "You gave him his mother's eyes! One of'em anyhow. I know you, *Ralse*. I'd know you anywhere."

The blast of pain was debilitating. All of Maxan's nerves screamed and gave out at once, jamming all their power to feel into the space living behind his golden right eye. He toppled backward over the bench, slamming against the table and dragging a heap of junk down with him to the floor.

Chewgar was up, shouting something, but so was Saghan. The light streaming from the windows was blinding. Maxan could barely see through the motes and stars that the green-scaled snake held the blade of his thin sword to the rhino's chest.

Chewgar picked up the wrench he'd spied among the clutter while the red snake ranted and raved. It was huge for any other species, equal in size to the snake's thigh and too heavy for anyone other than a rhino to be a decent weapon. Chewgar gripped it easily in one meaty hand.

More voices, and what sounded like laughter, but all Maxan heard was muffled sound. He squirmed around on the floor, both paws pressed tight to his head, the claws reflexively digging into his fur, as though they could extract the pulsating, painful mass of his brain. Maxan's body jerked violently, kicking out against table legs, sending beakers and apparatuses crashing to the floor beside him.

A hundred, a thousand, a hundred-thousand fragments of memories exploded vividly in his mind all at once. Places he'd been but never seen, words he'd spoken but never heard, animals he'd created in whose bodies he'd lived, and later died, customizing their genetic code to account for strength and prowess, weakness and deformity. He saw the faces of all those he'd killed, stabbed, burned, poisoned, hanged, strangled; the dead stared vacantly back at him, a feeling of pride and triumph welling in him at the perfect line of the slit throat. He was buying and selling and trading the armor and weapons he'd stripped from his foes, meeting and mating and marrying among his selected species: zebras, boars, rats, orangutans, tigers, jackals, sharks, sparrows, spiders, skunks, foxes. More and more visions flashed, feelings, scents, tastes. He was reveling in the heat of true and passionate loves, writhing in the freezing cold of bitter hatreds, reeling in the joy of mutual rivalry.

Within seconds, Maxan had relived a hundred lives of animals that he had never been.

Or had he? Hadn't he?

Control it.

"...how?" He managed to stammer. Behind the ringing in his ears, a muffled voice answered him. He felt the air shift. Someone was moving. Above all the outside noise, the inner voice was rising.

Stop searching for me. Stop expecting me to know what to do for you. Make your own choice, Max! And do it now!

"...get up..." Maxan softly ordered himself, rolling onto his back, releasing his head. Something huge moved in front of him. There was movement everywhere, shadows shifting all around. His paws swam blurrily before his vision. "Focus," he said softly, and his eyes obeyed. The pain receded.

"Max!" Chewgar was shouting. standing over him. "You all right?"

"Just the recall," Salastragore said matter-of-factly as if anyone else present would understand. "Our poor little fox has had to struggle through his short little life with the imprint of another mind crowding around in there, with all its own baggage. Thoughts, feelings, opinions. Memories. I can't imagine what those headaches must be like. Oh, Ralse, you lowdown beast! You actually did it, didn't you?"

Maxan blinked, and the sight of the red snake—hunkered down behind Saghan's waist, staring at him and clapping his hands—came into focus. Saghan stood rigid, his orange eyes and thin blade fixed on the hulking rhino standing before him, between him and the fox. And all around them dark shapes detached themselves from the jumbles of wires along the farther tables, materialized from the shadows between shelves, and dropped silently from the iron beams bracing the ceiling. Slender, Drakoran figures, clad all in form-fitting black armor, their faces shrouded, unsheathing the thin swords strapped tightly on their backs.

"Chewgar," Maxan said, sudden shock dosing his blood with adrenaline. Sudden sweat spread across his spine, matting his amber fur. "It's them."

"I remember," Chewgar said.

The memory this time was Maxan's own, of a rickety bridge, a mighty warrior standing against the assassins. Only Chewgar, not Yovan, was the mighty warrior.

"Well done, Ralse!" Salastragore went on, not even listening to their exchange. "Well done! This boy's brain was your final card to play in our little game. You, boy, did you think your immunity to this was a coincidence?" He clutched the chrome tube tightly in one hand, tapped it with a black nail, *tink-tink*. "The *Ay-Eye* in here goes haywire if taken from its housing, belching all kinds of signals that fry our normal little animal brains. But you made that one with a little extra room so that you could shield him. Clever, clever fox. As usual!"

"You have what you want," Chewgar said evenly, holding his free hand behind to help Maxan stand. The assassins had surrounded them now, standing on tables and closing off the aisle they'd taken to get here. "Let us go."

"Hmm." Salastragore rose to his full height, took a final, satisfied look at the relay, and tucked it into the wide chest pocket of his blacksmith apron. "Do you know how many I've had to kill? Can either of you even conceive of a number so large, I wonder. So, so, so many foxes. I eradicated them, all that I could. All the tricksters, deceivers, betrayers that I could get my hands on. I was perhaps too ... emotional, when I started that business. I've really regained my sense of composure since then."

"What about Rinnia?" Maxan said, his words feeling less fuzzy now leaving his mouth. He leaned on Chewgar's arm for support and drew his short sword, though it seemed to weigh a thousand pounds. "Why'd you keep her alive?"

"She would *NEVER* betray me!" Salastragore quaked violently with fury, squeezing both his hands into fists. "She's *mine*, Ralse. I raised her. I trained her. I gave her all the qualities you lacked! Honesty. Discretion... *LOYALTY!*"

Oh, how little you know her.

Maxan held the words back. The old con artist instincts knew saving them for later could be useful.

"Listen," the red snake said, inhaling and exhaling deeply, regaining himself. "*Maxan*, was it? Yes, Maxan, part of me is grateful to find you alive. I shouldn't be surprised, you had one of the craftiest old Monitors in there to guide you, lucky boy. And I want to let you go. Both of you. I couldn't care less if you go back to Leora and sit on the throne and do all you care to do with the time you have left. I really, really don't care. But there's just one problem. Maxan..."

Salastragore tapped the scar sealing his empty right eye socket.

"You're the key."

Maxan winced at the needlepoint of pain inside his skull. His right ear twitched as it flooded with a tinny noise. But he fought them down. *Control it.* He wasn't confused at all. He remembered Ralse had sealed the gate, but he didn't remember what it even was.

"Ah," he said, "uh huh." He gave his best impression of shocked revelation at Salastragore's pronouncement, all the while gazing about the benches and tables, the gaps between assassins, the slope that the mounds of junk made, the height differential of bookshelves, calculating if his paws could grip that chain over that other one, measuring the distance and counting the time it would take to reach the high window.

But what about Chewgar?

The route disappeared from his mind. He focused instead on his grip on the short sword. *I won't leave him.*

"For twenty long years, I tried to... to... *PLAN* my way around the gate!" Salastragore was pacing now. The assassins had made a kind of ring around the four of them in the workshop's center. Saghan and Chewgar, and Maxan also by the rhino's side, shifted their stances ever so slightly, but couldn't go anywhere. "Can you believe I was going to ride some rocket into the skies? Like a damned *bird!!*" Salastragore rocked with hysterical laughter. Another tear ran from his orange eye, and a thin line of blood darker than the red of his scales ran from the other. "I cut out my own fucking eye! Ha! Good one,

Ralse! One of your best jokes. Look at all the eyes I *made* down in the lab. The part you didn't set fire to, anyway. Trying to replicate the precise retinal code. But you knew I wouldn't get the variation, not in a million years. You deceiving, rotten bastard. You really got me good.

"Aaah... Hmm..." Salastragore settled down at last. "Saghan. Bring me the fox's golden eye, would you? And please..." He slipped a hand to his side and drew a ruby-encrusted dagger from beneath his robe. He flipped it, caught it by the blade, held it out to the green-scaled, younger version of himself. "Do it with this. I hope the symbolism isn't lost on you, Ralse."

But Saghan didn't take it. His orange eyes were dull. He stood like a statue, his sword held out to Chewgar, but there was no real threat there. No feeling.

"Don't forget who you are." Salastragore snapped impatiently, tapping the handle of the knife against Saghan's chest. "What you were made to do." His eye narrowed, the flame inside flaring. "How can I know you will do what must be done when I am gone, if you can't do what must be done while I'm still here?"

"You'll always be here," Saghan whispered, finally sheathing his sword and wrapping his slender fingers around the dagger's handle, "Father."

Maxan swallowed.

This is it.

"Saghan, listen to—"

Saghan darted right for him. Everything was a blur of motion. Maxan spun around to the rhino's side, ready for the move, and Chewgar had anticipated it also and brought the wrench down hard. Saghan's arms moved independently of each other, his left hand rising to catch the striking wrench with ease, his right swiping the ruby dagger at the fox by his side. Maxan leapt backward, narrowly avoiding the tip of the blade.

Chewgar roared and pressed on the wrench with both arms and all his strength, but Saghan's outstretched arm inched down only slightly.

The sight was unbelievable. The muscles beneath the green scales writhed like an angry nest of sightless worms exposed to daylight. The snake gazed apathetically at the rhino, spun the dagger around in his other hand for a different grip and would have slashed but for the sudden boulder of a fist slamming on his temple. He staggered, his grip wavering, and Chewgar punched him again, sending his long neck careening sideways. Saghan held onto the wrench but fell to his knees, slashing blindly, finding the rhino's belly, tearing through the soft tunic and thick skin below. The wound was no worse than a scratch.

Maxan screamed and charged, aiming his short blade at the kneeling snake's heart. Saghan spun defensively, his tail whipping out in a flash, cracking into the fox's ribs and sending him crashing over the bench, the hard wood digging into his back and nearly folding him over. His sword flew from his grip, and he sank against the stone floor, heaving for breath.

Chewgar drew back his fist, coming in again for another strike at the snake's head. The rubied dagger rose impossibly fast to meet it, its blade stabbing entirely through the skin and knuckles and out the other side like a fractured, metallic wrist bone. Their hands and weapons were locked in a kind of stalemate, but Saghan easily regained his footing, inch by inch, folding the rhino back as effortlessly as paper. Chewgar strained every muscle in his body to keep the snake down, his flat teeth grinding nearly to the breaking point. Saghan ripped the wrench free, sending it clattering across the workshop.

Maxan scampered up onto his knees, then doubled over wheezing when only half-breaths would come. With helpless horror, he watched Saghan advance on Chewgar, the dagger's jewel glinting high over his shoulder. But, just like Saghan and everyone else present, he'd forgotten that a rhinoceros was never truly unarmed and helpless.

The great horn crunched hard against Saghan's face, shattering bones audibly. With a monstrous bellow, Chewgar reeled back his head and brought it down again, brushing the curved horn uselessly against the Drakorans' armor, only to buck upward with all his strength, goring the snake through the layers of leather, skin, and organs and out through the snake's back in a gush of cold, red blood.

Saghan went limp instantly. The light gone from his eyes. The rubied dagger clanked on the floor.

With a furious huff, Chewgar surged forward, jerked his neck, and sent the lifeless body sailing across the workshop, where it slammed hard against the shelves and left a splash of red staining the schematics hanging there.

The massive rhinoceros warrior wheeled on Salastragore, his whole face slick with his enemy's blood but for the wide, wild eyes. Chewgar unleashed a thunderous roar and bent to charge, every muscle in his arms flexing, every vein pumping like mad under his skin.

Salastragore stood his ground, unflinching, grinning madly at this display of ferocity. Laughing. Maxan realized then that he'd been laughing the whole time.

Maxan got his low paws under him again at last. He stumbled forward, glancing about wildly, expecting the noose of assassins to finally close on them.

But the dark shapes had not moved. Chewgar was bent to charge, huffing and snorting furiously.

But something's not right.

The tense muscles in Chewgar's thighs quivered and spasmed uncontrollably, then slackened altogether. He crashed onto his knees, then pitched forward onto his hands, all of his great strength gone.

Maxan fell by his side, lifted the torn fabric of the rhino's shirt, and watched the black tendrils spreading rapidly along the razor-thin incision across his belly, like drops of oil in clear water. This wasn't bane. This was far worse. The black spread in his eyes. It blossomed in the backs of the rhino's big hands.

"Max, I can't… can't see."

"No," was all the fox could say.

"Max," Chewgar said, his voice cracking through the phlegm filling his lungs. He hacked and coughed, spots of blood mingled with the blackened spit. "You're crying," he said, the light gone from his eyes. "Max…?" It was a plea, a question.

What's happening to me, Max?

Maxan couldn't answer. The tears were choking him, closing his throat.

But it was answer enough. Chewgar's mind was being eaten, dissolved in the poison, but he understood enough. Chewgar grasped the last, truest part of who he was, the part that wanted to help, to save everyone. He scooped up the weight beside him and willed everything he had left to lift it and send it as high as he could.

Then, the great rhinoceros collapsed.

Maxan screamed his friend's name as he soared high over the workshop, thrown by the last burst of Chewgar's strength. He missed the high window by several feet, but he grasped one of the dangling chains as the arc carried him downward. Maxan swung the rest of the way to the pane of glass tilted open in its frame. He scrambled over and got his paws upon a narrow, pitched basin bolted along the wall just outside.

He'd found his breath again, the adrenaline pushing down the tears. He made to turn and peer back into the room below where he had left his dearest friend behind, the instincts overpowering his sense. He wanted to cry out Chewgar's name and go back and kill them all.

But he never got the chance.

A pair of claws had been waiting for him just below where he stood. They grabbed his ankles, tore him away from the workshop window, and tossed him out into space.

Chapter Seven

The Illusion of Choice

"After him!"

The hooded assassins obeyed, wasting no time, rushing to the wall beneath the window. They built a ladder of their bodies, five of them the base, while more and more clambered onto their backs and shoulders into a pyramid.

Within half a minute, Salastragore assumed the first of them would be out onto the storm drain braced to the wall, hunting down the fox. He smiled at how well he'd trained them all.

Then the smile vanished, catching sight of the great red splash staining his schematics. "So disappointing." His eye traced the line of Saghan's blood over the tables and piles of instruments and scrolls, back to where the rhinoceros had first gored the young, brash, incapable idiot. He lifted a spattered parchment and frowned at all the notations and scribbles that would have to be redrawn, the devices that would have to be cleaned.

His gaze came to rest on the melting pile of gray flesh at the center of his workshop.

"Oh, what a shame," he sighed.

Chewgar stirred. Somehow, despite the snake's best guess at the effect such a dose would have on a creature his size, the rhino managed to lift his head and glare at Salastragore, the blackening whites of his eyes ablaze with renewed fury. With a mighty huff from his nostrils, the rhino slapped his palm against the stone floor and pulled. He clawed his way to the snake, scraping his body inch by agonizing inch.

Salastragore drifted to a nearby table, utterly unhurried. He lifted a leather pelt and pressed a button on the device underneath. The thrumming of electricity confirmed that the thing was already almost at full charge. But it would still be a minute or so.

His long neck brought his eye to look back over his shoulder, checking on the rhino's progress. Fifteen feet, still some ways to go. "You could've been king of all Leora." He felt his old knees creak in protest as he lowered into a squat so he could speak eye-level with his honored guest. "Mighty Chewgar, they would've called you. In the arena, *the Gray Charger*, perhaps. A fine title. I don't know. I wasn't much for titles in my day."

Slap. Scrape. Slap. Chewgar's movements were punctuated by the rushing huffs of air in and out of his flaring nostrils. Trickles of black ran from each. Behind him, a long smear of wet black marked the progress he had made. It seeped from where the dagger had scratched his belly, now a wide-open wound.

"Man-eater," Salastragore said, simply. "Perhaps my greatest invention. A derivative of bane, though much, much deadlier. I very, very strongly suspect the antidote that Saghan and Sarovek gave you days ago is the *only* reason you've lasted *this* long, given your size. Initially, it seemed to overwhelm you, but now, I mean *look at you!* Like a resurgence of sorts. Fascinating…"

Slap. Scrape.

Salastragore hissed in pain as he rose, his old knees screaming at him. He glanced at the device. The sixth of eight lights had lit orange. Two green lights to go.

"You know, I've only ever used man-eater once before. I only ever hated one person enough in my whole existence to use it before today. But, like I said a moment ago, I had my doubts about the effectiveness of bane on your reinforced immune system. *Phew!* Things could've gone much, much worse for me."

Scrape. The rhino crawled onward. He was five feet away now. Very close. The seventh light came to the device. The thrum intensified.

"Who knows! You might even live through this."

Slap.

He saw that Chewgar's eyes were closed. Probably couldn't keep them open any longer. The poison had likely eaten its way up through his liver and diaphragm, spilled into his lungs, and even swelled in his sinus cavity. By now, it was gnawing his optic nerves to gritty bits of mud. He had, perhaps, a minute before it dribbled around the dome of his skull. Every slight movement was probably a lifetime's supply of suffering.

Pain had to be the rhinoceros' entire world surely at this stage. Then what could it possibly be that was animating him? What was pushing him onward, to seek out the source of the muffled sounds? For it was beyond certainty that Salastragore's words were incoherent puffs of cotton at this point.

"Hmm. It's rage." Salastragore nodded. "I understand you, friend. Believe me. More than you know. It's what's keeping me going too."

The final green light blinked to life.

"Aah, there we go." Salastragore stepped away just as the rhino's fist closed where his ankle had been. Five additional feet away now, he had his back turned as he tossed the covering aside and hefted the thing up with both his arms.

"Do you know why I call it man-eater? You have to first understand what *man* is. And I'm afraid you simply do not have the time for that history lesson. But, on a basic level, this poison eats you away—*so completely*—that I like to think there's nothing of your soul left to salvage. Nothing left for ... whatever comes next. Just ... ashes."

The fully charged weapon gave a high-frequency buzz. Its main capacitors were a patchwork of cells bolted meticulously together, with a network of wires soldered along its ridges that terminated in the long barrel of coils at its front. At its back, Salastragore decoupled the thick wire that served as its power supply, then slung the stock under his arm. He leveled the thing at the rhino.

Chewgar had stopped five feet away. Perhaps already dead. His body was a mess. Patches of his stomach had sloughed away and were now melting in the black trail he had made across the stone floor. His skin was black. It split like the skin of rotten fruit, spilling streams of black all around him.

"If only you knew what I know," Salastragore said, "you wouldn't have let the fox go. If you'd known who he really was inside, you would have killed him with your own hands." He let out the deepest, most regretful sigh, then stared down the plasma rifle's sights. "But some of us just can't handle the burden of truth."

For Chewgar, the white beam of light was mercy. With an ear-splitting *krraannggggg*, every molecule it touched flamed instantly into dust, leaving an enormous, round emptiness where Chewgar's chest used to be, boring through the floor and the walls at an angle. A spike of light cut straight through the castle, out beneath the lowest tier, across the lake, and into the cliff wall, atomizing everything in its path.

Salastragore peered over the rifle's sights at the smoldering damage. He let it hang lazily at his side as he picked up the animal's great, curved horn. He blew away the hot embers. The other traces of the rhinoceros—the arms and legs and head—were already sputtering in flames.

"Perhaps man-eater turns the blood flammable?" he muttered, watching them burn. "Hmm."

The plasma rifle clattered back onto the table, its steaming coils cooling from the colors of blinding morning sunshine to ruddy orange dusk. Salastragore crossed the workshop to the wall of bloodied schematics, absent-mindedly dropping the horn on one table along the way and retrieving a jar of pink powder from another.

He squatted over Saghan's corpse, his one good eye narrowing in utter disgust.

"Get up," he hissed, packing a handful of the panacea powder into the large hole in Saghan's abdomen. Already, even without the boost from the miracle concoction, he knew the cells were bubbling back to life, as they were engineered to do. This stuff would just make them bubble faster.

"Get up!" the old, red snake shouted, straining with the effort to prop his son's back against the shelf. He smiled when he saw the translucent brilles over Saghan's slitted eyes twitching. "You've still got some miles to go."

Maxan fell hard on his rump against the latticed metal walkway just below the rim of the storm drain. He did his best to roll backward with the force of the impact, but achieved only an awkward flop, ending with his snout and stomach pressed to the walkway, staring into a thousand feet of empty air and the lake below. He struggled through the searing pain in his back to rise, then froze in place when he saw who had dragged him down from the window.

"You!" It wasn't the sound of pleasant surprise. "*YOU!?*"

Rinnia held her paws out in a gesture of surrender. She wore the same burnt garb as the night in the Denland station, and spots of fur on her muzzle had been scarred permanently by the squirrel's fire, singed to red splotches of skin. Her eyes were as blue as he remembered, and there was a sincere plea in them now.

"Maxan, please. We don't have time."

"*Time?!*" He balled his fists, giving serious consideration to how best he could sweep her over the edge into oblivion.

Rinnia easily read the possible intention in his stance, shifting defensively away from the edge. "I'm not your enemy. You have to trust me."

"Trust you?! How can I trust you?"

"Who else is left?" She took a step forward, her paws still out. She wanted to scream in his face how they would be here in seconds, how they would separate his fool head from his body and salvage what they needed from his skull if he didn't do what she said right now. Instead, she swallowed her frustration, took another step, and simply said, "I understand, Maxan. You were right. We don't have to be killers. We can choose. You saved me. I know that now. And I'm here to save you."

Her paws wrapped around his, and she felt some of the tension leave his fists. Their faces were so close. "Please," she whispered.

Maxan relented.

Rinnia took his paw in hers and led him at a sprint down the length of the walkway and around the corner. The roof of the castle's lower, foundational tier sloped downward, thirty feet below. Just beyond its edge were the station's crisscrossed network of metal girders and smokestacks. Hundreds of feet further still, one of the bridges spanned the open space between the station and the encircling cliff.

But Rinnia didn't have time to explain their route. "We have to jump" was all she said, swinging a leg over the railing.

"Wait! Wait!" Maxan said, shaking his head. He wasn't going anywhere if she didn't prove, here and now, who she really was to him. "What happened to all of the foxes?" His claws shot out and gripped the clasp of her cloak, drawing her eyes closer to his. He'd asked her before, chasing her along the Crosswall rooftops, but never got an answer. "Tell me, Rinnia!"

"He killed them. All of them. Looking for *you.*"

She knew. She knew all along. Why didn't she tell me?

"I'm sorry," she said before he could ask. Suddenly, her gaze snapped over Maxan's shoulder, and she gripped his paw with both of hers and forced his claws open, making it look like he'd shoved her over.

Maxan leaned over the railing just as Rinnia's back slammed against the next rooftop hard enough to crack the tiles. She cried out, rolled painfully down the slope. He twisted back toward the corner they had just rounded and saw them coming. A line of hooded shapes drawing thin swords from their backs, running silently straight for him. Without thinking, he leapt after her. His impact was more graceful perhaps, but no less painful as he tumbled over and over again, a whirlwind of cloak and bushy tail, drawn by gravity to the bottom edge and then over its side, freefalling again, and finally colliding with the graystone surface below.

"Uhh," he groaned, pushing himself up, feeling the fresh scrapes and bruises on every point of his body. Rinnia leaned against a wall out of the assassins' view, similarly battered, clutching one of her swords. The other sword lay on the floor between them.

"Take it," she said, "and chase me. Now!"

He did as he was told, scooping up the weapon as he followed her down a flight of metal stairs that had been riveted into the side of the tower. They were past the castle's exposed foundation now, heading down the side of the station's flank. Rinnia ran as fast as she could, and Maxan put everything he had into his legs to keep up. When one twisting path terminated at an arched doorway cut in the iron, or a rising tower of welded metal beams, or some kind of machine with jumbles of wires and cables sprouting at every angle, she would turn and bound into the air onto the next open pathway, sailing across wide gaps. Along the way, they passed several crews of Drakoran laborers with dark glass masks covering their faces, their electric tools sparking against the surfaces they touched. Most didn't even look up as the pair of armed foxes sprinted, leapt, and tumbled right by. Maxan matched Rinnia's lead perfectly, vaulting over stacks of crushed pipes, spinning around carts of loose scrap, sliding around exposed vent covers. Every step drew them downward. One false move and either of the foxes would have plummeted to their death.

Maxan stole a look over his shoulder once they had landed on a long and narrow path. He saw the assassins flowing fluidly over the edges of the walkways, from one to another, like black raindrops. Once again, after all these years, he was the little fox boy in the forest. He was the living coward, watching them creep in from the dark to set his world aflame. Once again, he searched for a way out, but he knew there would be no Yovan for him to run into. He knew his only escape was Rinnia.

Rinnia's final leap took her onto another track of rails, just below the midpoint of the station tower, three hundred feet above the dark water. Her hind paws came down on the metal beams, and she tumbled into a roll to regain her balance. Every muscle in her abdomen, her thighs, and her hips were wrapped in searing fire, but she pulled herself up and ran on. In the pads of her paws, she felt the vibration on the beam and knew without needing to look that Maxan had landed behind her. They had made it. She ran a hundred feet onward, then slowed, then stopped in the very center of the bridge. She turned to face him, raising her one remaining short sword.

"Cut me," she told him.

"Wha—"

"*Cut me!!*"

Rinnia charged Maxan, bringing her blade out and across his throat. His own blade rose to meet it, battering it away. She could have spun with the parry and struck again, but she gave him the chance to retaliate.

He didn't take it.

"Dammit!" She spat, stabbing out at his shoulder, again locking blades, again being turned aside. Behind him, the assassins were already dropping onto the bridge. "There's no time! Cut me!"

Maxan saw them too. He understood, and he finally obeyed, striking at her shoulder, beating through her half-hearted defense, severing the fabric of her cloak, and slicing the fur and skin beneath it.

Rinnia shrieked in pain. She spun away from the wound, twisted into a crouch, and slammed her heel powerfully into Maxan's gut, sending him flying out over the edge into a free fall.

Had the wind not been entirely knocked out of him, Maxan would have screamed as gravity took hold. The only sound was the wind rushing in his ears. His claws scratched instinctively, searching for something they could hold onto. Rinnia's blade dropped from his grip. He managed to flip over legs-first before crashing into the frigid lake. He scrambled against the current to the surface. He came up gasping, flailing about wildly. High above, he caught sight of several black shapes along the bridge, looking down at him.

Something *plunked* into the water nearby. Then another *plunk*, closer. The onlookers were throwing knives at him. He spun wildly about, looking out across a thousand feet of open water.

Nowhere to go!

Nowhere but...

Something from the depths wound tightly around his ankle and dragged him down into the crushing dark.

The fifth and final assassin unfastened the weapon strapped to its leg and hurled it below. The blade disappeared at the exact spot where the fox had gone under an instant before, the best shot yet.

Rinnia clutched her shoulder and gazed down at the tumultuous surface. "It's done," she lied. "That last one struck him for sure." She knew without a doubt that Maxan was beyond the assassins' reach for now. She feigned a satisfied smile at their fine work and came away from the edge. She was about to pull her paw away and inspect the damage Maxan had done, but her eyes locked on a figure approaching from the castle side of the bridge.

"Good to see you, my dear," the green snake pronounced loudly. His eyes were a bright, glowing orange, and Rinnia knew it was not Saghan.

The hooded assassins knew it too, and they knelt as he passed.

The snake came to a stop a few paces away from Rinnia and scanned the dark waters below, his tongue flicking at the air.

"Master," she said. She did not bow like the others.

"Hmm. Did you get the fox?"

"Yes."

"Retrieve his body," he ordered the kneeling assassins, and they dove over the edge before he had hardly finished the command. The bright eyes flashed at Rinnia. "Now then, my girl. I knew you were outside the workshop. Watching. Waiting. I have an uncanny sense for these things."

"I was," she said, staring into those glowing orange orbs longer than she'd ever remembered staring before. She wondered if Saghan, her brother, was somewhere in there staring back, and what he would say to her then.

"You disappoint me, Rinnia."

Something inside her cracked, a numbness flooded down her spine. She knew then that he had figured her out. Her meetings with the octopus, her betrayal, her intention to take the red-scaled tyrant's life. How did he know?

She played off the fear that quaked in her as if it was shame, and she averted her eyes to the rails. Her claw inched closer to the lone sword at her back.

He gestured to the lake below. "You know as well as I that the boy lives," Salastragore hissed through Saghan's mouth.

A strange kind of relief swept over her. *He doesn't know I let him go.* She looked up at him. "Master, now that we have the relay, we can just launch the sky wing. We can let him go."

"No!" he snapped, the fire blazing in his eyes. "This score is far older, far more meaningful to me than the Aigaion." His hand cupped Rinnia's face under her chin, and his eyes drew close to hers. "I'll be going in a moment. Tell the *young Salastragore* to find the fox and bring me his eye. And you, get some rest, my dear. You look dreadful."

The orange fire swallowed her in its sight, inches away from her own. She hated herself for the fear, the helplessness she felt. Rinnia looked away, then he released her.

"And what about Maxan?" she asked his back as he turned away. "If he lives after... What should I tell Saghan to do?"

Salastragore closed his eyes, ignoring her question. He exhaled long, releasing the imprint of his mind on this vessel. When he opened them again, the bright orange fires behind the eyes had vanished. The green-scaled body belonged to Saghan once again.

The two Monitors, brother and sister, stared at each other in silence for several breaths, until finally Rinnia said, "He wanted me to tell you—"

"I know," Saghan cut in. His eyes lowered. His hand went to his abdomen, prodding at the hole in his blood-soaked armor. The scaled skin was new underneath. "He thinksss I don't hear, or see, or... feel any of it. But I do"

Rinnia heard the undeniable pain in his voice. "You never told him? That you're there for everything?" She took a step forward, wanting nothing more than to fold her brother in her arms and suffer it together with him, as they had when they were alone as children, far from their father's sight, when the snake boy would be punished for every tiny inadequacy in his father's eyes, while the fox girl was lauded for every trivial competency.

He held up a hand, halting her. "We all have our secretsss, sister." The pain was gone from his voice now, frozen by the chill of pure indifference.

"Will you go after Maxan?"

"What choice do I have?"

She understood his meaning all too well. There was nothing she could say that could change the truth of it. "Do you *want* to hurt him?"

"Who? The fox?" Saghan hissed a few notes of laughter. "What I want... What I don't want... What's the difference?"

"Saghan, I'm asking *you*."

"Don't call me Saghan. There is no Saghan. There never was." He turned his back on her and strode across the rails toward the castle, calling out over his shoulder, "Only him."

She watched her brother go, her mind clinging to the thoughts that had consumed her ever since she stumbled back aboveground, out of the station in the Denlands, and away into the night.

Maxan was right. I can choose what I am. Anyone can.

"There's always a choice!" she cried out after him, not caring who heard her. The sound of it circled the cliffs, echoing from the carved surface and coming back to her an instant later. Then it echoed again, fading into nothing at every turn.

Saghan did not turn around.

Chapter Eight

Old Four Swords

FACEDOWN ON THE SMOOTH PEBBLES, MAXAN CHOKED for breath. He coughed until his lungs and throat were raw, forcing spurts of putrid lake water out of his system.

Only moments before, as soon as his head sank below the surface, he had struggled against the current, fighting desperately against the flow to reach his ankle and pry off whatever had a hold on him. But the current was too strong, the thing was dragging him too fast, and he had no choice but to give up on that idea. For one agonizing minute more, Maxan focused solely on keeping his breath.

And then it was over.

Maxan's eyelids fluttered open. Before him, a curtain of white afternoon light shimmered on the water's surface, framed on all sides by total darkness.

Cave, he realized, his oxygen-deprived mind clinging to simple thoughts as it struggled to recover its awareness. *Rocks. Everywhere. Sharp. I can see the station out there. Across the lake. Was there a rope on my leg?*

He moaned, the sound escaping from his waterlogged lungs in a rattle. The pebbles crunched under his body as he twisted around and felt at his ankle. Beyond the shore, it seemed there was nothing but deep shadows, which not even the light from the cave's mouth could pierce. Maxan didn't need to see to know that something was there. The thing that had brought him here.

A darker shadow shifted above him. It slipped silently across the ground, closer, but far enough into the light to form the slightest outline around it. Maxan recognized the shape of its oiled cloak immediately, from when it had repelled the downpour of rain in Crosswall, when he had first seen the octopus wearing it. Those reflective silvery eyes leveled on him now seemed impossibly familiar to him, though he had never seen them up close before.

Him.

His name. Say his name.

What're you—? I don't know his name!

One of the thicker tentacles that served as the octopus's lower legs slid a step forward. Another, an arm, writhed beneath the front of his cloak, pushed a side of it up over his shoulder, revealing the handles of two of his four elegantly curved swords. The tentacle arm wrapped around the grip of one.

"The relay," the old octopus said simply, drawing the fine blade slowly with a pleasant scrape of metal that echoed within the confined cave.

You do know his name, Max! Say it!

Maxan's speech fumbled. Disoriented, his body still reacquainting itself with breathing, he managed to rise onto his knees. He held up a paw as the octopus brandished the full length of his weapon. "Wait, wait, wait," Maxan stammered, encouraged by the sight of the blade, thinner and sharper than a paper's edge.

"I-I-I know you…"

"The relay. Or your life."

"Wait! It's not about the relay anymore!"

"You have one chance." The tip of the tentacle holding the sword flicked a kind of switch on the weapon's handle. A small bead of light, similar to those on the relay, lit up green, and the cave was filled with a low, vibrating hum.

Think, Maxan! Remember!

I don't know who he is!

YOU don't. But I do.

Maxan looked away from the approaching length of shimmering steel and shook his head, trying to loosen the searing spear of pain splitting his thoughts in two. Half of his mind struggled to find the words to con the Peskoran into sparing his life, while the other tried to remember how he knew him.

"I know you," he said through gritted teeth. "From before. Twenty years…"

The third and final bead of light flashed on the sword's handle, red. The thrumming vibration peaked, and the blade almost appeared to be in several thousand places at once in the compact space above its handle.

"The war … the Monitors … *We* were Monitors…"

The octopus stopped, the blade just inches above Maxan's neck.

Suddenly, the pain dispersed. Maxan's mismatched eyes opened. He raised them to stare at his own reflection in the Peskoran's eyes.

"Zariel," he said. "Your name is Zariel."

The old octopus's silver eyes narrowed, then they looked beyond the fox's shoulder. A second tentacle arm emerged from beneath his cloak and gripped Maxan's shoulder hard. He pulled the fox up onto his feet and moved him around to his back. "Stand aside," he said, staring out over the water.

Maxan followed the Peskoran's line of sight and saw several dark things floating lazily in the water like pieces of driftwood, washing into the cave, inching their way toward the shore.

Odd how so much wood arrived all at once.

Odd how it all has eyes.

Oh.

Seven crocodiles rose in unison from the shallow water. They bent low at the waist, each holding a long, jagged spear level with their knees, readying for a fight.

Maxan's paw went to his side instinctively.

Before Maxan could recall how he'd lost it this time, before he could even finish thinking *Shit,* before the Drakoran crocodiles could land the first step of their frenzied charge, Zariel flicked his tentacle arm out in a swift, fluid motion, whipping the shimmering sword up and across in a half circle that cut through the air over the crocodile's heads.

The blade glowed like a rising sun on a distant horizon.

Zariel flipped the blade over and sank it almost fully into its empty scabbard at his side, leaving only an inch of it still drawn. The three lights on its hilt had winked out. The thrumming in the cave was gone.

The crocodiles had stopped. The movement seemed to have frozen them in the shallows, caught them in a state of panic. For a moment, Maxan wondered if the crocodiles who were there to kill him were thinking what he was thinking.

Ah... you missed.

A few of the crocodiles exchanged a nervous glance. One of them even chuckled. In some sort of voiceless battle cry, they sloshed their thick armored tails, churning the still water. The closest one took his first full step onto the pebbled shore.

Zariel slammed the handle home.

There was a stone-splitting crack loud enough to drown out all other sound, and the ceiling over the octopus's enemies became a boulder. It slammed on their heads, crushing them all with a force that could dent a mountainside. All light was snuffed out in an instant. The impact sent a shock wave of displaced air and energy that swept Maxan off his legs and flung him deep into the shadows of the cave.

Chapter Nine
The Crater City

WHO ARE YOU?

It's … complicated. I'M complicated.

And I'm tired of this. All this … thinking! Just once, I'd like to own my own thoughts! Stop talking to myself inside my head all the time. Just get things straight. Stop getting dragged everywhere and think like all the steps I take are by my own desire to put one paw in front of the other and look over there isn't that interesting? And know that it was myself and only myself that thought so…

What the hell are you asking exactly, Max?

Argh! This isn't making sense. TELL ME. Why do I suddenly know so much. Why do I… remember things when I know damn well they never happened?

They didn't happen to you, Max. It's recall. You've recalled my memories. Most of them.

All those… others. You lived in them. They were you. They had names, and faces, and voices.

Yes. I created them.

They had families.

Yes, I … started families.

How? How is that even possible?

The code, the signal. Epimetheus. The Aigaion. Anything is possible.

It was too much. Maxan's mind was literally split in two. The words and concepts and visions rushed out from one half like from a shattered tap barrel, and the other half was drowning in it. *Apt comparison there. My skull sure feels like a shattered tap barrel.* He pressed the heel of his paw into his eye. It did little to relieve the building pressure, but the inner voice was quiet for the time being. It must have known what the unlocked knowledge was doing. Maybe it felt it too.

He stumbled along half-blind in this way, for long hours and miles, following the squiggly outline of cloak and tentacles gliding ahead of him. The fox's lower paws plodded along, one step after another, automatically. The air in these tunnels was still, deathly quiet, but the noise inside his own head was deafening. He had no idea where the octopus was leading him, and he didn't care to know. At one point, he glanced at the scratches lining the walls and floor of the tunnel and knew Thraxians had made them, just like the ones under the Denlands that led to Drakora. He wondered where these led. Where was the octopus taking him?

Beyond the endless stretches of jagged gray stone and layers of gray dust, he could barely see anything in the dim glow of his leader's pinlight. Some uncounted hours later, Maxan was again completely lost in his own thoughts, absorbed by the inner conversation, determined to try again, to get an understanding at last. He was certainly no stranger to having half of his mind operate beyond his control; it's how he had lived most of his life. The only difference now was the awareness that there had apparently always been some reason for its freedom. Salastragore said something about his brain, how it was specifically made to hold…

Hold what? Extra space?

The Maxan-mind that had been born with this body *knew* now, forever, that the other-Maxan was not truly a part of him. It was a foreign object lodged in his consciousness. Something that was in hiding in those "sunless spaces between the synapses" as Salastragore put it. Something that had once lived its own life—*lives*—with its own emotions and desires.

And then it died.

Maxan felt it struggling to remember—or recall—its death now. He found that thinking actively about a thing dredged the subconscious memories. He could make the voice talk, have it describe what his mind's eye was seeing.

Being in that place again, it responded. *Seeing the station, the castle, the room. That was my room, Max.*

And below the station, there's the lab.

Was. There was the lab. I destroyed it. Or I thought I had.

It's where you…

Where I died, Max. For the last time. I didn't come back again.

But that's not true. You came back… in me.

Maxan nearly stumbled right into Zariel's back before he realized his guide had stopped abruptly. Zariel was rummaging through his cloak, saying nothing. Maxan's gaze drifted to the wall, scanning the telltale cuts and scores left by the Thraxians. One particular marking was more jagged than the rest. He reached out and felt its ridges, serrated like a knife. Although the two of them were on the run from the Drakorans that Salastragore had no doubt set on their trail, if he had time to ponder a mark left on the wall like this, then they didn't seem to be in much of a rush. Maxan reasoned it might have something to do with how the octopus had carved the cavern ceiling closed behind them, buying them a huge lead on their pursuers.

When Zariel's tentacled arms wriggled free from under his oiled cloak, holding some kind of orb, Maxan stole a look at the handles of the four curved swords, each with three unlit glass beads and a switch on their decoratively wrapped hilts. He remembered what Rinnia had said about this world, the stations, the Aigaion, and how the Monitors' principal charge was to keep secrets like these hidden. Weapons of terrible power. With those things in hand, a warrior could hack through a rank of armored soldiers, sever the lines suspending a bridge, or maybe even topple a tower.

Even just one of those things, Maxan figured, *could bring an army to its knees. And he has four. He has* four.

One of the old octopus's tentacle-hands squeezed around the pinlight, while another came away from his cloak with a small metal sphere stuck to its suctions. Zariel held the sphere in front of him. It looked similar to the bombs and other devices Saghan had kept in his satchel, useful for starting campfires, *and blowing enemy foxes out of windows.* A red light flashed at its equator like a waking eye then raced around its circumference. The sphere parted with a hiss of released pressure, then split open like a perfectly cracked nut. It opened into two halves, then a second smaller orb inside sprouted paper-thin wings and levitated out from the first. A dozen dull, red eyes came to life on this mechanical insect as it darted ahead and disappeared down a bend in the tunnel. A moment later, a ghostly blue, holographic light came into sharp focus in the air above Zariel's split sphere. As the winged insect flew further and further into the tunnels, a ghostly three-dimensional map expanded in front of Zariel.

And then, without a word, they were on the move again. A week ago, Maxan likely would have been rooted to the spot, his lower jaw hanging open in amazement. It might have taken several sobering slaps on his snout to convince him the sight of this thing wasn't a dream. But after the relay, the stations, the train, the swords, the very Aigaion itself, the mapping mechanism barely won any of his attention. All of Herbridia's hidden wonders had become as mundane as the air Maxan breathed. Even as the blue light grew, revealing an increasingly complicated network of twisting tunnels that must have represented dozens of miles in all directions, with two green blips at the center, the fox found himself yawning.

They walked—*or in Zariel's case writhed, perhaps*—for hours more, but counting the passage of time was futile down here. Occasionally, a red blip would form on the fringes of the blue map, and Zariel would slow the pace at which his tentacle legs flowed silently over the dusty ground. His tentacle arm would shift the open sphere left or right to scan for alternate routes, and then they would proceed down one branching tunnel instead of another, moving ever onward in one general direction.

Away. Always away.

Maxan was consumed by the need to remember things that never happened like a dreamer who was so convinced the images experienced in his sleep were real and somehow meaningful. But he found that trying to hold on to those images, trying to relive those memories, was like trying to remember that dream not just two days after it happened but two decades. And there was a part of him that knew exactly everything about who it was those dreams belonged to. His name, who he had been, who he was to Maxan. But Maxan didn't want to even think about it. He wasn't ready. The other fox no doubt felt Maxan avoiding this subject too but kept silent.

Over time, their path sloped gradually upward, and had Maxan paid any attention to the map, he would have seen their tunnel terminated half a mile ahead into a vast emptiness. As the two green blips moved onward, more and more of the blue light faded from view, and the dark of the tunnel enveloped them again. Zariel clicked off the pinlight with one tentacle and depressed a button on the underside of the sphere with the other. The holographic map began to shrink then faded entirely when the red-eyed insect buzzed back into view, settled back into its metal shell, and folded its wings. Zariel snapped the sphere shut and brought it back inside his cloak.

"We're here," the octopus said, the first words he had spoken since they had left the lakeside cavern.

"We're where?" Maxan asked, but he could see very well for himself where the tunnel ended just ahead and a colossal chamber began.

They stepped out into a field of broken rocks and arid weeds growing between the cracks. A midnight blue settled upon every jagged surface like dust, the light about as bright as one might expect the bottom of Peskora's ocean to be. Everything was so still and silent, the fox wondered for a moment if the ocean floor actually was where Zariel had led him. Maxan tilted his head back and saw the source of the meager light. The chamber's ceiling must have been a thousand feet high, at least, and studded with a million twinkling gemstones of all colors and sizes.

A chilling breeze wafted against him, and he suddenly realized the chamber was not underground at all. They had emerged into the bottom of a massive hole punched deep into the world, bigger than the cylinder surrounding the Monitors' castle, wider than the crater in the Denlands where they'd found Harmony waiting for them and later the Mind's Principals would clash. The gemstones high overhead were the stars, and the black rock where they were embedded was the emptiness between.

Maxan drew his cloak closely about him to ward off the chill. It was hardly any help, but thankfully, it had dried during their long trek through the tunnels. They made their way forward, but the ground here was not as level as it had been in the tunnels. They were surrounded by flat slabs of graystone that stabbed upward through the ground at all angles. Thickets of dry brush and stubborn weeds sprouted from the spaces between the rocks, waiting for years to snag a passerby with their skeletal thorns. Zariel glided around them easily enough, but Maxan sucked in his breath more than a few times whenever the barbs bit into the pads on his low paws. At times, piles of rubble several feet high and mountainous boulders blocked their path forward, and so they meandered their way left and right every ten steps it seemed. At one point, Maxan halted at the top of one of the highest mounds and scanned the immensity of the empty space all around him. They'd been wending their way in this wide-open place for almost an hour and were nowhere near even halfway to its center.

How many Crosswalls could fit in here? Is this still Drakora? Is this... Thraxia? We can't have walked that far. He wished he'd paid a little more mind to the holographic map.

He turned his attention to finding a way down the sloping mound where he stood, but remained still a moment longer, suddenly realizing that this place was not entirely a natural formation. Just below, Maxan spotted what appeared to be ten rounded slabs that might have at one time been stacked one upon the other in a column. He found another column in better condition a few feet away from the first. And just beside it lay a flat wall of a hundred bricks still bonded by the mortar between them, a testament to Drakoran masonry. Maxan narrowed his eyes, discerning that what he saw nearby was in fact an enormous oak door, with the metal hinges and bracing rusted, but still intact.

"This place is … a ruin." Although only a whisper, the sound of his own voice carried far through the stillness, loud enough for the octopus to hear.

Zariel turned about at the bottom of the mound. "Old Quwurth," he said. "Once the center of Drakora. Fallen in upon itself, which began the Extermination." The old octopus extended a tentacle and beckoned the fox to come down. "This place is a tomb."

"Old Quwurth," Maxan said slowly, running his paw along the weather-eaten surface of a stone nearby.

Hardly any Herbridian needed to study the words in one of the Mind's books to know what happened here. This was where the Thraxian War began. For years, perhaps longer, the insect race had bored their way under the ground, stretching a thousand miles from their hives in their arid desert homeland all the way to the Drakoran capital. And then they sunk it. A hundred thousand lives were lost in seconds as the weight of their city came crashing down upon them, and with the ocean of ants and insects streaming in from the tunnels all around—*like the one we came in from*—it had been easy to ensure not a single Drakoran of old Quwurth survived. The defeat here had been enough to unite the other three nations—Leora, Peskora, Corividia—under one banner, although by the time the allies truly mobilized their campaign to exterminate the insects, most of the Drakoran population had already been wiped out. Their swamps and river deltas were already being carved up and packed into new twisted hives to meet the demand for Thraxia's expansion. Throughout all of Herbridia's history, accounting for all of its bloody wars, there was no swifter, no bloodier moment of death than the fall of Quwurth.

Now, two decades after the massacre, by the direction of the Drakoran Council of Lords (and no doubt under Salastragore's influence) the Drakoran people had rebuilt their capital city as a ring around the Monitors' castle. And they kept the city's name, New Quwurth. But in the ensuing years, the reptilian species struggled to regain even a shred of their original numbers. Their spirits had been irrevocably damaged by the sudden, unexpected, uncountable loss of life.

Looking out now over the expansive wasteland, the despair was not hard at all for Maxan to understand.

We could be standing on the surface of Yerda for all I know.

He craned his neck skyward, hoping to catch a glimpse of Herbridia's enormous, broken moon hanging in the sky. The caved-in spherical body was nowhere to be seen among all the stars, but he did spy the trailing asteroids called Yerda's Belt. *She's probably drifting behind the high rim of this sinkhole.*

When Maxan's eyes returned to the broken city, he quickly realized he'd lost sight of his slippery, silent Peskoran guide. Instead of relenting to the sudden overwhelming panic, he tried to embrace the notion of loneliness, the insignificance of self when surrounded by something so, so incomprehensibly vast. He closed his eyes. He breathed slowly. He let the absolute silence and stillness envelop him. For a fleeting moment, he was the only survivor of a destroyed world.

The moment passed, and he was soon dashing to catch up to where he spotted Zariel squiggling up a slope made by two collided walls. In his haste, he hadn't seen the particularly strong vine waiting to snag his ankle and drag him down. With a curse on his lips, he twisted about and grabbed a hold of his ankle to free himself but froze in horror when he realized it was not a hardy weed that had tripped him, but the husk of a Thraxian pincer. He tried to kick the thing off his leg but only succeeded in splintering the natural armor into flakes. He recoiled from it, skirting on his rump along the path, right into the crumbling frame of a giant spider, with his head just between its jagged mandibles. Maxan turned about and peered up at a bed of a dozen shattered orbs, the creature's eyes that had fallen in on themselves. Had his stomach been full, he would have emptied its contents in that moment. A cold sweat soaked the fur along his spine.

"He cannot hurt you."

Maxan spun about and saw Zariel, standing like a statue that rose from the fallen rocks. The octopus' thick cloak concealed his whole body. Only his blue, bulbous head gave him away as something alive, floating amidst the sea of dead things in Old Quwurth. Maxan realized then that there were no scents whatsoever in this place. Nothing lived here besides wild vines and weeds. Nothing to breathe but dust and death. Mysteriously, even the damp-skinned Peskoran standing just a few feet away had masked his sea-salt smell. Maxan straightened, dusted himself off, and approached the octopus, doing his best to stop his paws from shaking.

"There was a great battle here. After the fall." Every other phrase in Zariel's speech was punctuated by the need for breath, as though talking at length gave him great pains. Each intake of breath seemed ragged and wet. The octopus's voice was nasal, and each word sounded like a quietly popping bubble. Maxan had never met an octopus, nor had he had any lengthy dealings with Peskorans come to think of it.

"One month," Zariel continued, turning about and gliding onward as the fox fell into step alongside him. "Was all it took. Before the other nations mobilized. And saw the threat. For what it truly was."

"I don't see any remains ... other than Thraxians. No weapons. No armor."

"We burned the insects." Zariel tilted his head back, his silver eyes full of glinting starlight. He gazed at the rim of the great cliff all around the deep ruins, far above and farther away. "We rained fire upon them."

A long silence followed as Zariel led the fox around the side of the largest mound of rock and ruins they had yet encountered. The path dipped beneath the remnants of a leaning brick wall. Two long, iron window frames that must have once risen at either side of some grand entrance had miraculously survived their fall into the pit. As they moved further in, Maxan saw that much more of this particular building was intact. They stood in an enormous domed chamber, though half of the dome was cracked wide open. The stars were the only source of light, but even in the nearly total darkness Maxan could perceive figures lined up along the wall. Statues of frogs, snakes, lizards, crocodiles, and other prominent reptiles and amphibians, all of them robed, the sculptor had long ago masterfully captured the essence of self-importance in their poses. Now most of them were decapitated with severed limbs and battered body parts strewn about among the dust. Only one statue survived perfectly intact: a thick, hard-shelled turtle.

The floor was uneven, pitched at an angle. Zariel led the way downward into a kind of hollowed-out hovel. The darkness inside the small space was absolute.

Then a spark flared where Zariel stood. And another.

He's lighting a fire. Or trying to. And failing at it.

Maxan drew closer to the old octopus and offered his paw. "Can I?"

He felt shadowy tentacles pass over his palm and heard a sticky uncoiling, popping sound as the things detached from their suction. He clutched the two stones, then got to work, crouching over a pile of dried brush and salvaged splinters of the ruins that had already been prepared at the room's center.

He's got swords that can cut stone in half. A metal ball that shows you where to go... And a little piece of flint. Such technological wonders.

We can't all start fires with our thoughts, the other voice reminded him. Suddenly, Maxan found himself missing Pryth. And Pram. Even Feyn.

And Chewgar.

All these hours, wandering in the dark, putting one paw in front of the other, interrogating himself, prodding at the subconscious, staring up at the ocean of stars, and he hadn't even thought about Chewgar. His captain. His best friend. His only friend. The last image he had of the mighty rhinoceros was how reduced, how blind he was, bleeding his poisoned blood on the floor of the workshop.

Maxan struck the flint harder and harder. He clenched his fangs, fighting back the flood of tears. Sparks flew everywhere, but none of them caught on the kindling.

I have to go back.

You know we can't go back, Max. We can't save him.

But I have to try. He'd go back for me.

Maxan. Please…

He made no reply. He felt but did not hear the other mind's unspoken final argument: *Chewgar's already dead.* But he refused to believe it was true. What good would it do to argue back? Here? Now? He'd already put miles and miles between himself and the Monitors' castle. He had to let it go. For now.

In the pitch-black dark, he let his paws fall to his lap. He knew the silver eyes of the octopus were upon him, observing, judging. But he didn't care. He took a deep breath, wiped the tears with his sleeve, and refocused, striking the flint a final time over the kindling. The flame caught instantly, and he breathed it to life. The fire was so close to his muzzle, the writhing dance of it reflecting in his mismatched eyes. He suddenly remembered that he hadn't touched flint and tinder in over five years. He sat back on his haunches and watched the small blaze grow, felt its warmth. He was no longer afraid of it. After everything else he'd seen, all the dangers that had tried to claim him, all the rescues, what did fire really have to threaten him with?

He envisioned the orange eye in the sputtering core of flame. He saw the intense rage fueling it. *Salastragore.*

Another identical eye blinked to life beside it. *Saghan. They're one and the same. The red snake made the green one. Grew him up in a glass jar like the one I saw in the workshop. A… clone. Of himself. With a special kind of brain. Maybe like mine. With extra space for an imprint.*

Maxan turned the small piece of stone over and over in his paw, staring vacantly at the eyes of the fire, lost in his own thoughts. From the very beginning, he never had a reason to trust Saghan. How many times had the snake tried to kill him? Twice? Three times? Or if not outright kill him, then leave him for dead at the very least.

But it wasn't Saghan. It was Salastragore. The puppeteer, pulling the puppet.

But not in the workshop.

It had all happened so fast. Maxan tried to remember everything. Salastragore gave Saghan the rubied dagger, and Saghan had come straight for him. And Chewgar had stepped in.

In the workshop, it was Saghan. He was in control of himself. He made the choice.

But what kind of choice, Max? Did he really ever have one?

Maxan narrowed his eyes, seething with sudden anger. The fire had swelled now, filling the little hovel with its light. Its heat boiled his blood.

I should feel sorry for him? He poisoned Chewgar! With bane, again, or something far, far worse.

The pain behind his eye speared him again, then faded almost immediately. It was the pain of another recall. He knew for certain then that it was indeed worse. Salastragore had once poisoned him with it too.

Saghan paid for it with his life, Max.

And there it was at last. The heat of his rage had burned away, revealing the utter disgust festering in his heart underneath. It wasn't Saghan at all that disgusted him. It was the *idea* of Saghan. The idea of Saghan having no control over his own destiny.

It was all Salastragore's idea.

I do, he admitted. *I do feel sorry for him.*

Maxan peered about the space in the growing light. There was a tightly tied bedroll leaning against a far wall, some more firewood (chopped into precisely straight wedges, Maxan noted) piled beside it, a few slipshod wooden crates, and nothing else but rubble and dust. Zariel wriggled out of his thick cloak and hung it upon a splintered beam jutting from the wall. The octopus wore a leather harness belted about his torso, which was attached to thickly oiled cloth that draped over his tentacle legs like a long skirt. The harness kept the grips of his four curved swords always at the ready, two at his hips, and two at his chest. The metallic map-sphere dangled from its hook on the harness as well alongside various other gadgets. Zariel's four bare, blue arms unfurled and slipped through the straps of the harness, then deposited his weapons and equipment gently against the wall. He glided to one of the crates, lifted its top, and tossed a canvas sack across the shelter to Maxan.

Food! He was so hungry that he didn't care what surprise was in store for him. Zariel could've tossed over a preserved scorpion bladder and the fox would've devoured it without complaint. Thankfully, what Maxan found in the sack turned out to be some kind of crispy, dried black leaf, rolled over and over until it was as thick as his arm.

"Seaweed," Zariel said, "from Peskora." The octopus lowered himself into a crouch across the fire from Maxan, the tips of his tentacles undoing the cord around his own bundle of the stuff.

Neither of them spoke. They simply watched the fire grow as they finished the dried seaweed. The octopus's body seemed to deflate into a puddle and change into the color of the graystone he sat upon, tinged by the shifting firelight.

"Huh," Maxan said aloud. Before, he'd only ever heard tales of octopus species' natural talent for camouflage, long ago perhaps, exchanging idle chatter with the other foxes of the Commune about what thieving might be like in other lands. And now, a thousand miles away, in a hole in the ground in Drakora, below a toppled palace or temple or something, huddled up with one of the old Monitors who'd escaped Salastragore's purge—the very last, in fact, now that Folgian was dead—he finally got confirmation that it was true.

"Epimetheus," he said, purposefully sounding casual and frank about their world's most carefully shrouded secret. He bit off another hunk of seaweed and formed it into a salty wad between his fangs, saying more as he chewed. "He gave you that gift. Nice."

Zariel's seaweed meal held by an invisible tentacle seemed to float in the air, half-finished. If Maxan hadn't known he was there already, he might've lost sight of him entirely. Except for the silver eyes.

"How did you come," his voice bubbled, then paused for breath and finished, "to know this word?"

"Would you believe me if I said it was in my head since before I was even born?"

Maxan shrugged, expecting to catch the octopus off guard with the rhetorical question, but the reply was quick.

"Yes," Zariel said. "There was some talk. Long before your time. Of avatars, that could house multiple imprints."

"Avatars," Maxan repeated, already aware of the knowledge unlocking itself in his mind. "Host bodies."

"It was theoretical. Experimental. We had other matters. Much more in need of our attention. The war, for instance."

They were quiet again, for a long time it seemed.

Maxan stared absently at the flames, glad for their warmth, his belly full, feeling the exhaustion gnawing at every bone in his body. Zariel's voice startled him awake.

"I am still deciding," Zariel said.

"What?" Maxan asked. He cleared his throat and rubbed his tired eyes. "Deciding what?"

The worth of my life probably. Whether I live or die. At least, I got something decent to eat.

"How did you know my name?"

The silver eyes were as unreadable as ever, shining back at him like mirrors, but Maxan felt the gravity in his voice easily enough.

"Rinnia told me," he lied, hedging a guess that Zariel would be too smart to take the con, but feeling the need to test the old Peskoran Monitor anyway.

"No," Zariel replied right away, coldly. "She did not. The truth, now."

"All right." Maxan spread his paws in a conciliatory gesture. "I heard your name in my head. Just before you were about to, well... Would you have actually hurt me back there, by the lake?"

"Explain," Zariel said, ignoring the question.

That's probably a No.

Maxan let out a deep breath. "For as long as I can remember, I've heard this voice in my head. I thought it was just me, thinking all the time. Second-guessing everything I did. Questioning my way through life. I thought I was smart, sly, crafty, careful, you know. Thinking things through. The voice kept me alive, kept me out of danger I didn't need to be in. Without it, I'd've starved to death in Crosswall. Or I'd've burned to death with my mother when..."

He looked across the fire, but all he saw was the small twin reflections of himself. Zariel was waiting for the answer Maxan hadn't given him yet.

"The voice has been with me as long as I can remember, to remind me there's always another way out of something that seems impossible to escape. And that's what it was. Rinnia kicked me off that bridge, and you dragged me under and pulled me out. I was practically drowned, and you had me dead to rights. No con could've gotten me out of that, and I heard the voice screaming at me to say your name. It knew your name was Zariel. And that's it. It sounds impossible."

"Impossible." The word slowly rippled out of Zariel's beak-shaped mouth, like someone who hadn't heard it spoken for centuries. In fact, Zariel had not. "Nothing is impossible. Not in this world."

Again, for quite some time, the only sound was the crackling of the fire.

Then Zariel spoke again.

"Three hundred thousand Drakorans. Lived here in Quwurth." The shifting camouflage of skin closed over both of the old octopus's silver eyes, deleting them from existence it seemed. It was the first time Maxan had seen him blink. They stayed closed as Zariel went on. "Can you imagine, such a number? Gone in seconds. But their deaths were not in vain. It sent a message. To Leora. Peskora. Corvidia. And it worked. Just as we planned it would."

"What?" Maxan blinked, not sure he was fully understanding what it was he just heard. "You planned what?"

The silver eyes opened again. "We directed the Thraxians here. To this very spot. Under the city. Hollowing it out for a year before the fall. It was all part of the plan. They had to die. A necessary sacrifice. To ensure the alliance.

Without the joined effort of mammals, avians, reptiles, sea-dwellers, the world would be overrun. Everything would crumble. You see, nothing happens randomly. Not in this world. At least not before."

As Zariel spoke, Maxan was transported to a grand hall of marble, a gathering of the ninety-nine of which he was a member, among Zariel, Folgian, Salastragore, all young, powerful, indestructible, and so many others whose names ran through his mind as he saw them. And there was also the one, presiding over them, raised on a dais. A robed turtle.

"Baaleb." He recalled the Grand Monitor's name. "It was his plan."

Zariel was struck silent.

He's probably wondering if he should just cut me in half at the waist and be done with all this.

Maxan shook his head, realizing then that he didn't actually care. He ignored the silver eyes and watched the dancing flames. He was absorbed with the puzzle pieces falling into place in his mind. "It was Rinnia," Maxan went on. "She once said to me that this whole world was all just a game."

He looked up again. Indeed, Zariel's eyes were open now, but the octopus said nothing. He also wasn't going for his weapons yet, so that was encouraging.

"She told me none of this is real," he went on, his heart racing, feeling all over again the worthlessness and frustration he'd felt when she'd jabbed her claw tip in his chest, in an empty alley of Crosswall, in the pouring rain. "She said that nothing we do matters. Even if we think we're doing good. Because everything's decided already. It was you, wasn't it, that told her so? The old Monitors' creed of controlling everything behind the scenes while all the animals' lives play out. Like some kind of game."

Maxan cut himself off before he could say more.

She got all of that from you, he thought, staring hard at the octopus' eyes, *when you met her. You got to her young, didn't you? Told her all this "truth." How once there were Monitors. Not like her, raised by Salastragore, but REAL Monitors. Guarding real secrets. Machines that could create life. Signals that could transport minds. Designing grand campaigns and adventures.*

"We called it The Animal in Man," Zariel said. "The game. Epimetheus. The great experiment. To save our species."

"Your species? Like... octopuses?" Maxan supplied dumbly, already knowing everything but purposefully setting the trap. And Zariel stepped right in it.

"Humanity."

For the last several days, the word had found its way into Maxan's thoughts a handful of times. But he'd never said it aloud, not to anyone.

"Humans," he said, then recited more and more. "Users. Their minds, lodged in our animal bodies, their avatars. Like… puppets."

Not puppets. He looked away, his paws balling into fists. *Slaves.*

One half of him already knew the facts, the history, the purpose. One half had forgotten and waited Maxan's whole lifetime to have this knowledge unlocked. That half felt indifferent, pragmatic, apathetic, as it recalled the centuries of bloodshed and war and murder, the atrocities of this world inflicted upon itself to satisfy the human need for violence.

But the other half, the half for whom all of this was new, the Maxan-half, was outraged. Maxan was overcome with anger. He wanted to scream at Zariel. He wanted the power of his voice to carry through all the Thraxian-made tunnels, crush all the buried, ruined stations under the pressure, and topple all the high towers of the Mind and the Monitors. He wanted them to know how evil they were.

But he said nothing. He felt nothing. He wondered then if Rinnia too had felt nothing when Zariel had first told her the truth. He wondered if he would let the truth beat him like it had beaten her, and if he would just be content to accept his nature as a killer, doing whatever Zariel directed him to do for the good of *humanity*.

Or, he wondered, *after knowing all that I know now, can I try to be something better?* He remembered Rinnia's words before they'd raced down the side of the Monitors' castle. *We don't have to be killers. We can choose.*

If she'd really meant it, then it proved a mind could be changed. Maxan had seen into her eyes back there. *She meant it.*

"You remember much." Zariel's low bubbling voice broke through his thoughts. "But do you remember why we play the game?"

"So that we don't forget… What we did to ourselves. What we did to the Earth."

Maxan stared at the fire. Once, years ago, he died in it. And he was born in it. He felt as though something in him had irrevocably switched, like gravity had flipped, that all the up was now down and it had been like that all along, but neither he nor anyone living had known. He felt like he had been flipping a coin all his life, and only now, at this moment, did it finally land, not on one side or the other, but on its edge. And the feeling stayed with him. He had caught it, and he had found that the only way to hang onto it was to let go.

He had spent countless nights atop the high, dividing walls between Crosswall's districts watching the outer asteroids of Yerda's belt float into view. Thinking of the brightness of Yinna's sunshine from somewhere beyond the horizon and how it limned her dark twin's broken body with light. But that light could not, could never penetrate the shadowed depths of the wound in Yerda's side. Maxan didn't remember where he'd first heard the names before, Yinna and Yerda, or who'd taught him. The mythology was the truth, unquestioned. But now, he realized that it was the Monitors' design. Some story to fool everyone, to distract from the actual truth.

"We destroyed it," he breathed the words. "We destroyed ourselves."

"It's in our nature."

No, Maxan wanted to say. But the other, the voice of reason, was a wall of doubt rising against him. He slammed full force against it and was stunned to silence.

"We made this world," Zariel went on, "to serve as a reminder. Of what we really are. Inside. What we really want. How we live to hurt. To hate. To kill. So we reshaped Luna, our moon. A paradise, to indulge our deepest desires, for the few of us still living on distant worlds. And the Aigaion, it was our doorway, through which we control the bodies, the actions and thoughts, of our avatars. So we designed the game, and we called ourselves—"

"Monitors," Maxan cut in. "We were the Monitors."

"One hundred of us. Builders. Game designers. Gods. Each with our own specialization. Do you remember who we were? What we did? I have forgotten our true names, our human selves, so long have I been trapped in this… *prison.*" Zariel's voice rippled in anger at the word, his tentacles rising and shifting wildly in the air above his slouched form, changing colors from gray and black shadow to orange and red firelight. "I remember only, what we call our avatars. Salastragore, he made things grow. Folgian shaped our cultures, our economies. And I… well…"

"Zariel," Maxan pronounced, his other mind recalling everything. "The weaponmaster."

The octopus seemed to calm. His writing mass settled into a puddle shape again. His bulbous head gave Maxan something like a nod. "And more of us still. And our director. Baaleb, above us all. He charted the course of history. Planned the great campaigns we would play. He wrote the great stories. He plotted the rise and fall of empires. The shared, collective experience of all life here. The ebb and flow of the users. All to keep the cycle of violence spinning. The game…

"Epimetheus' heart is rotten to its core. Epimetheus gave us differences, but it's differences that divide us. Differences for which we slaughter each other. Different species, different beliefs, different languages. And so we called on him again, when we saw only our own mutually assured destruction in our future. Project Epimetheus, we called it. A chance to put the ferocious beast in man's heart to sleep. But we were wrong. The beast never truly sleeps, Maxan."

"And so, we commit acts of violence *here*, in *this* world, so we don't... what? *Hurt* each other?" It was preposterous. Self-defeating. Maxan couldn't help but laugh at how violence could ever be conceived as a solution to violence.

"Man is the most violent animal of all," Zariel observed flatly, seriously. "With man, violence was never supposed to be, a part of our evolution. We hurt one another because we *want* to. Our minds are malleable. Tell a man enough lies, and he will believe the harm he does, is because he *had* to."

The thoughts tumbled through Maxan's mind like an avalanche, and he was at its lowest recesses, in the dark, grasping at boulders. He shook his head and gave up. "How does it all work? I mean, I think I know, but..."

He trailed off. It was another test, not a trap so much this time, to see just how much Zariel was willing to indulge the fox's curiosity. Maxan reasoned that if the octopus had truly meant to kill him and be done with it, he would've done so already. It seemed that Zariel was glad for the chance to explain, to spill all the secrets his order had made him guard for so long.

"Upon the death of one avatar. A user selects another. Our bodies procreate, according to nature, and species, but all by meticulous design. Offspring are born, ignorant, innocent, empty vessels. Tabula rasa. Waiting for the day when they will be controlled. The day when the Aigaion—our greatest creation, the mechanism of our control—it directs our minds to inhabit the body.

"But, as the centuries passed, fewer and fewer users were selecting Thraxians as avatars. The insect race, their greatest appeal, that of being the outlier, became the very reason for their downfall in the end. They have no real language. No real culture. No freedom. They serve only the will of the hive mind. To all others, they became monsters. And in the Thraxians' isolation, there was endless, endless growth. A population, soaring beyond the Monitors' control. We lacked ... the *foresight*."

Zariel paused at the word, his wet breath bubbling intensely for several seconds. Maxan realized it was the octopus's laughter.

"I... don't understand."

"The stories," Zariel sputtered, regaining his composure. "Epimetheus gave all living things, their differences. But he could not see how our difference could lead to our destruction. There was another. His twin brother. Who gave us fire. Fire, which was knowledge, and light. Fire, which was warmth. Safety. Fire, which was a test. For fire, also burns."

He's getting the story wrong, Max.

Maxan was aware already but listened anyway. *Not all living things. Epimetheus gifted the animals. Man alone was given fire, when there were no other gifts. And the Monitors believe he squandered it. Abused it. Nearly killed himself.*

Not nearly. He did.

No. We're still here. I'm still here.

He was aware of Zariel's silver eyes upon him, watching him silently fidget, blink, grimace at the argument playing out silently with himself. The fire was dim between them. Maxan busied himself by rekindling the flames with some of the precisely cut sticks nearby.

"The swelling Thraxian number was simply a flaw in our design," Zariel continued when Maxan had resettled. "Baaleb was the first to predict the outcome, but it was too late. If the Thraxian problem was not solved, the whole world, everything we had built, would be swallowed. Would perish. The game could not end."

"So he proposed a solution," Maxan said. It wasn't even recall now, just pure, cold rationality.

"Extermination." The octopus' voice sank very low. "And we agreed. All of us."

"Not all of us," Maxan said darkly. "Not Salastragore."

"The snake could not abide the slaughter of so many. Not even if it justified the survival of so many more. Not even if they were *insects.*" Zariel spat the word with derision, like a sudden splash upon a peaceful pond.

Maxan imagined Salastragore before the ninety-nine gathered in the grand marble hall, raving against the need for so much death. He felt pity for the young, red-scaled snake as the others laughed him down. The feeling belonged to the other fox residing in him.

"Baaleb directed us to our stations. There, we waited, as the war began, to protect the secrets. To abide by the first tenet of our brotherhood. And so we turned a blind eye on the snake. He relented to the master, to the necessity of the task, or so we thought. But all the while, Salastragore formed his plan in the shadows. He coded a virus into our systems. A poison, weaved into the signal itself. Undetectable. And so when he appeared at our stations, one by one, hunting us, we found our powers failed. And the dagger slipped easily into our avatars' backs. Only it was a death from which we could not be reborn."

"He killed all of you?"

"Not all of us," Zariel grumbled.

Maxan tried to calculate the odds, to conceive what it would take to betray your own brotherhood, all of them callers, masters, gods of Herbridia. "All by himself?"

Zariel rose, silently glided to the wall. "No," he said over his shoulder, his gaze locked on his four sheathed swords. "He had help. One who shared the snake's twisted ideology. The two of them believed it best to cut off the unseen hand of the Monitors, to set the avatars free, to end the game, to let the natural laws of the universe take their course. He was a fox."

Oh... Maxan heard the slow scrape of Zariel's steel. Part of him knew that if he turned now and bolted up the path out of the hovel, he might have a chance of escape. But the other part knew that his time was up, twenty years' worth. Choices had been made long ago. Events had been set in motion, and now the consequences of those actions would be felt.

"Me," Maxan said. The other voice was speaking too, a confession. "It was me."

He felt the other's guilt burst in his chest. "Ralse," he said. "My name, his name... It's the voice in my head."

"Your father."

Maxan had known it all along. It was the knowledge he had not wanted to accept as they walked in silence through the cave to come here. But to hear Zariel speak the truth so matter-of-factly, the weight crushed him. Maxan covered his face with his paws.

Zariel's bulbous head turned, and the silver eyes regarded the way the fox slumped over before the fire. The end of a tentacle wrapped around the handle of a sword, two inches of the blade drawn above its case, glinting in the firelight. He seemed to consider something for several long seconds, then slid the blade back home.

"The fox who sired you is dead. The body is dead. But the mind lives on inside your brain. Which, remember, was only theoretical. Salastragore and Ralse, together, they must have found a way."

But Maxan wasn't listening anymore. Not to the octopus.

He's right, Max. It's me. I've been here. With you. From the moment you were born.

But why? Why didn't you, I don't know... SAY something?

If I had, the recall would've crushed you. When you were a little kit. The knowledge would've killed you. So I slept, and I dreamed of a life, and that life was yours. And I forgot myself, for years. I forgot everything. I'm sorry, Max. I'm so, so sorry. I wasn't there for you.

So what am I? Your son? You, YOU, you weren't even a real fox! You're an imprint! That fox was nothing to you! So what am I? I'm not your son. I'm just, what? Another avatar? Another puppet?

No, Max—

ANOTHER SLAVE?!

"WHY?!"

The scream erupted from Maxan's throat, echoing around the ruined walls, sounding for miles out across the sunken city beyond. He was up on his hind legs, taking a menacing step toward the octopus, ready to scratch the old bastard's silver eyes right out of his squishy head if he had to, to get the answers. He was almost beyond caring about how Zariel had drawn his blade lightning quick and now held it at the ready. Almost.

"Why?" Maxan said again, stopping in his tracks. He let out a deep breath. "Why did Salastragore kill my father?"

"Sit," the octopus commanded, "calm yourself, and I will tell you."

Maxan did as he was told. He understood that Zariel wasn't his enemy. Zariel hadn't even been his father's enemy, not really.

"In the end, Ralse betrayed Salastragore. The fox locked the only gate that led to the Aigaion ... with no way to unlock it.

"Or so I believed," Zariel said quickly, seeing the fox squirm nervously, perhaps about to say what he knew about his golden eye. But Zariel already knew. "Rinnia told me about the fox she'd met in Crosswall. Not the first time, when you spied on us from on high. Later, after the battle below the station. I found her again. She told me about your eyes. One green, one gold. And that is when I knew. Because in this world, there are no such mutations. Not by accident."

Zariel sheathed the curved sword with a *clack*. But he didn't hang it again by the others. One tentacle arm coiled around its case firmly as his viscous body slumped beside the wall. He let out a long, bubbling breath.

Maxan understood how tired Zariel had to be. How old was the octopus body the Monitor's mind inhabited? Fifty years? Sixty? If the Peskoran avatar he'd fashioned for himself had been approaching middle age at least by the time the war started... Maxan watched the bulbous form rising and falling, catching its breath, and he pitied it. He wondered who the octopus would be, would've been, if the invading mind had never put its imprint upon it. How many thousands of animals had he met in his life who weren't truly themselves?

The old octopus regained his breath at last, his quiet, wet words breaking Maxan from his recollection.

"You see, genetic engineering was Ralse's specialty. It was Ralse who oversaw the design of all this world's creatures. He devised the original bio-mechanism, the mutation to our frontal cortices that receives the signal from the Aigaion. For him, tinkering with the code, which would become your eyes, while still in your mother's womb, was likely a trivial matter.

"My old knowledge of Ralse, together with what Rinnia told me about Salastragore's rage, at some *locked door*, that he'd tried, to keep secret from her... Young fox, your eye is one reason I decided not to kill you."

Maxan thought he would go on, but Zariel was apparently waiting for a response.

"Ah, all right." Maxan shrugged. "So what's the other reason?"

"I think you are sad. Pitiful. To be discarded as you have. Although your father killed all of my friends—"

"*Helped* kill them," Maxan pointed out, raising a claw tip, which Zariel ignored.

"He killed Baaleb, our master. With Salastragore, he *ended* the Monitors."

"Not completely. You and Folgian... Why didn't you join her? All these years."

"The bear and I had our differences."

"She told me she wanted to bury everything the Monitors ever built, along with all the truth of this world with it. Then build a new world, a new truth, on top of it. She was spending the end of her days dictating to scribes, writing down whatever she wanted the Mind to spread when she was gone. Rewriting everything. She said that education was our only salvation. But the whole thing was built on lies."

"Teaching truth, or lies, it would not have mattered. In time, without the signal to supply newly born avatars with imprints..."

"Everyone goes astray."

"Yes. The animals, without human minds to guide them, revert to their primal natures. What you call Stray cannot be stopped, so long as the signal remains... disconnected."

Maxan shook his head. Something wasn't making sense. "So why does Salastragore want the relay back? He means to carry it all the way back up there, but I didn't get the impression that he cares much for putting an end to the Stray and saving everybody."

Zariel was quiet. Perhaps he was thinking. His breaths came slowly, rippling softly.

Perhaps he's sleeping...? No. He's waiting. For me to say what it was I already know. What Ralse already knew.

"He means to control us," Maxan said. He thought of Pram, with the power to whisper wordlessly to her brother, to dominate a dying tiger and bend his every move to her will. All of it was possible when she called upon the Aigaion.

He means to control us. All of us. But why?

The red-scaled snake's single slitted eye burned brightly in his mind, the sight of Salastragore shouting at him, the sound of those words echoing.

WE ARE THE DISEASE!

"We're an army," he said softly, barely a whisper, inaudible against the crackling fire.

"What?" Zariel said. His body had once again disappeared involuntarily against the gray wall of rubble just under his hanging cloak and swords. The silver eyes were two points of glittering, fiery reflections.

"Ralse turned on Salastragore when he found out what the snake was going to do. It wasn't just to end the Monitors and let nature take its course. Don't you see? He's not done yet. He was so close to the final move. He's had to wait twenty years…

"We have to get out of here!" Maxan was on his feet suddenly, his eyes darting around to the path leading out, the crates of supplies, the swords, the half-seen octopus. "We have to get back and stop him!"

"Slow, boy." Zariel's body wriggled, and a pair of tentacles uncoiled, stretching out before him, like hands meant to hold the fox back. "We're not going anywhere but further and further away."

"What do you mean? He's on his way *up!* Do you understand? Once he gets there, it's all over!"

"Once he gets there…" Zariel said no more, letting the words hang in the silence, perhaps hoping the fox would see on his own. But the fox seemingly did not. "And how will he get there? On that rocket he's been building? Don't make me laugh. It must have been so agonizing for Salastragore to *know* for years and years how easy it would be if he had the right technology, yet he had to reinvent everything from scrap. And the Corvidian Houses that he fooled into paying for it, all of it. The snake preyed upon their false religion and self-fulfilling arrogance. And soon, they will come to destroy him.

"No, boy." Zariel allowed himself a few bubbling chuckles. "We will not be going back."

"You're so sure he won't succeed. And he's so sure he will. One of you has to be wrong."

"Even if I am wrong," Zariel allowed, clearly agitated by the notion, "you're forgetting that there is another. Close to him. Perhaps, closer than anyone."

"Rinnia."

"Your sister."

"So she… wait, *my what?*"

"If that's what you could call a clone of your father. Though female. She has Ralse's blue eyes."

The revelation struck Maxan to silence.

"Indeed. Ralse and Salastragore, together, thought to preserve their lives and fashioned for themselves superior avatars, Rinnia and Saghan, who would house their minds when their current bodies died. Only Ralse was killed, and apparently, he chose you. And cannot get out."

The inner voice, Ralse, confirmed everything Zariel said. *It's true, Max. It's all true.*

Why me? You could've just taken over Rinnia and been closer to Salastragore all this time, and then when the time was right … just put an end to all of it.

I couldn't. And you know why.

Because, you'd forget everything. Just like you did with me.

And it wouldn't have stopped him from finding you, and Vess, your mother. I thought maybe, if I could just somehow recall soon enough, maybe I could protect you. But I was wrong.

Maxan felt the weight of the other's guilt building inside him, swelling in the cavities of his chest until it felt like he would burst.

I… Maxan closed his eyes, not sure if he was ready for what he'd think next but compelled to say it anyway. *I forgive you, Father. For everything.*

Zariel had been studying the silent fox as he stared off into the gathering dark. The fire was dying. It would need to be fed soon. But the old Monitor was tired. He knew their advantage over the snake's assassins was wearing thinner by the minute, that the head start he had gained by caving in the lakeside entrance would shrink to nothing very soon. They would have to be up and out of Old Quwurth in a mere handful of hours. He yearned for rest. He could hold his eyes open no longer.

But Maxan wasn't sure he would ever close his eyes again.

"You're taking me west," he said softly. The mass of Zariel's body did not stir, aside from the rhythmic rise and fall of his breathing. "To Peskora. We'll skirt south first, throwing them off our trail, and avoiding the Thraxian desert wastes at all costs because you need water, don't you? You've little hidden caches all over the place. Been stocking up for years. Preparing. But your home is in Peskora. Under the sea. A station all your own where Salastragore hasn't found you. Or he has found you but can't get in because you've rigged it with traps. Either way, he doesn't care about you, Zariel. You think you're some powerful figure on the apoth board, but you don't see how useless you are to be running all the time."

Maxan sat, picked at his claws, watched the embers snuff out one by one, and thought. In the darkness and stillness, he thought about the game, Apotheosis. Only a few years ago, the Mind had handed out the game boards and first iron-cast champion figurines. Folgian, no doubt, had designed the game to serve as a kind of diversion. *Diversion from what?* The game simulated the glory of the combatants who earned their titles in the great arena at the center of Crosswall. After all, violence was the centerpiece of Leoran culture. When the great nation of mammals wasn't warring with the birds or fish or lizards elsewhere, it was warring with itself. As an undying Monitor who had witnessed violence—*no, not just witnessed, but orchestrated, participated, hungered for it*—Folgian knew that Herbridia, like the Earth, would be overrun by it in time. There was no stopping the violence inherent in sentient creatures, the old bear thought. She thought you could just mask it, hide it, ignore it, bury it.

Divert attention from it.

Divert our desire for true violence to a desire for a simulation of it. And that's all the animal in man is. And it will never, ever end.

Maxan rose in the pitch-black darkness. The fire was nearly gone. He stood over Zariel's sleeping form. He gently ran his paw over the beautifully etched designs on the hilts of the octopus's curved swords.

Rinnia is going to try and stop him. His paw closed tightly around the handle and drew an inch of the blade from its sheath. It was so easy. *She's going to kill herself.*

He thought about Chewgar, about the poison, the pain. He remembered how the unstoppable rhino had said his name, like a plea, even as his eyes turned black.

He sheathed the blade quietly. He stood for a moment longer, just breathing. Then he slowly, carefully, undid the fastening that held the sword.

Chapter Ten

Golden Eye

THIS IS CRAZY. I DON'T EVEN KNOW WHERE I'M GOING…

Sure I do. I'm going BACK. I'm GOING to wander in these tunnels until I find a way back to the castle, or a way up to the sunlight. I'm going back for Chewgar. And for Rinnia. And if anyone stands in my—

Wait, wait, wait. Wait! Hold on. I'm NOT going to hurt anybody, if I don't have to. I'm going to stick to the shadows. I'm going to be patient. I'm…

This will never work. I can barely swim, and that lake is probably filled with flesh-eating, fox-eating monsters.

Yeah right…

Seriously. Have you ever seen crocodiles' jaws? Of course, you have.

Stop it! Stop talking yourself out of it. You can do this. I can get over there, and once I do, everyone in the factory is so bent to their work, they won't even notice…

Or they're already rioting like the toad lord said they would. That was just one day ago! Or two days? I don't even know! Wait, did he say riot? Or strike?

In fact, the whole place could be empty. Riot or no riot…

But that thing's down there. The queen…

So why go inside then? Don't go inside. I climbed the pinnacle; I can climb the Monitors' station. Sure. No problem. Easy, really, with all the—ah, sharp metal and things sticking out everywhere. And assassins… Creeping in from every little crevice…

Right. Agreed.

Wait, who am I agreeing with?

Anyway, when I get there, best wait for nightfall. What time is it now? How long have I been walking?

Thoughts, thoughts, and more thoughts tumbled through Maxan's mind at every step. They had been assaulting him for hours and his sleep-deprived mind had nothing left to defend against them. Doubt, then determination. Fear, then tenacity. Hesitation, then certainty. The highest thrilling exhilaration, then lowest disheartening dread. He had as many emotions and arguments as a diamond had facets, and he stumbled through them all trying to find which one was truly leading him where he had to go.

Ironically, he sounded more crazy to himself now than ever before. The idea that he had been talking to himself all these years had turned out to be an illusion anyway; there really *had* been someone else in his mind. But this time was different. This time, he was *actually* talking to himself. The inner voice of reason, the other fox, the spirit of his father, the user-mind imprint, whatever it was, it had been silent ever since Maxan had crept out of Zariel's hovel and out into the pre-dawn expanse of the Old Quwurth ruins.

Maxan was jittery, mumbling incoherently, mostly in his mind, but sometimes in a gasp or explosion of hysterics that echoed in the darkened tunnels.

He had spent the first hours reviewing everything Zariel had told him. What he recalled from the other fox's experiences corroborated those truths. It was a wealth of knowledge Maxan had never rightly earned nor asked for. Rinnia had almost been right about much of it. She had told him that their world wasn't real, and he could see now that she didn't have the advantage of dormant memories to back anything up. Zariel had recruited her, manipulated her, used her, and now seemed fine with the idea of throwing Rinnia's life away. Because of what he'd told her, she believed that nothing mattered, that it was just a game. She'd told Maxan as much. She'd given in to despair, believing none of this was real.

But Maxan knew it was real. The lives of the Herbridians born on this world were real. They grew from cubs or hatchlings to children, to adults, to the elderly. They laughed, they loved. They worked and played and shared experiences. They had souls to call their own. They were all worth saving.

And with Chewgar and Feyn gone, he might've been the very last animal who actually thought they still could be saved.

Maxan came to a halt, aggravated by how he'd let the idea of Zariel's inaction and Rinnia's manipulation creep back into his mind. He stared ahead to where the path split in two. He swept the beam of the pinlight (which he had also lifted from Zariel's stash) from one to the other, hoping maybe Ralse could chime in, access some prior knowledge, say something, anything. Maxan let out a sigh when there was still no response. It was just a waste of mental effort. He knew exactly why Ralse was silent.

You're letting me make my way.

Guided by a slipshod sense of direction, he chose the tunnel where the light seemed to travel further in the same direction and resumed his pace.

His grip tightened around the handle of the elegant, curved sword he'd stolen from Zariel. Along with the pinlight, the katana hadn't been the only thing he robbed from the slumbering weaponmaster. He'd tried to unlatch the spherical mapping mechanism from the hook on Zariel's harness, but the thing had clicked and caused the sleeping octopus's skin to shift color. Maxan backed away slowly and settled for what he could find in the crate, just another bundle of seaweed.

Hours later, Maxan might have felt very lost and exceedingly exhausted, but the feel of one of the most devastating weapons the Monitors had ever constructed filled him with confidence and conviction. Maxan had always been atrociously bad at swinging a sword around. But with *this* sword, he was unstoppable.

I'm ready. I FEEL ready, but I still need to think through the first move.

His pace quickened. He had chosen tunnel branches that only sloped upward, always careful to aim his progress in the same direction. And suddenly, his efforts were rewarded. He smiled broadly as he ran his paw over the jagged, serrated wall he'd noticed when Zariel had first switched on the holographic map.

Probably halfway there. I can do this!

...Max.

It was Ralse's voice. Suddenly and unexpectedly. It raised the fur along his shoulders, spine, and tail. Something was wrong.

Turn back.

"Ha!" The single note of laughter burst from the fox's muzzle and traveled down the tunnel before him. "Don't think so."

No, Max, turn back! Something's coming!

The flare ignited like a new star born in empty space. Light exploded into brilliant life. The sudden, pink flash seared Maxan's vision. He leapt away from it automatically, throwing one paw up to shield his eyes, the other out to his side, readying the katana.

The snake waited patiently for his prey's eyes to adjust, watching the fox gradually lower his paw and catch his breath. He tossed the flare onto the tunnel floor where it smoldered in the graystone dirt. He stepped over it, a shadow framed in bright light.

"I watched you die," Maxan said. His eyes fixed on the hole punched through the red Drakoran leather armor and the deeper red of dried blood all around it.

"You did," Saghan admitted. He ran a hand over his belly, prodding the flesh beneath the armor, vibrant and healthy, covered in fresh, green scales. "But don't believe everything you see."

Maxan felt the edifice of determination he had built for hours start to crumble. He couldn't think of anything clever to say. His grip tightened on the sword.

"I sssee you've met the interloper." Saghan brought a hand up to rub at his neck thoughtfully, his forked tongue flicking. "I did too once. But he let you keep your head. And you stole one of his treasures in return. Well done, thief."

"I could steal one for you too." Maxan forced a smirk on his face, hoping it might help him hang onto at least a shred of his rapidly dissipating confidence. He twirled his wrist, spinning the blade in an arc at his side. It sang beautifully as it cut the air, but it also sliced awkwardly through the fringe of his cloak, missing his tail by less than an inch. "Ah," he said in shock, trying to recover. He held a thumb back over his shoulder. "Maybe we could go ask him to loan you one."

Saghan stood rigid, framed in shadow, his long neck curved down, his V-shaped head tilted up, his orange eyes dull, watching the fox indifferently. His forked tongue flicked the air. His fingers dangled lazily over the thin sword at his side. He looked bored.

No, Maxan realized. *Not bored. Just … tired. Defeated.*

"You know," Saghan said at last, pacing steadily from one side of the tunnel to the other, "my … *father* thought that Zariel was dead. When all this started. Twenty years ago, at the start of the war. There was a cave-in at his station. Salastragore had rigged bombs that could swim underwater, made especially for eliminating the Peskoran Monitors. He thought he'd got them all. But the octopus is a very cunning species. Zariel hid under the wavesss for ten years, you know, before finally resurfacing, with those blades."

Saghan stopped his pacing. He gestured at the weapon in Maxan's paw. "I saw what that did beside the lake. No doubt it left you ssspeechless. But I've seen its work for years. Zariel appears randomly, wherever the Monitors operate. He assassinates some magistrate or something, carves their bodyguards into a mound of severed limbs, then ssslinks away in some sewer. You haven't seen the bodies like I have, Maxan. Cuts so clean you could set your dinner table on their corpses."

Saghan paused for a few hisses of laughter.

As Maxan had listened to him talk, he'd been trying to recall just how far behind him the tunnel bent or branched, calculating if he could make it there at full sprint. Then Saghan had said *bomb*, and Maxan remembered the night they'd met at the Auroch's Haunch inn back in Crosswall. And he was suddenly aware of just how confined the space underground was. There would be no escape from the fire this time. There was no escape whatsoever.

He let out a breath, calming himself, abandoning the idea of retreat, resigning himself to fight. He relaxed his grip on the sword, aware of the tight cloth wrap of its handle against his palm. He imagined himself wielding it underwater, striking left and right fluidly, effortlessly. When he replied, he was surprised by the determined edge he heard in his own voice.

"Get to the point, Saghan."

Saghan smiled at that.

"I was jussst curiousss about Zariel. Why did he not just find a council or a king somewhere, in whose ears he could whisper? Just like the old bear did. Think of all the truth he held. All that potential *power*. Why did he hide it?"

Maxan gave no answer.

"You know why. Either he told you ssstraight, or you figured it out on your own. It's why you left him behind. Stole his sword. Betrayed his trussst."

"He wants to restart everything. Epimetheus. Just like how it was before."

"Yesss."

The snake drew his thin sword slowly, the steel slid from its sheath without a sound.

"Saghan," Maxan said evenly, drawing the calmness of water from the weapon at his side. "What do *you* want?"

Saghan's smile melted. The question ignited an angry glow in his eyes. "Sssame thing I've always wanted. *Nothing*." The snake ran his blade over the scales of his forearm, leaving a hairline cut. He watched it stitch together instantly.

"Can you kill me, Maxan?"

The fox understood the true desire in the words. "You can choose," he said. "Your own life."

"You're wrong. I *am* only what my father decides. You cannot understand."

"You have no idea," Maxan said, "just how *well* I understand."

"NO," Saghan spat venomously, his sword arm swinging wildly in the air between them, the tip of his blade scratching the scarred graystone wall.

Maxan's sword came up defensively, automatically. He inched lower, keeping his weight in front, readying himself.

"No," Saghan said again. The fire in his eyes swelled. "I killed him. I may not have wanted to. I may not have chosen to. But I slashed him open with the poison. And I watched him die!"

Maxan's heart fluttered, struggling to compensate for the sudden, flowing adrenaline. The beast held deep inside rammed against his ribs, clawing at the walls of the dark cave that held it, its prison. His grip tightened on the stolen sword.

"No," he said, his voice seething through his clenched, sharp fangs.

"And perhapsss," Saghan said slowly, pointing his blade straight at the fox, "I *enjoyed* it."

Suddenly, only the animal in Maxan remained. The fox launched itself forward, blindingly quick, sweeping the razor-sharp katana where the vile snake had stood only a split second before.

Saghan was not as prepared for the fox's speed as he'd anticipated. He evaded the tip of Maxan's strike by less than an inch but couldn't keep his thin sword from its ferociously sharp bite. Zariel's blade sliced Saghan's in two, effortlessly, silently, dividing it like paper. The fox's body whirled with its momentum, turning full circle in the gray dust, bringing the blade around again, this time lower, this time catching the snake in his belly, cutting through the Drakorans' armor like it was forged from air, opening a deep gash in the flesh below.

Saghan recoiled from the pain; he felt something slippery give inside his abdomen, as though the threads that sewed his organs in place had been cut. He tumbled over his heels, his long neck and tail forming a circle wheeling away. He came up in a crouch several feet from his enemy. His left hand tucked inside the hole in his armor, holding his guts together, and his right still clutched the hilt of his severed sword. The pain spread along every inch of his body, setting his cold blood boiling with hate. The snake's wide mouth opened reflexively, its twin fangs unfolded. A deafening hiss and a spray of bright green venom erupted from the reptile.

Fueled by rage and instinct, the rational minds had been overcome by the animals' beastial nature. And yet, they fought with weapons and techniques, actions and reactions, calculated movements and strikes. The two animals had an awareness of the other's capabilities and shifted their weight and angle to adapt accordingly. The fox recognized the snake's immense strength; it had seen it match the muscled arm of a rhinoceros. And the snake had felt the sharpness of the fox's weapon mere seconds ago, so it could not let it clash with his blade or his body again.

They were a whirlwind, a never-ending dance of limbs, dodges, steps, and spins. They kicked up a hazy cloud of dust leaping into and out of each other's range. The fox's katana cut across the rocky surfaces all around—scoring the rock, raining bits of rubble on their heads and shoulders—and missing the snake's lithe body by inches every time. The snake clenched tightly at his stomach, holding in his intestines, putting him off-balance just enough to slide away a half second too late. Its back collided with the wall. As the fox moved to rush in, its only option was to hurl the broken sword. It bought the snake just enough space to spin away. A chunk of wall clattered to the ground, sending up a burst of gray dust.

There was a pause.

The fox regained some of its rational sense as it breathed heavily and choked on the dust. It backed away a dozen steps, keeping the katana up defensively. A hissing breath swirled through the cloud. Two fiery orange lights burned at its center and lower, the red glint of the rubied dagger the snake's master had given it.

Within seconds, the snake shot through the tunnel, its dagger slashing at the fox's neck, weaving away in a feint, stabbing in again and again. It seemed that the reptile was first to pick up on the rhythm of their resumed battle, quickly seizing advantage over the mammal. Its flashing orange eyes read the flow of the fox's movements, the rate and angle at which it sent its sword striking in. The snake thrust its dagger at his enemy's shoulder with no intention of actually meeting its flesh. The fox rocked its hips just as anticipated, just in range of the fist thrust hard into its exposed flank.

The fox absorbed the crushing force of the blow and flew sidelong down the tunnel, slamming into a soft bed of gray dust ten feet away. If it had been only a few inches closer to the snake, its ribs would have split apart like dry kindling, and those fractured bones would have stabbed into his lung.

Maxan came up, leaning heavily on the wall, wincing as his paw clutched his side. Every gasp for air was a world of agony, and yet he couldn't stop heaving. The pain brought clarity to his mind. Whether driven by animal rage or invisible puppet strings, he realized just how reckless he'd let himself become. He resisted the animal urge to charge blindly back in.

"Is it… true?!" He wheezed, holding the point of the katana up toward the screen of swirling dust. The light of the pink flare was dying somewhere in the distance. The fiery eyes had vanished. "Did you… kill… my friend…" A shadow in the haze, and Maxan followed it with his weapon. "*TELL ME!*" he screamed, ignoring the agony it brought.

The only answer was silence.

Maxan coughed lightly, taking the hits in his side. The sword wavered in his grip, too heavy to keep up, and he was so tired. His arm fell. He sniffed and realized he was crying.

His fanned ears, twitching suddenly at the sound of a click from within the dust cloud. He recognized it from prior experience. It was the sound of the snake's spherical device arming itself. And then he remembered a device of his own. His claw brushed over the switch on his weapon's handle.

"Maxan." Saghan's words drifted softly through the tunnel. The snake must have also regained some degree of his senses, but each breath was labored, pained. "He killed *me*. He wasss ... a great warrior. I wanted it to be over. Once and for all. But I came back. I cannot change what I am."

A low-frequency thrum filled the tunnel. A vibrating pulse rattled the floating motes of dust, crashing them together, dispersing the cloud. A single green bead glowed in the haze.

"I cannot take back what I did."

Aside from the deepening vibration, there was only silence. A second bead, orange, lit up within the haze, and the sharp sound intensified. A second, more powerful pulse thrummed, and the dust fell to the ground like rain against glass, exposing the snake and the fox. The one with a razor wire bomb in his hand, the other clutching a katana with both paws. The air all around the blade's sides shimmered as it gathered energy. The rock beneath them rumbled.

Even if they'd wanted to speak more, their words would drown in the deafening vibration. Maxan's fangs buzzed in his head. His paws were numb. The third and final red bead of light came to life in the katana's handle, and the blade had all but disappeared, everywhere and nowhere, a thing of pure kinetic energy.

Then, everything happened at once.

The device flew from Saghan's hand straight ahead on a perfect course to collide with the fox. Its proximity sensors activated just as designed, its shell blew apart in a flash, and the web of filament within spread like a blooming flower.

And Maxan's paw was drawing upward, dragging the elegantly curved blade in a perfect arc, sending all its gathered force up along the length of thin steel and out into space. It felt like flinging a mountain. Everything that stood before it was divided by two, both the chain web meant to snare him and the hand that had thrown it.

The vertical shockwave shot forward through the tunnel. It cracked the ceiling and split the floor in a perfect line. The web came apart and spread harmlessly to either side of the fox, the ends of either half of it caressing his shoulders like breaths of wind as they passed.

The snake's left hand flopped to the ground, severed at the wrist. Its fingers twitched, striking up miniature storms of dust where it lay. A trickle of cold, reptilian blood spattered beside it. Saghan fell to his knees, letting go of his guts to clutch at the stump of his wrist, trying and failing to staunch the flow that gushed down his arm. His father's rubied dagger fell beside him with a puff of dust. Saghan did not cry out in pain. He was far too familiar with pain, merely a nuisance at this point. Instead, he hissed maniacal laughter at the stupidity of it all.

"Sssss-sss-sss! Clumsssy me!" he managed to say between fits of hysteria. He lifted the stump near his eye to brush away a tear with the back of the hand that remained.

Maxan emerged from the dark and laid the Monitors' Weaponmaster's razor-edged katana gently on his enemy's shoulder. Saghan enjoyed a final chuckle, then all was silent.

From above them, through the rock, there came a grinding sound and a low, continuous rumble, drawing both their gazes to the ceiling. Neither of them breathed. Somewhere in the vast subterranean network above, tunnels were collapsing under the pressure of loosened weight. After a moment, the rumbling faded, the tunnel settled to silence once more. Maxan let out a sigh, lowered his eyes, and found Saghan's staring up at him. The fires in them had gone out.

"Ssso... What now, Maxan?" The snake assassin sounded so tired. Defeated. It was the admission of an unstoppable force that it wanted to be stopped. It was a plea.

A plea that Maxan ignored. "Now you tell me straight." Tears welled in Maxan's mismatched eyes, a dam ready to burst. "Is he really dead?" Maxan pressed the flat of the blade so hard into Saghan's shoulder it nearly toppled the snake over.

Saghan's head dipped low.

"I'm ... sssorry."

Maxan's paw was trembling uncontrollably. The thin steel wavered atop the snake's shoulder. His fangs clenched. His throat choked. Finally, the flood of tears broke free and ran down his muzzle. He sucked in a sobbing breath and released a wail of agony that shook every shaft of the cave.

"I ... have no control," Saghan said. "I have nothing. I am nothing. I am not ... me. I never wasss. Never will I ever be." He released his hold on the bloody stump and let his arms fall to his sides. He glanced over at the severed hand, lying to his side in a clump of dust, muddied by his blood.

"Do it, Maxan." He met the fox's eyes again. "If you can, make it the lassst time. Pleassse."

Do it, Max.

It was a whisper. A voice from deep in his own heart. It was Ralse.

It feels good. It feels right. Because it is *good. It* is *right… It is justice.*

"You d-deserve it," Maxan stammered, fighting through his tears. "For what you did to him."

You want this. You hate him. You want it.

Maxan, suddenly, could swallow. His tears stopped.

What? He struggled to sort through his feelings. Did he hate Saghan? Did he? Did he hate this thing strongly enough to kill it?

I…

You know it's true, Max. You hate him. You want him to die. You can give him what he deserves. Justice. He's begging for it. Just do it.

"I didn't know," Saghan whispered, barely audible over the noise of Maxan's thoughts, "that the dagger was poisoned."

The next few seconds lengthened to a lifetime. Maxan believed choices were doorways, and he saw them stretching in an infinite line. Opening one and stepping through meant leaving all the others behind forever. There was no going back.

Zariel's sword ceased its wobbling. It slid from Saghan's shoulder and hung limp at Maxan's side. The fox wiped his tears and drew in the deepest breath he could manage.

"No."

He spoke to Saghan, on his knees, begging for a final death. But he also spoke to Ralse. And to Zariel, and to Rinnia. To Folgian, to Feyn. And to Salastragore. He didn't know who among them would bother to listen—to truly listen—if they'd actually been there, and he didn't care. All those fools thought they knew some kind of truth about how the world really worked, how the beast inside really worked. They thought they knew human nature. Hate, violence, revenge, destruction. So focused they were on these that they'd ignored the other side that could be decent. Maybe there was a ferocious beast in everyone's heart that could blind them, reduce them to monsters. But there was also the capacity to be more, to resist, to be better than the beast.

To be truly *human.*

Maxan did not understand what it even meant. But he would find out. When he did, he would remind everyone. And he would start right now.

"No," he said again, stepping away from the kneeling snake. "We can be better. *I* ... can be better. And, Saghan, so can you. It's so hard... but I don't hate you. There's a part of me that wants to, I feel it. But I can't."

The snake slowly raised his head. Listening.

"I'm going to stop him," Maxan said. "I'm going to set us free. You and me, the Stray. Rinnia. If I have to kill Salastragore, then he'll be the only one. Not because he killed my parents or burned everything I ever loved. Not because I hate him. Because I don't. If he doesn't stop, then I'll kill him because of what he's willing to do."

He held his paw out to Saghan. "But, ah, I could really, really use your help."

For a long time, Saghan examined the furless, scarred paw before him. His mind raced through his own lifetime of choices. When the other mind invaded him, he wanted to rip it out, regain control. He wanted to believe it was possible.

But he couldn't.

Saghan looked away. He closed his eyes. "Run," he whispered.

Maxan squinted at him, puzzled.

"Run. Pleassse."

It was too late. From the deep shadows beyond the nearly faded flare, a streak of silver flashed without a sound.

The fox grimaced. His paw lifted to the needle in his neck, already faltering as his muscles seized. His muzzle curdled into a snarl, and his fanned ears and bushy tail twitched and whipped about. His paws snapped open, dropping the old octopus's sword in the dust. His claws locked in a rictus of pain. He toppled over on his side, convulsing. Every wheezing breath clicked as the fox's tongue flopped in and out over the back of his throat, blocking the flow of air.

The shadows came into view, shrouded shapes moving against the darkening sides of the tunnel, coming to either side of their master.

Saghan watched Maxan spasming uncontrollably with a blank expression. He had tried to make a choice. He tried to help. He told the fox to run, and the fox would've run and been safe. Because he, Saghan, wanted Maxan to be safe. But did it matter? Not in the end. There, in the dust, writhing in pain before where he knelt, his choice had come to nothing anyway.

One of the hooded assassins drew its thin blade from its back and moved to finish its work. Saghan shoved it hard against the wall. The bones in its shoulder broke with an audible snap.

"NO!" he roared. Then he grasped the assassin on his other side and tossed him toward the fox. "Get it out of his neck before it kills him," he ordered evenly.

The second did as it was told. More rushed in soundlessly from behind, a few stooping over their crumpled comrade by the wall. One assassin stood over Saghan, observing him, noting the emptiness of his slitted orange eyes as they stared vacantly at the fox. It unlaced the ties around its neck and drew its black hood away, revealing a long neck of pure and red-patterned snake scales. A bloody skull marked the broad white space of her V-shaped head.

"Saghan," she said. He was aware of her voice suddenly. She might have been standing there saying his name for an hour, for all he cared.

"What?" His voice was hollow. The brilles over his eyes closed, blinking. His forked tongue flicked the air, taking in the familiar scent of the creature by his side. Something that might be like his sister, but that they were both genetically enhanced and identical clones of their creator, albeit with a few cosmetic differences. He said her name in reply.

"What, Selyen?"

"We're to bring the eye. And leave all else behind."

"K-k-kk-khhh…"

It was the sound of the fox choking on his own frothing spittle. He would drown in it, suffocating to death, in a minute or so. The assassin that had gone ahead to remove the poisoned sliver crouched over him, its reptilian hands searching through cloak and clothing.

Saghan rose, crossed to the fox's side and shoved the assassin over, not hard enough to break this time. He rolled Maxan onto his side, draining the fox's windpipe. The gurgling ceased, and the breaths steadied. Saghan noticed that Maxan was unconscious, and he was thankful he could give the fox that dignity at least.

His eyes found his severed hand in the dust nearby. He picked it up, turned it over idly, his tongue flicking. Then he threw it violently into the darkness. He retrieved the elegant, curved sword that had done the severing. Not a scratch, not a single speck of dust could cling to its perfect, polished blade. He stared into the orange eyes he saw reflected there.

"Saghan," the white snake hissed. She'd come to his side again.

He lay the wondrous katana by the fox's shoulder.

"We're bringing him back, Selyen. Alive."

"But the master said—"

"*I AM THE MASTER!*" he screamed, wheeling on her, backhanding her with the wrist where his hand had been, leaving a red streak of his cold blood across her face, marring the perfect red pattern in her scales. Saghan's strength could rival that of the monstrous behemoths that once roamed this world, amalgamations of genetic codes the original Monitors unleashed as final challenges in their campaigns. Saghan and Selyen were Salastragore's own amalgamations, the master's will made manifest in DNA.

The female clone was quiet, reclusive, while the male was inquisitive, genial. She was detached from their creator's affairs while he was constantly engaged. Selyen was perfect in their father's eyes, having only been alive two years, not long enough to feel the puppet strings at her back. Saghan knew she most certainly would. But in the meantime, he was the elder and she answered to him.

Selyen endured the blow without uttering a sound. She was just as strong and indestructible as her brother. She swung her head slowly back to face him, a look of pity in her red, slitted eyes. But behind them, he saw the look of disappointment only a father could have for a son.

He remembered then what she truly was. A monster. Just like him. And he pitied her too.

"Bring him," he said again. "Alive."

FILE: "FIRST CONFESSION"

Time: 003271/10/02-003271/10/03[23:58:05-00:11:51]
Location: Castle Tower
Begin audio transcription:

I think I've got it to work... Test. Test.

[bmmphff-bmmphff]

Well, we can troubleshoot later if it's not picking up. So...!

How do you like it? A little drafty up here, I know. But it was the best I could come up with given the level of security required. No doubt by now you've realized you've been cut off from the Aigaion. Probably my greatest invention. Made everything much, much easier.

Well, might as well give you the grand tour.

There's the only door. Hmm, I'm sure you've noticed already.

And you've obviously acclimated well enough to your cage. That's good, that's good...

And I've already introduced the audio device.

[bmmphff]

Well... Oh! Take a look up there. Do you see those braces near the top of the wall? They're drilled into the mortar, straight out the other side. There's this big ring of iron I slapped onto the tower, holding up eighteen inhibitors. Eighteen! One was probably enough, but let's face it. We both know what you're capable of. And please don't think their power supplies could ever fail. I've rigged solar and hydro, and I'm even paying one of my teams to crank the backup generator as part of their daily tasks.

So. Hmm. That's about it, I guess.

What'd'you think? A little sparse maybe, but I'm sure your brilliant mind will just fill this place to the brim with all your little plots and schemes. Well, once you've worked those out of your system—it may take years—you can, you know, talk about everything that's happened. ...how you really feel. It's okay to feel, hmm, a little bad about it.

...

Ah. Hmm.

Oh! I almost forgot! The crown jewel of the whole castle! Hold on. I have the remote device right... here. Just press...

[wwhhhrrrr]

There we go. Just a moment... Just a moment... Done. Look up there. I spent half a year redesigning and splitting the conical roof so it would open like that. Thousands and thousands of gold. One sad sack even fell to his death building it for me. Actually, for you, I should say. I compensated his family, of course. Anyway, take a look. There she is. In full view.

There's the glow at her center. The core. Still burning, like an eye. I remember you once told us that the Earth is watching us. That it was the whole point of the Project. That we should never lose sight of her. Hmm. Well, you'd be proud of me. I didn't. Never once. That little glow in there was the candle that lit my way in the darkness. And now I've come out the other side.

...

Hmm. Well... I think it's time I go. I believe it's past midnight now, and you must be exhausted. Listen, I'm leaving the audio running. Constantly. It's linked all the way down to the lab. If you ever feel like, you know... Well, I'm calling these "confessions," Baaleb. If you ever look at the ruined Earth and feel inspired to... confess something.

Feel free.

...Ha! That was a good one. Feel free...

Chapter Eleven
House of Saro

SAROVEK'S KEEN EYES SWEPT ACROSS THE FLAT LINE OF the northern horizon where the midday white of the sky clashed with the deep green-gray of the vast Drakoran marshland. Yinna hung directly over her in a cloudless sky. The heat of the daystar had dispersed the swamp mist but did little to eradicate the humidity. The sunshine beat down upon the hawk knight. She felt a dam of moisture break over her skin, and sweat ran like rivers between the forest of feather quills. Beneath the matted shirt and plates of armor covering her chest and shoulders, she rolled the joints as best she could to work away some of the weariness.

The hawk had set out from the castle the very next morning after her arrival, almost two full days ago. She had donned her full armor, despite not having the time to polish it back to its proud mirror sheen. She had set out an hour or so before Yinna rose to wake New Quwurth, not wanting to risk a confrontation with the animal laborers lining up on the castle bridge for another day of toiling in the factories, mines, walls, and railways that comprised the Monitors' network of power. But she'd miscalculated. Even at that hour, the tides of starving Quwurth commoners were already spilling through the grand entrance. They were too tired and desperate to confront anyone they might perceive as someone in charge. Regardless, her keen sight had detected the true, hidden feeling behind the desperation in their eyes.

Rebellion. If Lord Groak's warning the previous day was true and work on Salastragore's rail ladder was coming to an end, there would be bloodshed. If it came to that, there was little she could do to stop the Drakoran city from tearing itself apart against the Monitors' defenses. Little she could do *there*, anyway. There was something she could do to prevent at least some of the carnage. Her duty called to her from the north, approaching from the sky over the great swamps and bogs. Her twin brother Duke Sarothorn was coming, and with even a fraction of their great Corvidian house's fighting force behind him, he would bring doom to any Drakoran standing in his way.

When Sarovek had seen the first telltale glint of steel on the horizon, she knew. So she had stabbed her spear deep into the muck and stood as rigid and proud as her tired bones would allow, her pupils wide, flicking left and right at every shimmer of armor along the razor edge of the vast sky. She waited, and she watched. And she worried. There were more now coming into view. There was no doubt.

She was restless. Standing there, she yearned to spread her wings and blast into the sky to meet her brother and be done with it, regardless of the outcome. But her wings were still done up in bandages, held together by splints and gauze and pink pockets of panacea powder. Sarovek resisted the urge to lean on her spear. Principal Harmony and her agents had damaged her wings severely, but they had left her with her dignity. For a Corvidian, to be without wings was to be without honor. A grounded warrior made you no better in battle than the lowest species of Herbridia, what many in Corvidian society derisively called the dregs. Most, if not all, Corvidians believed they were superior by birth, just as Harmony had said before she died. Sarovek had learned much from the dead Principal's example.

"Tragic arrogance."

Sarovek muttered the words to herself. Like all the rest of her feathered race, she loved the feel of flying, the effortlessness of riding the currents of air, the heights from which one could see so very much. But after centuries of living above all other species, it had engendered a spiteful attitude throughout her beloved homeland that not only defined much of their shared history, it would soon enough shape the course of Corvidia's future. Despite the heat, a shiver ran over her skin and prickled the small feathers on her forearms and head. She swept her keen eyes once more along the northern horizon, hoping that future would never arrive, even as it approached, inexorable.

Sarovek believed every Corvidian could do with some time on the ground, trudging alongside the other species of this world. Sharing experiences and hardships. Forging friendships and earning respect. She thought of the callers Pryth and Pram, and to a lesser extent their Master Feyn. Their time together in the Denlands had been brief, but it had helped confirm a suspicion she had been harboring for some time now: the servants of the Mind, even those closest to the cult's supreme leader, were just as moral or immoral as the Monitors. And those two Crosswall guards that accompanied them, the rhinoceros and the fox, even though they had been dragged into this conflict—which had been waged without their or anyone's knowledge for decades—the two of them proved to be loyal beyond question and strong in their own personal ideals. They believed what they were doing was right, and Sarovek admired them both very much for it.

And Rinnia. Rinnia most of all. Sarovek had spent nearly every moment of her time among the Monitors in that fox's company. No one else in this world—not even her own twin brother—was closer to Sarovek than Rinnia. They had traveled impossible roads together, overcome physical cuts and spiritual wounds together. Rinnia, most of all, was responsible for dispelling Sarovek's Corvidian arrogance when the hawk had first arrived in Drakora.

Sarovek had learned not to ask her dearest friend about their "brother," the snake Saghan. The hawk knight suspected that he was haunted by some dark thoughts, perhaps some darker deeds. He was trying to escape something, as she had been once. Rinnia refused to provide more details, so she did not pry. Judging Saghan solely by his capability on a battlefield, she found pride enough in knowing him.

Though her own, true brother had sent her to Salastragore's employ nearly ten years ago—as a means to, in his words, "monitor the Monitors" and ensure the project funded by their and other Corvidian houses' significant wealth was going according to plan—Sarovek had learned nearly nothing about the red snake's ultimate goal. Nor had she learned much about the Mind's, for that matter. She knew enough about the ancient artifact that had fallen from the Aigaion, the so-called "relay"—and how possession of it was worth waging their secret war—but she had yet to discover what either of those factions planned to do with the actual world they would somehow reshape with its power. She hoped that helping all nations understand that they had to share this tiny world—including Corvidia—was part of their plans. And if it wasn't, she would remain wherever she could to best ensure it would be.

The translucent eyelids flicked over Sarovek's sharp eyes, moisturizing them. She looked away from the horizon. The black apertures of her pupils tightened reflexively, bringing the details of a patch of swamp several miles away into ultra-sharpened focus. Through a light veil of afternoon mist, she saw insects darting from reed to reed. One hapless hopper landed in the center of the web a spider had spun between two towering spires of thick grass, a monument that would have been obliterated in the first heavy wind, had there been any wind to speak of in this place. She saw the six-legged creature—no bigger around than her taloned fingertip—skitter toward its trapped prey, alerted by the vibration of its struggles.

The nostrils in her hardened beak took in a deep breath, and she smelled the stagnant, thick water and the putrescent mush that no doubt hid a fortune of medicinal and mind-altering plant life, a cache of resources that hadn't been fully tapped for more than a decade all across Drakora. Not since construction on the Monitors' rails to the sky had begun. And even if this nation's enterprising, industrious amphibians and reptiles thought to harvest the sunken bulbs and rotting reeds from under the muck, even if they knew what to really look for, all of the distillation and refining processes were the most closely guarded secrets of the Council of Lords in New Quwurth, of which Salastragore was beyond doubt the most influential and powerful. For now.

A loud croaking erupted behind her, bringing Sarovek out of her reverie. It was a noise like a cough and a snort and a belch all mixed in equally. She turned to regard the revolting cane toad that had released it, a Drakoran Lord himself, no less. While she did consider it important that all species of all races across this world learned tolerance of one another, just then she could easily think of at least one specimen who could challenge that notion.

"Mus*thpf*-t we wait in the open field, Lady St*hpf*-arovek?" Lord Groak grumbled. Sarovek doubted he suffered from the stench the same as she did, evidenced by the sound of his perpetually clogged sinuses that caused him to suck in and spew all his lisping breaths orally.

Sarovek had overtaken Groak and his small retinue of slaves and mercenaries just as the sun was setting the previous day. Had the light been better and had they not been raising the Drakoran Lord's silken tent on the other side of a low hill, she would have gladly avoided meeting him. Last night, it had been easy enough to deflect his invitations to exchange formalities and discuss their purposes for trudging northward (despite the obviousness) by blaming exhaustion. And by the following morning, words wouldn't have mattered much anyway. Sarovek knew why Lord Groak had lied about returning to the Council in Quwurth and come North. He was Duke Sarothorn's agent all along.

Just as her brother had once thought of his sister.

The fat, greasy cane toad watched from on high as four younger frog boys cleared the reeds and swept the mud below into a flat space wide enough to receive his litter. All the while, the team of six muscled lizardmen stood in the sweltering heat, keeping their lord (and his considerable girth) above their shoulders.

Sarovek clacked her beak shut, not even giving the Drakoran Lord a salutation when they'd all caught up. Ten minutes of the frogs' futile labor later, and despite his utter dissatisfaction with their progress, Groak's warted fingers wagged an order, and the lizards lowered the litter to the muddy ground.

"Would that a tree could grow in this abys*thpf*-mal bog and provide us with s*thpf*-ome more shade, no?" From under the comfort of his umbrella, he finished the complaint with a bulbous expansion and release of air from his throat.

Sarovek made no reply. Somehow, she even resisted the urge to clack her beak again. The silence, while it had lasted, had been enjoyable, and she hoped to encourage its return.

"Well..." Groak resumed, ruffling her feathers, "this*thpf is* Drakora. Flat. Wet. You can s*thpf*-log for a hundred miles before finding anything that ris*thpf*-es above your wais*thpf*-t. A was*thpf*-teland, don't you agree, my dear? Loaths*thpf*-ome place."

If Saghan had been here, he might remark how easy it was to find many things above Groak's waist, but few as wide around. If her beak could smile, she might have allowed it to do so. Instead, she turned about sharply, her eyes boring into the gluttonous bullfrog. "This is your home," she reminded him.

"Not for long," Groak croaked after a time.

Sarovek was grateful when the next silence stretched for half an hour with only minimal slurping and grumbling from the bullfrog lord. Groak permitted his frog servants to sit in his shadow while the lizards seemed content to warm their cold blood in the sun while propping up his umbrella and fan.

Sarovek's pupils constricted, her sight locked on the approaching flock still miles away, needlepoints of light shimmering like a slowly rotating gem. Something was not right. Sarovek blinked, incredulous. She could see the rhythm of their wingbeats. As one, they loomed like a shining silver arrowhead the size of a small city, resembling the Aigaion itself.

"Raptors," she breathed. There were hundreds of them, the Corvidian species of war. Eagles. Hawks. Falcons. Owls. Vultures. Kites. All of them were plated in polished steel with spears gripped in both talons and long swords at their belts. As the Corvidian force drew closer, Sarovek spotted ranks of lightly armored sparrows and kestrels and other smaller species with bows slung across their backs and quivers on their thighs. This wasn't just an emissary of the joint Corvidian Houses as Groak had intimated a day earlier. Her brother was not just here to check on the Monitors' progress, to talk, to make demands. This was a fighting force, to invade, to capture, to dismantle. She surmised that the Corvidians' supply caravan would be half a day behind the fighting force, perhaps more unless their scouts found a swifter route through the bog.

"What do you s*thpf*-ee, my dear?" Groak's body nearly rolled out of his chair. The toad stared myopically out over the expanse.

Sarovek made no reply. He would see soon enough.

Duke Sarothorn landed gracefully before her, his beak held high and proud. The raptor knights flew onward overhead, their polished armor shimmering like a million pieces of raining glass. He wore the same gleaming plates, adorned with robes spun with threads of gold. Even as he stood in the muck and mud of a Drakoran swamp, it seemed like nothing could tarnish the gleam of him, and the breeze would not allow his robes to touch the ground. Sarothorn's face was identical to his twin sister's in every regard, except for the ridge of his brown-feathered brow, which was harder, turned more sharply downward as though he was always in judgment of everyone and everything the bright eyes beneath them fell upon. Those eyes swept slowly over the flatness of land stretching in every direction, noting everything in existence ... except his own sister.

"What are you doing here?" Sarovek had to shout over the gust of feathered bodies passing overhead. The raptors were landing all around, sending bursts of wind rippling over the reedy grasses.

Behind her, Groak's bulging eyes narrowed against the unsettled dust and pollen. He raised a hand to prop up the eyelid sagging with the weight of its own warts. "My dear," he said, aggravated, "I told you. Duke S*thpf*-aroth—"

"What are *they* doing here?" Sarovek demanded, ignoring the cane toad. She lifted her spear skyward and swept it back, indicating the thousand raptor knights who had already occupied a great expanse of swamp within moments. The rush of their landings was fading to a rustle.

Sarothorn allowed the silence between them to stretch, surveying all but her.

"To collect what is ours." Sarothorn said at last. His voice was measured and deep. Its power resonated through the stillness of the swamp. It seemed he was not so much answering his sister as he was rallying his troops. "We will take it," Sarothorn went on. "Brick by brick."

Finally, his gaze fell on her. Sarovek knew the one thing her brother hated more than failure was waste. Waste of resources, labor, money. These were utterly deplorable. But above all, the Duke Sarothorn hated wasting time. That is what she saw in her twin's expression, the true message there only she knew how to read. His eyes told her that for ten years, she'd amounted to nothing more than a waste of his time. And her own.

Of course, he should've known his sister equally as well. Sarovek stood just as tall and prideful, gazing back just as hard, matching him in every respect aside from the polish of his armor, the glory of his robes, and the fitness of his wings. Who was he to talk down to her with his eyes? He had not fought, he had not bled, he had not suffered like she had. He had not witnessed the workings of the machinery deep underground or knew even a fraction of the truths that kept their tiny world spinning. He sat comfortably in plush chairs in halls of granite counting coins.

"You are too soon, brother." Sarovek's voice could carry just as much power and reach just as far as his. "The Monitors have yet to test the machine. After all this time, all this waiting, you arrive at the wrong hour. You are too soon."

"We are too late," Sarothorn corrected her. "For ten years, the snake siphoned our wealth, promising Corvidia the means to attain its birthright. Our rightful, natural ascension to our throne in the sky."

Sarovek's gaze snapped to the hazy, dark outline of shadow creeping along the horizon hundreds of miles away. The Aigaion had the uncanny ability to appear when spoken of. Or perhaps it was everywhere, always, yet unnoticed.

"And he lied to us," Sarothorn went on. "All the while. The so-called Master Monitor never intended to deliver the great Corvidian houses what they'd paid for. I sent you here, dear sister, to ensure he would."

Sarothorn's piercing gaze drifted from his sister and swept across the armored raptors ringing them. He opened his beak to say more, but a croaking voice cut in.

"Yours*thpf* was*thpf* not the only promis*thpf*-e St*hpf*-alastragore broke, honored Duke." Lord Groak gestured angrily at his lizard slaves to haul his litter closer to the hawk twins. "He st*hpf*-tood before the Drakoran Council of Lords, twenty years*thpf* ago, I remember well. He promis*thpf*-ed our nation would regain all it had los*thpf*-t to the insects*thpf*. He claimed our los*thpf*-t population could be recovered, through s*thpf*-cience! Rrr-hrr-grrhh! The arroganc*thpf*-e, the ridiculous*thpf*ness*thpf*! He told us*thpf* that he could *manufacture* Drakoran reptiles*thpf* and amphibians*thpf*. And yet, look around you, at all this*thpf* empty was*thpf*-te! *Three years*thpf, he proclaimed! And after five had pass*thpf*-ed, then ten, then fifteen. And s*thpf*-till no one here. Every time the Council convened in New Quwurth, we s*thpf*-wallowed the s*thpf*-ame promises*thpf*. The other Lords*thpf* were too scared to defy S*thpf*-alastragore."

Groak pretended to ease his bulbous body deeper into the cushions of his raised chair, dignified, with a look of self-gratification on his face. But, in fact, he was simply out of breath, exhausted, and grimacing. Nothing he said was new to Sarovek. She knew the Master Monitor had a stranglehold over all of Drakora, that the Council of Lords was nothing more than his puppet show to keep the citizenry entertained. And she knew her brother Sarothorn was already aware. After all, these past ten years, she'd been the one reporting as much.

Lord Groak regained his breath. He looked down from his raised litter at Sarovek, his throat bulging proudly as he said his next words. "It ends*thpf* now, my dear. Whatever s*thpf*-ecret the red s*thpf*-nake claimed to harbor, they lie buried beneath the fortress*thpf* that Drakora built for him. It is our fortress*thpf*. Once it is s*thpf*-afely back under our control, Corvidia can grac*thpf*-iously take what is theirs*thpf*." Groak shifted his weight in the chair, turning now to face Sarothorn. "Our aim is the same, Lord. Salastragore must be destroyed."

If Sarothorn was as repulsed by the bloated toad as Sarovek was, he didn't show it. Her twin brother's face was a mask of patience, of diplomacy. But she had known him since the day they hatched together. She saw the contempt and disdain deep within his eyes. Groak may be welcomed in the north as a defector and enjoy a splendorous reward for being Sarothorn's agent. But it would not last. Sarovek knew an unforeseen, fatal accident would be the slimy cane toad's final reward. And it had been decided just a moment ago. He had spoken too much, saying what was already known. He had wasted the Duke Sarothorn's time.

There would be little, if anything, Sarovek could do to spare the cane toad from his fate. (She wasn't even sure she wanted to.) But there might still be a chance to spare others. She turned wildly about, from Groak to her brother to his retinue, not quite sure who she was truly asking. "Will you slaughter what little remains of Drakora to destroy Salastragore?"

"My people will not impede the attack, Duke," Groak said, ignoring Sarovek. "New Quwurth is tired, worked to the bone, s*thpf*-tarving, going as*thpf*-tray. They will s*thpf*-ee your knights*thpf* as their saviors*thpf*, liberators*thpf*. They will not fight back. Only Salastragore's closest servants and soldiers remain, garriss*thpf*-oned inside the castle."

"How many?" A wispy, scratchy voice broke in. It belonged to Grandal, a broad-chested eagle that served as Sarothorn's right hand. He stood tallest among all the raptors, and his sun-gold feathers were flecked with white and gray. Grandal's house had once been prime among the rulers of all Corvidia until Sarothorn had challenged his authority in open court and slashed out the eagle's throat with his talons, leaving him clinging to life and unable to speak. Even after the crushing defeat of House Gran, honor dictated that Grandal and his remaining force serve the victor, the eminent House Saro. Now, more than a decade later, plenty had challenged House Saro but none had succeeded.

"I-I-" Groak stammered as the eagle approached. Even the lizards holding the cane toad aloft wavered, tipping the litter dangerously sideways. "I-I'm not… I cannot be c*thpf*-ertain, but I…"

"In *war*," Grandal hissed furiously at the toad, "it is unwise to deal in vagaries."

"Is*thpf* that what this*thpf* is," Groak replied, waving a hand at the armored host of knights and archers surrounding them. To his credit, the toad seemed to have recovered his dignity, enough to wag a long finger at the eagle. "Is*thpf* this*thpf* a war? Careful, Corvidian, what you s*thpf*-ay in the pres*thpf*-ence of a Drakoran Lord."

"Enough," Duke Sarothorn said, the practiced smoothness of his voice concealing his irritation. "This is a war, Groak. Yes. Though, we are not bringing it to you. We are not waging against Drakora. The war I'm speaking of has been here for years already. Decades. Skittering underground. Awaiting its final conclusion."

"The Thraxian abomination," Grandal added. "The last of their kind. In service to Salastragore."

"In s*thpf*-ervice to their *queen*," Groak corrected. Then he shrugged. "Who s*thpf*-erves the s*thpf*-nake, I do conc*thpf*-ede the point… But you've never s*thpf*-een or fought anything like her."

The eagle raised a sharp, black talon to point at Groak. If Grandal had wanted to, if his liege Sarothorn wold only give the order, he could pop the toad's belly like a soap bubble. "How many," he whispered hoarsely.

Groak's slimy forearms and fingertips wrapped around his girth and neck protectively. He flattened back in his high chair, shrinking as far from the eagle as possible. He finally regained enough of his dignity to stammer an answer. "It… it would be wise to atic*thpf*-ipate perhaps*thpf* a handful of s*thpf*-corpions, and a thousand ant drones*thpf*. I cannot be sure as they've made their hive deep in the tunnels*thpf* below the lake."

Grandal and Sarothorn both looked to Sarovek. She knew what they wanted from her, what they expected: loyalty. To her house, to her nation. She hesitated. If she confirmed Groak's estimation, she would be betraying her friends. Chewgar. Maxan. Even Saghan. And Rinnia. Her most of all. But it wouldn't matter. Her brother Sarothorn had already decided. Coming all this way just to turn about and fly home would be a colossal waste of time.

Sarovek nodded, more to buy herself time to think than to prove her loyalties. There had to be a different way. A move no one had yet considered.

Grandal turned his attention back to the toad. "And of the snake's personal guards?"

"You will face a few hundred. Armored, with s*thpf*-pears, s*thpf*-ome cross-*thpf*-bows, grrrgghhh." Groak croaked in contemplation, raising a finger to touch the side of his wide nose. "But it is S*thpf*-alastragore's elite you must be most wary of, my friends*thpf*. The shadows. They are unnatural beings. S*thpf*-trong, s*thpf*-wift. They move like water. Or... air, if you prefer." Groak's throat bubbled with croaking laughter at his own joke. Then he cleared his throat with a belch. "We don't know how many he employs*thpf*. My s*thpf*-pies' reports have been conflicting of where and when they have appeared within the castle, dropping from the c*thpf*-eilings and emerging from hidden pockets*thpf* in the dark corridors*thpf* at all times*thpf* of the day."

Sarovek had been silently counting the size of the Corvidian force as it swooped in and landed one by one in the swamp all around them. There were perhaps five hundred armored raptor knights and as many bowmen, and likely a few hundred more to follow in the rearguard with the supply train. She knew beyond doubt that every one of them would be a corpse within a day if they attacked the Monitor's castle.

"Sarothorn," she said, moving to stand directly in front of him. He had no choice but to see her now. "Brother. You will listen to me now. As equal. You will listen." She felt Grandal's immense size approach at her side, as if he would strike her down for her insolence, but she held her gaze steady on her brother. Sarothorn gestured to stop the big eagle.

"I am listening," he said honestly, returning her stare. Sarovek knew then that it was only the two of them, alone. Even with all those keen eyes upon the twin hawks, the rulers of Corvidia, none of them saw the true Sarothorn emerge.

"You will lose," Sarovek said flatly. "He has planned for this. You would wager so many honorable knights on the intelligence of this Drakoran Lord? This unloyal creature?" She ignored the croak of protest behind her. "He tells you what he thinks is the truth. But you do not know the Monitors. You do not know Salastragore. He plays the game always one move ahead. If Groak is giving you an estimation, it is because that is the estimation Salastragore wanted him to give you. You will lose."

As Sarothorn listened, his eyes locked on hers, Sarovek saw the title and prestige and weight of leadership melt away. As she finished speaking, her true brother was all that remained. It was a look filled with sadness. His eyes then told her how much he'd missed her, how much he regretted sending her away, how he would have given up all his power to have his sister back, if he could. But he could not. Sarothorn was there only for a moment, and then he was gone.

"Take her away," the Duke ordered as he turned away, and two knights of his retinue rounded his shoulder with iron manacles already in their grip.

Sarovek closed her eyes and took in a deep breath. She'd thought of the final move she could play in this game a few moments earlier, hoping it would not come to this. As the iron touched her wrists, she shrieked the sacred words, loud enough to carry across all the swamp.

"I challenge the rule of House Saro!"

With suddenly trembling hands, the two knights shrank away from her, the manacles dropping with a plunk into a muddy pool. Sarothorn stared at them in the deafening silence. Then he looked up at her. Honor mandated that terms of the challenge be matched. But he said nothing.

"And what do you risk?" Grandal was there, whispering intensely, standing between them, serving as arbiter. The eagle knew only too well the highest possible price for declaring a challenge to the ruling Corvidian House. It was how he had lost all control of House Gran alongside half the power of his voice. But a challenge issued from within a single house had never happened before. Not once in all recorded Corvidian history. Sarovek held no ruling power in Corvidia. By all reckonings, she was a pariah. And yet, she still carried the name. She stood tall and proud, armed and armored.

"If not by my house," she said evenly, altering the sacred words of the proclamation to suit the unprecedented situation, "then by my wings."

"Here, sister?" Sarothorn spread his taloned hands to indicate the expansive Drakoran wasteland all around them. The breeze had died to a stillness now that all of his fighting force had made their landing. The fringes of his fine golden robes had been soiled. His polished armor-plated boots were filthy. "Now?"

"Yes," she responded. She drove the blunt end of her spear deep into the muck. She drew her sword from its sheath and whirled it around at her side.

All of the raptor knights drew back. Lord Groak's crocodile and frog slaves teetered the toad's litter away to the edge of the widening circle of winged bodies. Only Grandal stood with the twin hawks, the arbiter who would finalize the terms.

Every thought in Sarovek's mind was screaming, doubting, seeking an escape from this pit she'd chosen to fall into. She was shaking, oppressed by heat one moment then assaulted by the cold of her sweat and fear the next. Her dented, tarnished armor was too heavy. Her sword, nicked and scraped from the last several days' battles, nearly fell from her grasp. She tried to stretch her wings, to take comfort in the feeling of air filling the downy pockets between feathers, but they winced away from the pain, held firm by the bandages.

But she had to try. For the lives of the knights all around them. For her brother. For Rinnia. The challenge was the only way now.

The real Sarothorn had returned now, and he did not flee. He stood in plain view, stripped of all the pretense of house honor and dignity and pride, no longer Duke Sarothorn. He was just her twin brother. He approached Grandal at the ring's center, who seemed all too eager to unsheathe his liege's sword and hold it with both talons before him. The blade was polished to such a mirror sheen that it glowed with the blinding white of the empty Drakoran sky. He turned his back on Sarovek and paced away, swished his weapon through the air a few times, then held it up and looked at her from its reflection.

Grandal backed away just to the edge of the wide ring of knights.

"On this day," the eagle began, even his hoarse whisper audible in the reigning silence.

"Save it" Sarovek shrieked at him, stifling the official proclamation with a resounding clack of her beak. She wiped sweat from the feathers of her brow. She bent at the knees, flexed her wings to hold them more tightly on top of her back.

Across the swampy field, Sarothorn stood as still as a statue, his back still turned to her, his wings relaxed and held apart, the glint of his blade rising above his shoulder.

"Begin," Grandal hissed.

Sarovek charged, her lower talons kicking up flecks of mud, pumping up and down with all the strength she could muster, resisting the suction of the swamp. Her brother stood rigid, his back still turned. For a brief moment, the thought flashed in her mind that maybe he was giving up, that he'd seen she was right all along, that he was underestimating his perceived enemy. The thought gave her hope, gave her strength. She extended her sword arm and cut hard just as she closed the distance.

With a strength and speed that far outmatched her own, Sarothorn's wings shot up then slammed down in a single, powerful motion, thrusting his body skyward and blasting a wave of air against his sister's attack. She stumbled back, missing the space he had occupied, while he soared over her back. Sarovek recognized his intention just quickly enough to save her life, spinning around and bringing her sword up to catch the vertical blow that had been meant for her wings. The clash of steel rang for miles around.

Miraculously, Sarovek's blade did not shatter to pieces. Numbness crept up her forearm, and her grip slackened. Her knees gave out beneath her. In less than a second, her brother's sword was raining upon her again, harder. He held it in both his talons. He battered her deeper into the mud, but somehow she held on to her guard. She told her muscles to rise, to meet him standing. Not like this. But it was no use.

Sarothorn's talon shot in, closing over hers, the tips of his claws piercing her flesh. He flung her sideways like a doll, ripping her sword from her weakened grip. It landed straight in the muck and wobbled, splattered with mud. He held on, crushing her talon in his grip even as she shrieked in pain. He twisted her arm, and she flopped over onto her broken wings.

Sarothorn stood over her, keeping her talon firmly in place, raising his sword, a great shadow surrounded by sunlight. He could strike and be done with it. He could chop her arm off or cleave her skull in two. But he hesitated. He let go of her.

Sarovek's sprained forearm splashed into a puddle at her side. She'd somehow lost control of her own body. The exhaustion and weariness sat in her bloodstream like hardened lead. She blinked, but she did little more than scratch flecks of mud across her eyes. She watched helplessly as her taloned fingers twitched in the puddle of mud. She heard herself sobbing, whimpering.

Then her brother was there. Not the Duke. Her brother Sarothorn by her side. He knelt beside her, soiling the perfection of his armor, close enough so only she could hear. His voice was soothing.

"Don't let them see you like this." He dabbed the clean, golden-threaded cloth of his robe against her beak to dry her tears. His gaze was gentle and warm. "I am sorry. For everything."

He did not know, but the last time—the only time—Sarovek had cried the first night she spent in the Monitors' castle ten years ago. Alone, cast out of her home, cut off from her family. She had stood in her drafty prison cell of a room and gazed at Yerda glowing outside the high window and let the tears go. Her brother had defeated her then too, his words were his weapons, rational and sharp, convincing their father that it should be Sarovek who joins the Monitors and ensures their wealth not be wasted. And then, all of a sudden, her tears had stopped. Sarovek decided from that moment on, her resolve would be harder than the steel of her armor. She would fulfill her duty to her great Corvidian House, learning what she could of the Monitors.

And she had indeed learned so much.

Sarovek drew in a deep breath and held it until the urge to cry was suffocated. She let it out, knowing she would never cry again. She clacked her beak and almost laughed in Duke Sarothorn's face.

"You ignorant fool." She would say more, but he was too much like their father. Brash. Bold. Stubborn. Sarothorn would no more listen to her than he had ten years ago. When she'd learned of his passing, she hadn't cried then either. "You arrogant, ignorant fool. You know so little about how the Monitors' world works. Everything belongs to them."

The warmth in Sarothorn's eyes chilled, his gaze hardened. By now, she was nothing more than a waste of time for the Duke, for all of Corvidia. He clutched her shoulders and lurched her up powerfully. He held her there with one talon, eye to eye, their beaks almost touching, then ran the other along the length of Sarovek's wing. She winced from the pain.

"I believe *these* at least, dear sister, belong to me." He tightened his grip, and Sarovek felt the fragile bones bending. She kept her eyes locked on his, breathing through the agony, as he went on. "And as for what I know, I know I told Harmony to spare you, against my better judgement. I knew then, and I am reminded now, just how stubbornly you would cling to your false loyalty and stand against your own kind. You see, I know about the artifact. I know it was taken, then hidden, then found and taken again. I know they call it the relay. I know that it speaks with the voices of gods. I know that if I bring it to that great castle in the sky, then I will hold dominion over all the lowborn, scrabbling species beneath me. Above all, I know that the shared dream of our superior race can at last be made reality.

"You see, Sarovek," he said, squeezing harder, twisting his wrist, and snapping her wings as she shrieked. "You could say, I know all I will ever need to know."

Chapter Twelve

The Last Living God

"Rise and shine. Oh, right. Well, look, I know I said last time would be the, hmm, *last time,* but this time I've got quite the surprise for you, old friend. A cellmate! Perhaps you already noticed? The guards dragged him in last night, but they said you were asleep. Who can really tell with you anyway?"

Not a dream. A voice… it's… Feeling in … stone. My face. My fangs. Feel it in my fangs. Throbbing… skull.

"Wait… are you awake now?"

Just a dream. Asleep. Tilt my… Turn my head. That smell. Awful… Feel my claws, scraping on stone…

"Hmm! What's this? Shhh. Quiet… The boy stirs."

My paws, so stiff. I can't…

"You are awake. Look at him. Do you recognize him? Take a very close look… Go on…"

Stone so… cold.

"I SAID LOOK GODDAMN YOU!"

Maxan's eyelid fluttered at the thunderous outcry. The light flickered just beyond a screen of drowsiness. His lashes dusted against the gritty stone floor. His muzzle was pressed against it, his upper lip held open, his gums dry. His tongue lolled between his fangs, numb and heavy.

"Aww. You woke him. So careless…

"Hmm? What's that, boy? Got something to say?"

What happened? Why can't I… move? Why can't I see? Why can't I do anything?

Maxan's mind felt in the darkness for his arms, found them, told them to flex. He had a vision of them pushing himself up off the floor, but it misfired. The most he could do was raise a paw weakly, but it flopped back to the floor, his claws clicking on the stone. The fluttering light in his vision intensified. But something was wrong with it. There was only a void where half should be.

"An introduction is in order, I think. This fine, strapping lad… *is Ralse's boy*! The fox's true-born son! I found him! Well, sort of, he came here, but anyway can you believe it?!"

For a moment, silence suffocated the room. When the voice spoke again, the mania was gone. It radiated heat, and power.

"Now I have your attention," it said. "This boy held the key all along, old friend. But now I have it. Now there are no more barriers. No more locked doors. Can you believe the irony? Rage is such a reckless, useless emotion. My burning fury nearly eradicated the very thing I needed all along. I didn't believe in destiny before, but now I see that this boy was meant to find his way to me. To slip through all the snares I'd lain. Year after year after year, I killed every fox I could find. And yet it is *this* boy, and *only* this boy, who survived. It's… breathtaking. That was his destiny. And now, this is mine. The universe chose *me*. Don't you see? It has given *me* the means to—

"Ohh! Whoa now! Don't get up so fast, you might—" The heat in the voice was gone; the hysterics returned. There was the sound of scuffling footsteps passing near Maxan's ears. "In your condition … I can see I've unsettled you." Then the sound of creaking knees. A sharp intake of breath.

"Ahh! Dammit… Hey. Hey, Is there something you want to say? I will listen. I've *been* listening. I've *been waiting*. Please… Please speak."

Maxan felt his neck tighten. He dragged his tongue in and shut his lips. He felt the warmth flooding his mouth. He felt his heartbeat. His blood was quickening after what felt like days, weeks, years of this lethargy. In truth, it had only been three hours. He released a guttural moan. The vibration in his throat sent shivers down his jaw and up along his skull, awakening the pain that had been drowsing there. His head moved reflexively, raising it off the floor. He felt something slimy creeping down the right side of his face. The dark void stuck there as he spun. Vertigo overwhelmed him, and he retched. His arms shot out and crashed against the floor, trying to anchor him to something solid.

"Ugh," the voice said, disgusted. "Had to ruin the moment."

Maxan's senses were returning faster now, and he had some understanding of the room he was in, though his addled brain could not yet conceive of a reason why he was here. He felt a draft of air stir the fur along his left arm.

He heard the scrape of receding footsteps. Then a longer scrape of those same feet pivoting about.

"Well," the voice said, "I'm off. This is goodbye. Really, this time. The last goodbye. Last chance for last words, old friend. If you beg me for death, I promise I will make it painless. I… You deserve that much, after all I've put you through. All you need do is ask…"

A painless death, Maxan thought. The idea relaxed him. The tension in his head and arms began releasing its hold slowly. *Is he asking me? Should I say… Is that what I want?*

Maxan, a voice spoke in his mind. Independent of thought. Subconscious. The sound of it echoed in his skull. It was Ralse. *We're not dead. Not yet.*

Maxan's green left eye rolled around behind his fluttering eyelid. His vision locked on a blurry shape, framed by a door, set in a stone wall. Again, the sense of wrongness and vertigo crept in, but he did not look away. The blurry figure boiled in a contrasting sea of darkness and light. He blinked, fought through the queasiness, until Salastragore came into view.

The red-scaled snake had changed from his workshop apron and fur-mantled robe into a form-fitting suit of armor that was darker than black; the velveteen material seemed to entice light closer only to murder it. Its ornate style was similar to Saghan's with a high collar to protect the snake's long neck. Salastragore stood with his hands folded behind his back, looking beyond where Maxan lay with his single fiery orange eye.

There's something behind me.

Salastragore's head drooped. He closed his eye. He paced slowly back into the room.

"*Twenty years* in this hell… And not a single word…

The snake again passed Maxan, stepping over him as if he was a pile of trash. His hands came around from his back, balled into fists. He struck his own face violently.

"Not a single word? You wretched bastard!"

He punched himself harder now. Maxan could not see, but he heard.

"I'll kill you, Baaleb! I'LL KILL EVERYTHING YOU EVER LOVED!! *AND STILL YOU'D SAY NOTHING TO STOP ME?!*"

The reverberating, thrashing cries of hatred flooded Maxan's blood with adrenaline. He twisted over onto his side. He no longer had to focus on keeping his eye open. He instinctively struggled to push himself away from the red snake.

Salastragore released his hands from the iron bars of the cage at the center of the circular chamber. He was looking down at a mound of rags within it. He chuckled, catching his breath. He straightened his back and sighed deeply.

"No. No, no, no, old friend." Salastragore breathed. "After all this time, I'm not letting you get in my head. No way. What's important is that you know I've won. And with that, this truly is... Farewell."

Salastragore turned on his heels and strode to the door. He didn't spare the fox a glance. Then he wheeled about. "Oh! One more thing!" All of the snake's scorching, abhorrent fury was forgotten. "I almost forgot! I've arranged a little... *entertainment* for you guys."

At the sound of his clapping hands, two crocodile guards emerged from the door, hefting a white sack trussed in thick ropes. They dropped the thing beside the wall and began cutting the bindings that held it together.

"Hey, you there! No, no, no! Don't cut it loose all the way. We have to make this interesting."

Salastragore stood over the white bundle after the guards had left the room. He prodded it gently with the tip of his red-scaled tail. "Watch this one *closely*, my friends. I want you to *understand*. One final reminder why I'm doing what must be done."

The heavy door crashed shut behind him, and the *clunk* of a heavy latch followed.

Maxan's lungs finally felt free of the lethargic after-effects of the assassins' poison. He heaved in several quick breaths, then groaned with the effort of pushing himself up to sit. He succeeded, but the pain in his head intensified; still, he managed to stay upright. The sight of a cloudless blue sky drew his gaze upward. And then he knew. The right half of his vision was simply gone. It had ceased to exist. The intangible dread twisted in his guts. Both paws groped at his face, searching for what he knew was no longer there.

"My eye," he muttered, his voice hoarse. The tips of his claws came away reddened with congealed blood.

Maxan slowly turned around, taking in his surroundings. It was becoming easier to focus, though he could not move quickly for risk of falling over. The cage Salastragore had clutched at the center of the circle was shaped like a cube, no longer or wider than six feet, no taller than four. The solid iron bars were welded into its solid iron floor, which was itself sunk into the slab below it. There was no apparent lock or hinges. Inside the cage, a stooped, rounded figure sat, watching him with weary eyes. His head was bent over, held closer to the middle of his abdomen than atop a set of shoulders. This animal had no shoulders. His gray-green face sagged, creased with more than a hundred years of wrinkles. What Maxan had thought was an enormous mound of rags was actually the species' most distinct feature.

A turtle's shell, Maxan realized. *An old... turtle.*

Baaleb, Ralse said in his mind. *The Grand Monitor.*

The white bundle beside the wall stirred, drawing Maxan's attention. It was growling low, roused from a drugged sleep by the commotion, or more likely the subtle scent of the fox's blood. The beast snarled. It rolled its shoulders and jerked its head violently, straining against the ropes that held its face down. The growling intensified with its frustration as it struggled more and more to free itself.

Maxan's legs were still heavy, numb, and half-petrified by the lingering effects of poison, but he managed to drag himself with his arms, inching closer to the turtle's cage.

The beast's head finally found its way through a loop of rope and swiveled around. The scarred white wolf bared its fangs, the telltale hideous pink line holding one side of its maw higher than the other. Feyn—the caller, the Principal—was gone. He had gone astray, and there was no coming back this time. Only the animal inside remained.

Oh shit.

Maxan lurched himself onward, still several feet away from the bars. Behind him, the white wolf wrangled his first paw free. It slapped and scratched the prison floor, then pushed itself up onto its hindlegs. The wolf barked and howled. It snapped at the air in Maxan's direction, sending gobs of frothy spittle onto the floor. It had only one impulse, hunger, ignoring all else, such as the ropes still binding its legs tight. The beast fell hard on its face against the stone.

Cold sweat drenched the fur along Maxan's spine and even colder fear threatened to freeze his aching muscles. But he wrenched back control of his own body and doubled his efforts, turning away from the wolf and hauling himself across the floor.

The turtle watched him from the center of the cage, a light brightening in his weary eyes at the animalistic spectacle playing out beyond the bars. Baaleb's ancient lips parted, for the first time in a year, or years. He had long ago lost track of the passing time. He moved his jaw as though to speak, but only a rattle escaped.

Maxan wasn't listening anyway.

Behind him, the writhing beast twisted about, searching for a way to free itself. Its jaws gnawed at the tightened ropes, ripping them apart. One snapped, and the wolf's second arm came down on the floor. The animal had intelligence enough to see its prey would soon be beyond its reach, so it scratched its way over the stone with its front claws, snarling and slavering, its hindlegs still bundled tight.

Maxan reached the bars but couldn't wedge himself through. He gripped tight and pulled, clenching his fangs hard enough to crack. His blood pounded in his temples. Pain stabbed behind his empty eye socket like a dagger. The clots inside split apart or dislodged, and blood ran like a stream of tears.

He pulled. Higher and higher. The hungry, hideous wolf scratched and howled for his blood. Maxan's paw grasped the top bar. He cried out with all his strength, hauling himself up. Behind him, a pair of razor-sharp claws reared back and lunged.

CHAPTER THIRTEEN
THE LEGACY OF REPTILES

SAGHAN SAT ALONE IN THE WORKSHOP. HE HUNCHED OVER on one of the many tables, his legs up on a bench, his tail dangling lazily behind him, and his elbows on his knees. In his right hand, he held a cylinder wrapped in paper and string. He idly turned it over, felt the ethereal weight of the thing inside floating, shifting, touching one side. Then he turned it over again and felt it touch the other. In his left hand, already fully regenerated, he held the relay, watching the golden beads of light racing one another in their perpetual circuit up and down the shaft of brilliant, shining chrome. His eyes moved from one object to the other, and he thought of what he had paid to bring each of them this far.

They were just things.

He was just a thing too.

Saghan wondered… what if he threw them out the window or down the fuming chute in the workshop floor? Would the things melt in the furnace? Could he crush them with all the strength he had been given? What if he dropped them in one of the jars of acid he knew was on the shelves just behind him?

He wished he could. Once, years ago, he might have. But now…

Saghan's gaze slowly crept along the floor and stopped where the stones had been stained black. The charred perfectly cylindrical hole where the light had punctured the tower. And the spread of the spilled blood beside it. Black blood. Nothing could get that color out.

"Hmm, good, you're here!" The pronouncement broke the silence, and Saghan looked up to see a redder, older version of himself strolling through the doorway at the other end of the room. The thing regarded him with the one fiery orange eye it had left.

"I had to tuck our guests in for the night. I believe they'll get along well enough." Salastragore stepped gingerly around the blackened stones and stood before Saghan. His father watched him patiently, waiting for the son to acknowledge him. Saghan felt the eyes of his maker upon him. He tried to resist but couldn't. He looked up into Salastragore's face but said nothing. For a moment, the two snakes simply looked at each other.

"You've done well," the red snake said. "Saghan. My son. You've done well."

It was the first time in a very long time Saghan had heard the old snake say his name. It was not the name he had been given when he was made. It was the name Saghan had given himself, years ago, as his only means of rebellion. Of course, the maker had found out eventually. And he had been furious. As punishment, Salastragore had given his son the worst kind of knowledge: the horrific truth of his very own nature, the true purpose for his existence, and the utter certainty that there could never be an escape from any of it. The knowledge inflicted pain beyond physical, though there had been plenty of that alongside it. It had changed how the young green snake would see his world and himself in it, forever.

And things between them had never been the same since.

Until now, it seemed. Salastragore put a firm hand on his son's shoulder and squeezed. His other hand stroked the scales at the side of his son's neck and head. A corner of Salastragore's eye wrinkled as he smiled at his son.

Saghan wanted to hate himself for smiling back.

Salastragore held out his palm, and Saghan placed the wrapped cylinder there. "What about the relay," he asked his father.

"Keep that." Salastragore crossed to one of the other tables, set the thing down, and lifted the plasma rifle with some effort, then slung it on his shoulder and around to his back. "I shall have my hands full as it is," he said, winking.

Saghan came down from the bench and approached his father. He unsheathed the dagger on his hip and admired how the ruby caught the afternoon light flooding in from the windows high above. He flipped it and caught the blade, then offered it to his father.

"No, no, my son. You keep that too. I won't be needing it back."

Saghan was overcome with emotion. Within the last two days alone, he'd died twice, felt his soul slip into the yawning black of oblivion, only to be wrenched back to consciousness. And he'd killed again, a warrior undeserving of death. And he'd watched as his father cut out the fox's golden right eye. He tried to be passive, indifferent, to feel nothing, to make himself as meaningless as all those things he'd suffered and done and witnessed. He'd always felt like he had no choice, but maybe that wasn't true. Maybe he was himself sometimes, behind his own eyes, a puppet in control of its own strings after all, doing all those things because *this* was all he wanted. He turned the dagger around in his fingers, watching the light streak brilliantly within its thousand facets. It was Salastragore's most prized possession. And now it was his. The jewel was the recognition of the son by the father. The pride swelled in Saghan's chest, choking him.

"Fine" was the only word Saghan could muster. He clasped the dagger back in its sheath.

The two snakes crossed the room to the circular platform at the workshop's center. Salastragore threw the switch, and the triangular iron teeth of the aperture in the floor cranked loudly open. The heavy chains ground into their housings overhead so fast they shot sparks in all directions, heating to an angry red glow. Then they slowed as the rising platform approached the top level and came to rest with a locking sound. They stepped onto it, and Salastragore threw the switch again. The chains clinked rhythmically, lowering them much slower. The sound faded the further they plunged into the cylindrical shaft cut into the center of the Monitors' castle, replaced by the clanking of gears along vertical tracks set in the graystone walls. Electric bulbs buzzed in alcoves every thirty feet or so.

Saghan could see a kind of anxiety growing on his father's face each time the light flashed by. Salastragore stared vacantly ahead at the bricks passing, his forked tongue flicking silently, shadows of apprehension and worry crossing his features one moment, then a glow of triumph and elation igniting in his eye the next.

"I built all of this," the old snake burst out suddenly without turning, "for you."

The pride, the smile, the moment his father had given him in the workshop just moments earlier had felt good. But they weren't enough to completely eradicate the doubt, the mistrust, the bad memories that collected in Saghan for years.

"You mean, for *you*," Saghan shot back. "For yourssself. Because when your body diesss..."

He had never dared say the words aloud before. Not to Salastragore. And only once had he spoken frankly to Rinnia of his deepest fear, that he would lose himself forever one day within his own scaled skin. He watched his father closely, waiting for the hand that would strike him for his insolence.

But it never came. Salastragore's eye looked downward, dimmed by what might have been a passing shadow of shame. "I know. I've been a terrible father. I've let my … *obsessions* destroy much of the life I should have lived for you. My son. I want you to know," he said, meeting Saghan's identical eyes as another electric light flashed by, "that when I am gone, when this tired old body finally keels over … I won't be coming back." The red snake stood off-center, hunched over, weighed down by the weapon strapped on his back, rickety joints and bent bones. He let out a deep sigh, and when he spoke again, his voice was very low. It was a voice Saghan had never heard before, that of his father, completely disarmed and sincere. "I'm so exhausted. I can't do this anymore. So it falls to you… All of this—everything I've built—it will be yours. The castle. The city. The station and all the tunnels. The ants and my armies. All of my wealth. All of my knowledge, all of my power. Everything. I entrust it all to you, Saghan. My boy. You're the best of me, son."

Salastragore's hand did move, not to strike Saghan's face in anger, but to settle on his son's shoulder in admiration. The older snake's glowing eye sought to meet his son's gaze.

But Saghan concentrated on keeping his eyes lowered. All at once, he wanted and did not want to smile, and to cry for joy, or perhaps simply cry. He did not want to believe that his only wish had come true. Because if it had, then he could be himself. He could keep his mind, body, and soul all for himself, and his father's spirit would never meddle with his consciousness ever again. His arm tensed under Salastragore's hand. He wasn't sure if he should respond. His eyes drifted to the wrapped thing in his father's hand.

"Is this … a tessst?" Saghan asked.

Then something vibrated against Salastragore's hip. Annoyed, the red snake rolled his eye, tucked the thing into a pocket hidden by the deep blackness of his armor. He unclipped a small, vibrating disc and held it in his palm. It unfolded like a tiny, metal spider's legs. The device was identical to the projector Saghan had used in the forest outside Renson's Mill but smaller, receiving only short-range signals.

"Speak!" Salastragore spat at it, even before the ghostly blue hologram could fully form into Selyen's face.

"Master," she said, the image sharpening to define the patterned skull on her forehead. "Corvidian knights approach from the North. One thousand in number. Fully armed. They will reach New Quwurth in an hour, perhaps less. Do we fortify the city?"

Salastragore scratched at the scales on the underside of his neck thoughtfully, his tongue flicking rhythmically. "I thought we had a little bit more time," he murmured. "At least a day." He scratched harder now, flaking away some shriveled red scales.

"What should we do?" The image of Selyen prodded when it was clear he wasn't going to answer her.

Salastragore perked up at the question. His eye ignited brightly. He turned it upon his son, smiling. He offered Saghan the disc. "Go on. You know what to do."

Saghan accepted it, cradling his sister's face in front of his own. He thought back to the time he'd contacted his father in the Denlands, just outside the station in Renson's Mill. He remembered Salastragore's exact words.

"Kill them all," he commanded. "They're not here for the city. They want the sky wing. The schematics and formulas. Hold the upper halls of the castle. Let them have the foundries. If the workshop is overrun, take the lift down to the station and join the Thraxians. The core is all that matters."

The skull-marked face of Selyen was passive. "I understand," she said. Then she added, "Master."

Before the projection faded, Saghan thought he'd seen her smile, but he wasn't sure if it was shaped from pride in his leadership or insolence. He recalled how he'd struck her in the tunnels, screaming at her. But in the next moment, he folded the spider-legged disc closed and realized he didn't care about Selyen or what she thought.

Salastragore was watching Saghan with admiration glowing in his eye. "You're the master now. Saghan. Yes, indeed."

"It'sss … so unfortunate," the younger snake replied, flicking his tongue. He was being intentionally vague, prompting his father's response.

"What's unfortunate?"

Saghan looked up, smiling. "Everything you've given me is about to go up in flamesss."

"Ha!" Salastragore rocked back on the platform, overcome with hysterical laughter. "Good one, son! Haha! Yes, I suppose you're right. Bad timing. But none of that stuff up there matters, my boy. Wait til you see what's in store."

The sounds of clinking chains and grinding gears grew quieter as the platform slowed near the very bottom of all the Monitors' grand enterprise.

"And where *are* we going?" Saghan asked.

"Up," Salastragore said, pointing down. He chuckled at his own cryptic joke.

But Saghan's scaly brows tilted in confusion.

"Oh, come on! You haven't figured it out by now?"

"If we're going where I think we're going, why isssn't Rinnia with us?"

All of Salastragore's apparent joviality vanished in an instant. The old snake whirled on his son, gripping the collars of Saghan's armor and shaking him violently.

"Are you stupid, boy! Do you think for a moment I would trust a *fox* to keep a secret? I made that mistake already! NEVER AGAIN!"

Saghan pried his father's hands off his armor, feeling the frailty in the old wrists. He could snap them like twigs if he had wanted. A day before, he would have. A day before he thought he understood his place, below Salastragore, below Rinnia, below even Selyen the newborn. But now he no longer knew where he stood.

"All the punishmentsss," Saghan hissed slowly, letting his father's hands go, "all the pronouncementsss, the promisesss. I thought she was your favored child. Dessstined to rule beside you."

The blazing fury in Salastragore's eye cooled as he listened, then died out completely. "Why do you think I was so hard on you? All this time. It's because the only thing I can really trust... is my own blood." He looked up. "*You*, Saghan. Quite literally. My own blood."

The platform had slowed to a crawl. There was a rush of air pressure as it lowered, exposing a massive underground cavern at the very bottom of the cylindrical shaft. Finally, the gears settled into their moorings with a heavy iron click. As it touched down, a line of dim glowing bulbs flickered to life, strung up on iron poles set at intervals along a winding path, disappearing into the enveloping shadows.

Saghan had never been this far down in the station before. Of course, he knew what was down here—the laboratory, and the hive—but he'd never expected he'd be allowed to see any of it with his own eyes. The lift in Salastragore's workshop was the only means of direct entry, but the Thraxian ants had no doubt carved hundreds of their own secret tunnels in and out by their master's design. There was a sound like rushing water coming from somewhere deep in the darkness.

Salastragore hopped lightly off the metal platform onto the gravel path, nearly falling over as his rheumatic knees buckled with the impact. The plasma rifle slung on his back spun around by his hip, dragging him over sideways. "Ahhh! Oughh," he cried out. There was no echo, all the sound eerily eaten by the darkness instead. "Not as young as I used to be."

Saghan stood over him, offering his hand. He was done with words. He was ready. Everything up to this moment had indeed been a test. His father might never say so openly. But his father had said enough. Salastragore accepted his son's help, rising, nodding at him.

Saghan's flicking forked tongue picked up the scent of rust, and soon enough, the meandering path brought them into a hidden valley where a squat iron-walled cube rested at its bottom. The same dim yellow bulbs burned in its sides all around, shining on the writhing sea of oily insect bodies. The sound Saghan had heard as the lift came to rest was not rushing water after all. Here, the insect horde's chittering mandibles and scraping pincers was a cacophony that drowned out all other sound. The Thraxians' movement in this pit had scratched at the rust that had naturally grown for decades in the dark and damp on the iron walls of the excavated station. The dim lamp light reflected off its metallic foundation like golden sunbeams through a dusty red haze.

Waves of ants no taller than Saghan's waste approached the two snakes but came no closer than the edge of the path. Saghan noticed a wire running from lamppost to lamppost along the ground. He felt a thrumming vibration in the scaled soles of his feet.

"We've nothing to fear," Salastragore said, almost shouting to be heard.

This deep, dark hole was the last Thraxian hive in existence. It was their promised land, which Salastragore had gifted to the last surviving Thraxian queen. It was the only home the insect race had left. In time, they could be reborn here, their population surging, digging its way out from under the surface, perhaps even returning to their homeland, rebuilding the foundations that the fires of war had made into desert. Until that day came, they would be patient, and they would serve as Salastragore's loyal slaves. Digging his tunnels, constructing his castle, hauling his metal tracks to and fro across the entire subterranean world.

What choice did their queen have but to obey? She had no choice but to believe the Master Monitor's words. Saghan knew that Salastragore had saved her from the extermination and rebuilt her years before he'd even drawn his first breath. He had rarely seen the gigantic ant queen but for the rare occasions she crossed the foundry floor on her way to the master's workshop for tuning. He had never heard her speak, but somehow the queen and his father had an understanding. It went beyond the parameters set by whatever control mechanisms he'd installed on her mechanical new body.

"She's not one of us, you know," Salastragore called back over his shoulder as if he'd heard his son's thoughts. Saghan was about to point out the obviousness of it, but he'd been mistaken.

"Rinnia," Salastragore went on. They were very close now to a gaping hole punched in the side of the rusted metal cube that served as the laboratory's door. The red snake stopped, turned to speak face to face. "I thought I could… I don't know, love her. Like a daughter. But she has his eyes. She *is* him, you know. An exact copy. I think I did a good job. I taught her everything. I gave her all the right ideas. But she's not my blood. She's not *our blood*. Do you understand me, Saghan?" His good eye was locked on Saghan. His voice had grown serious. He jabbed a finger against Saghan's chest. "If you think all I'm leaving for you is … *stuff.* Poisons, traps, lands, slaves. Bombs, guns, blades, books. Then you're a fool, boy. Let all of that stuff *burn!* Where we're going, what I'm about to show you, you'll see. Say goodbye to all the places you've been and all the stuff you've seen up there. You'll never go back; you'll never touch those things again. I'm about to give you *this world!*"

Salastragore gripped his son by the shoulders and drew him closer. "Do you understand?"

The younger, green-scaled snake was powerless to resist the drug of recognition. It spread in his chest, warming his cold blood. "I underssstand."

Salastragore retrieved the cylindrical thing from his pocket and tore away the wrapping, tossing it carelessly beyond the wire boundary of the path where it was lost in the writhing sea of insects. Inside the small jar of clear liquid was a severed eyeball, carefully cleaned of its gangly nerves. Its iris was a shade of gold, its retinal pattern unlike any other in existence.

Saghan had known all along what it was inside the wrapped up jar. He'd been there as Salastragore surgically removed it from the fox's skull. He'd held the razor-sharp instruments. He'd watched in silence, smothering all emotion, willing himself into a statue carved out of solid apathy.

The two snakes reached the end of the path and ducked into the hole at the side of the laboratory. Saghan noticed that the walls surrounding the entrance were charred black, which had made it appear larger than it actually was. There were no lights inside whatsoever. As he switched on his pinlight and swept it side to side, he saw there had once been electric lamps, but they had all been eaten by fire like everything else. Every surface was warped from heat and covered in thick black soot. Piles of decades-old ash had collected in every corner with blackened bits of twisted metal poking out like broken ribs of a corpse.

Salastragore seemed to know the path through the waste, stepping gingerly around sharpened metal bits and ducking under collapsed portions of the ceiling from which split wires and melted conduits dangled like intestines.

"Ahead of us," he called back over his shoulder, "there is a door I've never shown anyone. I could never open it, no matter how hard I tried."

They reached a long walkway that stretched far into the darkness beyond the reach of the pinlight's beam in Saghan's hand. The path was clear of debris, though stained just as black as everything else. Below, on either side of the walkway was a nest of twisted cables, pipes, and heaps of broken glass. To their left and right stood two rows of immense cylindrical braces, and Saghan quickly realized all the glass had once been the vats they held.

"Thisss place…" he hissed quietly.

Salastragore gazed over the wreckage too, finishing his son's realization. "Where you were born."

"What about Selyen?" Saghan turned the light on his father's chest. Salastragore's orange eye narrowed at the piercing strength of the light. "Are there others like usss?"

"No," Salastragore replied quickly. "No others. It took me sixteen years to replicate the technology that… *he* destroyed down here. Some of this place survived. The most important part. Come on. I'll show you."

The older snake spun about and continued on down the walkway. He'd been too fast for Saghan to read. Doubt once again crept in, gnawing at the confidence his father's recognition had only so recently formed. But then he recalled Salastragore's words. What did any of this stuff matter? So what if there were other laboratories and cloning vats? If all the secrets the Monitors had sworn to keep were exposed, none of it would matter anymore. Saghan was leaving it all behind.

He followed Salastragore. The walkway terminated into a rectangular shaft of wall-to-wall concrete. Running vertically through its center was a fenced elevating platform similar to the one that carried the Monitors between the factories and the castle, but it was inoperable like everything else here. The two snakes descended the metal staircase that wound around the central lift, delving a thousand feet deeper into the surface. The further down they went, the hotter the air, the more intense the pressure, the louder a rumbling noise grew. At the lowest possible level, the only evidence of fire was the wreckage of the lift that had smashed and exploded at the bottom of the shaft.

They picked their way over the mounds of twisted fencing and concrete rubble, exiting at last into an enormous chamber much like the one Saghan had led Sarovek, Chewgar, and Maxan through only a few days ago. An abyss of total darkness yawned below and all around. A bridge of steel girders and concrete ran from the shaft's exit to a colossal pillar of rock at the chamber's core, hundreds of feet away. Set into the pillar was a plate of chrome a dozen feet wide and twice as tall. Red lights glowed like eyes up and down its length, casting a blood-red haze throughout the chamber. Saghan recognized that hue almost instantly from an experience he had lived behind his own eyes when he had not been in control. It was the same red light cast by the relay when its signal was disturbed, the light of impulse and murder that had bathed the Crosswall inn where Maxan had stolen it.

The air was stiflingly hot, billowing up in pulsing waves from the abyss-like breaths. The only sound was the deafening winds from below. His father shouted something about machinery, failure, and time, all the while grinning maniacally. Saghan heard him say "doesn't matter." There was nothing to hold onto as the two snakes made their way precariously across the narrow bridge. If Salastragore's weapon had not been so heavy on his back, if Saghan's legs and muscles had not been so biologically strong, the hot wind likely would have blown them off into oblivion.

When they reached the foot of the great chrome door, the wind and its howling mysteriously vanished. They had moved into a pocket of regulated air pressure, balanced by the hidden machines embedded in the stone pillar. Salastragore lifted the glass jar and stared into Maxan's golden iris. It seemed for a moment that he would cry. But he did not. He held it aloft and the red eyes in the wall flashed blindingly bright all around, drowning everything in murderous red. Then the light waves collapsed, focused into beams that sliced the air and settled on the glass jar in the Master Monitor's hand. The eyes found what they were looking for, the unique code written into the pattern of the retina by Ralse's design. Then all the light winked out in a flash, leaving both the snakes in sudden and total darkness.

It felt like dying. Saghan knew it well. He was lost in complete oblivion. There was no sound, no sensation. The void seemed to stretch, one second, one hour, one lifetime.

But then the sun seemed to break on a vertical horizon before his eyes. The chrome door unsealed, split along its middle with a hiss of powerful pressure. The thick slabs of metal slid away slowly, flooding everything with a pure white light that dispelled the darkness.

Now Salastragore was crying. Truly crying. The old snake was on his knees, cradling the jar, staring at the fox's floating golden eyeball. He let it roll gently from his palms and clink on the concrete.

Saghan wasn't sure if he should go to his father, lift him up, comfort him, carry him on, or carry him back. But the next second the notion dissipated like mist in superheated sunshine. He couldn't keep his gaze away from what was happening inside the chrome chamber for long. It was shaped like a cylinder with walls of shiny clean chrome awash in light that came from nowhere. There was no apparent ceiling. Looking up, the light warped and stretched in such a way that turned Saghan's stomach, as if the light itself was being siphoned away into an infinity of shadow. At the chamber's center was a concave dip in the floor, and floating above it was a bead of complete darkness, no bigger than the tip of Saghan's black fingernail. A hole in the fabric of reality and space.

"What is thisss place?" Saghan whispered slowly.

Salastragore was at his son's side.

"The door to nowhere," he said, wrapping his arm around Saghan's shoulder. He wiped away his tears with the sleeve of his black armor. "And everywhere."

Chapter Fourteen

The Rose Tower

The white wolf's frothing fangs snapped shut powerfully, then pried open and snapped again, and again, blood-crazed, for the fox that had scrambled just out of their reach.

Maxan lay over the crisscrossed iron bars on top of the iron cage, huffing to catch his breath.

The wolf gave up momentarily and gave its full attention to the bindings still clinging about its waist and hindlegs. A constant growl rumbled in the beast's throat, punctuated by fits of enraged barking. It freed its legs at last and padded wildly around the cage's perimeter on all fours, seeking a better angle of attack, its animal mind unable to comprehend that no side of the square structure was any better than any other. If even a shred of Principal Feyn's rational mind remained, the beast might have easily reasoned that it could have placed its paws on the bars and climbed up the thing like a ladder. It might have remembered that it had once stood on two legs.

But Feyn was gone. There was only the wolf in him now.

Maxan had bought himself enough time to rise to a crouch. Although his ribs still stung from where Saghan's tail had punched him, and thick clots of blood still wept from his empty eye socket, he felt surprisingly invigorated by the adrenaline coursing in his veins, helping him to regain his balance. But he couldn't get comfortable on top of the cage just yet. The white wolf leapt and lunged, forcing Maxan to dance across to the opposite side.

His only escape would be wedging himself between the bars and dropping down beside the prisoner, but he wasn't sure if there was enough wiggle room there, or if he would be stuck, his top half devoured sickeningly once the wolf finally figured out how to climb. The beast's claws skittered across the stone floor as it raced around to follow the fox's movements, coming up to swipe at its prey's ankles only seconds too late. All around the cage, there was now a ring of scratches and spittle. It dripped from the beast's ruined, hungry maw.

"I know you." Maxan spoke to the turtle below him but kept his eyes on the pacing wolf. "You're Baaleb. I didn't need to hear him say your name. I know you because there's a voice in my—"

Maxan darted away from the snarling wolf's next attack, but too late. The sharpened claws snagged the ends of his cloak and brought the fox down. An iron bar sank into the small of his back, just above his tail. The wolf tugged at the fabric, tightening the cloak around the fox's neck, but gave up and ran around to hop up and swipe again closer to where the fox had fallen. Maxan flopped over reflexively, spinning away from the relentless wolf yet again.

I can't keep this up. Maybe if I can—

Got to try it, Max!

Maxan sprung to his hind legs, balancing precariously on the bars. In the precious few seconds before Feyn's next assault, he unfastened the cloak from around his neck and held it out. When Feyn came at him again, he kept his hind paws planted and swiped the thick fabric down to meet the wolf's claw. The maneuver managed to snag one of its arms; he felt the paw struggling against the bundled fabric. Maxan held on to it with both paws of his own and pulled at it, hoping maybe he could bind the beast to the cage somehow. But Feyn's free claw came up and sunk into the meat of Maxan's right arm and ripped four red lines into his furless flesh. Maxan let go of his cloak and fell back again, and his rump sank into one of the open squares on top of the cage. His bushy tail brushed against the turtle's shell below.

The wolf toppled to the floor, writhed wildly, recovered, and backed away with his prize. He shook his arm violently, slammed Maxan's cloak upon the ground, and pummeled it with both claws, tearing the fabric to shreds. When the beast realized there was nothing there that could satisfy its ravenous hunger, it gave up and howled at the fox atop the cage. What few patches of snow-white fur it had left bristled sharply along its spine.

Maxan struggled to free himself from the square gap in the bars he'd fallen into, but it was no use. Instead, he let out all his breath and relaxed his back and shoulders. A second later, the top of his head connected with the stone floor below, and the rest of him crumpled in a heap. He groaned, blinking the green eye he had left to dispel the swirling stars in his half-vision.

He sat up and caught his breath, then saw the fresh blood welling in the scratches on his arm. He was thankful that his nerve-dead flesh couldn't feel it.

Got that going for me at least.

Glad to see you have a positive outlook on the situation.

And I'm glad you're still here.

I can't tell if you're being sarcastic.

Outside the cage, the wolf raised its head from the tattered cloak, its nostrils widening, greedily sucking in the scent of fresh blood. The beast's eyes dilated, darting about for the source, finding it at the room's center. The wolf's slick, pink tongue lolled and the froth churned at the corner of its ruined mouth. It was overcome by the inborn instinct to alert the pack. It threw back its head and howled, a sustained peal of sound that reverberated in the bricks and burst into the blue sky above.

The sight of Principal Feyn reduced to an animal and the sound of his guttural howling harmed Maxan's spirit more than any claw could ever harm his body. He felt a sadness opening in his heart like a pit. As he scanned about the inside of the turtle's cage, dread and hopelessness flooded in. There was no way out. He would starve or bleed to death. And all the while the animal just beyond the bars would not stop its pacing, scratching, snarling, and howling.

This is it then, he told himself.

Baaleb had withdrawn his wrinkled face and limbs into the upright, rag-shrouded shell. Maxan couldn't see any sign of him. But even if he'd been there, what good would he be? Maxan grabbed a pawful of discarded rags and considered wrapping them around his fresh wounds. He sniffed at the years of accumulated dust and filth that had soaked into them and gave up the idea.

He lay back and stretched out as much as the cramped space would allow and stared into the vacant blue of the empty sky beyond. He knew exactly where they were: at the very top of the Monitors' castle, in the tallest tower with the flower-petal roof. Salastragore had opened it for the two of them—*correction: the three of us, technically*—so they could watch the show.

Can't be long now. He's going to fly whatever he's built straight into the sky, and that's that.

Maxan closed his eyes and thought maybe he could just sleep through it all.

You're forgetting something, Max.

Oh yeah? What's that?

Actually … someone.

Maxan swore he heard a *clink* from somewhere, the sound of metal locking against metal. Maxan cracked his left eyelid and swept his one good eye around the circular ceiling. Then he saw it. A hook, at the edge of the tower's rim, twenty feet above. Then a paw appeared beside it, its fur the color of amber, and another, pulling a pair of sea blue eyes up over the edge.

Maxan chuckled. Then he laughed. Louder and louder. The thunderous sound of his own laughter chased the despair out of his heart, hope returning. Even the wolf's snarling was drowned in the echoes of his relief.

"You climbed all the way up here!" He called to Rinnia. "You beat our record!"

Rinnia swung over the edge and dropped to the floor, rolling expertly with the force of the impact, tumbling into a crouch with her one remaining sword already drawn.

The white wolf's ears turned reflexively from the shouting fox in the cage toward the new commotion. It took all of one heartbeat for the predator to recognize the fresh prey that had quite literally dropped from the sky. The beast leapt into motion, its claws skittering madly across the floor.

Rinnia rolled aside, and it collided fangs-first into the wall. She came up into a full sprint toward the cage while the wolf shook the disorientation from its head. The hunger only intensified at the taste of its own blood. It wheeled about and charged, but Rinnia had already bounded up the bars and planted herself safely on top.

Maxan let go of the breath he'd been holding. He was about to laugh again, but the wolf had already lost its prey once and would not do so again. With a deafening snarl, it leapt into the air, just high enough for its chest to land against the topmost iron bar. Bent at the waist, its hind legs scrabbling below it, its claws swiped furiously for Rinnia.

Rinnia tried to cut at the wolf's incoming claw, but her awkward stance on the bars lent her strike no power. The wolf batted her sword across the room where it came to rest against the wall. She was caught by surprise, off balance, unprepared for the wolf's speed and ferocity. The next swipe caught her by the ankle and sent her stumbling backward, slipping from the bars, crashing to the stone floor on the other side of the cage.

Rinnia landed flat on her back, blasting all the air from her lungs. She did not cry out in pain or waste time catching her breath. All the years of relentless training kicked in by instinct, commanding her to ignore the pain and injury, to roll herself over and push herself up.

"Get in here," Maxan called out to her, even though he knew the narrow space between bars made that impossible.

The wolf was already rounding to Rinnia's side. She was bent over, tensed, her stance telling the wolf she would not just lie down for him. Its predatory mind read that easily enough, and it slowed, then stopped, lowering its head and shoulders, snarling and slavering. Rinnia crept backward slowly, inching toward the sword at the far wall. A trickle of blood ran down her ankle, spotting the floor. The beast's nostrils flared. Its dilated eyes locked hungrily on her.

Maxan could see she was done for. She would never make it. He hollered wildly at the wolf, but it was useless. The wolf had forgotten everything else that existed but the fox in front of him. Maxan scrambled around inside the cage, digging through the rags for something, anything he could use to throw at or distract or attack with. He uncovered only a glass box filled with sand and tiny insects. All dead.

"Help her!" he shouted at the turtle, tossing the box aside to shatter against the iron bars. "Help us! Do something!" Two small pinpricks of light reflected from his eyes inside the dark of his protective shell, but he said nothing.

The wolf was stalking her, closing the distance between itself and its prey, the cage and the other animals trapped inside completely forgotten now. Its paw pressed into the spot of blood the fox was dripping along its trail.

Maxan wheeled away from the useless old turtle and scanned around the circular prison cell with his eye. The motion flooded his head with an intense, sickening throbbing pain, but he ignored it. He saw something, the only thing, by the door. At once he rose to a crouch, then wedged one shoulder through the square hole overhead, frantically wiggling his way up and out.

Blood was flowing steadily now from Rinnia's ankle. The weight of her next step was too much for it, and she wavered painfully, wincing, drawing in a sharp breath. The predator saw its chance and pounced too fast for Rinnia to react. It crashed fangs-first into her, bringing her down. She had just enough time to jam her elbow into its skull, deflecting its fangs away from her chest. She struggled under the beast's weight, bracing her knees against its ribs, beating her fists against his flanks where she could.

But the beast hardly noticed. It wriggled its face left and right, its maw snapping in again and again, deflected each time. Its paws scrabbled and scratched, finding the fox's shoulders at last, pinning her in place at last. Then it lowered its body on top of her, crushing her, depriving her of the precious space she needed. Its frothing spittle dripped onto her face. Its fangs shot in again, closed upon the forearm brought in just in time to save her. The sharp daggers sank in to the bone and held there. Hot blood spilled into its maw and bathed its tongue. The beast released a guttural growl of glee, but the hunger wasn't satisfied. It could never be. The taste only intensified it. The beast twisted his head side to side, dragging the screaming fox across the hard stone floor, leaving a line of her blood on the stone.

It felt its prey weakening beneath it, its life draining out, its will to fight diminishing. It ignored all else in existence, even the sensation of something slipping around its neck, which then became a squeezing, a tightening, and a pulling. Its reflexive need for air rose in its animal brain, overcoming its powerful need for blood. Its reddened jaws released the fox's arm, but still it couldn't breathe. It stood up on its hindlegs, drawn back by the force of the thing pulling on its neck. Its claws reached up to touch it.

Maxan pulled as hard as he could, dragging the white wolf back with the impromptu noose he'd made from the discarded rope Feyn had been bundled in. The wolf toppled onto its back, writhing and twisting, choking and spitting. Maxan fell on his rump but held on tight. The wolf scraped its head on the stone floor, tugging at the rope desperately with its neck, trying to wedge its paw in the noose and gain back some life-giving air.

"Get in the cage!" Maxan called out to Rinnia, but she was already on the move.

The raging animal saw its prey slipping away. Its instincts were at war: to chase down the scent of fresh blood, to twist and flail about for air. Then it caught sight of the other fox with the suffocating, hateful rope in its paws, and all else was forgotten. The wolf sprang at it, careless if it choked to death.

Even with one eye, Maxan saw the wolf's intention clearly enough, rolling over and surging forward, still clutching the rope. He leapt at the iron bars of the cage, scrambled on top, and dashed on for the other side just as the wolf's slashing claws missed his ankles. Maxan slipped through the top bars—much more gracefully this time—and pulled at the rope just as the beast stumbled sideways, swiping one last time at the other fox who'd gotten away.

The wolf's claws missed Rinnia by less than an inch, as all its weight was dragged away by the tightening noose. Its tongue hung weakly from its mouth, red spittle and froth dripping. It leaned forward, pulling instinctively, trying to escape the thing killing it. The beast wanted to snarl, or to whimper, to relent to the greater force that had bested it but could only gag.

Maxan pulled harder, fighting against the weight on the other end of the rope. It was just an animal. A stray. Vicious. Unfeeling. Starved. It was just a scarred wolf with snow white fur. It had attacked him. It had attacked Rinnia. It would never stop until it had fed. Maxan had no choice. He had to kill it.

Maxan watched the beast crumple to the floor just inches from the iron bars, its claws scrabbling and scratching on the stone. He heard the wet, slimy clicking of its tongue and throat as it choked. He felt something break in his heart. He remembered.

It's Feyn.

He remembered the first time he'd seen the wolf's snarling face in the abandoned beast pen in the west district of Crosswall. But he'd learned the snarl was a scar. Feyn couldn't help it.

He tried to kill you, Max! The voice of Ralse flooded his memory with the image of a vortex of splinters and stone, of Principal Feyn barking an order to his black-robed counterpart, the great-horned owl Principal Harmony. *Kill them all, he said!*

But Maxan smothered the image. He saw instead the owl rising over him before a raging thunderstorm, calling the cobalt-blue lightning that would burn him alive. And he saw Feyn, behind her, calling on the fallen tree that would kill her.

He saved my life.

Maxan felt something touch his forearm. It was Rinnia, beside him in the iron cage. She cradled her other arm in her lap, and he saw she'd already filled the wounds with sizzling pink panacea powder. He read the words in her sea blue eyes.

Spare him.

Maxan let go of the rope. He crawled over to the still figure and reached slowly through the bars. His paws brushed over scraps of white fur and blistered skin, working to release the noose. Maxan felt Feyn's chest swell with the intake of breath. He was unconscious, but alive.

Maxan slumped back onto his elbows, finally allowing the exhaustion to spill on him like the crash of the tide. He noticed the prisoner, Baaleb, must have slowly retreated as far from the wolf as he could. The old turtle crouched at the opposite side of the cage, his back turned. Some of the ragged robes had slipped off his shell, exposing the natural hexagonal pattern. But there was one made of metal, bolted into the shell amid all the others.

Rinnia's paw stroked Maxan's muzzle gently, wiping away the thick clots of blood beneath his missing eye. He grasped her wrist and held it.

"You came back," he said.

"I came back."

"Zariel told me that you meant to… That you were going to try, one last time…"

That you were going to kill yourself, to kill Salastragore. He stopped himself from saying it.

It was clear Rinnia understood the implication. "I came to my senses." Her eyes fell to the floor, ashamed. "I'd been waiting so long for my chance. Years. And now it's gone. Salastragore's already gone. But I knew I couldn't do it, that it wouldn't matter."

Maxan gripped her wrist tighter, drawing her gaze back to his.

"He killed your father," he said firmly. Then he took a deep breath.

Time to tell her, Max. No time left.

"He killed ... *our* father."

Rinnia's brow furrowed in confusion. She looked away, stared vacantly at the floor as her mind worked, fitting all the pieces together, everything she knew about herself, about what Salastragore could do, about what Old Four Swords had told her. About Maxan, this idiotic fox that had interfered in her plans and her life, time and time again. About the other fox, whom she never knew, whose genetic code made her exactly who she was. Her father.

"Ralse."

But it hadn't been Rinnia that said his name. Both of the foxes turned toward the source of the dry, cracked whisper on the other side of the cage.

"His... children..."

The turtle's body had shifted around, and his head had emerged from his shell. Baaleb's ancient eyes blinked slowly. His cheeks wrinkled into a warm, affectionate smile.

Maxan waited, but the old turtle said no more. "And you're the Master Monitor."

Baaleb's smile faded. He closed his eyes and lowered his head. Maxan wasn't sure if his words had simply put him to sleep or suddenly killed him.

Did I say something wrong?

He's ashamed, Max. Look at him. Look at what Salastragore's made him. He's nothing now.

Maxan didn't need to recall any of Ralse's memories to understand how true it was. He looked to Rinnia for help, but she was already moving to the old turtle's side.

"I'm sorry for what he did to you." Her paw caressed the side of Baaleb's face. He shuddered visibly at the first touch he'd known in twenty years, but he said nothing. "I'm so sorry. All these years. I knew you were locked in here, but I couldn't..."

Baaleb's lips quavered. Both his arms emerged from his shell, little more than skin hanging from bone. He grasped her paw in both of his stumpy hands and held it to his face. His eyes squeezed tighter, and tears poured down his face.

"Please, child," Baaleb sobbed at last, his raspy voice cracking with emotion. "It's not your fault. When I saw you the first time, I knew I was not his only prisoner. I knew I was not truly alone."

Maxan saw the tears welling in her eyes, and it seemed for a moment that she would cry too.

But the moment passed. Rinnia sniffled just once, then stifled her vulnerability. "It's about time we got out of here," she said firmly, cupping Baaleb's chin and drawing his eyes up to hers. "Together."

Maxan spun his gaze around the inside of the cage. "There's, ah, no door," he observed. He gripped one of the bars sunk into the stone floor and tugged, not actually expecting to make a difference, only to illustrate his point. "The snake never intended to let you out."

"Death," Baaleb whispered. Every weary word came slowly, tiredly. "The only door open for me. His exact words. But… I chose to remain, living. At first, perhaps, from some sense of defiance maybe. But later… I… Because…" The final syllable drew itself out so long that Maxan thought Baaleb really had fallen asleep. "Because I knew," the old turtle said at last, "that this prison is where I deserve to be."

Rinnia shook her head. "Whatever you deserve, we're not here to judge you. Whatever punishment Salastragore gave you or whatever you've given yourself, you've served enough of it. We're going to stop Salastragore. We have to. Otherwise," she brought her head low, speaking inches from Baaleb's face, the sound of her bringing his eyes open again to stare into hers, "if he succeeds, then everyone will be punished. Everyone. Deserving or not."

"He told you?" Baaleb asked her.

"Zariel told me." Rinnia looked hard at Maxan. "He told *us*."

"How the world ends," he said. "Ralse didn't know how far Salastragore was going to go, after all the Monitors were gone. When he found out, he tried to stop it. Salastragore caught him. Killed him. And now that he's finally gotten the relay back, and he has the key, he's going home. To eradicate us. Every living thing. Because he believes life is a disease."

"Not life," Baaleb said. "Human life."

"And he's taking us," Maxan went on, reading the words on the puzzle as all its pieces assembled with blinding clarity in his mind. "All of us, the animals, to bring them war. The Aigaion. It's a ship. To sail between the stars."

"The *ark*."

The turtle's word was one Maxan had never heard, yet he recalled its meaning as if written into his very genetic code.

"We have to stop him," Maxan said, echoing what his sister said before, gripping the edges of the old turtle's shell and staring hard into his wrinkled, resigned eyes. The time for being gentle had run out. "*We have to stop him.*"

Baaleb smiled warmly, apparently unmoved by the gravity in Maxan's voice. "You both," he said, glancing between the two foxes, "you are like him in many ways. Salastragore was afraid of him. Respected him. His equal in every way. His only friend. The two of them, together, broke apart… Everything we had built. Everything that bound this world to the Monitors' will, like… chains. Which I, in my arrogance, had once thought unbreakable…

"Your father found me here, you know. He climbed, all the way up, like you, to see what Salastragore was hiding. And… I told him."

"You," Rinnia turned away from Baaleb. Her wounded arm lay useless in her lap. The other draped over an iron bar of the cage, her paw squeezing it. "You sent him to his death."

"Ralse believed they were building a better world. A free world, where these creatures could decide for themselves their own natures. Animal. Or Human. He told me, it was why he'd done… what he did. But your father didn't know how far Salastragore would go."

Baaleb turned his full attention to Maxan. "He sounded then just as you sound now."

I remember it, Maxan thought, the long dormant memory rising.

I said we have to stop him.

Before Maxan could open his mouth, Rinnia jabbed at the turtle's hard shell. "You made him hurry!"

"Rinnia," Maxan said, reaching for her.

She batted his paw away and struck Baaleb's shell with each shouted word. "You made him careless! Reckless! He could have survived!" The turtle suffered the blows, his wrinkled face a shameful mask again.

"Rinnia!" Maxan grabbed her shoulders and spun her eyes around to meet his. "It's not true."

"How do *you* know, Maxan?"

"Because he's not really dead."

"What?" She twisted out of his grip, her eyes blazing with incredulity.

Even Baaleb muttered a "What" of his own.

"Ah," Maxan stammered, aware of how crazy he was about to sound. "He speaks to me. He *has* spoken to me for almost as long as I can remember. In … here." He tapped a clawtip to his temple. "He somehow made me different. It's why the relay can't affect me … somehow. There's no more room. I can't be controlled like all the other animals. But I can hear him. All the time. Like an inner voice of reason. Like—"

"Like talking to yourself," Rinnia breathed. Her eyes darted back and forth across the stone floor. Maxan recognized the look in those sea blue orbs well enough. It must have been how he himself appeared no more than a few minutes before. Something had suddenly made a world of sense to her; some puzzle had just revealed its shape.

Tell her, Max. Please. What I've needed to tell her.

"I… No… He… he's sorry, Rinnia. Sorry he couldn't be there for you."

Save for the slow rise and fall of her breathing, Rinnia was silent. She had no mother, no family. She had never known her own father. She never thought she would ever hear him speak. But he had. And it was the words she'd needed to hear. Rinnia was frozen in place, staring at the floor.

"Fascinating," Baaleb marveled to himself in a whisper, observing this pair of foxes, brother and sister, and yet not related by the miracles of nature but by those of science. A golden glimmer of intrigue sparked in the old turtle's gaze. Maxan saw the machinations turning, devising, scheming. In truth, it was Ralse looking at his old master through his son's only eye, recognizing Baaleb's brilliant mind at work.

He's thinking of the game, Max. See him, even now. He's always thinking of the game. How it can be changed, innovated, improved. How it can better distract us from what we really are.

Maxan whirled about and grabbed the old turtle's shell, squeezing the edges so hard they could crack. The sudden motion and the seething anger in the fox's voice extinguished the spark in Baaleb's eyes. His arms withdrew into his shell, but Maxan caught him by the neck and held him. "You know why the snake kept you all the way up here, don't you? So you could see it. Every day. To remind you. It's true, isn't it? He wanted you look at the *Earth!* But did you ever actually *SEE* anything there? Did you ever *SEE* what it was the humans did? Don't you remember the whole point, why you made this world and started this game?" Maxan didn't care if shaking the frail old creature would break it or not. He nearly screamed into Baaleb's face. "They gained the power that ended their world. You swore—*the human race swore*—never to let that happen again!"

"Maxan," Rinnia tried to take his paws away from Baaleb's neck, but they didn't budge. When Old Four Swords, Zariel, had once told her his version of the truth—how the Monitors had transformed the Earth's moon into a place that gave life to chimerical monsters that would call it home—she had thought about strangling him too. She had understood how someone could once believe that all the wars waged here, all the blood spilt, all the slaughter, all of it could somehow serve a purpose. Mankind was a violent animal, the most violent of all. But could they disguise their own natures and hide what they really were from themselves? Could they create slaves and throw them in the fire for the rapture of watching living things burn? Could they spare themselves from their own destruction by destroying the Other?

But she could see that Maxan wasn't strangling Baaleb, wasn't harming the old Master Monitor. He was just holding him, not letting him escape, forcing him to see. Rinnia drew her paws away.

"The Monitors let the humans kill us by the millions," Maxan said. "They lost their minds in this sick game. Taking us over. The point of all this death was always to protect life. But you never saw that *we're alive too.*" Maxan slowly let go of the turtle's shell. "Do you see now?"

The ancient being, Baaleb—the first and truest Monitor who existed now only in the skin of the oldest living creature, the master, who once designed campaigns to wipe out hundreds of thousands and executed them with a wave of his scaly hand, the architect of so much death—suddenly, finally, felt the weight of truth. The guilt that Salastragore had tried to make him feel for twenty years this boy had brought upon him before twenty minutes had even passed. Both of Baaleb's old, yellow eyes welled with tears as he stared at the sky.

"You're right," Baaleb finally said. When he closed his eyes again, the tears ran down his wrinkled skin and dripped from his chin. "It's true. I am… so sorry. For all I've done." He slumped forward in a heap and wept, holding his face in both hands.

Maxan, the voice of Ralse resonated suddenly in his mind. He felt his fur prickling along his spine. *Maxan, he's coming.*

What? Maxan wheeled about in the cramped space, spinning his eye toward the door, as if expecting Salastragore to burst back through and roll one of Saghan's bombs through the cage's bars. *Who's coming?*

Salastragore. He's coming here. *To the Aigaion. Something just shifted. The gate. I can… feel something's different. I… We don't have much time left.*

The last thought filled Maxan with a sinking feeling. The words, spoken inside his own mind, filled him with dread.

He's coming, Ralse told him again. *Do you understand?*

"We don't need your words, Baaleb," Maxan said softly. His paws went to the old turtle's shell once more, this time consolingly. "We need your help." He nodded at Rinnia.

"I said before that we can't stop him," she said. "Not me. Not Maxan. Not alone. But we can stop him, Baaleb. If you help us."

"You… you have to leave me," Baaleb sobbed. "Even if I wanted to help you, child, there is no door by which I can leave. Only death."

Rinnia took Baaleb's wrinkled, blunt hand gently in her paw. His loose, hanging skin was paper thin. "Master Baaleb, he made you believe your powers had faded. That you couldn't call on them anymore. But it's not true. Your chains are gone. Nothing can hold you."

"My child… I don't believe you."

Rinnia let out a deep breath. "Belief is one thing. Technology is another."

Maxan's face screwed up in confusion, a question forming on the tip of his tongue.

"Would it help," Rinnia went on before he could ask it, "if I told you I sabotaged the inhibitor devices welded around this tower?" She looked up at Maxan's puzzled expression and shrugged. "I would've dropped in earlier, but it's not easy moving around out there."

Maxan could only see the back of the turtle's bald head, but he knew without having to see that Baaleb's eyes were opening. A few seconds later, the old turtle drew in a long breath and stretched his neck to its full height.

"Oh," he said quietly, a golden glow intensifying in his eyes. "Oh… my."

III

The Aigaion

Chapter Fifteen

The Sky Wing

"At the core of every world there is a point, infinitely small, and it is its own kind of world, with its own core, infinitely smaller, and so on, until you divide the universe by its own inverse and wind up with…"

A powerful gust of wind washed out Salastragore's voice as he turned his head toward the monolithic three-sided pyramid rising in the distance. Behind him, Saghan watched swords of thin, vaporous clouds slash uselessly against the structure's impenetrable walls, scattering themselves into rippling mists. Two other pyramids—identical in immensity and shape—stood equidistant at the opposite corners of the sprawling triangular plane where the two snakes had found themselves just moments before. It was impossible for Saghan to measure just how massive the three pyramids were. Their angular irregularity defied everything he had ever known to exist in his tiny world or could ever exist even in his wildest imaginings. He was dizzy, reeling in the wind and the eeriness, trying to keep up with his father. The floor beneath his scaled feet, and the walls of the three enormous structures were pure, starless obsidian black, although to witness them from up here underneath the pure dome of blue, they seemed to disappear from time and space as the world shifted around them, cutting the sky like mirrored blades. Saghan took every step warily, irrationally fearful he was stepping into a void of sky mirrored above.

The old red snake had waited several minutes already for his son to emerge from the existential shock of materializing on the raised platform at the very center of the triangular platform, itself at the very center of the three towering tetrahedron pyramids. Saghan's first sensation was the beating of his own heart, the gradual flow of the cold blood through his veins. Then he felt the sunshine on the scales of his long neck and on his back, warming him through his armor. When Salastragore sensed Saghan stirring, he started speaking excitedly, so eager to share where they were, how they got there, how everything worked. He'd gotten his son up off the polished floor and helped him limp off the platform, prattling on all the while about geometries, theories, relativities, orbits, gravitational alignments.

Salastragore swung his neck around again to call back to his son: "And so you wind up with… Ah, hell with it! You wind up going mad trying to figure these things out! Ha!"

The last thing Saghan had known before all of this was what his father had called The Door to Nowhere. The red eyes scanning the fox's golden eye, the chrome plate wall splitting open, spilling brilliant, blinding light. And the pinprick of total darkness suspended in time and space. As they approached, together the blackness swelled, yet somehow it did not move. Reality distorted around them, stretching at their sides and all around. Saghan stumbled, but his father dragged him on. Suddenly, he was no longer just looking straight, but sideways. They were no longer moving horizontally, but vertically. And all around, all at the same time. Nowhere and everywhere, like Salastragore had told him. The darkness enveloped them entirely. Within this oblivion, Saghan heard his father laughing maniacally. And then Saghan was free-falling through a universe of bursting kaleidoscopic color. His mind detached from his body, invigorated by the sudden knowledge it could be anything, go anywhere, but only in that moment, which stretched for eternity yet ended before it had even begun.

And then Saghan was through, his legs wobbling like jelly, his stomach retching, and his eyes rolling into the back of his head. His weight crashed upon the platform.

"I remember my first time through a gate," Salastragore called back again, smirking. They had crossed halfway to the base of one of the pyramids. "It's not so much the *space* you're feeling, though we've certainly moved across a vast amount of it, probably two miles. It's the *time*. Your body is trying to acquaint itself with the sensation of movement in space without having spent any *time*. Can you guess how much time has passed?"

"Time…" Saghan repeated softly, unheard against the crashing of the wind. It felt like he was a child, learning to speak all over again. He savored the feeling of his forked tongue against the roof of his mouth, the closing of his lips as they formed the final syllable. The vertigo was passing. He looked around groggily, observing the repeating geometries comprising the floor, the sloping walls surrounding them.

"Triangles," he said, ignoring his father's question. "Triangles everywhere."

"Saghan, you do know where we are, don't you?" Salastragore had come back, stood close, held his son by both shoulders.

The proximity to another and the steady grip on Saghan's shoulders helped to anchor him, and the vertigo abated at last. Saghan was suddenly very aware that the floor upon which he stood had vanished. And yet it was still there, holding him up. It was glass. Tinted darkly so that when viewed at an angle, it appeared black. But now he looked down past his feet, through the breaks between wispy white clouds, to the verdant green and mucky gray-brown of the Drakoran swamp lands and the black ribbons of river deltas that fed them miles below.

"I don't believe it," he muttered.

The old snake's smirk spread into a venomously wide smile. "Believe it or not, my son, we have ascended."

Days ago, when he had first witnessed Rinnia's sword ripped from her paw and buried inches deep in a solid wooden beam, then minutes later when the storm of air and force toppled buildings down upon him, Maxan had been unable to believe any of it had actually happened.

But experience is the greatest teacher, and so later, when he saw Pram animating a nearly dead tiger to protect her, and Pryth shatter Rinnia's sword to a hundred molten shards, and Harmony direct bolts of cobalt-blue lightning within a raging storm, the legend of callers became more than just stories. Their power was his new reality. Everything he had seen had taught him that the invisible forces with which the Aigaion exerted control over this world could only be touched for an instant at a time. Like a musician plucking a razor-sharp lute string, if he dared to strum for a lasting chord, he could lose a finger. Maxan had only ever seen the callers summon the Aigaion's energy in bursts. The only indication that its power could be held for a sustained period of time was when he saw Pram keep the tiger alive beyond death, and even then, the toll it had taken on her fragile mind and body had sent her into unconsciousness. All of these experiences had given Maxan an expectation for what it meant to be a caller.

Baaleb surpassed it in seconds.

The old turtle had asked that the two foxes crawl through the bars of his cage and stand back, his eyes glowing a shade of gold that reminded Maxan of the relay. While Rinnia retrieved the sword she had lost in the fight with Feyn, Maxan kept his one wary eye on the sleeping white wolf. Baaleb inhaled deeply, then simply lifted his hand, and the iron bars of his cage lifted with it in unison. The metal bars separated seamlessly and silently from the stone, as if the prison tower's floor was made of dust. With the power of the Aigaion once more bending to the true Master Monitor's will, perhaps all truly was dust. Baaleb sat comfortably at the room's center in awe at the sight of his own work. A subtle smile spread across his wrinkled lips. His mind commanded the fragmented metal to levitate slowly over his head, then to spin and flake away into pieces as it did, like ash in a gentle wind. Baaleb let out a gasp as he felt the Aigaion's power surging within him. His bright eyes followed the swirling storm of metal shards, coalescing in the air just above him until every gram of the matter that used to be his cage became a shining, perfect disc.

Baaleb's stumpy hand directed the disc to float gently to his side and come to rest flat upon the floor. The gentle scrape against stone was the first sound it made.

"Children," he called out to the foxes, who stood with jaws agape, "please help me up if you would." Earlier, the old turtle's voice could barely have risen above a whisper. Now, it was a different voice that spoke entirely. The reptilian body it belonged to was still decrepit and weak, disused, slouched, and wasted for two decades. Maxan and Rinnia rushed to his side, hooking an arm each and standing. "Oh," Baaleb grimaced. "Slowly please."

The turtle's short legs had been folded beneath him for so long that they had bowed outward. They dangled uselessly beneath him. Maxan was surprised by how light Baaleb's body was, lifting him easily with Rinnia's help. Most of the ancient caller's girth had wasted away on his prisoner's diet, and it took no effort to guide him onto the disc. There was just enough space for Baaleb at its center with a fox at either side clinging to his shell.

"Are you ready?" the old turtle asked, craning his neck skyward. It sounded to Maxan as though Baaleb might be asking himself. Without waiting for an answer, the disc began to lift.

"Wait," Maxan called out. The disc halted. Baaleb's mind held it suspended halfway to the wide-open flower-petal roof of the tower.

"What is it?" Baaleb said.

Maxan noted his impatient, slightly aggravated tone, as if the caller's rediscovery of his powers had changed the sound of his voice. He pointed below. "What about Feyn?"

The white wolf was stirring, pushing himself up on his forelimbs.

Maxan watched Feyn rising, wondering if he would stand as the former Principal of the Mind would stand. But then Feyn's hindlegs swept up beneath him, and he rose upon all fours, as an animal. The wolf shook its head, looked up at the prey that had escaped him, and snarled.

"We can't just leave him like this."

Maxan was surprised to hear Rinnia say the words before he could. He looked to her and read the concern on her face. She'd told him before that she believed the wolf was a monster—and perhaps Feyn had been—but Rinnia believed herself a monster too.

But even monsters can come back, Maxan thought. *And become someone better.*

Still, the voice of reason chimed in his head, *we can't take him with us. Not like this.*

Maxan pointed at the only door in the circular prison room. "Baaleb, let him out. Please. He may be caught, may be killed, but at least he'll have a chance."

"Very well," Baaleb said quickly. He glanced downward and raised a stumpy finger. The solid oak door exploded through the side of the tower in a cascade of bricks and concrete and steel, leaving an enormous hole with a clear view of the buildings of New Quwurth, the cliff, the lake far below, and just inside the wall, the staircase that led up here.

Feyn had skittered away cautiously to the opposite wall at the sound and fury of the ripping tower, but only a moment later the beast's mind had understood its only way out. The scarred white wolf raced across the room and disappeared down the stairs without paying the floating disc and its three occupants so much as a parting glance.

He's gone.

You hope he makes it, don't you, Max?

I do. And I hope he comes back. Somehow.

The disc floated over the topmost rim of the rose-petaled tower, and Maxan was struck with a sudden dizziness as he peered over its edge at the whole world falling away below. The sky above was a fusion of blues. Where Yinna hung halfway to the western horizon, her brightness overwhelmed everything to near white. To the east, the dark violet hues of evening approached, and the triangular black mass of the Aigaion dragged those colors over the world like a blanket. The fox's sense of time and space were severely impaired at this altitude, but he calculated the creeping, triangular tomb in the sky would arrive over the Monitors' castle in less than an hour. If they were going to get up there, somehow, they had to hurry.

His paws clutched the edge of the disc tightly. *The old guy could've thought up some handles on this thing!* The air up here was thin, frigid, and blasting in constant gusts. A sudden cold shuddered down his spine, setting every ruddy-colored hair along his tail on its end. He pulled his cloak about his shoulders, and the tattered and torn lengths wafted in the strong wind at his side. But even more than from the cold, he shivered from fear. He had never thought himself scared of heights until now.

"I cannot hold this aloft for long, children," Baaleb's voice rose above the rushing wind. For a moment only, Maxan had no idea how a body as light as Baaleb's could stay rooted to the center of the disc without being swept away by the powerful winds up here, then he realized Baaleb wasn't just *a* caller; he was *the* caller. "Perhaps, if I was younger…" There was a warm joviality to his tone that Maxan didn't particularly care for at that moment.

Of course, I understand why he must be feeling so great.

It's freedom, the voice of Ralse answered. *After decades. But it's more than that. Feeling his power again, after so long. You don't know what that means for a caller.*

Sure… But maybe he can enjoy the view later. From the ground.

"Don't take us up," Rinnia shouted over the rushing wind. She clutched the edge of the disc just as tightly as her brother. "We'd never make it. Down there. The lake. There's a way."

As she spoke, Baaleb's eyes never drifted from the Aigaion. When they first rose over the rim of the open tower, he had seemed so powerful, so determined. But now the disc wavered. Maxan could see the old turtle's hands poised just over its smooth surface, quaking as they tried to hold on to the invisible strings. Baaleb grimaced, drew his eyes away from the black mass on the horizon, and said at last, "very well, child."

The disc drifted lazily to the side, then descended only a few feet per second so as not to lose its riders. If he had wanted to, Maxan could have run his paw across the gritty graystone wall of the world's tallest tower, but that image only churned his empty stomach more. He wanted to shut his eye until all of this was over. Instead, it only widened at the sight of a shimmering swarm in the skies to the north. There were hundreds of them.

Wings, he realized. Even from this distance, Maxan saw the fading daylight glinting from their plated armor and deadly spears.

Rinnia saw them too. "Corvidians," she hollered. There was a deep dread in her voice, but the layer of frustration that rippled on its surface could not be denied. "Why now?" she called out to them.

"Didn't the toad say a few days?" he hollered back.

Ignoring him, Rinnia spun around on the frictionless metal disc toward Baaleb. "They've come to take the sky wing. We can't let them have it."

Maxan figured the old turtle had little idea what his sister was raving about, but Baaleb clearly heard all he needed to know from the desperation in her voice. He nodded and simply said, "Hold on." His stumpy fingers relaxed.

And then they plummeted.

Maxan gripped the side of the disc for dear life. His screaming was drowned in the air rushing past. All of his weight seemed to melt from around his bones. They dropped through a wisp of cloud that had obscured the twisted structures of the castle. And the battle that had already begun.

On top of every roof, outside of every window, along every walkway, in front of every door, the first wave of armored Corvidian knights clashed with black-clad Drakoran assassins. Not every Corvidian had landed to engage Salastragore's elite fighters; however, some of them circled the air in formations—units of ten or more—scanning for the pockets of fighting where they were needed, loosing volleys of arrows or diving to their comrades' aid with raised shields and drawn swords, taking the Drakoran assassins by surprise.

The incoming Corvidians had no time to process what had just shot by their wings, missing them by a hair's breadth. Baaleb's eyes were closed. The ancient, true Master Monitor spoke to the Aigaion, feeling the presence of all his world's matter in his mind. Stone, steel, flesh, and feather. His hands shifted smoothly side to side, keeping the disc level while guiding it left or right through the clusters of jutting structures and clashing bodies.

The disc rushed by the tall windows of Salastragore's workshop and the grated walkway skirting the graystone facade just outside of them. The place was overrun by Corvidian knights. They stabbed with spears and slashed with swords at enemies just within the workshop who Maxan could not see.

Maxan felt the explosion in his bones before he heard it. A massive ball of light and heat expanded from where three window frames had once been just as they dropped by them. Chunks of graystone and slivers of grimy steel shot through the air, seething with the lifeless, flaming bits of what had been living Corvidian knights a second before. The shockwave sent a shower of fragments raining over the lower tiers and lake far below. The force of the blast sent several knights over the railing, their wings in flames, dragged to their deaths by the weight of their armor. The disc wobbled and rocked against the invisible shockwave. Maxan and Rinnia miraculously held onto the edges, and even Baaleb had been thrown onto the back of his rag-shrouded shell but somehow remained on the metal surface. Miraculously, the Master Monitor kept his concentration.

Wiry, black-shrouded creatures slithered over the rubble and out onto the twisted remains of the walkway, leaping over sputtering fires, gouts of steam, and sparks from the ruined wires and pipes left in the explosion's wake. They set upon the few remaining Corvidians before they could recover. Three formations of knights wheeled about and beat their wings skyward, racing toward the workshop's level to join in the fray. One of these was coming straight for Baaleb's disc.

Maxan cried out a warning and waved his arm at the Corvidians, but they took no notice. He ducked and felt the rush of wind as most of the formation passed just inches over his head, but there was a resounding thud from the disc's underside as an armored knight crashed against the metal while his comrades sailed on through the air. Maxan dragged himself to peer over the disc's edge and saw the unfortunate knight sink to his doom, only to blast his wings apart just before impact, riding the gust out over the lake safely.

Maxan breathed a sigh of relief, then turned and shouted, "They can't see us!"

Rinnia propped the old caller to a sitting position at the disc's center, and Maxan saw his answer well enough within the vapid expression on the turtle's face. He was so absorbed within his own mind, reaching for and clinging to so much of the Aigaion's power that Baaleb was simply no longer there. Not only was he keeping them on course as they descended rapidly down the castle's second tier, but he was also clouding the vision of hundreds of creatures, all at once.

"There!" Rinnia cried out, pointing to their destination. It was the strange building at the end of the long pier, which Maxan had spotted when the Monitors' train emerged from its cliffside railway and circled the castle. He remembered thinking of it like some kind of shed; only now the rails lining the pier suddenly made sense. It wasn't built to house a boat, but an entirely different kind of vessel was kept there.

"*That's* the sky wing?" he shouted, more to himself than to the other two occupants of the metal disc.

Already, the pier was mobbed by a dozen squadrons of winged knights. This was the very thing the Corvidians had come to capture. The heart of the battle, it seemed, was being waged on that thin strip of railway, just planks of waterlogged wood bolted together by the metal beams laid across them, and no more than twelve feet wide. It was terrible terrain for the Corvidians' taloned feet, and they slipped easily on the slick metal rails, presenting the army of assassins and crocodile spearmen plenty of opportunities to fall upon them with deadly force. There was no wind to speak of down here in the cylindrical hole surrounding the excavated station, so the Corvidians' wings offered them little to no advantage. A few of them tried to fly away and come at their enemies from above, but it only made them easier targets for the crocodiles' spears. The waters at either side of the pier were stained red, littered with corpses of floating, feathered birds whom nature (and the Monitors) had designed to be only slightly heavier than air while Drakoran bodies sank easily enough below the depths.

But despite all of these strategic disadvantages, the Corvidians's battlefield discipline proved to be as legendary as all the stories claimed. Whoever among them had given the orders clearly recognized the value of this location and had somehow planned ahead for this assault. They pressed on in a tight line, surging down the pier toward the yawning entrance to the station. More and more formations were swooping in and landing behind this front line bolstering their ranks. For every knight that fell to a crocodile's spear or an assassin's thin blade, another would instantly descend to take its place. All the while, as the Corvidians received steady reinforcements, the trickle of Salastragore's extra fighters coming from within the station had all but ceased.

The disc, still invisible to all but the trio sitting on it, banked toward the end of the pier coming to rest at last on the thin walkway behind the structure there. The tension spilled from Maxan's limbs at once, turning them to jelly, and he rolled off and moaned, splaying himself out to feel the flatness and stability of the stone floor beneath him. The scent of brine and bloody water filled his nostrils. He sniffed and sneezed as Rinnia draped her arm around Baaleb's shoulder and hobbled with him away from the metallic disc.

"Get up," she scolded Maxan without turning, still on the move.

The two foxes held up the turtle between them and slipped around the side of the building, still unnoticed. Even with Baaleb manipulating their senses, all the Corvidian fighters' backs were turned. Their sole focus was resolving the battle in front before claiming their prize behind. Without speaking or even opening his eyes, Baaleb waved a hand and the thick chains holding the handles of the gigantic wooden doors disintegrated into a pile of sand. Maxan and Rinnia let the turtle sink to the ground gently, then each took hold of a handle and pulled with all their strength, the grinding of the sliding doors swallowed in the din of clanging steel and cries of agony.

Inside, Maxan beheld an incredibly complex clump of machinery. The two sets of wheels resting atop the rails were the only functional apparatus the fox recognized. Maxan could never have imagined anything like the sky wing in his wildest dreams. Not even Ralse's recalled memories could help him understand what his eye was looking over. His father's avatar had been slain long before Salastragore gave up on the idea of opening whatever gate the clever fox had sealed. And not long after, the snake had devised a way to bypass that barrier anyway.

This?

Maxan swallowed nervously as he examined the fruits of all Salastragore's meticulous design and craftsmanship. *This ... is how he planned to get up there?*

The sky wing's main hull resembled a Radilin river vessel with a pointed bow, sleek curving hull, and a widening aft, only it was a quarter the scale of a Peskoran trader's craft and fashioned entirely of lightweight materials the snake had spent years mining, smelting, devising, molding, and testing. A long, glass windshield was braced on its top, allowing the passengers who entered through the hatch in its side to view all around the craft. The wings themselves did not seem so long, Maxan thought at first glance. But when he saw a series of jointed hinges and bolts locking them in place, he realized that they were simply folded along its side, allowing it to pass through the door, and up through the guts of the station without fear of collision. Or so he hoped.

The nervous lump in his throat only seemed to grow larger when Maxan's eye wandered to the massive twin drums on the aircraft's back. An intricate series of pipes and wires wound their way around nearly every inch of the craft above the hull, all of them eventually terminating in the sides of those twin rocket engines. Through the glass shield, Maxan spied four barrel-sized cannisters bolted to the back wall, no doubt supplying the fuel for the sky wing's systems.

"*This?!* You're saying *this* is how we're going to catch Salastragore?"

"If you have a better idea, now's the time, Maxan!" Rinnia didn't wait for his response, even if he'd had one. She ran back to support the old turtle on his wobbly, emaciated legs, leaving her brother to stare in disbelief at the contraption.

"The Corvidians paid Salastragore to build this because they can't fly that high. This thing can. But please, interrupt their battle to double check. Maybe we can ask them to carry us! Or maybe they'll wait until Baaleb feels well enough to fly us two miles straight up." She hefted the turtle inside, then let him down as easily as she could against the hull of the machine. "Master? Baaleb? Maxan, look at him."

Maxan had already noticed how spent the old turtle was after landing the disc. The effort that must have gone in to calling on so much power, so soon after twenty years of being severed from it... Maxan looked at Baaleb, his shell propped against the hull, his legs splayed out on the floor, his eyes closed. He would have been certain, yet again, that the ancient creature was dead. But then Baaleb spoke.

"Something... Something..." The words came in airy breaths. Beads of sweat streaked down the turtle's bald head. "Something... is coming. I can... can feel..."

Baaleb said no more. His head lolled further out from his shell and fell against his chest.

"Is he dead?" Maxan and his sister exchanged a worried look. "I mean for real this time," he said.

Before Rinnia could respond, a screeching bellow tore through the air, sounding out over the water and all around the surrounding cliff. It came from the station entrance at the other end of the pier where the battle still raged. A hulking creature emerged from the dark, yawning mouth at the base of the station.

What little daylight there was down here glinted along the monstrosity's metallic limbs, running up and down the length of sharpened steel as they scraped and stabbed their way forward, bringing the bulk of its body step by deadly step closer behind Salastragore's assassins and soldiers. The few black-clad fighters that were left disengaged from their Corvidian enemies and hurried back. Several of the winged knights, for all their legendary fearlessness and discipline, broke away from the front line, wheeling about to run or fly as far away from the approaching creature as they could get, driven by another shrieking cry. Those among the knights who managed to get a hold of the deserters grabbed at their wings, pounded them on the chest, and shouted obscenities and orders at them until their fighting spirit returned.

With their line breaking, more than a few keen Corvidian eyes now spied the pair of foxes inside the shed.

Oh shit, Maxan thought, while Rinnia echoed the sentiment aloud.

I'm not sure which threat is worse.

The Thraxian queen's limbs stabbed their way forward, and within minutes she was swiping them left and right at the line of Corvidian fools who thought they could hold their ground before her. Her knives cut low, cleanly separating the knights' weaponry from the talons that carried them. They cut deep into the birds' bellies, splitting plates of armor like paper, spilling their intestines. The knives came again, higher, from the other side, carving their beaks, their throats, reaching far enough to sever the bones of their wings. She sliced them to pieces where they stood, turning all the air in front of her to a reddening whirlwind of blades, spurting blood, shards of metal, bone, and feathers. And yet, rising even higher than the screams of agony, the captains shouted for more reinforcements. More and more formations landed on the pier to bolster the line, even as the queen advanced through them like they weren't there.

Maxan watched the horrific display, paralyzed with fear. He failed to realize the three falcon knights trotting across the rails toward the shed. He failed to understand what was happening when dozens of smaller, brown-shelled monsters resembling the brilliantly shining queen swarmed from both sides of her and leapt upon the Corvidians who had somehow been spared from her knives. Maxan was enthralled by the display of incomprehensible violence and death. Because of the darkness that enveloped one half of his vision, he hadn't seen his sister draw her sword and rush onto the pier.

"No! Rinnia!"

"Get Baaleb in the sky wing!" She called back without sparing him a glance.

As Rinnia met the three charging falcons and danced and ducked and spun about to avoid their thrusting spears, Maxan reluctantly turned away to do as he was told. *She'll be fine,* both he and Ralse thought together, trying to reassure themselves with each repetition.

She'll be fine. She'll be fine.

She has to be fine.

Across the pier, with a slick, red trail of severed limbs and broken weapons behind her, the Thraxian queen reared up on her four back limbs. From above the carnage, she also spied the foxes and the open door where her master's sky wing sat exposed. She let out another air-rending screech, and the battle seemed to freeze. The line of Corvidians hobbled backward from her, tripping and slipping on the soaking planks and metal rails. Likewise, the mass of ants drew back to the sides of their queen. The only activity was the spinning female fox and the tireless falcons trying to skewer her, but even they disengaged when everything came to an inexplicable standstill.

Rinnia's three assailants turned to gape at the spectacle they had left behind, and Rinnia used the opportunity to take several steps back toward the shed.

It's not us that the queen's seeing, Max. She doesn't care about Salastragore's ship.

Why's she looking back here then? What's happening?

It's because of him.

Maxan felt compelled to look down upon Baaleb again. The ancient turtle slumped against the sky wing, utterly spent, exhausted. His eyes were open, though the golden glow was gone.

She sees Baaleb. She knows it was his order that wiped out her hive.

The queen's terrifying metal-plated mandibles parted, revealing a horrific opening in her massive head that must have once been her mouth. Now, after Salastragore's alterations, it served the same purpose as the rest of her body.

It was a weapon. The hole was deep, her throat lined with spiraling metal. There was some device built in, fused to the organic pieces of her that still remained. A bead of pure white light came to life at the back of the queen's throat, expanding into a sphere of energy. Its light reflected from the inner walls of her body, casting a flooding brilliance over all the battle before her.

Maxan scrambled to lift Baaleb to his feet, surprised by how heavy the turtle could be when hoisting him alone. But he knew, in the pit of his stomach, that it was already too late.

The beam of super-heated plasma erupted from the queen's mouth and burned everything it touched, reducing flesh, feather, and bone to molecular ash in an instant. There was no time before it lanced through the doors of the shed and struck both the ancient master and the fox that dove for him.

Except it never touched them.

Baaleb raised his stumpy hand, and the light refracted where he pointed. The line of white bent impossibly sideways and surged out harmlessly over the lake, cutting a line of molten rock across the wall of the cliff. The beam was continuous, slamming against the invisible bubble Baaleb had raised. He gently waved his hand and swept the melting plasma back toward the combatants lining the bridge, striking the far edge of the station first and burning straight through. The light cut through Corvidians and Thraxians indiscriminately, disintegrating anyone and anything in its path, leaving heaps of severed, charred bodies behind.

It was over in seconds. The queen swallowed the light just before it reached her. Her mandibles closed; radiant heat shimmered all around her head like a halo. Acrid white smoke spilled from between the seams of her mouth. With a loud *clank*, a spent energy canister unlatched itself from her back and shot into the air, a spiral of smoke trailing. It hit the lake water and hissed. Another canister rolled automatically into its place, locking itself with another clank.

Baaleb moaned, squeezing his eyes tightly, fighting against a sudden invisible pain wracking his body. The old turtle went completely limp in Maxan's arms, clearly blacked out from the effort of calling on so much power.

He's spent all the miracles he had left.

Maxan looked up and surveyed the smoldering, bloodied wasteland that was the pier. What little remained of Salastragore's assassins had withdrawn behind the Thraxian queen and disappeared into the base of the tower, replaced by a swarm of smaller insects that writhed at her sides. The dozen or so Corvidian knights had fallen back to the water's edge, as far from the sweeping beam of light as possible. Their reinforcements had scattered at the sight of the queen's power; their resolve melted.

Rinnia was at the middle of the pier, backing slowly away from the three falcons. They exchanged fearful looks, unsure if they should pursue the fox, regroup with their own, or fly away and never look back, saving themselves from all this madness.

The Thraxian queen released another deafening screech, expelling the excess smoke and heat from her throat. The ant drones at her sides stood their ground. She was the hive mind, directing the swarm to stay back and ignore the armored, feathered invaders. The overlapping plates of mirrored glass that hid her hundred compound eyes were focused on the reptilian creature and the two foxes that stood in her way. The queen's mandibles split apart once more.

"Rinnia!" Maxan called, though he did not know why he did nor what he would say if she answered. He gave up on the comatose turtle, letting him slump against the sky wing's hull. His eye scanned everything inside the shed. His mind raced with ideas and calculations. None of them good.

Bust through the wall. Or get on the roof.

What's the point of that when we're in the middle of a lake?!

Ah, true!

But anyway, no! I'm not leaving Rinnia.

Maxan stepped out onto the rails where his sister stood rigidly, her sword still raised defensively despite the distance from all their enemies. The acrid smell of seared flesh spread in the air.

I don't know what to do, Max. The voice of reason, Ralse, his father, spoke solemnly in his mind. *I know you won't run anymore, not even if I told you to. Not this time. It's not who you are anymore.*

Far ahead, Maxan saw the bead of white light expanding again in the queen's widening throat.

This is when you're supposed say, "Surprise, Max! I gave you a caller's brain too! You've had all those powers this whole time!" ...right?

Ralse was silent. The few seconds seemed to stretch.

Maxan watched the ball of light grow. He felt his sister tense at his side, unsure of what she was thinking to do and yet utterly certain it would make no difference. All around the pier, Corvidians were frozen in fear, and ants were kept at bay.

He stood his ground, surprisingly calm. High above their world, the Aigaion's edge crept just over the rim of the surrounding cliff. He closed his eye, took a deep breath, and raised his paw, as he'd seen Baaleb do moments before. He let his awareness of everything fade, focusing only on the feeling of the air in his fur, the solidity of the ground below him, brushed by his bushy tail.

Finally, the voice of reason replied.

...you can't be serious.

Then the plasma beam erupted.

Suddenly, a wave of shimmering energy rose like a wall from the water at the Thraxian queen's side, bending the lancing white energy, redirecting it sideways. The burst of invisible energy cleaved through the machine-insect's wide-open jaw and her two foremost legs, severing them cleanly from her body. Impossibly, her plate-armored limbs were nothing against whatever had cut up against her, as resistant as air against a cutting blade.

The white beam of light shot skyward at an angle, piercing harmlessly through the cliff and beyond through the sky, dissipating a hundred miles into outer space.

"*I... I!?*"

Maxan sputtered incoherent nonsense, examining his paw incomprehensibly, flipping it over again and again. He turned his good eye to his sister.

"*Did you—Did I—Did I just—*"

Rinnia regained her composure quickly enough to roll her eyes at him.

"Look!" She pointed to the lake.

A pair of writhing blue tentacles slapped wetly onto the pier, then hauled up the rest of the octopus's body. Old Four Swords, Zariel, the Monitors' Supreme Weaponmaster, rose to his full height and shrugged out of his dark oiled cloak. His other tentacles wrapped around the handles of the two other katana strapped at his sides and slowly drew them. He flourished the three blades elegantly, weaving them around his fluid body like a dance, all the while staring ahead at the Thraxian queen, watching her choke upon a jetting slurry of white liquid as it spilled from her severed maw onto the planks of the pier. The stuff hissed angrily and burned like acid straight through the wood, transforming instantly to a glob of pure silvery metal wherever it touched water. As it formed, the top of it stuck out above the lake's surface like an iceberg while the rest of its mass sank to the depths. She coughed out the last bit and lurched forward onto the stumps of her missing forelegs, all the energy that animated her cybernetic body draining with the sludge. Then she lay still.

With their hive mind extinguished, Zariel paid the horde of her chittering children no mind, turning his back on them. The octopus held one katana out to his left, one to his right, and swept the third slowly across the line of Corvidian knights.

"Leave this place."

Even from this distance, Maxan felt vibrations prickle the fur in his ears and recognized quickly enough that it was Zariel's weaponry. The air surrounding the blades shimmered, heralding the birds' doom.

The flock of warriors stood silently, clutching their own weapons, crude twigs by comparison. They blinked their sharp eyes at the old octopus before them. The katana he pointed at them intensified its hum, and whether it was because some deep understanding that this sound meant danger or because their legendary courage had finally, collectively failed them or simply because it was the strategically advantageous action to take at that time, the few knights that remained beat their wings one by one and flew away over the water.

Maxan frowned at his paw as if it had disappointed him. "Damn," he said aloud.

Once the last knight took to the air, Zariel glided over the bloody remains of their comrades toward the sky wing's shed.

Ah, why're his swords still drawn?

Because he's furious. At you. You stole one of them, remember?

Technically WE stole it, Maxan tried to point out, though he knew it wasn't true. Ralse was as silent now as he'd been when Maxan slipped one of Zariel's wondrous swords from its sheath and crept back to the Old Quwurth tunnels. He'd let his son decide his course on his own.

Ah, okay. Maybe I'll let you do the talking. You guys're old friends and all...

"You're late," Rinnia said dryly to the approaching Peskoran, saving Maxan the trouble.

Zariel said nothing. He passed between the two foxes without sparing them a glance. He stood over the turtle, and the thrumming of his blades faded. He sheathed all three swords without having to look for their scabbards and flattened himself into what must have been a crouch for an octopus.

"Master," he breathed wetly. The relief, the shock, and the anger in his voice all sounded simultaneously. "I am taking you from this place."

Baaleb stirred as the old octopus' four tentacled arms slid along the sides of his master's shell, wrapping around bunches of rags to pull.

"You can't," Rinnia said flatly. "We need him."

"*You knew!*" Zariel snapped at her accusingly. His voice exploded like a volcanic cataclysm that thundered around the deep bowl of the lake.

Maxan recoiled from the outburst, but as the echo died, he became aware of another sound, gradually building in intensity. He fanned his ears, turned them right and left, trying to identify what it was, where it came from.

Metal. Groaning metal.

He peered carefully at the heap of useless metal blades that had once been a functional Thraxian queen. *Not her*, he reasoned, seeing her laying still. *So where…?*

Without turning away from his master, Zariel let out a deep sigh, releasing the tension that had wracked his shoulders. "How long did you know," he demanded of Rinnia between rasping breaths, "that Baaleb was here?"

"If I had told you before, if you had dared come for him, Salastragore would have known I betrayed him." Rinnia's tone was even, sharp with defiance. Zariel could shout at her all day if he wanted, but he'd never convince her she'd made a mistake. "I didn't know who he even was," she said, gesturing at Baaleb. "Or what he'd done to the world."

The octopus was quiet for a long moment. The only sound was the angry groaning that seemed to come from nowhere yet echoed hollowly all around. Maxan's ears bent this way and that, his eye darting all about. Even Rinnia looked up from the old Monitors nervously.

"As I said," Zariel said at last, "I am taking him from this place." His fluid body expanded, rising to stoop over the old turtle and haul him up with surprising strength. Some of Baaleb's rags fell away, exposing the odd hexagonal plate bolted onto the turtle's shell. Zariel brushed it curiously with a tentacle but didn't comment. He focused all his energy on squiggling backward, dragging the turtle's body over the wooden planks, heading for the waterline.

Maxan abandoned his search for the sound and stood in his way. "You can't!" he shouted at Zariel's back. "There's no more time to hide!"

Zariel's tentacles unfurled from their grips on Baaleb, and he stiffened, rising to his full height to peer down at the fox. "If you don't move, I will end you." He shot a look at Rinnia. "Both of you." He turned his gaze back to Maxan and narrowed his silver eyes as if he'd only just seen the fox for the first time. He reached a tentacle to Maxan's muzzle, tapping just below the empty eye socket. "I see that you've already destroyed us anyway. Impatient. Insolent. Ingrateful. Just like your father."

"What do you think you can do," Maxan shouted defiantly, stepping forward to jab a claw tip against the thick apron covering the octopus's chest. "No matter how deep you go, the Aigaion will still reach you. He'll know where you are. You know it's true, don't you. But even then, he'll no longer have to *care* what you do. I'm really sorry about taking your sword," he lied, "but at least I *did* something! What are you planning to do? What did you *ever* plan to do? Sit back and watch every species go astray? Before that ever happens, Salastragore will take the Aigaion and watch this world fall to pieces behind him. You know it's true! Say it!" He jabbed the octopus again, harder.

"Say it!"

Zariel said nothing. While the insolent fox spat the words at him, the venerable weaponmaster had silently gripped two of his three swords, perhaps to fulfill his threat to end the fox. Yet, he made no move to draw them.

"We can DO this," Maxan went on. He ignored Zariel's menacing stance. He saw only himself—some bold, one-eyed stranger—reflected in the silver eyes. "The four of us. The old Monitors and the new. But we have to go. And we have to go, ah, on that thing." He gestured at the sky wing and huffed a nervous laugh. "And we have to go *now*."

The pervasive groaning sound built to a crescendo. Something was popping loudly, drawing all their attention suddenly. All around them the lake was still, as foamy and scummy as ever, aside from the churning of the water wheels.

Maxan's guts shrunk at the sight of them. At one side of the station, the wheels clanked and sputtered, breaking down. Fingers of undirected lightning arced wildly across the water and clawed up the structure's disjointed walls. Black smoke spilled upward from the wound in the side of the station. Whatever ancient machinery was housed within had been damaged by the queen's searing beam of white light that Baaleb had thrown back at her. The load-bearing columns inside had caught fire and slowly turned to slag. The groaning was the station itself, gradually failing to keep the colossal weight of Castle Salastragore upon its foundation. The whole great, towering structure was leaning, inch by inch, collapsing onto the scar in its side.

I mean… really? Could this get any worse?

Amidst the incessant, intensifying groan of the wounded station, Maxan's keen ears picked up a metallic clang at the other end of the pier. A corkscrewing, smoking cannister splashed into the water. The cybernetic Thraxian queen sputtered back to life, rising on the bladed legs she had left. The mirrored globes of her eyes flashed brightly, and a gut-wrenching shriek gurgled from what remained of her ruined throat.

Okay. Fine. Now it's worse.

"Oh, why not?" Rinnia echoed Maxan's attitude, throwing up her paw helplessly and shaking her head. "Sure!"

Zariel glided wordlessly between the foxes, his tentacles squiggling over the metal rails following their path to the queen. He drew his katanas and held them ready as before, two on either side, one leading the way. Against all the angry, ruinous cacophony of noise filling the deep bowl around the lake, Maxan again felt the thrum of all three weapons.

"Where are you going?" Maxan shouted at the octopus's back, only to realize how literally obvious was the answer.

The Thraxian queen hobbled forward awkwardly, then adapted to her handicap and simply dragged herself along the pier with the sharpened stumps of her two remaining forelegs. To either side of her, a blanket of skittering ants spread, keeping pace with their queen.

"To clear your path," Zariel called back. Then the old weaponmaster halted, paid the foxes a glance over his shoulder, his silver eyes impossible to read. "Take Baaleb with you. Finish this." And with that, he surged forward to meet with the monsters.

Chapter Sixteen

Ceilings of Glass

FROM BELOW, STANDING ON THE SURFACE OF HERBRIDIA and staring skyward, there was simply no way to see the Aigaion as anything more than a flat, black triangle. Even the near-blind, subterranean Leoran mole was no better than the high-flying, keen-sighted Corvidian in that regard. All of the dwellers of Herbridia were equal in their ignorance when it came to the colossal black object that had passed them over quietly day after day throughout their entire lives. For hundreds of years, Herbridia's denizens with even a passing fascination in the aimless monolith could only ever guess at just how high in the sky it floated overhead. In more recent times, the Mind's scholars had fashioned crude telescopic lenses and fixed them on the aimless wanderer for a better view, but they hadn't gleaned much to satisfy their curiosity.

From below, it was impossible to see that the Aigaion was actually not just a single, flat triangle, but four triangles. These pieces came together to form the single inverted, three-sided pyramid on its underside, while on its top, three smaller pyramids rose at each corner of the flat triangular plane, each made of the same glassy obsidian material, each one rising equidistant, a full half a mile into the cloying darkness of outer space.

"Actually, these aren't pyramids." Salastragore halted suddenly and brought a contemplative hand under his chin. The two snakes had been trekking across the Aigaion's smooth, central plain for quite some time. While Saghan had hardly thought to blink as he took in the sights of the eerily quiet, alien setting all around him, Salastragore had been filling the silence with idle chatter about the place.

"Long, long, long ago, the oldest pyramids actually had *five* sides. One base, four walls. These are technically *tetrahedrons*." His long neck brought his smiling face around to peer over his shoulder at his son. "Tetrahedrons, yes. I've forgotten much of the geometry of this place. It's so refreshing to see it all again."

His father had explained that each of the three structures had a name. A "designation," he'd said. The first behind their left shoulders was the House of Stability. Packed inside that tremendous tetrahedral volume were all the machinations and systems that generated and regulated Herbridia's atmosphere and seasons, its winds and precipitation, its tides and rotation. In the very beginning, the House of Stability had been the most vital of the three for reshaping the Earth's small, gray moon into a habitable, lush planet. The Monitors had commanded the Aigaion to level the moon's craters, to condense its dust into mountains, to carve its valleys and rivers, to spread the seeds and pour the waters of life, and the Aigaion obeyed. In the hundreds of years that followed, when the game called for a volcanic catastrophe to wipe out a Thraxian hive city, or a tidal wave to devastate the Peskoran coast, or a ceaseless flood to transform away the Leoran forests into a wasteland of silt and mud—all of which would claim the lives of thousands—the Monitors could achieve these disasters with the power in the House of Stability.

And to the snake's right, the House of Balance stood, where all the world's sentient life was conceived. It was here that the Monitors could refresh the populations of certain species if they so desired, or if more bodies were necessary to fuel a campaign until its completion. The Aigaion provided them with the tools to make their nightmarish imaginings a reality, giving rise to the monstrous behemoths that would serve as ultimate challenges for the game's players. Within the halls of this tetrahedral structure, endless rows of memory plates mapped the genome of man and all the Earth's other creatures that had ever existed. Genetic codes were separated or spliced, to ultimately design the walking, talking animal-human chimeras that would live, and fight, and die on the small world below, all to keep the never-ending cycle of simulated violence spinning. It was within the House of Balance that the Herbridians' unique brain matter was derived, made of a unique substance that conducted the signals of the Aigaion so that the avatars below could never detect, never escape the whims of their unknown, human masters.

It was impossible for Saghan to know which direction they were facing, since the Aigaion was kept in a constant state of imperceptible rotation, to "lace the beams," he thought his father had said. So many of the details Salastragore was spouting were lost on him. For Saghan, it was like walking inside one's own dream, never entirely sure if the experience was true or imagined. His mind was overwhelmed with trying to make sense of it all.

Saghan straightened his neck to see where the sky's blue deepened to night and faded to an abyss of diamond-studded black. The Earth, Yerda, hung in the V-shaped space between the apexes of Stability and Balance. Seeing that ruined world from this new angle, and through air this clear and clean, enthralled him. There was no daylight, no hazy atmosphere to diffuse his vision of the dead planet's massive wound. There was no denying the dim point of glowing fire that burned at the bottom of that pit. It was the Earth's exposed, dying core, and ever had it been bleeding layers of itself, which drifted into the great ring of asteroids surrounding it, Yerda's Belt.

Saghan's green-scaled eyelids hung open, against every impulse he had to close them, as he gazed at all this celestial wonder. Something turned idly on the periphery of his vision, no bigger than a speck, but in truth, it was a stray meteor probably twenty feet across. It hung in the space just above the Aigaion, slowly traveling in an arc. As he watched, the rock grew in size, and Saghan realized that it was falling directly for them.

He pointed at the incoming missile and wheeled about to his father, but the old red snake stood relaxed, arms folded across his chest, a wan smile stretching across his lips. "Just watch," Salastragore said, indicating the meteor with a wink of his eye.

Seconds later, the rocketing meteor collided with the invisible screen that encased all three of the Aigaion's grand houses and more than several miles of empty volume overhead. The hardened space rock broke apart like a ball of wet sand, its grains igniting in bright fires that splashed against a dome of thin air. The only sound was the sustained splitting of rock, muffled by the near vacuum around the point of impact. Saghan's jaw hung open in amazement as he watched the fiery bits swirl and separate into three distinct channels like rivers of orange light, each one absorbed into the apexes of the three black monoliths at the Aigaion's corners until nothing remained.

"Nevermind how the Aigaion sustains the planet below," Salastragore said, drawing Saghan's gaze. "It also protects it from the unseen dangers lurking above. Remnants of the ruined Earth, tumbling through space, drawn to the nearest gravitational force. They collide with the magnetic fields. They're pulverized to dust. The Aigaion recycles the energy and materials. All of it—gold, iron, copper, the very molecules that comprise the air we breathe and the water we drink, all the seeds, soils, microscopic organisms—all of it sealed inside the layers of hurtling stone and preserved in the frozen vacuum of space between. The asteroids are like little gifts. This machine takes them all, and the Monitors scatter them about Herbridia wherever, whenever, however we want."

Salastragore turned both his flickering orange eye up to the ruined world hanging in the dark of space, to gaze in wonder as Saghan had moments before. "With the Aigaion, we made a new Earth from the ashes of the old. With the Aigaion anything is possible."

Saghan heard the reverence in his father's voice, and the same feeling overcame him. It changed him, forever. Who he was less than an hour ago—the youthful, prideful, willful child, who before had wanted nothing more than to have his own identity, yet who had finally seen the true scope of the gifts his father was giving him—that version of Saghan was gone. The seething resentment for Salastragore that had once defined him had now transformed to an unpayable debt of appreciation. This, all of this, was Salastragore's gift. The Aigaion. The power. Everything.

Saghan observed his father—the pose he struck, the thin whip of his tail, the intricacies of his black armor, the scars and flaking scales of his age, the hollow of one eye, the fire burning proudly in the other—and he felt the weight of all the sacrifices the older snake had made. Saghan searched his heart for the words that could express the gratitude he owed—the sudden, blinding knowledge that all the feelings, all the reasons to hate, for all of those years—had only been lies. Ignorance and lies.

"The third house," Saghan said at last, unable to say anything else. "What's it called?"

"Huh?" The words broke Salastragore's trance. He tracked where his son's outstretched hand was leading, toward the tetrahedral monolith, the one they had been approaching. "Hmm? Yes, yes." He gestured to the two they had left far behind, naming each in turn. "Stability. Balance." He swept dramatically at the last.

"Manipulation."

Saghan's mind raced with the implication of these words.

"That's right," Salastragore said knowingly. "Control. Three forms of control. We thought ourselves so smart for coming up with that. Anyway, once we bring the signal back online, we control everything. Stability. Balance. Manipulation." The red snake snorted derisively and spat. "Just words. Meaningless words. Come. We're almost there."

As his father strode away, Saghan's hand tightened around the relay. It was the key, Salastragore had told him, to everything.

It had been impossible to see from the platform at the Aigaion's center where the two snakes had emerged from the gate, but now as Saghan approached the sleek, black wall of the three-sided monolith, he saw dim beads of golden light running in channels across the entire sloping surface. The lights turned at sharp angles and disappeared beyond the limits of his vision, only to be followed moments later by more in an endless circuit. The wall was made of the same clouded glass, perfectly smooth, perhaps a mile from its base to its apex. At the very center of the sloping wall, impossible to see at a distance, the two snakes slipped into a thin slice in the glass that served as the House of Manipulation's sole doorway.

Once, long ago, Saghan had been allowed to study a crystalline formation under a magnifying lens in his father's workshop, when Salastragore was deriving some new terrible strain of a poison. The twisting, inconsistent hallways within the pyramid instantly recalled the sharp edges and incongruities he had seen in the tiny crystals. Every surface was the same translucent black, slanted at perfect forty-five-degree angles, filled with the racing golden beads, which provided the only source of light. Their way forward would flash brilliantly gold one second, then snuff out to near darkness the next, then brighten steadily as a slow-moving bead passed along another wall, and flash again. Saghan's forked tongue flicked at the air incessantly, instinctively searching for some other sense than sight that could take hold and help him understand this place. It was no use. The lights' effects were dazzling, and combined with the irregular placement of steps and slopes and turns in the perceived path forward, Saghan stumbled several times.

"Move," Salastragore grumbled, hooking an arm under his son's after a particularly nasty spill. The older snake's mood mysteriously fouled once they entered the structure. He had been careless to slow their pace forward, to bask in the memory of this place and soak in the idea of the limitless power he had worked for two decades to regain. In his eagerness, he had nearly forgotten that his true work was only just beginning. "Get up! We're so close now!"

Saghan swallowed his question, knowing his father would only take it for a complaint. He swallowed his pride alongside it, willing himself not to wrench his arm from Salastragore's grasp, and instead he steadied himself against the wall and focused on following the red snake's tail as it whipped ahead through the twisting corridors.

All sense of time was lost to Saghan inside the Aigaion. It felt to him much the same as passing through the gate, only instead of an instantaneous tear from one point to another, his body was passing through space at a speed much slower than his perception could catch up to. It took him a moment to re-center his vision and feel the edge of the grand, triangular opening his fingers had just fallen upon. He let go and stumbled through. Now there was nothing to hold on to, so Saghan bent at the waist, his hands on his knees, his eyes spinning about. From somewhere further on, his father let out a shriek of elation, a peal of laughter. He called back something to his son, words muffled, but edged by a tone of disappointment. He did not want that, not ever again. He willed himself to swallow the rising bile, to stand straight, to feel his feet planted on the smooth, solid surface. When Saghan finally regained himself, he once again marveled at the alien wonder all around him.

The chamber was a massive, dark tetrahedral cavern. Saghan could see the base of each of the three sloping walls well enough in the dim light, but they disappeared high overhead as they stretched into thick shadows. He judged that the volume of this chamber alone must have taken up at least a quarter of the House of Manipulation's interior. Here, there were no disorienting, jagged edges. There were no other doorways besides the one that brought them here. But there were still the lights. They were everywhere, and here they all ran in the same direction toward the unseen ceiling, fading into the darkness as they climbed up the walls in their channels. Dozens of glass pillars jutted up from the floor like stalagmites in a cave, some rising no higher than his waist, some tall enough to merge with the overhanging shadows, but all of them encasing a single bead of light frozen in place.

He took another step into the chamber, then wobbled and nearly fell, his eyes sinking to the smooth glass beneath his feet. The floor was cloudy and dark but translucent like all the rest of the Aigaion. Through the glass, his eyes darted from bleak grayish brown bogs to fields of lush green to low-rising hills, across the terrain of all Drakora, stretching as far as he could see. A few breathless seconds passed, and Saghan realized that a flower-like object dominated all other sights below, rising higher into the sky than all the others. It was the tower atop the Monitors' castle. From here, its wide-open petaled roof appeared hardly larger than a mote of dust.

The tiny, golden lights raced through channels within the glass floor. He took a deep breath and put another step further into the room, his eyes following wherever the lines of light led them. Where the lights ran against the far wall, they turned sharply and flowed upward then cut across in ninety-degree angles, so that any two adjacent beads nearly collided before turning upward again and ultimately fading into the darkness. This repetitive pattern of their circuits created rectangular outlines in the wall. Saghan looked all around the chamber's three walls. The outlines were everywhere.

"Windowsss," he croaked, his throat sickeningly dry.

"Tombs," the voice of Salastragore corrected. It echoed from the irregular, angled walls. The younger snake wheeled about, unable to find the shape of his father amid all the dark glass in the eerie, golden glow.

"One hundred tombs," he heard it say, "for one hundred gods."

A hand clapped down onto Saghan's shoulder, bringing his slitted eyes swinging around to where they had seen only an emptiness before. His father's black armor absorbed all semblance of light, making him appear as no more than a disembodied, red-scaled head floating inches away from Saghan. He leered at his son. His good eye burned with a kind of rapture Saghan could only dream of feeling.

"We're *here!*" Salastragore cried out playfully, his long neck whipping his gaze all around. "I'm *back*, you bastards! Just like I promised! Can you hear me?! I've come to finish it!"

Saghan wandered away as if in a trance, feeling the weight of his father's hand slide from him. He stared ahead, drawn toward the murky shape just within the tinted glass of the closest rectangular outline. He stopped just before it. Inside, there was a creature. Hairless, draped in white robes, suspended upright, asleep. Its bare feet levitated just inches above the floor, and a halo of golden lights danced about its bald head. Saghan's palm pressed against the smooth surface and slid down. A new set of lights illuminated within the wall just to the side of the sleeper's pod. Saghan reflexively drew his hand away and peered at it. He recognized the letters and numbers, yet the language of it was incomprehensible.

"You know, I don't even remember their names." Salastragore was at his son's side, reading the indicators on the panel. "I mean their *true* names. Their human names. I only remember their avatars. And this one… *His* avatar," he said, wagging his finger at the figure floating inside the glass. "Breen was his name. A Peskoran. A shark. Very nasty creature, even without the terrifying skin he wore. I once watched him order a small fishing village put to the torch when the dwellers there refused to resettle. We were there for… Hmm. Actually, I don't remember why we were there, moving them out. Doesn't matter." Salastragore waved his hand dismissively, falling into a deep silence. His orange eye traced along the lines of the sleeping creature's smooth face. Its skin was the color of sand. Beneath the eyelids, its eyes danced about, eternally searching for an escape from its inescapable dream.

When he finally spoke again, Salastragore's voice was distant, reliving the memory of that day. "Breen caught as many as he could while they fled. Strung them to posts he had driven into the dirt at the side of the road. He ripped their guts out with his claws, gnawed on their arms, the blood staining his skin, his eyes dilating with madness as he looked in their faces. That terrifying mouth of his, with all the teeth, like razors, spreading in his … horrible, horrible smile. There were children too, strung up right alongside, watching, and wailing. Agony, and pain, beyond the physical. And Breen, the shark, he came for them last." Salastragore released a deep sigh.

Saghan wanted to ask why his father hadn't stopped the blood-crazed shark that day. But he knew all too well the feeling of having no will of your own. And he knew that in time his father had stopped Breen. He'd stopped them all.

"Why, Breen?" Salastragore's voice nearly broke to a sob. His eyes broke away from the creature's face as his fingers touched a series of glowing numbers on the console. Its eyes began to flutter. The golden lights of its halo faded. Slowly, its eyelids fluttered open, and the eyes within focused on the red-scaled monster on the other side.

Salastragore slammed his fist on the glass and leaned his reptilian face closer. The creature's eyes widened in horror.

"Tell me why!" Salastragore screamed at the creature on the other side. "Tell me why you *enjoyed it!*"

The human's eyes followed Salastragore's fingers as they touched a sequence of symbols on the illuminated console outside its pod. Its lips moved soundlessly. It lifted a wavering, weak hand to the glass as though trying to touch the animal on the other side. The window slid into the floor with a gentle hiss of pressure, and the human's frail body crumpled to the smooth floor at Salastragore's reptilian feet.

Saghan backed away as his father fell upon it, flipping the robed creature onto its back and wrapping both scaled hands around its neck. Salastragore's fingers tightened, the points of his long nails digging into the soft flesh at the back of the human's skull. "It doesn't matter now, Breen." The human's face reddened. Its eyes bulged. Its lips swelled. It flailed its flaccid limbs against the red snake's sides. The human's tongue swam around wetly behind its clamped, flat teeth. "Shhhh. Don't speak. There's nothing to say now. Shhhh."

The robed thing went still. Salastragore held on a moment longer, then finally let the neck fall from his hands. He rose, panting for breath, and yet surging with the adrenaline rush of pure murder.

Saghan felt it too. Saghan understood the feeling of his victim's final, heated breath brushing against the scales of his face. How many times had his father taken control of his own body? How many murders had his father committed with Saghan's own hands? How many lives had slipped through his own strangling fingers? How much had he hated it all, and hated Salastragore?

But now he understood all of it. All the death, all the murder. It had always brought them one step closer, together as father and son, to this place, the Aigaion, where the true Monitors—the true murderers—were trapped inside their dreams in the house of Manipulation. Before Salastragore had ever initiated the biological process that would give his clone life, the red snake had worked tirelessly to undermine them. He had found a way to lock them inside their avatars' bodies, to weaken their connections and reduce the powers they called upon. And why? Because humanity was a beast. This one's avatar, the shark called Breen, was only the mask the human beast hid behind. He deserved far worse than what he'd just suffered. Killing him had been a mercy.

Killing them *all* would be a mercy.

Every death… Every murder…

Saghan swept his gaze across the ninety-nine remaining glass tombs. "Thisss place," he hissed slowly. "It's a gift."

"Huh?" Salastragore's eye narrowed in puzzlement, but his maddened smile remained. "What do you mean?"

"We've come to make them all pay." Saghan clutched the relay at his side, his eyes lowering to follow the lights chasing each other in their never-ending circuit. "And to set the world free."

Salastragore stepped over the human's corpse and wandered along the row of pods. He peered at the faces beyond the glass, one by one, until he finally came to a halt in front of the dreamer he was looking for. "The slippery one," he said, pressing one hand firmly against the pod's translucent surface as before, the other reaching for the console that illuminated at his side. He chuckled. "Nowhere left you can slip to."

Chapter Seventeen

The Weapon Master

What little there was of Herbridian history—long before the Mind preached the necessity of records and furnished the tools to keep them—always centered on a singular theme: the might of arms, the elegance of combat, the titles passed down and the legends of how they had been earned. Herbridian history was a history of violence, after all. Not since the last great war, when the surviving nations banded together to exterminate the Thraxian threat, had there been any feats worthy of remembrance. In the relative time of peace that had settled on all the world in the decades that followed the fall of Thraxia, no single fighter had had the chance to truly display their prowess on the battlefield. The combat in the great arena of Crosswall and on Apotheosis boards across their tiny world were poor recreations of those true moments of glory, long forgotten.

But here, now, at the very bottom of the excavated station, on the artificial banks of the surrounding lake cut deep into the Drakoran land, Maxan was witnessing a spectacle of blades that he would never forget.

Zariel—the old blue octopus, the weaponmaster, the one Rinnia had once called Old Four Swords—faced down one of the world's last true behemoths all on his own, and with a quarter of his arsenal stolen hardly a day before by a conniving fox.

Before his squiggling tentacles had even brought him ten strides forward along the pier, the two rivers of the ant queen's children surged into one and crashed against him. His three wondrous katanas carved into the wave of ants again and again, from all angles, plucking their limbs and tossing them aside effortlessly. Their chitinous arms and heads and bellies blew away like ash in the wind, the edges of his whirling blades were the flame. Zariel's writhing body dipped low, sprung high, or bent to either side as his tentacled arms reached forth, back, and across. He gave them absolutely no ground, no mercy, and still they threw themselves at him. They clambered over the charred Corvidian remains and lifeless shells of their own brethren, only to join with the growing mound of corpses.

Then a pair of ant soldiers glided into the air, then arced down at their enemy's bulbous, blue head. Zariel was caught off guard momentarily but recovered his wits in time to whirl two of his three blades about his back—turning the edges around as he did—and bring them high and down in perfect unison. The two flying ants were separated clean down the middle, and the four divided halves sailed uselessly over Zariel's ducking head. The two ants' new tactic had forced the octopus to take a single, wriggling step back at first, then two more as the one blade remaining at his front had to contend with all the other targets at once.

But the little space the ants had claimed hardly mattered. The numbers of Thraxian drones throwing themselves upon the lone Peskoran decreased from a tidal surge, to a lapping wave, to a slow trickle.

Zariel cut the very last of them down with a sideward swipe of all three blades, slicing the creature to ribbons.

Far behind him, just inside the double doors of the shed that housed Salastragore's prototype sky wing, Maxan let out a cheer before he could stop himself. He lost himself in the thrill of a legend unfolding before him. But the more experienced half of his mind knew that the small army of Thraxians had only been a ruse, a sacrifice for time so the true threat could emerge.

An avalanche of brown husks slathered in slimy innards and green blood crashed against Zariel. The Thraxian queen charged ahead, shoveling the corpses of her children at the tentacled weaponmaster.

Zariel's two lower tentacles twisted below him as the four at his sides raised their weapons against the weight of the raining bits. He stumbled back, crossing two of his swords just in time to catch the bladed foreleg of the queen between them. The move was desperate, awkward, half-formed, and there was nothing Zariel could do to stand against the queen's monumental strength. She pushed the octopus as easily as sliding a figurine on an apoth board, right into her other chopping blade at his blind side. Some instinct in Zariel—born from hundreds of years spent in the skins of hundreds of warriors, and all of it in battle—solidified in him. He let go of his guard and drew his wriggling limbs into a ball, tumbling away on the ground, just under the queen's attack.

But Zariel was old, not as fast as he used to be. A sharpened length of steel found a squiggling tentacle as it whipped away. Half of one sword arm flopped uselessly upon the wooden pier, still wrapped tightly around the hilt of a katana. Thick, inky blood gushed from it, and it writhed with a mind of its own, jerking and clattering the sword against one of the metal rails.

Zariel came up in a trained fighting stance halfway back to the shed. Two of his tentacles pointed their swords at the Thraxian monster, while a third clutched at the bloody stump. The octopus was covered in a sheen of multi-colored blood, red Corvidian, green Thraxian, and black Peskoran. His natural camouflage flared sporadically trying to match the madness all around. Zariel's outstretched sword arms quivered.

The octopus drew in a deep, bubbling breath and shouted back at the foxes. "I told you to go!"

The queen dredged more of her spawn's corpses aside, clearing herself a path forward. Another gurgling shriek burst from her ruined maw, sounding out above the constant groaning and grinding of the collapsing tower.

Despite the clear danger, the impending doom, the gripping fear, and against the voice of reason screaming in his head and the octopus's direct order, Maxan felt compelled to rush in and do something. Then a paw fell hard on his shoulder and dragged him back.

"Get Baaleb inside!" Rinnia hollered in his face. "We can't stay here!"

There was nothing to say. There was no denying it. Maxan gripped one side of the old turtle's shell while Rinnia took the other.

The queen burst through the final mound of the dead, her cybernetic body buzzing with the renewed energy of her third and final plasma canister. The fuel pumped through the synthetic polymer veins inside her, electrifying the shock pads that Salastragore had grafted to the organs and ligaments sealed within the thick armor plating. The hulking machine he had made her into obeyed every furious command of the insect brain. The white substance dribbled from her mouth and sizzled upon the wooden planks beneath her. Without her lower jaw, the queen's monstrous face was held open in a silent scream of rage.

The mirrored globes of her eyes glared at her enemy. She knew the octopus was impossibly quick, yet she'd proven he was not invincible. The queen recognized this one. Once, long ago, he had come at the head of a hundred armies to exterminate her race, and he might have succeeded had the red snake not betrayed his own kind and shown her and her children the way to a hidden sanctuary. The snake had given her this body so she could protect them and protect the promise he made. That one day, Thraxia would rise again.

Zariel's own silver eyes reflected hers. He kept his last two swords leveled at her as he slowly glided to her side, hoping to draw her attention away from the foxes and his master. The only damage he had really done to her body was to hobble her movement, rob her of her primary bladed legs. But she still had four to spare beneath her, carrying her center of gravity.

The two foxes brought the unconscious turtle to the side of the sky wing. Rinnia unlatched a series of bars on the machine and threw open its oval-shaped dome. The hydraulic joints hissed as they eased the heavy glass windshield over onto its side. She grasped the edge of the thing's ramp and brought it to the floor with a thud. The space inside was cramped and crisscrossed with belts and locks for cargo. At the front, the lone pilot's chair was bolted to the sky wing's floor in front of a series of levers, buttons, and dials. Wires and pipes ran from the dashboard along the interior and disappeared into the rear paneling.

"Get him in," Rinnia shouted, "and get this thing in the sky,"

"What about you!"

But she'd already drawn her sword and darted down the pier to join Old Four Swords. The fur in Maxan's ears quivered with the familiar, vibrating thrum of the octopus's katanas.

They're going to be fine, he told himself, again and again, frowning at the tangled space of the sky wing's cargo hold and the old turtle he was supposed to shove in here. *They're going to be fine. They have to be.*

Back on the pier, the queen's armored head jerked to the side, drawn by something quick moving on her periphery. Zariel shot forward into the opening Rinnia bought him, predicting the queen's reflexes would unleash a sidelong slash of her bladed leg. The feint paid off, and her leg swept inches over his roll. He came up well within her striking distance, one sword leading the way, unleashing a wave of shimmering air that cut the bladed leg away at its root on her underbelly.

The queen's shriek of agony and anger was deafening. A gob of sizzling plasma belched from her ruined maw, spattering just inches short of her attacker. To swipe at the octopus with her other leg would put her off balance, so she simply lurched toward him, hoping to crush him beneath her tremendous weight. But the rubber-bodied creature sprang forward, straight into her, flipping mid-air and landing on her back. His tentacles writhed over her armor, gripped the sides and held him there.

Maxan pushed with all his might and finally rolled the turtle up the little ramp and onto his back within the hold. He sank into the pilot's chair and ran his paws over the dashboard, completely unsure of what to press or pull. The sound of crashing metal and furious shrieking pulled his eyes up.

The queen was wheeling about furiously, plowing waves of corpses aside into the murky lake, trying to dislodge the octopus suctioned on its back. Rinnia stood a dozen feet away, seeking an opening, dodging the crash of overturned insect and bird bodies.

The thrum of Zariel's swords intensified, then faded, then resurged as he was flung about. For the weapons to gather their decimating energy, they had to be held still, and all the queen's bucking and rocking made that impossible. One of Zariel's tentacled arms slipped, and half his fluid body flapped like a flag as the metal monstrosity spun about. Half a second later, a katana sailed out over the water and sank to the depths.

I have to help them! I can't just watch. I have to—

With a start, he scrambled up over the dashboard onto the nose of the aircraft. And then he froze, the tension bleeding from his muscles. Dread filled his heart.

Maxan… Listen to me… There's no time… It was Ralse's dread. The certainty of it flooded Maxan's mind. The overwhelming hopelessness paralyzed his body.

"Wh-what," Maxan stammered aloud. "What do you mean?"

I mean there's no time. For us.

A cold rush of sweat prickled his fur. The sounds of humming steel, groaning metal, and hollow screams all died. The vacuum opening inside his mind snuffed all his sense of the world around him.

"What do you mean?" he said again. Tears welled in his eyes. His chin quivered. He knew what it meant.

Maxan, my son. Listen… This is the end.

Away on the pier, the Thraxian queen reared on her lowest legs and jerked forward powerfully, flinging Zariel wildly forward. His old writhing body slammed hard and rolled like a ball over several feet of planking and lay still. His last remaining sword stabbed into the water-logged wood by the water's edge and wavered with the impact, its lights winking out, its thrum going silent.

Rinnia saw her chance at last before Old Four Swords had even hit the ground, leaping in to strike at the queen's metal joints. The monster spun frantically, fully anticipating the fox's attack. The heavy womb segment met Rinnia like a wall of steel, sending her reeling away.

Maxan slumped helplessly on top of the machine, watching all of this but seeing none of it; a part of himself was tearing away. He could not stop the tears from flowing. "What are you talking about," he said to no one.

I'm going away, Maxan. He's here. He's going to take me away from you.

Zariel's limp body stirred. The seven intact tentacles writhed blindly as the old weaponmaster seemed to inflate and rise to a crouch. His silver eyes came to rest on the katana by the rails, resting atop the dead tentacle the queen had taken from him. He scrambled painfully forward.

Blood streamed from Rinnia's nostrils and the split skin over her skull. Miraculously, she'd managed to hold on to her sword, and she used it like a crutch to rise. Then she collapsed to her knees, dizzied by the blunt force of the queen's body.

The last living Thraxian queen scraped the steel length of her foreleg on the metal rail of the pier, slowly, as she approached the battered octopus. She could not talk, could not laugh triumphantly. But she wanted the creature to know it was beaten. She wanted to savor the moment of its death. The octopus stopped wriggling, still several feet away. It flopped over and stared at her with its own set of silver eyes. She saw herself reflected in them as she neared.

A violent explosion blasted from the side of the tower, blowing one of the massive water wheels clean off. Sparks of fire and electricity glowed within the roiling column of smoke spewing from the structure's side. But the queen heard none of it, so focused as she was on ending her enemy once and for all. Nothing else mattered. Not even the intensifying, vibrating thrum as she finally closed the distance, raising her steel to strike.

Zariel's shimmering slash claimed the two legs beneath the queen's middle segment. She crashed sideways, her downward thrust missing the prone octopus by inches, the impact of her bulk cracking the wooden beams. The force of it rocked the whole length of the pier and into the shed, lurching the sky wing up and down like a boat on choppy water.

The motion didn't even register with Maxan. Nor had anything else. He drew up his knees to his chest and wrapped his bushy tail about him. And he cried, listening to the voice of reason, his father, saying goodbye.

Maxan, I can't stop what's about to happen, son. I want you to know—

"No!" Maxan cried between his ragged breaths. "You can't leave me! Not you too!" He was back in the dark forest by the river, watching the assassins cut his mother down. He was sobbing in both worlds—his memory, and here, all at once.

Another explosion thundered throughout the deep bowl of the surrounding cliffs, drawing Rinnia's gaze as a ball of fire burst from one of the station's upper levels, blowing away a cloud of metal bits and twisted machinery. The fire had eaten its way up through the inside of the station, consuming the factories and storehouses and everything. And still there were pockets of Corvidian knights fighting their way through the blinding black smoke, still seeking to strike down their foes, the last remnants of Salastragore's personal guard, still toppling lifeless to the water when they failed.

Rinnia wanted to laugh, but her chest hurt. Everything hurt.

She gawked at the leaning height of Castle Salastragore. A sudden vertigo washed over her. The vats of hazardous chemicals in the foundry must have tipped over, mixed, or washed up against a loose flame. With thunderous cracking sounds, fissures opened in the graystone like smiling mouths, tongues of the inferno flicking through all colors of the rainbow. Walkways and girders and scaffolds were ripped from their bolts and stretched out over the chasm, or they were torn away from the structure entirely, plummeting, crashing to the lake, sending up enormous gushes of frothing white water.

And then, above it all, looming directly above the castle, the Aigaion drowned the city and the pit and the whole world with its shadow. Beyond all the darkness, through all the smoke, Rinnia spied the rose-petaled tower, its side lit in the orange glow of twilight. She saw the rails bolted there, glinting in the dying light of day.

"No," she said, coughing. Rinnia spat out a broken fang and a wad of blood. Then she said it again, louder. "No. No! No!" She would not be beaten. Not here. Not like this. She repeated the word, again and again, moving a little more each time, dragging herself up, back to the shed. She limped by the twisted, ruined mass of the cybernetic Thraxian queen. She paid no mind to the tentacles dragging the octopus up on top of it, dragging a katana weakly along with it.

The queen was on her back, all but one of her arms and legs had been removed. The white plasma fuel spurted from her throat and the stumps of her severed limbs. She felt the octopus on her abdomen. She saw him rising over her. She knew she could not swipe at him in time to save herself. There was no time left.

Zariel pressed the switch by the handle of his sword. It would be only a moment now, and then he would cut her head off. The first green light blinked to life, then the second, and all the while the two creatures' reflective eyes mirrored one another.

The third, red light flashed to life on the hilt of Zariel's katana. The air around the blade vibrated so violently, the blade itself seemed lost inside an unseen pocket of space. Zariel raised the katana over his head, ready to unleash its energy.

Then, without warning, his body crumpled like a puppet.

Truly, a puppet was all Zariel had ever been.

His tentacles went slack, dropping the sword behind his shoulders and losing their suction on the metal plates where he stood. His bulbous blue head struck one of the rails, and an instant later, his wondrous, shimmering katana touched the wooden plank beside it.

The siphoned energy held in the blade released in a shower of chaos, boring through the pier and ripping ten thousand gallons of lake water into the sky all at once. Halfway back to the shed, Rinnia was blown off her hind-legs by an invisible shockwave and dropped onto the sky wing's metal hull. She slid off, her ears ringing, and saw a wall of white water hanging in the air, obscuring everything. Then the wall crashed down, washing the pier clean of all the dead.

All but one.

The ant queen's mechanical head lifted after the watery maelstrom had settled. The hole in her mouth had welded shut where the water had splashed against the leaking plasma. The mirrored domes of glass over her eyes had shattered in the shockwave. Half of her compound eyes had burst, though she could see the Peskoran's lacerated remains well enough by her side. Black blood oozed from a hundred cuts on its skin.

She put all the energy she had left into her last remaining leg, turning herself over, then rising slowly and dragging her bulk forward. Toward the other one. She hadn't forgotten the fox.

Maxan had seen Zariel fall. He had watched as if in slow motion as the wondrous, fully charged katana touched the ground. He felt the thud in the fuselage of the sky wing as the discharged energy flung his sister against it. His mind had processed all of these events. He knew what had just happened. He understood everything.

And yet, he could not will himself to move.

"Don't go," he whispered.

Maxan… You have to let me go.

"Don't go…"

Maxan… My son… I'm sorry.

CHAPTER EIGHTEEN
FINAL PARTING

SALASTRAGORE'S FINGERS FINALLY RELAXED. HIS COLD, reptilian blood boiled, igniting the terrible orange fire in his eye. Sweat streamed from the scaly furrows of his brow and dripped from his chin as he straightened his back. Whereas the death of the human he remembered only as Breen had been clean and quick, Salastragore had decided to extend the suffering of his next victim. He had savored every second of it.

And he had made quite the mess doing so. He drew his thumbs from the ruined eye sockets—the long, sharp nails at their ends slick with the human's blood—and wiped his hands on the creature's white robe, marring its perfection with streaks of red.

"Ahhh," he exhaled, then enjoyed a chuckle. "Bye, Zariel." He patted the corpse gently, as if to thank it for such a good time, then stood and strolled away, already putting all the years of aggravation the aged user had caused behind him.

"Now then," he called out to the silent chamber, lined with the oblivious dreamers in their pods. "Can we get a volunteer?"

After the echoes of his father's voice faded, Saghan still heard the second victim's screams resounding in his mind. He stood by, watching the murderous act with a cold air of indifference. For everything these humans had ever done, every one of them deserved this. Saghan questioned how much he also wanted to partake in the slaughter, but he was afraid of what finding the answer would make him. If these humans were the true killers, what was he?

So Saghan had simply watched, letting his father deliver "justice" with his own hands, content enough in the fact that his own hands were not being controlled.

Saghan's tongue flicked silently as he watched his father move from pod to pod. The younger snake's eyes had finally grown accustomed to the eerie flashing of the racing lights and the creeping vista of the world beneath his feet. As Salastragore walked along the wall in one direction, Saghan walked along the other. Now that he could feel the firmness of the floor beneath him and his sense of passing time had finally caught up with reality, he could clearly see the faces of each and every human on the other side of the glass. They wore identical clothing; their skin was of identical color—all a deep tan like sand under a shade. Every face was gaunt, furless, though some wore more wrinkles than others. They were aging within their pods. By his rough count, their number seemed equally divided among male and female.

His eyes came to rest on one pod in particular, and it took him a moment to realize the glass barrier had already been raised, but he had not seen Salastragore open it.

"Father," he spun about, calling out across the wide room, "thisss one is empty."

"Indeed," the red snake called back matter-of-factly without bothering to face his son. "It was mine."

Saghan examined the empty pod. "Yoursss..." Saghan's whisper was low, but the contemplative hiss at its end floated through the still chamber like a breeze. His forked tongue flicked involuntarily as his vision traced around the indentation where a human body should have been suspended, his mind racing with questions and uncertainties. Was Salastragore—no, the *real* Salastragore—was the old red snake's human user dead? He couldn't be. How else could his mind invade Saghan's body on a whim? Had all of it been lies?

He felt shame rising then in his throat. Had he not already set aside his resentments and doubts? He caught himself before most of these questions could slip off his tongue.

Instead, he simply asked, "If these are the Monitors, where are all the other users?"

"Far, far away. Mankind's last bastion in the solar system. What we call 'the red planet.' We shall be underway shortly, but first..."

Salastragore's voice trailed off as he halted at last beside a pod near a corner of the three-walled chamber. "I remember you, Folgian. So, the *bear* dies, but *the mind* lives on. Ha!" He wagged a finger at the sleeping human woman beyond the glass. "I met your pet wolf, you know. Was he the best you had? Your last hope? You should've sent a less incompetent assassin. Actually, you should've tried to stop me years ago. Ah, well… I'll come back for you, Folgian. In the meantime,… where's our blessed teacher, hmm?" His gaze slowly crept over nearby pods, scrutinizing each face within. "I know you two were … close."

Salastragore's eye roamed across the nearby pods, then locked on the one just after the turn of the corner.

"You," he said scathingly, pressing his forehead against its glass. The human male within seemed more feeble than the others and shorter. Its bare feet floated several inches more above the bottom of its pod. While every other Monitor Saghan could see had four golden lights revolving in their haloes, this one's halo had twice that many, and they were spinning about its bald head twice as fast. Salastragore seemed not to notice, his gaze locked on the creature's closed eyelids as if he expected them to snap open any moment now. The eyes within squirmed about more quickly and frantically, as if seeing a nightmare.

"Master… You're listening, aren't you? Always listening."

Salastragore punched a sequence into the console, then hesitated. "No," he said, his finger hovering over the final digit. "Not yet. *You* will be the last. When you see all your friends, all dead on the floor, *then* I will have your scream, Baaleb. *I. WILL. HAVE IT!!*" He drew his hand away from the console and stepped back, composing himself. "I will drown you in their blood," he said calmly.

The red snake's long neck whipped back and forth, his mind suddenly overcome with delirium. "I need to find her. I need to."

Salastragore jogged away from Baaleb's user, down the next row of pods, frantically peering at every face through each glass barrier. He stopped just a few feet from the empty pod where Saghan stood.

"Ralse," he breathed, a prolonged note of deep emotion rushing from him as though he had been waiting to say this very name in this very spot. In truth, he had. "Ralse. My friend."

Saghan inched closer to the pod, stopping just behind his father's shoulder.

The woman sleeping inside was *beautiful*, the angular features of her face transcending any species' definition of the word. And her eyes were open. Pale blue, like two calm seas.

"She'sss… awake."

As though she could hear the younger snake's whisper, those blue eyes shifted to Saghan, and bored into him. Deep in those seas, Saghan saw it. The truth. She knew him. Saghan could feel it. She knew about all he had done in his life. She felt the weight of all his guilt. And those eyes judged him. They gave him what he could not give himself.

"Forgivenessss," Saghan breathed, knowing it was what she felt for him but ashamed he could never feel it for himself. "She forgivesss me."

Salastragore was too absorbed in this moment and by this woman's presence to hear his son's words. He slammed a fist against the glass, smearing the blood of Zariel's human user over the glass like watery red paint, drawing her gaze back to him. The calm in her blue eyes ebbed away and fear flooded in. Salastragore pounded the glass again, and again, but it did not crack.

"Why did you do this to me, Ralse?" The red snake's face was a storm of conflicting emotions. Tears streamed from his fiery orange eye, yet his twin fangs were bared. His voice dripped with venomous anger at one word and sobbed at the next. "You betrayed me! I trusted you... *I TRUSTED YOU*!!"

The woman he called Ralse raised her hand, shuddering in fear, and pressed it to the glass as if to wrap it around the red snake's fist.

"No... No! I will not be tricked again! There is nothing left of me. There is nothing worth saving. All our worlds, all our games... All life... It all has to die, Ralse. Every cruel scar, every wicked stain on the universe mankind has ever left. I will erase it all."

Salastragore wiped away his tears and glared at how they dampened the scales of his palm. He growled angrily and wheeled about to his son, drawing the rubied dagger from its scabbard at Saghan's hip.

"And with it," Salastragore said, his finger touching the console with a deliberate slowness as he bit off every word, "will go all the hate. All the ferocity in our hearts. No more. Just peace... Just ... dust."

Ralse's blue eyes pleaded with Saghan. Even as the pod's barrier hissed and slid slowly into the floor, the soft tips of her raised fingers dragging across the glass, she was begging him silently. He could stop this, she was telling him. He could stop this.

Stop what?

Saghan felt the eternal battle raging in his heart. The fire against the ice. The compassion against the callousness. What was right? What was wrong? Was he alive, or was he dead? Isn't this all just a game?

Gravity overcame the woman's body, drawing her down onto the point of Salastragore's rubied dagger.

Saghan watched the red flower bloom across the white cloth along her back, and he did nothing.

Maxan… My little Max… Listen to me! This is serious. If you ever see anyone, you run. You get away. You hide. Look at me now, son. Do you understand?

Yes, mother.

"Show me, old friend… Show me which thing you love most, and I'll spare it."

Are you crazy, Max?! We can't go back for her!

I have to!

They're dead! They're all dead! Remember what mother told you!

SHUT UP!

Listen to me!

STOP IT! I have to go! I have to find Safrid!

You'll kill yourself! You'll die! They're still in there, Max! You'll burn! LOOK AT THE FIRE, YOU IDIOT!!

The snake's red scales were a camouflage against the dancing flames.

The fox's right arm had all but melted now. First, the ruddy orange fur withered to black. Then, the poison seared the exposed skin black, splitting it open like rotten fruit. All the bloodred flesh within bubbled to black. As the red snake spoke, Ralse watched in horror as the maneater glutted itself on his body.

"Fassscinating."

The fox felt the poison creep into his shoulder, infecting his muscles, biting the strands of them away sinew by sinew until they snapped. The maneater assaulted his bones. It bled between the vertebrae, seeping into his spine. Soon, the world would no longer make sense. But it made sense enough for him to want to laugh at the ridiculousness. The breath meant to be laughter burst from him in a huff, spraying the metal floor with a spatter of blood, spots of red, spots of black.

Be ready, Max. Be ready to run. Look at him, the big rhino. The guard captain. See how he's squinting down at you? He's trying to read you. He takes you for a thief.

I am a thief.

He's going to say, where'd you get this coin? Let's go, Max. Don't be stupid.

I was a thief.

No! Don't give him the coin!

No more.

Maxan, look at him. Don't turn away from his eyes. But be ready to run. See? He wants to ask you. Where'd you get this coin?

Wait. It can't be. It's the same rhino. From when… It is him.

Him who? Oh. Oh!

I'm not running. I'm done running. I've got nowhere to go. Nothing left. If this doesn't work…

No, Max. You can't think that way.

I don't care anymore. Not without her. If this doesn't work…

No, Max. You have to keep living.

"Show me which thing you love most, and I'll spare it."

Before the black poison blinded him, before it swallowed the rest of him whole, his green eyes looked at the enormous glass tank beyond the snake's shoulder, wreathed in flames. He wondered if she felt heat or pain. If she would ever know what happened.

"Your … *daughter* then?"

It took all the strength Ralse had left to lift his claw and touch the glass.

"I see. I will miss you, old friend."

Chapter Nineteen

Ascension

RINNIA'S FANGS GNASHED HARD ENOUGH TO CRACK AS SHE strained to pull both ends of the cargo strap together over the turtle's shell. The wolf's bite marks had already sealed themselves, and her strength in that arm had returned just in time. She heard the satisfying clink of the buckle and fell back onto her rump.

"Is he…" She peered at Baaleb's face, pressed against the floor of the cramped cargo hold. "Is he crying?

"No time for this, Rin! Dammit!"

She whirled about to face her brother. Maxan was slumped against the interior. She checked his nostrils, seeing that they still drew breath. His one green eye was open, staring vacantly ahead. A line of tears ran down his muzzle.

"Something's wrong," she muttered the obvious to herself. She shook him by the shoulders. "Maxan! Are you dead? HEY!"

Nothing. Maxan was lost inside his own mind.

"Not dead. Just useless…

"So, what else is new?"

Outside the sky wing's floating shed at the end of the pier, the world was literally falling to pieces. Fires spewed from the windows of the castle, charring its graystone walls to black. Ruined machinery and slurries of steaming chemicals tumbled through the passages right alongside the corpses of Corvidians and Drakorans that had given their lives over its treasures. All the wreckage found its way into the open air and eventually down to the lake, sending up great plumes of water as they broke the surface and sank to the deep.

Rinnia secured Maxan's catatonic body to the side with a final, whispered curse, then leapt over the back of the sky wing's sole pilot's seat and reached for the straps to secure herself. She froze, buckle in hand, her sea blue eyes locked dead ahead.

The ruined Thraxian queen dragged herself on the five nubs of her ruined legs. She anchored the tip of her last remaining, bladed limb into the wooden planks then lurched forward with all the strength she had left. The damaged compound eyes glared at the fox.

The queen was closing the distance rather quickly, Rinnia realized.

"Let's see if I can help you with that," she muttered, trying to make sense of all the controls on the dashboard in front of her.

"Pier's gone to shit. Rails are sliced to pieces. What hope you got, Rin?

"Hope. Funny. Just going to hope that the thrust'll be enough to… to…

The original wound Baaleb had made in the bottom of the station when he refracted the Thraxian's plasma beam suddenly crunched down with an ear-splitting boom, like a mouth biting so hard its teeth exploded. Whatever support beams were inside had succumbed at last to the incalculable weight bearing down upon them. On the other side of the station, a new split was forming all its own in the dark, grimy metal. The groan of warping and splitting metal was maddening.

The Thraxian queen's blade sunk again into the wood with a *thunk*, drawing her closer. She landed another short jump, shaking the end of the pier, thunked her blade again, only twenty feet from sky wing.

Rinnia frowned at the dashboard, shifting her paws about on the various controls, hesitating to turn any one of them for fear that what had happened to that monster's mouth would happen to all of them.

"This is stupid! What are you waiting for?"

She jerked a lever forward all the way and felt a vibration thudding through the bottom of her seat, growing in intensity. She cranked a small wheel and felt four clanks in unison under her low paws. She flipped open a plastic covering and flipped the switch she saw beneath. She spun dials to the right, then to the left, then halfway back, bringing a noise from the conical boosters that rose to a furious buzz, fell to a hushed whisper, then eased to a low murmur. Suddenly, on the outermost fringe of the dashboard, a red button she hadn't yet considered illuminated.

Her eyes lifted to the metal-plated monster outside, just as the thing's bladed limb fell upon the nose of the sky wing and drew away with a screech of steel against steel. It was enough to bring the queen's gaze level with Rinnia's.

The vibration and the buzzing were holding steady; the red button flashed. Rinnia reached over her head and tugged the oval-shaped dome of glass down with a hydraulic hiss, its latches locking in place.

The queen's ruined legs scrambled up onto the nose and flexed at their roots on the sides of her cybernetic belly, clamping herself firmly to the aircraft. She reared back, brandishing the razor-sharp blade.

"For Old Four Swords..."

Rinnia jammed her fist against the button and felt the whole world drag her away behind her.

The Thraxian's blade pierced straight through the glass dome, missing the fox's face by inches.

The sky wing screamed down the rails, plowing through whatever wreckage remained of the battles fought in the dying castle's shadow. The craft bucked up and down against the divots left in the rails, but by luck alone, its wheels clattered back home every time. Within three seconds, the sky wing had left the entire length of the pier behind.

Rinnia's body was pressed deeply into the pilot's chair. Her lips were peeled away from her fangs, and her eyes were held horrifically wide against her will. She wanted to shut them against this nightmare, against the glaring monster outside. She wanted to become blissfully deaf to the roaring of the dual rocket engines that followed her. But she couldn't. She had no choice but to watch the burning guts of the station whip by her on all sides. Inside, the rails sloped gradually upward, but the raw force of the rockets made Rinnia's eyeballs feel like they had just fallen through her skull and rolled to the tip of her chin.

The thing curved itself up.

Four more seconds of agony.

A bright window of light.

And then they were out.

The hawk's head twisted about over her shoulder. Her eyes blinked, magnified on the glimmering silver bullet shooting through the sky, picked out every shadowed line of the spreading white plume propelling it, pierced through that smoke to see the glowing line of white fire that sent it closer and closer to the impossibly long line of black hovering in the twilight sky.

Sarovek's escorts saw it too, the three of them freezing still in the Drakoran marsh.

A Corvidian's eyesight is far superior to its hearing, but no species in this world could deny the thunder that rumbled across all the land. They felt it in the murky ground beneath their taloned feet. The roar of the sky wing rattled in their bones.

Somehow, Sarovek knew who was aboard. Her beak parted slightly, and she breathed her name: "Rinnia."

But something was wrong. Something was angling the sky wing's trajectory away from the Aigaion, far too wide to bring it back on course as the aircraft crept to the monolith's edge. Sarovek blinked, refocused her razor-sharp vision, her pupils reflexively narrowing to needlepoints. There. On the side.

"What is that?" One of the falcons muttered beside her, though certainly not focused like she was on the Thraxian's metal body latched onto it like a parasite.

Until now, Sarovek had been wondering about the fate that awaited her back in her family's house. Would her twin brother condemn her to death as a symbolic gesture to restore the faith of the lesser houses? Or would he commend her for her show of honor and set her free?

But all those dark thoughts fell aside as she watched the silver thing miraculously, inexplicably curve itself back around toward the orange and purple ceiling above all the world.

"All our hope," she answered.

If Sarovek could smile, she would have.

Chapter Twenty

The Arc

Saghan stared at the pool of blood. It spread across the dark glass floor, smothering his view of all the world below in solid, glistening red.

His father sank the rubied dagger into the woman's heart one last time, then let his fingers open one by one, releasing the handle, drawing his quaking hand away. Then, the red snake was perfectly still. Straddling Ralse's human corpse, his long neck went slack, bringing his head down upon his chest. His one good eye stared down at the ruin his blade had written upon her body.

Ralse's blood crept to the edge of New Quwurth surrounding the Monitors' castle, bringing Saghan's attention for the first time to the enormous roiling black cloud. It was easily a hundred times as voluminous as the column of chemical runoff the foundry normally spewed. Tiny points of light twinkled across every wall. The smoke coiled around every side of it; from this distance, it was like seeing the Aigaion itself strangling the castle with one colossal hand.

"Father," he said, but Salastragore did not move.

Rising from the grasp of the great, black plume, Saghan could see the rose-petaled tower. Except… It was leaning precariously to the side.

"Salastragore," he called out, "something's wrong!"

The red snake's wide mouth parted. "What?" he spoke softly, with the tired voice of a sleeper who had not wanted to give up on his last dream.

"Look!"

"*WHAAAT?!*" Salastragore snapped awake, flailing his arms in annoyance, scratching his black-tipped nails in the air before him as if grappling with a phantom.

"The cassstle."

Salastragore followed the line of his son's pointing finger, his scaled brow furrowing in sudden concern. He wiped the human's blood away for a better look through the tinted glass floor.

Both snakes witnessed then the silver star of light emerging from the dark cloud of smoke. In its wake, it made its own streak of smoke, a line of white cutting against the strangling black.

"My, my, your child is persistent." Salastragore allowed himself a chuckle as he finally rose to stand over the bloody woman. Her lifeless, pale blue eyes stared at the shadows gathering at the chamber's top.

"Keep your eyes open, Ralse," the red snake said to the corpse, slinging his plasma rifle around to his front. "You're going to want to see this." He depressed a button above the device's stock, and the seams of it glowed with a pale, blue light. The barrel of the weapon ejected a pressurized steam and shot out to twice its length. He stepped away from Ralse, leaving bloody footprints on his way to the chamber's triangular entrance.

"What should I do?" Saghan called after Salastragore's silhouette as it retreated into the gloom.

The red snake's voice boomed back from all the tetrahedral tomb's three walls at once. "Reboot the signal. Put this world back on the leash where it belongs."

Saghan was alone. The sole animal among the humans. A puppet that dared rebel against the puppeteers.

The beautiful woman drew his gaze again. He shuddered and looked away from her empty eyes, watching her blood pool once again over the space his father had wiped away. Before it closed entirely, he saw through the tinted glass the rose-petaled tower topple at last. It blasted itself apart across a great stretch of the city and beyond into the surrounding marshland. The rest of it sunk into the rising coils of black smoke, igniting several balls of flame within. He felt the delayed popping of the explosions in the bare soles of his feet. Then the blood closed over his view, and Saghan recoiled from its touch.

He scanned around the room at all the worlds' masters surrounding him. Their eyes were closed, but somehow, he felt them watching, judging, waiting. They had been waiting so long.

For a moment, Saghan stared into the empty pod near where he stood, then his gaze settled on the two pods near the corner—Folgian, and the one his father called Baaleb. If they could speak to him now, what would they say? What would they tell him to do with the relay? What did he need to do?

What did he *want* to do with it?

Saghan knew where he had to go without having to be told. He raised the shining chrome relay before him as though it led his way through the dazzling golden fog toward the glass pillar at the center of the room. Unlike the other stalagmite-like formations, there was no light glowing inside, only a small opening that matched the relay perfectly. Every bead of light that ran beneath the floor of the house of Manipulation seemed to flow to this point, only to turn aside at the last moment as if searching elsewhere for what they'd expected to find.

"Thisss is meant to be."

He tried to convince himself it was the truth. What would his father say? Salastragore would agree. But what would the Mind's master tell him? Isn't this what the old bear wanted? An end to the Stray? An assurance that the world would not savage itself? Is that what this was?

What would Rinnia say? Or Sarovek. Or Chewgar. Or Feyn. Or…

"Maxan."

Saghan's hand clutched the relay, hovering just outside of the pillar where it belonged. What was it the fox had told him in the tunnels?

"We can be better."

Rinnia screamed.

The agony of the noise rattled in her skull, combined with the roaring rocket engines flooding the cockpit. She screamed, fighting the instincts to close her eyes, to sleep, to let her paws relax, to let herself melt against the pilot's chair, to simply let her spirit float away through her own back and be done. Just be done.

Outside the tempered glass, against the brilliant blend of purple, orange twilight sky, the howling wind blew patterns of crystalizing ice across the plated metal body of the Thraxian queen. The monster was helplessly anchored to the rocketing aircraft. Whatever was left of the insect mother willed herself to cling to life. Her eyes glared at the fox just a few feet away and yet entirely out of her reach.

Rinnia's lungs poured all they had, and when her scream faltered and died, her sensitive ears picked up a new kind of sound in its absence. Against the constant roar, something beeped rhythmically. She rolled her eyes around to the instrument panel, becoming aware of the pulsing green button that matched the beeping pattern. The tip of her claw fought against the amplified gravity, and she pressed it.

With a whirr and deafening clank of metal, her body abruptly lurched forward in the pilot's chair, slamming her against the harness strapped over her chest. The sudden force was enough to draw the queen's bladed leg back through the glass but not enough to dislodge her from the sky wing.

Rinnia sucked in deep breaths of the frigid, rarified air, letting out a series of gasps as her eyes darted about the cockpit to find what had changed. Outside the overhead glass barrier, she saw that two arms had thrust outward from the craft's sides, dragging chrome sheets of metal. The machine had spread its wings, and the added drag gave her the space to squirm about, albeit at an awkward, inverted angle, facing straight up in the sky, rocketing at impossible speeds toward the airless oblivion of the upper atmosphere.

To the west (just at her left shoulder), she saw the edge of the Aigaion pass her by. She saw its two foremost facades loom like two triangular shadows against the darkening field of blue along the far horizon. Behind them, the obsidian walls of the Aigaion's third structure captured and turned away Yinna's dazzling, fading sunshine. It mirrored the multicolored vistas as though it were a gateway to some inverse world hanging in the sky.

For an instant, time seemed to slow. The roaring of the engines died away. Rinnia simply lost herself in the wonder.

And then she was keenly aware that the sky wing was gradually sloping eastward to her right, making the captivating view creep away beyond her left shoulder.

"You."

She stared ahead at the queen, feeling the word form on her lips but unable to hear her own voice. Rinnia gripped the flight stick between her knees in both paws and jammed it as far to the left as she could. It moved an inch and did nothing to correct the craft's trajectory. She knew then that the monster's weight was dragging them off course, turning them toward a descent that would kill them all. Her eyes ran across the dashboard, searching frantically for anything she hadn't tried.

"I *can't*," she screamed to herself, knowing that she risked doing far worse to the sky wing if she flipped the wrong controls. It was the last rational thought she had.

Rinnia unbuckled herself from the harness and pressed her back up against the tempered glass ceiling. Her low paws kicked at the queen's wedged blade frantically, desperately. "GET OFF! GET OFF!" she wailed with each futile strike.

The air in the sky wing grew thinner still, colder; it seared the inside of her nostrils with its icy, vacuous touch. She opened her mouth to scream at the Thraxian but choked on the sheer emptiness filling her lungs. One of her legs rose halfheartedly in front of her, wobbled, and fell against the immovable metal thing skewering through the glass.

"Get… off…" She panted her final breath, feeling every inch of her body hardening in ice, the tendrils of it numbing her muscles, seeping in behind her eyes, caressing her brain. *Sleep*, the cold whispered softly in her mind. It snuffed out all the noise. *Just go to sleep. It's over.*

The twin engines sputtered. The bright white pillars of flame shortened, burned themselves down pale blue, then indigo, then nothing. The sky wing hurtled upward a final push, then seemed to hang in the frozen stillness of space just below the outermost ceiling of the world awash in a million twinkling lights. Yerda's river of gently spinning asteroids seemed to flow just outside the window. But Rinnia failed to see them. She failed to hear anything. She gave in and closed her eyes for good.

Leave everything to me, child.

Her fanned ears twitched against the intruding voice. A shudder of life traveled along her fur. The eyes behind her eyelids squirmed as if searching the cold dark for the speaker inside her head.

"Whaaa—" Her breath escaped in a prolonged release.

A crackling sound roused her. She thought perhaps to take one final, futile, curious peek at what had caused it.

Just outside the frosted glass, a cold line of diamond white stretched across the width of the Thraxian queen's bladed leg. A second later, the metal snapped apart, now more brittle than the thinnest sheet of ice. The monster's compound eye darted about, unable to see what was happening even as the same unnatural transmutation overcame the rest of its five ruined legs at the root of her abdomen. They snapped off altogether, and there was a shower of snow-like particles floating in the absence of gravity as her enormous metal body drifted away from the sky wing.

"Whaa-t-tt-t…" Rinnia's fangs chittered as she watched the Thraxian queen float into the stillness, the final rays of daylight casting her body in warm, shimmering gold. The last Thraxian hung in the emptiness for a moment, then plummeted from Rinnia's view as though dropped by an invisible hand.

The sky wing turned about gently to face westward, and the warmth of Yinna spread over the glass shield, dispelling the frost. The light speared through the circles of melting ice, striking Rinnia's legs, thawing the arms she had folded across her chest. She blinked, feeling it burn into her retinas.

"Wh-what?" She spoke more clearly now. She heard the sound of her own voice.

Rinnia moved about in the pilot's chair and saw first that Maxan was still asleep or dead, still slumped against the side panel where she had strapped him. She hadn't time to think about him, as her eyes widened to see the turtle standing upright in the back of the cargo hold. Baaleb held one wrinkled hand out in front of his chest, stretching his stubby fingers apart. His eyes looked past Rinnia, caught the flash of daylight, focused on the monolithic black object floating aimlessly in front of them.

"I have us now, child," the ancient caller said, guiding the aircraft straight for the Aigaion. "All will soon be set right."

Salastragore bound up the off-center staircase three steps at a time, ignoring the spearpoints of pain stabbing his aching knees. He rounded a corner, ducked under the sharp, jutting edge of the hallway to buy himself a precious half-second more, and ran down the final stretch toward what he assumed was the spot he hoped for. His memory of the house of Manipulation's architecture was tattered by years of neglect. Ever since Ralse had locked the gate, the snake's sole focus had been on devising a way to return here, to complete his work, to bring an end to the game. To answer the call of his destiny.

It was all so close now. But someone was coming to take it away. He knew exactly who it was. Who it had to be. Salastragore had killed Ralse once already. Twice, in fact. The human's blood was still wet on his wrist. Yet here he came again, all the same.

"Betraying me, again!" Salastragore's gibbering madness rang out hollowly throughout the eerie, crystalline corridors. "Another fox. Of course! The same fox. Same flesh and blood. Same scheming mind. Why'd I let him choose?

"Oh, Rinnia. Why didn't I let you burn?!"

Salastragore knew why but couldn't stand to hear himself answer. It was compassion. Such a simple, human emotion. The snake had allowed himself to feel it, to care. Even for the one who had betrayed him. Ralse, the human Monitor, even beyond the death of her fox avatar, had found a way to make him feel compassion, rising like an unsinkable stone from the ocean of hatred in the snake's heart.

He would not allow it to be his undoing. Not after all he'd done.

By luck or by instinct, Salastragore's memory served, and he skidded to a halt at the apparent dead end he'd been looking for. He smashed his fist against the panel he knew was obscured by the dark glass, and with a hiss of released pressure, two lines of white cascaded from over his head down to his feet, forming a triangular outline of light around the edge. The wall fell away before him and blended seamlessly with the smooth exterior outside, revealing an opening in the very center of the house of Manipulation overlooking the Aigaion's central plane.

He squinted his good eye, scanning the V of space between the two other tetrahedral houses, and all the horizon beyond. He didn't have to look for long. The machine he had agonized over for ten years—dreaming, engineering, gathering, bolting, welding, testing, failing, so many times failing—there it was, a streaking sliver of light against the oncoming night of the eastern sky.

"Now I have you."

His hand wrapped around the plasma rifle's grip, his finger resting against the trigger. He brought the weapon up, feeling the stock against his shoulder and the whirring energy of the battery pack, begging to be discharged. He had only one shot and no spare batteries—yet another lack of foresight he cursed himself for. The weapon was a crude, jury-rigged version of the wonders he could have made if his access to the House of Balance had never been severed.

"C'mon, c'mon," he whispered to his target across the chasm of open air, tracking it with his slitted orange eye along the rifle's iron sight. He knew the beam would cut straight almost instantaneously, but he had to account for distance, for speed… "Come back to your father, girl. C'mon!"

He just wanted it all to end.

"*C'mon, you bitch!*"

He shrieked in frustration almost squeezing the trigger.

Then, Salastragore's eye opened wide. He brought his head away from the sights, puzzled by the sight of the sky wing separating in two. He squinted at the dropping thing, followed it as it fell below the point where the Aigaion's triangles joined but had no idea what he was witnessing. The other silver thing hung inexplicably in the sky, unmoving. It was the perfect shot, but the old red snake was too awestruck to take it.

Then, he knew.

The scales of his face warped in the heat of his rage.

"Baaleb…"

Salastragore no longer knew who to hate most. Rinnia. Ralse. Baaleb.

Himself.

He had let the Master Monitor's avatar live. Why? Why did he spare the decrepit old bastard turtle? How many times had he asked himself that question? How many times had he failed to conjure an answer?

But he had the answer all along. He carried it with him all those twenty years. It had rooted inside his heart like a seed, and now, here, above all the world, it sprouted into a brilliant red flower that choked his insides. All he ever wanted was to hear Baaleb's confession. To hear him speak the truth: that mankind's heart was an abyss. That preventing death with more death would never fill that bottomless pit. That his capacity for evil had no limits.

The glowing outline of the sky wing grew larger. Salastragore heard no roar from the great rockets he built. He saw no lines of white fire, no cloud of trailing exhaust. It was Baaleb. It was all Baaleb.

The red-scaled snake's nostrils sucked in a deep breath of chilling air, and he held it in his lungs, lowering his slitted eye to the sights once again and steadying himself. He became a statue, perched at the center of that triangular monolith, waiting for the sky wing to glide closer, waiting for the shot he could not miss.

The beam of brilliant light streaked across the sky, catching the aircraft just off-center, disintegrating the molecules that fused its hull and starboard wing together. It was over in less than a second, the trail of white disappearing into the sky and outer space beyond.

The sky wing dipped into a sudden tailspin. For a few precious seconds more, Salastragore smiled maniacally, howling in pure ecstasy, more satisfied with this one action than he had ever been with any other experience throughout his thousand years of life.

But then the free-falling craft caught itself mid-air and came lurching back up, unable to completely wrest itself free from the grip of gravity despite the turtle's unmatched ability to call the Aigaion's guiding power against it. The sky wing was close now and drawing closer every second that Salastragore stood gaping at it. It left a trail of black smoke in its wake. It spat little wads of flame from its wounded, wingless side.

It was coming straight for him.

"Piece of junk," Salastragore sighed. He almost chuckled as he tossed aside the steaming plasma rifle. It struck the house of Manipulation's exterior wall and slid away.

He turned about and strode back into the triangular portal, then quickened his steps, then broke into an all-out sprint down the hallway as the sky wing crashed into the pyramid's side, shattering the obsidian glass into a billion unfixable shards behind him.

Chapter Twenty-One
Gifts of Epimetheus

Wisps of acrid smoke crept through the air, hanging low above the pulsing lights within the dark glass, spreading like a slow poison. They curled around the invisible heat, black shadows dimming the reds and yellows of slow-burning fires that clung to the wreckage in a hundred places across the floor.

Maxan jolted forward with a start, unknowingly drawing in a deep lungful of the stuff. Then he bent over at the waist as though kicked by a mad bovine, choking and retching, trying to rid himself of the caustic burn in his throat. He drew the edge of his tattered cloak over his muzzle, catching a cleaner breath, and peered through the smoke screen.

For a moment, he thought he was back in Crosswall's western district, feeling the press of the collapsed structure across his back. For a moment, it had all been just a dream. Seeing the miracles of the great-horned owl that called herself Principal Harmony had simply been too unbelievable. In the aftermath of the storm she called; Maxan's mind must have been swept away by the notion that there were uncanny forces asleep in this world, keeping him locked in falsehoods and lies, and he had been constructing all of this in his imagination ever since. Chewgar was alive and would likely reprimand him for venturing *that* far into Stray territory. He would say it was a lost cause. The guards would have been too late or wouldn't have come at all. Yacub would get away. No one would believe that the Mind had business with raiders. And the Aigaion would return tomorrow and every day after.

For a moment, Maxan felt the bliss of that dreamy ignorance wash over him. In that world where he had chosen to simply observe, report, and never engage, the fox shadow's life carried on as usual. In that world, he had chosen to look away from his first glimpse into something real.

But the moment didn't last long. He looked out across the central chamber of the house of Manipulation, and he knew exactly where he was. He had chosen to be here.

This time there was nothing holding him down.

This time, instead, there was fire.

Fire, Maxan realized, had been the last thing he saw in his father's final memory.

He lifted his right arm with some effort, expecting to find it blackened by the maneater poison or melted away entirely. But instead, he saw the furless, almost-human arm of his own body. He thought of the leather sleeve he'd worn for years, then tossed aside on the road outside the city. His arm was covered with spots of blood, and he saw but did not feel the dozen small cuts all down the limb.

He found the rest of himself was relatively intact. Sore, exhausted, but intact. Just like the collapse of the beast pen in Crosswall, he would survive this, wherever *this* was.

Maxan suddenly recalled his own final memory before his mind had swum with all the unbidden visions of Ralse. He recalled a battle at the bottom of a lake, a rickety pier, the bobbing of something beneath him like a wave. Rinnia. An octopus. A turtle…

The turtle!

He crawled over the mess of straps and buckles where he had last seen Baaleb in the twisted wreckage of the cargo hold and clambered over the edge of the sky wing's interior. The clear dome of hardened glass had become little more than a pile of jagged chunks beneath his lower paws. He flopped over into a wider open space outside the ruined craft right onto a pile of glass of a different sort.

Staring at the ceiling overhead, Maxan thought he was dangling over the edge of some deep pit of impenetrable shadow. Two of its three walls were illuminating at regular intervals with racing, golden lights. The third wall—the one the sky wing had smashed through—had winked out entirely, damaged beyond repair. Maxan rolled over and saw that the same lights ran in channels throughout the floor—inside what areas of it remained anyway—roughly ten feet from where he lay. The wreckage of the sky wing had pierced straight through the glass, cracking open a massive fissure that opened into empty sky two miles above their solid world. By luck alone, he had managed to roll onto the one side of the wreck that would not have dropped him straight into oblivion.

He pulled himself upright against the hull and found Rinnia slumped over in the pilot's chair. Her head was turned away from him, but he saw it was pressed against a length of metal that skewered through the glass barrier and the top of her seat. He recognized it as one of the Thraxian queen's bladed legs, and he couldn't recall exactly how it had wound up like this. The severed limb had effectively held the two parts of the craft, keeping that front plate of windshield upright, and likely saving Rinnia's life.

But then he recalled the genetic gifts Ralse had engineered in her body before it had ever drawn its first breath.

Wait. How do I know that? How… Oh…

There had always been a hollow in his mind. He never realized it was there until this sudden rush of insight, like finding a doorway disguised as a wall, opening it for the first time and letting the light spill through. The other fox had lived there, the puppeteer behind the curtain. The voice in his head. It would never speak again. Ralse—his father, *their* father—was gone.

But all his knowledge remained, stored within that hollow. Maxan knew that human users long outlived their avatars—their minds living on while their bodies died—but their actions and their language left impressions on the living host, an imprint. Who a Herbridian became was decided by the experiences directed by the hidden hand of the human. Maxan knew this because Ralse had known this. He had inherited all of his father's memories. His knowledge. His beliefs. All his fears and his regrets.

Was I your puppet? he asked the voice of reason. He called the question out within that hollow recess of his mind, but only thoughtlessness answered.

Doesn't matter. There are no strings now.

Maxan shook the thoughts from his head, stepping away from that open space and shutting the door. It could wait. It could all wait.

"Hey, Rinnia. Get up." He slapped his sister on the shoulder, bringing her head rolling away from the metal blade and the blood spatter where her face had smashed upon it. "Oh… Ah, well, you're always saying you'll be fine. I finally believe you. Now I know it's not *all* just an act."

Sure enough, the disabled fox in the cockpit groaned a moment later, raising one paw to undo the buckle at her belt while the other touched against the bloody gash across her temple. "You're… such an ass-huhh…"

"*Huhh*-hero," Maxan finished for her. "We'll see. Yours, anyway, for now."

She smiled at that, her sea-blue eyes flickering open.

Maxan hooked his paws under her arms and dragged her out of the wreckage. She drew a sharp breath when he set her down on her broken leg. "You'll be fine, remember?" He ignored the angry look she shot him but supported her all the same.

"Where's Baaleb?"

The two foxes hobbled further into the room—passing around the sputtering fires and through the veil of smoke curling near the wrecked aircraft—and came to rest only a few feet from the massive hole in the floor. The wide-open chasm did what it could to suck away the acrid fumes, so from there they had a much better understanding of the damage surrounding them.

The pyramid's hollow corridors that wrapped around this central chamber had slowed the sky wing stabbing through it, but the force had been enough to breach the last barrier. The twisted aircraft had erupted from one of the three interior walls, decimating a row of ten pods before lodging itself in the translucent glass floor. All of the lights running through that wall had extinguished from the damage, as had the lives of the ten human Monitors slumbering there. Their bodies had likely been crushed, killing them on impact, and were ultimately swallowed by the hole the sky wing had punched. Maxan wondered if any of those humans had survived long enough to awaken within the clutches of gravity just in time to see the ground of the fabricated world where they played their game rushing up to meet them. He shuddered at the morbid imagery playing out in his mind.

At the far corner where the ruined wall met the still-functioning one, the two foxes found the answer to Rinnia's question.

The Master Monitor stood with his back turned to them. His ragged prisoner's robes had all but fallen away from his shoulders, revealing the natural hexagonal patterns of his shell, and at the center of these, the single plate that had been bolted there. Baaleb stared at the dreaming occupant on the other side of the glass, silent, absorbed in his own thoughts. For him, it was like looking into a mirror.

The pair of foxes hobbled their way around the chasm toward the turtle but stopped short when an agonized groan reached them.

Salastragore rolled onto his side sending shards of glass tinkling to the floor. The red snake had dodged the initial bulk of the disabled sky wing as it bore its way through the Aigaion, but a cascade of broken glass had dragged him onto the path of its destruction and spat him out across the room. His dark armor had protected him from most of those jagged teeth, but some had still bitten through into his legs and more had buried themselves in the scaly flesh of his uncovered neck and head.

And his son, Saghan, had witnessed it all from beginning to end. He had felt the rumbling of the impact, heard the house's layers shattering, and seen the sky wing explode through the wall. Minutes before the chaos, he had wandered away from the central control pillar—which had miraculously been spared from the destruction—and sat against the furthermost wall, turning the relay over in his hands, entranced by the perpetual dancing of its golden lights. Even when his father tumbled through the wreckage and skidded to a halt a few feet away, even when the turtle emerged from it unscathed moments later and crossed the room, and the two foxes soon thereafter, Saghan sat through it all. Unfeeling. Uncaring. Cold.

"Uuuhhhh," Salastragore moaned, pushing himself up on his bloody palms. A slimy line of blood and saliva hung from his wide mouth. He leaned back onto his knees and felt at the pit in his gums where one of his front fangs used to be. A spatter of blood surrounded the orbital socket where one of his eyes used to be. "Dammit," he muttered. His other good eye narrowed into better focus and fell upon his son. "Saghan, help me up, would you?"

The green snake said nothing, only stared at the rhythm of the dancing lights in his grasp.

"Boy!" his father called, rising shakily on his own, "bring the relay to me! Now!"

"Salastragore."

The red snake's head spun about to the voice, widening the small cuts along his neck as he did so. He hissed at the pain it brought, raising a hand to the torn flesh reflexively. Salastragore's orange eye burned in the dimly lit room, brighter than any fire, brighter than any racing beads of light. His gaze shifted from his left to his right, from the turtle that had said his name to the two young foxes arm in arm at his side.

"Oh wonderful," he said, spitting another bloody wad from his mouth. "My three biggest mistakes in life have come back to haunt me." The ironic smile on the snake's face lasted only a single second, fading instantly when something serious dawned on him. "Baaleb," he said, shocked, "you spoke ... my name."

The withered old turtle broke away from his user's pod at the corner and shuffled toward the room's center. "Indeed."

"Oh... Hmm... Aahhh," Salastragore seemed struck by the master's voice, wavering on his injured legs, seeming on the verge of fainting. Then he sucked in a pained breath as his hand shot to his side feeling the fractured ribs through his armor and skin. "Well," he breathed, watching Baaleb approach the central pillar, which was hardly taller than the top of the turtle's curved shell, "I suppose you've come to apologize then?" Salastragore made himself laugh, but only doubled over from the exquisite pain it brought him. He fell back to his knees, struggling to control the waves of anguish pulsing in his chest.

"Give me the relay, child," Baaleb said, speaking past the red snake, addressing the green one against the wall.

Saghan looked up from the shining chrome tube and considered the turtle with a blank expression.

"Wait," Maxan called out, approaching Baaleb with Rinnia's arm still draped about his shoulder. "Wait, Baaleb. What do you intend to do?"

The old turtle turned his eyes upon the fox. "Re-establish the signal, of course."

Maxan could hardly believe this was the same wasted, ancient creature he had shared a prison with, albeit briefly. The turtle's old, sagging eyes flared with a renewed vigor that simply did not match the rest of his appearance. There was a determination in Baaleb's voice, a conviction that was worlds beyond the rasping resignation he had heard at the top of the tower. Simply put, the sound of it frightened Maxan.

"But that will let the users back in," Maxan protested. Now, it was the audacity he heard in his own voice he could hardly believe. He gestured at all the pods, all the white-robed humans dreaming, listening. "Whatever animals are down there, free, will be taken over again."

"And those you called *the Stray* will come home again, child." Baaleb's wrinkled mouth curved into a warm smile. "There will be no more stray when the human minds return. Isn't that what you wanted?"

Maxan would not let himself be fooled. The turtle's smile was the same as before, inviting, disarming, reassuring. But those eyes were cold. They were the eyes of a tyrant. Maxan felt the familiar conviction welling in his chest, realizing not for the first time that the Master Monitor would take his power too far. It was the same realization his father had come to when he had first heard Baaleb propose the campaign to utterly exterminate one of Herbridia's five kingdoms. It was why Ralse had joined Salastragore.

"No," Maxan said flatly. But then he stammered, "I… I don't know."

His eyes dropped to the floor, as though he could find the solution written in the racing lights. "There has to be some other way. The game *has* to end, Baaleb. It already *has.* It's *over.*"

Baaleb sighed deeply, his smile souring to a frown. "Oh, Maxan. You sound just like *him* you know. And I don't mean your father."

Maxan traced Baaleb's glance to the red snake wheezing on the floor.

"He'd destroy this world, you know. *Every* world. *Every* one of our games out there. He'd scorch every speck of dust man has ever pressed his heel upon throughout our solar system. Maybe even beyond. But just like Salastragore, you simply don't understand. Maxan, child, the *game is life.*"

"*WE*," Maxan yelled, pounding his fist against his own chest, "*WE* are alive too! You've spent so long inside that turtle that you've forgotten what *life* is! It's freedom! To choose! To decide for yourself what's right and who you want to be. That... that turtle's *skin* you're wearing—that body, that *slave*—he never got to choose."

Through the turtle's yellow eyes, Baaleb the Master Monitor expressed his utter disappointment. "Truthfully," he said slowly, managing to contain his annoyance, "this body will soon be free if it pleases you. And I shall take another. And I shall rebuild everything Salastragore and Ralse destroyed. I do hope you will help me, my child, when the time comes. But for now," the dam keeping his true emotions broke, flooding his glaring eyes with contempt, "you will *stand aside,* and you will *WITNESS,* and you will *NOT INTERFERE!!*"

Baaleb whirled about to the green snake, catching himself against the pillar before the weight of his shell toppled him sideways. "And *YOU,* boy! You will bring me the relay... *NOW!*"

Saghan rose to his feet without a word. His tail whipped side to side behind him. His forked tongue flicked steadily in and out. His slitted eyes roamed over his anguished father—the reptilian creature of which he was a copy—and finally came to rest on the furious turtle draped in rags—the decrepit husk that thought himself a god. His only response was to tighten his grip on the relay.

Maxan glanced about the room, calculating times and angles, searching for routes of attack.

Attack?! Attack who?

His mind raced with the possibilities, but his plotting was hampered by just how confused everything had become. Hadn't they come here to stop Salastragore? Was Baaleb his enemy?

And what hope do I really have against the world's most powerful caller, if I try to...? All of the scenarios, all the angles, all of it ended in his death. *There has to be another way out of this.*

He felt Rinnia shift beside him. He looked down to see her plant both her low paws firmly on the glass floor, unsure if her leg had healed itself by now, but certain that she was handling the pain well if it hadn't. He saw her free arm cross around her back. She might have been calculating too, might have wound up with all the same failed conclusions, but that wasn't going to stop her.

"Boy!" Baaleb hollered again at Saghan, raising a stubby arm to beckon him. "I will *take* it then."

"No, you won't..." Salastragore's voice rattled with the blood welling in his throat. It stained his clenched fangs. He coughed wetly, and it dripped and spattered to the floor. The red snake struggled to regain his footing, but could only gain one knee, as though kneeling in defeat before his old master.

The gesture seemed to suit Baaleb just fine, and the turtle lowered his hand to listen.

"No, you won't," Salastragore rasped again. "Let it be me. Please, Baaleb... Master... I beg of you, spare my son. He doesn't know your power, not like I do. All he ever wanted,was to be free. Free of me." The bloodied red snake fought through all the pain that wracked his body to lift his eyes to the turtle. "He is loyal, beyond doubt. A true monitor. Truest that ever lived. Give him a *controller's* mind, like Ralse gave these foxes, a new body all his own, and let him serve you. Let him live."

Salastragore's head slumped against his chest. He seemed too weak to hold his gaze up. He had not the strength left to face Saghan as he spoke next. "My son. Give me the relay, and the master will spare you."

All the half-formed plans of attack unraveled at once in Maxan's mind, when he saw Baaleb's intense demeanor soften at the red snake's words. The warm, gratified smile wrinkled the turtle's face. But Maxan found that he couldn't relax. He couldn't shake the uneasy feeling creeping down his spine, raising the fur along his tail on end. *Something's not right,* he thought, even as he watched the turtle nod, slowly blink his yellow eyes, and wait.

At his side, Maxan still felt his sister's body had not let up one degree of its building tension. Rinnia was still poised to spring, and Maxan felt himself readying to follow her if she did. He trusted her instincts more than he trusted his own, and that worried him.

All eyes but Maxan's were on Saghan. Even the green snake's bloodied, battered father managed to open his orange eye to meet his son's. Saghan's grip loosened around the relay at last, and he stepped forward and placed it into Salastragore's open palm.

The red snake grinned at his son despite the fresh sting of pain it ignited in his chest. His other hand wrapped itself tighter about himself, digging into the side pocket along his flank.

Maxan's instincts were of a different sort than his sister's; he had little sense for timing strikes or approaching a fight. But he recognized the strange angle at which Salastragore's arm pressed to his body. He saw the real face behind the smile the red snake wore like a mask.

It's a con.

"I know you have to kill me for what I've done," Salastragore said, turning back to face the Master Monitor. "I've… I've *wanted* you to kill me for so long. Just… please, Baaleb, say that part of me was right. Forgive me. Speak the words. Say you understand why I did… everything."

Baaleb shuffled closer to the kneeling snake. Salastragore was the youngest among the ranks of his Monitors, the brashest, the most passionate. While he, the oldest among them, had always admired the snake's cunning, the depths of his intellect, Baaleb could not help but remember all the good Salastragore had done, all the service, all the loyalty. It was incredible how he had devised this plan, how he had toiled, how he had never given up against all the impossibilities.

It all made Baaleb smile.

"I understand you, my child," the old master said. "And I… I am sorry you felt, perhaps, as deeply as you did."

Salastragore's single eyelid closed, and a single pure tear cut its way through the blood smeared on all his face. He seemed, for a moment, to have died.

The snake's reaction seemed genuine enough to stifle the warning formed on Maxan's tongue. *Maybe … this is true after all?* His fox's lips parted to speak, but no sound came. This solemn moment of Salastragore's absolution seemed to stretch. But then Salastragore's single slitted eye snapped open, blazing with an orange fire hotter than any of the light the old turtle could ever hope to conjure in all his thousand years.

"Well," he said evenly, all traces of his pain gone. "That'll just have to do."

Baaleb's body exploded in a shower of shredded skin, blood, and viscera. His ancient shell became shrapnel for the bomb that had long ago been embedded in his back, cracked into a thousand pieces by the ball of fire that ignited inside it.

Maxan and Rinnia were blown off their paws from the shockwave, though they were spared by the worst of the damage. In a way, Baaleb's shell had saved them, its curved shape cupping and redirecting the blast forward. Neither fox had lost consciousness, and in fact, the physical force had not been as tremendous as the mental shock. Maxan's back slammed against the floor only a few strides away, and he sprang back up easy enough hardly a second later. Near to the center of the micro-burst explosion, the hexagonal plate skittered to rest, blackened and slick with blood. A tiny teardrop of fire clung to it like a candle, then winked out.

Salastragore lowered the hand that held the relay. He had been the only one who knew what was about to happen and had thrown it up as a guard. Even his own son with the genetically altered strength to withstand much worse had toppled over from the blast. But Salastragore remained steadfast, bent on his knee. He was showered in blood, most of it not his own anymore. He spat the taste of it from his mouth. Then he laughed—a thundering, brutal, triumphant laugh—loud enough to rouse all the slumbering gods surrounding them if they had not been imprisoned in their dreams.

The red snake's concealed hand brought the detonator device from his pocket and tossed it aside. "Hmm! I carried that thing for almost twenty years, wondering if I'd ever have the will to use it." He shrugged, wiping away a layer of blood from his face. "I'm glad it actually worked!"

Salastragore rose easily to his feet and drifted toward the central pillar, paying the other three no mind whatsoever.

"Wait," Maxan called out feebly, unable to completely dispel his speechlessness at the horror that had just transpired. He thought perhaps Rinnia would have been upon the old snake by now. But she rolled about at his side, her leg still broken. Maxan took the first step forward. "W-wait," he stammered.

The command, awkward as it was, halted Salastragore in his tracks all the same. "Wait for what? Are you going to tell me *I can't do this*? It's already done, so do shut up already!"

Maxan was struck to silence. He watched helplessly as Salastragore took his final strides to the pillar and placed the relay back into the cavity that matched its shape perfectly. He drew his hand away, awestruck by the surreality of this moment. There were no sounds; there was no difference at all for several seconds. Then, the neutral golden color of the relay's racing beads brightened to brilliant blue. The beads emanating from the pillar's base matched its color, chasing away the last bits of gold through the channels in the floor, then up along the two undamaged walls, powerful enough to dispel the shadows at the room's apex. All the eerie, hanging glow of the room faded amidst the new, dazzling light.

It overwhelmed Maxan's half-dark sight, and he couldn't help but turn away.

"Baaleb was wrong, you know." The light flooding from the pillar was palpable, and for a moment longer, Salastragore's form was a shimmering silhouette folded into it. "He didn't know. Restoring the Aigaion's signal won't bring the human minds back. My virus locked them away from this place, forever. For them, there is no coming back. Now, I truly am the last."

The blinding light finally dissolved to a normal glow, and Maxan looked about at the chunks of blasted meat strewn about, and the horrifying truth finally sunk in. *Baaleb is gone. Zariel's gone. Folgian's gone. The Monitors—the real Monitors—all of them, are gone. There's no one left.*

"Only me," he muttered, somewhat impulsively. His father's spirit was gone, but Maxan was still in the habit of answering his own thoughts aloud.

"*What* did you say?"

The snake likes to talk, Maxan observed, *so keep him talking.*

"I said I wanted to know," the fox replied, even while his eye darted about searching for anything he could use as a weapon, "what happens now."

Rinnia had managed to rise and now came to his side, supporting herself on his shoulder, her sword drawn. Maxan thought the weapon was better off in her skilled paws, even with her crippling injury.

"What happens to *you*?" Salastragore clarified.

"To everything."

"Hmm." The snake seemed to ponder at that. He dislodged a brittle shard of glass from his neck and held it up between two black nails, then let it fall with a soft *tink*. "I suppose Baaleb was only half-wrong. You see, I re-engineered the system so other users could access the animals' minds. No user but me. Those below could carry on and die naturally, all on their own, without our influence. I let them free. *We* let them free. But it was never my intention to keep them off the leash for long."

"Ralse," Maxan cut in, finding the rest of the snake's story in the recesses of his mind where the spirit of his father had kept it hidden. "He didn't know what you were really planning when he helped you stop the Monitors. You're bringing the Aigaion's fire to the other worlds."

Salastragore gave the fox a sidelong glance, a wicked grin splitting at his mouth. "You seem to know an *awful* lot."

Maxan went on, hardly paying Salastragore any attention as he recalled the unlocked knowledge his father had left in his mind. "I know... that Prometheus gave man fire so they could learn."

"Oh please, boy," Salastragore scoffed. He spat another wad of blood and venom. "All man ever did with fire was burn his own house down."

"But his name means foresight. Man's time is not at an end. You're not seeing clearly, you old bastard. We're still learning who we are. We've made mistakes. We've killed each other since time immemorial, but we've loved each other too."

With Rinnia still at his side, Maxan had come several steps closer while he spoke. He spread his paws, pleading. "Mankind's story doesn't end like this. It doesn't have to."

Saghan too had crept closer, listening intently to the fox's every word. The younger snake stopped halfway between his creator and his creator's apparent enemy.

Maxan was uneasy with the way Saghan carried himself. He watched as the green-scaled hand he had severed himself just a day ago wrapped around the handle of the thin sword at his side. Maxan knew that if the snake came for him and Rinnia, there was little either fox could do to survive. His only play was to keep Salastragore talking.

"You think you've become a monster," he said evenly, his paws still spread. "But you're not. You still don't have to be."

Salastragore was quiet a long while, the cogs of his own history winding and unwinding in his thoughts. Nobody moved. Finally, he spoke. "If the poison hadn't paralyzed Ralse so quickly, if he'd been able to speak, I imagine he would've told me something like that. I've always wondered if he'd have tried to... stop me. Even after he saw how terrible I am. But he would have been wrong to try. As wrong as Baaleb. As wrong as you are now, boy.

"You see... I haven't *become ANYTHING* that I wasn't already!" Salastragore took a menacing step forward, arching his neck down to glare at the fox eye-to-eye, only a foot of space between them. "I've *embraced* human nature! All along, I've been the only one to see what we really are. *ALL* of us. We're *monsters.* We can't change what's inside us. I will see us all turned to ashes. All of man's monuments. All of the tracks he's scattered across the furthest paths through space. I will *kill EVERYTHING!* And then, when it's done, I will lie down and join him in oblivion."

Salastragore's palms came up in a flash and pressed into Maxan's chest, shoving him back with surprising strength. Maxan slid against the smooth floor, pushing bits of shattered glass and blood into a pile as the force carried him away.

Before her brother's body had even come to rest, Rinnia leapt into the pocket of opportunity, slashing her blade at the last Monitor's head. But the old snake's fighting instincts weren't as exhausted as she had assumed. Salastragore got a forearm up, matching the angle of her strike, deftly absorbing the weapon's edge and turning the strength behind it away harmlessly. He stepped back to create space, moving away as quickly as Rinnia moved in, except he had the advantage of two legs while she had sprung only on the strength of one.

Salastragore twisted his hips, bringing his tail whipping around to lash the side of her shin, breaking the fractured bone completely in two.

Maxan watched in horror as Rinnia's hind leg snapped like a twig, the bright white bone stabbing through her ripped flesh. The audible crack echoed off the three walls. Rinnia's scream drowned the sound out, but it was cut short as the red snake twisted again, punching her square in the chest, sending her flying back to land hard beside her brother.

Her sword clattered to the floor at the snake's feet. He bent to retrieve it, hissing at the pain in his arthritic knees. His orange eye looked the blade up and down with disdain, then he shrugged and tossed it into the gaping chasm the sky wing had punched in the floor. For a brief instant, the blade turned and glinted with the light of the chamber above, then disappeared into the gathering dark of night below.

"Saghan," he said in a labored breath without looking at his son, his eye glowering at the pair of foxes, "kill them, would you kindly?"

The green snake looked at them too, his emotions indecipherable. He brought his thin sword up, contemplating the meaning of its blade much the same way his father had with the other.

Then Saghan pointed its deadly tip at his father.

"Is it true?"

Salastragore emitted a deep sigh of intermingled disgust and annoyance. "Is *what* true?"

"What Maxan sssaid," Saghan replied flatly. "How you intend to kill everything. What you told me before. Before the gate. How you would... entrussst me with all your work." The icy, emotionless tone cracked slightly, revealing a thin line of the scathing contempt it tried to conceal. "Isss *any* of it true?"

Salastragore leered at his young clone. He threw his arms up in an exaggerated gesture of defeat. "So, you figured it out, hmm? Good for you. So, I never intended to let you live your own life. So what? I *made* you to *serve* me. You've always been my puppet. Just a newer, undeniably *better* vessel for *me*." He folded his arms over his chest and looked at his creation head to toe, shaking his head in disappointment. "I let you call yourself by that ridiculous name. I *humored* your little attempts to be your own self. But you're nothing! Safe on Saturn's frozen moon, my mind enslaves yours, controls you like a doll! There is no escape."

The words seemed to extinguish the building fire in Saghan. They hardened the icy shell where it used to burn. They cast him into an abyss from which there would be no coming back. The point of the sword wavered, then fell slowly by his side. Saghan's eyes lowered to the floor.

"Now kill them," Salastragore pressed on, "or I will take your hands and *make* it so."

Maxan had been holding his sister about the shoulders, the both of them seated on the floor, trying to quell the quaking agony that ran through her body. But as Salastragore's green-scaled puppet turned about to face them, Maxan rose to his feet. He knew he had no hope against Saghan. The foxes' only weapon was gone, quite possibly still sailing through the sky, still moments yet to strike the ground. The strength of Maxan's battered body was a fraction of what he knew had been coded into the muscles of the snake's frame. He thought maybe it could be his turn to call his sister useless, but this was no time for irony. All he could do, he did.

His paws came up, pleading with the green snake approaching. "Saghan. Stop. We can stop him. Together."

"No, Maxan." Saghan raised the thin sword, so very much like all the others that had cut down the fox's mother and all his species. "He's right. I thought there was nothing left of me, but the truth is, there's never been anything at all."

"Truth?" Maxan almost laughed. He backed away, each step buying a handful of seconds. "*Truth?!* From *him?!* When has he *ever* told you any truth? Listen to me, Saghan! We can stop him! I've lied, all my life, to keep myself alive. But I never lied to you." Maxan stopped at his sister's side. It was this, right now, whatever he was doing. Or it was nothing. "And I'm not lying now."

The blade came to rest just under Maxan's muzzle. Saghan looked deeply into the one green eye the fox had left, and he felt something stirring in his heart. He lowered the sword, grabbed its tip in his other hand, and broke the blade in two over his knee with a resounding snap. He tossed the pieces to either side.

"Oh, what a noble thing."

Maxan witnessed the birth of flame in Saghan's slitted eyes. Both of them welled with an orange glow at the sound of the mocking voice over his shoulder. Maxan slowly lowered his paws as Saghan's long neck drew them around to glare at Salastragore.

"What a noble, *useless* thing."

It wasn't so much that Maxan had doubted Salastragore's word; actually, the fox knew firsthand how true it was that the spirit of the red snake—the true, human user, wherever he was—could dominate the body of the green one. He had seen it happen in Crosswall, surrounded by walls of fire. He heard the truth of it now in Salastragore's voice, but Maxan's conviction held: *we will find a way to save you, Saghan.* No doubt could dent it.

Saghan stalked toward the one who made him.

"So be it," Salastragore said. He threw up his arms and smiled wildly, resigned to what he knew was coming.

The green-scaled hands wrapped about the red-scaled neck, the length of Saghan's black-nailed fingers just enough to meet above Salastragore's shoulders. Salastragore's hands shot up to his son's wrists reflexively, though there was no real fight in them. He was lifted like a rag doll, his V-shaped head bobbing with the movement of his clone's strides across the room.

Salastragore tried to laugh, but the air wouldn't come. All he could manage was a silent, mocking grin, spreading wider across his mouth than any other smile ever had.

Saghan came to the edge of the chasm, his grip as rigid as tempered steel, holding his father over the yawning abyss. His gaze searched the narrow slit of black splitting Salastragore's only eye, perhaps hoping to find regret, or compassion, or anything that a father might feel for a son. But there was nothing there. Only the arrogance of the player who knows he's already won the game.

Saghan said nothing. He simply let go.

The abyss accepted Salastragore, enveloping his form in palpable darkness. For a single second, the orange eye burned within those reaching shadows, and the rasping notes of wild, maniacal laughter reached the chamber above, ringing about its three walls. Then there was a hush. And the single point of orange fire faded from view.

Chapter Twenty-Two

Sins of Fathers

SALASTRAGORE WAS GONE.

And with him, for an instant only, had gone all of Maxan's worries, all of his fears. The creature whose hidden hand had hunted him all his life was gone. His father, his mother, the Commune, Safrid, Chewgar, Yovan, and even Feyn… All were avenged. All was right. And Maxan could move on.

But the instant passed. Salastragore was gone, but he would be back. The triumphant fantasy gave way to immutable reality, as assured as the solid ground would pulverize the red-scaled avatar to bits in the next minute.

Less than a minute.

Maxan left his sister's side and took a cautious step toward Saghan. He stood over the edge of the chasm, entranced by the dark of night and the invisible pull of the world below. There was no way Maxan could fathom the storm of emotions roiling in the green snake's heart, no way he could predict what Saghan would do next.

"I didn't do that for you," Saghan murmured over his shoulder.

"I know."

"You can't sssave me. It's not like you said."

"It might—"

"You *know!*" Saghan's words bit into Maxan's speech, halting the fox where he stood. "He'll come for me, and then I can't sssave you."

Saghan's head craned about. There was no sadness in his eyes like Maxan had expected, only a quiet resolve. "Thank you, Maxan. For showing me the way to find my own life again. These final moments, right now, are precious to me. But they can't last. You know what I have to do."

Maxan's eyes flitted to the abyss yawning before Saghan. "No. Saghan, listen. We—"

Saghan's foot shifted.

Time seemed to creep, then stop altogether, as plans and calculations exploded in Maxan's mind, even as he knew that a lifetime of his thoughts would never be enough to think of a way to tell Saghan he was wrong.

"WAIT!" he shouted all the same, seeing the snake's foot hovering over the drop.

He doesn't want to do this.

Just… just wait. Maxan squeezed his eye tight, purposefully bringing the pain rushing through his temples and thudding against his skull as though the sensation alone could somehow bring the dead back to life. Blood trickled from the empty socket from his exertion. *Ralse.* The name echoed in the chambers of his mind. *Ralse would know. So, I would know. Ralse would know, so I would know.*

His green eye snapped open suddenly, and he quickly abandoned the idea of the cautious approach.

Maxan's instincts were right about Saghan. The fox's sudden burst of movement didn't send him over the edge. His brow furrowed with a curiosity, and his foot settled back to the shattered glass floor as Maxan raced to the central pillar.

"What are you doing?"

"Saving your life."

Maxan's paw sunk into the space surrounding the relay, and his claws closed tightly around it, his frame blocking its brilliant white light and casting a gigantic shadow on the wall behind him. An unbidden memory visited him as he twisted the thing and pulled, as though he had stood in this very spot and done this very thing, long, long ago. The pulsing white lights in the pillar faded instantly to dull, glowing gold. They spread along the floor and up the walls, chasing all the brightness away.

"How can…" Saghan trailed off as the idea the fox had in mind dawned on him.

Only seconds left, Maxan knew, meeting Saghan's eyes.

"Remember where we first met?"

Saghan gave a solemn nod.

"I can't imagine what this will feel like, Saghan. But I swear to you, I'll come back for you. But you have to promise me something too."

The green snake turned away from the gaping abyss and nodded again.

Maxan smirked. "Pull your punches a little."

Saghan wanted to smile back, but his own will was simply no longer there. Something had just crushed it inside him. He was aware of it. He knew what it meant. He doubled over at the waist, falling upon his knees just inches away from the edge of oblivion. He fought to extend an arm to hold himself away from certain doom. He felt them, the dreaded fingertips creeping in from the base of his long neck, caressing his spine like the brushing of a hundred needles, flooding through his legs and pooling even in the tip of his tail. It pricked every inch of him with exquisite pain. The signal stabbed its way through his brain and burst out through his vision like baleful orange fires.

Saghan saw red. The world was drowned in it. His glowing orange eyes raised to the fox crouching before him.

Maxan had seen the transformation coming and didn't hesitate to bring the relay slamming down against the Aigaion's glass floor. He knew, because Ralse knew, that it had always been the sudden jolt of kinetic energy that sent the mechanism's systems spiraling toward the extreme. The relay was the safety valve of the signal. It was the lever with which the Monitors regulated the emotions of all the users' avatars. Whether their campaigns called for seasons of peace or for festivals of all-out slaughter, they need only turn the relay where it rested in the house of Manipulation. Salastragore had planned to wash all the animals in docility and march them aboard the Aigaion. When on Mars, he would turn the dial and unleash the true ferocity of their natures upon humanity. Ralse had robbed him of the means to do so.

Ralse knew this, so I know this.

The red beads of light overcame the gold, spilling like blood through the channels beneath his paws at one second, and enveloping the entire chamber in its dull light at the next.

He clutched the relay tightly in his paw, backing away from the rising, reptilian animal-man.

Okay, so, I've come to the hazy part of this plan.

He couldn't swallow the lump rising in his throat.

Saghan was gone. The look in the green snake's eyes was Salastragore. The body he wore stomped forward hard enough to crack the glass beneath his feet.

"YOU!!" Salastragore roared. He held both hands palms up at his sides, his black, razor-sharp nails violently scratching at the air. The will of the clone was shoved aside inside the reptilian beast's being, so strong was Salastragore's will.

But Saghan kept coming back.

At one moment, the snake's body would take another lurching step forward, and it would fall to its knees at the next, violently stabbing its nails into its neck to tear away wet ribbons of flesh. In seconds, the wounds would heal—the signal, the cells, the unstoppable desire of the user, all of it amplified a million-fold by the power of the Aigaion.

"I WILL END YOU!!" Salastragore pounded both his fists to wrest control of the clone's body once and for all, beating two more cracks along the glass. It seemed to work, and he sprang into a charge at the outline of a fox within the inescapable red haze.

Maxan dodged aside as Salastragore rammed into a dreaming Monitor's pod with enough force to snap the bones of his own neck apart. The glass barrier held, but the wobbling shock of energy rippled through the surrounding wall, sending fissures like lightning bolts shooting outward.

He can't break the pods. Maxan's thought was automatic. He hadn't the slightest idea why it had come to him when all his mental faculties were focused on calculating his next move. He rolled aside and kept low, hoping his figure would blend in with the sea of red light staining everything in sight. With half of his vision buried in a sightless dark, he felt more than saw the presence at his side. It was Rinnia. He turned to her and saw that she had crawled to him, leaving a fresh streak of her blood across the wreckage as it leaked from the bone stabbing through her leg.

"Max, help me!"

"Help you what?"

Even with half his normal eyesight, even in the terrible red haze, the rolling of her eyes was undeniable. "Hold here," she screamed at her brother. He did as he was told, wrapping his paws around her lifeless ankle. Rinnia clenched her fangs and pulled her knee up, stretching the muscles like flexing cords. She screamed through the pain as she wrenched the bone sideways back into place.

Maxan gladly let go of her, and she crumpled onto her back, panting, working through the agony with every heaving breath.

"RALSE! How many times must I kill you..."

The snake's action was somewhat similar to Rinnia's—*although twice as horrifying,* Maxan thought—as it reached its hands to its neck and snapped the severed segments of its spine back into place. Salastragore's head twisted around ferociously, beams of orange light poured from his eyes like the lidded apertures of a lantern. His sight roamed over all the wreckage as the rest of his body flopped over onto his belly. The reptilian nature overcame him, and he seemed to slither side to side as he moved through the reddened chamber.

The chamber was enormous, but the stalagmite glass pillars, the twisted metal of the sky wing, and the shattered glass of the third wall could only make so much cover for the foxes to hide behind. Salastragore missed them with his first sweep, then shuffled away behind a mound of wreckage.

"What's your plan?" Rinnia did her best to blend the whisper with the sonorous rushing of the air through the ruined hole in the floor.

"Working on it," Maxan whispered back.

Rinnia didn't bother chiding him. She rolled over and slunk away, disappearing into the red haze before her brother could tell her to stop.

Maxan froze, weighing the few options he had. He felt the relay still pressed into his palm. *Throw it over the edge?*

Sure, and leave the whole world below tearing each other's throats out.

Put it back in the pillar?

And Salastragore takes full control.

Hasn't he already?

I don't know!

...Remember the glass over the pod. What was it about the glass?

Maxan risked another look over the mound of bent steel he had crept behind, the wreckage of the sky wing. There were no cracks in the barrier sealing the sleeping Monitor away. His eye roamed around the room, viewing the pods and the forms of the sleepers within, all of them drowned in the same red light. Then his gaze came to rest on the one pod that was different from all the rest.

There was no Monitor inside. The barrier was open. The hole punched in the floor by the sky wing had missed its edge by inches. To its side, he knew that there was a control console hidden behind the dark glass.

Some door in his mind was creaking open. He glimpsed the plan forming on the other side.

Ralse knew, so I know.

Even in the stillness of the chamber, Maxan felt before he heard the presence rise up behind him. He knew it wasn't Rinnia.

He tried to twirl away, but the beast was too quick. Salastragore's stealth had earned him the precious half-second he needed to clip the fox's shoulder with a powerful fist. Maxan spun about and fell face first against the floor. He tried to push himself up and burst into a run, but the next blow fell squarely on his back, sending him to the floor.

Salastragore reared up again, laughing wildly, and brought his hand down again, nails leading the way, thinking to carve out the little animal's heart from between his shoulder blades.

Rinnia slammed both her lower paws into the snake's side before he could, sending him toppling over. She turned with the maneuver, tucking her shoulder in before hitting the floor, rolling across her hip, and halting herself in a low crouch.

Salastragore wheeled about and came at the foxes again, swiping left and right savagely with his claws.

But Rinnia had already been on the move, hooking Maxan under the arm and hefting him up, dragging him, cursing him, shouting at him to put his paws beneath him and run. "Useless idiot! Do I have to do everything?"

Miraculously, he had held onto the relay, and his arms had not broken from Salastragore's strike like he had thought. Maxan did as his sister told him, beating the smooth glass floor with his lower paws, feeling the beast break into a run right behind him, behind them both.

Rinnia tore away to the left just as they neared the open hole in the floor. She skirted around the edge of it and disappeared into the haze.

One, two, three strides brought Maxan straight up onto the top of the crashed sky wing. Another wide bound brought him to the opposite edge of the open cargo hold, and then, with a powerful propulsion of his legs, he was flying, straight up and over the yawning abyss below.

Maxan landed inches from the chasm's opposite edge and dropped into a roll. He slid around on his rump, craned his neck to the side, and first spotted twin points of orange light glowing through the red, then the rest of his pursuer's body arcing through the air just as he had a moment before.

Maxan tumbled away just as Salastragore's feet slammed into the already cracked glass floor, sending a chunk of it falling into the edge. The fox came up just in front of the empty pod, but not far enough away to avoid the scraping claws down his back. The snake's nails bit deep into his flesh, sinking in at the base of his neck and tearing a line of ribbons down to the base of his tail.

Maxan plodded a half step forward and crashed to his knees, both his shoulders jerked back in agony, as if they could press together and seal the blood from seeping through. He toppled over, squirming, kicking at the smooth floor, desperately trying to put more space between him and the maddened reptile looming over him.

There would be no more words. The spirit of Salastragore was driven to the extremity of fury by the relay. The orange fires in its eyes pierced through the red veil. The mouth of the snake spread wide, brandishing its twin fangs. Its head cocked back to strike.

"Wait! SAGHAN!" Maxan called the name not as a plea, but as a final con he hoped would buy him the seconds more he needed.

The green snake's coiled head froze, its mouth seemed to ease closed just an inch. If Saghan was in there, fighting like the fox had asked him to, then he had just won Maxan what he needed.

"Wait for what?" The beast with Salastragore's voice said.

For her, Maxan thought.

Rinnia crashed again into the snake's side, sending it straight into the open pod.

Maxan ignored the widening pain in his back and lunged forward. His paw pressed at the pod's side, and his claw points worked in the sequence.

Ralse knew, so I know.

Salastragore spun about, his nails scratching uselessly against the impenetrable glass of his old pod. The barrier glided down with a sound to match his hiss, blending seamlessly with the smooth wall.

The enraged orange fires blazed, flitting between the two foxes on the other side of the prison. The reptilian beast slammed his fists repeatedly against the glass, wobbling its material with each blow and sending a shockwave of energy through the air. The energy spread hairline fissures through the wall on either side, but the glass was unharmed.

Maxan punched in another sequence with a quaking paw.

The green-scaled snake ceased its writhing. The orange fires faded from its eyes.

Through those slitted windows, Salastragore's soul held the foxes in its withering gaze one last time. But even that faded away, overcome in the final moment by a different spirit housed in them. And then the slitted eyes rolled upward, the brilles and eyelids closed over them. The snake's slender body gently lifted a few inches from the floor. The halo of four beaded lights glowed into existence around its head, and they started revolving in a steady rhythm that matched the relay in Maxan's hand.

"Maxan!" Rinnia grabbed Maxan's wrist and hauled him up beside her. "The relay!"

All the room was still awash in the bloody, murderous red. And all the world below was going mad, Maxan knew. He had known all along that for the few minutes he had given the snake a chase around the house of Manipulation, the signal of the object in his hand was amplified ten thousand degrees across all of Herbridia. How many lives had been lost?

Without another thought, he let his legs give out from beneath him and fell with all his weight against the floor, crying out in desperation and slamming the thing against the dark glass floor.

"What do you think it's like for him?"

Maxan sat with his arm propped against the pillar at the center of the house of Manipulation, staring across the room at the creature trapped inside the Monitor's prison. He had restored the white light, and the green-scaled snake in the ornate Drakoran armor stood out like a stranger amongst the row of white-robed humans. But they all dreamed the same.

He sucked in a sharp breath as the tip of Rinnia's claw worked a few more grains of pink panacea powder into the line of gashes along his back. She only had a small vial of the stuff left, so she was careful to make every bit of it count. It wouldn't be enough to heal the scars entirely, but…

"You'll live," she said, ignoring his question but answering his pained breaths instead.

Her sea blue eyes were calm. They strayed from their work on her brother's back to the suspended body of her other brother on the other side of the glass barrier.

"I don't know what it's like," she said gravely. "Maybe like looking in one mirror and seeing another mirror behind you. Infinite space stretching out all around, and yet nowhere to go."

There was no set of knowledge the spirit of his father had left Maxan that could explain the experience of a mind trapped in a body, trapped in its own mind, trapped in a cell that could never be opened from the inside.

"Everywhere," he mumbled. "And nowhere."

"So long as it works."

"We can't leave Saghan in there forever. I promised him…"

Rinnia had no answer for that. She was still trying to decide who it was, really, they had just imprisoned. She had known as well as Maxan that during the few minutes the two of them ran around luring the reptile in this place, the whole world had likely been plunged into bloodthirsty chaos. And yet, the price of it was cheaper than what Salastragore had planned for them, and for yet more beyond the stars.

She tried to convince herself it was worth it while she worked another few grains of the wound-sealing medicine into Maxan's wounds.

Her wound had healed within minutes, without the need for panacea. Their father had given her the gift of genetic superiority. And to the brother she never knew she had—a secret she realized Old Four Swords could never have told her—Ralse had given him a different kind of gift.

"What was he like," she asked, changing the subject, knowing Maxan would understand who she meant.

Maxan thought for a while, even reaching out in the empty hallways of his mind, thinking maybe the other fox that had once lived there would respond. *What were you like, Ralse?*

But there was nothing.

"Annoying," he said finally. "Mostly annoying. But… he saved me."

Inside his mind, his thoughts stumbled in their search, like a wanderer who feels the sharp, painful press of a stone under his paw. "Hold on," he said. "Ralse was female? I mean the human, the user."

"Sure. Why not." Rinnia coaxed him, taking advantage of the fact her brother could not see the smile spreading on her face.

Maxan missed the playfulness of it though. "He—ah, I mean—*she* always spoke in my own voice. It was like—"

"Talking to yourself."

"Probably worse."

Neither of them spoke again until Rinnia's work had concluded.

By the time Maxan could stand again without feeling debilitating pain streaking along his spine, the Aigaion was creeping at last over an expanse of twinkling lights in the night sky below, most of them concentrated into the shape of a gigantic cross. They'd drifted hundreds of miles in just a single hour and were back where it had all started.

From up here, Maxan reflected, *everything looks so small. Actually, everything IS small. All the violence, all the wars and rivalries and bitterness, none of it matters when you see it from so far away.*

"How will we get back?" Rinnia's question broke his trance. She stared through the glass at the glowing shape of Crosswall as well. "And if we do get back, what do we do then?"

"I don't know," Maxan said truthfully. He looked down on a world full of problems. *Will the Stray return? Will Locain's army lay down their weapons? Did Pryth and Pram make it back? Did the Corvidians get what they wanted at the Monitors' castle?* These questions and more raced through his mind. The answers were down there, waiting.

"We can't go back," Rinnia said flatly after a time.

Maxan spun about to face her, his one eye narrowing quizzically. "What are you talking about?"

"I mean *us*. We know too much. We … *are* too much." She shook her head. "We can't go back, Maxan. We're on the Aigaion. This whole thing is *power*. Too much power. Power no one was ever supposed to have."

"Okay," he said, playfully nudging her toward the gap. "You jump first. I'll follow you; I swear."

Rinnia swatted his paw aside. "I'm serious."

Maxan looked away from her grave expression and decided to give being serious a try as well. Maybe there were bigger problems than the ones he knew were waiting below. If his experiences had taught him anything, it was that there was always something unexpected lurking in the dark places you never knew existed. Some danger. Something that was coming after you. His mother had told him to run. Yovan had told him to run. Even Ralse... How many times had his own *user* told him to run?

Thinking of Ralse shone a light on yet another unexplored hollow of inherited knowledge in Maxan's mind. He watched the haloed, green-scaled reptile floating in the glass prison, in a row of the white-robed humans. His green eye widened with sudden realization. He grabbed his sister's wrist and tried to drag her toward the triangular entrance of the house of Manipulation.

She tried to wrench her arm free, but Maxan's grip was a vise.

"What is it?" she called, again and again as they raced through the twisting, angular corridors of the tetrahedral monolith. Maxan turned around a series of corners, unexpectedly familiar with the layout of this eerie, unknown place.

By the time they emerged onto the central, triangular plane between the Aigaion's three looming pyramids, all the sky had fallen completely to black. Innumerable stars twinkled brightly above their heads, and their paws raced across their reflected images against the mirror-like glass below. Yerda, the Earth, hung in the sky just behind where they had emerged. The shadow of Herbridia, the tiny, terraformed moon where The Animal in Man was played, passed over that ruined planet's brown, lifeless crags.

The two foxes sprinted across the shimmering field of reflected stars for several minutes, approaching the very center of the Aigaion, before Rinnia finally regained enough of her senses to wrestle herself away and demand to know what had made her brother lose his mind.

"Where *is* Salastragore," he asked her frantically.

Her face screwed up in confusion. She slowly jabbed a claw over her shoulder, pointing back where they'd come from.

"No, no." Maxan shook his head, his paws danced about wildly trying to illustrate his point. "I mean the user. The *human*. The *mind* that's trapped in Saghan's body. See? Where is he? Where has he been? Where did he go?"

"Isn't he locked away with all the others?"

Maxan ignored the misinterpretation. "No. He's not there. He hasn't been there for twenty years."

"How do you even know?"

"I just *know*," Maxan said, thinking he could explain later if she chose to come with him. "He's... out there." His eye rotated up slowly, drawing a course between the distant lights in outer space. "On Saturn's frozen moon, he said."

Rinnia was speechless. Suddenly, quite unexpectedly, this raving idiot fox was making some sense.

Maxan went on before she could form a response. "You said it yourself. We can't go back down there. We can't let anyone up here either. But what if they do? The Corvidians? Or whatever Monitors are left, even ones you probably don't know about? What if they set him free?"

Rinnia was silent for a long time, gazing at the stars. Then, she said knowingly, meeting his gaze, "This is about your promise to Saghan."

"That," he said, nodding solemnly. "And more."

"What else is there?"

"What have they been doing for twenty years? I know there are humans who aren't locked in the game all the time. Ah, don't ask, okay? Don't give me that look. Not right now. What have they been doing, Rinnia? The other humans. Salastragore said it himself. On the red planet, do you think they'd just let Epimetheus die? This whole project? Would they just let him steal their signal and not plan to retaliate?

"Oh no..." Maxan's voice drifted off. A darker train of thoughts barreled suddenly through his speech, something much worse than he could imagine. "What if," he began slowly, "Salastragore planned an escape all along? What if his mind's not even in Saghan's body right now?"

"No." It was Rinnia's turn to correct him. "No. It's not possible. His mind is... it's... it's *looping* back in on itself. It has to be... Right?" She heard the faltering faith in her own question as well as Maxan. "Right?" she asked again, less steadily than before.

"Not if he *knew*, Rinnia. That he *could* fail. He planned for everything." His voice grew quiet. "Even Baaleb."

She let out an exasperated breath and threw her arms up in defeat. "So, what now, then?"

The Aigaion had left Crosswall behind in the west. It crept slowly over the winding Radilin River. It crossed the far, invisible border into Peskora. Below the foxes' paws, they could see the lights of the oceanic species' settlements lining their coasts and inland seas. Together, they both understood without words that the few minutes of red madness had not been enough to snuff out all the precious life in the world below. Not all the glowing fires they saw from above had been set to destroy. Some were set to ward off the chill of night. In Peskora. In Leora. In Corvidia and Drakora.

Without words, both Rinnia and Maxan knew that their world would never be safe unless they knew the ultimate fate of the one who threatened its existence.

"You said yourself," Maxan said at last, "we can't go back."

The instinct to roll her eyes at his dramatic tone was strong, but Rinnia resisted it. Slowly, she nodded her agreement.

Maxan drew his paws away from hers and approached the raised triangular platform at the Aigaion's center. He knew where to find the gate's controls. He knew the sequence that would bring up the hard light display. He knew how to read the map, and he knew how to find it there.

My father knew, so I know.

Rinnia watched it all silently, thinking that all her life she had known wonders the likes of which no Herbridian would ever witness. It had been the first tenet of her brotherhood. She had been a monitor. She was tasked with silencing anyone that stumbled upon such technology. And despite all her knowledge, the shimmering pool of light her brother summoned was worlds beyond her concept of reality.

Maxan's paw entwined with hers, bringing her back to awareness.

Together, the two foxes stepped into the light.

Epilogue

The figure in black robes was too small to fill the grand wooden rocking chair. Its delicate lower paws dangled over the edge, but the chair rocked back and forth rhythmically all the same. The fire crackled pleasantly in the hearth, chiseled to the shape of a monster extinct long ago.

The Mind's Supreme Master flipped through a few more pages of the book upon her lap, her eyes skimming the next subjects and crudely illustrated diagrams. She never thought she would have need to study battlefield tactics, specifically the chapters on combating winged foes. Arrows were the standard. Nets were something she hadn't considered, and the devices that utilized gears and pulleys to propel them into the sky had been an idea beyond her greatest imagination. Just moments ago, she had encountered a formula for a flammable mist—a substance so lightweight that it floated invisibly above the battlefield, yet so potent that it would ignite at the touch of the tiniest of flames. Such as a burning arrow.

Or, if her twin brother were anywhere around, maybe just a wink.

Pram envisioned the horror such a chemical weapon could unleash on the unsuspecting Corvidians as they swooped over the ranks of her Leoran infantry. Just at the right time, the flame would start, and all the skies would erupt in terrible fire. The cheers would go up. The birds unlucky enough to survive the initial blast would fall upon the waiting warriors' spears.

Pram closed the book with deliberate slowness, threw back the black hood of her Principal's robe and let out a deep sigh. She stared absently into the crackling flames in the hearth. Months ago, when she had first started accessing the old master's library at the top of the Mind's Pinnacle Tower, she found her eyes were always drawn to the statue of the monstrous, multi-species behemoth looming over the hearth, as though she expected it to come alive and take her life. Eventually, she'd grown used to it. In fact, she'd convinced herself it watched over her. She'd even dreamed it would come alive and protect her.

Lost in the dancing fires, Pram's mind wandered even further back, to the night she and her twin brother finally saw the great glow of Crosswall as they plodded along through the tall grass just off the eastern road. The city lit the sky for miles. They came to find that all the districts within, and throughout all the settlements clinging to its walls, everywhere in Leora, across all nations, there had been a horrifying purge of violence. For what might have only been a few minutes, the survivors generally agreed, all rational thought fell away. The lines of consciousness blurred. The beasts sleeping within Herbridian hearts were awakened. Blood fell like rain.

They called the event *The Frenzy.*

When it was over, the world needed answers. They needed the Mind more than ever.

And Pram and Pryth were there.

Taking control of the missing king's arbiters, advisors, and bootlickers had been trivial for her. Despite their high standing in Leoran society, their thoughts had been easier for Pram to crack than an acorn under a sledgehammer. Just a few days after the Frenzy, through her swift and subsequent decrees, Pram declared martial law. She organized the cleanup efforts and doubled the crews that were reconstructing buildings that had been demolished or burned. She suspended all trade and put all the traders' guilds to work reorganizing their stock and inventory for the greater good.

And, strangely enough, as those first days stretched into weeks it became clear that the animals in Crosswall were no longer showing signs of going Astray. In the time following the Frenzy, more and more Leorans wandered back to the city's center, starving, spattered with dried blood, draped in tatters or bereft of clothing entirely, abandoning the wilds of the western district's farthest reaches.

The Stray were coming home. However, they were not so easily accepted by the rest of society, so Pram had taken them into the Mind's collective ranks. Her advisors informed her of the shortage of green and blue dyes for new initiates' and students' robes. She ordered them to think of any other color and dismissed them.

The kingdom was still healing, but Pram doubted the greatest wound her people felt could ever be closed. The throne in the king's palace sat empty. The ultimate fate of Locain was a secret Pram and her brother Pryth never shared. For all intents and purposes, he had been killed by the Denlanders he had campaigned to slaughter. Pram knew well enough that Leora could live on without a king, but the people needed a symbol of strength, of justice, of majesty. The Mind could never be that for them.

Chewgar could have been all of those.

So it had been months and more months, and neither the fox nor the rhino had made good on their promise to come home. Pram doubted at this point she would ever see them again. They were dead. Pram knew, somehow, that Master Feyn was dead as well.

The calamity that befell the Monitors' castle went relatively unnoticed by the rest of the world. It was only after Pram's position as the Mind's new master was firmly secured that she thought to tap Folgian's disused spy network and investigate the rumors drifting west from Drakora. Weeks later, she heard their reports. There had been a battle between a small Corvidian force and a remnant of Thraxians dug out beneath the castle. All of the surrounding city had been evacuated, resettled a hundred miles away in the northern Drakoran swamps, suspiciously closer to the border with Corvidia. But the most disturbing part of the report was the looting. The Corvidians' official proclamation had been to finish the extermination that started decades before. Her spies informed her that this was not the case at all, having obtained a confession from a Drakoran noble involved that the birds had come for Salastragore's secrets, and that they had succeeded.

It was not long after that Pram's spies brought her new reports about the renewed construction of The Spire atop Corvidia's tallest peak, overlooking their great Lake Skymere. They were rebuilding the Monitors' monstrosity of a structure, brick by brick, in the heart of their homeland, and Pram knew exactly what they were trying to reach.

And that was how it fell to her, and her alone, to stop them. She had no choice. She had pored through page after page of Folgian's collected knowledge, always suspecting that there was something more sinister lurking between the words. The old bear master never mentioned the Aigaion directly, but Pram had seen the entrance to the stations, she had seen the relay and heard the others speak about its power. Pram didn't know how, but she knew beyond certainty that the Frenzy had been caused by the Monitors' meddling with those forces that should have remained beyond all the animals' control.

It would not be long now until the Leoran armies she'd gathered marched west to topple the Corvidian capital. Through the lost king's grand arbiters, Principal Pram had all of the battalions in her pocket. Rank upon rank of warriors who'd served in the Thraxian Extermination decades ago, even those who'd wandered back from the Denland purge, all of them eager to fight again. In fact, knowing she would need their arrows, she had the arbiters broker a treaty with the Denland rebels, ensuring they could operate as their city-state after the Corvidians' Spire was destroyed. She would lead all the massed fighting force herself, while her brother stayed at the Campus to tend to small but promising group of apprentice callers. He'd never agree.

Everything depended on Pram's success.

The reaching flames in the hearth were fanned sideways by a sudden gust of wind. Pram felt the chill seep through her Principal's robes. She wrapped her wide, bushy tail about herself and twisted about in the grand rocking chair to see that a window frame on the library's second floor had thrown itself open.

She ceased the focus she held in the back of her mind, and the chair stopped its rhythmic motion. She hopped down from the seat and held a paw up to the window, reaching with her mind to feel the metal frame, the delicate glass, the bolt and the latch that would keep it closed. Over the last several months, her powers had amplified. She found she could not control raw elements like her twin, but her command of physical forces and distant objects had bloomed unexpectedly. *Telekinesis* was the word she had read in the pages of one of Folgian's many books.

Pram turned about to the hearth, thinking to take the next book from the stack she'd made on the table beside the chair, but froze in sudden shock.

The slender figure was clad in armor so black that it seemed to absorb the glow of the flames and lengthen the shadows all around the library. It rose from a crouch and unlaced the bindings about its hood.

Pram had never known a Drakoran snake's scales could be so white. This one's were decorated with a repeating red pattern down either side of her neck, and something resembling a skull stained the space on her brow. Pram had never met the snake, but the gaze of those slitted orange eyes were well known to her. They were Saghan's eyes.

The white snake drew an immaculate, curved sword, its blade scraping slowly against the scabbard on her back. Pram assumed the deliberateness of the assassin's gesture was supposed to scare her. She scoffed at the snake.

"Before I make you throw yourself into the fire," the comparably shorter squirrel said evenly, "tell me what you've come for."

"You know," Selyen answered in a low voice, the blade of the katana resting against the length of her thigh.

"The Corvidians are paying you to take my life." It wasn't a question.

"Try again."

Pram felt a flush of annoyance bristle her fur. She made an effort to control the twitching of her nose. How easy it would be to just crack the snake's thoughts like twigs, to set fire to her mind from the inside like kindling... But she thought to at least try the more conventional means first.

After a moment's consideration, Pram said, "You want the Spire to succeed, and so, whether you're working *for* them or not, you've come to eliminate its greatest threat."

"Clossser," the snake hissed, curving her long neck to give Pram a sidelong glance. "But too small a scope."

"Do I get another chance, or can we just cut to it?" She pointed at the stacked books. "I've a lot more to read before morning."

Selyen lifted the katana and drew the tip of her black nail over the switch on its handle. A green bead of light glowed. A thrumming vibration filled the grand library. "Do you know this weapon?"

Pram shook her head. Her mind reached for the invisible strings attaching the sword to the Aigaion, but they were proving elusive. Perhaps because of the vibrations in its blade.

"With the power of the Aigaion," Selyen went on, "we can make more just like it. We can make weapons of unbelievable might. And we will need them to fight what's coming."

"And what, exactly, is coming?" Pram felt a bead of sweat form under the fur along her brow. She didn't dare reach up to wipe it. Her mind reached and reached, feeling blindly. Her neck stiffened with the concentration.

A second, orange bead lit in the sword's handle, and the thrumming intensified.

"Our doom," Selyen said, "from beyond the stars."

A trickle of blood ran from one of Pram's nostrils, and she released herself from the effort of grasping for the elusive object in space. "Heh," she breathed the note of laughter, a smile spreading along her face. "I'd ask you to tell me more, but I've run out of patience."

The white snake took a slow step forward.

Pram extended her paw toward the assassin's head to feel for the snake's mind.

Then, the squirrel's smile died.

There was simply nothing there to feel.

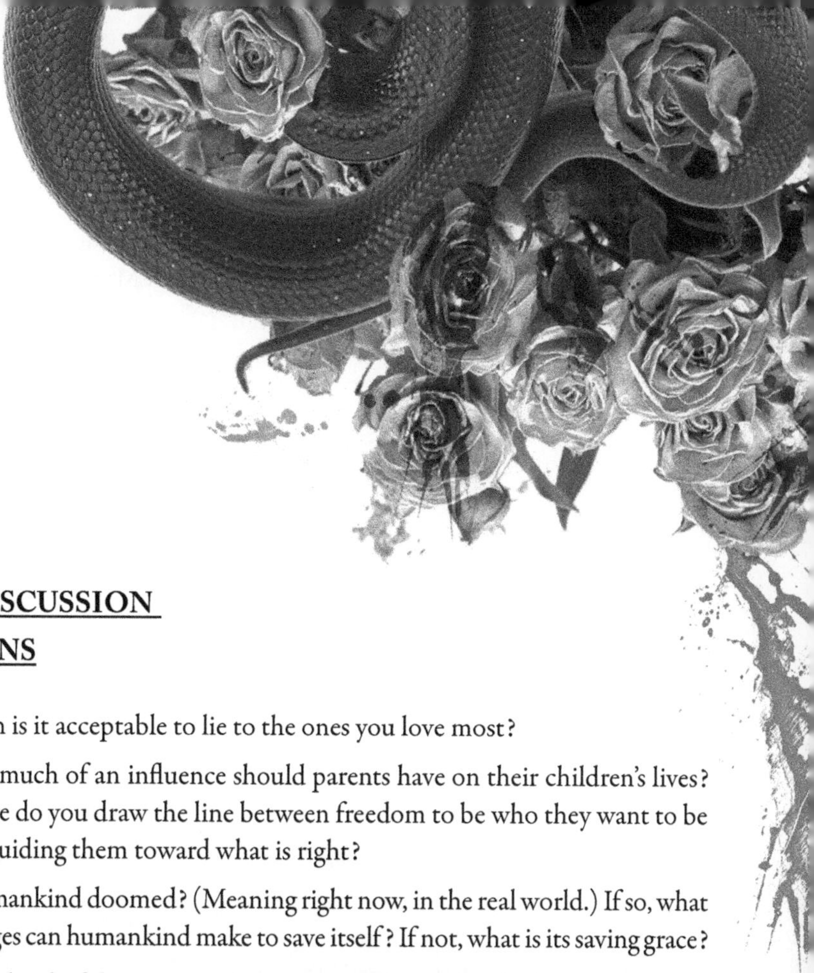

Book Discussion Questions

1. When is it acceptable to lie to the ones you love most?
2. How much of an influence should parents have on their children's lives? Where do you draw the line between freedom to be who they want to be and guiding them toward what is right?
3. Is humankind doomed? (Meaning right now, in the real world.) If so, what changes can humankind make to save itself? If not, what is its saving grace?
4. What kind of duty is most important and what kind is least important: Duty to your country? Duty to your family? Duty to work and team members? Duty to yourself? Why did you order these the way you did?
5. Design your own Castle Salastragore! If you could pick five commercial and/or industrial works in your dream fortress, what would they be and why? How would you let your friends get in? How would you keep your enemies out?
6. How many examples of the following genres can you come up with from the Ferocious Heart story: Fantasy, Steampunk, Science Fiction, Cyberpunk, Body Horror?
7. Was Salastragore's reaction (to plot the destruction of all humanity) to Master Baaleb's plan of exterminating the Thraxians justifiable? Is Salastragore right in labeling humanity as a "disease"?
8. After finishing the book, do you agree with Zariel's assertion, that it would have been best to hide the key in Maxan's eye, leaving Salastragore to

eventually destroy himself? Or was Maxan right to turn around and fight back? Who was right and why?

9. Predict what lies on the other side of the portal in the middle of the Aigaion. What awaits the two foxes in The Animal in Man part 3, Undying Soul?

Acknowledgements

HONESTLY, FIRST THINGS FIRST, THANK YOU FOR WAITING so long to get this book in your hands. I've seen you in multiple convention halls, I've talked over loud music in pubs, and I've sheepishly answered for years and years that it was still in the works; "moving at the speed of publishing," I'd say. But it's finally here, and thanks are due ultimately to 4 Horsemen Publications for believing in the quality of the story and the ability of its storyteller. (I may be presuming a bit with that second part.)

Thanks are also due to Alexi Vandenburg. Even though things didn't work out the way we'd hoped, I got to see you fight like hell for me and for this book, and I want you to know how much all your effort means to me. Thank you.

Thanks to Ben Goodin, Wesley Pender, Dale McKay, and Randy Buckley for playing Dungeons and Dragons with me in high school. The Animal in Man would never be a thing—since it began as a D&D campaign!—if it weren't for all of us shaping worlds and living other lives together all those late nights at Metropolis Comics. Thanks to Steve, the owner, for lending us the key.

About the Author

Joseph Asphahani is an avid video gamer, effective high school teacher, and enthusiastic candidate for whatever sort of cybernetic limb enhancement your megacorp is planning for the inexorable dystopian future. When he's not getting hopelessly lost in simulated worlds, he's often dreaming up worlds of his own. The world of The Animal in Man is his first and favorite, and *Violent Mind* is his first novel. He resides in Chicago with his wife and two children.

Milton Keynes UK
Ingram Content Group UK Ltd.
UKHW040334031224
452051UK00018B/452/J

9 798823 204804